LONDON BELONGS TO ME

BY THE SAME AUTHOR

Novels

ANNA
"I SHALL NOT WANT"
LOVE IN OUR TIME
FLAMES COMING OUT THE TOP
TRINITY TOWN
THE THREE FRIENDS
PENANG APPOINTMENT

Criticism

THE FACTS OF FICTION

LONDON BELONGS TO ME

by

NORMAN COLLINS

"London, thou art the flower of cities all"

WILLIAM DUNBAR

THE REPRINT SOCIETY
LONDON

FIRST PUBLISHED 1945
THIS EDITION PUBLISHED BY THE REPRINT SOCIETY LTD.
BY ARRANGEMENT WITH WM. COLLINS & CO. LTD.
1949

All the characters in this novel are imaginary. The London of the title is real enough—that's LONDON all right. But Dulcimer Street and the lives of the people in it, like the other lives which cross with theirs, are all fictitious. And so are the various Funlands, cafés, Spiritualist Societies, agencies, hospitals and institutions, with which the story deals

PRINTED IN GREAT BRITAIN BY RICHARD CLAY AND COMPANY, LTD.,
BUNGAY, SUFFOLK

CONTENTS

PREFACE

Getting to Know The Place

There may be other cities that are older. But not many. And there may be one across the Atlantic that is larger. But not much.

In fact, no matter how you look at it, London comes pretty high in the respectable upper order of things. It's got a past as well as a present; and it knows it. And this is odd. Because considering its age it's had a remarkably quiet history, London. Nothing very spectacular. Nothing exceptionally heroic. Not until 1940, that is. Except for the Great Fire and the Black Death and the execution of a King, not very much has ever happened there. It has just gone on prosperously and independently through the centuries—wattle one century, timber the next, then brick, then stone, then brick again, then concrete. Building new foundations on old ruins. And sprawling out across the fields when there haven't been enough ruins to go round.

In the result it's been growing up as well as growing. And it must be about mature by now. Even a bit past its prime, perhaps. Beginning to go back on itself, as it were. Maybe. But to see the people, you wouldn't think so.

Every city has its something. Rome has St. Peter's. Peking has its Summer Palace. Moscow has the Kremlin. In Madrid there's the Prado. In New York there's the Empire State. Constantinople has St. Sophia. Cairo has Shepheard's. Paris has got the Eiffel Tower. Sydney has a bridge. Naples is content with its bay. Cape Town has Table Mountain. Benares is famous for its burning ghats. Pisa has a Leaning Tower. Toledo has a bull-ring. Stockholm has a Town Hall. Vancouver has a view. But London . . . London . . . What *is* it that London's got?

Well, there's St. Paul's Cathedral. But St. Peter's could put it into its pocket. There's Westminster Abbey. But there are Abbeys everywhere; they're dotted all over Europe. There's the Tower. Admittedly, the dungeons are convincing, but as a castle it's nothing. Not beside Edinburgh or Caernarvon. Even Tower Hill isn't really a hill: it's only an incline. Then there are the Houses of Parliament and the

Law Courts. But they're merely so much Victorian Gothic—all turrets and arches and railings and things. There's Buckingham Palace. But that's too new; it hasn't toned in yet. It's just been planted there—a big flat-fronted palace with a made road leading up to it. No, it's the smaller, older palace of St. James's, just round the corner, with its grimy red brick and low windows and little open courtyards, that is nearer the real thing. Is the real thing, in fact. It's a positively shabby little palace, St. James's. And it's got London written all over it. And St. James's Palace—brick and soot and age—is written all over London.

Yes, that's London. Mile upon mile of little houses, most of them as shabby as St. James's. If you start walking westwards in the early morning from somewhere down in Wapping or the Isle of Dogs, by evening you will still be on the march, still in the midst of shabby little houses—only somewhere over by Hammersmith by then.

That's not to say that there aren't plenty of fine big houses as well. Take Mayfair. But even Mayfair is distinctly Londonish too, when you come to look at it. The mansions are all squeezed up there side by side, and in consequence they are rather poky little mansions, most of them; though the sheer marvel of the address—Mayfair, W.1—excuses any overcrowding. Not that Mayfair is all mansions or anything like it. It's Shepherd's Market, that hamlet of dark shops and crooked alleyways, rather than Bruton Street or Grosvenor Square, that makes Mayfair.

And what's more, it's Covent Garden Market and Smithfield Market and Billingsgate Fish Market and the Caledonian Market and Peckham Market rather than Shepherd's Market—which isn't a real market anyway—that makes London. They are a part of the people, these markets. And London is the people's city. That is why Petticoat Lane is more London than Park Lane. And that is why London is the Mile End Road and the Walworth Road and the Lambeth Road and the Elephant and Castle. Strange, isn't it, how much of the real London still lies south of the river, just as it did in Shakespeare's day, and in Chaucer's day before him? It is as though across the Thames—in London's Deep South—times and manners haven't changed so much as in the Parliamentary North.

But London is more than a collection of streets and markets. It's Wren churches and A.B.C. tea-shops. It's Burlington Arcade and the Temple. It's the Athenæum and the Adelphi Arches. It's Kennington gasometer and the Zoo. It's the iron bridge at Charing Cross and the statue of Eros at Piccadilly Circus. It's the Serpentine and Moss Bros. It's Paddington Recreation Ground and the Nelson

Column. It's Big Ben and the Horse Guards. It's the National Gallery and Pimm's. It's the Victoria Palace and Ludgate Hill. It's the second-hand shops and the undertakers and the cinemas and the obscure back-street chapels. It's the Waif-and-Stray Societies and the fortune-tellers and the pub on the corner and the trams. That's London.

And the people. They're London, too. They're the same Londoners that they have always been, except that from time to time the proportion of refugees has altered a little. At one moment the doubtful-looking newcomers are the Huguenots, at another the Jews, and it is the Huguenots who are the Londoners wondering whatever London is coming to. They're all Londoners—the French and the Italians in Soho, the Chinese in Limehouse, the Scotsmen in Muswell Hill and the Irish round the Docks. And the only way in which modern Londoners differ from the Londoners who have lived there before them is that all the Londoners don't live in London any more. They simply work there. By 8 p.m. the City is a desert. Round about six o'clock the trouble starts: the deserters leave. Everyone begins shoving and pushing to get out of the metropolis into the estates and suburbs and garden cities. There they sleep, these demi-Londoners, in their little Tudor dolls' houses, until next morning when they emerge, refreshed, ready to play at being real Londoners again.

Perhaps it is simply the size of London that makes its inhabitants seem somehow smaller. Dolls' houses appear to be the right dwelling-places for these thousands, these tens of thousands, these hundreds of thousands, these half-urban hordes. Stand on the bridge at Liverpool Street Station at a quarter-to-nine in the morning and you see the model trains drawing in beneath you one after another, and swarms of toy-passengers emptying themselves on to the platform to go stumping up to the barrier—toy directors, toy clerks, toy typists, all jerking along to spend the day in toy-town, earning paper money to keep their dolls' houses going.

Of course, there are still plenty of the other kind, too. Real Londoners who sleep the night in London as well as work the day there. Real Londoners—some in love, some in debt, some committing murders, some adultery, some trying to get on in the world, some looking forward to a pension, some getting drunk, some losing their jobs, some dying, and some holding up the new baby.

This book is about a few of them.

[illegible] Bow Bells and Big Ben and the Horse Guards. It's the Windmill Girls and Eros. It's the [illegible] second-hand shops and the [illegible] and the [illegible] of [illegible] back-street churches, it's the [illegible] and the [illegible] and the [illegible] on the corner and the [illegible]. It's London.

And the people. They're London, too. They're the same Londoners that they have always been, except [illegible]. Among [illegible] are the [illegible] and [illegible] the [illegible]. London is [illegible]. They're all Londoners — the [illegible] and the Italians in Soho and [illegible] in Limehouse, the [illegible] in [illegible] Hill and the [illegible] round the Docks. And the [illegible] Londoners [illegible] the Londoners who have lived here [illegible] for [illegible] the London [illegible] London [illegible]. They simply [illegible] there. [illegible] the City is a desert. [illegible]

Perhaps it is simply the size of London that makes [illegible] Dolls' houses [illegible] places for [illegible] thousands [illegible] hundreds of thousands [illegible] station [illegible] trains drawing in [illegible] passengers [illegible] clerks [illegible] typists all [illegible] to [illegible] their dolls' houses again.

[illegible] there are still [illegible] love, some [illegible] in the [illegible] and some [illegible].

[illegible] a few of them.

BOOK ONE

AN OLD-FASHIONED CHRISTMAS

CHAPTER I

I

It was four-thirty p.m. Four-thirty on Friday, the 23rd of December, 1938.

They hadn't done very much work in the office that afternoon because in their various ways they had all been getting ready to celebrate. Bethlehem now brooded encouragingly over London. And Mr. Battlebury, in his enormous greatcoat which looked as though it were lined with bearskin at least, had gone off importantly in a taxi at ten minutes to one, and had not got back until after three. In the interval he had visited Fortnum's in Piccadilly, where he had bought a large box of crystallised fruit not because he, or anyone else in his family, particularly liked crystallised fruit, but because it had been there on the counter and he was in the mood for buying things. After that he had visited the Goldsmiths' and Silversmiths' Company in Regent Street where he had bought Mrs. Battlebury a pair of small diamond clips to go with the crystallised fruit. And making his way through the crowds towards Oxford Circus—it seemed, as it always did on Christmas Eve, that the whole idea of Christmas had taken most people entirely by surprise, and they were now shopping frantically in an effort to catch up with it—he had gone into Hamleys to buy a drawing-room conjuring-set that was to convert Robert Battlebury, junior, into an astonishingly adept but rather boring amateur Maskelyne for a few weeks—after which the magic egg-cups and disappearing handkerchiefs would be put away for ever, and forgotten.

Finally, Mr. Battlebury had dropped into Scott's for a dozen six-and-sixpenny oysters and had ordered a bottle of Hock to go with them—which is why he arrived back in Creek Lane, E.C.2, carrying his gaily tied-up parcels, a lot later and a good deal more genial than he generally arrived.

Mr. Battlebury's staff had not gone so far afield. The typists had rushed off to the neighbouring Lyonses and Express Dairies and Kardomahs and Cosee Cafés (two flights up and mind the old oak beam), and had stuffed themselves with slices of rich dark pudding or hot flaky mince-pies. The male staff, of course, had made for the pubs. There, under festoons of paper flowers and silver bells cut out of cardboard, they had eaten even larger slices of pudding, with a mince-pie on the side as well, and had washed it all down with sixpenny beer and even, because it was Christmas, eightpenny whiskies-and-sodas and glasses of ninepenny sherry and sevenpenny port.

By the time they got back to their desks they were most of them comfortably mellowed and a little sleepy as well. And even then, they didn't honestly sit down to work off the effects as they would have done if Mr. Battlebury hadn't still been out of the office. Someone had been given a bottle of Happy Days, a ready-mixed, emerald-coloured cocktail in a fancy frosted bottle. The stuff was unstoppered with much giggling and they all—from young Harold, who stamped the letters, to the elderly Miss Unsett, who checked the *pro-formas*—had a sip out of their office cups.

The girls had most of them already exchanged Christmas cards. There was no obvious reason why they should have done so. They had spent the whole of the previous twelve months sharing the same office, and drinking tea together at eleven o'clock every morning and three-thirty every afternoon, and giving each other pieces of chocolate and aspirins. But for the past two or three days they had been behaving as though they had been parted for years. They had been distributing views of snow-bound coaches and lighted taverns and children tobogganing, and robins and boys bearing holly and old bellmen crying "Oyez," as though Noel and the eighteenth century were the same thing, and life depended on celebrating both.

The printed words inside the cards were as queer as the pictures. They all supposed a state of infatuation and a kind of agonised separation. There was a let-us-join-hearts-even-if-we-can't-so-much-as touch-hands note about the lot of them. And the less they cost, the more emphatic they became. For a penny you got a real heart-cry, with a quite decent quality envelope thrown in. All these cards were now ranged along the tops of the filing-cabinets and bookcases as tokens of popularity and good-fellowship.

Usually, everyone went off round about this time on Christmas Eve. But to-night they were all stopping on for the presentation. It was due to take place in the drawing-office at five o'clock. Mr.

Battlebury had said that he would be there; and that, of course, meant that everybody else had to be there as well.

In any case, it was going to be quite a big do. The collection had been made during the previous week. They had got together four pounds fifteen shillings between the lot of them. And with it they had bought a handsome clock, a mammoth marble affair with an eight-day movement. There was a pendulum that could be seen through a sunken glass peephole, and a striker that set up a low pulsating *booong* at the hours. It was an imposing substantial sort of clock, the kind of thing which looked as though it actually manufactured Time.

Everything was ready, so at five to five all the girls—except for Miss Unsett, who was still busy collating her *pro-formas* like a scholar—trooped up to the drawing-office. There was some pushing on the stairs and more giggling until they came to the frosted-glass door marked BATTLEBURY & SON, POWER SPECIALISTS, PRIVATE. ENQUIRE BELOW and then they all sobered down a bit. The drawing-office was a large room with charts and diagrams on the walls, and it did not encourage conviviality. There were no Christmas cards there, not even a new calendar. The green-shaded lights low down over the tables cast a dim aqueous glow as though the meeting were taking place at the bottom of an aquarium. The only concession to the season was a spray of rather faded mistletoe hanging from one of the beams. The drawing-office humorist had put it there. But it was not very festive.

The draughtsmen were mostly standing about smoking. They were in their shirt-sleeves as draughtsmen always are—as a race of men they do not appear to have a full suit of clothes among the lot of them—and the only sign of jollity was the cigar that the chief draughtsman, Mr. Bewley, had just lit. It was one of a box of fifty that Mr. Battlebury had given to him. Every year it was the same. Mr. Bewley industriously smoked a cigar a day until the box was used up. And then, sometime in early March, he went back to his pipe and felt better.

The girls had all managed to find themselves a chair—there was an empty place carefully being kept for Miss Unsett right under the mistletoe—when the door at the end opened and the counting-house staff filed in. They were a different breed of heroes from the draughtsmen. It was not only the devil-may-care shirt-sleeves that segregated the draughtsmen; there was something of the artist—the untidy collar, the puckered eye, the wisp of hair—about them as well. The book-keepers, on the other hand, were all smooth, precise little men wearing stiff collars and horn-rimmed spectacles and hair that was smoothed down like sleek fur. Unlike the draughtsmen, they didn't take off their coats when they were working and, in consequence, the most of them had very shiny elbows and slightly frayed cuffs. On the whole the draughtsmen looked as if they might provide the livelier company.

The young gentlemen from the counting-house perched themselves along the edge of the drawing-tables. And Mr. Veritter, the Secretary of the Company, a pale white-haired man with the thin anxious face of a whippet, sat himself down under the mistletoe in the place that had been reserved for Miss Unsett. There was further giggling when he did so—a half-suppressed, delighted chuckle, that ran right through the room—and Mr. Veritter's expression of anxiety increased. He had a vague unpleasant feeling that the laughter was somehow directed at him, though he couldn't imagine why, and his eyebrows contracted into a fixed nervous frown. He looked as though at any moment he might break out into a shrill frightened yapping.

Then Mr. Battlebury arrived. Even without his overcoat he was still a big man. He had a broad fleshy face, with heavy dewlaps and a long protruding nose that started too high up his forehead. What remained of his hair was crisp and curly and he wore it cut short except for a little bunch of the stuff that sprang out over each ear. The dome of his head was entirely bald—prematurely bald, that is—for Mr. Battlebury was only forty-three. Altogether his skull had a smooth glossy appearance as though it were regularly massaged, or even polished. Not that it seemed in the least out of place. Everything about Mr. Battlebury was rather highly polished.

"Well, well, well," he began, rubbing his hands together. "Are we all ready?"

He surveyed the room with a gratifyingly pleased beam through his horn-rimmed spectacles and then stopped himself abruptly.

"But where's Josser?" he asked.

There was just a trace of irritation in his voice as he put the question. Mr. Battlebury, it was apparent, did not like to be kept waiting even on purely social occasions.

He was not kept waiting for long, however. The door from the counting-house reopened and four large ledgers with a pair of striped trousers underneath them came into sight. The ledgers hesitated for a moment and then steered a swaying and erratic course towards the big steel safe on the opposite side of the room.

A voice from behind the ledgers said : "Just coming, sir."

Everybody gave a little titter. Then, as the walking ledgers passed the centre of the room, the owner of the voice came into sight. He was a small elderly man with a wisp of white hair that stood straight up like egrets' feathers. Under his black business coat, a blue knitted cardigan showed like an azure body-band along the back and seemed to divide him into two portions. When he finally reached the safe he tilted forward, swung the steel doors together, locked them and took the bunch of keys over to Mr. Veritter. There was something oddly mechanical about the whole operation. It was like that of an actor who has rehearsed a small part so thoroughly that he has forgotten what it is all about. It was obvious that Mr. Josser could have carried it all through blindfolded.

As soon as he had handed over the keys he began dusting his hands one against the other and addressed himself again to Mr. Battlebury.

"Sorry to keep you waiting, sir," he said.

Two of the young ladies exchanged glances. They were Miss Heyland, who hammered away for nearly eight hours a day at the invoicing machine, and Miss Woodman, who was Mr. Veritter's secretary.

"Isn't that just like old Josser?" Miss Heyland observed. "Still working."

"He *is* rather a *pet*," Miss Woodman admitted.

"Won't he miss it—after all this time?" Miss Heyland remarked sentimentally.

"Oh, I don't know," replied Miss Woodman. "Would you?"

Meanwhile, Mr. Battlebury was smiling again, now that he discovered that he wasn't to be kept waiting after all.

"Ah, Josser," he said. "Nothing like clearing up, is there?"

"No, sir," Mr. Josser replied dutifully.

"Well," said Mr. Battlebury, "we mustn't take up too much time because everybody wants to be off home. I'm sure that I do, and I'm sure Mr. Josser does. But I felt—we all felt—that we couldn't let our old friend go without making some little presentation to him. That's why we're all here now."

Mr. Battlebury paused and began rubbing his hands together again as though he were looking forward to Mr. Josser's departure and saw no point in concealing it.

"How long is it you've been with us, Mr. Josser?" he asked in the easy, deceptive manner of a counsel trying to draw out an uncommunicative witness.

"Forty-two years, sir," Mr. Josser answered.

The answer came pat because those forty-two years had been in his mind a great deal lately. Ever since his last illness Mr. Josser had found himself steadily re-living them. It was as though inside his brain someone were turning over the pages of an old photographic album with smudgy pictures of himself on every page.

But Mr. Battlebury had cheerfully taken up the thread of his address again.

"Forty-two," he remarked heartily. "Just about my age. Might almost be twins, Mr. Josser?"

He was smiling so broadly by now that Mr. Josser could see that he was meant to smile as well. He did so obediently even though he didn't feel in the least like smiling.

"So now our old friend is going to have the rest he deserves," Mr. Battlebury rattled on. "No more running for the early tram, eh, Mr. Josser? No more waiting about in the rain for the same old tram to take you home again. I'm bound to say I almost envy you." Here Mr. Battlebury shook his head as though the greater part of his life was spent in the rain waiting about for trams. "But the rest of us," he went on, "have got to put in a few more years before we can retire—that's so, isn't it, Miss Sweeting?"

Miss Sweeting was eighteen and had just joined Battlebury's straight from a Secretarial College. It seemed that the College had taught her everything about Pitman's Shorthand and touch typewriting, but nothing at all about large hearty men like Mr. Battlebury. She was a pretty fair-haired girl and she blushed.

"Definitely," she said, and tried to look older than she was.

"And now the time has come to make our little presentation to Mr. Josser," Mr. Battlebury continued.

He paused, and Mr. Josser shifted in his chair in embarrassment.

"Thank you, sir," he said awkwardly.

"No, no," Mr. Battlebury caught him up. "You don't have to thank me. They only asked me to speak because I've known you longest."

Mr. Battlebury turned abruptly towards the man on his right.

"Got it there, Veritter?" he demanded.

"Here it is, sir," Mr. Verriter answered, rising hurriedly.

He went over to a table at the back of the room, and picked up the big marble clock tenderly, as though it were a large stony baby. Then he placed it openly on the drawing-cabinet beside Mr. Battlebury and stood back. Up to that moment he had been trying to keep the whole thing out of sight so that he could produce it as a surprise even though Mr. Josser had been asked what he wanted and nearly everyone else had helped to choose it.

"Well," said Mr. Battlebury in a rising crescendo of heartiness, "this is the very handsome time-piece for which your friends have subscribed. And every time you look at it you can just sit back and remember that the rest of your time's your own."

"The rest of my time's my own," Mr. Josser found himself repeating silently.

He had got up and come forward. Now that he was standing up beside the majestic form of Mr. Battlebury everyone could see how small he was. How small and how shabby. Viewed from the front the effect of the blue woollen cardigan that Mrs. Josser had knitted him was even more striking. It buttoned up almost to the throat and made Mr. Josser look as though he'd dressed hurriedly and not put on anything underneath. The cuffs of the cardigan, which were too long anyhow, had been rolled up, and hung down outside the sleeves of the black jacket.

But it was his face at which everyone was looking. Behind the pince-nez glasses which lay aslant upon his nose—one of the springs was broken: it had been broken for years, seven or eight years at least, and Mr. Josser had never had it mended—large tears were forming. At last, one of them detached itself and slithered down his cheek on to the ragged grey moustache.

Mr. Josser took out his handkerchief and mopped about with it.

"Oh, look," said Miss Woodman. "He's crying."

"Sshh!" Miss Heyland replied sharply. "He'll hear you."

But Mr. Battlebury had picked up the clock by now. Formally and with a little bow, he gave it to Mr. Josser. It looked even bigger in Mr. Josser's arms than it had done in Mr. Battlebury's. Mr. Josser sagged right down under the weight of it.

"And now," said Mr. Battlebury, feeling in his pocket, "here is my own little contribution. I told you that I didn't have anything to do with the clock, that is entirely from the—er—staff."

He produced a flat white envelope as he spoke, and Mr. Josser mechanically caught hold of it.

Then Mr. Battlebury held out his hand for a cordial last handshake. But Mr. Josser could do nothing about it. The clock had just slipped alarmingly and he now had both arms gripped frantically round it. He seemed to be wrestling with himself. The envelope that Mr. Battlebury had given him was crushed and crumpled in his right hand. The other hand was clutching the clock.

And this was a pity: because in all those years of their association this was the first time that Mr. Battlebury had ever tried to shake hands with Mr. Josser.

It was very quiet now in the counting-house and only one of the lights was still on. The girls had left first, going off down the staircase in twos and threes, all chattering like a company of sparrows, and carrying their mysterious Christmas packages. The men had been rather slower about leaving. They had stood about first in groups, filling their pipes, and savouring the pleasant sensation of not actually doing anything. Then with a lot of cheery talk along familiar lines—"Have a good time, old man," "Don't eat too much," and "Be good," and "Keep sober"—they, too, had gone. Mr. Josser was left standing there.

He had shaken hands with all of them, one after another, until he was sick of shaking hands. He never wanted to see another hand again. And he had said "Happy Christmas" thirty-two times in all. But it was of neither of these that he was thinking now. He was thinking of the speech that he had just made. Ever since he had known that there was going to be a presentation he had been practising the little address—the few words—that he was going to give them. Among so many young people he suddenly felt like the ancient of the tribe, Old Wise Owl, and there was all manner of deep advice that he wanted to give them.

And what had actually happened? He had simply stood there facing the lot of them—even mere children like Miss Sweeting—and had remained silent, absolutely silent, for what must have been about thirty seconds. Then, in a thick unnatural voice that didn't sound in the least like his own, he had said all in one gulp, "Thankyouallverymuch," and had sat down again. Just that. No more.

The door behind him opened suddenly and Mr. Veritter stood there. He had got nearly as far as Cannon Street before he had discovered that he had left his reading glasses behind him in his desk. He started when he saw Mr. Josser.

"Hullo, Josser," he said. "You still here?"

Mr. Josser dropped his eyes to avoid Mr. Veritter's.

"Yes, I'm still here, sir," he answered lamely.

"Have all the others gone?"

"Yes, sir, they've all gone."

Mr. Veritter stood regarding him for a moment and then went through into his inner office. His glasses were there exactly where he had left them. Mr. Veritter shut up his desk once more and came back again into the counting-house.

Mr. Josser had not moved and Mr. Veritter became apprehensive for a moment—but not too apprehensive, as he still meant to have a slap at catching the 5.45.

"Feeling all right, aren't you, Josser?" he asked. "Chest's not troubling you again?"

Mr. Josser drew himself up with a jerk.

"I'm perfectly well, thank you, sir," he replied. And, after a long pause, he added, "Perfectly well," as though to settle the matter.

Mr. Veritter took one last glance at him and one glance at his watch.

"Well, good-bye, Josser," Mr. Veritter said hurriedly. "Happy Christmas. Come back and see us sometime."

"Thank you, sir," Mr. Josser answered. "Same to you, sir. I will."

Then, when Mr. Veritter had left him, he went on standing there as before.

It was the sound of St. Mary-Under-Cannon striking the half-hour that roused him. He went over to the hat-stand and took down his alpaca office coat. It rolled into quite a small parcel, and he wrapped it up carefully in a copy of the *Star* that someone had left in the waste-paper basket. Then he pulled open his drawer—the inside of the drawer that was the nearest that he had ever come to privacy in Battlebury and Son—and removed the things that belonged to him. There was a packet of pipe-cleaners, several empty tobacco tins, a collar stud, the end of a pair of braces and a box of iodised pastilles. He threw the tobacco tins and the brace-ends into the waste-paper basket, and shovelled the rest into his pocket.

Finally, with a feeling almost like relief, now that the moment had actually come, he put on his overcoat, wound the knitted muffler round his neck—it was blue, like the cardigan: off the same skein, in fact—clapped his hat on his head, gathered up the clock that was now back in the wrapping in which the makers had supplied it, took up his umbrella from the corner, turned off the light—with difficulty, because his hands were full—and closed the door behind him.

Mr. Josser and the fullness of life had parted company.

2

It was about twenty past five when Mr. Josser emerged into the icy coldness of Creek Lane and about twenty past seven when he came away from it.

At first he had intended to go straight home. But when he saw the glowing windows of The Bunch of Grapes and heard the sound of voices inside, he realised with a sudden pang that unless he went in there now, he might never go there again. True, the others, like Mr. Veritter, had all asked him to come back and look them up. But he knew in his heart that they didn't mean it. If he came back now he'd simply be an interruption. And by to-morrow the Grapes, so far as he was concerned, would be just something in the past.

So he went inside for the last time—edging his way carefully so as not to upset the clock—to have a farewell mild-and-bitter. Only it didn't work out that way. The saloon was crowded with old friends and familiar faces. Everyone had been celebrating a little already, and they seemed eager to include him in their celebration. They might have been waiting for him almost. Even the barmaid was pleased to see him. And, in the end, he had five half-pints—not because he wanted them—but simply because he got invited in as fifth man in a group of four and had to observe the convention of the thing.

When he finally managed to break away—Heaven itself, it seemed, could not have been more full of loved and dear ones than that bar—he found the swing doors more troublesome than ever. He was afraid of pushing with the marble corner of the clock for fear of breaking the glass. His umbrella was in the way. And his other parcel, his rolled-up office coat, was of no use as a pusher; it simply folded back upon itself, like a sponge. In the end, he went out backwards, disappearing into the night with alarming suddenness over the edge of the hearth-stoned step.

He recovered himself on the pavement and began the walk towards New Bridge Street. The doors of the offices were now all closed, and no lights were showing. The black brick precipices, where the firms huddled together by day like cave-dwellers, were empty, and their piled-up populations had departed. JULIUS F. GREENBAUM (STOCK AND SHARE BROKERS), F. MACREAGH (STIRLING), OIL FUEL ENGINEERS, WIGGINSON, WIGGINSON & CHEAP, SOLICITORS AND COMMISSIONERS FOR OATHS, had all gone away already, leaving the City to its cats and caretakers.

Every moment the clock seemed to grow heavier. It had been all right in The Bunch of Grapes. He had been able to rest it on a window-sill alongside a lot of palms in bright brass pots. But now that he had to bear the whole weight of it himself, it seemed more massive and marble than ever. And the office coat didn't help. On going out through the swing doors, he had caught the string on the knob of the handle and the knot had been loosened. As though encouraged by this fleeting grip, the office coat was now feverishly struggling to undo itself. One despairing arm had succeeded in forcing its way out of the end of the parcel, and it waved imploringly at passers-by.

By rights Mr. Josser should have had his umbrella up. But that was impossible. Unless he had been given as many hands as a Hindu goddess he couldn't manage everything. There was nothing for it but to trudge on, swaying slightly under the uneven weight of his load while the fine snow, or sleet, or whatever it was, came sifting down out of the dark sky and covered him. Under the street lamps the pavements gleamed and glittered.

When he reached New Bridge Street he crossed the Embankment to get his tram. And, as he stood there waiting for it, he suddenly found himself remembering Mr. Battlebury's words about no more waiting in the rain. He resented them. Why shouldn't he wait about in the rain for trams if he wanted to? Waiting for trams in the rain suddenly seemed entirely delightful and proper. It was part of the old order of things that he had wanted it to go on for ever.

He got a place on top, right in front on the curved seat above the driver. It had not been easy getting up. The steep half-spiral staircase had beaten him at the first two attempts, and only the conductor's hand in the small of his back had finally got him there. Then the long narrow gangway in the centre had been just as difficult. It seemed to be exclusively fat people who were taking a Kennington tram that evening. They bulged. In their heavy overcoats they were as shapeless as rows of walruses sitting there. But extremely sensitive walruses. The edge of Mr. Josser's marble clock roused them and broad whiskery faces turned menacingly towards him as he passed. When he reached his seat and sank down gratefully, easing the clock carefully on to his knees, he could still hear the distant growlings.

He had to sit tight because they have a style of their own, trams; especially four-wheeled ones. Their motion is a mixture of all known movements. On apparently straight stretches of level road they turn corners and mount hills. And the number EX lurched and vaulted along as though it were dodging things. Past Cleopatra's Needle and the Sphinxes it went, heeling over as though it were at sea with a beam wind blowing, until it came sharp to rest under the shadow of Hungerford Bridge like a horse that has been reined in too abruptly. Then the driver gave the tram its head again and it rocked and bounced its way up to St. Stephen's Tower, until the thing had to be curbed to take the corner that would lead it across Westminster Bridge.

It was then that Mr. Josser remembered the envelope that Mr. Battlebury had given him. He had simply stuffed it away in his pocket and done nothing whatever about it. For a moment he thought that perhaps he had lost it, and with his free hand—the one that was holding only his office coat and his umbrella, that is—he began feverishly trying to get inside his overcoat and into the pocket of his jacket. At the third attempt, when he was getting really frightened at not finding it, the man next to him complained and Mr. Josser had to proceed more gently.

Even when he had got hold of it—and the thing was apparently sticking straight up simply asking to be removed—he was not much better off. He had to put the envelope between his teeth and tear it open with his left hand in little snatches.

He was still only picking at it when the conductor called out "Oval." That roused him. Stuffing the frayed envelope back into his pocket, he began desperately making for the stairs. The tram was just starting again when he reached them. And if the top hadn't emptied considerably he would never have got as far as that. As it was, the conductor who had violently helped him up now had to prevent him from plunging with his parcels straight into the roadway. He was openly scornful about Mr. Josser's qualities as a passenger.

By the time Mr. Josser had recovered himself, the tram was on its way again, plunging onwards towards Camberwell and Brixton. The only thing that Mr. Josser had against trams was that they left you standing right out in the middle of the traffic like a sandbin. He started to cross.

It was a pleasantly rural spot where he had landed, a kind of woody oasis in the surrounding desert of cement and brick. The iron railings of Kennington Park ran beside him and the outline of the Prince Consort's châlet showed through the trees. But it was the other side of the road that he wanted to get to, the side where the shops were. He was going to do a little late Christmas shopping.

The first shop that he went into was a wine merchant's, and he bought a bottle of Fine Rich Ruby Connoisseur's Port. He paid four shillings for it and stowed the bottle away in the pocket of his greatcoat. Then he went next door into a tobacconist's and bought two eightpenny cigars—Pride of Perth (Havana) they were called. They were good robust-looking cigars with scarlet-and-gilt bands round them, and they looked as though they could stand a lot of handling.

Finally he went to a small shop a little further up the road and bought a box of floral crackers. His small granddaughter was coming to spend Christmas with them, and he foresaw the afternoon passing off more agreeably if she had plenty to play with—gilt whistles to blow, and tooters, and little glass cats that could hang on a watch chain, and dice, and toy fire balloons and puzzles. Mrs. Josser had already bought the child a fairy-doll, and Mr. Josser was really only being indulgent now.

If he hadn't bought the crackers he might not have dropped the clock. But the third parcel, and the big bulge in his pocket that the port bottle made, were too much for him. Almost as soon as he got out of the shop the trouble began. The office coat started slipping and Mr. Josser gripped his arms into his sides like a Guardsman to hold it in place. Then his umbrella, still hung over his arm, came obstinately swinging round in between his legs, and tried to trip him up. And then everything happened at once.

In trying to release the umbrella, the box of crackers got squeezed too tight and began to split open, and in seeking to protect the crackers he temporarily loosened his hold on the clock. The clock was far too heavy for anything but the firmest holding. For a single frantic moment Mr. Josser played with the thing like a juggler. Only not a good one. The trick just went to pieces before his eyes. Before he could stop it, the clock hit the pavement with the awful crash of stone on stone, and a long hollow *booong* rolled up into the night.

The clock itself was extraordinarily difficult to pick up—difficult, that is, for a man who is already carrying his office coat, an umbrella and a box of crackers. He would never have managed it, in fact, if a passer-by hadn't come along and offered to help him. With his aid, Mr. Josser finally got the clock up—there were queer jangling noises inside it as he moved it—and then the stranger piled the box of crackers on top of everything else. Mr. Josser was simply a pair of legs walking along under a large and awkward load. He was the man with the ledgers again.

By the time he reached Dulcimer Street and turned in at the gate-way to No. 10 he was sweating. Sweating on a night like this. And having reached No. 10 he was not much better off. There he was face to face with his own front door and he couldn't do a thing about it. He was an Englishman locked out of his own castle. His key was on a ring at the end of a long nickel-silver chain. And even if he hadn't been all loaded up like a camel he would still have had to undress himself to get at it. As it was, he had to proceed very cautiously, first of all setting the clock down on the stone balustrade, then balancing the box of crackers on top of the clock, and finally crowning the crackers with his office coat. What was more, as soon as he had opened the front door he had to gather the whole lot up again, and re-close the front door with his heel. But there was nothing very difficult in that: he had done it that way for years.

The door of the sitting-room in front of him opened and Mrs. Josser came out. She put her hand up to the chain hanging from the gas chandelier, and the hall was filled with a warm yellow light. The light showed Mrs. Josser as a small elderly woman with steel-frame glasses and grey straying hair. At first glance, she was extraordinarily like her husband. It was as though the two of them had agreed to share everything, including a likeness.

"Good gracious," she said. "I thought something had happened to you."

Mr. Josser shook his head.

"Just shopping," he said. "Just been doing a bit of shopping."

He bent forward and kissed her. It was a perfunctory, husbandly sort of kiss.

"You with your chest, hanging about on a night like this," Mrs. Josser went on.

"Sorry I'm late," he began.

Then he stopped short and gave a little laugh.

"Seems funny that it matters," he said. "All my time's my own now."

He paused because something else had come into his mind. And suddenly he went over to Mrs. Josser and kissed her again. He kissed her once on the forehead, once on the side of her face, and once full on her lips. It was no longer Mr. Frederick Josser, *retired*, who was standing there. It was the ghost of Mr. Josser, junior, the courageous young clerk who was getting married on twenty-five shillings a week and his prospects.

But Mrs. Josser did not realise that. She remained surprised, hungry and a trifle incredulous. Incredulous, but still flattered.

CHAPTER 2

I

STANDING at the corner of Dulcimer Street you can see down the length of the whole terrace. It stretches in an unbroken row from Dove Street at one end to Swan Walk at the other. And they are certainly fine houses. Or have been. They date from 1839, when the neighbourhood was still select, exclusive and sought after. They now front the street—solid-looking and graceful—receding in a gentle curve towards the river, like a monument erected to the good taste of our grandfathers; an inhabited historical monument with the history flaking off in great chunks of discoloured stucco that occasionally comes flopping down into the areas.

There had been changes, of course, during the last hundred years. And most of them had been for the worse. Down at the Swan Walk end, for instance, the large letters J. M. BILL & SONS, BUILDERS AND DECORATORS had been painted right across the frontage, and ladders and planks were stored openly in the basement. No. 24 next door was a normal private residence, a bit too thickly sublet perhaps, but a private residence nevertheless. Next door again, however, at No. 22 commerce had killed home life, and the look of the whole place was spoiled by a framed canvas screen let into the front window with the words A. LEVINE, HIGH-CLASS TAILOR, ALTERATIONS AND REPAIRS A SPECIALITY written there. The rest of the houses were private dwellings, with a vague and easily missed, but nevertheless real and important, social lift-up, as you got to the Dove Street end.

They all had three storeys above ground and one below. And they all had porches supported on slender imitation Grecian pillars, and high, rather steep steps—like the ones that Mr. Josser had floundered up two nights before—leading to the panelled and bevelled front doors with the fanlights over them. They were large houses with eight to ten good rooms apiece.

Across the road on the south side of the street it was different. The houses there had been built in 1888. They were simply six-roomed affairs in grey brick with small box-like bow-windows, and no pillars. The two end ones had even long since decided to give up even trying to look like houses, and had become shops—one a general grocery store and the other a newsagent's and tobacconist's.

The whole of the south side was mean, ungracious and undeniably depressing. And, of course, it was the south side that Mr. Josser saw every time he looked out of his window. It was at the south side that he was looking now, while he was waiting for the kettle to boil.

It was Christmas morning, and he had got on all his clothes except his collar and tie. His feet were encased in a pair of carpet slippers that had once been rich and plushy but were now bald and drab. And his blue cardigan was buttoned right up to the throat because it was chilly.

The tea-things were ready on the tray beside him, and he had mopped up the wet circle that the bottom of the milk-bottle had made on the kitchen table. Altogether, he was pretty expert at getting tea. It was the result of long practice. He always helped to soften the shock of each new day by bringing Mrs. Josser a cup of early morning tea. It was good strong stuff the way he made it. And it needed only a handful of fresh tea-leaves added to make it an equally rousing cup for breakfast-time. This small stratagem had the merits of economy, time-saving and *body*. Those cups of brewed tea fairly routed sleep.

But this morning he had more than tea-cups on the tray: there were two large parcels there as well. The parcels had labels on them, addressed in Mr. Josser's handwriting—high, cursive and flourishing. The labels read: "To Carrie, to wish her a Happy Christmas from Fred"—it was, he worked out, the forty-first Christmas present that he had given his wife; and "To Doris, with love from her Dad." He had bought Mrs. Josser a large Spanish shawl which in the shop-window he had seen described as a bargain and he had bought Doris an ornamental jar of jasmine bath salts.

It was the shawl that was worrying him. Now that it was too late to change the thing he wondered why he had ever bought it at all. For, when he came to think of it, he realised that Mrs. Josser never wore shawls. And, if she had done, she would have been certain to choose something rather quieter. Something in brown, or dark grey, or black even. But there it was. The kettle was boiling, and it was the shawl or nothing. He made the tea, gloomily pondering.

Mrs. Josser was already sitting up when he reached the bedroom. She had hauled up the Venetian blinds, and the blank morning light came seeping into the room through the lace curtains, revealing the red mahogany wardrobe, the wash-hand stand, the chest of drawers, the dressing-table.

"Happy Christmas," said Mr. Josser.

"Happy Christmas," Mrs. Josser answered.

Mr. Josser sat down on the side of the bed and carefully lowered the tray on to the counterpane.

"Got a little present for you, dear," he said, adding after a pause, "Always change it if you don't like it."

"What is it?" said Mrs. Josser, beginning to open the paper.

Seen against the pale blue of the quilt, the shawl looked even more lurid and foreign and exclamatory than Mr. Josser had remembered it. It seemed to be crying out for hot sun and a bull-fight. But Mrs. Josser did not waver. She gave the thing a twist as though she had been wearing shawls all her life and folded it round her shoulders. She even rubbed her cheek against it.

"It's a real beauty," she said. "You never ought to have."

"So you do like it, do you?" Mr. Josser asked, relieved.

"It's ever so nice," Mrs. Josser answered him. "Just what I wanted."

She paused and gave Mr. Josser a small flat parcel that she had been hiding.

"And here's a little something for you," she said. "You know you haven't got any."

Before he opened it, Mr. Josser knew what it was: it was handkerchiefs. It was always handkerchiefs. During the whole of his married life he had never bought any handkerchiefs himself, and never been without them.

"They've got your initial on them," Mrs. Josser told him.

Balancing the tray carefully with one hand so that the things shouldn't slide, he bent forward and kissed her.

"Thank you, dear," he said. "I was needing them."

He was sitting back, absent-mindedly sipping his tea—he had a noisy, rather succulent hiss that irritated Mrs. Josser at times—when he happened to glance up and catch sight of his wife's face. She was looking at the shawl and her expression had altered. She seemed to be taking the measure of the thing. Sizing it up like an enemy.

Mr. Josser leaned forward.

"You *do* like it, don't you?" he asked again.

"It's ever so nice," Mrs. Josser repeated with less conviction. "I said so."

There was a pause.

"You don't think it's too bright, do you?" he asked.

"It's a bit bright, isn't it?" Mrs. Josser admitted.

"Will it go with anything you've got?" he asked.

Mrs. Josser thought.

"I should have to try it," she said cautiously.

"Because I could change it," Mr. Josser went on mechanically.

Mrs. Josser did not reply immediately.

"Where did you buy it?" she asked.

"In the City," he answered vaguely.

There was another pause.

"Did you notice if they had any thick winter gloves?" she asked. "Knitted ones."

2

But there were more than the Jossers waking up to Christmas morning south of the river. There were even more than the Jossers in No. 10 Dulcimer Street.

Starting from the top of the house, with the attic suite, there was Mr. Puddy. Mr. Puddy was a widower, a morose, fattish man. Sometimes he said "Good evening" when he met you on the stairs, and sometimes he didn't. You could never quite be sure of him. In age, he was about midway across the grey wilderness between the fifties and the sixties. And he had known better days. Indeed, from the way he referred to it, he seemed to derive a gloomy satisfaction from the fact that he had come down a bit in the world. He was, as a matter of fact, still coming down. And, at his present rate, there would soon be no stopping him. At thirty-five he had been manager of a small dairy; at forty-five he had been reduced to a common roundsman; and at fifty the dairy had got rid of him altogether. Since then he had been employed on and off at various odd jobs—though sometimes for months on end Society managed to get along without asking Mr. Puddy to raise a hand to help. He had been caretaker to a succession of different firms and in his time he had taken care of ladies' clothing, celluloid combs—a lot of care was needed here because of the danger of fire—and gramophone cabinets. He had been hotel-porter, polisher in an undertaker's, dispatch clerk in a laundry and temporary postal sorter.

He was a postal sorter at the moment. But looking into the future, the very near future—next week, in fact—he saw another of his free periods looming up.

It was greatly to Mr. Puddy's credit that in all his ups-and-downs he had contrived to dress respectably. This was specially creditable as each new up started on the level of the last down. But it was also to his advantage. Because, if he hadn't taken pains about his appearance he would never have been seriously considered even for the skylight rooms. It was a very respectable house, was No. 10. As it was, however, Mr. Puddy used to go off in the morning to the most undazzling of jobs with the responsible air of managerial dignity still wrapped about him. And the house gained rather than lost by housing him.

He always, except on quite short journeys, carried an attaché case. Admittedly, nowadays his case contained nothing but his lunch. But stray passers-by weren't to know this. And they weren't to know that, in the really bad periods, Mr. Puddy, a man who liked his chop or steak and his boiled suet roll or treacle pudding, was sometimes reduced to several thick slices of bread and butter—packed face to face, so when he separated them they came apart with the sound of a long sticky kiss—and a piece of soapy yellow cheese.

Food and Mr. Puddy were in the same order of things. It occupied the place in his life which drinking occupies in some weaker natures. In consequence, he was almost always at it. On some nights he would go straight on with his evening meal, consuming a whole cold pie followed by slice after slice of bread and jam, or bread and syrup, or bread and fish-paste, until the loaf was a gaunt ruin, and Mr. Puddy was sitting back in his chair, his waistcoat undone, satiated, sickly, but in a dumb way happy and contented. One of the recurrent sadnesses of his single state was that boiled puddings no longer appeared on the table. On the other hand there was no one to expect him to talk at meals. And Mr. Puddy was against talking.

At this moment he was bending over the gas cooker on the landing shovelling rashers of bacon into a pan. He had broken two eggs into a cup and arranged a piece of fried bread alongside the rashers. On one end of the table the bread and butter and marmalade were set out in readiness and the milk-bottle was standing on the table. He had taken down the biggest teapot so that there should be no danger of a shortage and he was about to settle down to some pretty serious feeding. Luckily he was in the second shift at the sorting office and he had the next two hours entirely to himself—to himself and his breakfast.

Taken altogether it was about as good a Christmas as he remembered.

3

In the third floor back, it was being a very different kind of Christmas.

A single lady lived there and she was only just waking up. This wasn't surprising, considering the hours she kept. She never got back till about two or three in the morning, and by arrangement she let herself in with her own key and no questions asked. There couldn't really be any other way about it. She was a part of London's night-life and no one could be expected to sit up until the small hours simply to see that she got home all right.

It was the sort of life that parsons preach against that she was leading. There was danger in it. And temptation. By the time she got back to Dulcimer Street she was often a bit of a wreck. And into that sleeping thoroughfare she brought with her something of another and more glittering life. She was like an ambassadress from a different world—a world of blondes with their hair half-way down their shoulders and dark foreign-looking gentlemen and chemin-de-fer and champagne and lobster patties and the sound of saxophones. And every morning when she woke up she remembered that the two worlds did not mix.

She still called herself an actress. But there was not much sense in the term any longer. She was now simply the old girl with the dyed hair who sat behind the counter in the ladies' cloakroom and had a saucer, with a few pins in it, in front of her, ready to receive the tips. Her salary, even though the club was in Dover Street in a very select neighbourhood, was only a pound a week. And what she could make on the side. The latter was not much. It was astonishing how many Mayfair heiresses tried to get away without leaving even sixpence.

She was just beginning to stir now, pulling the muddle of bedclothes more closely round her shoulders because she was cold. And when at last she was awake she lay there without moving. After all, there was nothing to get up for. She wasn't expecting anyone. She wasn't late for anything. She wasn't even early.

After a bit she roused herself and thrust a thin ancient arm out of bed. The room was so small that the dressing-table was within arm's length, and she was able to reach the hand mirror that she had been groping for. When she had got it she simply lay back looking at her own image.

"Oh God, I'm old," she said to herself. "I'm the limit."

She tilted the mirror a little and raised her head so that the light fell across her face, showing up the wrinkles, the saggings, the loose pouches of skin under the eyes, the patches of last night's colour.

"Old," she went on. "Old, I'm just a bleeding sunset. I'm the afterglow." Tears came into her eyes as she remembered something unpleasant that one of the hostesses had said to her last night, and she continued her soliloquy unrestrained.

"She said it," she admitted. "I ought to be dead. I'm as old as Methuselah. As old as the hills. I'm the oldest thing left on earth. I'm as old as creation. I'm the space between the stars."

She was crying quite openly now.

"I haven't got any family. I haven't had any Christmas cards. I can't even remember the names of my lovers. I'm a week behind with the rent and this week will be due to-morrow. My new second-hand shoes hurt me. And I've got a pain in my side that won't go away. There isn't a man would look at me, not if he was ever so. I can't get my rings off because my knuckles are so swollen. I haven't got a winter coat. I haven't got a Christmas dinner. I haven't got any fresh bird-seed for Duke. I haven't got a box of crackers. I haven't even got a cigarette. . . ."

It wasn't much that she was asking: nothing that a Christian shouldn't have. A perishing post card would have been enough. And not even a real old-fashioned blush-raiser at that. She'd given up hoping for "To your brown eyes, Connie darling. May our two hearts soon beat together. How about next Friday? Cheerio, George;" and that sort of thing. Something far less would have contented her. For instance: "Just a line from your old Mum to wish you the kind of Christmas you'd wish yourself. Don't leave it too long before I see you again;" or "To our darling Mother in memory of the happy times she used to give us all;" or "To dear old Connie from the girls. May your shadow never grow less, Babs." Anything, in fact, to show that she mattered. That someone else couldn't get along without her. But what was the use of wishing? She hadn't got a mother. There weren't any children to make a fuss of her. And the only Babs she'd ever known was a dark girl from Middlesbrough who had a hasty temper and married a waiter. It was just silly imagining that she might get a post card from *her*. Or from anyone else.

She dried her eyes on a corner of the sheet.

"Now, Connie," she told herself. "Don't you let your imagination run away with you. There's nothing for you, dear. Nor will there be. You're washed up. You're high and dry. You're what the sea left behind it. You're on the rocks."

Then a change came over her and she brightened up. She had just remembered something that was in her handbag on the washstand. It was a nearly new lipstick in a silver gilt case. Brunette Rose, the colour was called. Connie had come by it the previous evening. One of the visitors to the night-club had left it for a moment on the counter, and Connie had popped it into her handbag. Then, when the lady had come back, Connie had helped her to look for it. She had even gone down on all fours. But it was hopeless, and she had told the lady so. She had repented afterwards. But not now. The lipstick was nice to have. Nice to have *something* new on Christmas Day.

She looked up at the bird-cage with the duster over it.

"Happy Christmas, Duke," she said. "Be a good birdie."

4

Come down one floor lower, and what sort of Christmas is it?

Perfect.

And that's because there are two people and not just one lonely one. Mrs. Boon and her son, Percy, are such a devoted pair. As is only natural, it is the woman who shows her feelings more than the man. He's tough. He works in a garage. And what with night shifts and rush jobs coming in at the last moment and delivering cars to purchasers in remote parts of London and evenings off at dance halls—and hasn't he earned them?—she doesn't see much of him.

But his mother doesn't mind. He's got his head screwed on the right way and at twenty he's doing better than any other young man she knows. You could tell that he was in the good money simply by looking at him. He's easily the best-dressed man in Dulcimer Street. Some of his suits even look a bit too good for the neighbourhood—his purple cashmere and his shadow check, in particular. But a nice-looking young fellow can carry a smart suit. And Percy Boon is certainly nice-looking. It's only his hands that worry Mrs. Boon. She used to be proud of his hands, so thin and long-fingered like his father's. Now they are rough and filthy with oil that the grease solvent only leaves more deeply imbedded. And the fingernails. They've practically gone. As a little boy he had the loveliest filbert nails. But with the work he does they're just torn and ragged. And they're stained too because he smokes such a lot. It's a pity about his smoking. He gets through packet after packet—Gold Flake, Player's, Top Score, Weights, Woodbines—anything that he can get hold of. Forty or fifty a day. Nerves of course. He isn't naturally a heavy smoker—of that Mrs. Boon is sure. And if the garage works him so hard that he has to smoke to soothe himself, it would have seemed only fair that they should keep him supplied with cigarettes. But they don't. And so Percy has to go on pushing out his sixpences and shillings simply to keep going. The only consolation is that, with the good money he gets, he can afford it.

If he didn't get good money he couldn't possibly have afforded a handbag like the one he's just given to his mother. It's a fine big handbag on any showing, with a lot of pockets and two silver-looking knobs on top and a mirror and a design like the rising sun let into the front in a different kind of leather. It's the sort of handbag that a duchess might carry. Indeed, the only thing that is wrong with it is that Mrs. Boon, who is a small woman, doesn't feel equal to the job of hauling it about.

She herself has given Percy a lighter. She had saved up for it for months, paring little bits off the housekeeping week by week—until she could buy the kind she wanted. They cost a lot of money, that sort. An awful lot. It had been silly, of course. It was too much to spend on any lighter. But why shouldn't she? she had asked herself. Wouldn't you, if you hadn't got a husband and every bit of pleasure and relief you got in life came from your son? Wouldn't you make a bit of a splash for his sake just once in the year?

They've just finished breakfast, Mrs. Boon and Percy. Mrs. Boon has been talking cheerfully all through the meal because she is happy. But it's been a one-sided kind of conversation because Percy has been reading all the time. Propped up against the marmalade pot he has got his copy of *True Adventure Stories*. His long legs are stuck out underneath the table, and the ash from his cigarette is dropping everywhere, on to the table-cloth, into his saucer, on to his plate, into the cup. Mrs. Boon doesn't like ash in the washing-up, and keeps on pushing a china Present-from-Weymouth ash-tray in front of him. But he ignores it. He is oblivious to ash-trays. He is not at the breakfast table at all. He is in a submarine. The submarine rests upside down on soft sand in forty fathoms, and the oxygen is used up. The port engine is on fire. The captain has gone mad and is threatening the crew with his revolver. Two of the plates have buckled and a thin trickle of water is entering the forward compartment. The chief engineer gives them another ten minutes of life. He is nonchalantly playing cards and all of the cards keep coming up black. . . .

"Oh, Percy, not in the butter," Mrs. Boon is saying. "It'll all have to be scraped off."

There is something in her voice that breaks the spell. Percy stubs his cigarette-end out on the first plate that comes handy.

"Gotter phone someone," he says.

"Not on Christmas Day," Mrs. Boon complains. "Won't they ever leave you alone?"

"Back in a minute," Percy answers. "It's a chap wants to buy a car. Only time I can get him."

He rises, pulls down his double-breasted waistcoat, gives a little tug to his dainty coloured handkerchief, lights another cigarette and goes out.

Mrs. Boon stands at the window wondering how long he will be out. She is sad that on Christmas Day of all days she can't have him entirely to herself. It is this sadness that is now showing in her face, making her eyes look deeper and more hollow, and the lines in her face longer. And this is strange because, with Percy about the house, Mrs. Boon is such a happy woman.

It's almost as though she's waiting for something sad that hasn't yet happened.

5

We've already met the Jossers, so we might as well go straight on down the steep flight of dark stairs leading into the basement.

Here in the nether depths it is Mrs. Vizzard who reigns. She, too, is a widow. But unlike Mrs. Boon she hasn't got a Percy. She's childless. And as much alone in the world as Connie. But better provided for. Mrs. Vizzard doesn't suffer any morning miseries. She can look in a hand mirror without wanting to cut her throat. She isn't the space between the stars. And that is because she is a woman of property. The house is hers. She had got her husband to make it over to her when she saw how things were going. And she had acted only just in time. When the Lord—impatient, it seemed, for Mr. Vizzard's company—had snatched him from her in his prime, the family business had yielded nothing. It was an upholsterer's, and even as far back as 1910 Mr. Vizzard had complained that people no longer wanted the good stuff, the horsehair, the leather, the cane bottoms. Already a weaker generation was demanding flock and velour and cretonne covers. And Mrs. Vizzard had watched the decline. She had seen Mr. Vizzard pale and hairy and distracted wondering where the next week's wages for his workmen was coming from. Then she had pounced.

In the result, she had one anxiety. The Lease. There was only another eighteen years to run. Eighteen years; and she was forty-six. She hoped to be comfortably dead in eighteen years' time. In fact, she was *counting* on being dead. But there was always the possibility that she might live on and on, right through the sixties and beyond, like a runaway. And after she'd got to sixty-four she would be living on her capital. That, in Mrs. Vizzard's religion, was the greatest of all sins. It loomed bigger than adultery. Bigger than stealing. Bigger even than murder. *They* were the unnecessary sins: if you read your Bible and took care not to lose your head in moments of excitement, you could avoid them altogether. But living on capital was different. It happened sometimes to the most respectable people. It was like secret drinking. Homes were broken up, lives ruined, neighbours mystified—and all because of living on capital.

It was to avoid these disasters, and this sin, that Mrs. Vizzard lived so carefully in a front basement even while the going was still good.

And in the result, never seeing any sunlight except what seeped through into the area, there had come to be a pale waxiness about her. A suggestion of Madonna lilies. Her hair, which was still dark, was worn so flat to the head that it might have been strapped there: it ended in a hard circular knob riveted into the nape of the neck.

No one could have said that she was not ladylike. She was positively steeped in a kind of austere, demure breeding. For instance, though she let rooms, she never hung a card in her window. Elsewhere Dulcimer Street was fairly decked out with such things—BED-SITTING-ROOM TO LET; FLAT TO LET; TWO GOOD ROOMS TO LET; ROOM FOR SINGLE GENTLEMAN; LIGHT BASEMENT TO BE LET. Even BED AND BREAKFAST, clumsily and inexpertly lettered by hand—but that was at the Swan Walk end. Mrs. Vizzard's own trade announcements appeared in the specialist pages of *Dalton's Weekly*. It cost more that way but you got a better class of tenant.

No one in Dulcimer Street knew anything about Mrs. Vizzard's private life. Indeed, at first glance, it seemed that there couldn't be any. But it was there, all right. And pretty highly coloured. Mrs. Vizzard was a Spiritualist. In the crumbling but imposing building with a wooden notice board outside announcing THE SOUTH LONDON SPIRITUALIST MOVEMENT, she conversed with Aztec princesses and Egyptian priests and Red Indian Chiefs. Conversed while the medium groaned and panted, and the table bounced about and shifted itself and luminous tambourines and trumpets drifted over her head, and the odour of violets filled the air and cold winds blew. It was all momentous and terrifying, and somewhere amid the hubbub and the confusion Mrs. Vizzard waited patiently for Mr. Vizzard's voice to come through. After fourteen years she was still waiting.

At this moment—ten forty-five on Christmas morning—she was sitting quite upright on one of the massive leather-backed chairs that was all that remained of her old dining-room. The table in front of her was arranged like a desk, and she was running over her rent books. There was something at once loving and superfluous about the operation. She knew them by heart already. And they were all in order. All except Connie's, that is. Connie's rent book remained the one disgraceful blot in that saga of sound finance.

Mrs. Vizzard sat there, pursing her lips over it, and wondering when to bring the axe down.

6

And, last of all, completing the census of 10 Dulcimer Street there was the back basement. It was empty at the moment and for some reason it was hanging fire. Mrs. Vizzard had even tried advertising in a spiritualist weekly, *The Spirit World*.

But, apparently, apart from herself, only spirits read *The Spirit World*.

CHAPTER 3

I

IT WAS being a good Christmas. The day had worn on light-hearted but exhausting. During most of the time Mrs. Josser seemed to have been either cooking or serving food or washing-up. The cooking alone had been tremendous. There was a kind of wholesale and Oriental magnificence about it; it might have been a company of satraps that she was expecting.

And this was remarkable because Mrs. Josser herself was a light eater. She would probably pick at a bit of turkey and crumble a mince-pie; but that would be all. And she admitted quite frankly that after doing a lot of cooking she felt less like eating than ever. But what was even more remarkable was that all over London other women, most of them fairy-eaters like Mrs. Josser, were similarly slaving away as chefs and pastry-cooks, every one of them obstinately convinced that Christmas without other people's over-eating wouldn't seem like Christmas at all.

Mrs. Josser was one of the comparatively lucky ones. She had her daughter to help her. And Doris did her share. But it was a small share. The most that could be got out of the girl was a little unenthusiastic bed-making and a certain amount of rather desultory washing-up. After that, Doris's domestic energy always flagged. It died away to nothing. And always, just when Mrs. Josser was expecting to have a nice cup of tea brought to her, she would find Doris curled up with a book somewhere. At times, the clash of interests led to unpleasantness between mother and daughter. The two of them would stare stonily at each other, and between the two generations there would be a gulf that would remain yawning and unbridgeable for a whole afternoon—usually a Sunday afternoon.

But, on the whole, Mrs. Josser was perfectly satisfied with things as they were. She had done her utmost, with the help of the Kennington Secretarial College, to make Doris a bit better than herself. And she felt that it was unreasonable to drag her back down again. As for Doris, she remained aloof, romantic and unsure of herself. Also a trifle ashamed of her parents, her brother Ted's wife and the whole background of Dulcimer Street.

But then they were all—except, apparently, Ted—ashamed of Ted's wife. At this very moment Mrs. Josser was sitting back, bitterly regarding the girl through half-closed eyes. She didn't belong: that much was obvious. There was something definitely dollish and un-Josserish about her. It wasn't merely her light golden hair worn longer than was decent for the mother of a child. Or her ridiculous childlike figure. Or her small slim hands with the two enormous artificial-stone rings on them. Or the piece of Burma jewellery worn glitteringly over one breast instead of in the centre where any sensible woman would have worn it. Or the shoes cut away so that the big toe was open to the weather. Or the clip-on ear-rings. (Mrs. Josser's own ears had been pierced and it seemed unreasonable that so much smartness on Cynthia's part should have been obtained at no pain at all.) Or the name Cynthia itself. There had never been another Cynthia in the Josser family. And it had injured Mrs. Josser more deeply than she could say that Ted's daughter, Baby, her own grandchild, should have been christened with the same absurd, irritating name. It was just one of those things that she didn't like and had to keep quiet about.

And this wasn't all. There was Cynthia's voice. And her laugh. Mrs. Josser was prepared to admit that anyone had a right to speak as he or she pleased. But giggling was another matter. Not to mince words, Cynthia was a titterer. And no Josser before her had ever tittered.

Even so she would have been prepared to overlook that annoying simpering laugh if only the girl's background had been better. But no amount of hushing it up was ever going to put that right. The plain fact remained that Ted had met her on her own ground in the one-and-threes. And not merely once, by accident. But night after night by arrangement and subterfuge. Sometimes seeing the same film three or four times over in the course of his fatal infatuation. Ted Josser, the pride of the family, the steady young man who at twenty-five had risen to be assistant manager in the fancy goods department of the local Co-op., had fallen for an usherette.

The afternoon, so far as the young people were concerned, had reached the stage of placid somnolence which is the result of plenty of food, and good fire and no windows open. Only Baby remained wakeful and energetic. The others were in a state not far removed from hibernation. Mr. Josser in his armchair kept dozing off and coming to and dozing off again. And Ted in his large, comfortable way undid several of his buttons and redistributed himself. Doris was reading. And Baby continued to destroy a doll.

Then Uncle Henry arrived.

He had been anticipated—his impending presence had hung over the party—but, in a way, not been expected. There was always something hauntingly uncertain about the exact moment of Uncle Henry's arrivals. He was a man of many engagements and much information. A greengrocer by trade—he had a shop with two assistants in Stoke Newington—he also cultivated outside interests. The chief of these at the moment was treasurership of the South London Parliament and Debating Society. And it was a long way from his business to the Parliament. In fact, it was only his bicycle that saved him. Independent of buses and trams, openly contemptuous of the Underground, he came and went on his green bicycle as his impetuous heart directed. It was nothing for Henry Knockell to turn up in his Norfolk jacket and cycling knickers at half-past ten on a Sunday evening simply because he had picked up a depressing piece of news that he wanted to share with someone.

Reliable information, dubious information, false information—it was all one to Uncle Henry. The only thing that he demanded was a steady flow of fresh sensation. Rumours about Continental Royalty, about reputable City companies hovering on the verge of bankruptcy, about impending changes in the Government, about corruption in the Metropolitan police force, about dissension among the Bishops—he was a free-thinker himself, and was particularly partial to ecclesiastical scandal—and about war. Above all, rumours about war. For the past seven years, Uncle Henry had been emphatically prophesying war. During times when trade had not been too good, it had been pretty much the only thing that had kept him going.

He had become worse, if anything, since Mrs. Knockell had died. With her had passed away the only modifying influence. It was she who had taken a supervisory interest in his clothing, not allowing him in her time to wear that ridiculous Norfolk jacket except when on holiday. But with his face, itself, she had of course been powerless to tamper. It was a startling and slightly alarming sort of face; the kind of face that is to be seen on the shoulders of dissenting ministers and patent-medicine pedlars in country fairs. The hair was grey and bushy, the cheeks lean and cadaverous, the chin long. An untrimmed moustache almost obscured the mouth. But it was the eyes that were the remarkable part. They were deep set and gimlet-like. Or at least one of them was. For, while the right eye was glaring incriminatingly, the left one was simply ranging playfully around as though looking for fun. Until you really got to know Uncle Henry it was all rather disconcerting.

He came straight in and sat down in Mr. Josser's chair, meditatively cracking his knuckle joints.

"You've heard about Hitler's latest?" he began.

Mr. Josser shook his head. So far as he and Hitler were concerned they seemed to get along without telling each other anything.

"He's castrating the Jews."

"I don't believe it."

It was Mrs. Josser who had spoken. As his sister she felt herself entitled to contradict him. And in all the years she had known him she'd never found him right yet.

"He wouldn't dare," she added.

Uncle Henry turned and faced her, cyclops-like.

"In every German hospital there's a special ward where . . ."

This was worse still, and Mrs. Josser roused herself. She looked meaningly at Doris.

"It's time that *somebody* got some tea," she said.

She didn't really expect Doris to get tea. After all, it was as much her Christmas as it was anyone else's. But what she did want was to have her *offer*.

As it turned out, however, it was Cynthia, silly fragile little Cynthia, who volunteered.

"Let me get it," she said with a giggle, as she got up. "I'm ever so good at getting tea. Aren't I, Ted?"

But Mrs. Josser had risen too. She had no intention whatever of allowing an ex-usherette to go chipping bits off her tea service.

"You sit down," she said firmly. "You're the visitor."

"But I like getting tea," Cynthia answered, still giggling. "I do reely."

Mrs. Josser skilfully changed her tactics.

"Mind Baby," she said warningly. "She's going over to my work-box again."

The giggle changed to a little shriek of anxiety and Cynthia rushed over to her daughter.

"Nasty pins," she said. "Box full of nasty pins."

But pins apparently were exactly what Baby wanted. She was a substantial and determined sort of child. Taken over all, she had the appearance of a small but thick-set policewoman: if crossed, it seemed that she might start blowing a whistle or applying a half-Nelson. At this moment, she was stretching both hands grimly towards the work-box and pushing out her nether lip to indicate her feelings in the matter.

"I know," Cynthia said quickly. "We'll take her in the kitchen with us."

It was obvious that she was anxious to avoid any direct clash of wills with her daughter.

But Mrs. Josser wouldn't hear of it.

"And let her get herself scalded to death with the kettle?" she asked scornfully. "Not in my kitchen, you don't."

With that she left them. And to distract Baby, Cynthia was now making a new doll walk along the floor towards her, Mr. Josser was blowing out a paper squeaker that expanded to nearly three feet when fully inflated and Ted was trying to dance her up and down on his foot.

Baby, meanwhile, was still trying purposefully to get over to the work-box.

2

After so much pandemonium, the kitchen at the other end of the passage seemed wonderfully quiet and civilised. Mrs. Josser let out a long "Ah" of relief when she got there. Compared with what she had been up against, the task of cutting bread and butter single-handed was nothing.

She had not been out in the kitchen long, however, before she heard a sound like that of someone crying. It was faint, but unmistakable. Quite unmistakable. There is something about human misery that is sharply and insistently recognisable. Ordinary conversation, or laughter even, in another room passes unnoticed: the ear simply doesn't trouble about it. But with crying—especially the low sobbing kind—it is different. The misery communicates itself. It is impossible to work within ear-shot of it. Mrs. Josser put down the bread knife and listened.

It couldn't be Doris who was crying because Mrs. Josser had seen her only a moment before. It wasn't coming from Mrs. Boon's room because, if it had been, it would have been louder. It wasn't coming from Mrs. Vizzard because it was coming down and not up. It couldn't, even if the sex of the sound had been right, have been coming from Mr. Puddy because he was out. That left only Connie.

Mrs. Josser opened a jar of fish-paste and set out six little paper d'oyleys on the tray. Connie's unhappiness, she told herself, was no affair of hers. And, in any case, she wasn't the sort of person to go pushing her nose into other people's business.

But the sound of sobbing, faint and almost imperceptible, at times, continued.

Mrs. Josser had finished cutting the bread and butter. She opened half a dozen small buns that she had bought, and put jam inside them. Then she took the Christmas cake out of the tin and stood back admiring it. It was a handsome, solid-looking cake, reinforced within by raisins and cherries and sultanas, and covered with a thick blanket of marzipan paste and pink-and-white icing. It was while she was still looking at it that she became uncomfortably aware of the sobbing again.

She hesitated. Hesitated quite a long time, in fact. Because she didn't really approve of Connie. Then, irritably, she decided that something must be done about it. She just couldn't bear to have another human being in the house so miserable as all that. It spoilt everything.

All the same, as she mounted the top flight of stairs she felt a bit dubious: she had known Connie before. And when she came to the door she paused. She raised her hand to knock and then let it fall to her side again. There was no doubt about it, however, Connie was in a pretty bad way. Now that she was so near to it, Mrs. Josser could hear that it was the sort of sobbing that began high in the throat and ended somewhere deep inside the chest. It was the real thing, all right.

And it was so loud that Connie didn't even hear Mrs. Josser the first time she knocked. Then, when she had knocked the second time, there was a sudden alarming silence. It was as though Connie had died abruptly in the middle of her misery. Mrs. Josser turned the handle of the door and walked in.

It was obvious from the first glance at her that Connie must have been crying for a good long time. For even longer than Mrs. Josser had heard her. Her eyes had bright red rims to them and the tears had been coming so fast that she had been unable to catch all of them. The bosom of her pink silk blouse was splashed and dappled.

Mrs. Josser stood in the doorway regarding her.

"Connie!" was all she said.

But Connie was apparently in no mood for answering. She just buried her face in her hands and seemed to be trying to hide herself.

"It's nothing," she said. "There isn't anything anybody can do about it. It's just the way things are."

And the sobbing started up again.

"But it must be *something*," Mrs. Josser pointed out.

Having come up all those stairs, she wasn't going to be put off with that sort of reply. In any case, she didn't propose to go back down again until, somehow or other, she had stopped the noise that Connie was making.

The sobbing ceased abruptly.

"No, it isn't," Connie persisted. "It isn't the first time I've skipped a meal because there isn't anything to eat. I'll get over it. I'm slimming."

"Nothing to eat?" Mrs. Josser demanded.

Connie shook her head.

"And nothing that'll fit the meter," she added. "If you'd like to eat a raw potato on Christmas Day, you're welcome."

Mrs. Josser regarded her suspiciously. For a person who had just been howling her head off there seemed to be an unusual amount of spirit left in her.

"Didn't you know there wasn't anything?" she asked.

"Of course I knew," Connie told her. "I've known all the week. I've seen it coming." She gave a gulp as though the sobbing were about to start up again. "It was me, or the rent. And the rent won. Mrs. Vizzard saw to that."

Mrs. Josser's lips had been drawn in tightly while she was listening. Then she relaxed them again.

"I'll send you something up," she said.

Connie tried to clasp her hand.

"I wouldn't let you," she replied. "It'd be sponging. Connie hasn't come to that yet. Just because someone unnamed is after the rent, it's no reason why . . ."

"I've told you what I'll do," Mrs. Josser reminded her.

Connie gave another gulp. A more confident one this time.

"In that case, if you insist, I'll come down and fetch it," she said. "Just because you're the Good Samaritan, there's no reason why you should have to run up and down."

She began remodelling herself as she was speaking. She went over to the chest of drawers and removed a bright yellow handkerchief. As a turban, it covered up the disordered hair completely. But it also gave her a startled, unnatural look. There didn't seem to be any connection between the turban and the face beneath.

"Just you wait a moment," she said. "Then I'll come down to you."

Her eye-black was there already on the dressing-table. She applied some shamelessly, with Mrs. Josser standing by watching. And then she went round her cheeks with the rouge-pad. Finally, she took out her surprise lipstick and gave herself a new mouth.

"Just in case I meet anyone on the stairs," she explained.

It was silly, of course, for Connie to make a mistake as soon as she got to the Jossers' floor. But it was just like her. Instead of waiting for Mrs. Josser in the kitchen she went straight into the living-room instead.

As soon as she saw her mistake, she apologised. Apologised to everyone. But by then it was too late and the harm was done.

"What is it, Connie?" Mr. Josser asked, starting up.

Connie looked down at the carpet and began shifting her feet.

"Mrs. Josser very kindly offered to give me some tea," she said.

"Mum!"

It was Doris who had spoken. Up to that moment, she had remained completely detached from everything—detached from Baby tumultuously entertaining herself on the floor; detached from Ted who, in a dreamy vacant fashion, was stroking Cynthia's hair in a way that made Mrs. Josser squirm every time she looked at him; detached from her father who was sitting smoking beside the fire, beaming contentedly on his family circle; detached from Mrs. Josser who still hadn't quite forgiven her for not offering to help; detached from the madness of Uncle Henry. Certainly detached from Connie. She couldn't imagine whatever her mother could have been thinking of to ask her. Connie was just the last straw in a perfectly awful afternoon.

Mrs. Josser thought so, too. She drew her lips in again.

"On a tray was what I meant," she told Connie.

Connie gave a great gasp of embarrassment.

"Oh, but that's what I meant, too," she explained hurriedly. "I wouldn't dream of breaking up a family party. One more can be one too many even if she is only a little one."

"Well, wait here till Mother's got something ready," Mr. Josser suggested.

That did it. There was no getting rid of her after that. As soon as Mrs. Josser returned from the kitchen, Connie began admiring everything that she brought with her—the thinness of the bread and butter, the variety of the biscuits and the extreme richness of the cake. She was talking so hard that no one seemed to notice when Mrs. Josser passed her a cup of tea without saying anything more about the tray.

Not that it really mattered. There was something else to think about—Mr. Josser's clock. There it stood on the mantelpiece—handsome, dominating and useless. There wasn't much to show from the outside what had happened. It was simply that the carved bronze figure on the top had lost the trident that she had been holding, and now faced the world unarmed but still defiant. Inside the clock, however, things were different. Something had gone wrong with the striking part. Every few minutes, the clock roused itself as though it were going to play a full carillon, then paused for a moment and uttered a single hollow boom before relapsing into silence. That solitary boom, no matter how often it happened, was the signal for everybody to start laughing. The whole thing might have been devised simply for their amusement. And once when the clock struck, and then did it again almost immediately, it was too much for them. Mrs. Josser had to sit back and wipe her eyes.

"That clock'll be the death of me," she said.

Mr. Josser himself was rather hurt by this attitude. As he saw it, people weren't being nice about his misfortune. So far as he was concerned, it was his clock and he had been unlucky enough to drop it, and that was all there was to it. But the others couldn't see that. It seemed to them almost too funny to be endured, simply sitting there waiting for the thing on the mantelpiece to misbehave itself.

The clock had just struck again—one of its even funnier double booms, this time—when Uncle Henry suddenly returned to the conversation.

"No one but ourselves to blame," he said. "When the Japs went into Manchuria did we raise a finger to stop them?"

"Not a finger," Mr. Josser agreed placidly.

He was in no mood to be drawn into an argument this afternoon, and he was careful to keep on the same side as Uncle Henry.

"Or Abyssinia? Did we stop the Eyetalians?"

Mr. Josser shook his head.

"And what's the outcome of it all going to be?"

Mr. Josser paused. He was sure that he had the answer somewhere, because he'd heard it so many times from Uncle Henry before.

"I know. Chaos," he said. "World chaos."

Uncle Henry turned and fixed his sound eye on Mr. Josser. The other caught Cynthia for a moment and she giggled. This simple fact stimulated Uncle Henry. In his philosophy, levity was as good as opposition.

"You may laugh," he said. "But are you familiar with what is happening in China at the moment? Ten thousand dead in one air raid. That's the scale of things. There's your brave new world for you. Ten thousand killed and forty thousand wounded. Planes coming over night and day for twenty-four hours. That's the state we've brought things to."

"How?" Ted asked.

It was the first thing that he had said for nearly two hours, and Cynthia was surprised at him: it seemed to her simply fatal to encourage Uncle Henry when he was in one of his silly moods.

But there was one person in the room who didn't mind how much he was encouraged—Connie. She was enjoying everything. The warmth, the close intimate atmosphere of a lot of human bodies all together in one room, the brightness of the light, the noise of voices, the good tea she was having. And she was picking at the marzipan icing on her plate like a bird.

Also, she wasn't listening to a word that anyone was saying. She was carrying on a private and largely congratulatory conversation with herself.

"You're in clover, Connie, old girl," she was saying. "You're where you meant to be."

She allowed her eyes to wander round the room and saw Cynthia happily clasping Baby to her and allowing herself to be hit repeatedly and cooingly in the face.

"You got caught, you poor thing," she reflected. "With hair like that you ought to be enjoying yourself, same as I did at your age, not sprawling about the floor to amuse a blooming baby. You haven't got any self-respect: that's your trouble."

She finished the marzipan, and sat there rattling her cup on the saucer until Mrs. Josser silently filled it for her. Then she took a long deep drink, folding her lip round the edge of the cup.

"And as for you,"—she was looking in Doris's direction now—"if you were my daughter, I'd take your nose out of that book and pull it. It's not natural, seeing a girl reading."

But there was a distraction. A little piece of the marzipan had gone down inside her blouse somewhere and she was trying to get at it.

3

They'd all gone now. Connie, a good Christmas tea inside her, had left for her night-club. Ted and Cynthia had gone off for their bus, with Baby, placid and inert at last, sleeping in Ted's arms; even Uncle Henry had finally departed, a rather seedy-looking Job, with his coat collar turned up and his head buzzing with Eyetalians and outrages in China and wars that would scorch the heritage of man. Mr. Josser heaved a sigh when he had gone. He supposed that he was fond of his brother-in-law. But he was, it had to be admitted, really more of a Lenten figure than a Father Christmas.

After the party, it was pleasant for Mr. and Mrs. Josser to be alone together for a few minutes. The remains of the evening were still spread out all round them. They hadn't attempted to clear up yet and the empty port glasses stood about in a litter of paper caps, mottoes and the remains of a large paper bell that Baby had discovered. The Jossers were just having a cup of tea before they got down to things.

They didn't say very much to each other. Instead, they just sat there, sipping their tea and staring disinterestedly into the embers that were dying in front of them. Once Mr. Josser took out his pipe, but when Mrs. Josser said, "Oh, Fred, you've smoked enough for to-night," he put it away again without seeming to notice.

Up on the mantelpiece the clock, worn out at last by its own enthusiasm, had stopped altogether. Mr. Josser got up and went over to it. He seemed apprehensive of touching the works in any way at all, and contented himself with running his thumb-nail down a vein in the marble.

"I should take it along to the watchmaker's on Tuesday," Mrs. Josser recommended. "They'll be able to fix it up for you."

Mr. Josser stood there without moving.

"It's a nice clock," he said slowly.

Mrs. Josser felt suddenly ashamed that they had made so much fun of it.

"It's a beautiful clock," she agreed with him.

"I wasn't expecting anything, you know," he went on.

Mrs. Josser pursed her lips, but didn't say anything. There was another long silence and Mr. Josser came back and sat down again. He was apparently deep in thought about something.

"Seems funny to think that I shan't be going back there any

more," he said at last. "You'd better remind me on Tuesday just in case."

"You won't need any reminding," she told him. "You've done your bit."

Mr. Josser did not reply immediately. He was busy taking off his collar and tie. When he had undone them he laid them carefully on the chair beside him and twisted his neck from side to side to ease it. The new freedom seemed to bring a return of energy.

"First thing in the morning I'll start writing round," he said.

Mrs. Josser shook her head.

"You know it's no use," she answered. "It isn't fair on Doris."

"I don't see why not," he persisted. "Plenty of other girls come in every day."

"And waste all that money on fares?" Mrs. Josser demanded.

Mr. Josser considered the matter.

"Wouldn't cost any more if we *buy* a cottage," he pointed out. "There won't be any rent then."

There was a pause. Mrs. Josser had just poured herself out another cup of tea—it was practically a twenty-four-hour service in this household—and went on stirring it long after the sugar had dissolved.

"I'm not so sure that I want to live in the country myself," she said. "And I'm quite certain Doris doesn't."

Mr. Josser put his cup down.

"But . . but it's what we've always said we'd do," he told her. "It's what we saved up for."

"I know it is," she answered. "And it was all right while we were only talking about it. Now it might really happen I don't know I'm so keen."

"Well, there's no harm in writing," he said, "perhaps . . . perhaps they haven't got anything."

To change the subject a little—only a little—and put a more cheerful aspect on the evening, Mr. Josser started talking about the cheque. He still had it in the envelope in which Mr. Battlebury had handed it to him.

"That's another thing I've got to do in the morning," he said. "Pay in that cheque. Come in very handy, twenty-five pounds, if we *do* move."

"*If* we do," Mrs. Josser said grimly.

But Mr. Josser wasn't to be depressed.

"You could have knocked me down with a feather when I saw how much it was," he said. "From Mr. Battlebury personally, too. Not from the firm at all."

"He could afford it," Mrs. Josser answered. "It didn't hurt him."

The tone of her voice shocked Mr. Josser. It seemed ungrateful somehow, so disloyal.

"Generous I call it," he said. "That's what I call it. Generous."

"Well, I don't," said Mrs. Josser. There was something surprisingly heated in her voice as she said it, and she was sitting bolt upright in her chair while she spoke. "After the way you've slaved for them."

"But what about the pension?" he was saying. "Two quid a week just for doing nothing."

Mrs. Josser didn't hear him, however. For some reason, she was crying. Not loudly and emphatically like Connie. Just silently and privately crying.

Mr. Josser was astonished. He just couldn't make sense of it all. Apparently, Mrs. Josser was crying because Mr. Battlebury had given him twenty-five pounds as well as a pension. Her whole body was trembling. She seemed to be shivering as well as crying.

Mr. Josser got up and went through to the bedroom next door. He brought the shawl back with him. Mrs. Josser had her handkerchief up to her eyes and didn't notice as he spread the thing out and refolded it cornerwise. The first thing that she knew was that something icy cold was being wrapped round her and tucked in uncomfortably underneath the arms.

"There," said Mr. Josser triumphantly. "Now you'll feel better."

Mrs. Josser reached out her hand to him. She was sorry now about the little outburst. For nearly thirty years she had been meaning to utter her feelings about Battlebury's and, having uttered them, she felt better.

But she wasn't going to admit it.

"Oh, Fred, you know, they won't change it if it gets all creased," was all she said.

CHAPTER 4

I

Percy Boon had been depressed all day. And this was strange because there was no reason for it. He'd been paid the first five pounds commission on the little job he'd done on Christmas Day—balance on completion of sale—and he was looking round for another little job just like the last one.

"Free lance," he said, because he rather liked the word. "Free lance, that's me."

There was a fun fair just opposite the garage, and he wandered over to it for ten minutes. This was one of the nights when he didn't get off till midnight, and he felt he needed a little relaxation just to keep going. But somehow delight was absent. Everything was flat, and the fun fair didn't seem funny. He went aimlessly from machine to machine in search of happiness, and couldn't find it. Even the pin-tables had lost their magic. The little steel balls careered madly about, striking first one kind of obstacle and then another, lighting things up on their zigzags, flashing up the score in thousands and tens of thousands—and he was just too bored to count. Then he tried the Electric Crane which looked as though it could scoop up watches and fountain pens and cigarette cases as often as you cared to put a penny into it. He'd wasted ninepence and gone back for more change before he decided that happiness didn't lurk in the Electric Crane either. So, finally, still searching as hard as ever for something to make him forget himself—he sauntered over to the peep-shows, He knew them all by heart, of course. They were an old selection. and the peep-show in England is an art form that hasn't renewed itself with the times. But he put his pennies in dutifully and saw the old faded sets of post cards flicker past again—the Honeymoon, Milady's Toilet, What the Butler Saw, The Artist's Model and Greek Statues. They didn't, however, rouse him to-night. They simply left him depressed and dejected. He felt he needed something stronger.

To give himself a test of skill and to get some kick out of having come over to the place at all, he played a solitary round of Radio Billiards. But the machine wasn't working properly. One of the magnets was stronger than the other and kept pulling the balls sideways. After the third miss he gave it up and walked over to the change-desk to have another look at the girl inside.

She was new there. The previous girl had been rather a fat girl with red hair. This one was quite slim. And blonde. Not real blonde —Percy could tell that straight away—but blonde nevertheless. The bright, shining sort. She wasn't good-looking, judged by the top standards. But she was all right. And she looked as if she might be adaptable. He went over and leant against the desk.

"Hallo, beautiful," he said. "You new here?"

The girl looked at him for a moment before answering.

"Fresh, aren't you?" she answered.

Percy didn't mind this reply. It was all part of the pattern. And in any case he didn't like girls who gave themselves away in the first five minutes.

"I noticed you as soon as I came in," he said.

"I dreamed about you last night," the girl told him.

He grinned politely.

"Ever have any time off?" he asked.

The girl shook her head.

"No, I go straight on. All day and all night."

"What's your name?" Percy asked.

"Oh, call me Mrs. Simpson," she replied.

"Like to come out some time?"

"Yes, but not with you."

"Fond of dancing?"

"Never heard of it."

"Like to go somewhere on Saturday?"

The Blonde handed a shilling's-worth of change to another bored, lonely youth like Percy, and then went on staring vacantly into space.

"What about the Palais?"

"What about what?"

"Pick you up about nine."

"Pick yourself up if you're not careful."

"Take you there by car if you like."

"Thanks. I'd rather fly."

Percy smiled and lit a cigarette. He offered the girl one. She took it.

"That a date then?" he asked.

"Oh, forget it," the girl answered. "You make me tired."

She handed out two more piles of coppers and scratched her head absent-mindedly with a knitting needle. In her lap lay a pink jumper that she was finishing.

Percy straightened himself up and began to move off. He certainly didn't intend to stop there any longer and make himself cheap.

"See you later," he said over his shoulder.

"Don't hurry," the girl called after him.

There were two customers waiting at the garage when Percy got back and he had to tell one of them where he got off. He was a Jew who seemed to expect service at an all-night garage whenever he chose to drop in for it.

But it was quiet enough now. There was a mechanic working

somewhere in the rear and there was a boy in front to look after the pumps. Percy himself was odd man out. There was nothing for him to do, and he stood in the steel and glass box that was the office, a cigarette between his lips, staring out along the tramway track. His head was sunk forward a little and there was a dreamy far-away look in his eyes. He had moods like this sometimes.

"If I had a thousand a year, on the level," he was thinking, "I'd be O.K. I'd know where I stood. I'd know what to do with it. I'd be O.K. I'd get a house out Purley way with a garage. I'd have a radiogram and a cocktail cabinet. I'd stop mucking about with blondes and marry some girl or other. I'd have a home cinema. I'd spend every week-end at Brighton. I'd learn French the easy way by correspondence. I'd buy a ukulele. Then I'd be O.K. in the evenings. If I wasn't working in a garage I'd have a manicure every week from a different girl. I'd wear one of the new low-curved bowlers. I'd carry a gold cigarette case. I'd make my wife put on evening dress every evening. I'd have a Riley's home billiard table and have friends in. I'd be O.K."

As he was thinking, his hands were plunged deep into his trousers pockets and the fingers of his right hand were fiddling with something. It was a knuckleduster. And rather a good one, too. It was called the Hedgehog. Instead of the outer band's being smooth, there was a kind of blunt spike in between the knuckle joints, so that anyone getting hit with it would have to take quite a lot of punishment. He'd never actually used the knuckleduster. He didn't, in fact, even know anyone who had ever used a knuckleduster. But it was nice to have one all the same. Especially a good one like that, with a guard for the thumb and everything.

And he knew other people who *carried* knuckledusters; ordinary plain ones. Most of the boys who hung around Smokey's Café in the evenings carried them; and he'd had one or two of the real gang-fighters pointed out to him. But you couldn't be sure. There was always a lot of loose talk and boasting at a place like Smokey's. And nothing much ever seemed to happen there.

The smooth steel of the knuckleduster seemed to seep up into his brain as he fondled it. He began to think about other of his toys as well. The knuckleduster wasn't the only thing he'd got. He'd got a cosh too. It wasn't a real cosh. But it was good enough. It'd lay a man out all right. He'd say it would. And he grinned as he remembered how he'd got it. It was a present from the Underground. He'd pinched it off the Morden tube late one night when he was the only passenger in the compartment. And it had been difficult because, of course, he'd had to lay off at stations. It was just one of the solid rubber knobs on a long springy stalk for standing passengers to hold on to. All the fellows were carrying one.

There were other kinds of weapons of self-defence, too, that some of the fellows carried. But he hadn't got any of them. Not in his line, really. Too dangerous. There was an Italian from Clerkenwell who'd come south of the river on a job. Razoritti, people called him. He always carried a razor in his trouser pocket.

At the thought Percy idly went through slashing motions in the air.

"If I had a thousand a year, I'd be O.K.," he said again dreamily. "I'd learn tap-dancing."

But what was the use? He hadn't got a thousand. And remembering that he hadn't, he became depressed again.

2

It must have been something in the air because Doris was depressed, too. Depressed and disappointed. She had allowed herself to get very excited about the cottage—not because she particularly wanted to live in a cottage—but because she had finally decided she didn't want to go on living in Dulcimer Street. And then Mrs. Josser had put her foot down. She had refused, obstinately and absolutely, to have anything to do with cottages. Dulcimer Street, she said, was where she had made her home and she didn't see why she should be turned out of it. . . .

Doris looked at her watch. It was eight-thirty. To be really early it should have been eight-twenty-five or even eight-twenty. It was going to be a rush. Not that it mattered. She felt in an angry, rushing sort of mood, and being late was just part of it. The other people in the tram looked sullen and rather sleepy: they might have been a race of liverish ghosts returning to their morning graveyards. It was Monday morning. No mistaking it.

She got off at the Temple and started up Norfolk Street. It wasn't a bad sort of morning really. There was a sparkle of sunlight in the air that helped to clean things up a bit, and the cold wind had dropped. It no longer came driving through the cañons of brick and concrete like an invisible avalanche that had started somewhere near the Pole. Altogether, as Monday mornings in January went, it might have been worse.

But Dulcimer Street couldn't have been worse. It was bad enough living in Kennington. Bad enough living *anywhere* south of the river. Nobody who was anybody lived there: she had long ago realised that. In the best of circles to say Dulcimer Street, S.E. 11, when you were asked for your address, was as bad as saying that you slept out on the Embankment. And, as she walked along, she began once again going over the whole complicated business of being born in the wrong place. And on the wrong side of the river. As she saw it, she'd missed her chance by a mere couple of miles or so.

She knew the solution, of course. Had known it for the last six months, in fact. And the only reason why she hadn't done something about it was that she'd been afraid. Not afraid in one sense—it wasn't a crime to go and share a flat with a girl friend—simply afraid of all the fuss and commotion that it was going to cause. She knew just what her mother was like when she drew in her lips because something had upset her. And to suggest leaving home would be just about the biggest upset that Mrs. Josser had ever known. It would be every bit as bad as when Ted had married Cynthia.

But she'd decided now. Or rather it was Connie who'd decided her. The memory of that awful Christmas party with Connie sitting up at the table like a tarnished old idol, dipping the corner of her cake surreptitiously into her third cup of tea, still rankled. And she wasn't going to risk another Christmas like the last one. Doris Josser, in fact, was walking out on Dulcimer Street.

As soon as she got to the office she phoned Doreen about it. And Doreen seemed quite excited. But she couldn't stop then because one of the partners wanted her, and she was *frightfully* behind with his stuff already. In the end, it wasn't until lunch-time that they could talk about it properly. And even then Doreen really wanted to talk about the simply gorgeous week-end she'd been having. It had been divine, perfectly divine, with lots of cocktails and music and young men. It was the kind of week-end that might have been staged in Hollywood and put down all ready cast, in Belsize Park.

As a matter of fact, she was now showing the strain of it. She was a dark handsome girl like a well-bred gipsy. But at this moment she was a slightly frayed and ravelled-looking sort of gipsy. There were deep shadows under her eyes and she still seemed a little dazed by remembering how utterly marvellous everything had been. She would go on talking about it. First of all she'd gone to a simply heavenly film with a young doctor friend who was only twenty-six but was doing absolutely marvellously, and then they'd gone on somewhere to dance and the doctor had danced divinely. On Sunday morning she'd had to go home, which was a frightful bore anyhow; but they were really awfully sweet and darlings really, even though they did make her want to *scream* sometimes. Then another friend—in the Navy this time—had suddenly turned up from nowhere and had rushed her down to the West End where everything had been simply too marvellous and divine; they had fed marvellously in an adorable little restaurant in Soho and then, most marvellous of all, this rugged seaman had turned out to be as divine a dancer as the doctor. They had finished up round about one-thirty in the morning, *this* morning it was, at a simply wonderful coffee-stall near Baker Street Station where the most incredible people had gathered. Then, when they couldn't get a taxi, the naval officer had offered to carry her.

Doris listened, enviously and a little stunned: it was obvious that her friend Doreen had just emerged from something terrific, and was adjusting herself only slowly and with difficulty to ordinary, unmiraculous existence. And then she remembered that life for Doreen was always pretty much like that. That was why she wanted to join her, in fact.

She was interrupted in her thoughts by Doreen asking if she'd got an aspirin. After searching about in her bag for a moment Doris found the small Bakelite holder and tipped one of the tablets out into the palm of her hand. There was only one other tablet left in the case. And, as Doris dropped it back in again, she couldn't help remembering that Doreen had had all the other eleven on previous occasions when life—her life—had proved too much for her. She didn't mind, however: some kind of sedative was obviously needed if Doreen was to be kept going at all.

"I do hope it isn't my eyes," Doreen was saying. "I'm too scared to go and see an oculist in case he says I need glasses. I should look an absolute fright in glasses."

They had finished their lunch by now. And because there were two other girls standing behind their table they got up and went out.

"I don't know why we come here," Doreen said as they went down the stairs. "It's always so hideously crowded."

Doris didn't attempt to make any reply to this. She knew perfectly well why she went there and she intended to go on going. It was because she got a perfectly good meal for one-and-three, with coffee and roll and butter thrown in.

But Doreen's quick mind was already working.

"Of course, it wouldn't be the least bit of good suggesting my present flat. There wouldn't be room for two people to turn round in it." She paused. "But there's a perfectly marvellous flat in Adelaide

Road," she went on. "I saw it when I took mine. It's right at the top and it used to be a studio. We could make a simply divine living-room out of it." She paused again. "How much can you afford to pay?" she asked.

"I give them a pound a week at home now," Doris told her.

As she said it she felt uncomfortable. It seemed one of those family secrets that are better kept inside the family.

"We might just manage it," Doreen said dreamily. "It's a heavenly room."

They went on up Fetter Lane together. And Doreen, who evidently was something more than just a dreamer, put another question.

"How much furniture can you bring?" she asked.

"I . . . I haven't got any furniture of my own," Doris answered.

Doreen gave a little laugh: it was a dry husky sort of laugh.

"Oh, my pet," she said. "Then how are we to manage? I haven't got enough."

"There's my bedroom furniture," Doris replied doubtfully. "They wouldn't want that if I leave home. At least I don't think they would."

Doreen, however, didn't seem to be at all impressed.

"But we can't have *that* sort of furniture," she said. "There wouldn't be room for it. All the other rooms are frightfully small. They're just boxes. I meant divans and rugs and easy chairs and that sort of thing."

As she said it Doris was glad that she had never actually taken Doreen back home to Dulcimer Street. She'd debated it a lot of times. But always at the last moment she'd decided against it. If Doreen had ever been there she would have realised that divans and Dulcimer Street just didn't go together. She felt re-humiliated. And she wanted to do something to re-establish herself in Doreen's eyes.

"I tell you what," she said. "We could *buy* some."

Doreen raised her eyebrows. She seemed interested again.

"How much do you want to spend?" she asked.

"Oh, about twenty pounds," Doris said airily.

She had got precisely twenty-two pounds, four and six in her Post Office account. And she felt safe enough in saying about twenty. She only hoped that Doreen didn't think she meant twenty-five, or twenty-four, or even twenty-two pounds, five shillings.

"That'd be marvellous," Doreen told her. "We could get a lot with that. Second-hand, of course. But I adore old furniture. And we might have my big divan re-covered. It's all falling to pieces anyhow."

They'd reached the office by now. It was a tall sooty building, sublet into business suites. But Doreen made no attempt to go up for the moment.

"There's only one other thing, my lamb," she said. "If we're going to live together you'd better know the worst. I've got rather a lot of friends and some of them stop quite late. I hope you're broad-minded."

"Oh yes," Doris answered.

And, because it didn't sound convincing, she added, " Very."

3

The third person to feel depressed was Mr. Josser. And that was very unusual in him.

It had all started very early—as Doris left the house, in fact. Everything was still all right as he sat watching her gulp down her cup of tea. Then as the front door slammed after her—there was no time for proper good-byes in this regular morning rush—he suddenly felt sorry for himself. As he sat there and realised that he need never go again unless he wanted to, he felt old. Very old. And useless. Except for the pension, he was just a dead-weight in the family.

The feeling passed off, of course. He got over it during the day in a placid, odd-jobbish sort of fashion. There were any number of things that he'd been meaning to do for years. And he had at last started—in a fiddling, desultory way—on several of them. Twice he'd had all the things out of the kitchen tool-box and twice he'd had to put them all away again because Mrs. Josser had a meal ready for him. As a result, he'd got nothing done and was already a bit late for his appointment.

It was quite a big do, this evening. It was on Wednesday that the South London Parliament and Debating Society had their meetings. And to these meetings the fanatical and persevering Uncle Henry had committed him. Not that he really minded any more. At first he had resented trailing to Camberwell to hear a discussion on "Evolution or Divine Creation?" or "Bi-Metallism the Way Out." But after a bit he had got used to it. Provided that he got a seat in the corner somewhere towards the back where he could smoke, it was not really so very different from spending an evening at home. Simply because he was adaptable and unresistant Mr. Josser became one of the best-informed men in London. For five seasons he had barely missed a debate. And in the result he acquired views—both for and against—the League of Nations, State Medicine, Sport for Girls, the Colonies, Compulsory Religious Education, Free Trade and Cremation. But as Mr. Josser was the last person in the world to want to impose his views either one way or the other on anybody, that was the end of it. It was simply that, as views went, he had a great many of them.

And then, just when Mr. Josser had got used to listening to all these subjects, there came the fateful change in Uncle Henry. He suddenly switched over from general knowledge to politics. He left the Camberwell Debating Society to look after itself and went into the South London Parliament. The ragged moustache, the open sports collar, and the glittering and unfocused eye became familiar symbols of the Front Opposition Bench. And all the things that Mr. Greenwood and Mr. Attlee left unsaid at Westminster, came booming out just one postal district away.

Mr. Josser, however, had got into the habit of debates. He couldn't give them up. And everything would have been all right, except that Uncle Henry couldn't give up Mr. Josser either. One night just as he was setting out to hear "Flats or Houses? The Architect's Viewpoint," Uncle Henry called at Dulcimer Street to intercept him. Flats or Houses, Uncle Henry explained, was just playing with life. It was Capitalism or Socialism that really mattered. And questions like that, real burning questions, were settled in Parliament, not in debating societies.

All that had been four years ago. And for the last three, Mr. Josser had represented Bolton in the Conservative interest.

The actual business of election in the South London Parliament was comparatively simple. In the first place, the seat had to be vacant—that much was obvious. Secondly, if you were an arch-Tory, you couldn't represent a constituency that was notoriously Socialist. And thirdly, you had to take your job seriously. It was no good, as it was just across the river in the other House, getting yourself elected and then turning up only when you felt like it. The Honorary Secretary—a Mr. Linnet—took a weekly census of all attendances. And as elections were annual there had been more than one frivolous young politician who had found himself round about the beginning of March without a seat simply because he had relapsed into going to the pictures when he should have been shadow-governing his country. So far as Mr. Josser was concerned, his own seat was almost uncomfortably secure—with Uncle Henry in the background prodding him it could scarcely be otherwise—though he consoled himself with reflecting that it was always possible that there might be a landslide up at Bolton.

The Ministers of the Crown were elected annually as well. Even the Prime Minister had to take his chance with the others. The reason for this was of course perfectly simple. You just couldn't expect a self-respecting man to turn up indefinitely as Chancellor of the Duchy of Lancaster or Minister without Portfolio, without the hope of anything better. And so it was that towards the end of February the seals of office were all handed in and a new Government was formed. The P.M.G. was given India, the Treasury swapped over with the Foreign Office, Health went across to the Dominions, the Colonies gave way to Education and Scotland did a deal with Transport. All anyhow. Just like the real thing, in fact.

To-night, everything began smoothly enough. Mr. Muspratt, the retiring P.M., sank his pride and expressed himself perfectly content with being First Lord. And Mr. Plumcroft, a retired gentlemen's outfitter, who was almost the father of the House, got where he had always wanted to be. Mr. Josser had known Mr. Plumcroft for years, and he was delighted to see his old friend in Downing Street at last. Mr. Plumcroft was a more genial manner of man than Mr. Muspratt, as well as more substantial—Mr. Muspratt was only a booking clerk on the Southern Railway—and under Mr. Plumcroft's captaincy it seemed certain that they were in for a good year of common sense, retrenchment and sound finance.

Mr. Plumcroft's essential conservatism—it wasn't just a label with him, but something fundamental like his stiff cuffs and his butterfly collar—was evident in the men he picked for the key jobs. There weren't any exactly young ones to choose from. But there were at least some who weren't so old as the others, including one really brilliant orator, a Mr. Whipple from Barclays Bank, who emphasised his points most effectively with a pair of gold pince-nez whenever he spoke in public. Mr. Plumcroft, however, passed him over without a thought. He chose discreetly, cautiously, unadventurously.

Mr. Josser wasn't exactly listening when Mr. Plumcroft called his name. He was, as a matter of fact, thinking of something entirely different: he was thinking of a new and rather complicated clothes-airer that he was going to fix up for Mrs. Josser if the kitchen ceiling was strong enough. And then quite suddenly through the maze of pulleys and strings and lengths of rope with which his mind was full he heard himself addressed.

It was quite understood that anyone could refuse, if he wanted to do so: in any Parliament there are always some who prefer to remain back benchers. On the other hand when the entire Conservative Party is only fifty-four strong and there are the usual number of offices to be filled, it isn't very helpful if members don't rise to their responsibilities.

Mr. Josser rose and cleared his throat.

"Would the right hon. member for Birmingham Central mind repeating what he just said?" he asked.

Mr. Plumcroft obliged.

"I nominate the hon. member for Bolton for the post of Secretary for Foreign Affairs."

Mr. Josser felt an icy shudder run through him. The only views he had on Foreign Affairs were those he had absorbed from Uncle Henry. And though Uncle Henry made them sound so convincing that disagreement was unthinkable, he had rather gathered that they weren't what the Conservative Party believed. Looked at either way there would be trouble. If he said what Uncle Henry told him to say the Party Whip would only discipline him for it afterwards. And if he took the orthodox Central Office line—that Hitler only wanted to restore German self-respect and tidy up some of the weak points in the Versailles Treaty—he would get in trouble with his own brother-in-law.

So he tried to wriggle out of it.

"The right hon. member is paying me a big compliment," he said gratefully, "but . . . but it isn't quite in my line."

The sentence had started off in the true Westminster manner, but had tailed off somewhat disappointingly towards the end.

Mr. Plumcroft, however, had set his heart on Mr. Josser and he meant to have him.

"The hon. member is not doing himself justice," he said flatly and emphatically. "I've considered the matter in all its aspects and I still ask him."

He spoke as though Mr. Josser, though not perhaps quite *persona grata* in Moscow, was nevertheless a name to conjure with in the Wilhelmstrasse—and still acceptable in the Quai d'Orsay.

Mr. Josser shifted from one foot to the other.

"I . . . I'm not much of a speaker," he said diffidently.

But Mr. Plumcroft only smiled.

"I think we can safely leave the oratory to the hon. member for Spen Valley," he said blandly.

Mr. Plumcroft had spent nearly seventeen years on the Borough

Council and he had an easy way with him in Committee or out of it. He had ingeniously turned an objection into a pretty compliment to his colleague, the Home Secretary, Mr. Beeman—of Warbell and Beeman, Estate Agents and Auctioneers.

Mr. Josser looked down at his feet. He disliked these occasions when everyone was staring at him. If it hadn't been for Uncle Henry he would simply have chucked up the whole thing and gone back to the Debating Society—or even have stayed at home. But as he was there, he couldn't let everyone down.

"Oh, very well," he said rather sulkily, "if you insist, I accept," he said. "But I'm sure there are others here who could do it better."

Secretary of State for Foreign Affairs! It appalled him. It was enough to appal anyone. And at such a moment, too. Admittedly Munich had saved the peace. But there was still a pretty nasty undercurrent of talk about the State of Europe. It said in the morning's papers that President Hacha had been summoned to Berlin. And when Hitler invited someone to come and stay with him, it didn't usually end there. Before Mr. Josser knew where he was he might find himself . . . No: it was no use imagining. He must keep his head, read through the reports of his Ambassadors and trust to Providence.

Mr. Josser and Mr. Chamberlain were in the same boat now.

Up in the Gallery, a fattish rather bald young man was writing rapidly. He had a black leather folder of squared paper, and he was diligently making notes of the proceedings. The folder was full of his clear angular handwriting. The young man was Dr. Otto Hapfel of the University of Heidelberg. He was at present engaged in a post-graduate course at London, and he was writing a thesis on English political institutions. It was his Professor who had suggested that he might care to add a section on the local parliaments. Dr. Hapfel, who liked being told by his superiors exactly what he should do, was delighted. He was also delighted by the South London Parliament itself. It provided an excellent footnote to a chapter already entitled *The Leader-Principle in Amateur Democracy: England as an Example.*

CHAPTER 5

I

CONNIE was being raided. . . .

It was at the Moonrakers, of course. You got to the place through a narrow front door that led straight out of Dover Street. It was a respectable-looking sort of door, in between a military tailor's and a bespoke shoe-maker's. And judged by the concentration of expensive personal trades in Dover Street the door might merely have led to a firm of select and exclusive hatters. But you would have noticed the difference the moment you got inside. No reputable hatter would have had an entrance hall with daffodil-coloured walls covered with drawings of Apaches and Hawaiian dancing girls and bull-fighters in scarlet cloaks.

The entrance hall was confined. And, once the front door was closed, it was completely unventilated. A slightly suffocating odour of face powder and stale scent filled the place, as though actresses had been caged here. In the wall facing the entrance hall were the double mahogany doors of a small passenger lift. The doors had been smart and highly polished when new. And the upper portions, except for the finger-marks, still were highly polished. It was only in the lower portions that the smartness had worn off a bit. The bottom panels were heavily scarred all over, and it was evident that patrons growing weary of waiting had used their feet in an effort to attract attention.

In a strange way, the same mixture of smartness and shabbiness was repeated in the upstairs rooms. There was the same daffodil-coloured paint everywhere, and more of the same sort of drawings. But round about waist height the yellow paintwork was smeared and dejected-looking as though generations of customers in rather greasy clothing had rubbed against it. Some of the drawings had been almost effaced, in fact.

It could not exactly be said that upstairs the atmosphere was the same as downstairs. Because here it was so much stronger. It was the original form of the smell, in fact. What you smelt as you came in was simply what had leaked down the lift shaft. And mingled with it up here in its primitive form were the characteristic odours of several dozen different forms of alcohol, cooking, the close foxy stuffiness of two cloakrooms that were often so full that some of the hats and coats had to be arranged along the occasional tables in the passage, and whatever fresh perfumes the ladies had happened to introduce into the room that night.

The plan of the club was very simple. It was merely the top floor of two identical houses. This meant that there were two large rooms on each side, as well as a couple of smaller ones. One of the large rooms was the restaurant. This was entirely Spanish, with massive metal grilles over the windows and little balconies built out from the wall and stuffed birds in wicker cages and a bogus well-head with a piece of mirror at the bottom, right in the centre. The tables were of chromium and scarlet wood. Out of this led the *salon de danse* with its radiogram, painted scarlet like the tables, and kicked about the base like the lift doors.

On the other side of the hall were the card-rooms. One of these was an innocent-looking, conventional sort of place with wicker chairs and green baize tables. Only a large velvet spider suspended from the middle of the ceiling added the authentic night-club note. The other room was a very different affair. It had a big gold chandelier and was hung with a lot of rather dubious tapestries. The rest of the room was taken up with a long polished table with large glass ash-trays on it. Except for a roulette wheel in the centre and the flimsy little gilt chairs, it might have been the board table of a city company. It was in this room that the serious business of the Moonrakers went on. Eating and dancing and bridge, even poker, were only pastimes to keep the patrons cheerfully occupied until their turn came. In the name of Charity and the Voluntary Hospital movement as much as six thousand pounds had changed hands in the tapestry room in the course of a single night.

And this evening everything was warming up nicely. The dining-room was full of prosperous-looking men, and sleek-haired women all wearing that season's fashionable haggard expression. The women were mostly rather younger than the men and the most of them looked as though a course of good nourishing food might still be able to put them on their feet again. The men on the other hand all looked as though if they went on as they were going they would soon be off theirs for ever.

Even though it was still quite early—not yet midnight, in fact—the *salon de danse* was packed full with lumbering couples dutifully grasping each other. In the tapestry room a nearly bankrupt peer and a well-to-do stockbroker were leading about a dozen other players in a friendly game of faro.

Outside in her little cubby-hole Connie was all right, thank you.

She had come to terms with one of the waiters and he had brought her the better part of a round of chicken sandwiches and a cup of soup that was still quite hot. Connie was doing fine.

Then in the midst of all this simple amusement, one of the customers—a tall strapping fellow half-way between a moon-calf and a Guardsman—extricated himself from the scarlet table-legs and going over to the window opened it, and began blowing a police whistle into the darkness. His two companions got up in the same unhurried way and stood at the entrance to the lift.

"Nobody to leave, please," they said mechanically, while they were getting out their notebooks.

It took Connie next to no time to realise what was happening, even though she was stuck away in a corner and couldn't see anything. This wasn't her first raid. And she knew just what to do. It was quite like old days diving for the main switch and flooding the whole place in darkness.

And after that the fun really started. Even the two detectives at the lift-head started blowing their police whistles as well, and their mates down below kicked at the already damaged double mahogany doors in the entrance hall just to let the raiding party upstairs know that support was at hand.

The customers for the most part took the raid rather as people at a picnic take a sudden thunderstorm. One or two of the men complained that it was a bore, and the various women who were out with other people's husbands wore a vexed expression. Only one girl broke down. She was a slim pretty thing, and slightly drunk. She was the daughter of Mr. Veesey Blaize, K.C., and therefore of news-value in the popular press. She didn't want any more paragraphs about herself at the moment while her fiancé was away. So putting her golden head down on the table amid the litter of coffee-cups and cigarette-ends, she wept. She was still weeping when the police located the switch and put the lights on again.

Meanwhile Mr. Vercetti, the manager, had been active and resourceful. Avoiding the beams of the policemen's torches which were making darting criss-cross patterns across the room like the novelty illuminations on a carnival night, he was gently ushering his most important customers to the fire escape at the back. There was one chance in a hundred that way, he explained. But, as it happened, it didn't quite come off. The police knew at least as much about raids as Connie and Mr. Vercetti, and they always reckoned to pick up a handful round at the back. Down there in the backyard among the dustbins they gathered together an outside broker, a peer's nephew, a

South African business man, a member of a South American military mission, a lady of title, an actress and two young women who spent quite a lot of time accounting to the police. It was a good haul and rather fun for the police just waiting there for the flitters to come down one by one into their arms out of the darkness. Mr. Vercetti himself was past caring: he had merely tried to do his best by his customers.

But he was hurt, bitterly hurt. It seemed to him that he might as well give up trying to amuse a race so illogical as the English. In their despondent Anglo-Saxon fashion they flocked to a night-club to enjoy themselves. Then a lot of policemen, as despondent as the revellers, came in and raided them. And neither side really seemed to mind. In Mr. Vercetti's country the police would either, for a consideration, have been ready to leave him alone altogether or, if political personages had been involved, there would have been shootings, gunfire in the street outside, knives, vitriol-throwing and prison sentences for ten, fifteen, twenty years. As well as one or two suicides.

Then, quite suddenly, Mr. Vercetti's temper gave way. He went up to the original whistle-blower and addressed him.

"This issa da outrage," he shouted. "I will ruina you. I demanda my lawyer. I demanda you to stop."

The tall policeman put down a glass he was sniffing, and turned towards one of his men by the lift.

"Take him downstairs," he said. "First car."

The rest went very quietly after that, with the exception of the pretty girl who was still weeping with her head on her hands. Her two companions had got up with the rather sheepish expressions of people who are told to stand in line like children, and left her. She remained a lonely pathetic figure by the bogus well-head. One of her shoulder straps had slipped, leaving the pale young flesh with the red weal where the strap had been. There was something appealing and virginal about her. The sub-inspector, or whatever he was, came over to her.

"Have to come along now, Miss," he said.

The girl did not stir, and the policeman tapped her on the arm.

The indignity of it, the miserable sordid indignity of being tapped on the arm by a policeman for the second time in fourteen days—it was only a fortnight ago when she had been among those rounded up at the Dishwashers—overcame her. She remembered her father's good name, the money that she had lost, the inevitable paragraphs in the popular press, her fiancé. When the policeman's hand descended on her, the second time, she turned sharply round and bit it.

That was why Celia Veesey Blaize—the one customer who had lowered the tone of the place by violence—went down in the small box-like lift with two policemen all to herself.

Connie was one of the last to leave. By then, she'd seen the leader of the gang go round putting a seal on the drink cabinet in the bar and, after he'd removed the roulette wheel and the faro board, even putting a seal on the tapestry room itself. By the time he'd finished sealing up everything, the Moonrakers looked as though a mad solicitor had been let loose in the place.

The journey to Vine Street was quick and well conducted. The driver of the Black Maria knew the way and they were all quiet in Connie's car, including Connie. Only two of the passengers, indeed, showed any agitation over the whole affair. One was Mr. Vercetti; he was still crying out that it wasa da outrage and that he would smasha da sergeant and ruina him. And the other was the fair girl. The cold night air had gone to her head and she was imploring her gaolers to let her out. She said that she had had enough of it, that she felt sick and that she wanted to go home. Then she was sick.

As for Connie, she was in the first cubicle on the left as you go in. And provided the policeman in the gangway didn't stand bang in front of the door she kept getting little glimpses of London life through the grille at the back. She found them rather exciting—the flashing signs, the statue of Eros with the lights shining down on him, the crowds. Because, though Connie spent every single one of her nights here in the centre of things, she was too busy to see any of them. And it was a funny thing, now that she recalled it, that she had once made almost this identical journey already. It had been at the end of a stag party in Half Moon Street when some Army chaps had invited a few girls in afterwards, and a brunette had been hit with a champagne bottle. The only difference was that the Black Maria had been horse-drawn then.

All the same, the fun seemed somehow to have leaked out of the thing by the time they got to Vine Street. It had been raining—still was raining, in fact—and the pavements were cold and messy. They couldn't all go into the little yard because there were too many of them and some of the cars had simply to draw up outside, like limousines arriving for the Opera. The policemen on duty were brusque and businesslike and, though Connie tried to keep up her spirits by blowing a kiss at the solitary spectator, there was a kind of soullessness hanging over the whole proceeding.

Once inside, there was the distempered unhomeliness which is peculiar to police stations. Against the setting of the dark green paint, the white waistcoats of the men and the evening frocks of the ladies showed up startlingly.

Immediately in front of Connie in the queue was a tall young man with vague purplish pouches under his eyes and a straggle of honey-coloured moustache across his upper lip—he was the peer's nephew—and his companion, a dark melancholy-looking girl with green finger-nails.

"Frightful bore this," the young man said whenever he caught her eye.

"Can we smoke?" the girl asked.

"Not a hope," the young man answered. "Frightful bore, I'm afraid."

"How long shall we be here?"

It was her first raid, and she felt tired.

"Oh, hours probably," the young man answered. "They've got to write down all our names and addresses. They're always fearfully slow. Can't really write, you know. Frightful bore, waiting."

"Can we go home then?"

"Oh yes, rather. We'll be released, on bail."

"Can *you* arrange it, or do we have to get Daddy's solicitor?"

"Oh, I'll fix it. Bit of a bore, but it's nothing really. Providing we're both here in the morning, doesn't really cost anything."

"But I'm meeting Mummy in the morning. She's coming up specially."

"Have to put her off, I'm afraid," the young man comforted her. "Frightful bore. Don't know why we had to go there. Too sickening they should have chosen that one. Frightful bore all this, I'm afraid."

Connie despised the dark melancholy-looking girl because in the ways of the world she seemed no better than half-witted. But she liked the perfume that she was using, and she kept coming up close to have sniffs at it. When the girl found out what was happening, and looked round to find Connie's little withered face pressed up against her collar and the old nostrils distended like a horse's, she gave a little grimace and took half a step forward. But they were packed too close for easy movement and a little shudder, half jolt, half ripple, passed right along the line of arrested revellers, as though a shunting engine had butted into the back of a goods train.

After this rebuff Connie spent her time discreetly going over the contents of her moire handbag just to be sure that there was nothing in it that she would have preferred the police not to question her about. But it was quite all right: everything in the bag was hers.

The queue got smaller and smaller, and Connie was finally brought face to face with the sergeant. He was still scratching away in his book like the Recording Angel. One after another the gentlemen in evening dress had put a price on their own head and on the head of the lady who was with them, and one or two of the ladies who were without companions had opened up their sequin pouchettes and produced a visiting card. Of course there were some who had earlier in the evening made Mr. Vercetti a present of most of the ready money they started with, and there had to be a bit of telephoning. Taxi-cabs kept arriving with surprised friends arranging to go bail. Then Connie's turn came.

"Name?" said the sergeant.

It was the forty-seventh name that he had written down, and he had given up saying "Please."

"Victoria Regina Coke," Connie told him.

It was her real name that she was giving: Connie was only a pet name that she had given herself because Victoria Regina had seemed a bit too formal among friends. Also it went so well with Coke.

"Address?"

"10 Dulcimer Street, S.E. 11."

"Occupation?"

Connie disliked everything about the sergeant. He was large, disinterested and foxy-featured. And she wondered if he would have behaved in that off-hand manner if she had been the one with the pen in her hand and he had been standing against the rail almost up to his chin.

"Hostess," she said firmly.

The sergeant wrote it down without raising an eyebrow.

"Anyone to go surety for you?"

Connie drew herself up and flashed her little yellow teeth at him.

"I can go surety for myself, thank you," she said and handed her bag across to him.

The sergeant opened it, took one glance at the broken comb, the match-box with cigarette-ends in it, the chipped mirror, the bus tickets, and began counting out the odd coins.

"Only three-and-eight here," he said.

"There was a five-pound note there when you had it," she said.

"Want to make a charge?" the sergeant demanded, leaning forward across the desk.

Connie shook her head.

"No use," she said. "I may have spent it at my milliner's."

"Anyone you can phone up?" he asked.

Connie thought for a moment.

"Only the Lord Mayor," she answered. "And he's probably in bed."

"Then we'll have to keep you here, Mum," he told her.

"Who are you calling Mum?" Connie demanded.

But he ignored her. He raised his hand and beckoned to one of the waiting policemen.

"Down below," he said. "Look slippy."

Connie avoided the constable's arm and went off in a kind of mincing tripping walk that was meant to convey light-heartedness. But on the way one of the green-painted doors down the bleak corridor opened, and Mr. Vercetti appeared. He had been taken into one of the private rooms for questioning. Connie greeted him eagerly.

"Oh, sir," she said. "I've come out without any small change and they won't let me go. I don't want to spend the night in a cell with my rheumatism."

But Mr. Vercetti was too much agitated to take any notice of her.

"Getta out of my way," he said to Connie and turning to the Inspector he resumed the conversation where it had been left off. "I admitta nothing," he declared loudly. "You is notta so clever as you think you is. Ina morning you will find out. I will grilla you. You will be ruina. . . ."

And with that Mr. Vercetti, his own surety in £50, went out into the night, and Connie went down into the cells. She spent her time demanding rugs, a hot-water-bottle, a light over her bed, privacy, an aspirin, something to drink, and a Bible. She said that she wanted the Bible to kill the miscellaneous vermin with which, so she threatened to tell the magistrate in the morning, the cell was swarming.

But her real anxiety was for Duke. It was because of him that she cried.

2

In the half-light of the basement—a more extravagant woman would have lit the gas by now—Mrs. Vizzard was seated at the mahogany dining-room table, going over her budget. There was everything set out there in the smallest and minutest detail. "Fish, fourpence; stamp, penny-halfpenny; milk, threepence; tea, sevenpence; soap powder, twopence-halfpenny; pair of quarter-rubbers, ninepence; beetroot, threepence." Her eyes fixed themselves in a frightened stare as she gazed at the figures. It was terrifying, positively terrifying, the way things mounted up. Money seemed to be slipping, slipping from her all the time.

With a sick feeling of alarm, she remembered the lease. Eighteen years. It wasn't long, was it? And after that . . .? She shuddered at the thought of it, and returned to the column of household expenses in front of her. The beetroot, for instance. That had been simply a piece of idle indulgence. She could perfectly well have done without beetroot.

The bell of the spring bracket outside the door suddenly began pealing, and Mrs. Vizzard started. For some reason it alarmed her. She caught her breath and sat there for a moment without moving. By the time she had recovered herself and got up the stairs, the rusted wires were already scraping once more on their pulleys and the bell was beginning to ring again. Mrs. Vizzard quickened her pace.

But she was taking no chances. Before she laid a finger on the door-knob she made sure that the safety latch was in place and she put down the lid of the letter-box as an additional precaution so that nothing could be thrust at her from outside. Then, having flattened out the corner of the door-mat that always jammed when the door was opened, she turned the handle.

It was not yet quite dark. And in any case the street lamp was only just opposite. It threw a pool of milky light over the doorstep. Standing there in the cold was a man. And rather an unusual-looking man. He wore a broad black hat like a priest's or an actor's, and a heavy overcoat that was too large for him. It hung straight down almost to his ankles. On the step on either side of him were two battered, dumpy suitcases. Mrs. Vizzard sized him up at a glance and judged him to be trying to sell something. She made ready to close the door again.

But the man on the doorstep was speaking.

"You have a room to let?" he asked vaguely, in a faint hollow-sounding kind of voice. "A furnished room, I believe."

Mrs. Vizzard kept the door half open. She was undecided. Horribly undecided. What she had been looking forward to was a young single business gentleman: it was, in fact, what she had specified in her advertisement. The man on the doorstep might have been single. But he certainly didn't look businesslike. There was an indefinable suggestion of moth-balls and the rag-bag about him.

But, at least, his voice sounded educated and refined. It was even possible that he might be a gentleman.

"You saw my advertisement?" she asked non-committally.

The broad black hat stirred in silhouette.

"The advertisement? Yes . . . yes, of course. The advertisement."

The voice under the hat was hesitant and unassured. It was almost as if, having actually come to the house in search of lodgings, he had at that moment been thinking of something else.

Mrs. Vizzard pursed up her lips. She had to admit that she didn't like the look of the man. But she couldn't keep him waiting on the doorstep indefinitely. And that back basement room, unlet and unearning, was a constant reproach to her.

"Would you like to see the room?" she asked.

The black hat nodded.

"Thank you," the man said. "Thank you very much."

When the safety chain was undone, he followed her into the hall and put his bags down against the small bamboo table that supported the fern. The bags collapsed inwards upon themselves as soon as he let go of them as though there were practically nothing in them.

"It's downstairs," said Mrs. Vizzard grimly. "If you wait here I'll go and put a light on."

It was not only thoughtfulness that made her do this. She wanted to keep a safe distance between herself and the stranger until she knew a bit more about him. It wouldn't have been the first time that defenceless elderly ladies had been slugged on their own back-stairs.

When she had lit the gas she called out to him to come down. She had half hoped that he might be disinterested when he found that the room was downstairs. But the man gave no hint of minding. He followed her as though he had been going down basement stairs all his life.

The room even with the gas lit was scarcely cheerful. The bamboo table in the hall upstairs was only a small side shoot of the original bamboo forest that sprouted in the basement. Everything down here was of mottled, banana-coloured bamboo. There was another occasional table, with a red-fringed cloth spread cornerwise, obscuring most of the little criss-cross pieces, but under the cloth the tell-tale ridge of the wood showed unmistakably. There was a bamboo wardrobe, ingeniously strengthened with angle brackets, also of bamboo. There was a bamboo wash-stand. There was a wicker-and-bamboo easy chair that sagged suggestively as though very fat men had been sitting in it for years. And there was a bamboo-and-shell overmantel.

The bed was the one entirely bamboo-less object in the room. It was of iron and brass, set high with its casters in separate glass bowls, either to save the oilcloth or because, with so much bamboo about, Mrs. Vizzard had unconsciously grown to fear the depredations of white ants.

But the stranger scarcely seemed to notice the furnishings.

"Thank you," he said, in the same hollow voice that she had noticed on the doorstep. "Thank you very much."

Down here between four walls it sounded more hollow than ever: it was like reverberation in a vault.

"You mean you *like* the room?" Mrs. Vizzard asked.

She was frankly incredulous. In all her years of experience in letting she had never known anyone like the room before.

"Thank you," the stranger said again.

But this was too easy. It revived all her suspicions.

"You know the rent?" she asked.

"The rent. Ah yes, the rent."

Again it was as though the man was mysteriously thinking of something else, as though he wasn't paying proper attention to what was going on. He passed a limp hand that carried a long frayed cuff with it across his forehead and seemed to recover himself a little. "Ten shillings a week, I think the advertisement said," he added.

"Without service."

"Without service?"

"And in advance," Mrs. Vizzard reminded him.

There had been nothing in the advertisement about payment in advance. But the stranger didn't seem to mind.

"In advance," he replied. "Yes, yes, of course. In advance."

"With references," Mrs. Vizzard added meaningly.

The stranger was silent for a moment. The limp hand and the frayed cuff straggled across the forehead again.

"Would rather an old one do?" he asked apologetically. "You see I've been moving about rather a lot lately."

"When do you intend to come?" Mrs. Vizzard asked.

"Intend to come?" The stranger gave a little laugh that sounded more hollow than his voice. "Oh, I've come," he said. "I shan't be going away again."

He unbuttoned his coat and drew out an envelope containing two one-pound notes. He handed one of them to her.

"For a fortnight," he said again. "A fortnight in advance."

Mrs. Vizzard hesitated. While the stranger had been standing there, Mrs. Vizzard had been inspecting him. It wasn't merely that his coat was long. It was the ghost of a coat that had once been magnificent. A complicated brocaded arrangement of frogs ran down the front of it, and the collar was of astrakhan. The buttons had once been covered in the same material as the coat itself. But these had worn threadbare by now, leaving only a pattern of small wooden discs.

But now that his hat was off, it was his face that fascinated her. It was a swarthy, dusky face, almost like an Indian's. Under the eyes were two half-moons that were faintly bluish. But the eyes themselves were dark and brilliant.

"Like a mesmerist's eyes," Mrs. Vizzard told herself. "The sort of eyes that could hypnotise you and make you do things you didn't want to."

Across the stranger's forehead a lock of lank black hair fell forward. Mrs. Vizzard shivered slightly. She was aware that the man was smiling at her.

Slowly she stretched out her hand for the note and her fingers closed on it. It crackled authentically and she felt temporarily reassured.

"Are . . . are you connected with the stage?" she asked.

"The stage?" The stranger shook his head. "No, I am quite unconnected with the stage," he assured her.

"And will you be out all day?"

"No," he answered, the dark eyes still smiling at her. "I shall be in. In all day."

Mrs. Vizzard began backing towards the door. She wanted to shut it. Shut it between him and her, and decide what to do. Call the police seemed the sensible thing. Get rid of him before he could make trouble. But on what evidence? The police wouldn't arrest a man for answering an advertisement. Or offering to pay his rent in advance. So she tried to keep her head, and be businesslike. With her hand on the door-knob—somehow the very feel of the thing gave her confidence—she raised her eyes to him again.

"The name," she said. "I didn't catch it."

"I didn't give it to you," he answered. "It's Squales. S-Q-U-A-L-E-S. Henry Squales. And now if you'll permit me I'll get my bags and unpack."

Back in her own living-room, under the portrait of the departed Mr. Vizzard, Mrs. Vizzard shut the door and locked it. She felt safer that way. But not much safer. The newcomer was too near to her in the back room for her to feel altogether safe. "Suppose he tries to hypnotise me through the brickwork?" she asked herself. "Or taps on the wall at night when everyone else is asleep. Or bores holes in the skirting and spies on me. . . ."

Her thoughts were interrupted by the sound of the front door opening. It was followed by footsteps, quick athletic ones mounting the stairs two steps at a time. She recognised them at once. They were Percy's. He was bolting upstairs to his old mum in just the way a good son should. Then she heard another door, an upstairs one, bang and she knew that he was home. She'd always liked the lad and now she was positively glad of him. It was comforting to have anyone so strong and vigorous about the place.

She glanced towards the wall that separated her from the back room. Behind the wall she could hear the man moving about shifting things. The old feeling of timidity returned to her, and she shuddered.

"I hope I've done the right thing," she told herself. "It wouldn't surprise me to find we'd got a murderer here. A murderer here in No. 10."

3

And what about Connie? How's she been getting on?

Lumme, she didn't half have a time of it at Vine Street. It wasn't no bed of roses being shut up in that cell worrying about Duke all night. And she didn't exactly look at her best when she came before the beak in the morning. By the time she got the mug of police station tea at breakfast she wasn't much more than yesterday's buttonhole.

But she wasn't going to have a lot of flatties putting anything over her. Not likely. That was why she kept on insisting on her rights just to show them that she was a human being and not some kind of a horse. First of all she told 'em she wanted a chair. And, when they asked her why, she said mysteriously that it was because of her condition. Then she wanted to report the night wardress for sticking her nose up against the grille of the cell door and making faces at her every time she'd just been dropping off to sleep.

Nothing came of that complaint. But it was funny while it lasted. And it established her. She spoke in a carrying sort of voice, and everyone who was waiting to go up into the court room could hear her. She was the life and soul of the party downstairs.

"Just you ask the sergeant to step along this way," she began again after a pause. "Tell him I was at College with his sister. And if he's out having a quick one, send the inspector. The good-looking one. Tell him it's a matter of life and death. But don't say who for. And if he doesn't come, say I'll report him to the magistrate. If you think that was tea you gave me just now someone's been robbing you. There's a lot going on around here that needs showing up. I'll give you five minutes by my gold wrist-watch and if nobody's been to see me by then . . ."

But the constable outside didn't even let her finish. He just opened the cell door and waited there.

"Come along," he said. "We're ready for you."

"About time, too," Connie answered, and joined the little queue that was going upstairs.

They went through the narrow oak door that led into the court, and it was then that Connie had her first big disappointment. She'd rather been looking forward to being a member of a big happy family, all peers and stockbrokers and pretty ladies, with Mr. Vercetti himself, the dirty Eyetie, as centre of the picture. She hadn't half been wanting to see him get it in the neck from someone without being able to answer back. But apparently that part of the circus was already over, leaving Rex *v.* Victoria Regina Coke to come on separately. It was flattering, but not so friendly.

Just to keep her spirits up she had a good look round the court while they were getting things ready. It would have been nice to see even one friendly face in all that crowd. But she couldn't find one. She'd never seen a more awful-looking lot of dials in all her life. The policemen all looked hot and beefy, as policemen always do without their helmets on, and the other people in the body of the court might have been borrowed from a mortuary.

Her second big disappointment was the magistrate. He wasn't the regular one and that made things more chilly and impersonal. There had been a time—during Connie's gay period—when the magistrate had been like an old friend to her. Rather a spiteful and vindictive one at times, but still friend. Whereas this cheesy little man on the bench might have been an elderly dentist. He didn't look as if he could be a friend even to himself.

"I wonder if anyone at No. 10 has noticed that poor old Connie didn't get back last night?" she was thinking again. "I wonder if Duke's had his water changed. . . ."

Then the usher called her name and she went into the box.

The magistrate and his clerk had a whispered conversation and then the clerk, very rapidly, began intoning.

". . . charged with obstructing the police in the performance of their duties in that she did switch off the . . ."

"Oh, I never," Connie exclaimed.

The magistrate took one glance in Connie's direction and told her to keep quiet. Her turn would come in a minute, he said. From his voice he seemed a quiet, unemotional sort of man.

". . . when the police entered, with the intention of impeding them in their lawful duties."

The magistrate looked at his finger-nails for a moment and then turned to her again.

"Do you plead guilty or not guilty?"

"Not guilty, m'lud," Connie answered. "It's a lie."

"Call the inspector."

The big young man like a moon-calf was called. He took the oath with an expertness that left Connie aghast.

"Give your evidence," the magistrate ordered him.

"At 11.30 in accordance with my instructions," he said almost as though he had spent the earlier part of the morning in learning the part, "I visited the Moonrakers Club and secured entry. Alcoholic liquors were being served and in an inner room card games were in progress. . . ."

"Yes, yes, we've heard all that," the magistrate interrupted him. "We've heard all that."

But the moon-calf did not seem in the least put out by the interruption. Still in the same over-rehearsed monotone he continued.

"At 12.5 as ordered I rose from my table and opened the window so that my police whistle could be heard outside. The prisoner then appeared from a side passage marked 'Cloaks' and operated the electric light switch connected with the mains. In the darkness a number of those present attempted to escape."

"You're quite sure that this is the woman?" the magistrate asked.

The policeman took one look at Connie.

"Quite sure, sir," he said.

It was her turn now. The usher handed her a Bible and she took it with the easy nonchalance of someone who is used to Bibles.

". . . the truth, the whole truth and nothing but the truth so help me God," she said, speaking almost as fast as the inspector.

The magistrate looked even harder at Connie than the policeman had done. He was, in fact, staring at her so hard that Connie felt uncomfortable. Because he was staring, she began shifting from one foot to the other.

"Is the prisoner sitting down or standing?" the magistrate asked at last.

The policeman who had handed Connie the Bible answered for her.

"She's standing, sir," he said.

The magistrate, however, appeared unconvinced.

"She seems very short," he remarked resentfully. "I can scarcely see her."

For a moment he regarded his finger-nails again. Then he turned to Connie again.

"You have heard the evidence," he said. "Have you anything to say?"

"Only that it's all a lie, sir."

"You mean that you didn't turn off the electric light switch?"

"Not deliberately."

"Then how did you turn it off?"

"I slipped."

There was a titter from the public gallery when Connie said this. The magistrate removed his horn-rimmed glasses and placed them on the desk in front of him.

"This is a court of justice, not a pantomime," he observed in the same cold lifeless voice. "If I hear more laughter I shall order the court to be cleared. I am frequently amazed that there should be so many idle persons who apparently have nothing better to do than to sit in court deriving merriment from the misfortunes of others."

The magistrate—who was quite famous for that kind of thing—waited long enough for the reporters to get down his saying-of-the-week correctly, and then resumed.

"I am expected to believe that suggestion about slipping?" he asked.

"It's God's truth, sir," Connie answered.

The fact did not seem to impress him unduly.

"I trust that it's *all* God's truth that I've been hearing," he said. "You have been on oath ever since you entered the box, remember."

"I'll remember, sir," Connie answered contritely.

The magistrate replaced his glasses and contemplated her solemnly.

"And what did you do with your arms when you were falling?"

Connie thought for a moment.

"I held them in front of me to break my fall," she said.

"Do you remember what it was you fell over?"

Connie thought again. She felt that there was a catch in it somewhere.

"My feet, sir," she replied at last.

At the reply a titter started up again in the body of the court. But the usher was up on his toes all ready, and the laughter died away before it had really come to anything.

As for Connie, the magistrate appeared to be satisfied with her for the moment. He asked her to stand down and invited the moon-calf into the box again.

"How high on the wall is the switch?" he asked.

"Seven foot, eight inches, your worship," he answered.

That was all from him. For the magistrate called Connie once more. It was to be the last time he would worry her.

"How tall are you?" he asked.

"Five foot one, sir," she told him.

"Yet you invite me to believe that in falling you became entangled with an electric light switch nearly a yard above your head." He paused: "Even if you had extended your arms to their full length it would still have been a remarkable coincidence if you had worked the switch. It must in fact have been either a very extraordinary switch or a very extraordinary slip. But your arms were not extended above your head, you say. On the contrary, on your own oath, they were held in front of you to break your fall. In the circumstances I can only conclude that you did turn out the light. Possibly it was *before* your fall. Indeed, your fall may have been the result of putting out the light. . . ."

"Silly old buzzard going on about my fall," Connie was thinking. "They go on about anything you tell them."

But the magistrate was still speaking.

"There is nothing in the evidence to show why you extinguished the light," he continued. "I will conclude that you did so under instructions. Fourteen days. . . ."

The magistrate had removed his glasses and was now sitting back once more. The bench in fact was feeling a bit peckish and was just about to go over to the Club for its lunch.

But Connie had not moved.

"Fourteen days," she repeated incredulously.

"Fourteen days," the usher repeated and tapped on her shoulder.

"But . . . but I've got a dependant," she said. "I can't leave him."

The magistrate regarded her for a moment without his glasses and then regarded her again with them on.

"You wish to say something?" he asked.

Connie nodded.

"I've got a dependant," she said again. "There's no one to look after him."

"Is it your husband?" the magistrate asked. "Is he an invalid?"

"No, sir, he's quite all right. That is to say I haven't got a husband."

Again the titter. And again the usher up on his toes.

"Then who is this dependant?"

"He's a canary."

This time it was more than a titter in the body of the court. It began somewhere with a loud guffaw and broadened into a general murmur of laughter.

The magistrate rapped on the desk.

"My orders have been disregarded," he said. "Usher, clear the court."

Next morning, Mrs. Josser received a cheap-looking Government envelope containing a letter in a ragged, unreliable hand like a child's. It was on the notepaper of Holloway Prison.

"*Dear Mrs. Josser,*" it ran. "*Owing to a slight misunderstanding, I shall be here for fourteen days. Please ask Mrs. Vizzard to on no account let the room which I shall be requiring. Tell her the rent will be attended to prompt on my return. Also please look after Duke. His water will need changing. The birdseed packet is in the top drawer with my hair-brush. Give him enough to cover a penny. Please tell Mrs. Vizzard it's only for a fortnight or sooner if I can get solicitors. If it gets very cold please have Duke down with you. Again thanking you and apologising for bothering you, and hoping that you and Mr. Josser are both well.*

Yours truly

Connie.

"*P.S. Please don't on no account let Duke out of the cage even if he asks, he's very uncertain. Tell him we'll stretch our wings together when I get home.*"

CHAPTER 6

THEY had finished with Mr. Puddy at the sorting office. With the pay-packet they gave him a little slip telling him that he wasn't needed any more. To soften the shock of dismissal, however, there were a few lines in italics at the bottom of the slip to say that in case the Postmaster-General should want Mr. Puddy to help him with the next Christmas rush Mr. Puddy might in due course get in touch with him. Mr. Puddy took the pay-packet and the slip with the philosophic detachment of a man who for years has been plunging in and out of employment like a porpoise. So far as he was concerned it simply meant that this was another of those occasions when he was temporarily tail up in mid-air.

It was twelve noon when the slip was handed to him—he had been working only morning shifts ever since Christmas—and he told himself that the best thing would be to go and get a bit of lunch. In success or failure, Mr. Puddy remained faithful to his food. He thought of the Marquis of Granby up the street. But he dismissed the idea because they never served enough pastry with the steak-and-kidney pie—and he had already decided in his mind on steak-and-kidney. Then he thought of the Pillars of Hercules. But somehow nothing at the Pillars of Hercules was ever really hot. The Irish stew there came out with small eyes of fat like ice floes floating on it. A bit further afield, there was the Rose and Crown which had everything—huge chunks of pastry, soup so hot that men like Mr. Puddy who wore glasses had to keep on taking them off and wiping them, and boiled syrup roll that swam lazily in a treacle sea. But the trouble there was the waitresses. They were overworked and that meant that he would be kept waiting. Also, the waitresses had their regulars and reserved the best portions for them. Mr. Puddy had to be in a specially good mood not to mind that happening. And somehow to-day he felt that it might upset him. So, in the end, he went to the White Rose Eating Rooms just opposite.

The time was half-past twelve when he got there, and at five-and-twenty to two when he emerged he was a replete and contented Mr. Puddy. What he would have liked best would have been to loosen his boots, remove his collar and have forty winks. A sense of duty, however, overcame him. A sense of necessity. There was nothing for it but to go off straight away, all heavy and sleepy as he was, and start looking for something to fill in the awkward gap while he was waiting for next year's sorting rush to begin again.

There was always the Labour Exchange, of course. But Mr. Puddy felt himself a cut above that. The Exchange was all right for men who were in grooves already, men like paper-hangers and bricklayers and carpenters. But for a man of Mr. Puddy's sort who had ranged the whole world of possible employment it was mostly pretty fiddling stuff that the Labour Exchange had to offer. Nearly all their jobs meant clocking-in, a practice that Mr. Puddy detested.

The place that he was making for was Bert Bowman's Employment Agency in the High Street. It cost money to go to Bert Bowman's. But there was the satisfaction of knowing that having gone there you had done the best by yourself. If Mr. Bowman didn't know about a job there probably wasn't one going. But there was no fear of that. Mr. Bowman was bristling with jobs. A small board at the foot of the stairs advertised a whole host of tempting occupations.

Mr. Puddy mounted the stairs, his breath coming in short, after-luncheon gasps, and then had to wait for nearly half an hour for Mr. Bowman to get back. While he was waiting, Mr. Puddy read the testimonials of satisfied clients and employers which plastered the place like wall-paper. The letters all seemed to have been drafted by the same pen, even though the handwriting was different, and all mentioned Mr. Bowman's name somewhere in the body of the message. "So thank you, Mr. Bowman, for finding me my niche. Your fees are most reasonable," or ". . . I am glad, Mr. Bowman, once more to be able to thank you for helping me in my recent labour difficulty." "Your fee, as always, Mr. Bowman, was strictly reasonable. . . ."

Then Mr. Bowman himself came in. He was wearing a black coat and striped trousers and a butterfly collar with a bow tie. He was brusque and very businesslike.

"Take a seat, please," he said, even though Mr. Puddy was already sitting. "The fee is five shillings."

Mr. Puddy counted out the coins and handed them over the desk.

Mr. Bowman, who had got his coat off by now, promptly shovelled the fee into an open cash-bowl in the drawer.

"Name an' address," he asked.

Mr. Puddy told him. He was rather hurt that Mr. Bowman didn't remember him. He had been there often enough.

"What can I do for you?" he asked bluntly.

Mr. Puddy explained his position carefully. He wanted something senior and responsible, something that brought good money and prospects with it. He was a man who could look after things, he said, and supervise other people.

"Ever done any waiting?" Mr. Bowman demanded. "Public banquets and that sort of thing."

Mr. Puddy shook his head.

"Mind living in?" Mr. Bowman asked. "House duties?"

Mr. Puddy went back over the ground again and painted in his own past life so impressively that he scarcely recognised it. It was like talking about a man of the same name who had been a success at everything.

Mr. Bowman turned furiously through the pages of his ledger. "Cooking for four hundred in a large institution? No good no experience. Foreman in a big cabinet-makers? No good no experience. Brewer's representative? No good no connections. Animal trainer in a private circus? No good no experience. Cutter in an artistic furriers? No good no experience. Sewing silks traveller? No good no connections. Optical lens polisher? No good no experience. Ah . . ." His finger remained poised over one entry rather far down the page where Mr. Puddy couldn't see it. "Ah," he said again. "I have it."

Mr. Puddy felt his heart pounding against all that lunch inside him.

"What is it?" he blurted out.

"Night watchman in a tea warehouse, respectable, sober, live out," Mr. Bowman recited to him. "Must be of large build, under sixty-five." He paused and looked up sharply. "That all right?" he asked.

"I'be under sixty-five if thad's whad you bean," Mr. Puddy admitted grudgingly.

His voice was flat and adenoidal. It made him sound as though he were grumbling even when he wasn't.

"Salary two pounds five a week to right man. References taken," Mr. Bowman continued.

He picked up his pen again and began rapidly copying the address on to a gilt-edged card bearing the words "With Bert Bowman's compliments to introduce."

"First week's salary comes here and we give you back half," he said. "After that the prospects are what you make of them."

He had risen from his seat by now and was holding out the little card to Mr. Puddy.

"Better get along straight away," he added warningly. "That sort of post doesn't remain vacant long."

"Is . . . is thad all you've got to offer?" he asked.

"Come and see me if you're not suited," was all he said.

For Mr. Bowman had ceased to be interested in him. Another elderly man, slightly flushed from coming upstairs, had just entered, and Mr. Bowman had fixed him with his horn-rimmed spectacles.

"Take a seat," Mr. Bowman was saying. "The fee is five shillings."

CHAPTER 7

I

It was Saturday afternoon, and Doris and Doreen were on their way up to Hampstead together.

"*I* think it's rather a pet," Doreen was saying above the roar of the Underground train. "But you may feel it's perfectly loathsome. You must promise to say so if you do."

But Doris was perfectly sure that the flat was a pet and not in the least loathsome, because Doreen had been telling her so all the week. An artist had lived there, it seemed, and his studio was going to be their living-room. The little cubicles that had led off it would make the simply sweetest bedrooms, Doreen said. And above all things, the flat had got character. From the way Doreen spoke of it, it might have been smoking a pipe when they got there.

They had reached Camden Town by now and Doreen started pushing her way towards the door. It was not easy. The whole of London was going home to its half-day off, and most of them seemed to live somewhere on the Hampstead and Highgate Line. They were ranged all down the carriage like a submarine crew at action stations. And getting out on to the platform was as difficult as escaping under water.

"But I thought this train went on to Hampstead," Doris said once they could talk once more. "It said so on the indicator."

Doreen seemed vexed at her for mentioning it.

"It's a different part of Hampstead we're going to," she told her. "You can see the trees of Primrose Hill from our windows."

"Our windows," she said, Doris noticed. It was evident that she had already decided on the flat.

They went up the escalator and came out into the High Street. Doris hadn't been to Camden Town before. Just opposite was a splendid concrete-and-plate-glass emporium, a kind of lesser Selfridges; and all down the street outside on either side was retail commerce, a bit lower down in the scale of grandeur—greengrocers, butchers, tobacconists, fish shops, with a flourishing rival trade in fruit and flowers being carried on from the road in barrows. The pavements were packed with people as though a big excursion steamer had just berthed somewhere up Park Street, and a small body of disabled ex-soldiers stood politely in the gutter playing jazz instruments to amuse the trippers. A little further up the street was a super-cinema all chromium and carpet.

Doris was a bit disappointed. It was all exactly the same as the Elephant and Castle on her side of the river. It didn't seem likely that this was the way freedom and the gay life would lie. But Doreen was impatient. She was lugging Doris across the road in front of the ploughing army of trams and buses and private cars.

"It's always simply frightful here on a Saturday afternoon," she was saying. "I don't know where the people come from."

They got into a 31 bus and started along a road that seemed to Doris to get steadily drearier, like penetrating further into a rather murky dream. The tram-lines made it bumpy and after they'd shot under a railway bridge the bus ran beside the grey walls of a goods yard. It was as though somehow they had got round to the back of the stage by mistake, and Camden Town or Primrose Hill or wherever they were was showing them the side that wasn't really meant to be looked at.

Then the conductor said "Primrose Hill Road" and Doreen dragged Doris out of the bus again.

"We'll just go and get the key from the agents and then in five minutes we'll be there," Doreen assured her. "He's an absolute little lamb the agent, I know he'll let us go in alone."

They had to wait some time for the key, however. The absolute little lamb was still out in the meadows somewhere having his feed, and a cardboard notice stuck in the door said "Closed for lunch." By the time the little lamb had returned, wiping his moustache, it was nearly three o'clock.

When they reached the house, the afternoon had already darkened appreciably. The sun had disappeared entirely and all the sparkle had gone from the day. It was as though someone had deliberately smeared a wet dirty cloth across the sky. But Doreen was not in the least dispirited. On the contrary she seemed to take the weather as a kind of challenge.

"Of course, if it looks even the least bit all right on a day like this you can imagine what it would be like on a sunny day," she said.

The house in front of which they were standing was large and detached and of yellow stucco; a real plaster castle. But whatever family of local barons had inhabited it, they seemed long since to have abandoned it, and discharged the serfs. In the result, the privet bushes that sprouted out of the black earth in the front garden were ragged and untidy, and the lawn with the round flower-bed in the middle was gradually reverting to open heath.

They went up the stone-flagged path, past the iron gate that had come off its bottom hinge and now rested permanently on the stonework. But at the tall flight of steps leading up to the massive important-looking porch, Doreen turned to the side, through the green wooden doorway that was marked "Tradesmen."

Doris felt a little abashed at this, but Doreen seemed to be delighted.

"We've got our own separate little entrance, you see," she said over her shoulder.

They were at the side of the house by now, standing on a short path that was made up of two drain covers and an inspection slab laid down by the electric light company. Above them loomed the blank, stucco wall and up this zigzagged a cast-iron fire escape.

Doreen patted it affectionately.

"This is my little surprise," she said. "I wouldn't have given it away for the world. I told you we had our own way in but I didn't say how."

They went up the fire escape together. And at the top they came out on to a large balcony that was really the top of one of the second-floor bedrooms. Round the balcony there was a trellis that needed nailing up in places; and one or two tubs with the skeletons of plants in them stood about in the corners. But right in front of them was what they had climbed for. It was a yellow front door quite newly painted, bearing the words "The Studio." Beside the door was an ornamental bracket supporting an old-fashioned storm lantern.

"I really can't imagine how anyone can have left a darling thing like this—simply walked out and left it, I mean," Doreen exclaimed. "I went absolutely crazy when I saw it."

Doris put her hand up to examine it. But already Doreen had found something else to be excited about. She had got out her key and was opening the yellow front door....

"It's a marvellous colour, isn't it?" she said.

Doris followed her inside and stood there looking round her. Apparently the storm lantern on its hanging bracket wasn't the only thing that the late tenant had left behind him. Inside the front door was a cardboard box containing a pile of old newspapers, two beer-bottles, one arm of a pair of tongs and a lady's shoe. Next to it stood a brown earthenware teapot without a spout, and a further huddle of bottles.

But Doreen didn't stop to notice things like that. She had gone on ahead and opened the door in front of her. As the wall opposite was nearly three-quarters window a great rush of dampish yellow light suddenly seeped into the flat; it was like being transported into the middle of a cloud. But there was no doubt about it; it was certainly a fine big room. The walls were sky-blue and the doors scarlet. And it was so high it was nearly cubical—a cube with the top corners knocked off where the roof slanted sideways. There were no other windows except the enormous tall one. But, on the wall facing it, someone—possibly the late tenant—had *painted* a window. It was a window complete with a flower-pot on the window-sill, lace curtains and a view of trees beyond. It had been slapped on in good bright colours like the back-cloth to a child's ballet.

"That's something else I hadn't told you about," Doreen shrieked at her—she always raised her voice a little when she was excited. "That's what comes of taking a flat from an artist."

It occurred to Doris that the man who had drawn the window couldn't have been a very good artist. But as Doreen seemed to like it all so much she didn't mention it.

"My goodness, it's cold up here, isn't it?" was all she said.

"But look at that marvellous big stove over there," Doreen went on. "Just imagine when it's actually been lit."

Black, and about the size of a pillar-box, the stove stood on a little brick dais all its own. A large flue like a drain-pipe rose from the back and mounted mysteriously through the ceiling. Written across the front of the stove in large letters were the words "POELE ALBERT FRERES."

Doreen pointed to them in triumph.

"You see," she said. "French."

She spoke as though, alone among the nations, the people of France had thought of the idea of warming their rooms, and she seemed to be proud of being associated with such a people. She opened the door of the stove, and a lot of ash and the remains of a wire flue brush fell out on to the floor.

"Of course the whole place needs cleaning up," she said. "It's just as it was left."

Doris agreed with her. It was rather as though the artist tenant had absent-mindedly set out one day and forgotten to come back again.

Behind the stove was a large pile of old newspapers. And there was just a hint of a rough-house before he had walked out. Over in one corner stood a bed with a broken spring mattress and its casters off, and underneath the painted window a chair with three legs had collapsed on to its side. More cardboard boxes, containing saucers, electric light bulbs, nail-brushes, bits of cloth, china ornaments, a sink tidy and a comb with most of the teeth missing, stood about on the floor. On either side of the window, two long curtains striped like zebra-hide hung down on a tilt because the rod had come off the support on one side.

The window worried Doris because there was so much of it. She raised her eyes to the discoloured, sloping ceiling above it. Then a thought struck her.

"Supposing there was a war," she said suddenly. "Wouldn't this be an awful place in an air raid?"

"Oh, my pet, don't think about such things," Doreen told her. "I shall positively always be thinking of air raids now."

They went on into the other rooms and found more evidence of the sudden flight of the late tenant. There was a cupboard with some ties hanging on a wire, a pullover on which moths had been gorging, another shoe—a man's shoe this time—more newspapers, more beer-bottles and a box of night-lights. In the kitchen there was a toothbrush on a hook on the wall, a saucepan still cemented to the gas stove by something that had boiled over on to it—milk probaby—and in a zinc meat safe fixed on to the wall there was the bluish green wraith of what had once been half a loaf of bread. There was even an old newspaper inside the safe as well, as though the previous occupant had been a connoisseur of such things and had put his extra choice specimen—it was a copy of the *Daily Mirror* for the 23rd of September, 1938—inside for special safety.

"Well," Doreen was saying. "Now you've seen it all. And I want you to say just what you think of it. I shan't mind a bit if you simply detest it. I only want you to say so."

They were back in the big studio again with its sky-blue walls and scarlet doors and Doreen was standing there with her eyes half closed and a dreamy look spread across her face.

"As I see it," she went on, without waiting for Doris to speak, "we don't want a lot of furniture in here. Only a great enormous divan with a lot of cushions on it over by the stove, and perhaps an easy chair or two, and a little flat table for drinks and some of those big glass ash-trays and my gramophone." She broke off suddenly in delight. Her voice rushed up half an octave and she began shrieking again. "Just imagine having dances up here. We could have the most marvellous dances."

"Do you think the floor's level enough?" Doris asked.

It was a bare board floor with wide cracks between some of the boards, and the heads of rows of small nails as though scores of tenants, one after another, had laid down oilcloth and then ripped it up again.

But the question had offended Doreen.

"You've been simply horrible about my darling little flat ever since you came here," she said. "You haven't said one nice thing about it. If you don't like it, I wish you'd say so. You know I shan't care. It's no good setting up somewhere Dutch-treat unless we both like it. If you'd rather go on as you are, I shall quite understand."

But Doris was remembering Dulcimer Street. Remembering Uncle Henry in his cycling stockings. Remembering the smell of cooking from Mr. Puddy upstairs. Remembering Connie. Remembering a lot of things.

"Oh, but I do like it. I do really. I like it very much," she said.

2

They had said good-bye and gone their separate ways—Doreen to a perfectly marvellous show at the Cambridge with a friend of hers who was doing a terribly important job and doing it frightfully well but was really a perfect dear and screamingly funny when you got to know him. And Doris back to Dulcimer Street.

But she didn't go straight back.

She was too much preoccupied and jumpy about things. There she was with one half of an expensive new residence on her hands, and only twenty pounds in the Post Office. It was like getting married in a hurry and ruining herself. And whose idea was it, she asked herself—hers or Doreen's?

It seemed that she had merely mentioned quite casually that she didn't like living at home and the next thing that she had known was that she was being whisked off to that bare, bleak-looking barn of a place with its silly painted window and hideous scarlet doors somewhere under the roof-tops.

That window that looked as if it were tumbling back into the room still worried her. But so did a lot of other things as well. She was worried about her share of the rent. About the furniture. About the awful iron staircase up the side of the house. About who would wash up and get the evening meal—somehow she didn't see Doreen doing it. About the electric light bills and the gas and the water rate. About getting the place cleaned. About buying an alarm clock so that she could get to the office in time. Also, about telling Mrs. Josser.

She'd been putting it off because there hadn't seemed to be any point in breaking the news until she'd actually seen the flat. But now that the time had actually come, she felt more strongly than ever like putting it off again. That was why instead of turning down Kennington Lane in the direction of Dulcimer Street she went along to the Toledo instead.

The Toledo was new. It had only been open for a couple of months. And she was using it for the very purpose for which it had been erected—as a retreat. It was a huge ferro-concrete refuge from the cares and troubles of life, complete with a marble fountain in the forecourt, carpets like bog-moss, the largest organ in South London, attendants like chorus-girls who went up and down during performances with the latest kind of antiseptic scent-spray, an ice-cream fountain, Acousticonaids for the deaf, Synchro-Harmonic Reproduction, and deep rubber-padded chairs for the refugees. It seemed just the place to go and forget about having to tell Mrs. Josser.

And as it turned out, she didn't go alone. She had just left the pay-box when someone spoke to her. It was Percy. He was in his smartest suit—the purplish one with a shirt and handkerchief and tie to match—and it was obvious that he was at a loose end. Also it was obvious that he wanted to be friendly.

"Mind if we see this together?" he asked, in the easy manner that he had been cultivating.

"No-o-o," said Doris.

He liked her for accepting it that way. It was all so simple and straightforward. Most of the other girls he knew always fooled about first before accepting anything even when they wanted it. But Doris was different. She was ladylike.

The girl with the antiseptic scent-spray had just passed down the aisle when they reached their seats, and their nostrils were full of the musty fragrance of peach and sandalwood. It was like a trip out East for nothing. Percy distended his nostrils and sniffed. Then another girl, a twin sister of the first one with the scent-spray only clothed all in white this time, came along selling ices, and Percy bought two threepenny cartons with flat wooden spoons. When he had finished his, Percy took out a pocket comb and combed his hair. He always tried to keep himself looking nice when he was out anywhere.

On the screen a lot of well-developed girls of the kind that Percy usually liked looking at were singing a song called " Lido Blues." They were dangling their legs over the edge of the swimming-pool and wearing very tight-fitting bathing costumes. Every so often—the song was a long one—one of the girl would throw up her arms and dive out of sight.

But Percy wasn't looking at the film at all. He was looking at Doris. He could see her profile silhouetted against a distant illuminated "Exit." It was a nice profile, something he liked looking at. Not exactly his type, he told himself. But all right. Very much all right. She was O.K. in a quiet way. He wondered vaguely how much she knew about things. It was something that he always wondered when he went out with a girl.

The Blonde from the fun fair had been a failure. She had known more about things than Percy did. And she was married. She'd told him that while they were parked in the car under the trees on Wimbledon Common. Even up to that moment it had not been a good evening. They'd gone to the Palais de Danse, and the Blonde had been a positive menace. "Don't be afraid," she kept on saying. "Go on: hold me tighter. I don't bite." In the result his arms had ached and he had got a lot of lipstick smeared across his collar. And then on top of all that, after he'd gone to the trouble of borrowing somebody's car from the garage to make everything cosy for them both, to have her tell him that she was married. A bit of a moralist in his way, he dropped her on principle as soon as he found out.

But he was looking at Doris now and had forgotten the Blonde. Or, at least, she and all the other blondes in the world had become merged. It was Doris versus the All-Blonde.

"If I had a girl like Doris, I'd be O.K.," he was thinking. "You can see she's all right just by looking at her. She's not like those mucky blondes. And she's just a little girl. She needs looking after. She needs someone to look after her who knows his way about. She doesn't know anything. She's the sort of little girl who'd get hurt just because she doesn't know what's bad for her. She's only a baby."

Because he felt sentimental he reached out and tried to take hold of her hand. At first she thought that he wanted her to pass him something. But when she discovered what he was up to, she avoided the hot groping hand that had come working its way towards her. She just sat there as she was, her hands clasped in her lap and her bag over them. Her refusal hurt Percy. Hurt him more than he cared to admit. It was the first time that anyone had ever declined to hold his hand in a cinema. And it hurt him still further to think that after the way so many women had been ready to grant him so much he should trip up over a little thing like this. But perhaps that was the whole point, he told himself. He'd been going about with the wrong kind of women. The cheap sort. *They'd* let you do anything; and Doris wouldn't. That was just the difference. That was what made her worth while.

"If I'd got a decent girl like Doris, I'd be O.K.," he thought again. "I'd be in clover."

He stared at the screen for a moment—the swim-and-sing girls had changed into sombreros and cowboy suits while he wasn't looking—and then stared back at Doris again.

"If I'd got a girl like Doris," he told himself, "I'd buy her a cocky little hat and a lot of smart stuff from the Burma Gem. That's the way brunettes look best—with jewellery on. *She* ought to wear ear-rings. And a diamond clip. She needs more lipstick." He eyed her up and down in the half-darkness, thinking of ways in which he could improve her, and fell back on his old thought again. "She's only a little girl," he told himself. "She's only a baby really."

Then a new idea struck him.

"I'd give her a good time," he told himself. "I'd take her round and show her places. I'd watch her come to life. I'd stand by and see her unfold. She'd go places with me."

Percy Boon was no longer thinking that he'd be all right, O.K., if he had a girl like Doris to take about with him. He wanted Doris herself. Wanted her desperately.

"If I had her," he went on, "I'd give up all those peroxide blondes. I'd leave them to the chaps who want them. They'd have to get along without me. Doris and me would be different. We'd go to the Palais and the cinema, of course. But everything quite open. Everything O.K. from the start. I'd take her up the river to Hampton Court. We'd go punting together. I'd buy a portable gramophone to take along with us, so we could have dance tunes. We'd go ice-skating. I'd give her a pair of skates with white kid boots and everything if she'd come skating with me. She'd wear a short skirt with a lot of pleats. And a tight jumper. I'd show her what money can buy. I bet she's never had a real day of it, with a decent sports car and drinks on the way and all that. We'd go to Brighton. I could fix the car all right. I'd get hold of something snappy. I'd attend to everything. Leave it all to Percy."

The film was drawing to its close now and Doris let him help her on with her coat. It was just the moment he had been waiting for. His arm went round her and he was most unnecessarily tender. As he was bending over her, his cheek brushed across her hair and he sniffed expectantly. But he was disappointed.

"She doesn't know anything yet," he told himself. "She doesn't use perfume. She doesn't even use a strong shampoo. She doesn't know anything yet."

CHAPTER 8

MRS. VIZZARD was off to enjoy herself. But somehow her appearance didn't suggest enjoyment. At least there was no hint of the riotous about it. The whole effect was formal and rather frigid. She was dressed all in black, with a large shiny black handbag. It might have been something rather sedate in the way of funerals that she was going to attend.

And that was just how Mrs. Vizzard liked to dress. Modern women, girls especially, slouched their way through life. Without corsets and sometimes even without stockings, they slopped. Whereas Mrs. Vizzard carried herself. She was upright and un-sagging.

At the moment, however, she was nearly out of her senses with anxiety. And all because of Mr. Squales. She had already gone round once, locking everything up. But, now that she remembered him, she made another inspection, pulling at the drawers of her desk, at the cupboard door, at the lid of the coal-bin just to make sure that the catches had caught. She had turned over in her mind the idea of fixing a piece of stamp paper across the outside door to see if Mr. Squales had equipped himself with a skeleton key—a whole bunch of them possibly—which enabled him to break in whenever he fancied.

Finally, she could bear it no longer. She went and stood for a moment outside Mr. Squales's door, listening. But she wasn't quite sure what it was that she expected to hear. Whatever it was, she heard nothing. The sense of mystery deepened. Why should he go out only at night-time? she asked herself. It was almost as if he were afraid to face the daylight. He was never out for very long on these furtive evening sorties. It was usually well before midnight when he got back. But whatever went on in those intervening hours was evidently strangely wearing. She had met him once when he was coming in, and seen his face in the downward shaft of light from the gas bracket in the hall. It was the face of an exhausted man—with beads of perspiration all along the forehead.

A burglar? Could that be it? It would explain everything. A burglar here in the next room beside her. And a murderer, too, for all she knew. Either that or someone who preyed—she didn't know how—on women. Whichever of these he was she resolved to get rid of him.

But there was something else to-night to occupy her mind. For she was on her way to keep an appointment. And no ordinary appointment at that. Nothing less than one with the late Mr. Vizzard, in fact. For a few tense privileged moments she was going to be allowed to peep behind the veil, to penetrate, to voyage astrally. And all for half a crown. The members of the South London Psychical Society had been specially circularised for the occasion. The new medium was as gifted as he was reluctant, it seemed. The recipient of frequent and informative messages from the Other Side, he was perfectly content to remain in exclusive possession of them. Nothing less than two guineas would persuade him.

There were half a dozen of the subscribers already arrived by the time Mrs. Vizzard got there. And Mr. Chinkwell, the secretary, was passing with bright birdlike movements from one to the other, a tray of sandwiches in one hand, a plate of bridge-rolls in the other. He was a quick nervous little man, always up on his toes and anxious to make a success of things. Full of new ideas, he was always proposing fresh schemes—visits to neighbouring psychical societies, pilgrimages to the homes of famous mediums, trips to haunted houses.

Altogether, he was the driving force in the Society—very different from the decayed and unprofitable clergyman, Dr. Glassey-Whyte, who had preceded him. Dr. Glassey-Whyte's exclusively theological training had finally landed him into trouble on the financial side—there was nearly fifty pounds' worth of subscriptions that could never be traced—and he had resigned. But little Mr. Chinkwell was a born accountant. Under his guidance, the spirits showed a profit.

Mr. Chinkwell hopped forward to greet Mrs. Vizzard.

"Good evening," he said. "I'm so glad that you were able to come. The medium has not arrived yet. But I'm told that he is never late. Fish-paste or sandwich-spread?"

The other women who were there were already munching. They were building up their strength for the experience. And Mr. Chinkwell was plying them. Between single ladies and light refreshments there is, he had discovered, an irresistible attraction. And though they paid sixpence a head for them, on top of the half-crown, they still liked to have the plate passed to them and say "Thank you," as though it had all been a friendly charity of Mr. Chinkwell's. What was more, they ate heartily. Even Mrs. Jan Byl. A widow of great wealth from Knightsbridge—it was her car that stood outside as glittering and imposing as a hearse—she tucked into the sandwiches along with the rest.

By five to eight there were thirteen of them there and Mr. Chinkwell was getting worried. But at eight o'clock sharp—it showed an almost psychic awareness of the time—the door-bell rang and it was the medium, the great Qualito. There was something strangely electric about his coming. One of the members, a schoolmistress from Sydenham, said that she could positively *feel* the man: it was, she said, exactly as though someone had run a long, cold thumb-nail along her spine.

But even so that didn't mean that the séance could begin at once. Mr. Chinkwell brought back the message that Qualito was resting and did not wish to be disturbed. He had asked for a cup of coffee and a cigarette, and it seemed that there was no possibility of rushing him. The Sydenham schoolmistress declared that a sudden loosening of the tension in her spine denoted that the medium was probably dozing.

But at eight twenty-five everything was ready, and they all trooped through into the séance room. It was a bare lofty room, sparsely furnished with a long oval table. A small red-domed light glowed in the middle. The table was surrounded by deal chairs. And a second-hand sideboard supported the apparatus—a megaphone, a canary-cage with a white silk handkerchief inside, a planchette, a pair of tambourines and a deep bowl of mercolised wax. Most of the objects were painted with luminous paint so that the spectators could keep an eye on what was happening to them once the light had been turned out. But the mercolised wax was for examination afterwards. It was there specially for those mediums who produced spirit hands out of themselves and tantalisingly re-absorbed them.

The idea was simple but effective. The medium was invited to materialise the ectoplasmic hand inside the wax. Then when the séance was over a cast of the pseudopod could be cast in plaster and the investigators could examine this hand from nowhere. It was all very modern and scientific and advanced. And Mr. Chinkwell had calculated that he could sell plaster casts of pseudopods for five guineas apiece to no fewer than 137 corresponding societies. The only thing so far that was lacking was the medium who could produce pseudopods.

But sometimes at dull séances, when Mr. Chinkwell should have been thinking of the Other Side and the Dawn Lands and the Happy Vale, he just sat there multiplying 137 by 5 and adding in the odd shillings.

Qualito, as it turned out, was one of those mediums who couldn't stand a strong light even before séances. He had apparently been sitting in total darkness upstairs for the past ten minutes. So the lights in the séance room were turned down in readiness and only the red light on the table—a kind of satanic night-light—was left burning. Then the door at the end opened and Qualito was led in. He sat down in the big armchair at the head of the table with Mrs. Jan Byl on one side of him and Mrs. Vizzard at the other. The schoolmistress had asked to be allowed to sit up there beside him, but Mr. Chinkwell had been compelled to refuse. If she felt long, cold thumb-nails running up and down her spine when she was in another room, he did not like to think what she would feel when she was actually touching him.

Qualito himself seemed admirably composed. He had already changed into slippers and now he took off his collar and tie and loosened his waistcoat. Then sitting back limply in his chair he hung his hands over the side as if they didn't belong to him and in a deep un-English voice addressed the company.

"Let us form a leeving circle," he suggested. "Circles are so strong."

The schoolmistress almost swooned when she at last came into contact with this powerful man even though he was seven places away from her. It was as though invisible sparks, as she described it, leapt from the finger-tips of her two neighbours, and kindled something inside her.

For quite a time, however, absolutely nothing happened. Qualito seemed merely to be resting at the Society's expense. And for all the good he was, he might have stayed away altogether.

It was the alert Mr. Chinkwell who was the first to notice that his breathing had changed. It was now deep and laboured as if instead of just sitting there he were running, actually running. And it was getting more laboured still. It was as if the man were choking. Finally he said something, something so muttered and indistinct no one could catch the meaning. It was obvious, however, that the man was speaking. But was it? It didn't sound like his voice at all. Qualito's voice was smooth, like olive oil, and this other voice was higher and *older*. It was as though a man of seventy were in the chair with him.

Then quite suddenly the voice, whose-ever voice it was, came through quite clearly. It spoke to them. There was Qualito, low in his chair, moaning and shuddering, and there was this voice speaking through him.

"I am Pi Yam," it said. "I greet you. I cannot see you plainly. But I greet you."

There was a pause after this, and Mr. Chinkwell, after allowing

Pi Yam a few seconds' grace to see if he wanted to add anything, addressed him.

"Where are you, Pi Yam?" he asked.

"Among the mountains," Pi Yam answered.

"What mountains?"

"High mountains."

"Are you alone?"

"Yes."

"How long have you been there?"

"Time has no meaning where I am. There is no sunrise and no sunset. It is always morning. It is very beautiful."

"What do the mountains look like?"

"They are snow-covered. Like clouds seen from far off at sea."

"Is it cold?" the schoolmistress asked in a tense voice charged with emotion.

"There is neither heat nor cold where I am," he reproved her. "Heat and cold are diseases."

"Isn't even the snow cold?" Mrs. Jan Byl asked.

But this time Pi Yam declined to answer.

"What were you on earth, Pi Yam?" Mr. Chinkwell put in hurriedly.

He didn't want the evening spoiled for the others simply because Mrs. Jan Byl was badgering their visitor with awkward questions. On the other hand, he couldn't afford to offend Mrs. Jan Byl.

"I was dedicate. A Lama," Pi Yam said simply. "Tibet was my home. I lived in a monastery with two hundred other Lamas. My earthly name meant Water Stillness. I was renamed when I came here. My new name is Brightly Shining. But they call me Messenger."

"I thought you said you were alone."

It was Mrs. Jan Byl who had spoken.

"I am."

"Then who is there to speak to you?" she demanded.

Pi Yam was silent for a moment, almost as if sulking.

"The birds," he said at last. "And the flowers."

"Flowers up there among all that snow?"

"Snow-flowers," said Pi Yam tartly and refused to be drawn further.

"Have you any message for anyone here?" Mr. Chinkwell enquired.

"I have a message for everyone," Pi Yam replied. "Confucius gave it to me. It is this: an eagle falling from a great height may capture a young lamb, but a lily gathers sweetness without moving."

"Is that all?" Mrs. Jan Byl asked pointedly.

"Only by realising our All-Oneness shall we attain Peace," Pi Yam continued as though he had not noticed the interruption and were speaking to himself now. "Speed is no substitute for contemplation. The love of mother and child is no more gracious than the lust of a serpent for its victim. The stars show us the way but we do not follow them. Our pride is like slippers of lead upon our feet. Even the All-Nothingness is a part of the All-Oneness."

"Will you speak direct to one of us?" Mr. Chinkwell suggested. "Bring us tidings perhaps?"

He knew how much these personal messages were always appreciated.

Pi Yam considered the point for a moment.

"There is one here who is unhappy," he said at last. "A woman. She is like an empty bottle containing no wine. She is desolate. She longs for the wine, but it is withheld. She has searched for truth but been disappointed. She seeks for a strong arm to rest on, but she cannot find it. Her breasts ache. She weeps for her misfortunes. I tell her to be happy. She is like a harp that the wind plays on. The music is faint and far off. But somewhere there are ears which hear it."

The schoolmistress from Sydenham gave a great gulp and because her hands were engaged and she could not get at her handkerchief she sat there sniffing. She could hardly bear to have him go on.

But Pi Yam apparently had finished: his message was delivered. It was Qualito and not the Tibetan Lama who sat there. And as the spirit left him he began twitching and jerking so violently that Mrs. Vizzard and Mrs. Jan Byl could scarcely hold him. There were those shuddering groans again. And, as he jerked his head, little flecks of sweat from his forehead fell on Mrs. Jan Byl's expensive skirt. Then the breathing quietened and Qualito's real voice spoke to them.

"Give me light," he said anxiously. "Give me light. I am frightened."

Mr. Chinkwell had been ready for this moment. He leant forward and kicked on the switch with his foot. In the sudden blaze no one could see anything for a moment. They screwed up their faces and shook themselves. One or two wiped their foreheads. Then everyone turned towards the medium who was lying back in his chair exhausted.

Mrs. Vizzard was one of the first to turn. And when she turned she saw that it was the hand of Mr. Squales that she had been holding.

"It's my belief," Mrs. Jan Byl was saying in a Knightsbridge whisper, "that the man's an impostor."

CHAPTER 9

Interlude with Dr. Otto Hapfel

IN HIS single bed-sitting-room in Coram Street, Dr. Otto Hapfel, the young man who had visited the South London Parliament, was writing a letter. It was a long letter, and he was taking immense pains over it. For it was no ordinary letter. He had written a weekly document of this kind ever since he had been in England. And it had finally become the very centre of his life. Even his studies were now only of secondary importance compared with it. He spent nearly the whole week, when he was not at lectures, going to the theatre, the football matches, to restaurants, to religious services, to public meetings, painstakingly observing the strange British race and making notes on its behaviour. It was his fervent hope, his prayer, that somehow or other he might hit on some single aspect of English life that had never been scientifically isolated before, something that might provide the essential key to the national character.

On the face of it the effort was not wasted. The recipient of these six- and seven-page letters—he was Dr. Karl Anders, senior history master at the Gymnasium at Krefeld—had hinted that the letters did not remain unseen by other eyes. He had even taken the liberty of having copies made. And he had shown them in the right quarters. In the result, they had gone high. Very high. Exactly how high Dr. Hapfel dared not ask. But there was a suggestion of ultimate elevation that made it possible for Dr. Otto Hapfel, writing away in the rosy glow of his shilling-in-the-slot gas fire in Coram Street, to imagine that passages from his letters—certain skilfully chosen sentences—might eventually find their way upwards and upwards until finally no less a person than the Führer himself. . . . But this was absurd. Dr. Hapfel was allowing his imagination to run away with him.

All the same, was it really so absurd? If it hadn't been for those letters why should he have been invited to the Embassy in Carlton House Terrace? There must have been a reason, a special and distinctive reason, something that had singled him out from all the other members of the German Students' Club who hadn't been invited. The Ambassador didn't go about offering his hand to every German post-graduate who was quietly pursuing his researches in London.

"Heil Hitler!" he began his letter. "I trust that our beloved Führer enjoys good health. May he prosper!"

There were two perfectly valid reasons for beginning his letter in this style. In the first place, it was only fair to Dr. Anders as the envelope was sure to be opened by the postal censors as soon as it got into Germany. And secondly he really felt that way. During the whole of his year in England he had felt himself mysteriously supported or assisted by the divine—yes, divine wasn't too strong a word—love and strength that emanated from one man, and reached across rivers and mountains, over frontiers and continents and oceans to others of German race no matter where they were. It was exciting, like living in the birth of a religion while the Saviour—was still alive.

Dr. Hapfel gave the knob of his stylo a little twist and continued with his letter.

"*I have been to many theatres and cinemas lately,*" he wrote as solemnly as before, "*and I thought that you might be interested to hear how the audience behaves when the National Anthem is played. It is highly instructive to observe the devices which are adopted to avoid testing the patience of the public too strongly. Sometimes a few bars only from an electric recording are played at the very beginning of a performance so that people can come late and so avoid hearing it altogether. Many adopt this pitiful subterfuge. In other theatres and cinemas, it is played in the same shortened form at the end. But the effect is much the same: many leave deliberately before it. Everyone is, of course, expected to stand at attention whenever it is played but, at the end of a performance, only some High Tories observe the convention. Others button up their overcoats, feel about for their gloves and reach for their umbrellas. Singing of the anthem is rarely heard except on Boat Race Night. The Boat Race, you will remember, is an intercollegiate race rowed in tidal water on the Thames between Putney and Mortlake and as the British are a sea-power nation much popular enthusiasm is released by this demonstration of water fitness. At religious services in those denominations which I have attended the anthem is not played at all. At large football matches, called Cup Ties, the anthem is both played (generally by compulsory military bands) and sung; but at cricket matches it is rarely heard. I have been to Lord's (the principal cricket stadium in London) three times without hearing it once.*"

Dr. Hapfel gave another twist to the knob of his stylo so that the ink should flow really freely and went on with the second page. And with the third. And with the fourth. And with the fifth. And with the sixth. And with the seventh. When he had finished, he was quite exhausted. He sat back in his chair wondering how a race like the English which had once been so vigorous and ruthless could have decayed so rapidly. He thought that perhaps it had something to do with the women. English women, he had already noticed, habitually smoked in public, wore their hair short and arranged their own marriages.

The clock in St. Pancras Church at the bottom of Southampton Row chimed midnight and Dr. Hapfel put away his writing materials in the flat zip-fastened brief case that he always carried about with him.

When the room was tidy he stood at attention and saluted the Führer's photograph on the mantelpiece.

Then he started to undress.

CHAPTER 10

1

MR. AND MRS. JOSSER were sitting facing each other.

Mr. Josser, his waistcoat undone and his feet up on the fender, was the more placid figure of the two. Spread out on his knees was a copy of the *Homefinder*, and he was buying cottages. One after another, he marked them down. "Delightful secluded cottage residence. Old-world garden. Main water. 1 mile from good bus service;" "Genuine Elizabethan snip. 5 good rooms. 15th-century well in garden;" "For lovers of the antique, sit. outskirts small country town, thatched barn converted into labour-saving *pied-à-terre*"—the list grew, and Mr. Josser went on buying.

The matter of price was a difficulty, of course. All the cottages that he liked seemed to cost between five and six hundred pounds, and Mr. Josser had only got five hundred altogether. But he had long since passed completely out of the world of reality. He was now in an enlarged dream state in which he bought everything that took his fancy. Thatched, Elizabethan, Cotswold-stone, brick-built, ivy-covered, Queen Anne—it made no difference. For the past half an hour he had been living in Essex, in Hertfordshire, in Middlesex, in Bucks, in Kent and in Surrey.

Glancing up he saw Mrs. Josser regarding him. And rather self-consciously he tried to conceal what he had been reading. But he need not have troubled: Mrs. Josser wasn't thinking about cottages.

"If Doris was so unhappy here that she wanted to leave home, why didn't she say so?" she demanded. "I shouldn't have stopped her."

"But that's just what she has done," Mr. Josser answered. "She's said she wants to go."

"It's no use *now*," Mrs. Josser replied, scornfully. "She ought to have said so before."

"When?"

"When she first thought of it."

"But she hadn't got anywhere to go to."

"She was planning, wasn't she?"

It was no good. They'd been over it all before. Mrs. Josser was offended. Bitterly offended. She found it difficult to forgive her daughter for this piece of family treachery. It savoured of everything that was scheming, underhand and deceitful. She drew in her lip as she thought about it.

"If she goes," she said suddenly, "I'm going to find a p.g. I'm not going to leave that room standing empty."

As Mrs. Josser didn't appear to be inclined to go on with the conversation, Mr. Josser returned to the *Homefinder*. Of course, if you were prepared to go as far away as Cumberland there were waterfalls, and uninterrupted views of magnificent, unspoiled mountain scenery (bus service, one mile) to be had simply for the asking.

"It's my belief she was influenced," Mrs. Josser said suddenly.

"You mean . . . ?" Mr. Josser began.

Mrs. Josser nodded.

"I mean that Doreen person," she said. "She's at the bottom of it. She's the one I'd like to talk to."

"Then why not?" Mr. Josser asked innocently. "Get Doris to bring her here."

"Have her here?" Mrs. Josser answered. "Not likely. She's done enough harm already, hasn't she?"

"Then how are you going to talk to her?"

"I'm not. I'd only like to."

Mr. Josser was silent again.

"You know, Mother," he said at last, "it isn't anything very serious she wants to do. Plenty of other girls have done it. She only wants to leave home."

"*Only!*" Mrs. Josser repeated, raising her eyebrows a little.

"Well, you'd have left home yourself if you'd had the chance, wouldn't you?" Mr. Josser asked her. "You often said so."

Mrs. Josser turned on him. To throw the past up in her face in this fashion was intolerable. So she denied it.

"What? Me leave home?" she asked. "Never!"

With that, she got up and went round the room, tidying. Tidying—particularly tidying of this kind—was always an indication that she was badly upset. She jerked the corner of the hearthrug straight, thumped up the cushions and rearranged the ornaments on the mantelpiece.

Mr. Josser sat watching her.

"There's one thing, Mother," he said. "In a way it makes it easier, not having to consider Doris. You were against her making the journey, remember. If we've only got ourselves to consider we could have a cottage *anywhere*."

"And leave Doris with that Doreen person," Mrs. Josser replied over her shoulder. "Not likely. If Doris goes, we let her room and stop where we are."

2

Percy was flat on his back underneath a car thinking about Doris.

"This is love," he kept telling himself. "This is the real thing. This isn't just something passing. This one hurts. This is the real thing."

He removed the last nut and the silencer fell down on him, spattering bits of dried mud and rusted metal into his eyes and hair. He could hear the burnt-out baffle plates rattling about against each other.

"This'll be a spot-welding job," he told himself.

As he worked his way out from under the chassis he was still thinking about Doris.

"She's different," he began all over again. "She doesn't know anything. No one's woke her up yet. She's never been kissed. She's just an ice queen." And then, as though defending her, "But that's because she's just a kid. She's got a heart all right. Only it's hidden. She's afraid of love. She needs teaching. Someone's got to show her how."

It wasn't any use leaving the silencer there on the ground, and

Percy went through into the workshop with it. He'd have to write out a repair ticket. As he went he sang:

"Little girl Blue,
Is it a ghost, or is it you,
That haunts my dreams that never come true,
Little girl Blue?
Is it a moth on my lips I feel
Every night in the darkness, or something real,
Little girl Blue?"

A lump came into his throat as he thought about the words. That was him all right. It was at night that it got him most. Late at night. Two o'clock in the morning. That sort of thing.

"I'll give her chocolates in round boxes. I'll buy her a hundred State Express. I'll take her to get her photo done. I'll show her where life begins," he went on to himself. "She'll wake up and think she's still dreaming. She'll think Father Christmas did it. She's just Cinderella. She's never been kissed."

Never been kissed! Something hot and uncontrollable ran through him. And he wanted her.

"I'd kill any man who got her first," he said aloud in the empty workshop with the motor tyres and the headlamp bulbs and the cheap accessories all round him. "I'd kill anyone who looks at Doris."

He wrote out the repair ticket, and went upstairs again. It was his last job. And when it was finished he was through. He didn't intend to take too long over it.

"Perhaps I'll meet her on the stairs as I go in," the thought struck him. "Perhaps I'll be close to her. Perhaps she'll say something to show she cares. Perhaps I'll meet her on the stairs as I go in."

Then he had a new idea. He had got the end of the silencer off by now and taken a look inside. Two new baffle plates would make it O.K. again. It'd last for years then. Last as long as the car. But they'd have to be spot-welded. And it would all take time. His time. What was the big idea behind it anyway? He wouldn't make anything out of it. It was just his job. Nothing on the side. And no commission. Someone must think he was a sucker. Or was he?

Picking up a monkey wrench he did a bit of work inside the silencer and held it up to the light. The light came shining through in places and he widened one of the places with his thumb.

Then he put the silencer up on the bench as evidence.

"Bung on a new silencer in five minutes," he said. "It's sweated labour anyhow."

It was eleven o'clock when he left the garage.

Outside the public houses groups of people were standing as though, having spent the rest of the evening together, they could not bear to part so abruptly now. But elsewhere the streets were deserted. There were stretches of a hundred yards or so without anyone in sight. Kennington in fact had put itself to bed, leaving Percy, one of the world's workers, without anything to do.

He thought for a moment of the All Night Café in Brixton. But it seemed a long way to go simply on the off-chance of meeting someone. And it wasn't adventure he was wanting to-night: it was Doris.

"Anyhow, Mum'll be pleased to have me home early for once," he told himself.

So he crossed over and stood waiting for a bus. He was still humming "Little Girl Blue" and he felt in a romantic exalted sort of mood. He wanted to go upstairs on a rainbow and dream. Then suddenly the mood changed and he began feeling feverishly through all his pockets. He was afraid he'd run clean out of cigarettes and all the bloody shops shut. But he was O.K. He'd got a packet of twenty not started. He'd just recovered from his anxiety and was back upstairs on the rainbow again when a voice greeted him.

"Hallo, Perce," the voice said. "I hoped it was you."

He was aware of a strong waft of perfume as he turned, a mixture of shampoo and cachou and scent and fancy toilet soap. He knew before he saw her that it was the Blonde from the fun fair.

"Hallo," he said unenthusiastically.

"I was horrid to you the other night," the Blonde said. "I've been sorry ever since. I teased you."

"Teased me?" Percy repeated coldly. "Did you?"

"Don't you remember?"

Her voice was husky and she seemed undecided whether to be relieved or offended that he had not remembered.

"Can't say I do."

She came nearer to him.

"You know. About me being married?"

"Oh, that."

He could feel her arm pressing up against his and he told himself that she could save herself the trouble. Because of Doris, neither this blonde, nor any other, had any meaning for him. He could have found himself on a desert island full of blondes and he wouldn't have cared.

"It doesn't matter," he said loftily. "It doesn't matter in the least."

The Blonde drew in her breath quickly.

"In that case it doesn't matter to me either," she said. "I only thought that perhaps it might."

Percy wasn't even looking at her now. He was looking down the Brixton Road. And he saw what he wanted.

"'Scuse me," he said. "This is my bus."

He pulled his hat down a little more firmly over one eye and stepped into the gutter with his arm raised. He liked getting on a bus that way—simply slowing it down a bit and then jumping on as it was going. It showed you knew your way about.

"Good night, Perce," the Blonde said, and there was a little break in her voice as she said it. "I'm sorry I spoke to you. I just didn't understand."

"That's O.K.," Percy answered, and made the mistake of looking back at her.

If he hadn't looked at her he wouldn't have known that she was in tears. And then he would have been on the bus all right, instead of simply looking after its red tail light vanishing down the long street. But for as long as he could remember he'd always been weak on tears. They got him right there, and he couldn't stand up to them. So he let the bus go by and asked her what was the matter. She was only a little thing, about Doris's size. And already he felt sorry for her. He couldn't help feeling sorry when women cried because of him.

But the Blonde was already perking up a bit.

"I didn't mean to start crying," she said. "I don't like girls who cry. It was only that you were so cold I couldn't help it."

Percy remembered his bus again.

"Well, what's the trouble?" he asked. "I haven't done anything, have I?"

"Only come into my dreams," she said, more like her old self. "That's all you've done."

She took hold of his arm and pushed it through hers. "I can't make you out," she said. "Honest I can't. You're so funny I reckon you must be afraid of me. You didn't seem to be the other night and now you are again."

Percy looked down at her. He was right: she wasn't bad-looking. And she'd had her hair brightened up again. She was almost a real blonde now.

"Why should I be afraid?" he asked defiantly.

"You shouldn't be," the Blonde answered, brightening up again. "Come and buy me a cup of coffee, and I'll tell you all about yourself."

There was a coffee-stall opposite the Oval, and they went towards it. After the cold deserted expanse of the Brixton Road it was like stepping suddenly into a farm-house kitchen. The tea-urn sparkled like a fireman's helmet and reflected the pile of ham sandwiches and the thick slabs of fruit-cake and the coconut macaroons. They both had two cups and a hot meat-pie apiece. And then because the coffee-stall was crowded they crossed over to a neighbouring doorway where everything was private.

"Put your arm round me," the Blonde said. "I'm cold."

He did so and held her pressed up close to him. He kept on pretending that it was Doris whom he was holding.

"You do believe me, don't you?" she asked anxiously.

"I believe you."

"I only said that I was married just to tease you," she said. "Honest I did."

"O.K.," Percy told her. "Don't go on about it."

"Well, kiss me. Just to show we're friends."

It was the Blonde who prolonged the kiss. It was her kiss, in fact. But Percy got something out of it all right. Towards the end it was O.K. so far as he was concerned as well.

And then the Blonde told him what she had brought him there to tell.

"Don't let's hang about out here," she said in a whisper. "What's wrong with my flat?"

"O.K.," said Percy hoarsely.

It was no use pretending about Doris any more.

It was one-thirty a.m. and the streets were quite empty now. Cherry Street, where the Blonde lived, was simply a blank brick chasm with lamp-posts down it. And the Brixton Road itself was a dead watercourse with the glitter of tram-rails under the moon where the river should have been.

Coming down the Brixton Road was a man. He was the only living thing in sight. And he was hurrying. Darting along like a fox in a desert.

"If I had a girl like Doris," he was saying under his breath, "I'd give over mucking about. I'd get a house out Purley way with a garage. I'd have friends in in the evening. . . ."

Mrs. Boon had lain awake for him.

"That you, Percy?" she called out.

"Yes, it's me, Mum," he answered with his fingers on the handle of his door.

"D'you want a cuppa tea, or anything?"
"No thanks, Mum."
"Come and kiss me good-night."
"Coming, Mum."

CHAPTER 11

IT HAD been arranged. Doreen was coming, and Dulcimer Street was getting ready for her.

It was already after tea-time and Mr. Josser was standing in front of the little mirror in the kitchen, shaving. This was one of the little things that he had got slack about, shaving. Every morning except Sundays for nearly forty years he had shaved, hurriedly and uncomfortably, while the early tea-kettle was boiling. But now he was taking things a bit more easily. Every day was a Sunday, in fact. He just pottered about, reading the papers and getting in the way, until about the middle of the morning and then borrowed a jugful of hot water wherever there was any going. Sometimes there wasn't any and Mrs. Josser told him that he should have asked for it earlier. But it didn't matter: there was no fixed time for it any more. The only way in which he was strict with himself was in looking spruce and respectable by the time Doris got back. It was a point of honour not to do anything that would lower him in his daughter's eyes. Least of all to-night.

Not that he'd have her much longer. It was a sad business. But apparently she'd set her heart on that flat of hers. He couldn't blame her, he admitted. After all, it was her life and if she preferred spending it in a half-converted attic in another part of London, there was nothing that could be done about it. He had hoped—before Mrs. Josser stepped in and stopped it—to tempt her with the offer of a cottage in the Chilterns with an old-world garden and a good train at five to eight in the mornings. But that simply wasn't the way her mind was working. With her, it was the attic or nothing.

He was only sorry that Mrs. Josser was still taking it so badly. In her view the whole plan remained a subtle and deliberate slight. He could see her in the corner of the mirror as he stood there shaving. It was no more than a small glimpse of her back and shoulders. But there was something unmistakably uncompromising about it. The hard line of the backbone radiated hostility to attics.

Then, quite suddenly, Mrs. Josser turned on him.

"And what's going to happen if either of them's ill? Who's going to do the looking after? Just you tell me that."

It was unfair, Mr. Josser thought, that Mrs. Josser should tax him with it as if it had been all his idea. But he tried to pass it off smoothly.

"It'll work out all right," he told her. "Things always do."

"Always do what?" Mrs. Josser demanded.

"Turn out for the best," he persisted. "You see if they don't."

Mrs. Josser drew in her lips and declined to answer. This wasn't the first time she had been disappointed in him. It was like going into battle with someone who didn't care which way the fighting went.

She glanced up nervously at the clock.

"You'd better get dressed," she said. "They'll be here any moment now."

Mr. Josser had finished shaving by now and he pulled out his own watch to satisfy himself.

"Oh, not yet," he said. "It isn't six yet."

But Mrs. Josser had already left him, and he was simply talking to himself again. It had been like that all the afternoon. Ever since lunch-time Mrs. Josser had been darting about doing things. First of all, she had cleared up all the papers and magazines—they were *Home-finders* mostly—from the little table beside Mr. Josser's chair, and carried them mysteriously into the bedroom. Then she'd gone round swooping on things, even quite ordinary things that had a right to be there, like Mr. Josser's carpet slippers and his pipes, and she'd carted those away too. By the time she'd finished, the room had a bleak, unaccustomed look. It was as though looters had been round the place.

Mr. Josser put his collar and tie back on and went through into the drawing-room to see if he could help. On the way he met Mrs. Josser carrying in the fern that had always stood on the window-sill in the passage. She put it down where the papers and magazines had been.

"What's that doing there?" Mr. Josser asked.

"Nothing," Mrs. Josser answered promptly. "It's just that it looks bare without anything."

"But why bother just because Doreen's coming?"

It was a foolish, untactful question. And it got Mrs. Josser on the raw.

"Bother?" she demanded. "Who's bothering? She's got to take us as she finds us. I'm not bothering."

Then she caught sight of Mr. Josser's suit.

"And you needn't imagine you're going to wear that," she told him.

Mr. Josser had, as a matter of fact, been wondering about it. It was a suit he was very fond of. His favourite suit, in fact. But the trousers belonged to a different suit altogether. And it was apparently this that rankled with Mrs. Josser.

"What sort of people'll Doreen think we are?" she asked.

"She isn't coming here to see my trousers," Mr. Josser objected. "She's coming to see Doris."

Mrs. Josser refused to argue.

"She's coming here to meet me," she said tersely. "And I'm relying on you."

So, in the end, Mr. Josser went through to the bedroom and changed. He put on his new black, the one that made him look like a mute. He looked in fact so funereal when he saw himself in the mirror that, without being asked to do so, he changed his tie. The one he chose was a brightly striped one that he didn't often wear. And it certainly altered the whole effect. He still looked like a mute. But a mute on a Bank Holiday.

When he had re-dressed himself he went down on all fours and dragged out his carpet slippers from underneath the chest of drawers where Mrs. Josser had hidden them. They were loose and comfortable, and they seemed to make the whole evening easier. He was in a good temper again when he returned to the front room. Having given way, he had the gratified, indulgent feeling of a man who has done something to please a woman, even though he knows that it is silly. He almost expected to be thanked for remembering to change his tie. It was all the more hurtful, therefore, when Mrs. Josser wouldn't allow him to wear his slippers. But she was adamant about it. Apparently between the Best People and Mr. Josser's slippers was a gulf that was unbridgeable. Mr. Josser said nothing and thoughtfully put his boots back on again.

Mrs. Josser followed him into the bedroom and then asked him to leave her for the next ten minutes while she slipped something on. She made it quite clear, however, that there wasn't going to be any dressing up on her part. From the way she spoke Mr. Josser had been pestering her to change.

"It's all right for you," she said over her shoulder as he went out. "You haven't got to do the dishing-up. I'm not going to spoil my best frock to please anybody."

In the end she was away rather longer than ten minutes, and Mr. Josser without his *Homefinder* was left with nothing to do. He lit a pipe and went moodily over to the window, staring out into the street. But it was more than Doreen that was troubling him.

A great deal more. It was his forthcoming speech on foreign policy.

So far he had managed to get through the present session without doing more than express the Government's misgivings over the fact that Hitler should have decided to cross the Czecho-Slovakian frontier and set up a Protectorate there. It had been a carefully guarded speech, because he hadn't known at the time that Mr. Chamberlain was going to be so outspoken over at Westminster the very next day and openly accuse the Führer of breaking his word. This was a side, the angry indignant side, of Mr. Chamberlain's nature that he hadn't met before, and it warmed his heart towards him.

All the same, matters had been steadily going from bad to worse since then, and it seemed that perhaps Mr. Chamberlain hadn't used that tone of voice soon enough. The climax came when Germany refused to accept the British note of protest. And at this point, to Mr. Josser's relief, Mr. Plumcroft decided to take over in the House. In the result, Mr. Plumcroft made the best speech of his career. From the Front Bench he had spread peace and tranquillity over the agitated assembly, like an ointment. He was as calm as he was confident. And it nearly broke Mr. Josser's heart a couple of days later when Hitler (who had evidently missed what Mr. Plumcroft had been saying) demanded Memel and got it.

He had already got the opening sentence of his address pretty clear in his mind when Mrs. Josser came back into the room. She was wearing her afternoon frock with the sleeves that were a shade too tight, and she had pinned on a cameo brooch that she hadn't worn for years.

Mr. Josser regarded her for a moment.

"I thought you said you weren't going to wear that dress," he remarked.

Mrs. Josser turned on him.

"And why shouldn't I wear it if I want to wear it?" she demanded.

It was Mr. Josser's second mistake already that evening and he wanted to do something to make amends for it. He asked Mrs. Josser if there was anything that he could do to help. But it made no amends. It only aggravated her.

"I don't know what's the matter with you this evening," she said. "You aren't usually like this. Why don't you sit down and read something?"

Mr. Josser sat down. But as there was nothing left to read, he sat there picking absent-mindedly at a loose place in the upholstery, and thinking about his speech. Mrs. Josser sat down opposite to him and began to sew.

About six-thirty Mr. Josser's clock struck, and Mrs. Josser started.

"That clock makes me jump," she said. "I'm sure there's something wrong with it. Nobody could have meant a clock to be as loud as that."

Mr. Josser looked up in astonishment.

"I thought it sounded just about right," he said.

There was silence between them after that. Quarter to seven struck and then seven. And each time Mrs. Josser looked up as though the clock had hit out at her. It was not until quarter-past, however, that she actually spoke.

She let the boom die away and said a trifle anxiously, "I hope nothing's happened to them."

That was all she said. And she did not speak again until the next quarter-hour. This time the note of anxiety in her voice had increased noticeably. But there was something else as well. This time there was an unconcealed jumpiness.

"It . . . it was to-night Doris said, wasn't it?" she said.

Mr. Josser thought for a moment.

"Either to-night or Tuesday," he said at length. "I don't really remember." He paused. "But even if Doreen isn't coming," he said, "where's Doris? She didn't say she was stopping out, did she?"

"She'd better not with all that ham and tongue," Mrs. Josser replied, and went on with her sewing.

At quarter to eight, she could endure things no longer. She glared at the clock waiting for it to strike and, when it had done so, she turned to Mr. Josser again.

"If they're not here in a moment," she said, "we start. You don't catch me waiting for anybody."

"Give 'em till eight," said Mr. Josser. "No point in getting two meals in one evening."

"There aren't going to be two meals," she said briefly. "When we've had what we're going to have, the table'll be cleared."

Then at eight o'clock everything happened at once. The clock struck, Mrs. Josser sprang sharply to her feet, and Doreen and Doris came in together.

Mr. Josser smiled indulgently.

"There you are," he said. "I knew they'd be here by eight."

Mrs. Josser smoothed down her dress and went out on the landing to meet them. As she did so, she sniffed. But it was nothing from her kitchen that she could smell. It was something going on upstairs on

Mr. Puddy's gas ring. And Mr. Puddy was in charge of that smell. He had been cooking himself a nice piece of cod when the fat had caught. The staircase was now full of dense blue smoke and Doreen and Doris came upstairs, their eyes streaming.

Mrs. Josser had already decided that the ladylike thing would be to ignore it. She was holding her hand out in readiness when Mr. Josser's voice came through from the front room.

"There's something burning, Mother," he said. "It must have caught while we were waiting."

And Doris didn't make it any better either.

"Good gracious," she said. "What a smell! Have we got to eat it? Mother, this is Doreen."

"Pleased to meet you," said Mrs. Josser, studying her hard.

"D'y'do," said Doreen.

They went into the front room into which blue tendrils of Mr. Puddy's cod were already penetrating, and Doris introduced her father.

"Pleased to meet you," said Mr. Josser.

"D'y'do," said Doreen.

"Sorry if I've made Doris late," Doreen said in a sudden apologetic rush as though she had noticed a coldness somewhere. "We had a most hectic time getting here."

"Are you late?" Mr. Josser asked politely. "We were just sitting here talking and didn't notice."

Mrs. Josser caught his eye as he said it, and Mr. Josser looked down at his feet again.

"Well, I expect you're ready for a meal, now you are here," Mrs. Josser observed.

"I must do my face first," Doreen said. "I'm sure I look a perfect fright."

"Take her along, Doris," said Mrs. Josser. "It'll be all ready when you get back."

As soon as the door was shut, Mrs. Josser turned to her husband.

"I've met her type before," she said.

She did not say where. Nor did she say what type it was. It was apparently sufficient that it should be at once a type and familiar.

"She's a nice-looking girl, isn't she?" Mr. Josser observed. "A good bit older than Doris I should say."

It was some time before they started. But apparently the wait hadn't given Doreen an appetite. She refused the ham altogether and took only a small section of the bottled tongue. Mrs. Josser apologised for the potatoes which had boiled themselves into a paste but

Doreen said that she simply didn't ever dare to eat potatoes they made her so fat. She'd like just the weeniest bit of bread instead.

"Do you good to eat potatoes," Mr. Josser said in an indulgent sort of way. "A big girl like you needs building up a bit."

"Please don't call me a *big* girl," Doreen exclaimed. "It makes me feel absolutely *enormous*."

"I don't see why," Mr. Josser answered. "We can't all be the same size."

Doreen did not attempt to reply because she got a curious impression that the light was going out. Gradually at first, but rapidly quickening up, the darkness was descending. It was already dusk in the room.

Mrs. Josser was the first to speak. She turned to Mr. Josser.

"Didn't you do what I asked you?" she said coldly.

Mr. Josser shook his head.

"I forgot," he said.

"Well, do it now," she told him.

Mr. Josser thrust his hand into his pockets one by one. But they were empty.

"It's in my other suit," he explained.

By the time he left them the little party at the table were in almost total gloom. Only Doreen's white silk blouse could be seen gleaming in the firelight. And in the darkness they gave up attempting to eat. They just sat there, wondering.

Then, with a rattle of silver on the landing, the light shot up again, and Mr. Josser came back in rubbing his hands.

"Where was Moses?" he asked pleasantly.

After the interruption, they ate for some minutes in silence. The going down of the light seemed temporarily to have damped everybody's spirits, and Doreen appeared frankly sceptical about the whole affair. She kept glancing up at the red-shaded chandelier again. It was obvious that she wanted to know where things were in case the light should suddenly go out again.

When they had all finished Mrs. Josser looked round the table.

"Will *anybody* have some ham?" she asked pointedly.

"Oh, I really couldn't," Doreen answered. "Not after what Mr. Josser said about me being so simply huge already."

"You could leave the fat," Mr. Josser suggested.

But Doreen was not to be tempted and Mrs. Josser turned to Doris.

"Bring in the jelly," she said. "It's in the kitchen with the pineapple. Don't forget the cream."

To Doris's astonishment, Mrs. Josser didn't move. She just sat there ordering her about. And there was nothing that could be done about it. Not until later, at least. Doris gathered the plates together—she positively snatched Mrs. Josser's from in front of her—and piled them up on a tray. As she went out of the room she heard Mrs. Josser talking confidentially to Doreen.

"I don't know what I should do without Doris," she was saying. "She helps me so in the house. I could never get along without her."

It was a cold night, and the fruit jelly and pineapple had an unusually chilling look about them. Even the pineapple seemed sub-Arctic rather than tropical. The little cubes slid icily on to the plates as Mrs. Josser spooned them out. Doreen begged Mrs. Josser to give her only the teeniest little bit.

Doris wasn't eating properly either. Some sixth sense told her that Mrs. Josser was about to get on to the subject of the flat. And she was right.

"Doris was telling me all about this scheme of yours," she said suddenly, turning to Doreen, "and I don't . . ."

She got no further, however, because there was someone at the door. Whoever it was knocked twice, like a postman.

"There's someone there," Mr. Josser said unhelpfully.

"See who it is, dear," Mrs. Josser said still without rising. She turned to Doreen. "We'll talk about this flat idea later," she said. "I want you to hear my side."

When Mr. Josser opened the door, he was quite surprised to see Percy. And a very much embarrassed Percy. He had been holding himself back for the last half-hour until he was perfectly sure that the Jossers would have finished supper. And now here he was at a quarter to nine gate-crashing right into the middle of it. Because it had been Doris whom he was going downstairs to see, he had taken pains with himself. He had thrust a new crêpe de chine handkerchief into his breast pocket and he was wearing his yellowest shoes—the pair that were so tight they wouldn't do up properly. He hadn't gone so far as to change his suit as well. And—until you noticed his hair—it seemed a rather stained and oily figure that was standing there. But the hair was immaculate. He had just rubbed a handful of brilliantine into it and he came forward into the room smelling like a conservatory.

Half-way across, however, he stopped dead. He had caught sight of Doreen. She was resting her chin on her hands and staring at him. He became aware of dark-lashed eyes, a fringe of gleaming hair and a pair of dangling jade ear-rings.

"She's O.K. She knows her way about," he thought hurriedly.

It was the first time, so far as Doris could remember, that Percy had come down to see them in this way. She was puzzled. But she didn't want to seem put out by it.

"Oh, this is Mr. Boon," she said. "You haven't met my friend, Miss Smyth."

"Hahjahdo," said Percy, stretching across the table to shake hands with her.

"D'y'do?" Doreen replied politely.

After that there was a pause. Percy felt awkward. He just stood weaving his hands together.

"Did you come down for something?" Mrs. Josser asked unencouragingly.

"I . . . I wanted to know if Doris was doing anything. Next Saturday, I mean. I thought we might have gone to the Palais," he replied. And then, because it sounded a bit flat and not the way a man of the world ought to talk, he added, "Just the usual hop, you know. Nothing special."

"Oh, I can't, thank you ever so much," Doris answered promptly. "I'm going out with Doreen. It's all fixed up, isn't it, Doreen?"

Doreen was quick on the uptake for that sort of thing. She understood at once.

"Such a pity," she said. "If only we'd known we could have put it off. But we can't now we've asked all those people."

Percy stood there looking down at his feet.

"Well, I suppose I ought to be going in that case," he said.

"What's the hurry?" Mr. Josser asked. "Why don't you come and sit down."

"Thanks," said Percy.

He sat down in Mr. Josser's chair, and took out his cigarette case.

"Mind if I light a fag?" he asked. Then he remembered his manners.

"Anybody else have one?" he enquired.

"We haven't finished yet," Mrs. Josser told him.

But apparently Doreen didn't mind in the least not having finished. From the way she took the cigarette it was apparent that it was the one thing for which she had been longing. She left the two cubes of pineapple and the iceberg of jelly on her plate untouched, and took a cigarette holder out of her bag. Then she sat there blowing out slow coils of smoke across the table.

Mrs. Josser said nothing. But she made a note of it—both of smoking at table and using a cigarette holder. She had already made a note of the way Mr. Josser had invited Percy without consulting her.

But Mr. Josser seemed unaware of having done anything wrong. He was talking to Percy in a familiar, friendly fashion as though Percy often spent the evening with them.

"How's everything at the garage?" he asked.

Before Percy could answer, Doreen had interrupted the conversation. She turned her back on Mrs. Josser (which was another thing that Mrs. Josser made a note of), and suddenly became quite animated.

"Oh, are you one of those marvellous people who know about the insides of cars—valves and things?" she asked. "I think they're terribly clever. I'm quite sure I shouldn't even know one end of an engine from the other."

"She's a bouncer. She is a lady. She's hot stuff. She's the only girl I know who uses a holder," Percy was thinking.

But he didn't know how to answer. She talked too quickly for him.

It was Mrs. Josser who answered for him.

"It's not your job: that's why you don't know," she said.

She herself could see absolutely nothing marvellous about young Percy, and she didn't see any use in pretending that there was anything.

Doreen turned towards her just long enough to give offence again.

"Oh, I don't know," she said. "I think it's absolutely wonderful being able to do things with engines. Men are *so* much cleverer than women. Don't you think so, Mrs. Josser?"

Mrs. Josser drew in her lips. It was obvious that she did not think so.

"Will anybody have some cheese?" she asked.

"Oh, I couldn't, thank you," Doreen answered. "I've eaten a gigantic meal."

"Then I'll give Doris a hand with the clearing away," Mrs. Josser offered.

Outside in the kitchen mother and daughter scarcely spoke. It was not until they were going back into the front room that Doris said anything.

"How long do you think Percy's going to stop?" she asked.

"All night if your father has anything to do with it," Mrs. Josser replied. "And I want to have a private word with that Doreen of yours before she goes."

It was even worse than they had feared when they got back. They found that Mr. Josser had suggested rummy. Obstinately misreading the nature of Doreen's visit, he was trying to make things go with a swing. He was counting out little heaps of coloured tiddleywinks, saying humorously, "Five pounds ten for Miss Smyth. The same for Mother. Same again for Percy. Ditto for Doris. And what's left for me. No cheating, mind."

This was too much for Mrs. Josser. She had no intention of sitting down to rummy with young Percy.

"Where's your mother, Percy?" she asked.

"Upstairs."

"Did you tell her you were stopping?"

Percy shook his head.

"Don't you think she might be lonely?" she said pointedly.

A pleased, unself-conscious smile spread across Percy's face.

"You mean bring her down?" he asked. "Thanks ever so."

There was a rather strained silence when he had left, and Doris turned to Mrs. Josser.

"Oh, Mum, why did you?" she asked.

"Me?" Mrs. Josser replied indignantly. "I didn't do anything. It was your father."

"Never opened my mouth," Mr. Josser answered, still arranging the chips. "You asked her down yourself."

"I didn't," Mrs. Josser said emphatically.

"Well, she's coming, that's the main thing," Mr. Josser replied. "We shall be a big party before we're finished."

But Mrs. Boon evidently needed a bit of persuading. Five minutes passed, and then ten, and there was still no sign of either her or her son. Finally Mr. Josser insisted that they should begin without waiting for them. Mrs. Josser, however, seemed reluctant even to pick up her cards. It was not, indeed, until she had actually got them in her hands and begun studying them that she seemed to enter into the spirit of the thing. Then something happened. She adjusted her spectacles, frowned, made little clicking noises of disapproval at the luck of the deal and began arranging her cards into a fashionable fan-shaped pattern. In her youth she had cut a pretty good figure at the whist table, and she still knew how to hold her cards.

But before the round had reached her there was another knock on the door. Mr. Josser put down his cards and glanced across at Doris.

"That'll be them," said Mr. Josser. "Now I'll have to re-deal."

But it was not Mrs. Boon. It was Mrs. Vizzard. She was obviously agitated. And standing there in the dark passage with the light on her face she seemed pale. Unnaturally pale. Almost like a spirit herself. Doreen sat watching her, bewitched. She wondered how many more people were going to arrive.

"Is your mother there?" Mrs. Vizzard enquired.

Mrs. Josser put her cards down and got up.

"You wanted me, Mrs. Vizzard?" she asked.

She had a respect for Mrs. Vizzard and was even prepared to interrupt the game for her. After all it wasn't every night that Mrs. Vizzard paid them a visit.

"I wanted a word with you *in private*," Mrs. Vizzard began in a mysterious whisper, and then stopped herself. She, too, had become aware of a strange young lady at the table who was staring at her. "I'm sorry," she said. "I didn't know you had company."

Doris recognised this for another occasion when poise was called for.

"Oh, Mrs. Vizzard, this is my friend, Miss Smyth," she explained.

Mrs. Vizzard's hand seemed like cold ivory. It was like shaking hands with a dead duchess. Doreen felt a kind of icy chill rising up her spine at the contact. It quite upset her.

But Mrs. Josser could not bear to be kept waiting any longer to hear what Mrs. Vizzard had to tell her.

"Come outside," she said in a whisper of the same mysterious hoarseness that Mrs. Vizzard had used. "We'll talk *out there*."

Doreen turned away and picked up her cards again. The game of rummy was beginning and breaking up again so frequently that she was losing count.

And even now Mrs. Josser and Mrs. Vizzard got no further than the door. For at that moment Percy was coming back in with his mother. He was rather self-conscious about being there at all. And so was Mrs. Boon. They sidled in rather than walked. And Mrs. Boon began thanking Mrs. Josser straight away.

"It was nice of you to ask me down, Mrs. Josser," she said. "It can be a bit quiet, you know, just upstairs by yourself."

Percy had warned her about Doreen. But the presence of Mrs. Vizzard was an entire surprise. She realised now that the Jossers must be throwing a party. What she didn't realise of course was that half the party was trying to go into the passage for a secret session. She led the way over to the fire and the other two followed.

"Oh, I do hope we're not breaking up your game, are we?" Mrs. Boon said apologetically.

She had a way of regarding herself as the least important guest wherever she was and therefore kept on excusing herself.

"Quite all right," Mr. Josser told her. "If you ladies want to talk we'll make up a four with Percy. It might as well be whist as we're the right number."

Doreen started and looked around her. Except for Doris, she didn't seem to have any connection with the evening at all. And until Mr. Josser actually named it she had never suspected anything quite so awful as whist. The very worst that she had feared was Auction.

There was a distraction, however. A very effective distraction. She became aware that the three women behind her were talking earnestly in low whispers. And if there is one form in which the human voice carries better than another it is the low whisper. Sitting up at the table waiting for Mr. Josser to decide whether to throw away a two or come thumping in with a trump, she found herself in the middle of a shadowy conversation that fascinated her.

". . . nowhere else to go if you do turn her out," Mrs. Josser was saying.

". . . poor old thing. I'm quite sorry for her." That was Mrs. Boon's voice.

"But not"—Doreen recognised Mrs. Vizzard's voice—"after this. She can come back for one night to pack her things. But after that she goes."

It was Mr. Josser who interrupted Doreen's eavesdropping. In the middle of the fourth round he suddenly forgot what trumps were, and had to ask. And then when they told him he wouldn't keep quiet about it. Mr. Josser was a man who enjoyed a good game of cards. But in particular he liked the lighter side of it. At this very moment he was going through a cheerful little pantomime, first of all pretending that he hadn't got any trumps at all and then that his hand was full of them.

". . . . of course she must have deserved it to get it. Magistrates aren't monsters." This was in Mrs. Vizzard's voice again.

"Fourteen days isn't a very long time." (Mrs. Boon.)

"It's quite long enough for me with my good name to think of." (Mrs. Vizzard.)

"But if we're prepared to overlook it. . . ." (Mrs. Josser.)

The rest of the sentence was entirely lost because Mr. Josser, finding that his pipe wasn't drawing properly, had removed the mouthpiece and was blowing noisily through the stem.

"There's more than ourselves to consider. There's the reputation of this house." (Mrs. Vizzard.)

Then Percy cut in.

"Have another fag, Miss Smyth?" he asked.

He was holding out his cigarette case. It was one of those neat little toys in which the cigarette comes popping up like a small Jack-in-the-box when the lid is slid off.

"Thanks," she said and thrust it into the holder that had overwhelmed him earlier.

Percy turned towards Doris.

"It's no use offering you one, is it?" he asked.

Doris shook her head.

"Why not?" Doreen asked. "She smokes. At least she does in the office."

"Do you, Doris?"

Mrs. Josser had abruptly disengaged herself from the whisperers and was addressing her daughter directly. Everybody stopped talking for a moment.

"Sometimes," Doris answered uncomfortably.

"Well, please don't do it here," Mrs. Josser told her. "If you get among that sort at the office that's your affair. It's different in your own home."

Doris didn't say anything. But she was angry. She felt herself blushing.

"Thank you, Percy," she said. "I think I will."

He whipped out his cigarette case again and the cigarette came bobbing up as briskly as before. Then he produced the lighter that Mrs. Boon had given him for a Christmas present. It worked at the first flick, and Doris sat back defiantly trying to blow the smoke out through her nostrils.

"Well!" said Mrs. Josser.

It was Mr. Josser who was the first to speak after that.

"What's trumps, Percy?" he asked.

"Still hearts," Percy said.

But his mind wasn't in the game really. It was on Doris. And Doreen. For a start it was pretty exciting sitting down with a girl like Doreen at all. He'd dreamt about her sort. She looked the kind you saw pictures of in the *Bystander*. She had class. And a haughty voice. And long red nails that didn't look as though they had ever touched a typewriter. She knew her way about, all right: you could tell that. But what had really gone to his head was seeing Doris blush. He'd been imagining it as he came home to-night. It had been just one of those things. And now he'd seen it. There was something oddly rousing about it. To cover his confusion he pulled up his trouser leg and began scratching at his calf.

The next couple of rounds passed off smoothly enough, except for

Mr. Josser taking Doreen's Queen with his King. It was an awkward sort of situation. But Mr. Josser managed to extract some fun from it. He gave his own hand a reproving slap, and looked across at Doreen to see that she had appreciated the significance of it.

Meanwhile the whispering had begun again.

"When she comes I shall tell her," Mrs. Vizzard was saying. "It won't be pleasant, but it'll be better for all of us."

"But don't you think . . ."—Doreen missed this bit—"just for a bit while she's making fresh arrangements."

"She's made her fresh arrangements, so far as I'm concerned."

"It's to-morrow Connie's coming out, isn't it?" Mr. Josser asked suddenly, making no pretence of not having been listening to what the ladies had been whispering about. "I thought we might get things a bit ready for her—it can't be much fun coming home from . . ."

"This is a private conversation we're having," Mrs. Josser told him tartly. "Mrs. Vizzard came up to see *me*."

"All right," Mr. Josser answered good-humouredly. "You can tell me afterwards."

They had finished the game by now and Mr. Josser sat looking at the clock. It was just on ten o'clock and he was waiting for it to strike. It was a good long chime at ten, and he enjoyed every moment of it. When the last note had died away, he stacked the cards in front of him and addressed Mrs. Josser.

"What about a cup of tea, Mother?"

The suggestion was the signal for Doreen to start saying that she had to go. She'd had a perfectly marvellous time, she said, and she'd simply love to stop, but there was that awful journey. She spoke of the journey as though there would be St. Bernard dogs out looking for her before she was finished with it. But Mr. Josser wouldn't hear of it.

"Can't go out with nothing," he said. "Mother'd never forgive me if I let you."

Doreen was still saying at intervals that she would have to be going. But she saw that it was useless.

"Oh well," she was thinking. "I'll just gulp a cup of tea and then dash off. Heaven knows when I shall get back to Hampstead."

She felt sorry for Doris. But also resentful. She felt that Doris ought to have warned her what the evening was going to be like. If Doris had said to her: "Doreen darling, I'd love to take you home, but I just can't because everything's too impossible," she would have understood. She could have forgiven her for it. But as it was, Doris had just made her ridiculous. It was really unthinkable that she should have been expected to spend an evening playing whist with people like Percy and Mr. Josser.

"Thank God it's nearly over," she told herself.

Nearly over, but not quite.

She was just searching in her handbag for a last cigarette when there was a strange scuffling noise on the stairs outside. It was the sort of noise that furniture removers might make when carrying something heavy round an awkward corner. And it was a swaying kind of scuffle. It died away completely for a moment and then returned louder than before. There was the sound of someone coming down two stairs at once, probably backwards. Then there was a heavy thud, followed by a groan.

"Careful," a voice said. "Mind her head."

Mrs. Josser got up from the china cupboard and looked accusingly at Mr. Josser.

"What's going on out there?" she asked.

Mr. Josser put his pipe down on the table and got up.

"Better go and see," he said reluctantly.

But he was too late. Mrs. Vizzard had already risen. The good name of No. 10—already sullied—was at stake. And in front of a stranger, too. She was in no mood for trifling. It might be, she reflected, that others beside Connie would have to be asked to leave.

But she was quite unprepared for what happened. As she reached the door, it flew open and she was swept back into the room by a sudden rush of bodies. She gave a little scream and retreated hurriedly behind the table. Doreen, who had thought that she was ready for anything by now, screamed too. And even Percy felt instinctively in his pocket for his knuckleduster. . . .

But there was no need for it. It was only Mr. Puddy and Mr. Squales. Mr. Puddy, Mr. Squales and another. The third figure, who was precariously supported between them and was still kicking out vigorously with her legs, was only half the size of the others. She was a small elderly lady with dyed hair.

It was Connie come home. Come home before the welcome was ready for her.

"Lumme," said Mr. Puddy, trying to recover his balance.

"What is the meaning of this?" demanded Mrs. Vizzard.

Mr. Squales passed his hand across his forehead, thrusting back the lock of lank hair that hung there.

"Perhaps I should explain that our friend here is not . . . not well.

She came home unexpectedly and this gentleman"—he indicated Mr. Puddy—"found her on the stairs outside her room . . . er . . . crying."

"They've asshaulted me," Connie broke in.

She said it very indistinctly, however. It was obvious that the poor old thing was quite used up. She swayed from side to side as she stood there.

"Pounshed on me, they did," she went on. "Out of the dark. Like tigers."

Mrs. Josser was regarding her closely.

"Sit down on one of these chairs," she said. "That is if Miss Smyth wouldn't mind moving."

Doreen obliged by moving as far away as possible. And it was then that she noticed that the small elderly lady's hands were clasped tightly together in front of her almost as though she was holding a prayer-book. Even the fact that she was supported underneath her armpits didn't make her separate her hands. But when the two men—the fat puffy one and the dark aquiline one like an actor—lifted her into the chair something happened. The hands came apart for a moment and for the second time that evening Doreen screamed.

Out of the clasped hands, a small yellow bird shot upwards and began flying wildly in circles round the gas chandelier like a large saffron moth, while the little old lady struggled frantically to get at it.

"Duke," she was screaming. "Duke. Don't you know me? It'sh your mother."

The canary hit the chain that dangled from the chandelier, and Connie put her hand over her eyes.

"He'll burn hish wings. The little angel'll scorsh himshelf," she was sobbing. "It'sh shuichide."

CHAPTER 12

I

ITALY had invaded Albania. And Uncle Henry had been suspended.

The two facts were connected. Closely connected. And the unfortunate part was that Mr. Josser, innocent and unsuspecting, got wedged in between. At first when he heard the news about Albania, he didn't believe it. Couldn't believe it. But the B.B.C. news-reader said it calmly and confidently as though he'd been keeping his eye on Albania for some time, and Mr. Josser supposed that he *had* to believe it. Then he got angry. Very angry. It seemed that Mussolini really was what Uncle Henry had always said he was. And on a Good Friday, too! That was really shocking. There was only one consolation. But it was quite a sizable one, when you came to reason it out. Mussolini had struck East, and not West: that was the point. His ambition had carried him into the Balkans. And the Balkans were always at war about something. If it had been France, for instance, that Mussolini had attacked then the fat would really have been in the fire. But the very fact that he hadn't done so showed that he daren't. He'd gone, typically enough, for the little chap. And even if he got him down, Europe—or at least Mr. Josser's end of it —would still be all right.

It meant writing a new speech, of course. Because the P.M., Mr. Plumcroft, was down at the moment with a quinsy. The quinsy was still intact and unsloughed, and not so much as a word could be choked out of him. But Mr. Josser had intended in any case to begin by saying: "We are living in a page of history in the making . . ." And if you *are* living in a page of history, a footnote or two on the way is probably inevitable. He had spent a lot of time getting his facts right. He had looked up Albania on a map—and found it. And he had checked the number of bayonets that Mussolini had behind him. The general outlook, he admitted, was certainly dark. Entirely dark except for that one ray of light about striking Eastwards. When he went along to the South London Parliament, he was deeply conscious of the fact that to do justice to a speech like this someone in the top flight—a Mr. Whipple or a Mr. Beeman, at least—was needed.

The first person he met when he got inside was Uncle Henry, who thrust a piece of paper into his hand. Mr. Josser thanked him for it and then started to read. The paper said in large rough capitals—the whole thing had been hurriedly Roneo-ed—"THIS IS WAR. GET READY!" And underneath it there was a lot about Sanctions and Guarantees and Hopeless Isolationism. Mr. Josser folded it up and put it into his pocket to read afterwards.

There was a full house to-night, and Mr. Josser led off straight away. He was speaking by ten past eight. He could see Uncle Henry sitting on the front Opposition bench just opposite and he smiled nervously across at him. But Uncle Henry was in no mood for smiling. He looked madder than ever to-night, Mr. Josser thought. And he was on his feet even more than usual. "Had His Majesty's Government already signified that they were going to the aid of Albania, and if not what was the cause of the delay?" "Were arrangements being made for the intake of refugees?" "Where was the Navy?" Mr. Josser tried to deal with the points one by one as they came up, but they were troublesome and distracting. He was tired already by the time he came to his point about war in the Balkans not mattering so much as war in Western Europe. And he was just beginning to prove that the storm would blow over as storms always do when Uncle Henry leapt to his feet and began waving a bundle of his little pamphlets in Mr. Josser's face.

"There are times," he began, "when blindness is not an affliction. It is a curse. And more than a curse it is a sin. There on the wall before us is the writing, and we are so criminally blind that . . ."

Here the Speaker interrupted him.

"I'm afraid that the Hon. Member is attempting to make a speech," he said. "That is not what was intended. He may only ask a question."

Uncle Henry paused. Then he turned towards the Chair.

"Are you aware," he asked, " that within the next few months—weeks possibly—we shall be fighting for our lives? The dead bodies of our young men will be . . ."

The Speaker rapped sharply with his hammer.

"Now you are addressing questions to me," he told Uncle Henry. "I cannot allow that either."

A good background of vestry-work had prepared the Speaker for most awkward situations and he was as calm and unrattled as Mr. Plumcroft in the face of crisis. But he wasn't prepared for Uncle Henry.

Nor was Mr. Josser.

Suddenly pointing full at him, Uncle Henry raised his voice until he was shouting.

"Mr. Speaker is a fool," he said. "An ignorant, credulous fool. . . ."

The Speaker brought down his little gavel as though he were cracking nuts.

"I cannot allow such language to be used," he said. "It must be withdrawn before you can continue."

"Withdraw nothing," Uncle Henry shouted back. "He's more than a fool. He's a murderer. If we enter this war unprepared. . . ."

"I have no alternative but to suspend you from the sittings of this House," the Speaker said sternly. "And stop pointing your finger at me!"

The House adjourned shortly afterwards because, by then, feelings were running dangerously high on both sides.

And Uncle Henry did not stay behind as he usually did. Having stalked out of the Chamber with his arms full of his alarmist pamphlets he had apparently mounted immediately on his green bicycle and gone pedalling off home alone.

That was a great pity, Mr. Josser thought. And a mistake. Breaking up a regular weekly party was carrying your convictions a bit too far.

It was the worst of cranks: they spoilt things.

2

Young Percy was on to something pretty hot. It was, in fact, about the hottest thing that he'd ever handled on his own. That was why he was smoking faster than ever and the cigarette-stubs were scattered all round him on the floor of the compartment. It wasn't a smoking compartment. But what the hell? He was worried, wasn't he?

Not that "worried" quite described it. He was excited. And jittery. But something else as well. He was flattered. Flattered, because he'd been picked out for the job. Somebody—he didn't know the man yet—must have asked: "Do you know anyone big enough to fix a thing like this?" And the answer had come slap out: "Percy Boon." That was the advantage of having connections. Without them, he would have been missed, passed over. People—particularly the big people—just wouldn't have heard of him. They'd have had to go elsewhere to get their jobs done for them. And what would have become of his percentage then?

It had been in Smokey Joe's that he'd first heard of this particular little bit of business. And it was his friend, Jack Rufus, he had to thank. Apparently a friend of a friend of Jack Rufus's—Jack Rufus was a man of many and far-reaching friendships: they made a constantly changing zigzag pattern right across the population of London—was on to something good just at the very moment when he couldn't avail himself of it. *They*, Jack Rufus had explained in the undertone in which he conducted all his conversations, were watching him and he couldn't move. He didn't say who *They* were. And he didn't have to say it. Percy understood without being told. *They* was just an impersonal, almost inhuman force. A hostile influence. Like Fate. Something that was forever interfering with an easy living in a free country.

Percy had been cautious at first. Flattered, but cautious. Just because a man of Jack Rufus's size had asked him, he wasn't going to give everything away at once.

"What do I get out of it?" he had asked.

And when Jack Rufus had told him, he had laughed.

"Chickenfeed," he had said contemptuously, turning down the corner of his mouth. "Just chickenfeed."

The phrase and the facial expression were something that he had practised. It was a proof that all the years at the films hadn't been wasted.

And Jack Rufus had come up step by step just as Percy knew he would. By the time Percy and Jack Rufus had separated, the job was worth fifty pounds to Percy. No, not fifty. A *cool* fifty. That was the word that Percy kept repeating to himself. A *cool* fifty.

"Easy as walking off a plank," he kept telling himself. "Easy as breathing. And a cool fifty at the end of it."

It was the biggest single sum of money that he had ever earned. And it seemed to hold out the promise of even bigger and sweeter things.

"All I need is a bit of capital. Then I can get started on my own," he repeated over and over again. "If I had a thousand a year on the level I should be O.K. I'd marry Doris. Not some mucky blonde."

The hot job was getting rid of a stolen car. In the ordinary way this was easy enough. Austins and Morrises changed hands like sixpences. But this was different. This was a Bentley coupé that was waiting to be delivered. And Bentleys were tricky cars to handle. Too classy and ultra. They were almost as bad as a Rolls. People noticed them. You couldn't leave a Bentley in some cheap lock-up somewhere until things had cooled off a bit without people beginning to get talking. The insurance people were always after missing Bentleys like a pack of bloodhounds. Little private investigation agents in grey trilbys and greasy raincoats went round garages and lock-ups, sniffing. In Percy's own personal circle of friends there were two reliable men who had got in bad simply because they'd started fooling about with Bentleys instead of sticking to Austins and Morrises and Fords.

But it was a cinch, this particular Bentley, Jack Rufus had assured him. The buyer was already waiting for it, and no questions asked. So long as he got the car and a pair of perfectly good number plates he wasn't the suspicious sort. All that Percy had to do was to drive the car over from Brook Green to Kennington and get to work on it. If anyone said anything he could say he was doing it for a customer. One of the great advantages of a lad like Percy was that he had such a nice open face and the police hadn't got anything on him yet.

All the same, when Percy saw the car he thought twice about it. It wasn't just an ordinary Bentley. It was a Cambridge Blue town coupé with one of those fancy bodies that looked as though they had come out of a Lord Mayor's Show. There was bassinet work down the sides and a pair of silver coach lamps with blue glass in them, standing out on little brackets. The radiator cap was fitted with the glass statuette of a dancing girl.

Percy shook his head and sucked in his teeth.

"Too risky," he said. "Get stopped before the next corner."

Jack Rufus's friend's friend, the man who couldn't move because *They* were watching him, shrugged his shoulders. If Percy didn't want to make a bit of easy money, he said, he wasn't going to help him. As a matter of fact, he'd been able to tell from the moment he saw him that Percy wasn't the right man for the job. He was too pansy altogether. Too pansy. And just a bit yellow.

Percy didn't like that, so he compromised a little. He offered to take the Bentley away if he could put in a couple of hours of work on her in the lock-up beforehand. But that was exactly what Jack Rufus's friend's friend wouldn't hear of. He said that he wasn't going to have anyone fooling about with the Bentley while it was still on his premises. It had got to be a clean job, or nothing.

Percy lit another cigarette—the old one was only half smoked through—and thought the matter over. It was silly to be in any doubt with the cool fifty just sitting there waiting for him. But *They* were waiting for him, too. So far, he and *They* were strangers. And he wanted to keep them so.

But another thought was going through his mind all the time. "Nothing venture, nothing gain." It seemed like a challenge. Something showing him which way his duty lay. He remembered the cool fifty. He remembered the thousand pounds capital that he needed. He remembered Doris.

"O.K.," he said. "I'll do it when it gets a bit darker. Have you got a shuvver's hat anywhere?"

The friend was able to fix him up with that all right. He ran a hire service on the side, and he had quite a collection for Percy to choose from. While he was trying them on the friend told him that he knew all the time that he'd do it. He said that you couldn't be in his game for long without becoming a pretty good judge of character, and he'd known what Percy was worth as soon as he'd clapped eyes on him. All the same, he made Percy sign a delivery chit for the Bentley before he let him take it away. For himself, he didn't mind, he said. But there was more than him in it. It was a syndicate.

And he couldn't, he explained, have Percy Boon or anyone else going off with a valuable car without signing for it.

It was about five-thirty when the doors of the lock-up were swung open and Percy wearing a chauffeur's cap drove out. Dusk had already come down, but it would have needed more than dusk to kill the magnificence of that Bentley. In the twilight, the long pale blue bonnet glittered like a satin dancing slipper.

He avoided main roads so far as possible. *They* were sure to be hanging about on the main roads and he didn't want to run into them. And, on the whole, he was successful. It was only once that he got himself into a tight spot and felt the sweat all ready to break out down his backbone. That was when he had to draw up in a traffic block right alongside a policeman. There was a street lamp exactly overhead and the Bentley seemed every moment to be growing longer and lower and shinier. It was like sitting in the middle of a shiny coloured supplement in a motoring paper. Percy didn't shift his eyes. He just sat there without moving, the motor running and one foot ready on the accelerator. He was all ready for a quick getaway. The policeman turned his head and inspected the radiator for a moment. Then he ran his gaze along the bonnet. He seemed interested in what he saw. Very interested. He sauntered up in a suspiciously slow and casual kind of fashion. Percy just sat there without moving. He was sweating now. He could feel the drops forming.

"Nice car you've got there," said the policeman.

"It's O.K.," Percy answered.

"What'll she do?"

"Ninety."

"Keep it up?"

"You bet."

"Ever get a chance to let her out?"

"Not often."

The lights changed and Percy revved up a bit. He let the car slide forward without even saying good-evening to the policeman. The policeman *seemed* harmless enough. He was evidently just a motoring enthusiast. He'd have been interested in any Bentley, and not in this particular pale blue one. All the same, Percy wished that he hadn't spoken to him. *They* could be at their worst even when they were apparently only being friendly.

Just to be on the safe side he kept glancing into the driving mirror to see if he were being followed. But there was no one. Absolutely no one. It was fifty pounds for sweet Fanny Adams.

He had reached the garage and was just congratulating himself on having got there without having been recognised when a voice hailed him.

"Hallo, Percy," it said. "I was wondering if I should see you."

It was the Blonde. She was standing right at the bottom of the ramp, just where he had to go down to second to go up the slope. He hadn't seen her until she stepped out into the glare of the flood-lighting.

"Hallo," he said, without even turning his head to look at her.

He had got rid of the Blonde. She had looked like stopping. But he had been cold with her. Very cold. He'd frozen her out of the garage by just not speaking to her. She didn't know but he was waterproof against blondes by now. Because of Doris the Blonde could jump into the river for all he cared.

And he'd been busy. If the previous owner of the Bentley had come in now he wouldn't have recognised it. The headlamps and the pass light were off, and he'd removed the statuette of the dancing girl. He was standing there with it in his hand.

"Look all right, on the mantelpiece," he told himself.

And then he remembered Doris.

"Give it to her for a present sometime," he decided. "Make some little joke about it, and give it to her for a present."

But the practical side of him re-asserted itself.

"Have to get a capital 'B' to put on instead," he went on musingly. "If the owner's looking out for a glass dancing girl and he sees a capital 'B' instead, where is he?"

He put in about another half-hour's work on the car and then stepped back again and looked at it. The silver coach lamps were off by now, and he'd got the radio set out as well. Altogether he was pretty pleased with what he'd done.

"Spray her over in navy," he was thinking, "and she's a different car. And pick her out in something. Doesn't matter how bright, so long as it's different."

Before he stopped for the night he removed the floor rug from the well of the coupé. It seemed too good to leave there. And in any case all the fittings would have to be changed before the new owner took over. You wouldn't get anyone in his senses driving around with a lot of other people's stuff still in the back.

In the end he took both the rug and the glass dancing girl home with him. The glass dancing girl he put away in the drawer of his dressing-table until later. But the rug he gave to his mother.

Mrs. Boon was delighted. The sad expression left her face for a moment as she stroked the rich deep pile.

"Oh, Percy, you are good to me," she said. "I don't know any other son . . ."

"S'nothing, Mother," he cut her short.

CHAPTER 13

I

MRS. VIZZARD was attending to her little bit of unpleasantness with Connie. She had declined to take the chair—her chair—that Connie had offered her. And, in consequence, the interview was stilted and formal. Connie perched herself on the corner of the bed and sat looking down at her old feet in their swansdown bedroom slippers. And Mrs. Vizzard stood over her.

". . . never had anything like it happen in this house before," she was saying.

"Same with me," Connie told her. "Victimised. That's what I was. Victimised."

"Your private life is no concern of mine," Mrs. Vizzard went on. "It's no part of my business to speak about it."

"I see your point," Connie agreed with her.

She was swinging her foot as she was talking and this time the swansdown bedroom slipper dangled for a moment and then fell off. Mrs. Vizzard waited for her to replace it. It took some time, however, as several rolled-up bits of old newspaper which Connie used for stuffing up the toes—the shoes were a full size and a half too big for her—came tumbling out, and had to be gathered up again.

"But remember it's my house and I can't have goings on here," Mrs. Vizzard resumed.

"I'll remember," said Connie contritely. "I was canned. I don't deny it."

While she was remembering how canned she had been, she started to hum. The humming annoyed Mrs. Vizzard.

"I shall have to ask for your room," she said.

Connie started.

"You mean you want me to hop?" she asked.

Mrs. Vizzard merely nodded. She disliked vulgarity on all occasions and she wished that Connie could have avoided it now.

"I mean I shall have to ask for your room," she repeated.

Connie gave a little laugh.

"And how d'you think you'll get your money if I buzz off?" she sked her. "There's three weeks now, isn't there?"

She hadn't originally intended to mention it. She hadn't, in fact, hought that there would be any need as Mrs. Vizzard would do so. But she was playing for time now.

"I'm quite aware of how much is owing," Mrs. Vizzard answered. 'And I'm prepared to forgo it."

Connie raised her eyebrows.

"I always said you were a generous woman," she told her.

Mrs. Vizzard sniffed.

"I don't want to be hard on anyone," she said. "But I've got my wn interest to look after."

"Are you *sure* you won't sit down?" Connie asked her.

"I've got nothing to sit down for," Mrs. Vizzard answered. "I've aid what I came to say."

"Have you got anyone else in mind?" Connie enquired. "It'd e a shame to have this beautiful room standing empty."

"What I want is to have this room available by Saturday," Mrs. Vizzard replied. "I'll attend to the rest."

"Saturday night?"

"First thing Saturday," Mrs. Vizzard answered. "And I want it eft clean and tidy."

It looked as though it really were the end this time. All that she ould do was to admit defeat. But it would be nice to admit it sportngly. With a bit of a flourish, in fact.

So she kicked the swansdown slipper off again—right up in the ir in Mrs. Vizzard's face.

"O.K.," she said. "See you on the Embankment."

As the door shut she thumbed her nose at Mrs. Vizzard's retreatng back. She stood there like that for a moment. But it only elieved her feelings temporarily. It didn't really comfort her. She at down on the bed again.

"Connie, my old dear," she said. "You're for it. Better pack our toothbrush and your tiara. To-morrow to fresh woods and astures new."

Then, because she couldn't help feeling miserable at the idea of eaving, she began to cry. The tears ran down her cheeks, carrying mudges of eye-black with them. But she was past minding. It was o fun—no fun at all—starting afresh at her time of life.

2

Mr. Squales had bought a bunch of violets.

Alone in his room, and with the door locked, he was playing with them. He was practising concealing them about him—in his armpits, stuffed into the waistband of his trousers, inside his shoe—and withdrawing them with one sweep of the hand. He had been distinctly amateurish at first. But as the morning wore on he improved. In the end, underneath his collarband *at the back* turned out to be the best place. Three times in succession he was able to produce them almost spontaneously from there, and send them flying across the room with a little flip of his fingers. After the third success, he sat back satisfied. Producing flowers from nowhere was now something else that he could do. And he was determined that his next séance should be a flowery one. The only thing he needed was a fresh bunch of violets.

It has been a funny life, his, when you came to think of it. He had done so many things. So many, and so different. Phrenology, for example. Reading bumps on people's heads. He'd still got the charts and the diagrams in one of his bags somewhere. And the skull. It was rather a good skull, complete with all the teeth. A child's. Somewhere between twelve and thirteen. He'd paid two pounds ten for it. And if the phrenological text-books were correct, in life the child had been by way of a musical genius with a flair for agriculture. Indeed it seemed sad that anyone so remarkably gifted should have died so young. Not that the bumps were really anything to go by. He'd run his fingers over scalps that had disproved everything the experts had written—Guardsmen and ex-sergeant-majors with strong maternal instincts, and women tied by unsuspected cravings for adventure and the open sea.

In those days he had occupied one of the little kiosks on the West Pier at Brighton. His cloak and broad black hat had once been a familiar sight on the Front and his practice had brought him in a steady six or seven pounds a week from May to September. If it hadn't been for the remaining seven months of the year when it brought in next to nothing, he might have been a Brighton Front phrenologist still.

Then there had been the short experiment of palmistry. He had taken a room in Westbourne Grove and done a little discreet advertising—YOUR HAND IS YOUR FORTUNE and LET PROFESSOR X READ THE LINES OF YOUR LIFE. But it wasn't serious, like phrenology

The clients who called on him always wanted to know when they were going to get married and how many children they were going to have. So in the end he'd told them—promising flat-chested spinsters tall, dark husbands with a small private fortune and a knowledge of foreign parts, and telling tired unhappy men in their late fifties to expect a young golden-haired bride with small teeth and violet eyes. Just sex, that was all it was. And in the end it disgusted him.

It might, all the same, have been very paying if only the fat, stupid-looking female who pathetically wanted to know about her love chances hadn't in the end turned out to be a policewoman. After that, they had closed him down. So all his acquired knowledge of the human hand had gone the way of his knowledge of the head, and he had turned to astrology instead.

The stars, for a time, had seemed unusually encouraging. For a start, the police couldn't get at them. And, though it was illegal to tell a smouldering, red-faced girl that there was a clean-shaven young seaman with robust biceps somewhere around the corner of the year, it was perfectly in line with the public interest to predict wars, train disasters, shipwrecks, fires in orphanages and pit explosions. But, of course, all that meant a lot of study, too. You couldn't set up in astrology without being familiar with Scorpions and Bulls and Fishes and Water-Carriers and that sort of thing. It wouldn't stand a chance.

The top men, the Sunday-paper astrologers, the real modern Merlins, were solid with real sound knowledge—all book stuff—from the neck up. They could cast a horoscope with their eyes shut. That was why they commanded such enormous salaries—as much as a Cabinet Minister, some of them. But somehow Mr. Squales had never managed to get himself into the Big Money class. All down Fleet Street there were men foretelling floods in China and Royal divorces—some of them charlatans too—and drawing their two or three thousand a year for doing so, while the best that he could get was a syndicated half-column in a group of local papers at a couple of guineas weekly.

In the end, the sheer hard work and the lack of recognition had led him to abandon astrology as well. He had turned over a lot of other possibilities in his mind. There was psychology, for example—but there was a lot of reading in that, too. And the market was crowded. Or nude photography. A good glossy nude called "Eve" or "Bubbles" was always a profitable property. You paid the model a guinea and you could go on selling prints of her to art students over eighteen for ever. But he didn't know anything about photo graphy. He hadn't got a camera. He hadn't got a model. He hadn' even got the guinea.

Then massage and chiropody suggested themselves. But ther again there were difficulties. The L.C.C. took a close interest. An granted licences—or didn't. Mr. Squales thought of setting u quietly without a licence and relying on personal introductions fron friends. But he abandoned the idea as too risky. Besides, he had s few friends.

So finally—after nearly two months of living on his savings—hi cigarette case, his watch, his fountain pen, his cuff-links had all gon —he decided to pool all his talents and go in for spiritualism. At th time, it had seemed like the finger of God pointing.

Not that it was easy. There was a heart-breaking fortnight whil he rehearsed. Rolling back his eyes and going off into trances, an that sort of thing. And that was only the elementary stage. He ha to practise voices as well. A variety of them. In fact, it was lik learning to be Houdini and Hamlet at the same time.

But the real trouble was supply and demand. Even without him the market seemed overcrowded. Neat, efficient professionals wit their prayer-books and bits of cheese-cloth in little attaché cases wen about from séance to séance picking up their three guineas a time leaving no room for a newcomer. No room at least for an *ordinar* newcomer.

As in all other professions, however, there was always room at th top. Always room for someone who could produce spirit faces an ectoplasmic hands and strange scents and sudden drops in temper ature. Even a few mysterious flowers arriving suddenly from no where in the centre of the table was a good deal better tha just plain voices. That was why Mr. Squales was not sparin himself.

He was going to practise with a concealed scent-spray as wel to-morrow.

3

And Connie?

She hadn't been wasting her time. Bless your heart, no. Tha wasn't Connie's way of doing things.

At the moment she was busy in front of the mirror. She'd alread brushed her hair down very flat, smothering out the little curls tha were so difficult to make, and now she was fairly plastering th powder on her face. It was a dead white powder and it gave her a startling corpse-like appearance. Even so, the result was not yet to her liking. She went over to the wash-stand and came back with a small sponge in her hand. Then holding back her head she allowed a few drops to fall on each eyelid. It was magical. Down the wrinkled chalky face large tears were running once again, carving their channels through the thick layers of powder. By the time they had dried, Connie was just the way she fancied herself. She might have been in mourning for mankind.

"Go on, Connie dear," she told herself. "Give 'em a turn. Get downstairs and smash 'em."

She selected two depressed-looking handkerchiefs from her bag and left the room, her shoulders heaving. By the time she reached the Jossers' door she was right inside her part and the sobs were uncontrollable. It was like an encore to her Christmas performance. She felt almost sorry for Mrs. Josser, knowing that the spectacle of tears always broke her good kind heart.

But it was not Mrs. Josser who answered when she knocked. It was Mr. Josser. He'd been sitting with his feet up on the fender and a copy of *Popular Gardening* open on his knees, and he was appalled by this spectre of desolation that had suddenly crept in on him.

"Why, what *ever's* the matter, Connie?" he asked. "I've never seen you this way before."

"I've never felt this way before," she told him between sobs. "It's the end. It's my swan-song."

Mr. Josser drew another chair over to the fire, and Connie sank gratefully into it. But only for a moment. Almost as soon as she had sat down, she began climbing up again.

"But I mustn't be stopping," she said miserably. "I told myself I wouldn't. I didn't ought to go about pestering *happy* folks."

"You sit there until you feel better and then you try and tell me," Mr. Josser advised gently.

There was a pause while Connie was too muffled up with crying to be able to answer.

"It's no use," she said at last. "All I came down for was a good cry on another woman's shoulder."

Mr. Josser got up and stood over by the mantelpiece.

"Better get it off your chest, Connie," he said. "We're all friends here."

The gentleness of his voice, the fact that he called her his friend, were too much for her. There were fresh paroxysms, interrupted by odd phrases ". . . one of Life's unfortunates . . . not wicked just because I'm poor . . . never harmed a fly."

In the end Mr. Josser had to ask her to start again.

"I'm being turned out," she said finally, as soon as she could speak properly. "Turned out because I've been to prison."

Mr. Josser shook his head sadly. He was shocked but not surprised. Mrs. Vizzard had certainly taken the whole matter very much to heart.

"Not that I bear her any grudge," Connie went on as though reading Mr. Josser's thoughts. "She'd got herself to think of. And if everyone complained about me I don't see that she had any choice."

"Complained about you?" Mr. Josser repeated. "We didn't do any complaining."

"I'm sure you didn't," Connie answered. "You're both of you much too kind. It was probably that Boon woman."

"No," said Mr. Josser firmly. "She was on your side like the rest of us."

Connie pursed up her lips.

"Then it must just have been Mrs. Vizzard's spite," she replied. "She thinks she can treat me this way just because she's got a hold over me."

"Got a hold over you?" Mr. Josser asked unguardedly.

"The arrears," Connie told him. "Three weeks at seven-and-sixpence. It's blackmail. And me with only ninepence."

"But couldn't you come to some arrangement?" Mr. Josser suggested. "You know—so much a week until it's all cleared off."

Connie gave a contemptuous little laugh.

"Not with her," she said. "Not with Mrs. Shylock. I'm her pound of flesh."

"Did you try?" he asked.

"I did," Connie answered. "I grovelled and she spurned me with her foot."

There was a pause, a long awkward pause, during which Connie glanced once or twice in Mr. Josser's direction. When she saw that he did not apparently intend to add anything more in the way of consolation, she rose weakly and remained standing with one hand on the arm of the chair.

"I only really came to say good-bye," she went on. "I didn't want to leave all my old friends without seeing them. I knew there wasn't nothing you could do to help me—not with all that money hanging over me."

She went limply towards the door and stood there holding out her hand from which the bangle drooped like a hoop-la quoit.

"If you don't never see me alive again don't think too badly of little Connie. Tell Mrs. Josser I tried to say good-bye."

Mr. Josser came over and shook the hand that was held out to him. It was a small and feeble hand like a child's. The feel of it broke down something inside him.

"Do . . . do you think Mrs. Vizzard would let you stop if you could pay her?" he asked.

"She'd let Jack the Ripper stop if he could pay," she answered. She broke off. "But what's the use of talking about it?" she asked. "I haven't got it, and that's that. Under the stars for me to-morrow if I'm still here."

"Just you wait where you are for a minute," Mr. Josser said. "I'm coming back."

As soon as he got outside he told himself that he was making a fool of himself. But that didn't stop him. He went through into the bedroom and shut the door behind him. In the little pink vase on the mantelpiece was a key. He tipped the vase upside down so that the key spilled out into his hand and then went over and unlocked the top drawer of Mrs. Josser's dressing-table. In a tin box with "Cash" written on it were two one-pound notes. They were Mrs. Josser's emergency hoard. She kept them there as a kind of charm against sudden disaster.

Mr. Josser took out one of the pound notes. He had a strangely guilty feeling as he did so.

"Go round to the Post Office first thing in the morning and draw out a pound to replace it," he told himself.

Then he felt about in his trouser pockets and extracted half a crown.

"Now she's all square, the poor old thing," he reflected.

Connie was waiting there obediently when he got back. He could tell from her face that she had no notion of the good fortune that was coming to her. She was so completely unaware, indeed, that Mr. Josser found great difficulty in giving her the money. He simply thrust the note and the half-crown into her hand—luckily her hand was open—and stepped back.

As soon as Connie felt the convincing stiff paper of the pound note against her palm the fingers closed together like a bird's claws. There were real tears in her eyes this time.

"You're a corker," she said. "You're a real Good Samaritan, you are. You're just about the kindest thing in trousers I've ever met."

To Mr. Josser's embarrassment she took hold of his hand and kissed it.

"Don't say anything about this," he asked. "Just let it be private between the two of us."

"Mum's the word," Connie promised. "Sealed lips, that's me."

CHAPTER 14

I

Mrs. Vizzard glanced at her clock. It showed a quarter to four. Because she was eager and impatient she went straight over to the sideboard and took out the best table-cloth. When she had smoothed out the folds, she set it elegantly cornerwise so that four little triangles of dark mahogany were left at the corners. Then she got out the best cups—the ones with a voluptuously opening rose painted passionately on the side—and the silver teapot. By the time she had put the cake rack on the table as well it was evident that she was doing things in style. The table was laid significantly for two.

Finally, she went through to her bedroom and changed her lace cuffs. The new pair looked exactly the same as the old ones. But Mrs. Vizzard was very particular about her cuffs. "No lady," she remembered reading as a girl, "will ever tolerate soiled lace." She had remembered it in fact right through from 1890 until 1938, until she was almost the only person left in London still wearing lace cuffs.

When she changed her cuffs, she studied herself carefully in the mirror. There was a wisp of hair out of place and she shackled it with another hair-pin. Apart from that there was nothing that needed doing. The face that gazed back at her was as smooth and unwrinkled and expressionless as it had always been. The long dark hair, plaited tightly in the nape of the neck, was so smooth that it might have been melted down and poured on.

But it was still too early. Four-thirty, she had said, and it would be unthinkable to make it earlier, to *appear* impetuous. As it was, she was growing apprehensive again. The folly of what she was about to do became apparent to her, and she half regretted it. But only half.

To occupy the time, to kill the intervening twenty minutes, she took out a cushion cover that she was embroidering. The design, like that on the tea-cups, was a rose; a rose so full blown as to be almost wilting. With quick deft stitches she began filling in the red unfolded heart. But her mind was too full of other things this afternoon to concentrate. And finally she gave up the attempt. Thrusting her needle right in up to the eye she sat back, pondering.

"It may be foolish of me," she admitted to herself. "It may even be rash and indiscreet. But I have no one but myself to consider in the matter. And no one need ever know. It's only because he's lonely that I'm doing it. And he really is rather distinguished. I've never known one socially before. It will be very stimulating. I wonder if I shall find that I'm sensitive to anything."

She looked at the clock. It was four-thirty now.

"No one need ever know," she repeated. "It is only just this once. And it will be quite private."

All the same, as she realised how close the moment was, her heart was fluttering a little. And it was pounding and thumping most remarkably as she got up and left the room. Outside Mr. Squales's door she paused, hesitating.

"But this is absurd," she rebuked herself. "I'm getting myself into a state just like a girl."

Controlling herself, she knocked.

"Mr. Squales," she said, trying to keep her voice steady and natural-sounding. "Would you be free to join me for a cup of tea?"

The reply was not so prompt as she anticipated. She had expected that he would rise at once and open the door to her. Instead, there was a grunt and the scraping of a chair—of two chairs—almost as though he had been asleep in the deep armchair with the broken springs with his feet up on the hard Windsor one opposite. There was a further sound of scraping as though he were searching about for his slippers and then the door opened and a squalid and tousled Mr. Squales stood there. His black cravat was undone and hanging downwards. And his velvet jacket was secured by the wrong button as though he had pulled the thing hastily together whilst he was still rather muzzy. On the mantelpiece behind him stood a beer-bottle and a dirty glass.

"Dear me," he said. "So late already. I'm afraid that I must have dozed off for a moment. You were asking to . . . to take tea with you. How delightful—how very delightful it would be."

Mrs. Vizzard re-inspected him, and then averted her eyes.

"In . . . in ten minutes' time?" she suggested.

"In less, in five," he answered. "Almost straight away. I'm practically ready."

Mrs. Vizzard returned to her room and stood there for a moment motionless.

"It *was* wrong," she confessed. "I've lowered myself and I've been punished for it. Mr. Squales is not a gentleman. No gentleman would have been in such disorder."

But five minutes later when he arrived, he certainly *looked* a gentleman. His hair—except for the lock that naturally hung downwards—was sleeked back across his head and his cravat was now tied up with a flourish. He had buttoned his jacket up properly, and put on a pair of shoes in place of his slippers. Also, his manners were perfect. He came in diffidently, apologetically, as though he knew that he was in disgrace.

"I shall never forgive myself," he said. "Never. I had been working and I fell asleep. I can only say that I was very, very tired."

Mrs. Vizzard accepted his apologies. It was flattering, decidedly flattering, to have a professional medium, an international one even, paying so much personal attention.

"I shall ask him," she thought, "what it feels like to be a medium, what are the sensations of being one of the spiritually chosen."

But all that she said was, "Do you take milk and sugar, Mr. Squales?"

And, in a way, Mr. Squales's reply rather disappointed her.

"Milk, please, and two lumps," he said. "I like it very sweet and rather milky."

There seemed something oddly unspiritual in such an answer. It was almost as if Mr. Squales were a greedy man. And he certainly made an uncommonly good tea. He sat there wolfing scones, bread and butter and two kinds of cake.

"Poor man, he's ravenous," Mrs. Vizzard reflected. "It's more than a pleasure. It's a *duty* to feed him."

And Mr. Squales seemed to repay feeding. Under the influence of food and several cups of his specially sweet milky tea, he lost the reserve that had hung over him and been so chilling. But his manners remained perfect just the same. He asked Mrs. Vizzard's permission before he smoked his first cigarette. Apparently, he smoked a lot of cigarettes. His fingers were stained and discoloured right up to the nails.

"Now," thought Mrs. Vizzard. "I'll put my question to him."

But Mr. Squales spoke first.

"Have you lived in this house long, Mrs. Vizzard?" he asked.

Mrs. Vizzard dropped her eyes.

"I came here as a bride," she said.

"So-o-o-o."

Mr. Squales very deliberately prolonged the word. He made of it a sound that was at once infinitely understanding, sympathetic and consoling.

"And now you are alone?" he went on.

"I'm a widow," Mrs. Vizzard told him.

"Sad. How sad," Mr. Squales replied. "In the midst of life, as the poet says. . . . And is it long since Mr. Vizzard died? . . . passed on, I should say?"

"Nineteen-twenty-two," Mrs. Vizzard answered. "Michaelmas Quarter Day."

She had a concise and businesslike mind even in matters of the heart. She remembered dates just as she remembered figures.

"Since then you've been alone?" Mr. Squales persisted, as though the loneliness of Mrs. Vizzard held a special fascination for him.

"I've had my guests," Mrs. Vizzard replied sharply. "From the time I took matters into my own hands I've never had a room empty."

It was not true, as Mr. Squales knew. But Mrs. Vizzard was quick to answer any aspersion. She had, however, misunderstood the observation.

"No, no," said Mr. Squales, brushing the point aside with tobaccoey fingers in the air. "Not in that sense. In the more important one. You have been alone in the world, I mean?"

"I've had my Faith," she told him. "I only really learnt to know my late husband after he went across."

Mr. Squales drew himself up sharply.

"Ah yes. The other world. What a comfort it can be," he remarked. "What an awakening!"

A dreamy look came into Mr. Squales's dark eyes, and Mrs. Vizzard drew in her breath expectantly. Now was the moment. Without any prompting from her, Mr. Squales was going to talk about the Life Beyond. But in this she was disappointed. At least for the time being he seemed entirely preoccupied by things on This Side.

"I have a curious feeling," he began, "that it was no accident that brought me here. I had other addresses, other houses, to go to. I knew no one. Yet I came. I knew from the moment you answered the door to me that there was no need to go further. There was something that told me that I had arrived."

"I . . . I'm glad you're comfortable," Mrs. Vizzard faltered.

Mr. Squales's eyes were cast full on her.

"I am more than comfortable; I am at home," he assured her.

For some reason Mrs. Vizzard found herself blushing. It was an unfamiliar sensation. Rather unpleasant, as though hot ants were running over her. And she was aware that Mr. Squales was still looking at her. Looking at her hand, and smiling. The ants began to run round in circles.

Mr. Squales cleared his throat.

"It's very strange," he said. "I see now how wrong I was. When I first saw you I took you for a much older person. I took you for a woman already middle-aged."

2

Percy was feeling pretty good. Quite O.K., in fact. He had got himself just where he liked to be—right in the ringside seats. And there was no doubt about being in the thick of things. Trainers and managers and press-men kept pushing past him. And, when one of the boxers managed to get the other up against the ropes it was as though the fight was not merely going on in front, but actually on top, of him. Only two seats away, another gentleman, a big man in a light grey suit with a carnation in his buttonhole, had burnt himself on his own cigar when a feather-weight had come slithering out of the ring on his back into the midst of the spectators. It was life all right, hot life, where Percy was sitting.

Next to Percy was Mr. Josser. They hadn't just met there by accident either—Mr. Josser wasn't the sort who went about to prize fights. It had all been a part of a carefully thought-out scheme, a plot almost—of Percy's. He'd told himself that the best way of getting to know Doris was to put himself on easy terms with her family. And it was because he didn't know how to tackle Mrs. Josser straight away—he couldn't, for instance, ask her to put on a dance frock and come along with him to the Palais—that he'd begun on Mr. Josser.

Even then he'd been cautious. The one thing that he wanted to avoid was being obvious. So, in the end, after paying five shillings each for the seats he'd told Mr. Josser that they'd been given to him. It gave him a pleasant sensation of well-being—he'd already got twenty-five pounds in advance on account of the hot Bentley—to be able to lay out half a quid for the sake of the girl he loved. And Mr. Josser had quite innocently accepted.

He'd never seen a boxing match before. He didn't, indeed, particularly want to see one. But it seemed so nice of the boy to have thought of him that he was afraid that he would be disappointed if he refused. Mrs. Josser remained frankly disapproving of prize fights. And Doris was cross with her father for going at all. It seemed to lower his dignity somehow.

The only person, other than Percy, who was thoroughly delighted by the arrangement was Mrs. Boon. She gave a great sigh of relief when she learned who her son's companion was to be. It was the first time she could ever remember since Percy had grown up when she had really known where he was going and with whom.

The fight was taking place at the Baths. And about four hundred people were watching it. It was, of course, only the ringside seats that were so expensive. Elsewhere in the house the prices of admission went right down to a shilling—for standing room, of course. But there were plenty of people in the middle income classes, people who were ready to pay two shillings or half a crown to sit in one of the galleries, craning their necks round the ornamental iron pillars, to see the pugilists, from that distance looking no larger than frenzied pygmies, hammer away at each other about thirty feet below.

The air was thick with tobacco smoke, and blue spirals of it went drifting in little eddies across the brilliant block of light that was shed by the shaded lamps above the ring. By now the lesser weights, the trivial stuff, had frisked and feinted and glissaded and were over. Percy and Mr. Josser had watched a fly-weight, a feather-weight, a bantam-weight and a cruiser-weight. And they had come at last on to the serious business, the real purpose, of the evening. Tiger Stoneman (of Stoke Newington) who turned the scales at twelve stone seven was about to put himself to the supreme test of strength against Battling Charley (of Balham) who was a full thirteen stone one. It was to be a battle of the giants, and most of the audience was outside priming itself on beer to be ready for the ordeal.

There was, indeed, something pretty impressive about the way in which since seven-thirty the spectacle had been devised in a mounting crescendo of calves and biceps. Starting off with agile, flimsy creatures like fierce dwarfs it had now got itself among the Titans. And it looked like going on in that way. There was the half-veiled hint behind the arrangements that if the display lasted for even another half-hour gigantic monsters about ten feet in height and weighing twenty stone would trample their way into the ring like dinosaurs.

In the meantime, Tiger Stoneman was quite big enough to please Percy—and even the bantam-weights had been enough to satisfy Mr. Josser. The Tiger entered the ring in his celebrated striped dressing-gown, allowed his seconds—two bullet-headed thugs like escaped convicts—to disrobe him as though he were too well-bred to do that kind of thing for himself, and stood there, like a cockerel, turning himself about for people to admire him. This performance was interrupted at last by the arrival of Battling Charley. An older man and clad in a very drab sort of wrap, he aroused no enthusiasm until he showed his chest. Then he got a round all to himself because he was so hairy. Mr. Josser was amazed. Battling Charley did not look like a man at all. He was simply something from the trees that had come down to earth for half an hour to make mischief. And at the sound of the clapping, the great ape began grinning. He swayed backwards and forwards enthusiastically shaking hands with himself above his head.

"Nah you'll see," said Percy delightedly. "This'll be murder."

It seemed to Mr. Josser that Percy was very nearly right. Quite early in the first round Battling Charley darted into his opponent's face with a straight right, that everyone except the Tiger seemed to have been expecting, and his glove came away scarlet. After that it was sheer jungle stuff. Every time he touched the Tiger's body, even if it was only a jab, he left a small red print like a penny stamp. It seemed that bright terrible wounds were being opened at random all over the beautiful white body of the boxer. By the time the gong went at the end of the second round, the Tiger looked like a medieval martyr. And Mr. Josser was feeling sick.

The rest of the evening was no more than a jumbled pageant of horrors for Mr. Josser. Assault and battery, attempted manslaughter, torture, disfiguration, death itself it looked like, were all staged before his nose for him to laugh and wonder at. Great ham-like fists thrashed the air and divided it. Eyebrows were cut clean open. Dust rose up in clouds from the flooring. And the sound of massive, hunted breathing filled the place. Altogether he might have been back in the red dawn of history.

Out of all that brilliantly lit spectacle of commercial courage—there was prize money of fifty pounds for one of them—only two sights remained clear to Mr. Josser afterwards. One was of the smaller of the two thugs who were the Tiger's handmaidens, clad in a pair of dirty grey flannels, white tennis shoes and a singlet. The creature was bending forward over the Tiger, pouring drops of collodion into an open gash in his forehead. It was First Aid at its most brutal and elementary. And apparently the Tiger didn't like it. He kept shaking his head and growling. About the whole proceeding there was the suggestion of a piece of intricate brain surgery being performed at the hands of a butcher's boy.

The other sight that remained with Mr. Josser was a self-contained nightmare. Battling Charley had worked his man into a corner and was getting ready to eat him like an ogre when the Tiger suddenly caught him full in the mouth with a half-hook. The effect was appalling. Battling Charley was rocked backwards on to his heels and when he recovered himself what seemed to be his entire set of very white front teeth fell out on to the floor and were trampled on.

Young Percy leant over affectionately, and thrust his mouth against Mr. Josser's ear.

"There goes his gum shield," he said gloatingly. "I told you there'd be murder."

But Mr. Josser was past caring. He was sitting there with his eyes closed and his hand up in front of his face so that Percy shouldn't notice. Even with his eyes shut, however, he couldn't keep himself cut off entirely from what was going on behind those springy ropes. For shutting his eyes didn't keep out the sounds. There was the soft sinister thump of the punches when they hit the body, and the sharp click when the jaw or the forehead caught it. There was also a whole host of other horrid little sounds as well. He now recognised every one of them. He knew the noise that wet towels make as the seconds flap them in the faces of their wilting pets; the glug-glug-glug of water being drunk from a bottle—apparently it would have been unseemly for a pugilist to be caught drinking from a tumbler; the rough friction of hairy muscular legs being massaged.

And it would have been absurd, when the climax came, to pretend that he hadn't heard *that*. There was a bang that seemed to shake the whole Baths and somebody began counting "One-two-three-four" quite slowly. Mr. Josser opened his eyes. Battling Charley, the hairy one, the old man of the trees, was lying flat on his back with his knees drawn up almost to his chin, and Tiger Stoneman, the young, the twelve stone seven, the beautiful, was standing beside him, wearing a slightly dazed and self-conscious expression as though he wasn't altogether sure about the politeness of what he had just done to the older man.

Young Percy, Mr. Josser noticed, was nearly hysterical with delight at the outcome. And when the referee finally counted Battling Charley out—small desultory movements of the legs indicated either that the hairy body was still alive or that at least the muscles were still twitching—Percy's feelings became almost uncontrollable. Taking his soft green felt in one hand he smashed it flat with the other.

"Oh, boy," he said over and over again, "was that a punch? Just you tell me. Was that a punch?"

It was only a quarter of an hour's walk from the Baths back to

Dulcimer Street, but Mr. Josser was grateful for every minute of it. He felt the need for fresh air, and he went along drinking in the night in great gulps. In a sense, it was taking Percy even longer to recover. A small envelope of violence still surrounded him. As he walked along he fought shadowy battles with himself. He made sudden, darting side steps as though to avoid imaginary adversaries, brought up short left jabs against chins that only he could see. He shook his head helplessly when some spectral invisible blow, harder than the last, landed full on him.

"Oh, boy," he repeated from time to time. "Was that a punch? Tell me, was that a punch?"

And then a strange mood of shyness overcame him because he remembered Doris. He was being led back to the house in which she lived. And by her own father, too. He was practically one of the family.

"Come in and have a bite of something," Mr. Josser suggested when they got back to No. 10. "I could do with it."

"O.K.," said Percy, and then paused. "Think it's all right, me coming in like this, without knocking?" he asked.

Mr. Josser regarded him in astonishment for a moment.

"Why ever not?" he said. "It's Liberty Hall."

Mrs. Josser seemed, however, a somewhat severe custodian of so much freedom.

"Good gracious," she said. "You're back early. Did the police stop it or something?"

Mr. Josser didn't reply. He hung his hat up on the hook outside and forced his companion into the room in front of him.

"I've brought Percy back with me," he said. "We've just . . ."

But he was cut short.

"Oh, Dad, you haven't."

It was Doris who had spoken. She was kneeling in front of the fire and he hadn't noticed her until that moment. Apparently she had been doing something to her hair. A brush and comb and a bottle of setting lotion was spread out on the rug beside her. Her jumper was off and there was a towel wrapped round her shoulders.

"You'd better go through to the bedroom, Doris," Mrs. Josser told her meaningly.

"Sorry if I'm disturbing anyone," Percy said gallantly.

"Oh, you're not disturbing me in the least," Doris answered. "I was just going, I assure you."

She got up very red in the face from hanging over the fire, and pushed her way past him. Percy was aware for a single moment of a delicious nearness, and the odour of the setting lotion. And then it was all over. The door shut behind her and she was gone.

Mr. Josser went over to the cupboard.

"Cuppa tea, Percy?" he asked.

But Percy scarcely heard him. He was thinking ruefully of the whole wasted evening. It had been all right while the boxing had lasted. But after that—nothing. He had simply chucked away ten bob on giving Mr. Josser a private treat. So far as his stock stood with Mrs. Josser he was down lower than ever.

"I've been made a sucker of," he thought miserably. "That's what's happened. I've been made a sucker of."

CHAPTER 15

I

It was Saturday, the day of Doris's move. After dawning hopefully with a clear sky, it clouded over by breakfast-time and by ten o'clock it was raining. The rain was still coming down by midday. And at twelve-thirty, when the move was due to begin, it was a downpour.

Because the furniture had to arrive from two different places it was complicated enough anyhow. Scouts had to be posted at Kennington, West Hampstead and Adelaide Road in an attempt to synchronise the various movements of furniture. And, even so, things went wrong. In the first place, the van that was calling at West Hampstead for Doreen's settees and cushions and mirrors arrived early, and the van that was collecting Doris's solider stuff from Kennington arrived late. This meant that Doreen's boudoir was already *in situ*, drawn up alongside the kerb in the rain, while Doris's bedroom was still trundling over Lambeth Bridge on its journey northwards.

It was Mrs. Smyth, Doreen's mother, who had agreed to act as co-ordinator. A large, imposing woman who always wore pearls—big pinkish ones for preference—she had promised herself an easy, rather queenly afternoon simply presiding in the flat until the girls arrived. But, unfortunately, things weren't working out that way. There was a sudden rush in the office and there were Doris and Doreen, hammering away at their typewriters, when they should have been lugging chairs about and trying out the new window curtains. In the end they got off at a quarter-past one, ate a sandwich in a milk-bar, drank a foaming raspberry drink called a Special and fought their way on to a No. 31 bus to Chalk Farm. They were both of them very excited, very impatient and slightly apprehensive.

They arrived to find a row going on with the moving-men from West Hampstead. It was the iron staircase that was the cause of the trouble. Apparently the estimate would have been different if the firm had known about the staircase. And from the way the men spoke they made it clear that the difference would have been in blood money. Nor were the men from Kennington any more encouraging when they turned up. They were dark soured little fellows, and they had all the heavier pieces. They kept going round to the back of the house to have another look at the staircase, and each time they returned shaking their heads. Then the foremen said something about tackle, and the two teams went into a huddle to discuss it. The main difficulty seemed to be that neither side had brought any tackle with them. They were clearly in favour of calling off the whole operation and going quietly home.

It was Mrs. Smyth who finally over-awed them into action. They emerged from their interview with her with the appearance of men who had drawn lots, and both lost. They turned up their coat collars, and, inverting their pipes to keep the raindrops from spoiling their tobacco, consented to climb up aloft once more and see for themselves. Mrs. Smyth put up her umbrella and climbed with them. It was her second view of the inside of the flat, and it confirmed her first one. She was horrified. It seemed incredible that, because of Doreen's mad infatuation for this girl from South London, her daughter should be sentencing herself to live in such a place. She kept on glancing at the painted window with the sloping window-sill, and glancing away again.

But at least it was dry. After the streaming rain that had slanted down the outside staircase even the bare boards and discoloured walls of the flat seemed luxurious. And from so much security, Mrs. Smyth refused altogether to be budged. She simply begged the men to hurry, telling them that they could see for themselves that the outside staircase was nothing, and stayed where she was.

After another pause that drove Doreen nearly frantic—she didn't attempt to conceal that she blamed Mrs. Smyth for the delay—the moving-men came staggering up like small storming parties. The furniture had been swathed in layers of dust cloths to protect it from the rain, and wet figures appeared suddenly in the doorway carrying large shapeless cocoons.

It was here that Doreen's nervous energy showed itself. She

rushed at the men as though attacking them and began tearing the winding cloths off the furniture. A moment later she was trundling chairs and settees across the floor, and standing back with half-closed eyes to see how the room looked that way.

By four o'clock the last of the storming parties had retreated and only the hard work of getting things tidied up remained. Here Doreen suddenly went under. Probably as a result of so much effort, one of her headaches came on. Whatever caused it, it came. And it laid her out. All the time while Doris was opening packing-cases and trying to get the kitchen in order, poor Doreen couldn't do a thing. She just lay back on her own settee with her own cushion under her head, giving advice and promising to help as soon as she recovered.

She was still lying there when Mrs. Josser arrived. Doris hadn't told Doreen anything about Mrs. Josser's visit, and Doreen seemed to resent it. But when she found that Mrs. Josser had brought tea with her—she was carrying a large wicker basket full of cake and buns and biscuits as well as a bottle of milk and a bag of sugar—Doreen, who was feeling hungry by now, softened a little in her attitude. She recognised that in a humble, rather pathetic way, Mrs. Josser distinctly had her uses. And in the result she sat up and ate a good tea. So did Mrs. Smyth.

But not so Mrs. Josser. Having carted the food all the way from Dulcimer Street she just drank a cup of tea and nibbled at a biscuit and said nothing. It was the first time that she had seen Doreen's mother, and she was having a good look at her. In the result, the study was not half so unsatisfactory as she had anticipated. Admittedly, Mrs. Smyth was smart and well-to-do-looking with her big pink pearls and a large crocodile-skin handbag, and a fur strung over one shoulder. But there was something about her that Mrs. Josser detected almost at once. Detected and liked. Underneath all that magnificence, Mrs. Smyth was common.

And Mrs. Smyth, taking things more easily, had arrived at her own estimation of Mrs. Josser. There was no point in denying that she cut a pretty unfashionable figure as she sat there. Any woman who cared for her appearance would long ago have changed those grim steel spectacles for something smarter in tortoise-shell or coloured bone. But there was character there undeniably. And sense. Mrs. Smyth felt more hopeful about the future.

Finally, she came over and sat beside Mrs. Josser on the settee that was to be Doreen's bed as soon as Doreen had decided where she wanted it.

"What do *you* think of this flat?" she asked in a whisper.

"I wasn't asked," Mrs. Josser snapped back at her.

"But now you have been," Mrs. Smyth said coaxingly, "you can tell me: I won't pass it on."

"I think it's a mistake," Mrs. Josser said briefly. "A terrible mistake."

"Oh, I'm so glad," Mrs. Smyth answered. "I think it's awful. Do you think they'll be happy here?"

"Not if I know them," Mrs. Josser answered.

Mrs. Smyth seemed delighted.

"I do so agree," she said. "It's what I've been telling Doreen. Is Doris headstrong too?"

"So so," Mrs. Josser answered.

"And what a time to choose," said Mrs. Smyth suddenly. "Supposing there's a war, they can't live on the top floor then. It wouldn't be safe."

"Oh dear," Mrs. Josser agreed wearily. "I do so hope something goes wrong and they get tired of this flat idea."

"I couldn't agree more," said Mrs. Smyth. "For a start, Doreen isn't strong enough. . . ."

The headstrong and delicate Doreen had, however, apparently recovered considerably by now. She was going about the flat rearranging things. Shrill shrieks of disappointment or delight indicated in which of the four rooms she was at any moment to be discovered.

"Horrid flat," Mrs. Smyth said suddenly. "So dirty."

Mrs. Josser turned on her.

"That it isn't," she said. "I scrubbed it out myself."

"Did you really?" Mrs. Smyth said. "Couldn't you get a woman?"

"I didn't try," Mrs. Josser told her. "I just came and did it."

It was nearly six now and Mrs. Smyth said that she would have to be going. Doreen put down the two lampshades that she was carrying and came forward, open-armed, to hug her mother. It was a demonstrative kind of parting heavy with kissings and promises and squeezes.

"You've been an absolute angel, mummy dear," Doreen told her. "Thank you so much for coming over and doing everything."

Mrs. Josser beckoned Doris to come to her.

"Here," she said. "You may want this."

She handed Doris the basket from which the tea had been produced. Apparently there was still quite a lot in it.

"There's half a leg of cold lamb in there," she went on. "And a peach flan. You won't be feeling like doing much cooking tomorrow."

Doris caught her mother's eye as she said it. They were not an emotional family, the Jossers. Beside the Smyths, indeed, Mrs. Josser and Doris seemed unnaturally frigid and aloof. But for a moment mother and daughter smiled at each other. It was an understanding smile. Mutely it expressed the simple truth of the situation—that though they might get on each other's nerves to screaming point if they ever had to live together again, they would miss each other like mad if they were actually separated.

The moving in was now finished, and there was nothing for it but to leave the girls to the discomforts of their new home. They made a very charming pair, Doreen and Doris, as they stood at the top of the staircase waving. But the staircase was far too tricky for there to be any turning and waving back. Neither Mrs. Smyth nor Mrs. Josser was prepared to risk a header even for the sake of a daughter.

"How perfectly awful," Doreen exclaimed as she came back from the front door. "I thought they were *never* going."

Doris looked uncomfortable. For some reason or other she was suddenly feeling sorry for her mother. Not grateful or dutiful or anything like that, just plain sorry. And she didn't like to hear Doreen saying that she was glad that she had gone away again.

"It wouldn't have mattered," she said.

"Not mattered?" Doreen shrieked at her. "You must be mad. It would have spoilt everything."

As she said it, Doreen came to life again. What she had shown up to now was just a little eddy of energy. But this was the real full hurricane. There was something positively alarming about so much dynamism let loose in such a confined space. She went tearing about from room to room carrying even quite small things, like a cigarette box or a travelling clock, and putting them down somewhere different.

But there was a reason for the rush. She had—it was one of those brilliant ideas of Doreen's that came from simply nowhere—hit on the notion of throwing a moving-in party. It wasn't going to be a big affair, she had explained to Doris, and she wasn't going to take any special trouble over it. All that she had done was to invite a few of the chaps round for a drink—and it was a part of the scheme that they should bring the drinks with them. In her enthusiasm, she rattled off again a selection of the fellows that she had invited. There was Tony and Christopher and Donald and Bill and Maurice and Hilary and Bernard. She couldn't stop now, she said, to tell Doris anything about them. But they'd all said they were absolutely crazy to meet her.

There had been a careless generosity about the manner of inviting them. They had all been asked to bring along with them any other chaps who might happen to be free that evening. In less than a couple of hours' time, it seemed, dozens of unknown men, at least half of them strangers to each other, would be piling into the place. Doris asked Doreen if she would like her to go out and find a shop where she could buy some more food. But Doreen wouldn't hear of it. She said that it was far more important to get the studio—it was "the studio" that she had decided they should call it—looking respectable. In any case, it was drink, not food, they'd be wanting, and she had told them to bring that with them.

She went on to say that if only they were on the phone up there she could have doubled the number that was coming. She must have been mad, quite mad, she decided, to have left out all her very oldest friends. There was Hughie and Valentine and Frank and Quentin and about a score of others whom she'd only just remembered. . . .

By nine o'clock one out of the multitude had actually turned up. He was Bill, a quiet, rather serious-looking young man wrapped up in an enormous striped muffler. He came in carrying a quart bottle of beer and saying that he hoped he wasn't late. While they were waiting for the others to arrive, the time passed rather slowly because Bill, though friendly, wasn't much of a conversationalist. Even the best subjects simply died on him. He was a Bart's man, a medical in his final year, and the most engaging thing about him was his grin. It appeared suddenly, almost without warning, completely transforming his whole face, and suggested a broad vein of sheer idiocy running somewhere right through him. Doris found herself rather liking Bill and wondering if all the other young men were going to be as nice. In whispers, in the kitchen, Doreen promised her far better: Bill was quite a pet in his way, she said, but it was Tony, his best friend, who was the real scream. He ought to be along almost any time now, she said.

But she was wrong. Tony didn't come. Nor did the others. Nobody came. By ten-thirty there was still only Bill, and by then they had finished the beer that he had brought with him. They waited until eleven to see if there was going to be a chance of anything else to drink, and then Doris suggested that they might have some sort of meal. She produced the leg of lamb and the peach flan that Mrs. Josser had left behind, and between them they polished it off.

The one who didn't make a hearty meal was Doreen. She was too busy explaining.

"What a joke," she kept on saying. "I've only just remembered —I don't believe I gave any of them the new address. If only I could see their faces now. You imagine how you'd feel if someone asked you to a party and then moved away without telling you."

She was still saying something of the kind when at midnight Bill announced that he had got to be going. He left assuring the two girls that he had had a wonderful time, and disappeared heroically down the iron staircase, his muffler flying. His "Cheerio" sounded up from the darkness somewhere down below.

"I wonder what did happen to all the others," Doris asked, as soon as they were alone together. "They must have known that it couldn't be the old address if this was a moving-in party."

"Oh, them. I've forgotten about them," Doreen told her. "They were drunk probably. In any case, I shan't speak to any of them again."

2

Percy was depressed again.

He'd shifted the Bentley. It was off his hands by now. But what had he got out of it? Just half what they'd told him. He'd been paid of course for the work he'd actually put in on it—the re-spraying, the new bumpers, removing the fancy coach lamps, toning down the pretties. But all he'd got for *doing* the job was just twenty-five pounds, instead of fifty. It wasn't good enough. And it hurt. Hurt right down where he was tenderest. Hurt so much, in fact, that he'd decided to do a bit of lifting on his own account.

"Free lance, that's me," he said to himself over and over again because it was his favourite word by now. "I'm just wasting my time playing in with those boys if they won't play fair by me."

Not that he was going to do anything silly. He wasn't going to rush things. He was going to use his head. Stealing a car was a serious job. It needed brain-work. And planning.

Because he was worrying about how to begin he stood there, biting his nails. It was an old habit that he'd retained from childhood. Mrs. Boon had always known just how he was feeling from the way he kept bringing his fingers up to his mouth. He was like that now. Leaning up against the petrol pump marked COMMERCIAL, he gnawed away at the quick—the nails of all garagemen are short enough, anyhow—and began straightening things out in his mind.

For a start it was no use doing things entirely single-handed. Too risky. If the police were out for stolen cars they'd go straight for any man who was driving solo. A couple of people up in the front seat was safer.

It looked too social somehow to be involved in crime. And if one of them was your grandmother you'd be able to drive right through a cordon. But supposing your grandmother wouldn't play, who then? Certainly not the Blonde. The police knew all about blondes. And suspected them. Besides, the Blonde might talk. She had never seemed to Percy the intellectual type. And she looked the wrong *sort* anyhow. Even if she'd been brunette the police would still have suspected her. What he wanted was a nice quiet girl with not too much make-up on, and not in a fur coat. Fur coats were suspicious too, especially half-length ones with the tails hanging down. He wanted someone more the quiet kind. The difficulty was that he didn't know any of that class of girl. They just didn't interest him, somehow.

Of course, there was Doris. But he was going to keep Doris right out of all this.

"Your little hands must be kept clean, my darling," he began thinking. "Let Percy do the rough work. You keep yourself all sweet and lovely for me. I want you to keep your little hands clean."

For a moment he peered into the future. He saw himself sitting side by side with Doris on a Knole couch in a good-class drawing-room with a radiogram and big Chinese vase full of tulips and long velvet curtains up on pelmets and a pretty maid bringing in a tray of drinks. When the maid had pranced out of the room again on her high heels, Percy put his arm tighter round Doris and told her his secret.

"You remember all those cars I used to collect with you on Saturday afternoons when we were engaged," he was saying. "Well, they were all hot. Every one of them. We'd have done three years both of us if I hadn't been careful. . . ."

But that was all wrong: it was just what he wasn't going to do. It was dreaming. It had always been his bad habit, dreaming. Besides, he'd got it all worked out by now. He was right on to the big idea. At this very moment there was someone driving about in a car that wouldn't belong to its owner by to-morrow night. It would belong to Percy. Percy Boon, Esq., Hot Car Specialist. And the way he had planned it there wouldn't be any danger. Any real danger, that is. Of course, in all professions there is always an element of risk. You can't get rich and play safe at the same time.

"Cut it clean out and don't be a fool. You're playing with fire, Percy," Voice No. 2 suddenly said inside him.

Voice No. 2 always broke in about now. It was a dreary, cautioning sort of voice. Like it might have been his father's. It warned him against things. Not just hot cars. But blondes as well. And places like Charley's Bar and Smokey's. And little things like fifty cigarettes a day, and betting on the dogs. Percy didn't know where it came from. But it was always there, ready to say something spoiling just when he was beginning to enjoy himself.

Then Voice No. 1 chipped in. Voice No. 1 was a very different kind of voice. More like some of the voices he'd heard on the films. It was an Edward G. Robinson voice that made you sit up. And the advice it gave was different, too.

"So you're backing out, are you?" it asked. "You're content with things as they are? You haven't any ambition? You want to stay a garage-hand?" Voice No. 1 paused for a moment almost as if taking a deep breath. Then it fairly bawled in his ear. "Go on and do it, you lady's man. Show you've got guts. Let 'em know who's the clever one round here."

It was funny having these two voices inside him all the time trying to make him move in different directions at once. No wonder he had headaches. And where did he come in? he wondered. Which of them was really him? Or wasn't he either of them? Was he just the one that did the listening?

In any case he couldn't help hearing. Because the voices were right inside him. And Voice No. 1 was so loud. Right against his ear. And it did something to him, too. It was Voice No. 1 that had urged him on to handle the hot Bentley. It was Voice No. 1 that had told him to go after blondes and reminded him that if he didn't somebody else would. It was Voice No. 1 that had told him to be a Free Lance and use his head. In its time Voice No. 1 had led Percy into a lot of trouble.

But now it was helping him. Helping to fix up the details of the first little job on his own account.

"Easy as falling off a log, if you use your head properly," it was saying. "All it needs is timing. Pick your moment. Don't force things. And look out for a nice lock-up somewhere off the beaten track. Don't go too fancy. Don't go too high. Choose something that the cops won't turn round to stare at. Then you'll be all right. Make it a Morris or an Austin, and Bob's your uncle."

"And what about your poor old mum if you slip up somewhere?" Voice No. 2 said as soon as Voice No. 1 had finished. "Have you thought about her?"

3

Connie was downstairs seeing Mrs. Vizzard. Mrs. Vizzard hadn't asked her to sit down and Connie stood there on the hearth-rug twining her little yellow fingers in embarrassment.

"I've done my best," she said. "And that's the most anyone can do." She gave a little sniff that turned into something like a sob before it was finished, and held out three half-crowns in her hand to Mrs. Vizzard. "All I could raise," she added. "The widow's mite."

Mrs. Vizzard had been prepared for this. She made no attempt to take the money.

"I've told you before," she said. "It's not your money I want. It's the room." She paused. "And I want it by to-night. You know that."

"I could pay off the other two weeks bit by bit if you didn't mind waiting," Connie suggested. "Sixpence a week'd clear it all up by Christmas. Then we could all start fair and square again, the way I like things."

Mrs. Vizzard did not waver.

"You're wasting your time, Connie," she told her.

There was silence between them, broken only by the quick sound of Connie's breathing.

"And what about my feelings?" she asked suddenly.

"They're your affair."

"And supposing I won't."

"Won't what?"

"Won't go."

Mrs. Vizzard drew herself up. As she was always a bolt upright ramrod of a woman, this only meant that she raised her chin a little higher. But it was enough. It gave her just that bit of extra confidence that was needed to ensure that the whole situation didn't get out of hand and become vulgar. A row with a lodger would have been unspeakably degrading.

"Don't be silly, Connie," she said. "You'll go if I tell you to go."

"I wouldn't be so sure, if I were you," Connie answered. "I'm not."

There was another silence. But not a complete one. Connie was humming now.

"If you don't go of your own free will," Mrs. Vizzard said in a low steady voice, "I'll have you put out."

"Meaning the police?"

"Meaning the . . ."

As she came to the word Mrs. Vizzard checked herself. It was something that she didn't like to hear from her own lips. That single word stood for everything that was sordid and unpleasant in life.

"Meaning exactly that," she corrected herself.

Connie stopped humming.

"They'll be needed," was all she said.

Somewhere in the back of one of the sideboard drawers was a little book, *The Law of Landlord and Tenant.* Why hadn't she re-read it in preparation for this kind of thing? Mrs. Vizzard asked herself. Memorised it even. She had studied it carefully enough when she bought it. It had been her first primer in self-supporting widowhood, in fact. But ever since then it had lain there, unread—and unneeded. There was one chapter entitled "Rights of the Landlord," that had been specially written to help with people who are being difficult.

"If assistance has to be sent for," she said at last, in the same steady voice, "that's only the end so far as the landlord is concerned. You'll have been in unlawful possession of premises, and you'll have to bear the consequences. And if you try to resist arrest. . . ."

"What about squatter's rights?" Connie demanded. "I've seen my solicitor and he says . . ."

Then Mrs. Vizzard did a bold thing. She took up her hat from the chair where she had laid it, and went over to the mirror.

"I am going to the police station now," she said.

Police station! The horrid word had slipped out despite herself.

"See you when you get back," said Connie.

"You'll see more than me," Mrs. Vizzard answered.

"It's the third floor back you can tell 'em," Connie advised Mrs. Vizzard. "The one with the door locked."

Mrs. Vizzard's hands shook visibly as she thrust back a strand of hair.

"And while you're down there, tell 'em to bring an axe with 'em. Because once this door's been locked, it stays locked."

"They'll know what to do, without me telling them," Mrs. Vizzard replied over her shoulder.

"You bet they will," Connie answered. "It's just what flatties love, smashing up other people's property. It won't be only the door that gets broken if I have anything to do with it. There's furniture in the room, too."

"Do you . . . do you want to get yourself *handcuffed*?" Mrs. Vizzard asked her, her voice rising a little as she said it.

Now she really had been low and outspoken. She had threatened.

Threatened, but not intimidated, Connie gave a little laugh.

"You've got it," she said. "Handcuffed and carried. If they can hold me. You can tell 'em from me I'm a struggler. I'll scream, too, if they don't put a gag on me. Tell 'em that as well from Auntie."

Mrs. Vizzard picked up her gloves and began slowly thrusting her fingers into them. Her movements were not so rapid now and she appeared to be thinking.

"It'll be a scene all right when it happens," Connie went on. "If I were you I should stop out for it. And if any of the others give you notice on account of the noise, you've only yourself to thank for it. There'll be a crowd outside before I'm finished with. When I start screaming people hear me. They'll remember the day little Connie said good-bye to No. 10."

Mrs. Vizzard was motionless. Her left glove—it was black shiny kid—was half on, and she made no movement to draw it on further. Then, abruptly she pulled it off again and turned to face Connie.

"If I let you stop, will you have learnt your lesson?" she asked.

"By heart," Connie answered, contritely.

"And there won't be any more of these goings on?"

"Not likely," said Connie. "If you were in my place, would you?"

"Very well," Mrs. Vizzard told her. "This time we'll agree to overlook it. But you've been warned, remember."

"Then I can stop?"

Mrs. Vizzard bowed her head.

"Bless your dear kind heart," Connie said complacently. "You've done your good deed all right for to-day." She turned and started for the door. "And may you never regret it more than I shall," she added.

"And what," Mrs. Vizzard asked, "about that seven-and-six?"

Outside Connie paused and drew a deep breath.

"Saved again in the eleventh hour," she told herself.

Then she remembered the seven-and-six, and she shook her head.

"Dear kind heart nothing. One pound of flesh, please, and I want it by lunch-time: that's more her mark."

Then she smiled. It wasn't really so serious even about the seven-and-six. After all, Mr. Josser had given her the full three weeks. And she supposed that she was really one of the lucky ones. Lucky to have a roof over her head and a bit on the side to see her through this little bit of trouble.

4

Mr. Josser had got himself another job. Tired of his retirement, he was now a rent collector. And, after four and a half months of doing nothing, it was like emerging from the gloom of the chrysalis into the full sunlight to realise that he was a free man no longer.

Because he'd only had the job for the last three-quarters of an hour he was excited as well as pleased. Pleased that he should have got the job at all when London was full of old clerks, all of whom wanted something part-time, something not too strenuous. And so excited that he wanted to tell someone. Admittedly, there had been wire-pulling and a word or two on the side to help him. The Under-Secretary for the Colonies had spoken to the First Sea Lord—in his civil capacity, of course—and that had fixed it. But, influence or not, the simple fact remained that he had been interviewed by strangers and found worthy. That was what had been bothering him. After all those years at Battlebury's Mr. Josser hadn't really known what the outside world would have to say about employing him.

He was still bubbling over with his new importance when he got back to Dulcimer Street. A pound a week the job was going to bring in. And, coming on top of the couple of pounds he was drawing as a pension, that made three pounds. It was as much as he had got married on. And there had been the children as well to bring up then. At the thought of the bright future, the roseate prospect of the ensuing years, Mr. Josser began whistling. He was still whistling when he got out his door-key and went inside.

Went inside, and stepped right into the middle of a crisis. It was Baby who was the centre of it. In perfect health and high spirits at breakfast, she had been sulky and fretful by lunch, and by tea-time spots had appeared. And Cynthia—silly little giggling Cynthia, who looked too young to be a mother, anyhow—had lost her head at the sight of them. She had rung Ted up at the Co-op., thereby interrupting its important retail affairs. And Ted, like the sensible fellow he was, had come straight round to his mother as soon as the stores had closed. He was sitting there now, morose and preoccupied.

The effect on Mrs. Josser, however, was magical. She responded to crisis as to a tonic. It braced and stimulated her. There was a passing flattery in the implicit acknowledgment of the fact that even a small child nearly three miles away in Balham couldn't come out in a rash without her having to be sent for.

And in her new role of indispensableness Mrs. Josser became dictatorial and overbearing. She told Ted point-blank that if there was serious illness in the house the best thing he could do was to keep out of the way for the time being. This was an affair for Cynthia and herself, she said. Illness, particularly the sudden illness of little children, it seemed, was something far too big for any man, with the exception of the doctor, to get mixed up with.

So she began by insisting that Ted should stop on at No. 10 for a meal while she went over to Larkspur Road herself. There was nothing, she explained, more upsetting for a woman when there was illness in the house than to have a man hanging about wanting a meal—or worse still getting it himself. In time of sickness the whole sex in Mrs. Josser's eyes became superfluous. And to prove its uselessness, she started to get a meal ready for her two waifs before leaving. She was away only about five minutes. But she returned, with her hat already on, carrying a loaded tray.

Having placed it before them, she refused to eat anything herself. She seemed, indeed, shocked at the suggestion that she, a woman, should even think of eating at a time like this. Instead, she shot straight off, carrying a shopping bag containing a thermometer in a little metal case, three Oxo cubes, a box of night-lights, a Seidlitz powder and a packet of cotton wool. There was always a tendency on Mrs. Josser's part to dramatise these occasions.

Ted was the first to speak after Mrs. Josser had gone.

"I dunno that Cynthia'll be very pleased to see Mum if she's expecting me," he said.

"I thought of that," Mr. Josser answered. Ever since he had got back he had felt like a man who sees an avalanche descending without having been able to warn the people down in the valley below.

"But it wouldn't have been any use trying to stop her," he added. "No use at all."

After that they ate in silence for some time. Then Ted spoke again.

"Spots aren't dangerous, are they?" he asked.

It hadn't occurred to him until that moment that they might be. But something of Mrs. Josser's reaction had now seeped through to him. He was a great pal of Baby's and he couldn't bear to think of anything happening to her while he was just sitting there eating.

But Mr. Josser reassured him.

"You both had 'em," he said. "And you got over 'em."

After that conversation died away again. Even when the cheese course was reached and Mr. Josser lifted the floral china lid of the dish, he just shook his head. Under the strain of emotion he had already been unusually eloquent and he was back to normal again now. He was thinking of the affairs of his department. They'd been two shillings and sevenpence short in the cash-desk when he'd come away and he was wondering if they'd find it.

Mr. Josser cleared his throat. It was the moment, the postponed moment, that he had been waiting for.

"I'm going back into harness," he said. "Start again next Monday. Three days a week."

Ted showed no astonishment. All that he revealed was a certain calm apprehension.

"What does Mum say?" he asked.

"She doesn't know yet," Mr. Josser admitted.

Ted paused.

"Is your chest strong enough?" he enquired.

"Oh yes. My chest's all right," he said. "The doctor says so."

As he spoke he raised his hand automatically and felt the pad of Thermogene that he always wore there.

There was another pause.

"What is the job?" Ted asked at last.

Mr. Josser told him.

When Ted didn't say anything, didn't even ask how much the job was worth, Mr. Josser felt rather hurt. But Ted was hurt, too. He supposed that it was because his parent was hard up that he had done this thing. And that made him more silent than ever. He thought for a long time before he said anything.

"Is this because Doris has gone?" he asked at last.

"Oh no," said Mr. Josser emphatically. "It's nothing to do with that. It's not because of Doris."

Ted thought again.

"Is she still allowing you anything?" he asked.

It was the first time he had ever actually asked in this way. Family finance is always a delicate matter. And ever since the conference that had been held when Battlebury's had decided to pension his father off, he hadn't referred to it again. It had been agreed then that he should give them ten shillings a week and that Doris should contribute a pound and live at home. On any showing she had probably been a dead loss from the start. But it had sounded fair enough at the time.

And Ted simply hadn't enquired about what allowance she was making now that she had left home. It hadn't seemed any of his business. But now, abruptly, he saw it in a new light. Just because she had chosen to set herself up in a fancy flat somewhere, his father —her father, too, for that matter—had got to go out to work again. It wasn't good enough, and he determined to talk to her about it.

But Mr. Josser was looking at him in surprise.

"Doris?" he asked. "She wants to give Mother five shillings a week. I won't let her." Mr. Josser paused. "It's not fair," he went on. "A girl paying out like that and getting nothing for it."

"Well, I'm going on," Ted said sullenly.

Mr. Josser played with his pipe, fondling the warm bowl in the palm of his hand.

"No, you're not, son," he said. "I've had it quite long enough. Time to stand on my own feet now."

"We'll see," Ted told him.

Mr. Josser rubbed his hands together.

"We haven't touched our capital. That's one comfort," he said.

Then they both sat there, Mr. Josser on one side of the fire not saying very much, and Ted on the other side, saying nothing at all.

At eight-thirty, when the clock struck its sombre Westminster chime, Ted got up and said that he'd have to be going. It had been an unsettling kind of evening.

It was not until nearly eleven that Mrs. Josser returned. She looked tired and put out about something.

"How were they?" he enquired.

"How was what?" Mrs. Josser asked irritably.

"The spots."

"Gone," Mrs. Josser told him. "Not a trace. It must have been something she'd eaten. Either that, or Cynthia imagined them."

In the circumstances, Mr. Josser decided that it would be better to wait till later to say anything about his new job.

BOOK TWO

THE CRIME ON THE COMMON

CHAPTER 16

I

WAS six-thirty in the evening now. Six-thirty on Sunday evening. ercy was getting ready. Up in his room with the door locked he as going over all the things he'd be needing. They were spread ut on the bed in front of him. There was his knuckleduster—the edgehog. And a pair of kid gloves that wouldn't leave finger-rints. And a screw-driver. And a pair of dark glasses that might come handy. And his cosh. Last of all there was his bunch of car keys.

"Only fools carry a gun," he said to console himself for not having ne.

When he was ready he put on an old raincoat and a scarf and got own his second-best trilby. It was a soft one with a snap brim that ould come right down over his face if necessary. He hadn't done uch all day except dress up. He'd been too jumpy. He'd started ff in his best purple with a nice brown tie and a pair of near patents. hen he told himself that there weren't very many of that type of iting about in London. And what was the use of making yourself eyeful when you wanted just to be one of the crowd? So he anged into his light check. That was better. A lot of gentlemen ore light checks, especially with summer coming in. But all the me it was conspicuous. Not actually an eyeful like the purple, ut still conspicuous. And that wasn't what he wanted. So he anged a second time. He was now wearing his old blue pin-ripe. That was all right. Half London wore old blue pin-ripes.

As he came out of his room, Mrs. Boon saw him.

"Oh, Percy," she said. "Not going out."

He sidled past her.

"Shan't be long, Mum," he muttered.

But to-night of all nights, when his hands were trembling so much already that he had to keep them behind his back, Mrs. Boon cho to be difficult.

"I never have you at home, Percy," she said. "You're alwa going somewhere."

"No, I'm not," he answered sullenly, not looking up into h face as he was speaking. "Just want to get some air."

"But what are you wearing those awful old clothes for? Yc look . . ."

"Because I gotta go into the garage on the way, that's why," told her. "Can't a chap take an interest in his job without . . ."

"Oh, all right," Mrs. Boon answered. "But I never know wi you, I don't really."

And as he went on down the stairs, he heard Mrs. Boon askir when he'd be back. But he was too far down to make any rep Better pretend he hadn't heard her.

Outside dusk was gathering. There was still some light, but t edges of everything had been blurred. Softened. At that mome Kennington wasn't in brick any longer: it was in crayon. Some the windows had lights in them, and the interiors looked cosy ar inviting. His own window was shining when he glanced back up it. But what caught his eye was a flock of pigeons wheeling rour in the sky above Dulcimer Street, catching the declining sun they turned. Each time their wings were lit up coral-coloured for moment and then turned grey again.

Percy extended his forefinger like a pistol and pointed it at ther "If I had a gun I could get one of them. Get the whole lot if had a gun."

But he wasn't serious. Only fooling. He'd just said that to ta his mind off his mother. What right had she got to question him He'd never done her any harm, had he? There he was, setting out do a job, a hot lift, and he'd been scolded by his mother. It mac him look silly.

It meant, too, that he couldn't keep his mind on his business. H had to keep on *reminding* himself where he was going. Even when got on to the No. 3 bus and booked right through to the Cryst Palace it seemed that this was just some ordinary jaunt that he w out on. He didn't feel any different from the other people on the bu

But he *was* different, Voice No. 1 reminded him. Very differen They hadn't got any ambition. They were just ordinary. They' stick where they were, while he climbed upwards. He wouldn't riding in buses much longer. He'd be going about in a car. Not just lifted car, either. His car.

When he got to the end of the journey, he looked about him for a bit. It was the sort of district that he liked. Nice class. With detached villas and neat gardens and little garages. He could just see himself setting up in one of those with Doris. Perhaps they'd join a tennis club. He'd never actually played tennis but he could learn, couldn't he? All the same he mustn't start dreaming now. He'd got work to do first.

The light was just right for him as he walked along to the Carlton. Not too dark for him to see what he was doing and dark enough for other people not to see him. It was a big new cinema, the Carlton, with a large car park beside it. From the look of the place there were a hundred different cars that he could choose from. He strolled along on the opposite side of the road and hung about as though waiting for someone. Nothing out of the way in that. Outside cinemas there are always chaps hanging about for their girls. And in any case, it was essential to the plan. He couldn't afford to pinch a car just when the owner might be coming back to get into it. He wanted a car that had only just been left there. One with the driving seat still warm. Something that would give him a clear three hours if it was a long picture before the alarm was raised. So he leant up against a wall and watched.

First of all a small Morris with dented wings came along, keeping very close to the opposite kerb as though avoiding him. It turned and made its way into the car park in the same furtive manner, like a cat squeezing into the pantry. Percy let his eyes rest on it for a moment and then looked away again. There'd probably be better later. And sure enough there was. A natty little Riley with its radiator all covered with the badges of Continental touring clubs drew up at the barrier. Percy ran his tongue across his lips: they were dry. Then he pulled himself together. The Riley was no use to him. It bristled. He wanted something a bit smoother.

And while he stood there, along it came. An almost new Austin 12.

"Like a lamb to the slaughter," he told himself. "Like a bleeding lamb to the slaughter."

He ran his tongue across his lips again. His heart was thumping now.

"It's yours," said Voice No. 1. "Don't do anything silly. Think first. And it's yours."

"Suppose they get you," Voice No. 2 came. "You'd be for it, you would."

But it was too late now to listen to No. 2. Percy came forward, still keeping in the shadows, to see whereabouts in the car park th Austin was going to be put. And it couldn't have been better. It owner went right down to the far end—the dark end—and backe carefully into a vacant space, coming out again once or twice so a to do the job properly.

"That's right," Percy thought. "Don't scratch it. Leave it al nice for me like Mother makes it."

He watched while two people, a man and a woman, got out o the car and went into the cinema arm-in-arm. Their heads were clos together and they were talking.

"Give you something real to talk about," he thought. "Just yo wait till you come out again."

The couple came out of the car park by the side entrance and wen up the broad marble steps into the cinema. Percy fell in a few pace behind them. They were evidently pretty well-to-do folk. The bought two-and-sixpenny seats. Percy bought the next one an followed them up the stairs. His feet sank into the deep moss-lik carpet.

The half-crowns were right at the back of the circle. Nice seats Percy would have liked to spend the rest of the evening in them. I looked a good film, too—girls dancing and hot trumpeters an rhythm. But the usherette was trying to put him right alongside th couple that he was shadowing. And that would never do. He'd go to go outside again, long before they did.

He stood back, and the usherette flashed her torch on to one o the seats in the row behind. This was perfect. Percy sat there, his ha in his lap. He could see just what he wanted to see. The head of th Austin owner showed up like a dark blob against the lower part o the screen.

"I'll let 'em get settled first," he decided. "Let 'em get properl settled, and then I'll leave 'em here to enjoy themselves."

It was hot in the cinema, and the palms of his hands were sticky He undid his raincoat and watched the whole of the next numbe right through. It wasn't until the illuminated clock over the exi showed eight-fifteen that he got up. As he went he turned and looked over his shoulder. Mr. and Mrs. Austin were snuggled dowr in their seats as if it were a sofa.

"Say good-bye to baby," Percy said under his breath. "And ring up the insurance in the morning. Do you good to have a nice walk."

Nobody seemed to notice that he was leaving the cinema almos as soon as he had sat down. Why should they? They were all far toc much interested in the crooner on the screen. And no wonder. He could see every detail of her face. It was about six feet across, and every inch of it was pretty. But Percy wasn't taking any notice of it. He was on the job. He was one against ten million. He was a free lance.

And he was being careful. He deliberately didn't put his hat on till he was outside. It would have been a mistake to let other people see him wearing it. He wanted to be two quite different people now. There was the quiet young man without a hat who had taken himself to the picture and then slipped out again because it was boring. And there was the young dare-devil with a snap brim trilby low over his eyes who drove stolen cars across the plains south of London. And because he was clever Percy didn't even leave by the same door. He went down to the exit right in the front of the house. It was the exit leading straight into the car park.

During the last fifteen minutes something had happened outside. It was a good deal more than dark now, it was slightly foggy. A thin yellow haze had been smeared over everything. And it just suited him. There were no lights in the car park and a street lamp opposite merely picked out the shadows of the cars. Shadows, that was it. His little bit of business was best done in the shadows.

Beside the exit of the cinema there was a large notice printed in black letters on a white ground. It announced that cars in the car parks were left entirely at the owners' risk. Percy grinned when he saw it.

"That's O.K. by me," he thought. "And what I'm doing is O.K. by them. So why worry?"

But his body wasn't as brave as he was. It was trembling again. And he was cold suddenly. So cold that he buttoned his coat right up to the neck to protect himself. As he did so something thumped up against his hip. It was the Hedgehog.

"Now or never, Percy," Voice No. 1 said to him. "This is your big chance, chum."

The lock in the car door gave him a bit more trouble than he had expected. None of the keys he'd got were any good for it. And the windows were shut fast to keep the flies out. But that didn't stop him. If you couldn't open a car any other way you just took the handle clean off and the lock came away with it. It was easy. He'd got the screw-driver with him and he began using it. All the same this was the part where he'd have to go carefully. It was one thing to go up to a car and unlock it. It was something quite different to be seen tinkering.

He'd got all the screws loose and was just getting ready to do what he'd come for when the exit door of the cinema opened again and a couple emerged into the car park. They came straight towards him. For a moment Percy thought that they were Mr. and Mrs. Austin. His mouth went dry.

"Careful," Voice No. 1 warned him. "Take it easy. Act natural."

That was the important thing: to act natural. He thrust his hands into his pockets and began to saunter off. But it wasn't anything. No need to get jumpy. The couple got into a battered little Ford and shot away from the Carlton as though they were inside a rocket. All that they left behind them was the smell of oil. Percy went back to his work, though he was still trembling.

It was easier now. With a bit of a tug the lock came away with the handle and there was nothing between him and what he wanted except a door that hung open on its hinges. Even so he hesitated a moment before he actually climbed in! He was more nervous than he had expected and his mouth kept going dry.

"It's you I'm doing it for, Doris darling," he told himself. "It's going to be our nest-egg. It's you I'm doing it for."

Once inside it was child's play. He knew all about starters. And this wouldn't be the first time he'd started a car when he'd left the key behind him. Everything was in nice condition, too. The batteries were full and the engine started almost as soon as he touched it. It was only the door that was a trouble. It was still standing open as if inviting the whole world to get in after him. But it wasn't the first missing lock either that he'd known. He made a wad of newspapers that Mr. Austin had left behind him in the car, and jammed the door with it. Now he was ready.

Getting past the man at the gate was the first difficulty, but it wasn't a serious one. With his hat pulled down over his eyes, Percy lowered the window a little and held out threepence. And threepence wasn't a guess either. He'd studied how much to give in car parks. More than that might have raised an eyebrow and less might have led to a few sarcastic remarks. Threepence was just right. The attendant took it and even went out into the road to see that there was no traffic coming. Percy gave a little salute with his free hand by way of acknowledgment, and the journey home had begun.

Simple, wasn't it?

2

Now that he had actually done it, now that he was riding high he didn't feel nervous any longer. He drove carefully, of course—it was practically a new car: scarcely run in, he should reckon—and he didn't want to spoil it. But he felt quite at home in it. It might have been his for years and not just for the last five minutes. And because he was driving slowly it gave him plenty of time for thought. He drove along contemplating the future.

"And this won't be the only one," he told himself. "There'll be others too. Posh ones, some of them, as soon as I get things re-organised. Bentleys and Lagondas. And I'll get someone else to do the dirty work on them. Keep my hands clean as soon as I get a chance."

He was rummaging about in the front pocket of the car and found the remains of a packet of cigarettes that the previous owner had left there. And Percy lit one with the lighter his mother had given him.

"And I shan't go on lifting cars once I'm married. Not when I've got Doris," he continued. "I shall be on the level then. I'll run my own garage. I'll do high-class hire work on the side. And have a second-hand department. I'll be a Morris agent. I'll sell car insurance. I'll have a hydraulic jack and hot air for drying. I'll do repairs and re-boring. I'll charge 'em plenty. I shan't go on lifting cars after I'm married. Not when I've got Doris."

He was in a stream of traffic by now. He couldn't drive fast even if he wanted to. But it didn't matter. Twenty-five miles an hour was good enough for him. And in any case this was where he turned off. This was where the road led towards Wimbledon. Wimbledon was important—he'd got it all argued out. Supposing some chap was lifting some car from anywhere to take it to some place, would you expect him to start off almost in the opposite direction? Of course you wouldn't, not unless you were screwy. And suppose some cop saw you driving it in the opposite direction and remembered you, and suppose things got hot afterwards and they started asking you questions, you could prove it wasn't you because you weren't going your way. See?

But Percy's mind wasn't on coppers for the moment. It was on pleasanter things.

"Or I might get clean out of the garage line altogether," he promised himself. "Build sports cars. Boon specials. And race 'em.

Have my own team. Pick up some of the big prizes and put Boon specials on the market. I might get clean out of the garage line."

Then a more tender and sentimental mood came over him.

"My little darling," he thought. "You're my Destiny. You're the girl of my dreams. You'll look all right in furs. You'll walk beside me. You'll have a dressing-table with a glass top. You'll dwell in my secret heart. You'll use scent I choose for you. You're my Destiny, my little darling."

He could almost feel her sitting there in the seat next to him. He'd only to lift his hand off the gear lever for it to come to rest on her knee. The silk stocking would give a little squeaky thrill as he drove.

"Oh, Cripes," he thought suddenly. "Let her like me a bit. I'm not good enough for her, but let her like me."

He was getting into Wimbledon by now, and so far there hadn't been a single hitch. Everything had worked out exactly according to plan. In consequence, he was feeling better.

"Cool as ice, that's me," he told himself. "Trust Percy."

Just in front of him stood the Duke of Marlborough. It was at a cross-roads and from the way it dominated the place it might have been the civic centre of those parts. It was flood-lit to show up the modern Tudor beams. And in the flagged courtyard there were cars, parked in a double row. A space in the front one gave him an idea. It wasn't nine yet, and the film, the big film, wouldn't be over till ten-thirty. He'd got all the time he could want. So, waving on the rest of the traffic, he turned into the courtyard. He was just in time to capture the empty parking place from a thirsty little Hillman that came sneaking up.

Inside, the Duke of Marlborough was pretty high-class. Percy liked the lounge. It was a large impressive sort of room with light oak panelling and lots of little separate tables with green leather chairs. The decorations were high-class, too. There were long velvet curtains that might have come off a stage and some nice pieces of china on a shelf running round the walls. The whole place had just been rebuilt, which was why everything was so new and fresh-looking, even the old parts. The antique copper jugs that hung in a row over the bar were brand new, every one of them. And even the stag's head that was mounted over the door was bright and glossy as though it had been shot specially for the opening.

The lounge was full to-night because it was Sunday. And it was hot. Almost as hot as in the cinema. And noisy. Between sixty and seventy people were crushed in there, all talking at the tops of their voices. Above the noise they made was the constant chink of glasses, the rattle of the cash-register madly recording the shillings and pennies, and the tinkle of a small bell, like a fire alarm in a doll's house, as someone scored a lucky shot in one of the pin-tables. Business was certainly brisk and change was being passed over the counter in wet handfuls.

It was some time before Percy could get served. And in the interval of waiting he changed his mind several times. Originally he had just meant to order a bitter. Then he thought of a Guinness. Then a whisky-and-soda. Finally, the man in front of him ordered a large pink gin. And Percy asked for the same.

It might have been far better if he'd stuck to a bitter. But of course he wasn't to know that at the time. And because the pink gin seemed just what he needed—"I've earned it, haven't I?" he asked himself. "I'm only human, aren't I?"—he made his way to the bar a second time and ordered himself another one. It was about nine-fifteen by now and after he'd finished it he decided that he might as well be going. No hurry. You understand. Just getting the job over and done with.

He couldn't get out immediately, however. The party at the table behind him was just breaking up and the man with the crushed-in sports hat and the roll-top pullover was just leaving.

"Ta-ta," he said to the girl at the table. "You'll be hearing from me."

"Ta-ta," the girl answered.

Percy found himself looking at the girl. And then suddenly he realised who it was he was looking at. It was the Blonde. At the same moment the Blonde looked up and saw him.

"Hallo, Percy," she said, smiling at him under her eyelashes. "Fancy meeting you."

He paused.

The Blonde stroked the empty chair beside her.

"Come and sit down," she said.

He took a step, but no more, in her direction.

"Just going," he told her.

"What's the hurry?"

"Nothing," he replied grudgingly.

That was just the point: he couldn't *admit* that he was in a hurry.

"Well, come on then."

He came over, and sat down on the extreme edge of the green leather cushion. It was obvious that he didn't mean to stop long.

"You are matey," she said.

Over by the door, the man in the crushed-in sports hat turned and waved. Percy just caught a glimpse of him and then he was gone. He envied him being able to walk out like that.

"Aren't you drinking anything?" the Blonde went on.

"Finished," Percy told her. "I was just going when I saw you."

"Well, have another one with me," she invited him. "A short one. Then I'll be coming along, too."

He thought rapidly, going over all the possibilities in his mind. He needed time to figure things out. It was no use simply standing there.

"O.K.," he said feebly. "What's yours?"

"Same as before," she answered. "Gin and orange."

When he got back, the Blonde moved her chair closer to his. She let her hand droop down so that he could hold it.

"Going straight back?" she asked him.

"No," he said. "I've got to go to . . . to Victoria."

The Blonde pouted.

"I thought perhaps you might have dropped in to see me if you felt that way," she told him. "But it doesn't matter."

Percy felt his heart begin to thump as she said it. He forgot all about Doris for the moment. But he was careful. He wasn't going to let himself go all to pieces just because he'd been invited.

"No good to-night," he said. "I'm delivering a car for someone."

The Blonde pouted again and clearly didn't believe him.

Percy was angry. Now that he'd got over the invitation he wanted to be going.

"It's outside in the car park."

But the Blonde wasn't giving anything away.

"Well, you drop me on the way," she said. "I didn't mean anything. Just thought you might like to."

This was worse. She looked more of a blonde than ever to-night. She'd had her hair done, and her head was covered in a thick fancy work of little yellow curls. If a policeman saw her in a tram-car he'd guess she'd stolen it.

"Not supposed to in customers' cars," he blurted out.

Then the Blonde got up-stage.

"Oh, of course if you don't want to, it's different. Sorry I spoke. If you don't want to be seen with me . . ."

This wasn't any better, either. The last thing he wanted was to have her think that he was keeping anything from her. So he grinned politely.

"I'll risk it," he told her. "Only get hanged once."

"That's more like you," she said.

She was smiling again now.

As soon as he got outside he realised that the worst had happened. Those three gins had been just one gin too many. He was muzzy. Not badly muzzy. Not swaying or indistinct or anything like that. But definitely not at his best.

"I've got to go carefully," he told himself. "I've got to mind my step. I've got to go carefully."

And a silly thought came to him.

"Suppose when I get back to it the Austin isn't there? Suppose somebody's pinched it? Suppose it isn't there?"

But it was there all right. Over two hundred pounds' worth of it.

The Blonde made her way round to the far door, but Percy stopped her.

"That door's jammed," he said. "You slide over."

When the Blonde had settled herself in, Percy slammed his door after her. Then he began fiddling about under the dashboard because he'd disconnected the starter.

"Want a hair-pin?" the Blonde asked.

Percy shook his head.

"It's O.K.," he said. "There's a repair job in this."

Because he was afraid that he was muzzier than he really was, he was clumsy. He made a mess of getting out of the courtyard. His rear bumper got under somebody else's mudguard. It made a noise like a tin bath tearing.

The Blonde gave a little titter.

"That's another repair job," she said.

But nobody paid much attention, and Percy didn't trouble to get out and investigate. He didn't want to get drawn into a long argument because he hadn't got time. It was just too bad for someone.

When he got the nose of the car out into the main road he looked carefully both ways before edging into the traffic. The little incident of the mudguard had rather unnerved him.

The Blonde noticed this.

"Why don't you have 'L' on the front?" she asked him.

"Not my car," Percy told her. "That's why I'm being careful with it."

"Do you mean you've pinched it?" she enquired.

She was lighting a cigarette as she was speaking and when it was lit she passed it over to Percy. He took it from her without saying anything and, as he raised it to his lips, he noticed the broad band of lipstick round the butt. Because he was thinking of Doris at that moment, the sight of the wet red cigarette that the Blonde had handed over disgusted him and he wanted to throw it away.

The fog had thickened by now. It was damp and clinging. He started up the windscreen wipers.

"If I hit anybody I'm finished," he kept saying to himself. "One tap and I'm out. A ruddy dog'd be enough. If I hit anybody I'm finished."

"You talking to me?" the Blonde asked, and Percy realised that he'd been saying those things out loud.

He shook his head and drove on more carefully than ever. If he was saying things out loud it showed that he must really be muzzy and not just imagining it.

They had reached the outskirts of the Common by now and the silver birches showed up in the headlamps of the car.

"This is where I can let her out," he told himself. "This is where I begin to drive."

The needle of the speedometer started to swing round. Thirty-five. This was more like it. Forty. Forty-five. It didn't matter to him if the car hadn't been run in yet. He wasn't going to keep it, was he? Besides this was the authentic thrill of motoring. Nearly fifty. Real open road stuff. Over fifty wouldn't be safe with this fog about.

"Look where you're going," the Blonde advised him. "You've got me in the car, remember."

Percy started. She'd been quite right to warn him. He'd simply been driving with his eyes fixed on the speedometer: he hadn't been looking at the road at all. So he stiffened up in his seat and stared grimly out through the windscreen.

Then he saw what the Blonde had really warned him about.

Right in front of him, only fifty yards or so, stood a policeman. And he was flashing his torch at him. Dot, dot, dot, the little beam of light went. Percy felt his jaw drop. Then it tightened again. So They'd got on to him, had They? Somebody had put the word round. They were after him. Well, They weren't going to get him. Not without a chase. If They wanted him They'd got to come for him. He pressed his foot down on the accelerator and drove straight on.

"You gone crackers?" the Blonde asked. "He's trying to stop you. There's been an accident or something."

An accident! He didn't properly hear the words until he was right on top of it. And by then there had very nearly been another one. All he saw was a man lying stretched out flat on the side of the road with his collar open and the two ends sticking up, and his hat all smashed in, lying beside him. That—and the policeman jumping to one side as Percy and the Blonde shot past him.

He felt sick when he realised that he'd nearly killed the policeman. Suppose he had? But it was bad enough the way things were, wasn't it? The cop would be bound to report what had happened. He might even get a patrol out. Then Percy'd be in the gravy all right. He'd have something to think about.

As it was, the Blonde was behaving queerly. Under that hard exterior she'd got no nerves at all. She was screaming at him to stop.

"Let me out," she was saying. "I don't like it. Let me out."

"You shut your trap," he told her. "You get out when I say so."

He was still driving fast and the fog or mist, or whatever it was, was thicker. He turned his headlamps off. The fog was hitting back at him and he didn't want to go about with a bleeding halo round him. They would be after him now for sure.

"Let me out."

The Blonde was clawing at him by now, and the time for politeness was over.

"If you don't shut up, I'll make you."

"You try!"

She caught hold of his collar and pulled. She'd got her fingers down inside his neck. She was throttling him. Just as the stud broke and the collar went loose again, he got his hand free and shoved it in her face. The car gave a nasty swerve as he did so. But it taught the Blonde a lesson.

She started whimpering. Then, suddenly, in front of her in the dashboard pocket with the cigarettes, she saw a spanner. It was a large one with a head like a battle-axe. She grabbed at it and held it over him.

"Now will you let me get out?"

It was the sort of moment Percy had often read about—when everything depended on keeping calm.

"All right," he said. "Do it. Then we'll both be killed."

He accelerated again as he said it. He knew she'd never dare. But at the last moment just as she hit him he knew that she was going to. His left hand helped to soften the blow. Even so, the spanner went right down into his hat. It hurt, and because it hurt he forgot No. 1 had always told him about keeping cool. Driving with one hand, he wrenched the spanner from her, and hit back. She was trying to stop him, wasn't she?

And he got her all right. He felt the jar run right up his arm as the sharp end of the spanner caught her. She simply folded up away from him. And that was the end of her. She fell back against the door and the little wad of paper came out. The door swung open and a moment later Percy was in the car alone.

This time he didn't care who was following. He just jammed the brakes on and brought the car up rocking. There were nearly twenty feet of skid marks in the road behind him. And almost lost in the mist the Blonde was lying all doubled up just as she'd fallen. He started to run back. When he got to her—it surprised him to find what a long way it was—he saw that she must have rolled over and over when she hit the road. Everything on her was torn.

What was worse was the way she was lying. Her head was twisted right back. And she was looking up at him.

Looking up at him with a dirty lifeless face down which a thick dark caterpillar of blood was crawling.

"I'm getting out of this," Percy told himself. "I don't like it. I'm getting out."

3

That's what it was like on the spot. But come up a bit higher, get an angel's view as it were. What's it like now? Well, travelling across the South, the red foothills of Surbiton give place to the grey brick forests of Wimbledon. And then, like the primitive jungle itself criss-crossed with tracks, the Common—Wimbledon Common—comes right up against habitation. There are no outposts. It is simply there. You can't see much of it because of the mist. It is only in patches that the ground is showing. And in one of these patches where the road is gleaming, a crowd is gathered. It is quite a big crowd with two policemen and a tall white ambulance. The ambulance is for the Blonde. But she doesn't know it. They've put a blanket over her.

Then the crowd divides because there is something coming. It is a police car. The police car stops and three men in raincoats get out. The fourth continues to sit there in the back with his ear-phones on. The others say something to him and begin to move off across the bracken to where an abandoned car is standing with its side lights still on.

Silly, wasn't it, of Percy, to leave the lights on? But he couldn't really be blamed. He'd lost his nerve by then, and wasn't responsible.

Further over among the bushes a policeman who has found Percy's snap brim trilby is blowing his whistle. Coming out of the darkness the policeman's whistle sounds like some melancholy nightbird.

Is there anything else of interest to report? No, everything else is lonely and peaceful. It might have been primeval England, that bit of Common. Until you come right up to the north-west corner of the Common, almost into Putney. Then there's something. It's the figure of a man. He is running, darting from tree to tree, seeking cover all the way. He's milky pale and down his face the sweat is coursing. He hasn't noticed that there's blood on his collar. But there is: the Blonde splashed over him when he hit her.

And while he runs he keeps muttering something to himself. It's indistinct because he's out of breath. But it sounds like this:

"Oh, Mum, I didn't mean to. I never meant to hurt her. I didn't mean to, Mum."

Percy is in real trouble now.

CHAPTER 17

I

It was just a week later. Sunday had come round again. And Sunday is always a good time for finding people at home.

Over at the studio flat in Adelaide Road Doreen was sitting up in bed reading the paper and drinking a cup of tea that Doris had made for her. It was a bright sparkling kind of morning. There had been rain in the night. But now the sun was shining and all the surrounding roof-tops—there was a good view of these—looked as clean and fresh as though they had been scrubbed as well as drenched. Doris was sitting on the end of Doreen's bed, drinking a cup of tea herself and smoking a cigarette. There was something pleasantly idle and luxurious about it all. Because it was Sunday it wouldn't matter if they just messed about in dressing-gowns for half the morning and then had a sort of combined meal later, half breakfast and half lunch. It was, in fact, exactly for such a morning as this that she and Doreen had set up house together.

Because Doreen had been the one to grab the paper, she was the first to see the headlines about the dead girl on Wimbledon Common. She adored all crime. And she started to read automatically. But there weren't many details to go on. It was too early for that. The headlines, in fact, were the best part. TROUSERED BLONDE DEAD BY STOLEN CAR, they ran; and below them in smaller type, MOTOR BANDIT'S DEATH RIDE. The news of this affair was really very scanty. All that it said was that a blonde, with coloured toe-nails and extensive head injuries, had been found dead close beside an abandoned car belonging to a Crystal Palace accountant. The car, which had been stolen less than two hours before the occurrence of the crime, had since been identified by P. C. Grubb (inset) as the vehicle which had been driven head-on at him when he signalled it to stop. The police had removed the stolen car on a lorry so that they could examine it for fingerprints.

Fingerprints! Doreen curled up her toes as she read. The word always gave her a delicious little shudder. She was very comfortable and this was really the ideal way to enjoy a crime. It had always seemed a funny thing to her, the way there were two kinds of people in the world—those who went about murdering and getting murdered, and those who just read about it. She had, however, read so much about crime that she was sure, absolutely sure, that she knew *exactly* how murderers must feel after they'd killed someone. Sooner or later, if she could find someone to go with, she meant to get into the Old Bailey sometime and sit right through a murder trial. She had never actually seen a murderer.

She looked up for a moment.

"Doris, my lamb," she said. "Do be an angel and give me another cigarette. I wasn't going to, but yours smells so divine I simply must."

2

Back in Dulcimer Street, Sunday morning was proceeding very much as usual. Starting from the top flat, Mr. Puddy was doing quite nicely, in a quiet bachelor way. He had just finished a piece of best end haddock and was going on to the bread and butter and marmalade. The only thing that rankled was that there hadn't been enough haddock, or at least not so much as he had expected. He'd chosen the bit of fish himself—chosen it carefully—and they couldn't have given him the bit he'd picked. His bit had been nearly twice the size.

There was only one other thing that was wrong. Because the haddock had been rather on the salt side—tasty, but decidedly salt—it meant that Mr. Puddy kept on wanting cups of tea. He had to go over to the gas ring twice for more hot water. And all that jumping up and down wasn't doing him any good. He couldn't digest properly when moving.

Mr. Puddy read about the girl on Wimbledon Common, too. He sucked at his teeth as he read it, and wondered if P.C. Grubb was any relation of a man who had once been with him in the milk round business. But he didn't linger over the case. There was nothing particularly interesting about it so far as he could see. Nothing that made it stand out. Now, if the policeman had been fired at, for instance. . . . Or if the dead girl had been *inside* the car, and if the bandit had set fire to the car.

As it was, Mr. Puddy's thoughts reverted to the fishmonger and what he was going to say to him.

Down below, Connie was already up and about. She wasn't looking her best at this moment. She hadn't dressed yet. Or washed. Or done her hair. With last night's make-up still on she had the look of a battered, rather dissipated doll.

She was clad only in her dressing-gown and her swansdown bedroom slippers. But she was busy all right. She was doing a letter, she was. A very important letter. And it wasn't easy. The sixpenny pad from Woolworth's—the Goldonia—was half used up already and nothing to show for it. This was to be her last attempt. And, if it didn't come out right this time, she'd decided to chuck the whole thing and try again later. But everything was now ready for the last attempt. She'd cleaned the nib and drawn half a dozen faint lines in pencil to keep the writing straight.

The letter was addressed to the Secretary of the Actors' and Actresses' Benevolent Fund. "*Dear Sir or Madam,*" it began, "*Like so many members of our Profession I have fallen upon evil times, owing to me having been in the club business prior to our licence going. I have lost most of my old stage connections and I am too short for the films. I am now entirely without funds and the rent keeps coming round as usual. Anything that your Society could do in the way of a small pension or loan, or put me in touch with someone with a view to an engagement either backstage or cloaks, would be gratefully appreciated by Yours truly, Connie Coke. P.S. The play's the thing.*"

She sat back and read the letter over. Nothing had gone wrong this time, and what she had written was about as good as she could hope to get it. There was an envelope already addressed and Connie folded the letter, kissed it and popped it inside.

Then she got up and poured into her hand a little heap of crumbs from a paper bag that had contained biscuits.

"It's in the laps of the Gods, little Dukey boy," she said.

And taking a mouthful of the broken biscuits, she pressed her face up against the cage so that Duke could peck the crumbs one by one out of her pursed-up lips.

In the Boons' front room everything was still very quiet. Mrs. Boon had been up early as usual and had gone round to St. Joseph's for eight o'clock Mass. It was silent and detached and peaceful, and, at the same time, snug inside St. Joseph's. Those thirty-five minutes on Sundays were like a rest cure. They did her real good. It was funny the way just going round the corner for half an hour before most people were up could make you feel calm and contented all the rest of the week. And it was a pity that Percy was too tired to come with her nowadays. But he was all in by Sundays.

She was back now and had taken Percy's morning cuppa into him. That had been nearly an hour ago. And there was still no sign of him. It seemed to Mrs. Boon that the garage worked Percy too hard. And those odd jobs they gave him, like last Sunday night. He had been worn out by the time he got home. She was quite worried about him.

She didn't want to start breakfast without him because that would destroy all the cosy feeling of Sunday morning. Besides, Percy didn't like it either, that way. That was because they were such chums, her and Percy. He wasn't like a son the way he went on. He was more like a husband really. And always thinking of her in his own way, too. There was that lovely blue rug he'd given her. It made her feet tingle just to touch it in the mornings.

And only on Thursday he'd talked about a holiday for her that summer. "Somewhere good, like Clacton," he'd said. "Book up at a boarding-house. Have someone to wait on you for a bit." And he'd said that he would try to get hold of a car to run her down. It was just too lovely to think about. So lovely, that perhaps it was wicked. In any case, she was sure it wouldn't come true. Percy would be too busy, or he would forget, or something. All the same, she kept on thinking. She couldn't help it. It was wonderful to think of four square meals a day appearing punctually on the table without having to cook any of them.

She glanced at the clock. It was after ten now. Percy was even later than usual. She put out her hand and felt the teapot. Cold. Very nearly stone cold. But that was her fault. She'd heard a sound earlier that she'd thought was Percy dressing, and she'd made the tea without calling through to ask if he was ready. Of course, as soon as Percy showed up she'd have to make a fresh pot—he couldn't be expected to drink stuff like that. And he'd probably want some fresh bacon as well. It would have to be a new breakfast, in fact.

While she was sitting there, she poured herself out a cup of the dark tepid brew that had been quietly stewing itself, and drank it quickly, furtively. She didn't want Percy to catch her at it. It would have looked so greedy, not waiting.

. . . At Clacton, too, there would be pleasure cruises and chara-banc trips. Round the lighthouse and mystery tours of East Anglia with twenty or thirty other happy, carefree mothers. Perhaps she could persuade Percy to come with her on one of them. Only Percy hadn't said anything about going to Clacton himself. Only about sending her there.

One floor below, Mr. Josser was getting ready for his new job. He had just taken his fountain pen to pieces. For some reason or other the ink wouldn't flow properly. And he'd removed the nib. Now he was engaged in taking everything else out as well. It was a messy job. Messier than it need have been perhaps. Apparently there was still some ink left in the barrel. Because, just as he was removing the sac, a great gobbet of ink, like a wet black egg, came squirting out through the hole where the nib had been. A little of it went on his sleeve, but most of it spattered on to the newspaper that Mrs. Josser had made him spread out before he started. Mrs. Josser was a woman who was deeply convinced of the precautionary merits of newspaper.

He was due to start to-morrow, and had spent all yesterday as well putting things in order. On the table in front of him were the list of addresses, and a little pad of blotting-paper and the spare rent books in case new ones were needed. He'd put in a lot of time, too, on the confidential notes that the firm had given him. Pretty nearly memorised them, in fact . . . No. 22 Reginald Buildings: *slow payers, accept no promises* . . . No. 17 Guinevere Street: *out till seven, all day Saturday* . . . No. 143 Arkley Rents: *Charge 2/6 for new rent book if old one still missing* . . . No. 1 Cranmer Terrace: *Knock loudly, very deaf*. . . . It seemed that once you became a tenant of his employers they knew as much about you as though they were members of your own family.

Then, as Mr. Josser was absent-mindedly jigging the little filling lever of the pen backwards and forwards to see how it worked it came clean off in his hands. Apparently he'd shifted the little catch inside that was meant to hold it. This was a pity, a great pity. Because, of course, it meant that the pen was no use any longer. And he needed a fountain pen more than ever now. He couldn't go walking up to people's front doors with a penholder in one hand and a bottle of ink in the other.

He was still trying to get the little lever back into place again when Mrs. Josser came in. She was as neat and brisk and businesslike as usual. In her hand was a large china mug.

"Stop playing about with that pen," she told him. "Here's your shaving water."

"It's broken," said Mr. Josser, looking up suddenly.

Mrs. Josser came over and inspected the inky mess in front of him.

"I told you not to," she said. "Fountain pens aren't meant to be taken to pieces."

"It isn't the bit I took out that's broken."

"Well, you'll have to dip it, that's all," Mrs. Josser replied. "And don't let the water get cold."

"I've had that pen a long time," Mr. Josser said slowly.

In the front basement, Mrs. Vizzard had already done all that she had to do. The breakfast things were washed up and put away, and the table had been polished. Altogether, it was as neat and tidy as any room you could find in South London. Mrs. Vizzard herself was taking things easily for a moment. She was sitting bolt upright in the tall armchair, reading a magazine.

It was her favourite reading that she was absorbed in. Luckily, *The Spirit World*, a sixpenny, came out punctually on Saturdays, ready for its Sunday morning treat. And it was certainly full value. Every issue spoke straight to hearts that were broken or in disrepair. There were messages from the dead, dozens of them, and through the closely printed pages, subscribers could keep in touch with other people's sweethearts, children, parents, even pets—all recently passed over. As well as these there were communications from ancient priests, medieval Doges, Emirs from Afghanistan and deceased clergy of all sects.

This week's issue contained one special attraction. It was a long spirit letter, astonishingly mature in manner from one so young, from an unborn child. The recipient, a mother of three other children, chose to remain anonymous, but was vouched for by a vicar, a faith-healer and a Captain, R.N. (Retired). Mrs. Vizzard had saved this to the last. It was too good to be squandered lightly by rapid reading. The mere address from which it was written, "Inside Limbo," was enough to send shivers of anticipation running through her.

"*I know my name now, dear mother,*" the missive began, "*the name that you would have given me. It's Daphne. I repeat it to myself sometimes because it helps me to remember you. But in the spirit world we have our own names—names that cannot be expressed in words. Beautiful, luminous names. . . .*"

But, for some reason, Mrs. Vizzard wasn't thinking of the spirit world any longer. She was thinking of Mr. Squales. It wasn't as though he were a failure, an actual failure, she told herself. He just hadn't succeeded, that was all. But there was still time. He hadn't reached his prime yet. Not a man's prime, that is. He couldn't be more than forty-two or forty-three at the most. And that was where a man was so lucky: in his forties, he has another fifteen or twenty years in front of him before people even begin to think of him as getting elderly. Whereas a woman . . .

Mrs. Vizzard got up and stood in front of the mirror overmantel. She studied herself, slowly and critically. But so far from being depressed, she was actually reassured. There was nothing actually *wrong* with her face that she could see; nothing that she couldn't alter if she wanted to. Lifting her hands, she loosened the dark metallic hair a little at the temples so that the hard lines of the forehead—it was a bleak uncompromising forehead—were concealed. Then abruptly she turned away from the mirror in disgust.

"Don't be a fool, Louise," she said bitterly. "You ought to have more pride."

At the same moment, Mr. Squales was lying on his back in bed in the next room staring up at the ceiling.

Because he hadn't shaved, the sides of his face and chin were dark and bluish-looking. But that was only natural. Even when shaved, Mr. Squales's complexion was still distinctly olive. Almost Levantine, in fact. And in the early morning it was more Mediterranean than ever. He was smoking, of course, because he always did smoke either in bed or out of it. And, because the stub was just burning his lips, a supple, dusky hand emerged from the bed-clothes and crushed out the cigarette-end in the saucer on the chair beside the bed. Then the hand began groping for the packet.

But the packet, when the hand found it, was empty. There wasn't even a half-smoked one stuffed away there. So there was nothing that Mr. Squales could do but draw the hand back under the bed-clothes again and go on lying there, gazing at the grey discoloured ceiling and thinking.

"It'd be a solution," he told himself. "One way out of this mess. At least it'd be security."

But his spirit, the unquenchable part of him, rebelled against it.

"I must have sunk pretty low. I must have come down further

than I realised," he went on. "If I hadn't, I wouldn't even be considering it. Probably I'm not well—I haven't felt well lately. If I was myself, I'd turn it down without a thought." He paused. "And how do I know I can't do better?" he continued. "Much better. After all, there's something about me. Something the others haven't got. I know. I can tell from the way women look at me. I've seen a light in their eyes that shouldn't be there."

The line his thoughts were taking helped to brace him.

"*If* I did it," he continued, "I should be throwing myself away. I should just be squandering myself." He squared his shoulders on the pillow. "No, it's not good enough. I may come to it. Or something like it. But not yet. Definitely not yet."

His courage was returning to him in great waves. He laced his hands behind his head and sat up in bed a little. For a moment he was resolute, confident, resourceful; almost young again. But it was a mistake all the same sitting up in this way. For his eyes fell upon his clothes spread out over the armchair by the fireplace. And there was nothing in the least reassuring about his clothes. The frayed turn-ups, the tattered lining of the jacket, the shirt with its tail cut off to make new cuffs, the blue socks darned with black, the shoes that had collapsed sideways over the worn-down heels—they weren't the clothes of a success in life.

"Even my fur coat is going back on me," he told himself. "The collar comes out in tufts if you forget and pull at it."

His courage was leaving him again now, ebbing away as though some mysterious tide had turned inside him. He felt weaker. Curiously weaker. And the taste of that last cigarette returned to his mouth, making him long for another one. It was possible—just possible—that there might be one in his coat pocket. But he felt too feeble, too feeble and depressed, even to get up and see. He just lay there limp and inert as though he were sleeping. Even his eyes were closed now.

He wasn't asleep, however. He was simply exhausted. His mind hadn't stopped working. The front part of it, the part that ached for a cigarette, had given up. But from the back there came the gleam of distant flashes. Strange, disconnected glimpses of things that might have been part of a pattern of which the whole was withheld from him. And not pictures only. Voices, too. Unfamiliar, discordant voices. Voices that poured out confidences. Voices that left him aghast and frightened. There was one of them speaking now. It was a girl's voice.

"I suppose I'd got it coming to me," it was saying. "I took risks.

I had to. I was one of the lonely ones. I don't blame anyone. Not even him. We both of us lost our heads. That's all it was. And it was nice while it lasted. I'd have done anything for him. He knew it. I'd have kept myself for him, if he'd wanted me. I only filled in with other chaps when he wasn't there. I did really." The voice became choked with crying, and Mr. Squales missed a few words. He had lost the thread of what it was saying, and could understand less than ever, when it resumed. "But he didn't ought to have done what he did. He didn't ought to have hit me. Not even if the cops was after him. He wouldn't have hit me with the thing if he'd loved me. But don't let them hang him. I wasn't dead when I fell out. It was the fall what did it. We were doing sixty. . . ."

Mr. Squales roused himself with a start. It wasn't the first time lately that these queer fits of abstraction had come over him. And it was always the same. First the pictures. Then the voices.

"I'm not well," Mr. Squales repeated. "Perhaps I'm really ill. Something serious, I mean. Like a breakdown. If I could raise the money I'd see a specialist."

And what about Percy? After all, it was his morning as much as anybody's else. How is he getting on by now?

Well, take a look in his bedroom and see for yourself. There he is lying curled up, like a baby, fast asleep. It's the sleep of the just he's sleeping. He's enjoying the rest that comes of a clear conscience. You can see that. But wait a minute. Appearances don't prove anything. It was after three before he had drowsed off into the light slumber that grew deeper as the morning came. And if you look closer you'll see that his hair is all damp and matted where he's been lying on it. And the pillow's damp too.

That's because Percy cried himself to sleep again last night. And that makes a whole week of it.

CHAPTER 18

I

THEY WERE on the phone now. It had been Doreen's idea. But as Doris was paying half of everything she had to contribute her share, of course.

At the start there had been some friction about it. Doris said outright that they couldn't afford it and added that, so far as she knew, there wasn't anyone who would want to ring her up. Doreen, however, was set on the thing. It would drive her to the brink of suicide, or over it, she declared, if she had got to live forever, completely shut off from the whole world simply because Doris wouldn't ever agree to anything. And she went on to say that Doris had no conception, literally no conception, of what she was missing by not being on the phone. There were always dozens of people ringing up dozens of other people, she said, to fix up last-minute engagements that simply couldn't be arranged in any other way. She made it sound as though, simply by sending a couple of men along to connect the thing, the Postmaster-General could convert their life overnight from an affair of Lyonses and milk-bars into a whirl of Berkeleys and Savoy Grills.

It hadn't, as a matter of fact, quite worked out like that. They had been on the phone for just over three days, and so far the bell hadn't rung once. But it would begin to ring in earnest, Doreen persisted, as soon as people realised that they could get them.

This afternoon—it was Saturday—was quiet enough in all conscience. Doreen had gone out with a middle-aged someone called Monty, and Doris was all alone. Before she had left Doreen had explained all about Monty. He was, she said, absolutely mad about her and was always sending her flowers and ringing her up at the office, and things. She didn't herself, it appeared, care for him in the least: it was simply that sometimes she *had* to accept his invitations just to pacify him. All the same, he was rather a pet, she admitted. He always bought her a rose or an orchid or something and laid it beside her place on the table whenever they were dining out anywhere.

Compared with the sort of time Doreen would obviously be having with Monty, the flat seemed strangely silent and unexciting. Doris had washed up the breakfast things that made a little slum of their own in one corner of the kitchenette, and was standing by the window, staring across the roof-tops to the trees of Primrose Hill. The tops of the houses were sharp and regular and looked as though a child had cut them out of creased cardboard. It was while she was standing there that she suddenly confessed to herself that she was homesick. She had been suspecting it for some time and now she knew. For a moment she considered the idea of going over to Dulcimer Street. But she couldn't do that, she realised. She had been home last Saturday, and she didn't want her mother to get the idea that she wasn't enjoying being free and independent up at Hampstead.

She was still standing there at the window when the phone bell started ringing. Doris started. Adelaide was not an automatic exchange, and the rings were long and sustained with a suggestion of fire and panic about them.

But it was only Bill. And it was Doreen, of course, that he wanted. It wasn't anything important, he explained. It was simply that he'd lost his hat and was ringing up to see if he'd left it there last time. When Doris told him that they hadn't got his hat he didn't seem surprised—it was evident that he had lost hats before—and he was just ringing off again when he suddenly stopped himself.

"You doing anything?" he asked.

"Me?" Doris answered.

"Yes. Like to come out somewhere?"

"I would rather," Doris told him.

"Got to be cheap," he warned her.

"I don't mind," Doris answered.

There was a pause during which he seemed to be thinking. She could hear him patiently breathing into the mouthpiece.

"Any idea?" he asked at last.

"Oh, just anywhere."

There was the sound of further breathing.

"Well anyhow, I'll come along and pick you up," he said. "We'll decide where to go to, then."

In the end it was the Zoo they decided on. Bill seemed rather surprised when Doris suggested it. But it was certainly a relief. He'd only got ten shillings until Monday and if Doris had suggested going down West, he wasn't sure how they'd get back again.

They set off up the Adelaide Road arm-in-arm—Bill had taken hold of Doris's arm and shoved it absent-mindedly through his almost as soon as they left the house—and climbed the steep path leading to the top of Primrose Hill.

Then, if you had stood there on the summit under the pink hawthorn, looking out over London—almost standing on top of it as it were, with St. Paul's and Big Ben underneath your feet—you would have seen Bill and Doris going down the long walk on the Regent's Park side. They made rather a gay pair—Bill in a green sports coat and grey flannels and Doris in a yellow dress. Somehow they made everyone else who was out that afternoon seem rather heavy and middle-aged.

When they arrived at the North Gate they found that they were not the only ones who had thought of going to the Zoo. Simply because it was the first hot day of summer—it would be June to-morrow—half London had turned out to drink bottled lemonade and consume great slabs of Nestlé's chocolate and study natural history. There was a queue at the gates already, and the turntables were clattering with the noise of broken farm machinery. Then the turnstile clattered personally for Bill and Doris, and they were swept in with the dispersing crowd.

Once inside the difference was amazing. The temperature seemed to rush upwards. It was as though within those revolving iron gates everyone had been suddenly transported into the blazing tropics. Men, quite respectable men with stiff collars, were going about with handkerchiefs tied round their heads to keep off the sun and mothers of families were loaded up with surplus clothing like a race of female umpires. And the queer thing was that, in the midst of this sun-baked crowd that milled round and shrieked with delight at the monkeys and chattered, there were little pin-points of another life, impinging. From the back of dim cages, strange quiet eyes looked out at the human jungle and small furry backs turned themselves contemptuously.

"Bit of a crush, isn't it?" Bill remarked.

It was the first thing that he had said for some time and Doris was almost surprised to find herself still with him. Now that she really looked at him she was surprised to notice how shabby he was. Not shabbily shabby. But shabby in a cheerful, unminding sort of way. His green sports coat was bound up in leather at the cuffs and elbows, giving him a kind of amateur vanman appearance. And his trousers weren't any better. They were very light, but also very dirty. They looked as if he made a special point of wearing them whenever he was oiling things. Even his shoes seemed to have suffered. They were of dark chocolate suède with deep spongy soles that opened out—"like a camel's," Doris thought suddenly—every time he set his foot down.

Then she forgot about Bill, and went on rediscovering the Zoo. It was years since she had been there. And the astonishing thing was that the place hadn't altered. It was simply stuck there in time. Everything was just as it had been when she had first gone there as a little girl. The bison, in his eighth of an acre of rolling prairie, was leaning up against the bars to have his forehead scratched, and didn't look any older. The sea-lions were the same. And coming up the path towards her was a schoolboy carrying the same peacock feather which she had first seen stolen when she was eleven. There was even the same old man, with the round blunt face—rather like one of the great cats himself—who was tickling the same cheetah in the same spot under the chin.

"What about some tea?" Bill asked, abruptly coming back into her life again.

They went into the restaurant. And there were the same plates with the same lion stamped on them. . . .

When they came out of the Zoo, they made their way across Primrose Hill again back to Adelaide Road. They were tired, now. The tropical life inside the Gardens had exhausted them. Bill was so done in that he wouldn't come up with Doris. He said the stairs were too much for him, and just slouched off on his camel's feet.

But Doris wasn't alone. Doreen had got back by then. She, too, was exhausted. But with a different kind of exhaustion. She was dazed. Mr. Perkins, it seemed, had been more than usually indulgent. They had drunk champagne at lunch and he had given her an enormous cart-wheel box of chocolates and asked her to marry him. The only thing that upset her was that she had left the chocolates in the taxi on the way home.

Doris's afternoon rather amused her.

"Did you go alone?" she asked.

When Doris told her, Doreen wasn't pleased. She blew out a cloud of cigarette smoke and looked straight at her.

"Look here, young lady," she said, "don't you start stealing my friends, or there'll be trouble."

2

Percy was in the washroom at the back of the garage. A new edition of the evening paper had just come out and he wanted to go somewhere private and read it.

But there was nothing about him in it. There hadn't been for three days now. It was as if they had forgotten him. It was just as though it hadn't happened. That was the funny thing about it. Simply going on living, simply waking up with another night gone by, made it seem that there was nothing behind him to be afraid of. Nothing that shouldn't be there. Nothing that made you jump when you remembered it. It was still less than a month since That Night, but already life was becoming clean again.

Monday had been a black day. The *Evening News* had printed a paragraph about him then. It was only four lines. But it said that an early arrest was expected. Just that. Not a hint of how much They knew, or when They were coming for him, or even if it was him at all. Merely that an early arrest was expected. His heart had hammered as he read it, and he had to take a glass of water out of the washroom tap marked NOT FOR DRINKING because his throat had gone so dry. Those four lines upset him properly, they did. He went on feeling faint even after the water. And he felt sick. His stomach seemed to have dropped right down to his knees somewhere.

Just thinking about the *Evening News* was bad enough. The words kept on repeating themselves whisperingly in his ear when he wasn't expecting them. But it was all right. He'd got a charm against them. Something that he'd cut from the *Star* last Saturday. It was in his pocket-book now. Putting the catch up on the door so that no one should disturb him, he unbuttoned his coat and pulled out the cutting. It had been opened up and flattened out so many times that it almost broke into three pieces where the folds had been. And the type had become smeary. But the message was clear enough. There was hope and freedom and salvation in that piece of newspaper. ". . . shortly before the crime was committed," the extract ended, "the murdered girl was seen in the company of two men, one aged about forty and heavily built, wearing glasses, and the other tall, grey-haired and walking with a slight limp. The police believe the shorter of the two men may be able to assist them in their enquiries."

Percy knew that sentence by heart. But he read it again just the same.

"If it's two men they're looking for," he told himself, "I'm O.K. If it's either of them, I'm still O.K. They don't sound like me. They're not my type. And if it's two men They're looking for, I'm O.K."

But you couldn't be sure. Perhaps the *Star* reporter didn't know. Perhaps it was just something that he'd made up in the way journalists do. Or perhaps They had told him that just to put the real murderer, the man They wanted, off the scent. Perhaps the *Star* and the *Evening News* were both saying the same thing only in different ways.

Well, he couldn't stay there all day. They'd be asking him if he'd taken something. Because he should have been out on the pumps really. So he folded up the piece of paper and stowed it away in his pocket-book again. But with the thought that it might just be a piece of bluff, something They'd put over him, all the magic had gone out of it. That sick feeling in his stomach had come back again.

On the way out he caught sight of himself in the little circular mirror engraved with the words JEYES FLUID, that was stuck on to the washroom wall. He paused and regarded himself. Somehow the sight comforted him. He still *looked* the same. Taking out his pocket comb he ran it once or twice through his hair, so that the wave showed. It was almost corn-coloured, Percy's hair.

"If it's two men They're after, I'm O.K."

CHAPTER 19

I

THERE IS a lot in rent collecting. More than Mr. Josser had realised. It is the sort of profession that you can take up in youth, and still be finding out more about it by the time you have reached middle age. Some men never become good collectors.

The trouble with Mr. Josser, of course, was that he had started too late in life. Sixty-three is old to begin learning new tricks. And some of the tenants weren't slow to notice it. In consequence, they tried all the old dodges. And succeeded. When he called, they were out. They were ill. They were indifferent. They were destitute. Those careful notes of the previous collector turned out to be no use at all to him. Instead of presenting the problem as it really was, they skirted it. Take No. 8 Reginald Buildings, for instance. You could go there at any time in the twenty-four hours and you wouldn't find a soul. It was a posse of sheriffs and not one elderly collector who was needed to track down a tenant like No. 8.

All the same, Mr. Josser was enjoying the work. He was doing something, that was the point. Earning his own living again. Not being a drag on anyone.

It meant more than he had realised, having a definite job in mind when he got up in the morning. Not that any man in his senses would want to go out on a morning like this. Mr. Josser, surveying it from behind the long curtains of Dulcimer Street, saw that it was real dirty weather. He'd heard the rain rattling on the window during the night. And now that the downpour had stopped temporarily, the whole of London was steaming like an equatorial forest. You couldn't see the sky. In its place was a low sponge-like blanket that had descended to the height of the roof-tops, and was hanging there, caught up in chimney pots and telegraph wires. The other end of the street just lurked in the mists, sweating unhealthily. Pedestrians were swallowed up as they approached it as if they had passed through a curtain.

The nature of the day hadn't escaped Mrs. Josser either.

"If you want to go out, I can't stop you," she said. "But it'll probably be your last. You and your chest on a day like this."

It was, in fact, the third time that she'd said it. And she took an entirely unrealistic view of the whole affair. It was as though Mr. Josser's job, his pound-a-week employment, were some kind of silly hobby like butterfly hunting, that could be indulged on fine days but not on wet. The fact that to-day was a Friday and that Friday was a big day for rent collecting apparently meant nothing to her.

"You and your chest," she said again. "It's just asking for trouble."

But Mr. Josser was determined. He'd got seventeen addresses to visit, and he didn't want to take all day over them. So he finished his last mouthful of cold sausage, drank another cup of strong, sweetish tea and went through to the bedroom for his goloshes. He hadn't worn them since the winter and had forgotten that they had a hole in them. All the same, they were rubber, and they gave him confidence. Then he put on his raincoat, fastened his little strip of scarf round his neck to keep the drips out and hung his umbrella over his free arm.

When he went to say good-bye to Mrs. Josser, he found her sulking.

"I'm the one that's going to have all the trouble when you're in bed again," was what she said to him. "You don't ever think of me when you go out on these jaunts of yours."

And when Mr. Josser tried to reason with her, she abandoned logic altogether.

"They found somebody else to collect their rents for them before you came along, didn't they?" she demanded. "Well, why can't they find somebody else now?"

Because she was in that sort of mood, Mr. Josser didn't stop to argue. He just left her and started on his rounds. And, apart from the weather, it was one of the most successful mornings that he could remember. The first six numbers were all in and had the money ready waiting for him. Merely collecting it and putting his initials into the rent book seemed the sort of work that a child could do. But it would have been rather a wet child. For the rain was coming down hard again by now. It was as though someone had given the sponge a final extra squeeze. Altogether, Mr. Josser was pretty damp, all over, despite his umbrella and his goloshes.

And there was one little incident that made him wetter still. No. 23 Birkbeck Street refused to pay up because the back kitchener wasn't working properly and the Society hadn't sent anyone to look at it. Mr. Josser by now had become familiar with this excuse. He disputed. He cajoled. He threatened. And all to no avail. No. 23 simply wasn't paying. And when he went on elsewhere in search of easier rents, he realised how very wet his trouser legs had become. All the time he had been standing on the doorstep, the rain had been driving full at him.

At eleven-thirty, he went into a Lyons' for a cup of coffee. The whole place was full of moist, steaming people all gulping something hot. While he was drinking his coffee, he tried to dry his trouser legs up against a gas radiator. But he might as well have given it up. There was a lot of water soaked up into the blue serge and all that happened was that a little of the moisture on the outside turned to vapour. Soon his legs were enveloped in a kind of tepid Turkish bath up to his knees.

Even then he might have been all right if he hadn't left his umbrella on the tram. He had carried that umbrella about for years—for nearly twenty years, in fact. He had carried it through summers so dry that people with gardens were being told not to water their lawns. He had carried it when there wasn't a cloud in the sky. He'd carried it out to lunch and back again. He had had it re-covered twice because the seams had been worn out with simply lugging it about with him. He had even had the handle refixed. And now, on the day of the deluge itself, he was without it. In consequence, he had the lost, hopeless feeling of a sentry who has inadvertently mislaid his rifle.

All the same, there were the remaining addresses to be visited. And he didn't feel like giving in. So he simply turned up his coat collar and, with his goloshes oozing, he went padding round the streets. It was the top flats of the tenements that tried him most. He was a pretty breathless angel of debt by the time he arrived at those top landings, and asked huskily for the rent book.

Seventeen is a lot of addresses. It was after six by the time he had visited the last of them and collected the final driblet. The rain had stopped by then. But it had got colder. Much colder. Absurdly cold for June, in fact. And in the cold his wetness seemed to get wetter. Even his chest, that precious delicate part of him that Mrs. Josser insisted he should guard like a talisman, was wet. And because he was wet and cold, he was shivering. His teeth chattered as he turned into the Brixton Road. If it hadn't been for the fact that he now had over twelve pounds on him he'd have gone into a public house for a nip of whisky. As it was, however, he kept on. Cold or not, he wasn't going to risk being robbed of a fortune.

The only indulgence that he allowed himself was a bag of peppermints. He went into a small confectioner's and bought twopennyworth. They were certainly warming. But not warming enough. Going home in the bus he breathed peppermint all over the other passengers—and went on shivering.

In the night Mrs. Josser, magnificently justified in her predictions, had to rub him with embrocation. And in the morning he was running a temperature.

2

Percy had been on the pumps for nearly two hours—they were the old-fashioned sort where you really did have to pump, not just press a button like the new ones—when the two men came into the garage. He'd noticed them even before they began to mount the ramp up from the pavement. And he didn't like the look of them. There was something about them that was wrong. They looked like police officers. Like detectives. Like Them.

Percy took another glance, and his stomach sank still lower. They were both dressed in fawn raincoats and flannels and they had very ordinary cloth caps pulled down low over their foreheads. Well, what of it? Half London, or at least half South London, dressed that way, didn't it? Nothing to worry about in that. But it was their size that gave them away. They were six-footers both of them. And they strolled rather than walked. It was as if they wanted to take as long as they could to get over to him.

Percy knew this was the moment, before they even spoke. The palms of his hands had gone messy and he rubbed them off against the trousers of his boiler-suit.

"Can you spare a minute?" the front one asked, giving a little backward jerk of the head as he said it, as though he expected Percy to come over to him.

"You want summing?" he asked without moving.

He'd got his back to the door of the little glass box with the till inside and he wasn't shifting unless he had to. After all, he didn't *know* that they were police.

"Just want to make a few enquiries," the man went on. "If you get any customers you can serve them. We aren't in any hurry."

This was It, all right. This was what the *Evening News* had been talking about. But he wasn't going to show that he knew it.

"What sort of enquiries?" he asked. "Want to buy a car?"

The man shook his head.

"Just routine enquiries," he said. "We're checking up on things."

Percy sucked in his lips.

"Are you Petrol?" he asked.

"No, Police."

"Got your cards?"

The two men in the fawn raincoats produced their wallets. They carried their cards like season tickets.

Percy examined them both, not actually taking hold of them because his hands were shaking.

"O.K.," he said.

"You been here long?" the first one asked.

The other stood by, not saying anything. He might have been dumb for all the use he was.

"About three years," Percy told him.

"Know most of the people round here?"

"Some of 'em."

"Ever go over to the fun fair?"

Percy felt his heart give an up-and-down beat as the man said it. It was as though one of the valves had seized up for a moment.

"Which one?" he asked.

"Funland," the man answered. "The nearest one."

"Oh, Funland." Percy was thinking fast. Very fast. "Yes, I've been over to Funland." He paused. "Not lately," he added.

The man in the raincoat seemed interested.

"Stopped going there?" he asked.

Percy was cautious again. He wished he had left out that last bit.

"Never went much," he said.

"Know any of the people there?'

"Only by sight."

"D'you know her?"

Even though he was a six-footer, the man in the fawn raincoat was nimble. He brought his hand round from behind his back and Percy found that he was looking at a picture of the Blonde. It was an old photograph that he knew. It used to stand on the little table beside her bed. In the photograph she was wearing a bathing costume. The valve in Percy's heart seized up again.

He shook his head.

"No savvy," he said.

"Then you can't help us," the man said, putting the picture away again.

"Can't I?" Percy answered.

His mouth was so dry again, that it didn't sound like his voice as he spoke. He had to keep on running the tip of his tongue across his lips. Even after the man had put the photograph away again he could still see it. The eyes kept looking up at him and he remembered her as he had last seen her. It brought it all back again. But he was trying harder than ever now to show that he didn't care, that he hadn't anything to worry about.

"What did you want to know?" he asked.

"Who killed her," the man in the fawn raincoat replied. He'd taken out a cigarette case and was offering it to Percy. But Percy shook his head.

"No thanks," he said.

He was afraid of fingerprints if he touched the cigarette case.

And he was getting confused too. He'd just been shown the picture of a murdered girl and he hadn't even seemed surprised. That might look a bit fishy.

"Who is she?" he asked.

"Cashier from Funland," the man answered. "Name of Watson."

"And she's been murdered?"

"Don't you read your papers?"

It was the second man who had spoken now. He'd come sidling up and was almost on top of Percy when he said it.

Percy was thinking again.

"Yes, I did see it," he said at last. "I remember now."

"It was all there," the second man went on. "Picture as well."

"I wasn't specially interested," Percy told him.

"Perhaps she came after you'd stopped going," the first man suggested.

"Yes, that's right," Percy answered. "She came just after I stopped."

"How do you know she came, if you'd stopped going?"

This was the second man again. He'd got a lower voice than the first man. It was a soft, quiet sort of voice.

"Musta done," Percy said quickly. "Or I'da known her."

"Perhaps you saw her and don't remember," the first man put in. "We don't expect everybody to remember everyone they've ever seen."

"I maya seen her," Percy answered. "I just can't remember."

"You didn't write her any letters?" the first man asked.

Percy's heart bumped upwards again. No. He was quite sure he'd never written to her. Thank God, he hadn't.

"I never wrote her nothing," he began.

"How could he?" asked the second man. "He didn't even know her, did he?"

"So you didn't miss her when she'd gone?"

Percy shook his head and didn't say anything.

"You used to go over regular once, didn't you?" the second man asked.

"Pretty regular."

"Why d'you give it up?"

"Too busy."

"Been over there since she's gone?"

"No."

He blurted that out at once. Better to tell the truth whenever there was a chance of it.

But the second man—he might have been the superior from the soft way he spoke—didn't attach any importance to his answer.

"How's he to know if he's never seen her?" he asked. "He doesn't even know when it happened."

The first man stood corrected.

"Thanks, chum," he said. "Just ordinary routine, you understand."

Percy squared his shoulders and tried to stroll slowly down the ramp beside them.

"Let me know if I can do anything more to help you."

"Thanks," the first man answered.

Percy ran his tongue across his lips again. They were so dry now they were cracking.

"Hope you get him," he said.

"Don't worry," the second man replied. "We will."

CHAPTER 20

I

Dulcimer Street was at its most peaceful on these summer afternoons. The plane trees in the vicarage garden at the corner gave a pleasant flicker of green against the dirty stucco and the grey brickwork, and the everlasting pigeons were making big sweeping patterns in the sky. Some of the peacefulness of the scene, it must be admitted, lay in the absence of children. Dulcimer Street was just a cut above such things. It was left to side turnings like Dove Street, Water Street and Swan Walk to provide playgrounds for the next generation.

Most of this generation was missing, too. There was only one pedestrian coming down Dulcimer Street. He was a young man. A young man in flannel trousers which were too short for him, and a cheap sports coat. Every time he turned his head—and he kept on turning it because he was looking for a number—the sports coat went into a deep ruck between the shoulder-blades. The thing, in fact, was too tight for him. It was only by wearing it unbuttoned that he was able to get into it at all.

When he got to No. 10, he paused for a moment and inspected it. It wasn't noticeably different from No. 8 or No. 12 on either side of it. But the young man evidently wanted to know all about it. He might have been learning it by heart. When he had surveyed it from top to bottom for the second time, he went up the steps and rang the bell. It was the Jossers' bell that he rang.

And it was Mrs. Josser who opened the door to him. She stood there in the protection of the hall peering out into the bright sunlight with the cautious, suspicious expression that comes natural when nearly every ring at the bell means that it is someone who wants to sell something. But the young man wasn't a seller: he hadn't got a non-electric vacuum cleaner or a fancy line in tin-openers with him. On the contrary, he was a buyer. He had come after the room, Doris's room. That was why Mrs. Josser stared at him even harder. It was one thing inserting an advertisement in a local paper and quite another meeting the person with whom you might actually have to share your bathroom. The most that she would concede him at the moment was that he *looked* all right.

And then a strange misgiving came into her mind. As she showed him the room, it struck her for the first time that it was rather a shabby little room. She was ashamed of it. When Doris had been in there it had been a family affair. The fact that the curtains had once been a bedspread hadn't seemed to matter. But now it was a stranger who was seeing them. And somehow they looked more like an old bedspread than ever.

But the young man wasn't particular. He was thoroughly easy and accommodating. He simply needed somewhere quiet to sleep. He was on the night shift at Battersea Power Station, and he wanted to be able to get a bit of rest by day. After about half-past seven every evening his room would be empty, he said, and they wouldn't see him again until breakfast-time.

He didn't even need very much in the way of service. Provided he could get his bed made for him that was all he wanted. He understood perfectly well that he couldn't expect Mrs. Josser to provide him with a hot dinner at eight-thirty in the morning, and he explained that he did most of his eating out anyhow. All that he wanted was to move in. His present landlady was going away and he couldn't stay there any longer. He gave her name and the power station as references. The latter would have been enough by itself. It was like having London Bridge or the Marble Arch as a guarantor.

And he was ready to pay the rent that Mrs. Josser was asking. He'd have paid in advance if she'd pressed him. Five minutes after he'd arrived, he'd agreed to take the room, bedspread curtains and all, and move in next Monday—assuming that the power station didn't know anything to his discredit. Altogether, he seemed the ideal tenant. His name was Todds.

After she had shown him out, Mrs. Josser went back upstairs, her lips pursed tightly together. There was victory in that face. Victory, and the promise of further victory. She'd had Mr. Josser in bed for more than a week now and for about eight hours a day she'd been telling him that he'd have to give up all thought of going on with his rent collecting. The lodger was a brand new argument. Mr. Electrician Todds' weekly contribution would just about square things.

2

Mr. Squales was sitting up in bed reading a letter. He was wearing his long flowered silk dressing-gown—the one with the stains of previous breakfasts all down the big flaring lapels.

The letter was from Mrs. Jan Byl. And it did Mr. Squales good just to feel the expensive, deckle-edged notepaper between his fingers. The sound which it made as he smoothed it out flat was almost like the authentic crackle of a Bank of England fiver. Absent-mindedly, scarcely aware of what he was doing, Mr. Squales went on reproducing the sound. *Crrck—crrck*, it went.

Not that Mrs. Jan Byl was not an engaging letter-writer—Mr. Squales had to admit as much. There was a brusque, overbearing manner about her as though she were taking up the references of a new chauffeur. But, in the circumstances, he was prepared to overlook it. After all, she was very rich, and very rich women were often a little brusque and overbearing in their manner. It was practically an occupational disease with them. The simple fact—and it was enough—was that she had written.

Smoothing out the crisp paper, Mr. Squales re-read what was there. "*Dear Mr. Squales,*" it ran, "*I could see you at four o'clock on Thursday afternoon at this address to discuss a séance which I am thinking of holding. My regular medium, Chakvar Ali, is indisposed and I urgently wish to get into touch with my deceased husband. Mr. Ali has been most successful at previous séances for which I have engaged him and I have no wish to make any permanent alterations in my arrangements. However, I am perfectly prepared to give your talents an open test and anything you can do to enable me to correspond with Mr. Jan Byl will not be forgotten. I shall probably wish to hold the séance on next Saturday or Sunday evening at about nine o'clock. If you are not able to attend here at four o'clock next Thursday please telephone to my secretary and I will endeavour to suggest another time. In replying, please mention the fee for yourself and assistant, if any, which you have been accustomed to receive. Yours truly, Emma Jan Byl.*"

Well, there it was. An engagement. Definitely an engagement. And there were two things about the letter which were oddly flattering. In the first place, Mr. Chakvar Ali was right at the top of the tree among mediums. He was one of the few. There was therefore the pleasing implication that Mr. Squales was another of the few. It was as though a violinist in a second-rate palm court somewhere had received a letter saying: "*As Yehudi Menuhin is unable to be present at the Albert Hall on Sunday, would you please come along instead.*" And then there was the bit about suggesting the fee. Mr. Squales lit a cigarette and thought it over. It could, within reason, be almost anything. He could name five shillings, five pounds, or even twenty-five. Mr. Ali probably received the latter—but then he was able to produce, apparently at will, a strong and unmistakable odour of lilies of the valley, and feathers floated down from nowhere. That sort of thing always commanded a bonus. So, in the end, Mr. Squales compromised on five guineas. And a guinea for the assistant. It sounded a respectable, professional kind of fee. Like Harley Street. But he wasn't out of the wood yet. There remained the question of the assistant. Who on earth? he wondered.

And the notepaper. Mr. Squales remembered gloomily that he hadn't got a decent sheet in the place—nothing that had a printed or embossed heading to it. That meant that he couldn't reply in writing. And this was a pity because Mr. Squales's handwriting had character to it. Give him a broad nib and a bottle of violet ink, he often told himself, and he could produce something that no penman need feel ashamed of. As it was, there was nothing for it but telephone and let his voice do the trick. The one thing, he reminded himself, was to avoid the jangle of pennies at the beginning of the conversation. By pressing button A while he could still hear the ringing tone, he would be able to conceal the fact that he, Professor Enrico Qualito, the co-equal of Mr. Chakvar Ali, was ringing up from a common call-box.

And now that he had settled the fee in his own mind, he surveyed the larger question: "What precisely is it," he asked himself, "that the old girl *wants* to hear?" If he could find that out, the séance was half-way to being a success already. It might, for example, be her re-marriage—for all he knew she might be amorous as well as wealthy. But, after reflection, he decided against such a possibility. Most women in the circumstances would want to forget their previous husband and not go trying to talk to him. Or was there something on her conscience, something that was haunting her? Yes, there might be. But what? Even a hint, no matter how small, would be useful.

He only wished that Mrs. Jan Byl was more the kind of woman who would take a man into her confidence. If only she'd tell him what she wanted the late Mr. Jan Byl to say, Mr. Squales would make it his business to see that Mr. Jan Byl damn' well said it. As it was, he was perfectly ready to admit, the whole thing might turn out a perfectly dismal failure. Even a bunch of flowers suddenly plopped down on the table from nowhere might be out of place at the kind of séance on which Mrs. Jan Byl was counting.

This was direct-voice stuff, or nothing.

3

Connie had sunk her pride. She was back with Mr. Vercetti again. And Mr. Vercetti had sunk his pride, too. He was no longer the proprietor of a flourishing night-club. He was only the manager. There was a Mr. Scala, or somebody they all called Mr. Scala, he now worked for. But Mr. Vercetti didn't mind. It kept him in touch with his old customers and made things easier for the moment when the Government was ready to forgive him and he could open up once more on his own account.

Mr. Scala's night-club was called The Turban. Except for the fact that it was in the basement, instead of on the roof, it might have been designed by the same man who had designed the Moonrakers. There were the same canary-coloured walls that were not much more than sparrow-coloured in places where the customers had rubbed against them. There was the same box-like lift that was so small that the occupants got to know each other by the end of the journeys. And there were the same foot-marks on the doors as though the patrons habitually opened them with their feet. But that was only a small difference. The real difference was that the lift went down instead of up. The leather and chromium furniture, the glass and chromium tables, the plywood and chromium bar, were the same, too. Even the toy tarantula stuck in the middle of the ceiling, was the same. And so was the card-room behind the curtained door. Mr. Vercetti, in fact, had every reason to feel at home at The Turban.

And so had Connie. The ladies' cloakroom was a small, brick cavern that branched out from the passage that led into the restaurant. It had once been the coal-hole. There, seated behind a counter (plywood, like the bar) with a saucerful of pins in front of her, sat Connie. By screwing her head sideways, she could just see into the room beyond and catch a glimpse of the gay life being lived. But, for the most part, her time was spent in giving rich girls sixpence change for a shilling, or running her hand lightly over the coats to see if anything interesting had been left in the pockets.

It was her second night at The Turban and it was getting late now. Very nearly three o'clock. The crowd, except for a small group in the card-room industriously ruining themselves, had dwindled away to nothing and half the waiters had put on raincoats and made off to their families in Balham or Mornington Crescent. Connie herself would be one of the last to leave. So long as there was even one lady—other than the professional hostesses, of course—left in the club, Connie would have to be there. After all, manners apart, she was responsible for the clothes they had come in.

Not that they were really so bad, those late hours. You got used to them. And they were all friends together at The Turban. Only just now, the bar-tender who had been with her at Mr. Vercetti's other club had slipped her a Manhattan that had been scarcely tasted, and she had been making up on oddments all the evening. A little earlier she had eaten the better half of a chicken sandwich, only slightly covered with cigarette ash. What was more she had got her shoes off underneath the counter, which meant that she could stretch her toes a bit. Connie, in fact, was doing fine.

She got off finally at about three-thirty. It was a fine moonlit night and the streets had that dignified, civilised appearance that comes of being empty of people. Regent Street, as she turned into it, was a white-walled ravine gracefully lit by hanging lamps all down the sides and centre. And Piccadilly Circus had the quietness of a country fairground. The electric signs had all been switched off and Eros, very Greek in inspiration but decidedly Edwardian in treatment, pointed his bronze bow blankly at the stars. It was late even for him.

Despite a slight uncanniness about the place, Connie rather liked London this way. There was a pleasant feeling of importance about having the Haymarket all to yourself as though you were a one-horse Royal procession. And she turned into Cockspur Street with her high heels setting up a kind of kettle-drum accompaniment from the echoing walls of the tall steamship building. But by the time she reached Trafalgar Square, the echoes just died away into space. The Square was too big for one woman to have all to herself. It was like taking a midnight walk on the moon. It gave Connie the creeps. It wasn't far now, however. She had only got to cut down Northumberland Avenue and she was where she wanted to be—on the Embankment. She could get her all-night tram from there.

She dozed right off in the tram and it was only the conductor calling out "Oval" that roused her. It had been a nice little nap. She'd even managed to fit in a short dream. She'd dreamt that she was an aeroplane. Not *in* an aeroplane. But actually the aeroplane itself. She was in the midst of a giddy series of loops and side rolls under her own power when the conductor roused her. She was just the teeniest weeniest bit tiddly.

But she got off the tram all right. And here, out at Kennington, it was even quieter than in the middle of the town. When the tram had gone swinging off into the night it seemed that she was the last living thing left in London. No, not quite the last living thing. There were the cats. Lots of them. Up in the West End there were always one or two peeping inside the lids of dustbins. But here there was a whole sub-jungle life going on among the bits of privet. There was prowling, love-making and assault to be discovered in those sleeping front gardens.

But when Connie got to Dulcimer Street there was a surprise waiting for her. She had just turned into the gate of No. 10 and was preparing to mount the steep flight of steps when she saw that the door was open and there was someone standing on the top step. The porch cast a dense black shadow and she couldn't see who it was.

But what she'd seen was enough. In all the years she'd been

coming back to Dulcimer Street in the small hours she had never known anyone else in No. 10 still about. It smelt fishy. Distinctly fishy. So, hitching up her dress, she darted up the steps like a ferret. And when she got to the top, she found that it was Percy.

Breathless as she was, it was Connie who was the first to speak.

"Wotchu doing at this time of night?" she asked.

Percy paused. He was careful now to pause before answering any question about himself. It was only this afternoon that the two policemen had called on him at the garage.

"Just slipped out for a breather," he said. "Couldn't sleep. Got heartburn."

Connie walked up the stairs beside him.

"Next time you've got anything on your conscience just come up and tell your Auntie Connie," she said cheerfully. "She'll put things right for you."

As a matter of fact Percy was nearer telling her than she realised. He had been standing out there for nearly half an hour looking down the empty street, trying to sort things out.

"If only I'd got someone I could talk to I'd be O.K.," he'd been thinking. "If I could get it off my chest, I'd go back to bed again. I'd go off to sleep. I'd feel fine in the morning. If only I'd got someone I could talk to, I'd be O.K."

4

The proudest man in London at the moment wasn't a Londoner at all. He wasn't even an Englishman. And, for that matter, he wasn't in England. He was Dr. Otto Hapfel and he was standing on the German soil, the sacred German soil, of the Embassy.

It was the first time that he had ever been inside. On other occasions he had simply stood at the top of the Duke of York steps, looking at the large yellow building that was so like all the other buildings in Carlton House Terrace. So like, but so utterly unlike. More than once the sight of that black-and-white flag with the Nazi swastika on it had brought tears into his eyes as he saw it there, prophetically fluttering in the very windows of the King-Emperor's palace.

There had been tears in his eyes again to-night. But that had been different. That had been when he had shaken hands with the Ambassador, *had shaken the hand that had shaken the hand of the Führer.* But he had pulled himself together hurriedly. It would have been un-German to weep publicly. It would have been Latin. Worse, it would have been positively Jewish. And after he had made his bow and stepped back so that he could look at the rest of the assembly, he saw how unthinkable emotion would have been in such a company.

Such a company. With the exception of little Dr. Hapfel himself, they were all magnificent men who were gathered there. Magnificent men and blonde, motherly women. Only the Ambassador himself looked a little worn. He had pouches under his eyes like the abdicated English King-Emperor. But the Military Attaché was superb. He was a Siegfried in the shining armour of a boiled shirt and tails. As he regarded him, Dr. Hapfel tried to comfort himself by reflecting that Dr. Goebbels was of small stature also: his heart was larger than his body, people said. Or the Führer himself for that matter. But that was a silly thought. It was irreverent. It was blasphemous. The Führer was beyond all size. He was not a man at all. He was a vibration, a radiation. . . .

One of the footmen was standing beside him. Dr. Otto Hapfel, Secretary of the Overseas German Students' Federation (London Branch), was being offered champagne. He sprang to attention. And carefully so as not to disturb anything, he selected one of the tall, gilt-rimmed glasses. But having taken it, he made no attempt to sip it. He had drunk two glasses already and he was cautious. Only a moment ago he had caught himself staring at his own reflection in a mirror as if he had been a stranger.

It was now three-quarters of an hour since anyone had spoken to him. All that time he had simply been alone in his corner, watching. Not that he felt miserable, or neglected. On the contrary, Dr. Hapfel, Ph.D. Heidelberg, was blissfully, rapturously content.

"Happiness," he was telling himself, "is not necessarily perfect only in retrospect as the books say. It is perfect also, provided the subject experiences it in mental solitude. If I were distracted by speaking to someone I should not realise how happy I am."

But the two earlier glasses of champagne had loosened something inside him. It now seemed selfish to remain silent. Dr. Hapfel looked round for someone to speak to. Beside him was a very large man, a visiting industrialist perhaps, also alone. Dr. Hapfel addressed him.

"It is very agreeable, is it not," he asked, "to hear nothing but the German tongue spoken?"

The large man raised his hand.

"Quiet, please," he said. "Excellency is about to say something."

Dr. Hapfel blushed and spilt a little of his champagne in his agitation. Then he raised his eyes. . . . At the far end of the immense room—more immense it seemed because of the severe German style of decoration which had covered up the English decadences of the architecture—Ribbentrop was standing. Above him hung the crossed Nazi flags which, with the Führer's portrait in the middle, were the only decoration in the room. He was speaking to the German correspondents in London.

"Less than a year ago the Agreement of Munich was signed," he was saying, "and the peaceful restraint of German foreign policy was again demonstrated. Less than three months ago our Führer assumed the Protectorate of Slovakia and a storm centre of European chaos was reduced to order. Memelland is now German territory. Has there been war? Has one drop of blood been spilled?" The Ambassador paused and coughed into a handkerchief. "But it would be idle to ignore that we have enemies. Powerful enemies. Certain politicians are anxious to surround the Reich in an intricate meshwork, a barbed-wire barricade I will call it, of pacts and guarantees. Take the French and British guarantees to Poland, Roumania and Greece and the signing of the Anglo-Turkish Pact. Such indications cannot be ignored. That is why the World Powers of Germany and Italy, bound in inalienable ties of affection and respect, have concluded last week in Berlin a solemn military alliance. And to extend protection to smaller states imperilled by the frank imperialism of certain of our neighbours not entirely unconnected with the New Jerusalem" —Ribbentrop smiled suddenly, and all the reporters smiled too— "this week Denmark and the Reich have signed a pact of non-aggression. Again I remind you in this 'off the record' chat, would a nation which wishes to wage war sign such a pact? The pact has already been circulated to the news agencies and our Press Attaché has advised you how to handle the London reaction. . . ."

If only, Dr. Hapfel was thinking, my schoolmaster, my Professor of Systematic Philosophy, my mother and my two sisters, could see me now. In the German Embassy. Representing the Students' Federation. Listening to our Ambassador. The list of those present. I am by so much more than any who are absent. . . .

It was nearly one o'clock when Dr. Hapfel came away from Carlton House Terrace. It was a pale June night and London looked very beautiful. Beautiful and defenceless.

CHAPTER 21

I

It was Sunday evening and Mr. Squales and Connie were on their way to Hyde Park Drive together. They were in a taxi now. But they'd only climbed into it for appearance' sake a hundred yards or so up the road. And the earlier part of the ride had been slower and less fashionable. Much slower, because Dulcimer Street and Hyde Park Drive were remote islands in the complicated archipelago of London. There was no direct channel joining them.

There could be no question about it, it would have been easier by Underground. But the Underground was no good for Connie: she couldn't stand the feeling of being buried. It was just one of those things. There were, in fact, so many of those things with Connie that Mr. Squales wished already that he hadn't brought her. But it was too late now, and he had to endure it.

All the same, there remained the question of her clothes. Because it was a warm night, Connie had come out in something that she called her summery-mummery. It was of brightly flowered voile and very thin. And it was the thinness that was the trouble. It was absolutely transparent. Beneath the short ruffed sleeves could be seen a thick ridge of what looked like sensible winter underwear.

Not that Connie hadn't taken trouble with herself. When Mr. Squales told her that her arms—her thin wrinkled arms—looked too bare she had gone straight upstairs and borrowed a pair of long lemon suède ones from Mrs. Boon. Mr. Squales made no comment on the gloves. What he had really meant was a coat.

And another thing was that Connie *would* talk to him. She had a high piercing voice, rather like an agitated child's, and it jarred. At one of the changes he bought an evening paper and gave it to her. But it was no use. She read him all the tit-bits aloud as she came to them.

As soon as they were in the taxi, Mr. Squales took the paper away from her again and addressed her.

"Now, Connie," he said firmly, "I want you to remember everything I told you. This is really a very solemn occasion, not a funny one. An unhappy widow is trying to get in touch with her dear departed—keep on trying to think of it in that way. And you're there to help me. If Mrs. Jan Byl asks how long you've been working for me—you'd better seem to be trying to work it out and then say something about how exhausted I am after every séance. Something about fainting in the taxi on the way back would do. And don't forget: when I raise my foot, you say, 'He's off.' That's important. We don't want to be there all night." Mr. Squales paused. "I'll give you your half-guinea to-morrow," he said. "Don't ask for it in front of Mrs. Jan Byl."

"Ten and six it is," Connie answered.

They had reached the house by now and Mr. Squales had just rung.

The door opened and he gave a little bow.

"Professor Qualito and assistant," he announced.

2

They made rather a lonely little group as they sat in the big drawing-room waiting for Mrs. Jan Byl to arrive.

Fortunately, they were comfortable. Mr. Squales's chair was so deeply upholstered that his knees were above the level of his chin, and Connie was lying practically full length on a deep rose-red couch. The room was undeniably well furnished. Indeed, it was more than furnished: it was appointed. The inlaid desk with the gilt legs and enormous claw feet, over by the window, was obviously Loowee, Mr. Squales told himself; obviously genuine French Loowee. And the porcelain shepherdesses on the side table were obviously genuine Dresden. Or Wedgwood. Mr. Squales couldn't quite remember which. But whatever they were, they were clearly genuine. Indeed, this quality of genuineness ran right through the room. Even from where he was sitting he could see the hall-mark on the period ink-well.

But it wasn't at any of these things that he was looking now. He was looking at the photographs. There were a lot of them all over the room, mounted in elaborate silver frames. And they were all of the same man. Mr. Squales went round and inspected them in turn. So far as he was concerned they were so many clues, staring at him. There was not much to be gained from them, however. It was a flat, unexciting kind of face—a Dutch face, in fact—with a pale drooping moustache and a small pointed beard.

"So that's what you looked like, is it?" Mr. Squales said musingly. "I'd pictured you a bit larger."

Only this morning he had been doing some research work on Mr.

Jan Byl. He had looked up his obituary notice in *The Times*, and by now he was by way of being quite an authority. That melancholy visage with the dark pondering eyes was the picture of the man who had made a corner in the soft cheese market and had left a hundred thousand pounds to a chest hospital.

Then, while Mr. Squales was still studying one of the photographs in fact, Mrs. Jan Byl came in. She was an impressive woman. And she dominated. Mr. Squales had risen as she entered, but Mrs. Jan Byl waved him back again into his chair. It was a gesture at once casual and imperious, a mere backward flip of the fingers as though to warn him that if he didn't move out of her way she would run him down. And having cleared a path for herself, she passed him with the rustle of silk and a strong waft of perfume and sat down in the big throne-like chair with the lamp beside it. Getting out her lorgnette, she scrutinised her visitors.

Mr. Squales disliked being examined through a lorgnette: it made him feel inferior. He longed for the monocle that he had worn with the light check suit during that happy summer down at Brighton. But he doubted whether even the monocle would have been a strong enough magic to save him. It was one thing using a monocle on a lot of defenceless natives. But Mrs. Jan Byl's lorgnette was of inlaid tortoise-shell on a gold chain. It was colossal.

"There's a dressing-room next door if you want to change, Professor," was all she said.

But Mr. Squales only shook his head. He had no intention whatever of leaving Mrs. Jan Byl and Connie alone together.

"Then shall we begin?" Mrs. Jan Byl asked impatiently. "I'm quite ready as soon as you've composed yourself."

The only light came from a shaded standard lamp that cast a small circular pool of brightness on the polished floor. All round, the shadows gathered mysteriously.

Mr. Squales was reclining on the couch, his head supported by a cushion, his eyes shut. Opposite to him sat Mrs. Jan Byl. She was in a small semi-circular armchair that fitted her so tightly that she seemed to be wearing it. Her head was bent slightly forward, and there was a tense, alert kind of expression on her face, as though she were ready at a moment's warning to jump up, chair and all. In between them, on a kind of footstool, perched Connie.

Mrs. Jan Byl leant over and whispered to her.

"Is he quite comfortable, do you think?" she asked. "Is there anything he'd like?"

For a moment Connie studied the slowly breathing form on the couch.

"He might like another drink," she said.

As she said it a quiver ran through the medium almost as though the moment of possession had come to him. But all that happened was that he raised one of his long sensitive hands and waved it reprovingly.

"Nothing at all now, thank you. Nothing at all. But please go on talking. It helps me."

There was a pause.

"We shouldn't have asked him," Connie observed. "We should just have put it by him."

"Chakvar Ali always fasts before a big séance," Mrs. Jan Byl replied.

Connie raised her eyebrows.

"Some like it one way, some like it another," she replied. "I've had to help Mr. Squales out of the taxi before now."

Another quiver ran through the medium, and Connie corrected herself.

"Not what you mean either," she said to Mrs. Jan Byl. "Just exhaustion."

It was Mr. Squales who interrupted them. He was anxious to bring the conversation to a close.

"Quiet now, please," he said, his voice fading away to nothingness. "I feel myself drifting . . . drifting . . . drifting."

"You watch out," whispered Connie. "You're in for something good. It's the surprise of your life you'll be getting."

After that the room was silent except for the sound of Mr. Squales's breathing. It was a low regular sibilance that seemed different from ordinary breathing. It was deeper and slower. The breathing of the profound sleeper, of the exhausted lover, of the man near to death. And it should have been pretty good breathing: Mr. Squales had been practising it long enough.

Then a change came over him. He was restful no longer. He was choking now. Just lying there in front of them, throttling himself. The air that he was swallowing might have been in solid chunks from the way he was biting at it.

Very slowly the left leg rose into the air. . . . But Connie wasn't looking at the moment. She had never imagined that Mr. Squales was such a good actor, and the whole performance made her feel quite queer.

It was after the left leg had raised itself for the third time that

Mrs. Jan Byl called her attention to it. Connie pulled herself together hurriedly.

"That's his signal," she said impulsively. "He's ready."

Even so they had to wait for a minute, two minutes, three, before anything happened. And then a voice began speaking. It wasn't like Mr. Squales at all. It was very low and guttural. And it spoke in a faint foreign accent.

"Good evening, loved one," it said. "How I miss you. I cannot tell you what separation means. It is like having a knife passed through me. It makes me bleed."

The voice ceased for a moment, and Connie could hear that Mrs. Jan Byl was breathing heavily too.

"But in a way I am happy, too. The air is like balm and I draw in sweet breaths of it. I suffer no pain."

"Go on," Mrs. Jan Byl commanded.

She was leaning right forward now so that the chair seemed no more than a tiny bustle behind her.

"And I'm happy because I see your dear face all around me. It is in the flowers, in the clouds, in the stars above me. . . ."

"He's certainly going it," thought Connie delightedly. "She'll burst her bodice in a moment."

But before the voice could speak again, Mrs. Jan Byl had asked it a question.

"What was your mother's first name?" she asked.

The voice hesitated.

"Wilhelmina," it said, uttering the only Dutch name that it knew.

Mrs. Jan Byl drew her lips in tighter.

"And when was your sister born?" she demanded.

"In . . . in The Hague," the voice told her.

"I said *when*," Mrs. Jan Byl reminded him.

This time the voice didn't answer immediately. It just stayed somewhere inside Mr. Squales saying nothing. When at last it came through it was distinctly petulant.

"But these are trivial questions," it complained. "They are frivolous. I have a message for you. A great message. Something that is like a shaft of light through darkness. I am a light-bearer."

Mrs. Jan Byl had sat back abruptly in her chair. Reaching over her shoulder, she pulled the pendant switch in the tall standard lamp. The bright light made Connie blink. When she could see she looked in Mrs. Jan Byl's direction. She was sitting there with her arms crossed.

"You mean you're an impostor," Mrs. Jan Byl contradicted him. "I've had plenty of your sort before. You can get up now. You're only wasting my time lying there."

There was a silence. A strained awkward silence. Even the breathing on the couch seemed to have stopped.

Connie roused herself.

"Don't do anything," she advised. "Maybe there's been a bit of a mix-up. Perhaps the late lamented'll be coming through in a minute."

Mrs. Jan Byl rounded on her.

"And you're an accomplice," she said. "I ought to make the pair of you over to the police. You're nothing but a pair of cheap charlatans."

A faint sound from the couch—a sound like a dry, rasping cough—made them both turn round. It came very obviously from Mr. Squales's direction. But it hadn't come from Mr. Squales. His lips were still closed. And, while they listened, the sound, the husky hollow cough, came again. Mrs. Jan Byl gripped Connie's arm.

"What's that?" she asked.

"Search me," Connie answered.

They went across to the couch together and stood over Mr. Squales. Even in the half-light he looked somehow different. His chest with the broad black stock flowing over was no longer rising and falling as it had been. It seemed to have stopped altogether. And his face was now chalky pale. It was like the face of a comfortably dead man. The lower jaw had dropped down, and his upper denture was sagging. All Mr. Squales's self-respect had gone from him.

"Get up," Mrs. Jan Byl said roughly. "Get up and leave the house."

But Mr. Squales apparently couldn't hear her. He just lay there and while they looked his eyelids slowly rolled back into his face and his eyes stared upwards at the ceiling. The pupils had contracted, and the light catching them made them glint as though they were luminous. Mrs. Jan Byl drew back a little.

"He's . . . he's fainted," she said falteringly.

She turned away to ring the bell. But before she could reach it someone addressed her peremptorily.

"Stay where you are," she was told.

And it was not Mr. Squales who had spoken. His lips were still drooping. And, in any case, the voice did not even seem to be coming from him. It came from a point about two feet above his placid figure. It was a voice without a body. An invisible mouth opening in the air.

And the room had suddenly grown cold, unutterably cold. It was as though a frigid, unboisterous wind were blowing through the closed doors and curtained windows, freezing everything; as though slow waves of iciness were emanating from the body of the silent medium. Connie shivered.

Then the voice began speaking again.

"Why can't you leave me alone?" it asked again. "Won't you ever leave me alone? Not even now?"

It was a flat, weary voice that was speaking. The voice of a man who had had all the sparkle trodden out of him.

"I didn't want to come when they sent for me. I was better off where I was. A lot better off. I just wanted to be left alone. . . ."

The voice paused, interrupted by the same recurrent cough.

"I don't believe you ever knew how much I got to hate you," it went on. "You and your grand ways and everything about you. That's why I left all that money to the hospital. You did your best to stop it. But I was ready for you. I left everything tied up. If I'd been a bit braver, I'd have left you. Not gone after another woman. Just left you. Just walked out and left you sitting here. I thought about if often enough. I just hadn't got the courage."

"Stop him," Mrs. Jan Byl cried out. "Don't let him say any more. He doesn't know what he's doing."

But the voice didn't seem to hear her. It went on in the same flat voice as before.

"And do you know what the first thing was they said to me up here when I told them? They said: 'Well, why didn't you? It's too late now.' That's what they said. They don't think much of me up here." The voice was getting fainter now but they could still hear it speaking. "Don't send for me again," it said. "I don't want to come. I've had enough of you. . . . I just want to be left alone. I want to think things out."

The voice had stopped altogether. And the room seemed to grow warmer. Connie took a deep breath and glanced across at Mrs. Jan Byl. But Mrs. Jan Byl was past noticing. She was lolling back in the tight armchair, crying.

They were in the taxi going home now. Connie had pretty nearly carried Mr. Squales downstairs and lifted him into it. He just sat there passing a handkerchief across his forehead and shivering. It must have been one of those unaccountable attacks that had come over him. He'd certainly have to see a specialist if they went on.

"Was . . . was I a success?" he asked feebly.

Connie gave a little giggle.

"A success?" she answered. "You were a knock-out."

CHAPTER 22

I

PERCY WAS standing at the window looking out across the street. Just standing there. He'd been like that for nearly five minutes. He didn't go out so much in the evening now. It felt safer indoors.

Mrs. Boon looked up from her mending. Her face for some reason looked sadder than ever to-night. An expression of resignation and defeat seemed to have settled down on it.

"Why don't you do something, Percy?" she asked. "Just standing there."

He was so jumpy that he started when she spoke to him. But he couldn't admit that he was jumpy. Couldn't admit that there was anything wrong with him. He felt betrayed that his mother had even noticed that there was anything wrong. It was as though she weren't on his side after all, as though he weren't so safe with her as he'd thought.

"I'm all right, Mum," was all he said.

Mrs. Boon continued to stare across at him. There was something about him that reminded her of him as he had been when he was a little boy. She never saw him as his real age. He was fixed in her mind, photographed as it were, somewhere round about the age of seven or eight—rather as a delicate little boy, tall for his years, in a jersey and blue corduroy trousers. He'd had these silly, difficult fits even then.

"Why don't you go out for a walk?"

"Don't wanna walk."

"You used to like it all right," Mrs. Boon went on. "You weren't never in."

She was no longer looking at him. Her eyes were down on her mending again.

Percy turned on her.

"Oh, shut up, Mum, can't you?" he said. "First you nag at me because I'm always out. And now you're nagging at me because I stop in."

"Oh, Percy."

There were tears in Mrs. Boon's eyes as she spoke. She couldn't help it. It was silly minding about Percy like that. But he was all she had. She couldn't bear it when he was cross with her.

But Percy had turned his back on her again. He was looking down the street once more.

"There isn't anything worrying you, is there?" she asked.

Percy shook his head.

"I'm all right," he said.

Then Mrs. Boon screwed up her courage. She had to do so: she and Percy never discussed his private affairs together.

"Not a girl or anything, is it, Percy?"

She was sorry as soon as she had said it, because she was afraid that it would make him angry. But she hadn't anticipated that it would make him as angry as all this.

He rounded on her.

"Wotta you going on at me for?" he demanded. "I asked you to shut up, didn't I?"

Before Mrs. Boon could answer he had crossed the room and gone over to the door. He stood there for a moment, his hand resting on the handle.

And as Mrs. Boon looked at him she noticed again how ill and pallid he seemed. There were dark circles under his eyes. Too much smoking. That was it. Or not sleeping. She'd heard him tossing about at night lately.

"All right," he said abruptly. "I'll go out if you don't want me here."

It was about eight o'clock when he pulled the front door shut behind him. And he went straight down the steps even though he hadn't yet decided where to go. He was feeling anxiously in his pockets for his cigarettes.

"Perhaps I'll feel better if I get a walk," he told himself. "Get a walk and have a drink. Go to the pictures if it wasn't so late. Go to the pictures if they'd got anything decent on." He looked at his watch—the rolled gold wrist-watch that Mrs. Boon had given him—and then pulled his cuff down again. "Reckon I'll just go for a walk," he decided. "Just go round the streets and try to walk it off. Perhaps I'll feel better if I get a walk."

He'd turned automatically in the direction of Dove Street. But on the way he stopped suddenly. Stopped suddenly and drew himself up flat against the railings so that he shouldn't be noticed.

And all because he'd looked ahead of him and seen two men in sports coats and flannel trousers standing at the street corner in front.

He stood there without moving long enough to see the two men saunter slowly off towards the Oval. It looked O.K. But how was he to know that they hadn't spotted him before he noticed what was happening? How was he to know that? And it couldn't just be a coincidence. He was always seeing men in sports coats and flannels nowadays, men in proper plain-clothes uniform, standing about where they could see him. There'd been a man that he hadn't liked the look of, standing outside the garage for nearly an hour this morning. And two nights ago someone had followed him home. He was sure of that. He'd noticed him right up by Kennington Park Road, and he'd still been behind him by the time Percy had turned into No. 10. That man, whoever he was, knew where Percy lived all right.

So he turned round and walked off quickly in the opposite direction. If those two narks thought they were going to pounce on him as he came round the corner they were in for a big disappointment. He'd like to see their faces.

Then as he walked on—"I mustn't look back over my shoulder. That'd give them something on me," he told himself—he realised how foolish it all was. There weren't any men waiting for *him* at the corner. *He* wasn't being followed. It was just nerves that made him imagine them. Why should anyone be following him? He was just Percy Boon, one of the ten million. His little Bit of Trouble was a secret between himself and Percy Boon Esq. And if Percy Boon Esq. didn't feel like talking that was that, wasn't it? And where did they go to from there? Ha! Ha!

Then he remembered the drink that he'd been going to have. Perhaps it was what he needed, perhaps it would do him good. Other people had drinks and felt better for them. But what was beer anyway? It hadn't got any kick in it. What he wanted was something hard. Large gin and a baby tonic, or a double Haig and soda. Something with fireworks.

Over on the opposite corner stood the Clachan. Percy crossed over and went into it. Almost as soon as he went inside he knew that he'd done the right thing. The saloon-bar was full of noise, cheerful noise. There was a loudspeaker up on a shelf among the bottles, and a shiny cascade of hot dance music was bubbling out of it. Over in the corner a couple of pin-tables were pinging and clattering, and all round the bar there was a huddle of drinkers talking about happy things like dog-racing and a Big Fight, and themselves.

"I done the right thing coming here," he repeated to himself. "Better'n outside. I done the right thing."

But had he? he wondered almost immediately. There was one big difference between him and all the others. He wasn't really one of them. They were all in groups of twos and threes. And he was alone. He was the only person alone in all that bar.

"I oughter brought someone along with me," he told himself. "I oughta brought someone along to talk to. No fun in drinking by yourself. Not even whisky. I oughta brought someone along with me."

He was so lonely he didn't even want to drink. Usually whisky was reliable: it made you feel different while it was still going down. But to-night it didn't. It just reminded him of things.

"It's Doris I want," he told himself. "Little Doris here beside me. My little darling with her arm through mine. I'd do anything for Doris. Only got to ask for it and it's hers. I'd buy her a Bronx or a Passion Fruit Nectar or a Pimms No. 1. Or soft, if she'd rather. She knows that. She knows I'd give her the moon if she cried for it. I wouldn't mind what it cost if she asked for it. It's Doris I want."

Then an appalling thing happened. Because he was so lonely and because Doris was over at Hampstead in that flat of hers, he began thinking about the Blonde. For a moment his mind was divided right down the middle. Cut clean into two parts. And one half didn't know what the other half was up to.

"Why shouldn't I go along and see her?" he asked himself. "She likes me. She'd be there waiting. Why shouldn't I go?"

Then there was a click and the two halves came together again. He realised what he'd done. He'd been planning a date with a dead girl. . . .

That shook him. Shook him badly. Made him lose confidence, in fact.

"Going balmy, that's me," he told himself. "Going balmy."

But he was all right now. He could afford to laugh—but not much—at his mistake. And that wasn't because of the whisky, either. It was because a real good idea, a proper brainwave, had just come to him. *Why shouldn't he do what he really wanted? Why shouldn't he go and see Doris? There wasn't any law against it, was there? Why shouldn't he?*

All the same, it needed a bit of face to do it. Because Doris didn't know how he felt about her. Or did she? Women were supposed to know when men Felt That Way. It was some sixth sense or something. And he'd *got* to see her. Got to. He'd go mad if he didn't.

He glanced at his watch. Eight-thirty. That was all right. If he went now he'd be up in Hampstead by nine. And in his excitement he could picture it all happening. He'd rung the bell—rather a posh sort of front door bell in a big block of mansion flats—and Doris herself was there to let him in. "Why, Percy! This *is* a surprise. Come in. . . ."

Quickening his pace, he set off.

It took a long time on the bus. Longer than he had reckoned. And the funny thing was that the excitement suddenly wore off. It just evaporated. At one moment the bus was toiling along past the Black Cat factory in the Hampstead Road and there he was in a front seat all sticky and eager, thinking: "I'll be seeing you, my little darling. We'll be together again. You'll be mine for keeps one day. I'll be seeing you, my little darling." And, at the next, he was wondering why he'd come. Just like that. Perhaps it had been the whisky after all.

But he wasn't going back now. Not after he'd come all that way. It wouldn't make sense. In any case, he liked it over this side of London. There wasn't anyone who knew him there. It was *safer*. If it hadn't been for his old mum he'd have taken a room over at Camden Town and made a fresh start.

He was still thinking about that when he found that he wasn't going right. The bus had turned off suddenly and he was actually being taken away from Chalk Farm Station. As soon as the conductor told him what was happening he did one of his flying get-offs and started to walk back. And it was a long way. Chalk Farm itself was far enough, but the Adelaide Road only started there. There was miles of it. And it wasn't quite so good-class as he'd expected. O.K., but not Ritzy.

And the flat itself wasn't in the least what he'd imagined it. Even after he'd reached the house, he couldn't be sure. Twice he got to the bottom of the flight of iron stairs and each time he went back round to the front to see if it really was the right address. Then on the third attempt he plucked up his courage and began to mount in the direction of the little sign that said "STUDIO." His heart was hammering again by now.

Because they weren't expecting him he had to ring twice before anyone answered. Then the light came on and the door was opened to him. It was full in his face, the light, and for a moment he couldn't be sure who was standing there. Then he saw it was Doreen.

"Hallo," he said awkwardly.

Doreen stared.

"Who is it?" she asked.

"Don' 'spect you remember me," he explained. "Met you over at my place when you came to see Doris."

"Oh, it's Doris you want, is it?" Doreen asked.

Very cool. No invitation in her voice.

"Thasright," Percy told her, smiling politely.

It wasn't easy. He was having to be pleasant for both of them.

"As a matter of fact, you're unlucky," Doreen said, still in the same off-hand manner. "She's out."

Percy paused. He hadn't allowed for this one. For the moment Doreen had floored him.

But only for the moment.

" 'Specting her back—soon?" he asked.

"Y-e-s," Doreen answered, doubtfully. "She shouldn't be long. Would you . . . would you like to come in and wait?"

"Thanks," said Percy. "Don' min' if I do."

As he said it, he was aware that she was pouting at him. She was cross about something. But she couldn't go back on her word. She'd invited him, hadn't she?

And then as soon as he got inside he understood everything. She'd got a man there. Percy saw his hat and gloves—canary yellow ones—on the table by the door. He'd broken in on something. And as soon as he saw the way the cushions were on the couch, he knew what.

The man was Mr. Perkiss. He rose as soon as Percy entered and stood there waiting to be introduced. He was a pale, rather seedy-looking little man with thin silver-grey hair very neatly brushed and a thin summer suit, also very neatly brushed, of the same colour as his hair.

"Oh, Monty," Doreen said. "This is Mr. . . . What is your other name?"

"Boon."

"Mr. Boon. He's a friend of Doris's."

"Any friend of Doris's is a friend of . . ." Mr. Perkiss began. But he was interrupted.

"Hot en it?" Percy remarked, fumbling with his cigarette case.

"It's June, you know," Mr. Perkiss told him. "Flaming June, remember."

"Smoke?"

He had offered Doreen a cigarette before he noticed that she was already smoking. She'd got that holder of hers. He turned to Mr. Perkiss.

"No, no," Mr. Perkiss told him hurriedly. "You're *our* visitor. Have one of these. They're Turkish."

Percy took one and then wished he hadn't. It would have looked more independent, more man of the world, to have had one of his own. Or would that have been bad manners? He didn't know.

"Nice little place you got here," Percy observed.

"Delightful! Delightful," Mr. Perkiss answered. "Such character."

That was where Percy stopped. He didn't know what Mr. Perkiss was talking about. There was a long difficult pause. It was Doreen who broke it.

"You're something to do with cars, aren't you?" she asked, when the silence couldn't go on any longer. She felt like screaming already.

"Thasright," Percy replied again.

"Not . . . not a racing motorist?" Mr. Perkiss enquired. "I have always had such an admiration . . ." But again he was interrupted.

"I'm in the garage business," Percy told him.

"Garages!" Mr. Perkiss repeated. "Then you're one of those wonderful men who know all about the *insides* of cars?"

Wonderful men! Was he getting at him? Percy wondered. Or was that the way he always talked? He couldn't make it out.

"I know a bit," he answered.

There was another silence. Percy couldn't think of anything to say. The silence seemed as though it would go on for ever.

"I had my car stolen once," Mr. Perkiss said at last.

Percy whistled.

"Lot of it about," he remarked. "What was it?"

"A Hillman Minx," Mr. Perkiss told him. "A blue one."

Percy nodded his head knowingly.

"They're easy," he said.

As soon as he had said it, he wished he hadn't. He'd be giving himself away if he wasn't careful. And the worst happened. Mr. Perkiss became very interested at once. Then Doreen sat up and opened her eyes.

"Do you *know* about stolen cars?" Mr. Perkiss asked. "How exciting! I've always wondered how they manage about the number plates. I find criminology so fascinating."

"I don't know anything. Not personally," Percy answered.

There was silence again. And to his irritation, he realised that he was blushing.

It was during the silence that Doris came in, with Bill's arm round her shoulders.

It was after eleven when he got back to Dulcimer Street. He hadn't wasted any more of his time up at that flat. As soon as he saw how things were he had walked out on them.

"Second time I've been made a sucker of because of Doris," he told himself ruefully. "So that's why she wanted to leave home, was it? Second time I've been made a sucker of."

As he turned in at the gate he met the Jossers' lodger coming down the front steps. They hadn't met face to face before. As things were, with Percy out at the garage all day and the lodger on the night shift at the power station, it was pure accident that they should have met now.

" 'Evening," said the lodger.

" 'Evening," Percy answered.

And then as he went on up the steps it suddenly occurred to him that he had seen the lodger before somewhere. He turned and looked over his shoulder.

What he saw was a plump, heavily built young man wearing a sports jacket and a pair of flannels.

CHAPTER 23

Mr. Puddy was on guard. Theoretically on guard, that is, not actually. He wasn't standing at the foot of the stairs with a drawn cutlass, or anything like that. He was, as a matter of fact, sitting beside a gas ring waiting for his kettle to boil. But he was there on the spot in case he was wanted: that was the point. He had just completed his midnight tour of the premises of the company, and he had popped into his little cubby-hole in the basement to snatch a bite of something before going off on his rounds again. While he was waiting, he was glancing through yesterday's paper.

And what he saw had upset him. There was too much happening for his taste. Reading the papers nowadays you might think that journalists were in charge of things instead of simply writing about them. There was a fresh surprise every morning. Missions were going and coming all the time. Pacts were being signed and repudiated. And to show that Mr. Chamberlain had really meant what he had said about compulsory military training the first batch of conscripts who had registered at the beginning of June were being called up to-day. There was a picture of one of them receiving his papers. He didn't look much older than a schoolboy.

"Caddod fodder," Mr. Puddy said to himself, shaking his head sadly. "So buch caddod fodder."

He was glad for his own sake that he was fifty-six. It wasn't likely that they'd reach the fifty-sixes. They wouldn't want men of his age in the trenches. Besides, they were doing away with trenches this time. If there was going to be a war it would all be fought in the air. The papers said so. And he couldn't fly. He was safe enough: this was going to be a young man's war. The papers said that also. But supposing they should try to rope him in, he'd got an answer for them. His feet. It was his feet that had saved him last time. Even an Army doctor could tell that they were impossible. With feet like this marching was out of the question. If any general in the British Army had wanted to start up something in a new sector he'd have had to send a car for Private Puddy.

But getting killed in the trenches wasn't the only thing that could happen to a man in wartime. Particularly in World War II. Civilians weren't going to be any safer than soldiers this time. Take air raids: before he was through with it his own little cubby-hole might have to be turned into a shelter. Or poison gas on all the big cities. Or germ warfare. Or invasion. . . .

The kettle boiled up suddenly and put the gas out, and Mr. Puddy made his tea. He was still depressed and apprehensive. And as he stirred he thought.

"Blogade," he reflected. "That's adother danger. Hundreds of subbarines blogading everything. Dothing cubbing id. Just whad's left in the shobs."

The thought was so awful that he put his cup down and sat staring straight in front of him. This peril—and it was the likeliest of the lot—was the one that haunted him most. From the way things were going, he might before next Christmas be *slowly starving to death*. He went clammy at the thought.

And all through the night the terror preyed on him. It came to him in a dozen different forms. He remembered stories of shipwrecked sailors, just skin and bone by the time they were rescued:

of elderly neglected invalids discovered by welfare officers; of natives in famine areas; of sentences of slow death in the Middle Ages.

When morning came he was down in his cubby-hole again. Only this time, he was writing. On the back of a post card he was jotting down a list. It read:

6 tins condensed milk.
8 lb. sugar.
3 packets Quaker Oats.
2 marmalade.
2 jam.
2 Bovril.
6 tins salmon.
2 pineapple.
2 peaches.
3 lb. rice.
1 tongue (Lazenby).

After the last entry he drew a line and started off in a different category. He wrote:

2 pr. pyjamas.
2 pr. thick socks.
2 wool combs.
1 pr. gloves.
1 blanket.

Next to starving, being cold—really cold, the freezing-to-death stuff—had always seemed to Mr. Puddy one of the most terrible ends that could happen to any man.

CHAPTER 24

I

Mr. Josser had been in bed all this time. Ever since his soaking he had been up and down. Better one day and worse the next. And this evening Mrs. Josser didn't like the look of him at all. He had a pain in his side every time he breathed and his temperature was mounting again.

Taken altogether it had been the most trying three weeks that she could remember, with Mr. Josser more peevish than she had ever known him. And then, on top of everything, the regular panel doctor had to choose this of all times to go off on holiday, and Mr.

Josser refused point-blank to see his *locum tenens*. Not that Mrs. Josser blamed him. The *locum tenens* was a woman.

At about nine-thirty, when Mr. Josser was breathing nineteen to the dozen and groaning with every lungful, Mrs. Josser could stand the strain alone no longer. She arranged with Mrs. Boon to sit with the invalid while she slipped outside for a moment, and she phoned up Doris. It was the first telephone call from her family that Doris had received.

"But, my sweet, you can't think of going now," Doreen said when she told her. "Not with all those sandwiches to eat. You simply can't. And you know how alarming everything always sounds over the phone. It's probably nothing really."

She was speaking at the top of her voice because she was excited. But she was also annoyed. The first time they'd ever had anyone to the flat something like this would happen to Doris. At the present moment there were eight cheerful young men in the room—which in itself was something of a scoop with so much competition about—and when the phone started ringing, she had thought it was going to be the ninth explaining why he wasn't there already. In fact, she'd gone over to the instrument expecting Mr. Perkiss and had found Mrs. Josser instead.

"I think I ought to go," Doris said quietly.

Doreen leant over and grabbed Bill by the arm. She had to do something to attract his attention. He'd been taking no notice of her all the evening.

"Tell her it isn't anything to worry about," she said. "Tell her she's just getting panicky."

Bill thought for a moment.

"Shouldn't think it's serious," he replied at last. "But it might be. You can't tell without seeing him." He paused and looked across at Doris. "She'd better go if she wants to. There's no harm in finding out."

Doreen dropped Bill's arm again.

"I think it's monstrous," she said, "trailing across London at this time of night, simply because someone phones."

She was speaking louder than ever now. Her colour was higher, too. And she seemed in danger of bursting into tears at any moment. Then somebody behind her—it was Clifford, the one who could do Hitler, and was such a perfect scream with his imitations—put his arm round her waist and pulled her back down on to the settee beside him.

"You still have *me*," he said in his Boyer voice. "Take life by the throat, little girl. Don't be afraid of love."

Doris had gone out of the room by now. Simply walked through into the bedroom and left them there. And a moment later she came back. She had got her handbag under her arm.

"Please don't anybody move," she said. "I'm terribly sorry breaking up everything like this."

She'd gone half-way to the door. Then suddenly Doreen jumped up and flung her arms round her neck.

"I've been a pig," she said. "An absolute pig. Of course you've got to go if you're worried. We all understand."

But she'd spoken a moment too soon. For Bill had got up too and was standing staring at Doris again.

"I'll come with you," he said.

It was touch-and-go for a moment. But Doreen realised that she mustn't lose her temper in front of all those people. So she gave a little laugh instead.

"Now I understand," she said. "It's just a blind for you two to get off together."

"No, it isn't," said Bill. "I only just thought of it."

But Doris was already in the tiny hall, opening the yellow front door.

On the way down together they met Mr. Perkiss toiling up the iron staircase. He was carrying a bottle of Scotch and a bunch of dark red roses. His patent leather shoes twinkled. But he was obviously out of condition. By the time he reached them, his mouth was hanging wide open.

As soon as he saw Doris, however, he drew himself up and tried to look like a youngster who had just come bounding up the whole flight.

"My dea-ah young lady," he said. "Not going? Not leaving your own party?"

"Her father's ill," Bill told him. "She's just going over to see him."

"And a very charming visitor for a sick man to have," Mr. Perkiss replied. "I only hope that if I should ever be ill . . ."

"Good night," said Bill, who didn't like Mr. Perkiss.

"I feel awful dragging you away like this."

It was the dozenth time that she had said it since they had left the flat. And Bill made his usual answer.

"My idea entirely," he said. "Just thought I'd like the ride."

They were nearly there at last. The sun had gone out of the sky by now and was setting amid the smoke of Hammersmith. The whole western quarter of London seemed to be ablaze, and the windows of Whitehall glittered back at it. Ahead of them, Westminster had caught the glare and was shining. Then when they came to the bridge they saw the river on fire; a great flaming tide flowing seawards under their feet. The walls of the Embankment had turned from grey to pink and were smouldering, and little burning wisps carried high into the air sparkled from the tops of railings and lamp-posts. St. Paul's itself carried a lighted faggot shaped like a cross on its summit.

Bill surveyed the scene for a moment in silence.

"Going to be a fine day to-morrow," he said.

There was a pause.

"You'd better get a bus back from the Oval," Doris suggested.

"We're not there yet," Bill answered.

There was something obstinately faithful about him. It was a following, dog-like quality. He was clearly determined not to allow Doris out of his sight if he could help it.

In consequence, there was quite a scene outside the Roebuck when the bus put them down there. Doris wanted Bill to go back, and Bill wanted to come on.

"Can't drag a chap all this way and then send him home again," he kept saying. " 'Tisn't good enough."

The trouble was that Doris couldn't explain why she didn't want him. There were two reasons. In the first place, she was worried about her father. And secondly, she was worried about her mother. She had planned to take Bill over sometime, and she didn't want him dropping in unannounced like this when everything was bound to be a bit upset anyhow. She hadn't forgotten that awful evening when Doreen had paid her first visit to Dulcimer Street.

Dulcimer Street itself looked unusually drab and shabby when they got there. Now that the commotion of the sunset was over and done with, the whole of London was glowing no longer. It was grey. And south of the river greyness seemed thicker and more opaque. There was none of the pearly greyness of early morning about it. It was a flat, dirty grey that seemed compounded of equal degrees of soot, nightfall and the littleness of man's ambition. After the clear air of Primrose Hill it was too abrupt, this descent into the gathering darkness of the London jungle.

They had reached the house by now. And Doris suddenly repented. She held out her hand to him.

"It was ever so sweet of you to come with me," she said. "It was really. I'm sorry I was so cross."

"Hadn't I better come in and see if I can do anything?" Bill enquired hopefully. "Bit of medical advice and all that."

Doris shook her head.

"Some other time," she said. "Not now. Mother's sure to be worried."

Bill remained there silent for a moment. The faithful dog-like expression was more noticeable than ever. Then something crossed his mind. He gave a little grin—a mere tremor of the tail as it were—and thrust his hands into his pockets.

"Tell you what," he said. "I'll wait outside. Just in case I'm needed. You may want something from the chemist's. I'll give you a quarter of an hour and then if you haven't sent for me, I'll go home."

"Good night, Bill," she said to him.

"Good night, Doris."

"He's asleep at the moment," Mrs. Josser was saying. "Just dropped off before you got here."

"But how is he?" Doris asked.

Mrs. Josser drew in her breath.

"Not himself," she answered. "He doesn't complain much because he isn't that sort. But he's not himself. You can see for yourself he isn't."

Just as they reached the bedroom door, Mrs. Josser laid her hand on Doris's arm.

"Try and get him to see a doctor," she said. "I've been on at him all day. He may take more notice of you."

Mr. Josser was awake again by the time Doris got to the bedroom. He was propped up by so many pillows that he seemed to be almost leaning forwards. And there was something anxious and staring—frightened even—about him. His eyes were scared. And across his forehead the beads of perspiration were standing out.

"Doris," he said faintly. "What are you doing here?"

"How are you, Dad?" she asked, trying to keep her voice level and casual-sounding.

She went over to the bed and bent down. His face felt rough and burning as she kissed him. And, as Mr. Josser raised his lips to hers, she was aware of something oddly disturbing about it. His kiss was at once passionate and feeble. It was as though he had been carefully saving up just enough strength for that one kiss and even then had found that it was too much for him. The kiss died away before i could come to anything.

Then Mr. Josser smiled. The odd frightened look disappeared fo a moment from his face, and then returned.

"Just my old chest playing me up again," he said. "Just something wrong with the bellows."

Because he felt that it was expected of him in front of Mrs. Josser, he attempted a little laugh as well as the smile. But it was a mistake. It made him cough. And it was a violently painful cough. He helc his hand to his side as though he'd been wounded. When he hac recovered, the beads of sweat on his forehead were reinforced with new ones.

"That's the second time this evening," Mrs. Josser reported. "H was like this earlier."

"I . . . I'm all right if I sit up," Mr. Josser assured them. "It' only that it catches me sometimes."

"Hadn't we better get the doctor?" Doris asked him.

Mr. Josser shook his head.

"Not to-night," he said. "Not as late as this. Wait till Dr. . . ."

"But you've got a temperature," Doris told him. "You're eve so hot."

She was fondling his hand as she spoke. It was a dry rasping sor of hand.

"We've had all that out earlier this evening," Mrs. Josser saic grimly. "I tried to take it, but he wouldn't let me."

Mr. Josser looked from one to the other imploringly.

"It's nothing," he explained with a little gasp in between th words. "Just being shut up in this room all day."

As he finished, Doris got up and faced him.

"Well, I think it's something," she said. "You've got to see a doctor and I'm going for him."

Mr. Josser roused himself for a moment and tried to stop her. Bu the pain in his side was too sharp and he had to sit quiet again. H muttered something about a lot of women fussing over him.

Mrs. Josser turned to Doris.

"You go right along," she said. "And don't come back withou one."

2

From behind the long hanging curtain in the front room, Percy stoo staring down through his squint into the roadway below him. He had see it twice already. And as he waited he saw it again. A young man—

heavily built young man—in flannel trousers and a sports coat was patrolling up and down outside the house, going two doors in one direction and then turning and going two doors on in the other. Every time he paused, the street lamp outside lit him up like an actor on a stage.

"That's Them," he said helplessly. "They're watching me. They're playing cat-and-mouse. That's what They're doing. Cat-and-mouse. They know it's me and They're waiting. There'll be someone there all night just to make sure of me. And when They're ready They'll pounce. That's Them. They're watching me."

3

Bill was still there when Doris got back down to the street again. He had the manner of someone who was prepared, if necessary, to stop until morning. Even so, he didn't seem surprised when Doris came up to him.

"Want some throat lozenges?" he asked cheerfully.

But Doris wasn't a bit cheerful.

"Oh, Bill," she said. "I'm worried. I've got to get a doctor. Quick."

"Me come too," Bill said, and fell into step alongside her. "What's gone wrong?" he asked.

"I . . . I don't know," Doris answered. "I think it's pneumonia or something."

"Who's your doctor?" Bill asked.

"Oh, he's away or something," Doris told him. "I'm just going to get the first one I can find."

"What about me?" Bill suggested.

"But you're not qualified."

"I'm as good as."

Doris paused.

"Would you know what to do?" she asked.

"Can't tell unless I see him," he said. "Better let me have a look."

He took hold of Doris's arm as she spoke, and steered her back round in the direction of the house.

"Nothing to worry about in pneumonia nowadays," he assured her. "M. and B.'ll fix him."

Bill took a bit of explaining to Mrs. Josser when they got back. He didn't look in the least like any doctor she had ever seen. The whole thing seemed like a put-up job to her. And she remained suspicious and unconvinced. But as Doris had brought him straight into the bedroom there wasn't much that she could do about it.

What was more, Bill had taken matters into his own hands. He was over by the bed talking to Mr. Josser. The two of them seemed to have developed a rapid and intimate friendship. They were whispering together and Bill was doing something to the top button of Mr. Josser's pyjama jacket. This only made things worse in Mrs. Josser's eyes. She had always regretted her husband's readiness to make friends with anyone. First of all Percy. And now this strange young man with the baggy flannel trousers and the extraordinary tie.

When Bill had lifted Mr. Josser's pink-and-white pyjamas, he got round behind him and pressed his ear against his back. As he did so Doris noticed how thin her father was. His backbone made a hard knobbly ridge with the hot skin stretched over it.

"Just take a breath as far as it will go," Bill was saying. "Don't strain at it."

Mr. Josser drew in his breath and winced as he did so.

"Ah," Bill said approvingly as though the pain had been his own idea. "Do it again."

Mr. Josser sucked in the air again—his mouth was hanging open slightly all the time from the strain of breathing—and again he winced before his lungs were half full.

"That'll do for now," Bill said.

But he hadn't finished. Laying his hand on Mr. Josser's back, he began percussing him. There was an intent, absorbed look on his face that Doris had not seen before. He seemed for the moment someone apart from the rest of them, someone remote and vastly important. When he had done, he tucked in Mr. Josser's pyjamas carefully all round as if he were arranging a baby, and wiped his hands which were sticky. Then he stepped back.

"Just you sit up and enjoy yourself," he said, "and I'll tell you what's the matter with you."

"Is it . . . is it bad?" Mrs. Josser asked.

She caught Mr. Josser's eye as she said it and then looked away again as if ashamed of herself for asking.

"Not if we do something about it," Bill told her. "You've got a touch of pleurisy. That's all it is. You'd better let me do a paracentesis. . . ."

"What's that?" Mr. Josser demanded.

"Just tap the left lung and let the fluid out. That's what's causing the pain."

But it was not so easy as all that. Mrs. Josser came over to Bill and stood in front of him.

"Are you qualified, young man?" she asked.

Bill paused, and hoped that Doris wasn't going to say anything.

"Yes," he answered.

"Hm."

Mrs. Josser was obviously still dubious. But she didn't say anything. Instead, she went across to the bed and began stroking Mr. Josser's forehead.

"Don't worry, Fred," she told him. "You'll be all right."

There was something protective in her attitude, as though she were defending him from any rash assault that Doris's young man might attempt upon him.

And Bill took advantage of it.

"That's right," he said. "Keep the patient comfortable while I go and collect my bag. Back again inside half an hour. Not too much excitement, mind."

Outside the door, Doris caught hold of Bill's arm.

"Oh, Bill, are you sure you can do it?" she asked. "Are you certain that he'll be all right?"

And because it was dark on the landing and because she was close to him, he kissed her. It was a rapid, clumsy sort of kiss. A kiss hastily inserted into the momentous business of the evening.

She followed him downstairs without speaking.

"Don't get run over, Bill," she told him.

In the end, he was away for nearly an hour. First he tried a friend at St. Thomas's which was near. But the friend was away somewhere. Then he tried the Westminster where he vaguely knew the house-surgeon. But the house-surgeon was unimpressed by the whole proposal. He recommended calling in another doctor and rang off. So there was nothing for it but to go right over to Charing Cross where he belonged. And there was a night sister there who gave him what he needed. She was a calm, sensible sort of woman.

"And if anything goes wrong, don't forget that you came in and took the things when my back was turned," she said. "I don't want to go losing my job because of you."

Bill smiled at her.

"Sister," he said. "I'll make you matron one day. And now have you got an attaché case or something? I can't walk about London looking like an emergency."

He blewed two shillings on a cab on the way back, and Doris was waiting for him down in the street when he got there.

"Oh, Bill," she said. "Do hurry. He looks so awful."

When Bill had got on his long white coat Mrs. Josser seemed more ready to believe in him. But by now Bill had ceased to take any real notice of her. There was that intent, absorbed look on his face again. He asked for a saucepan of water and stood there impatiently while it was brought to him. And then, without asking Mrs. Josser's permission, he lit the gas ring by the fireplace and placed the saucepan on it. Then he unpacked his case, thoughtfully, counting out the contents.

"One hypodermic," he was saying to himself. "One bot. iodine; one packet swabs, one pump, suction; one vacuum jar; one bot. novocaine; one trocar; one pair surgical forceps."

He took up the hypodermic syringe in the forceps—it was noticeable that there was a kind of expert daintiness about him now, quite unlike his usual clumsiness—and lowered it into the saucepan. Then again without asking permission, he went over to the wash-basin and started scrubbing his hands. He looked more professional still as he stood there. And he was certainly more authoritative. He turned to Mrs. Josser.

"You look tired," he said. "Just you go and sit down and leave this to Doris and me."

Mrs. Josser pursed up her lips.

"I'm stopping here," she said.

"In that case perhaps you could give me a couple of clean towels," he asked. "Just to save the sheets, you know."

He went to the bed and stood over Mr. Josser.

"Do you mind sitting round this way a bit?" he asked. "The light's better."

Then he beckoned to Doris.

"Come over here," he said. "I shall want you to hold things."

Mr. Josser tried vainly to protest.

"Leave it . . . to . . . the morning," he began. "I . . . don't . . . want . . . Doris . . . to . . . have . . . to . . ."

"Quiet, please," Bill told him. "This won't hurt. It's only iodine."

He felt Mr. Josser's back like a masseur and, just below the point of the shoulder-blade where the thin back fell in again, he painted a little medallion with the iodine. It stood out startlingly bright on the pale flesh, like dark blood. Doris wondered suddenly if she were going to faint.

Then Bill returned with the hypodermic syringe, and filled it from the little bottle.

"This'll be just a prick," he said. "You'll hardly feel it." And pinching up the skin between his thumb and forefinger he thrust in the needle.

"Didn't hurt, did it?" Bill asked.

Mr. Josser shook his head gratefully.

"And the rest's easy," Bill went on.

He took up the forceps again and went over to the saucepan where the other, the aspirating, syringe was being boiled. This syringe was an altogether bigger and more formidable affair than the first one. It had a needle like a dagger. It seemed impossible that Mr. Josser could endure having it thrust into him.

Bill caught Doris's eye.

"Can't hurt," he said, understandingly. "I've given him a shot of something."

He prodded the dark medallion with the point of the needle and waited for Mr. Josser to complain. Mr. Josser, however, continued to sit there, staring in the direction of the fireplace, unnoticing.

Then, spreading out the skin between the first two fingers of his left hand, Bill thrust the needle right home. There was something brutally deliberate about the whole performance. A severe professionalism had set in and it was obvious that the idea of sensitive protesting flesh didn't concern him in the least. All that he had in mind was the needle, and the way he wanted it to go. This time there was nothing in the syringe when the little circle of brown skin was punctured. But as Bill drew back the plunger, the small glass cylinder became filled with a straw-coloured fluid. It was as though the tip of the hollow needle had somehow landed into a pot of freshly brewed weak tea.

Bill said, "Ah."

It was, as remarks go, thoroughly unrevealing and non-committal. But at the same time it was involuntary. It confirmed what for the past hour Bill had been doubting—that there was any fluid there at all. He now felt himself a wizard among diagnosticians, and he got ready for the next part of the operation.

First of all he removed the syringe altogether. Then he crossed over again to his conjurer's table and came back with a large jam-jar-looking thing fitted with taps and with a length of rubber tubing attached to one of them, and a still larger syringe. And there was more to it than that. He had a small suction pump in his hand as well. It was a chunky, solid piece of work that might have belonged to a garage or a workshop. Bill gave one or two vague sucks at the air with it to satisfy himself that the instrument was working properly and then attached it to the spare tap on the jam-jar and began to pump out the air. He gave twelve strokes and the thing was ready. There was now forty pounds' pressure in the jar, and it was going to be applied to the inside of Mr. Josser's lungs.

"Can you pass me the jar?" he asked Doris.

He reached out his hand without even looking at her. And Doris passed the suction jar without looking at Mr. Josser's back. She felt sick. Very sick. And she had seen enough. She was dimly aware that Bill was connecting a dangling piece of tubing to the tap on the jar. The piece of tubing was connected to her father. Then Bill turned the other tap ever so little and more of the same straw-coloured fluid came splashing into the jar. The level in the jar surged up, leaving a little scum of froth on the sides. Bill adjusted the tap and the rush dwindled to a trickle.

Doris glanced across at Bill. He had eased his bent back a little and was resting the jar on a folded-up pillow.

"This is where we take it easy," he said. "This takes some time." He put his spare hand on Mr. Josser's shoulder. "You'll feel better almost any minute now."

Then he looked round at Doris.

"Take her into the other room," he said to Mrs. Josser, "and tell her to sit with her head between her legs for a bit. Then she'll feel better, too."

It was two-thirty in the morning now, and Bill was sitting propped up in one of the two armchairs in the Jossers' front room with his feet up on the other one. He had Doris's coat across his knees. And not because he was cold but for quite another reason he pulled it up to his chin and rubbed his cheek against it.

"Three pints of fluid . . . no cardiac collapse . . . patient breathing comfortably . . . and I shall see Doris at breakfast," he was telling himself sleepily.

CHAPTER 25

I

CONNIE HAD just had the thrill of her life. And all of it through the crack in her bedroom door which had just happened to be ajar at the right moment.

She liked having her door a bit open because it kept her in touch with what was going on in the house. Even if she herself were less private, there were recompenses. Like this afternoon, for instance. She'd heard one of the doors on the floor below open and shut itself and she'd thought that it was Mrs. Josser pottering about at something. But as soon as she listened to the footsteps, she knew that they weren't Mrs. Josser's. They weren't even a woman's. So they must belong, she realised, to Mr. Todds, the dull hard-working young man who was on night shift at the power station. There was no rule so far as she knew why he shouldn't move about in his own house if he wanted to, but a sixth sense, a kind of supernatural hunch, told her that there was something unusual going on. And when she heard the footsteps *ascend* the stairs instead of going down them she felt sure that she was on to something. Very neatly she hid herself behind the curtain.

The footsteps—was she only imagining it, or did they really sound muffled?—came on up the stairs and paused for a moment outside the door. Actually paused there, as though Mr. Todds was going to pay her a visit. But he didn't come in. He just stood there, and Connie could almost *hear* him doing nothing. She remained quite still where she was, behind the thick curtain with the red plush pile hanging in folds all round her. Then she heard her name called. And it was called twice, quite distinctly. "Miss Coke. Are you there, Miss Coke? Is anyone about?" But it was called so softly that she knew that she wasn't meant to answer. Knew that nobody was meant to answer. And, in any case, she couldn't very well come out now. She didn't want Mr. Nobby Nightshift, whatever he was up to, imagining she spent her time playing peep-bo with herself behind the curtain.

And it was just as she had expected. When she didn't answer, he went on. It was perfectly plain that he'd never had the slightest intention of coming in anyhow. Mrs. Boon's was the door he was really making for. And when he reached it, he knocked quite openly and stood there waiting as if expecting someone to open it for him. But it was a very subdued kind of knock. The kind of knock that you wouldn't hear unless you were actually inside the room—or straining your ears to listen, like Connie.

And that wasn't all. Wasn't even the most important part. The big interest, the real hanky-panky stuff came in now. She heard Mr. Todds knock a second time. And then she heard him open the door and close it again. He was still standing there on the landing, and it was obvious that he'd simply stuck his head in the room to see for himself. After a moment, she heard him move across to the other door, Percy's door. And the same performance went on. He knocked, waited, knocked again, and then looked inside.

Risking everything, Connie stuck her head round the fringe of the curtain and took a peep. She was just in time to see Percy's door closing.

Mr. Todds, sneak-thief, was inside.

As soon as he got into the room, Mr. Todds turned the key in the lock behind him, and got busy. He began straightaway searching through the things in the cupboards, in the hanging-places for clothes behind the bit of cretonne, in the dressing-table. He was very quick and expert about it. But somehow not in the least hurried. He took as long as he wanted to take about everything. When he was examining Percy's clothes, for instance, he first of all ran his eye rapidly along the lot of them like a second-hand wardrobe dealer, then he felt them over to see if there was anything in any of the pockets and, finally, he carried one pair of trousers over to the window to see them by a better light.

It was the same when he came to the dressing-table. He was so cool that he might have been rummaging through other people's drawers all his life. He inspected everything—the jumble of fancy ties, the bottles of hair lotion, the steel-and-spring chest expanders, the packet of art photographs hidden away at the back. And he evidently didn't think anything of any of them. It wasn't until he got down to the second drawer that the quiet Mr. Todds, the borough servant with the good references, came on something that took his fancy. And that was the blue glass lady from the radiator of the hot Bentley. It was love at first sight. He grasped it, handled it lovingly, and held it up to the window so that the light shone through the robes and seemed to kindle them. Then, without pausing for a second to consider whether it was wrong or not—whether it was stealing—he thrust her head downwards into his side pocket, and went on poking about. There was something else in the drawer below that interested him just as much—and that was the pair of silver coach lamps that Percy had removed and kept. Mr. Todds took them up and inspected them. Evidently, like Percy, he had a taste for expensive knick-knacks. But he didn't keep the coach lamps. After he had finished fondling them, he put them back again.

Even after he'd been right through the dressing-table, drawer by drawer, he wasn't satisfied. He went over to Percy's raincoat which hung on a hook all by itself beside the wash-stand, and thrust his hand into the pockets. He found one oddment that made him pause. And that was Percy's cosh. He evidently liked it almost as much as he liked the blue glass lady. Because after one or two tries with it in the empty air just to see how heavy it was, he pinched that too.

Finally with one last quick look round to make sure that he hadn't left anything out of place, he leaned his weight against the door so that the catch would come back quietly—it was obvious that he knew all the tricks—turned the key and stood there listening for a moment. When he didn't hear a sound, he opened the door a crack and listened again. There was still silence. That was good enough. Without more ado, he stepped out, closed the door behind him and went downstairs again.

Smart, eh? Smart nothing. He hadn't even worn gloves. There were fingerprints everywhere for anyone who was looking for them. And—though of course he didn't know it—there was Connie behind the curtain watching him as he came out on to the landing.

She was nearly swooning from the suspense.

When Mr. Todds' own door—the only door that he had any right to open—had closed after him, Connie came out from her hiding-place. She was hugging herself with excitement. To have a sneak-thief under one's own roof was a piece of luck that didn't come to everyone. And to be right on top of him—that was the real fun. And at the beginning, too. It might lead anywhere. Even into the police court, with Connie in the witness-box instead of in the dock, and the beak congratulating her on having caught her man red-handed.

She turned a number of schemes over in her mind and then chose the simplest. She got her handbag and taking out a sixpence—it was lucky that this should have happened in a week when she could spare it—she went over to the light and scratched a cross in the middle of His Majesty's right cheek. Then she laid the sixpence scratch downwards on the mantelpiece and left it there. There was nothing like marked money for trapping smarties.

"You whistle, Dukey boy, if anyone comes for it," she said to the canary.

Not that she really liked leaving her room wide open for Mr. Todds to prowl about in. If he was the sort of easy-fingers who wasn't above pilfering from people like the Boons, how did she know that her own pink satin shoes would be safe? She was in no doubt about what the Boons had in their rooms because she'd taken the liberty of having a little innocent look round once or twice herself, when there had been nothing else to do.

And if Mr. Todds was after that sort of stuff, he'd take anything.

2

And Percy?

He was out at the back, polishing a car, at the time. But his mind wasn't on his job.

"If They come for me," he was thinking, "I'm not stopping here. I'm getting out. I'll go some place. They'll have to start looking if They want to find me. They'll need bloodhounds. And fast cars. They'll have to draw a cordon. And you won't catch me waiting for Them. If They come for me, I'm not stopping here."

He paused for a moment and straightened his back. The car that he was at work on glistened where the wash-leather had been over it. It might just have come out of the showroom. But there was a hell of a lot of it still to be done. The far side still had the spray from the hose congealed all over it. The car was an American; and, like most things American, it seemed a bit larger than life-size.

"Or suppose They come on me sudden," he went on. "Suppose They break in when I'm having supper. Just let Them try to lay hands on me. Just let Them try. They'll find out. They'll learn Their lesson. They'll get Their fingers burnt if They come on me sudden."

The hard edges of the Hedgehog in his pocket were sticking into him as he bent over; and the blunt points—not *so* blunt either—made him feel better, safer. He began polishing again.

"The trouble with me," he resumed, "is I think too much. I'm getting nervy. I'm seeing things. Just let Them try to lay Their hands on me. Just let Them try."

CHAPTER 26

I

THERE WAS no longer any question about it. Uncle Henry was going mad. Always a bit odd and peculiar, he had gone clean over the edge lately. And it wasn't even one of those comparatively simple cases of insanity where it is the little things that count. No, Uncle Henry was going big mad on the big scale. And what was more, he was doing it in public.

The form it took was . . . but to get the full picture of it, it is necessary to go back to early April when Uncle Henry and Mr. Chamberlain started writing to each other. Even that isn't strictly accurate, however. Looked at dispassionately, it was a decidedly one-sided correspondence from the start, with only two formal acknowledgments from the Downing Street end—and then nothing. In fact it was the eventual silence that got Uncle Henry's goat. The exchange, the one-way exchange, became fiery and abusive from then on. And still Mr. Chamberlain kept his temper and held his tongue.

The deterioration of confidence could be traced from the style of the letters, of which Uncle Henry kept copies in a spring-back folder. The first one read almost like an echo of the eighteenth century.

"*My dear Prime Minister,*" it began, "*I hesitate to approach you in person and not through the agency of the gentleman who has been freely elected by the people to represent the constituency in which I reside, but events are grave and time is fleeting. Europe, nay civilisation itself, is at this moment tottering and we look in vain for the props. Sir, you with so many calls upon your time have no doubt to rely upon advisers. It is against these advisers that I write to warn you. They do not advise. They betray. Your own good name is at stake. At the time of Munich . . .*"

Altogether it was what Uncle Henry called a "diplomatic" letter. It was a piece of Machiavellian infiltration. Relying on flattery, it contrived to get the rapier thrusts home between the compliments.

The second letter was shorter and more terse.

"*Dear Mr. Chamberlain,*" this one ran, "*I note that my letter will duly be considered. But what exactly does this mean? While insults are being hurled at our heads by Franco and his Fascist minions, and Germany and Italy is arming to the teeth in readiness for the death stab, has your government done anything about it? No, sir. Your government has done nothing, is doing nothing and apparently never will do anything. . . .*"

Even the signature was different this time. "Yours disgustedly" the missive ended. From then on the gloves were off. Uncle Henry hit hard, and hit often. In one week, Mr. Chamberlain got a letter from Uncle Henry *every morning at breakfast time*. But it was worse still when Uncle Henry switched over to post cards.

There was a double cunning in this. In the first place, a post card

—especially when the message is written in large red ink capitals—cannot escape the eye of the recipient. And secondly, there is always the possibility that it may convert the postman as well. After all, the messages the post cards contained were simple and memorable like—WHERE IS ALBANIA NOW? IS YOUR TIN HAT BOMB-PROOF? WOULD YOU GO TO MUNICH AGAIN? and IS HITLER A GENTLEMAN? One of them, in particular, stuck in Uncle Henry's mind after he had posted it. Not one of his best possibly, it nevertheless continued to excite him. All that it said was: HAVE YOU FORGOTTEN MANCHURIA?

It was the subsequent revelation that everybody had forgotten Manchuria, and the final discovery that half the big stores in Oxford Street were displaying Japanese-made goods, that unbalanced Uncle Henry. He started writing round to the shops, and protesting. But Oxford Street was less accommodating than Downing Street. The big stores simply ignored him. They passed his letters on to their counting-houses, found that he had no account there and that was the end of it. Thereupon Uncle Henry threatened to boycott the whole lot, even though he had never been into any one of them in his life. And finding that this too left them contemptuous and outwardly unshaken, Uncle Henry went over to the attack. It was war. War between Uncle Henry and Oxford Street. He resolved to picket the whole stretch between the Marble Arch at one end and Oxford Circus at the other.

And because there was no time to recruit an army—the only possible conscript that he could think of was Mr. Josser, and he was clearly unequal to it at the moment—Uncle Henry decided to go into battle alone. He constructed himself two large posters covered with such phrases as MADE IN JAPAN MEANS MADE BY MURDER and FANCY GOODS DRENCHED IN BLOOD. The posters, four feet by two feet six inches, were pasted on two large pieces of cardboard that had originally been lime-juice advertisements, and Uncle Henry rigged up a kind of harness out of an old pair of braces. Then, armed like a sandwichman, he started off on his lonely patrol, wheeling his green bicycle beside him. At one time he had thought of cycling with the posters. But it was no use. The harness kept on getting tangled with the handle-bars.

Even walking, it wasn't much of a success. Part of the trouble was that by the time Uncle Henry had shut up his greengrocery establishment for the night, Oxford Street had shut up too. If any pro-Japanese shopper had wanted to buy a shilling tin tray for sixpence he couldn't have done so until nine o'clock next morning. And

Uncle Henry was simply picketing a lot of drawn blinds. But the real trouble was that he didn't cause half the sensation that he'd expected. Evening strollers simply took one look at him and then went on. It wasn't until he had stood in the entrance to Bond Street Tube, distributing small handbills entitled MERCHANTS OF DEATH, and a policeman had told him to move on because he was causing an obstruction, that Uncle Henry felt that he was even beginning to get anywhere. But even that wasn't what he had really wanted. He didn't want to cause obstructions: he wanted to create disturbances. Bricks through plate-glass windows, fancy ash-trays and cheap celluloid toys trampled to bits on the pavement by an enraged democracy—that was the kind of thing Uncle Henry was after. And he was still as far away from it as ever.

He had been on patrol for the better part of a week now, and he was growing sick of it. What particularly discouraged him was to find that this evening he was in competition with a larger and better organised attack on the public conscience. The Salvation Army, emerging from their advanced headquarters on the south side of Oxford Street, were filling the air with an uproar of religious martial music, and Uncle Henry was nowhere. Even the posters and banners of the rival force were larger and more striking. THE WAGES OF SIN IS DEATH, they proclaimed loudly, and some of them were held aloft on velvet-covered poles and had yellow silk tassels dangling beneath them.

"Time to pack up," said Uncle Henry crossly as the big drum suddenly started up again close beside him. "Might as well go over and see how they're getting on in Dulcimer Street."

2

Bill and Doris were at Mr. Josser's bedside. But it was a very different sort of party from the midnight one, the pleurisy party. Mr. Josser was sitting up in bed now. He'd shaved and, except for the fact that his hair was a bit long, he hardly looked an invalid at all. The only thing that gave him away—and that might have been simply his age—was the puckered chicken throat, seen through the open neck of his pyjamas.

"It's a funny thing," he was saying. "I feel all right. I look forward to my food. I'm sleeping properly. And I don't cough any more. But I can't stomach a pipe. After all this time I just don't feel like it any more."

"You will do," Bill told him. "Get away for a bit, and you'll be back to an ounce of shag a day."

"That pipe was at the root of it all," Mrs. Josser interposed. "He'd just been poisoning himself with it for years."

She was used to having Bill in the house by now. And she was used to contradicting him. An undeniably clever young doctor he might be. But it seemed to her that he was altogether too young, too cocksure and too much accustomed to riding rough-shod over other people's opinions. He hadn't got any of Ted's natural steadiness, and he didn't dress so well.

But Bill knew Mrs. Josser, too. And he no longer made the mistake of answering her. Instead, he went straight on with what he was saying—which annoyed Mrs. Josser still further.

"That's what you need now," he continued. "A fortnight at the seaside. Somewhere not too far away. Like Brighton."

"The East Coast's more bracing," Mrs. Josser observed.

"And have a drink or two when you feel like one," Bill went on. "Tone yourself up a bit."

"He isn't fit to travel," Mrs. Josser put in.

"And play with the slot-machine on the pier. Have a ride in a charabanc. Go to the Pavilion."

Mr. Josser had not replied until now. He was wearing the resigned, contented smile of someone who is the helpless centre of conversation.

"I'm all right," he said. "I don't need a holiday. Give me another week or two and I'll be on my feet again. Besides, I can't afford it."

Mrs. Josser pursed her lips.

"Of course you can afford it," she said. "You're going away as soon as the doctor says you can."

"And what about the Building Society?" Mr. Josser asked. "They're keeping the job open for me until the end of the month."

Mrs. Josser's lips contracted again.

"I married you, not the Building Society," she said firmly, as though the remark made sense.

Mr. Josser leant back again. "Well, well," he answered. "We'll wait and see."

He was in that placid, slightly aloof state that follows long illness. He really rather enjoyed talking about a seaside holiday so long as he didn't have to go to the trouble of actually having one. It seemed to him lying there that he was the one sane, contented person in a chattering, impatient world. It was Doris now who wouldn't leave him alone.

"No, we won't wait and see," she said. "You'll do just what Bill says. You'll go straight off."

"That's right," Bill urged him. "You go to Brighton and I'll bring Doris down to see you."

At that, Mrs. Josser's lips came together like elastic. This was the last straw, Bill's suggesting that he, of all people, should help to keep the Josser family together. She wondered that Doris didn't say something to show that she resented it.

But Doris, instead of saying anything, was looking at Bill in one of those strange dark ways in which young women sometimes look.

It was at this point that Uncle Henry arrived. Not an ideal sick-bed visitor at any time, he came in to-night straight from his defeat by the Salvation Army, and aching for an opportunity to air his latest grievance. And at the first pause in the conversation, he took it.

He turned suddenly towards Bill and addressed him.

"Have *you* forgotten about Manchuria?" he asked.

Bill looked surprised.

"Give it up," he said. "You tell me."

3

Percy had come to a decision. A big decision. He'd ruled Doris clean out of his life. And, in consequence, he was feeling better. So much better in fact that he was falling in love again.

Of course Doris still occupied a large place in his thoughts. But the thoughts themselves were different now. He'd turned against her, in fact. Or told himself that he had, which came to the same thing anyway.

"She'll be sorry," he kept repeating. "Throwing herself away on someone just because he saved her father's life. That's not love. That's infatuation. She'll be sorry. He won't be able to give her what I could give. She'll have to do without. She'll never know what love means. She'll be sorry."

It seemed in his mind now that he and Doris had meant a great deal to each other once, and that she had been unfaithful to him. He saw himself as single purposed and unchanging, someone who was ready to dedicate his whole life to one lucky woman. And because there had to be one lucky woman in his life—and because there was one again now—his self-esteem was returning. He was a different man. His hair was a bright glittering pad again. Also he'd bought himself a new tie and handkerchief set. They were bluey-mauve, with a satin stripe in them. And it made Mrs. Boon happy just to see them. It showed her Percy was returning to normal. He'd got over his bit of trouble, whatever it was.

And now that he'd got interested in this new girl, he didn't spend so much time worrying about Them and what They were planning to do with him. He went out again quite openly in the evenings, and even passed policemen, and men who looked like policemen, without glancing over his shoulder after they were behind him. Occasionally, he told himself: "Doris'll be sorry. She doesn't know what she's doing." But most of the time he was thinking about the new girl. She was lovely. He didn't know her properly yet. All that he knew about her was that her name was Jackie—there was something oddly exciting about having a girl with a boy's name—and that she had red-gold hair—natural, no colouring. She worked in an all-night café at Victoria, and that was where he had met her. He ate most of his meals at the café now, hanging about outside if all the seats at her tables were occupied. As soon as he saw his chance he was going to take her out somewhere and spend money on her.

Spend money! That made him pause and think. He wasn't making much money nowadays. Not money that was worth calling money. You couldn't make enough to keep a girl contented on what you picked up in a garage. It was special jobs, assignments on the side that counted. And he'd been missing these lately. Ever since the scare, he'd backed deliberately out of the sort of company where you heard about what was on. And unless he was going to be content to live forever on thirty shillings and tips, he realised that he would have to get back into the running again. He'd have to start paying Smokey's and the All-Star Café a visit or two. It was in Smokey's that someone had put him on to the hot Bentley.

And at the thought of another job of that sort and the money it would bring in to him, his spirits mounted. Those two voices, Voice No. 1 and Voice No. 2, began speaking again. "Go steady, Percy," Voice No. 2 warned him. "You don't want to go getting yourself into further trouble." "Trouble!" Voice No. 1 repeated. "What's wrong with a bit of trouble if you're strong enough to ride it?" "Never get a second chance in this world," Voice No. 2 advised cautioningly. "One more slip and you're out." "And who says you're going to make another slip?" Voice No. 1 asked him. "You've got brains, haven't you? You've got intelligence. Go right in and show them. Make circles round them. Keep 'em guessing.

Become a big man. Get on to the job before someone else chisels in on you. Get on with it."

The funny thing was that the incident of the Blonde troubled him so little by now. It didn't really seem his affair any more. The details of it had grown blurred and confused inside his mind, so that it was by now like something that he had seen or read about. Not like something that had actually happened to him. After all, it was over two months ago that it had happened. Over sixty days and nights since he'd been mixed up in it. And a fellow can't go on thinking about the same thing for ever, can he? Percy Boon and the affair on Wimbledon Common were fast becoming separated.

He was on his way over to Victoria now. The bluey-mauve handkerchief was sticking out of the breast pocket of his dark pin-stripe and he was wearing his pale grey hat with the black band.

"I look O.K.," he'd said to himself as he passed the tobacconist's plate-glass mirror with the name SALMON AND GLUCKSTEIN stencilled across it. "They done this suit well across the shoulders. I look O.K."

He had to wait for a tram. But he didn't mind. It wouldn't be a tram for long that he'd be using. Something low-swept and sporting like an Alvis. Or one of those big Americans with feather-springs and air conditioning and finger-tip gear-change. Not by himself either. The red-gold girl would be beside him. She'd be seeing life for the first time. She'd be going places. She'd be learning. And he'd be teaching her. He'd have his hand on her knee while he was driving.

"She'll understand me," he began saying. "She'll understand even if I tell her everything. She's been through things. She's suffered. You can tell by her eyes she's suffered. She deserves to have it all come right. And she'll look O.K. anywhere. You wouldn't have to worry about her. She'll be a help too. Not just a bleeding drag. She knows a thing or two already, not like Doris. She'll understand even if I tell her everything."

With the discovery of the red-gold waitress, the Blonde was really dead now.

CHAPTER 27

THE JOSSERS' going away wasn't only just their own affair. The whole of No. 10 was in it. Mrs. Vizzard, Mrs. Boon, Connie, even Mr. Squales and Mr. Puddy, all gave help or advice. Everyone, in fact, except Mr. Todds, the sub-lodger, got drawn into it. As the day grew nearer, the tension mounted. And on the morning of the departure—it was the 10.10 from Victoria that they were planning to catch—excitement reached a high peak. After all, there was a reason for it. Mr. Josser in health was Mrs. Josser's affair, and nobody else's. But Mr. Josser, convalescent and still feeble, belonged to the whole lot of them. He was *their* invalid.

The first sign that the awaited hour was really on them was when Mrs. Boon, still with the same sad expression on her face as though at any moment she expected to be made unhappy, came downstairs carrying a tray with tea-things on it and a plate of fancy biscuits. She knocked respectfully and went into the room where the bags, carefully locked and strapped as well against disaster, seemed to take up most of the floor. There were only three of them—three and a straw bag of the kind that game is sent in—but they looked more somehow. Perhaps it was the piled-up look that came from Mr. and Mrs. Josser's umbrellas planted sideways across the top so that they shouldn't get left behind.

"I just brought you down some tea," Mrs. Boon explained. "I knew you wouldn't want to be making any at a time like this."

She spoke in her usual hushed voice, but there was a distinct hint of big things impending in the way she put it. She might have been talking to the wife of Moses on the morning of Exodus.

Mr. Josser was the first to speak. He was sitting propped up in his armchair with a tea-cup in his hand. But he didn't allow himself to be the least bit embarrassed.

"Now if that isn't real nice of Mrs. Boon," he said. "I could just do with another cup."

Mrs. Josser drew in her lips.

"It's very kind of you. Very kind indeed," she said.

She was at once flattered and vexed by the amount of attention that she had been receiving. As a forthright and independent woman she found it both touching and galling to be treated as though she herself were an invalid. It was silly, too, because she felt confident that, if the occasion had arisen, she could perfectly well have shepherded the whole of Dulcimer Street, children and all, to Brighton alone, single-handed and unaided.

As the fresh pot of tea was there, however, there was no point in not using it and she accepted the cup that Mrs. Boon poured out for her.

"Nothing to eat, thank you," she said. "We've got something with us for the journey."

Something for the journey had been Mr. Puddy's idea. From the moment that he had heard that the Jossers were going, the ordeal of the trip had haunted him. And when Mrs. Josser had finally told him that they were taking sandwiches, he knew that his worst fears were really justified. Sausage rolls, he said, were the thing. Sausage rolls and a couple of hard-boiled eggs apiece. Anything less for a journey of that length was simply asking for trouble.

They were still sipping the tea that Mrs. Boon had made them, when they heard steps coming up the stairs from the basement. They were hard staccato steps as though there were no spring, only impetus, behind each footfall. Mrs. Josser knew the step. It was Mrs. Vizzard's. And, when she entered, she was carrying two neat brown paper packets tied round with fine white string. She went over and whispered in Mrs. Josser's ear.

"Just a little something in case you should want a snack in the train," she said. "It's only bridge-rolls and cress."

Mrs. Josser thanked her and put the packets in the straw bag on top of the other things. Made nervous by Mr. Puddy's warnings, she had packed rather a lot of food in there already.

Then with all that fresh tea going she offered Mrs. Vizzard a cup.

It was probably the chink of the tea-things that brought Connie down—the chink of tea-things, and the smell of human company. It was early for her, after her late hours at the night-club. But she was dressed all right. She was wearing her red velvet house-dress—the one with the lace collar and turnback cuffs—and she had even made her face up. In the cold morning light it was more doll-like and startling than ever.

"All ready?" she asked cheerfully. "Remembered your bathing costumes?"

Mr. Josser laughed. He liked Connie. Especially the way she always had the right thing ready to say at the right time. But Mrs. Vizzard simply ignored her. Their little piece of unpleasantness was still too recent in the memory—it was, indeed, ineffaceable—to be passed over in easy banter. And in the end it was so obvious that there was coldness between the two of them that Mrs. Josser was forced to do something about it. So she got down another cup and saucer. She didn't want Connie there. Wished that she hadn't come. Would have preferred that she went away again. But, after all, she couldn't send the poor old thing back upstairs without giving her anything, could she?

"Cup of tea, Connie?" she asked brusquely.

"Cuppa tea," Connie answered. "That's me."

She glanced down at the cherry Madeira cake as she spoke and then looked round at the company.

"Everybody got what they want?" she enquired meaningly.

This time, however, Mrs. Josser was too much preoccupied to notice. She kept glancing nervously at the marble clock on the mantelpiece as though she suspected that if she took her eye off it for a single moment it might begin playing tricks on her. It had become a part of their life by now, that clock. They no longer hung round nervously waiting for it to strike. It boomed and blasted its way past the hour, and they ignored it.

"I hope Percy's not going to be late," she said suddenly. "I wish now we'd ordered a cab like I said."

"Percy's never late."

It was Mrs. Boon who had spoken. The obvious untruthfulness of her remark passed unnoticed in the fact that she had spoken at all, and spoken so forthrightly. And having said what was in her mother's heart, having defended her offspring, she withdrew into obscurity again.

"I only meant that something might stop him," Mrs. Josser said lamely. "It's very good of him saying that he'll take us at all."

Mrs. Boon nodded her head in that slow sad way of hers.

"He's a good boy," she said placidly. "He'll be here."

"He's a son to be proud of," Mrs. Vizzard said charmingly. "So handsome, too."

She was feeling at her most gracious this morning, and it pleased her to be able to pay a compliment in this way. It helped to keep the atmosphere of No. 10 refined and as it should be. Also by addressing herself to Mrs. Boon it served to exclude Connie from the conversation.

But not entirely. At the mention of Percy, she screwed up one eye into a wink and wagged her forefinger in Mrs. Vizzard's direction.

"Now, remember, no cradle snatching," she said.

It was three toots on the horn that interrupted them. Mrs. Josser hurried over to the window, and there below them was Percy getting out of a large Daimler. Inside, the car was a bit tatty and threadbare. But from above it looked magnificent. It was as though a small battleship had berthed herself alongside.

Mrs. Boon smiled contentedly.

"I knew we could rely on him if he promised," she said.

As a matter of fact, she was thinking of something else that Percy had promised—her own holiday at the seaside. He hadn't mentioned it lately. But she was sure that it was in his mind all right. She wasn't worrying.

Mrs. Josser in the meantime had taken charge of things. A mood of desperate action, of panic almost, had taken possession of her. At one moment she was sitting there talking quietly to them, and at the next she was struggling with the cases. It was Mr. Josser's umbrella that was the trouble. Lying sideways across the string bag with the provisions, the handle had caught itself on to the arm of a chair. From the way Mrs. Josser was behaving she seemed ready to cut her losses by sacrificing the chair.

Mr. Josser started up.

"Wait a minute, Mother," he said. "There's no hurry. We've got an hour yet."

He was very fond of that umbrella and it hurt him to see the way it was being jerked about.

Connie, however, interrupted him.

"No, you don't," she said. "You're an invalid. This is where you need Connie."

She removed the two umbrellas—though Mrs. Josser's was shorter, and wasn't really in the way at all—and Mrs. Boon took the smallest of the three cases. Then with Mrs. Vizzard in the rear they all went downstairs together. Mr. Josser descended shakily, one step at a time, like a child. He was still very weak.

When they reached the downstairs passage, a voice greeted them. It was Mr. Squales's.

"Might I, a mere acquaintance, say *bon voyadj*?" it asked. "May I wish your invalid a speedy recovery?"

Mr. Josser was really touched. He had never liked Mr. Squales, and now felt sure that he must have misjudged him.

"Thank you ever so much," he said.

Mr. Squales stood there smiling and bowing in that charming half foreign way of his.

"My love to Brighton," he said. "It knew me once in happier days." His eye caught Mrs. Vizzard's and he paused. "In *former* days, I should say," he corrected himself.

By the time they reached the car, Percy had everything ready for them. He had a cigarette in the corner of his mouth but, apart from that, he was very much the professional chauffeur showing what he could do. He even held out a large moulted rug which he insisted on wrapping round the Jossers once they were inside.

"Getcher there in a jiff," he said.

Connie looked at the seat alongside the driver.

"Who's going in there?" she asked.

"No one," Percy answered.

Connie's eye brightened.

"O.K. if I don't talk to the driver?" she asked.

That was how it was that Connie became mixed up in the start of the Jossers' holiday. Naturally Mrs. Josser objected as soon as she saw Connie sitting up in front as a kind of second coachman. But by then it was too late to do anything about it. After all, it was Percy's car, and if he cared to pick up passengers on the way it was no affair of hers. What really irritated her, however, was the way Connie leant over the side waving to Mrs. Boon and Mrs. Vizzard as though she were going with them all the way. And, when she squirmed round and remarked through the glass partition that they were off at last, Mrs. Josser simply didn't answer.

They had just over half an hour to spare when they reached Victoria. And Mrs. Josser had got the tickets in advance. So naturally they went into the tea-room under the clock and had something to keep them going. It was not a restful meal, however, as Mrs. Josser was in a twitter in case the time should somehow slip past without their noticing. In consequence, Connie had to wolf up her Banbury cake and leave half her tea untasted. And when they emerged again there was still more than twenty minutes before the train was due to leave.

Mr. Josser used up quite a lot of this time at the bookstall. He went right round it from the Book-of-the-Month at the lavatory end to the second-hand political biographies on the other side. And he ended up by buying *Popular Gardening*, and a kind of rubber strap for carrying library books. Mrs. Josser followed him round urging him to hurry. She, too, examined everything, and it was a *Daily Mirror* that she bought finally.

There was a bit of a scramble at the last moment. Mrs. Josser suddenly looked at Platform 2 and saw a train standing there. The four of them were making slowly towards it when Mrs. Josser saw a porter going along closing doors. The sight shook her. It seemed that at any moment the green flag might be waved and the train draw away without them. In consequence she made a dash for it. Laden as she was, she ran. And so did Connie. Together they pounded up to the barrier. But Connie of course couldn't get through without a platform ticket. There was some unpleasantness about that, and by the time Percy and Mr. Josser had caught up, Mrs. Josser was already on the platform telling the guard that her husband was an invalid and that it was no use telling him to hurry because he couldn't. But at last when Mr. Josser, rather grey-looking in the face and breathing heavily, arrived leaning on Percy's arm, the crisis had passed over. The train standing there wasn't the Brighton train at all. It was all stations to Redhill. They stood back and let it go without a pang.

At the last moment Bill and Doris turned up. This was an entire, a carefully concealed surprise. It had been planned and executed all in secret. They arrived just five minutes before the train—the right train—was due to leave. Which was perfect. There was just time to say everything and there were no awkward pauses. The only person who was put out was Percy. He kept glancing at Doris and then looking away again.

"She doesn't mean nothing to me now," he told himself. "Doris doesn't. I've learnt my lesson. I've found someone who understands me. I've got the real thing now. Doris doesn't mean nothing to me."

Then the guard, a quiet steady-looking sort of man, came up behind them from nowhere and blew a whistle that he'd been hiding under his moustache.

It was the signal for the final good-byes.

"Mind the crabs when you're paddling," Connie shouted.

For no reason at all—except that he was sentimental and easily moved—two large tears ran down Mr. Josser's cheeks as he sat there.

Then he roused himself and thrust his head out of the train window.

"See you all soon," he said. "Be good."

CHAPTER 28

We really are somewhere now. Not that it looks anything very much at first glance. It's a high, bleak room with bare distempered walls and a dark green dado; the sort of room that might have been designed by an architect who specialised in booking-offices or hospital corridors. In short, it's a room to be occupied rather than lived in. And this is evidently the case at the present moment. Four of the five men sitting there—the fifth, whose room it is, is facing them—have got their hats with them. Three trilbies and a bowler are resting on the top of the steel filing-cabinet just inside the door, and an umbrella hangs down with its crook inside a wooden tray marked "Out."

You couldn't at first glance tell what manner of business it is that goes on in this office. It's evident enough that the customer doesn't ever come here or there would be more effort to impress. And it's evident, too, that the business is a sound old-fashioned one. There's almost an ancestral note about the rubbed arms of the bentwood chair behind the desk. And the desk itself has clearly seen a lot of use. Round the wooden ink-stand, the ink splashes have hardened and congealed into a permanent dark stain. The fact that the pins and the paper clips are in the upturned top of a tobacco tin shows that no money has been wasted on office furnishings. On the other hand, there are three telephones beside the ink-stand—which shows that business must be pouring in pretty steadily.

But take a look at the framed photograph over the nest of drawers. That ought to give a clue. It's a close-up of a winning team in the Metropolitan Police inter-divisional sports for 1903. And it's the only piece of decoration in the whole room, except for a large street map of London, with the Thames winding like a thick blue snake through the middle of it.

Then, for a moment, the door opens—and the whole show is given away immediately. It's a policeman—a policeman without his helmet—who has come in. He gives a buff envelope with "G.R." on it to the man behind the desk, and withdraws again. It's plain enough now that we're in a police station. But not just an ordinary police station—not the sort of place where the drunks and pick-pockets get taken. This is Scotland Yard, the Buckingham Palace of police stations, the real House of Lords of crime. It's here that the big things get attended to. And it's all departmentalised like the head office of a chain stores. On the floor above is the Counterfeits and Forgery department. But that doesn't take up the whole of the floor. There is also the Prostitution and White Slavery section. The Burglary and Breaking-into room. The Crimes with Violence room. The Aliens and International room. The Gang room. And the Confidence Trick room. Each with its resident specialist. Nothing has been forgotten. The fingerprint laboratory is one floor higher still—and everything is ticking over as smoothly as clock-work. Knock a man on the head with a jemmy, draw a cheque on somebody else's account, or be an unregistered alien, and there'll be a neat little dossier in a buff folder, the same colour as the envelope, all to yourself and neatly filled in with a space left in the front cover for the name.

But come back for a moment to the room with the five men sitting in it. What's happening in there? It's the time for the young one on the right to speak. He turns towards the man behind the desk and as he does so you can see his face. What's more you know him. It's Mr. Todds, the night-shift worker at the power station, Mrs. Josser's p.g.

So Connie's marked sixpence has done the trick, has it? But surely they wouldn't bother Scotland Yard with a special interview about a thing like that. No: Mr. Todds hasn't got himself into trouble. He's getting someone else into it. Not spitefully or maliciously. Just in a quiet matter-of-fact sort of fashion, because it's his job, and because he's good at it and wants promotion.

He's one of Them. "The owner identified the radiator figure, sir," he is saying, in a smooth sing-song voice as though he's memorised his speech before saying it, "and I've since replaced it. I described the lamps on brackets and they tallied with his memory of them. The salesman from Jack Barclay's was also present and confirmed the owner's impressions. Similarly with the car rug being used as a mat in the other bedroom. It's a special body on the Bentley and the measurements should confirm it."

"Have you got the measurements?"

"No, sir," the man answered, and looked abashed.

"Don't you carry a measuring tape?"

"Not in those clothes, sir."

"Then take this for a lesson. There's men back on point duty because they didn't carry measuring tapes."

"Yes, sir."

The man behind the desk is obviously thinking whilst he is talking. He is drawing round smudgy daisies on his blotting pad.

"So you want a warrant?"

"Yes, sir."

The man at the desk draws one more daisy.

"All right," he says at last. "You can have your chance. Report back here when you've picked him up."

CHAPTER 29

IT WAS lovely at Brighton. The weather was perfect. And the wind came blowing up the narrow streets from the front with a whiff of old rope, fish and sea-weed that made you glad to be alive, and proved once again that there's nothing like the ocean for a tonic.

But it takes more than sea air to make a holiday. There's eating. The old rope, the fish and the sea-weed give you an appetite and, if there's nothing to satisfy it but cold ham and a plateful of pink blancmange with a square of cheese afterwards, you're worse off than if you hadn't come at all. And that's where the Jossers were lucky. They were at the Medusa Private Boarding Establishment—actually they were at the annexe across the road: but that didn't matter because they ate in the main dining-room with the twelve separate tables and the sea-shell overmantel—where the food was famous. Other visitors who didn't know Brighton and stayed at places like the Barbados Private Hotel, the Cyril or the Ogilvie Pension cast envious eyes on the Medusans when they heard of the standard of living that went on behind that neatly clipped privet hedge, those green-painted railings, and the white front door.

The Jossers were lucky, too, in the bedroom they'd got. It hadn't actually got a view—except the Medusa Private Boarding Establishment opposite—but it had got a balcony. It was a large airy room with a double bed, an easy chair with a pull-out flap so that Mrs. Josser could put her feet up, and a shilling-in-the-slot gas meter in case it turned cold in the evening.

You could tell that the Medusa was good class simply by looking at the wash-stand. The toilet set was a collector's piece. Gracefully rounded and flounced round the top edge, it was new-looking and unchipped—though obviously it came from the classic age of such things. And the flowers on the side—peonies in full splendour—might have been painted there only yesterday. The jug with its delicate Grecian handle that didn't look strong enough to support even its own mass of earthenware when empty, was the sort of thing that you picked up praying that you wouldn't knock it against the toothbrush holder, or the soap-dish or worst of all the side of the basin. Mrs. Josser took one glance at it and decided that she'd do the pouring out herself for both of them.

Mr. Josser didn't take very much notice of the bedroom the night he got there. He was pretty badly knocked out by the journey, and he went straight to bed as soon as he arrived at Medina Road. It was not until next morning that his holiday really began. But it began early. Round about six-thirty, because he still woke up at his old hour as though there were a tram for him to catch. And, once awake, he simply lay in bed, thinking. Mrs. Josser was still fast asleep beside him, and there was no interruption to his thoughts. He recognised for a start that he was lucky to be there at all. It had been touch and go this last time, all right. Bill had come along only just in time. He liked Bill, and supposed that Doris was going to marry him. The idea was rather flattering: he'd never imagined that he'd have a doctor for a son-in-law.

From thinking about Doris his thoughts turned to Ted for a moment. He was certainly lucky in both his children. All things considered, Ted was about the steadiest young man he knew. He'd got himself well up the ladder and if he just went on being steady for a few more years he'd be a manager one day. And after that there was really no end to what steadiness could do for you in the Co-op. line. . . .

But he forgot about Ted and began thinking about the cottage instead. He had changed his mind on the way down, and decided on Sussex. He had even changed his mind as the train ride itself proceeded. First of all he'd fixed on the North Downs, which wouldn't be too far away from the rest of the family. Then he'd gone for the Weald because he liked it better. And finally he'd decided on the South Downs because he liked them better still. The trouble was that Mrs. Josser still didn't want to leave Dulcimer Street. She'd said that nothing would induce her.

Thinking about the cottage made him remember how much money he'd been spending lately. The illness had cost him something already. And now there was this holiday which they'd all recklessly insisted he should take. He was glad for Mrs. Josser's sake that they'd come away: she needed a holiday. As for himself, he could perfectly well have afforded to do without one. And he couldn't forget it was costing him five guineas a week—for the two of them, of course. Five guineas was a lot of money. And it would be ten guineas by the time the fortnight was over. That meant that he'd have just £492 left—and he'd always prided himself on being over the £500 mark.

A stirring beside him told him that Mrs. Josser was waking. She always gave a series of little shudders almost as though someone were shaking her and then finally a bigger one as she actually woke up.

Mr. Josser turned towards her.

"It's a fine morning, Mother," he said. "It's going to be a fine day."

"Mmmm," replied Mrs. Josser, drawing the bed-clothes round her again. There was a shuffling movement, a kind of shudder in reverse, and she was asleep again.

The fact rather pleased Mr. Josser.

"It's the sea air," he told himself. "It's doing her good. She's the one that really needs a rest. Not me."

And lying there on one elbow he looked out of the window at the day that was getting finer and brighter every minute.

CHAPTER 30

I

It's a mistake that people always make. They imagine that when they've come away from a place the life they've left simply stops dead with their departure.

Even Mrs. Josser fell into this error. For the first two or three days, of course, she worried about things in London—whether Doris was all right up at Hampstead with that girl-friend of hers, whether silly little Cynthia was giving her Ted enough to eat, whether the arrangements would work all right for Mrs. Boon to give Mr. Todds' room a once-over, and whether Uncle Henry had been run over yet while he was wearing those ridiculous placards. By the end of the first week, however, London had ceased to exist for her. She didn't worry about it. She didn't think about it. She didn't even remember it. But that didn't mean that there weren't a lot of things—important things—still happening.

For a start, Ted's promotion had come. Within eighteen months of having been made a sub-manager of soft goods, he'd been put temporarily in charge on the hardware side. It was a bit of a wrench having been switched from soft to hard just like that, and it meant saying good-bye to all his old friends in the department. But Ted felt equal to it. After all there was another twenty-seven-and-six a week in it straightaway, and, with Cynthia's birthday on the way, that was exactly what Ted wanted. It wasn't bad, he told himself, six pounds five a week at thirty-four: it was better than he had ever hoped for. He was careful, however, to keep that side out of it when he was finally called before the board and offered the position. On that occasion, all that he said was: "I appreciate very deeply the confidence you have shown in me and I shall do my utmost to justify it." What was more, he meant it. For a man who has been inside the movement all his working life, it's a solemn moment coming up before the full board. Like going to Rome. Or being inspected in the Territorials. At that moment, hardware, particularly Co-operative hardware, seemed easily the noblest end in life.

It wasn't until he had actually got the job that the hidden side of Ted's nature showed itself. As soon as he had come down the steps of the head office, it asserted itself. Instead of going straight back to his branch as he was supposed to do, he cut loose. Ted Josser, the new deputy-manager, went on the spree in his employers' time.

He went first into a chemist's shop and bought a round flowered box of toilet-powder called "Allurement." Then he called at a tobacconist's and asked for Abdulla Turkish—the kind to make a room smell as though incense and orchids and dancing-girls have been shut up there. And still he wasn't satisfied. He continued down the street until he came to a large corner-shop, all of plate glass and chromium. The lights were on in the windows, great rows of them, even though it was still broad daylight outside. Ted stood for some moments on the pavement, undecided. Then, having made up his mind, he went in.

"I want one of the nineteen-and-eleven nightdresses," he said. "The black kind with the lace on it."

As he paid for it, his conscience smote him. It was the most reckless thing that he had ever done, spending his first week's increase before he had actually got it. And that wasn't all. He was spending it outside the Society—there was the taint of disloyalty in it. But it couldn't be helped. Black silk nightdresses edged with pink lace aren't the sort of thing that a hardware manager can afford to be seen buying in his own store.

And every man has the right to a little private life sometimes.

2

If it was Ted's big day, it was also Mr. Todds'. He'd got everything ready. When he pulled down the blind of his back bedroom and raised it up again, his two friends who were waiting round the corner in Burma Street would take it for a signal and come along to No. 10. The drawing of the blind would mean that Percy Boon had just come in.

Everything was ready from seven o'clock onwards. It was Thursday. And Thursday was one of Percy's early nights. Not that there was any accident about that by now: Mr. Todds knew about as much—just as much in fact—about Percy's arrangements as Percy himself knew. After all, he'd been studying nothing else for the past three weeks. The bit about Battersea Power Station had been all eye-wash.

Mr. Todds had been on C.I.D. work long enough to be pretty hard-boiled about it in consequence. Even so, he couldn't help feeling sorry round about seven-fifteen when he heard the front door slam, and Percy came upstairs, two steps at a time, whistling

"Little Girl Blue." He was a natural whistler, was Percy, and he got plenty of tremolo into it. Sounded like a professional music-hall turn, in fact. But Mr. Todds only shook his head.

"You'll be whistling a very different tune in a moment," he told himself, as he drew down the blind.

Mr. Todds went down himself to let his friends in. And after he had gone upstairs with them to show them which was the Boons' door, he left them to it. He still had some nice feelings in the matter and it was better that he should leave the final stage to strangers. After all, he had done all that was necessary. He had warned the inspector that Percy was dangerous and might put up a fight for it.

All five of them were now bowling along to the police station together, the four cops and Percy, sitting between two of them, in the back seat. It was a very quiet and well-behaved little party. There hadn't been any violence: no knuckleduster stuff or attempted escape across the roof-tops.

When the inspector had explained what he had come for, Percy had just put down his knife and fork, and fainted.

CHAPTER 31

BRIGHTON had done the trick and Mr. Josser now looked a different man. From the way he squared his shoulders, as he marched along the front, there was really nothing to show that less than a month ago he'd been a dying man with his family gathered round him. He'd even bought himself a walking-stick. It was a thin pliable sort of cane, in some dark mysterious wood that still had a hint of the jungle about it, and it carried a little silver shield for initials on the front. The stick had cost four and six, and been worth it.

Mrs. Josser looked better too. She had allowed herself once each day to be taken by Mr. Josser into the Old Ship and given a glass of port. Except on holiday it was a thing that she would never have contemplated: she despised and disapproved of women who went into public houses. But here at Brighton it wasn't quite the same. There was a freedom in the air that excused such behaviour. Even so, she hadn't got the same swagger in her walk that Mr. Josser had acquired. But perhaps that was simply because of her shoes. A fancy pair, with a bit of white suède let into the sides, she'd had them for seven years and worn them only on holidays. Too tight when she had bought them, they had already bitten into six holidays and were now in process of biting into the seventh.

But it was only her feet that were troubling her. The spirit inside Mrs. Josser was rekindled and unconsumed. With twelve good days at the seaside behind her, she had now reached the stage of buying presents. The purchase of post cards had been an earlier phase. Almost as soon as she had arrived, she had gone into a stationer's and then into one of the glass-sided shelters on the front and had written to everyone she could think of—to Doris, Uncle Henry, to Ted, to Baby—the last in large block capitals as though in expectation that Baby would somehow astonish them all by being able to read it—and to Mrs. Vizzard. Then, recognising the way jealousy spreads like a fire inside any household, she had written to Mrs. Boon and Connie as well, reassuring them about her safe arrival. On the first day of Mrs. Josser's holiday the Brighton postman had tottered back to the sorting office carrying a pile of coloured post cards, all saying the same thing to different people.

But this bout of buying was on a larger scale altogether. More time had to be spent on it. More thought. And more money. Not that Mrs. Josser made a labour of it. On the contrary, she did her best to minimise the whole undertaking so that it shouldn't seem to be interrupting the holiday.

"I've just got to get a little something for Doris," was all she said. "Just a little something for Doris. And something for Baby."

The idea of something for Cynthia hadn't crossed her mind at the time. It cropped up only when she saw a small battlemented castle of shiny porcelain with an ink-well in the middle of the castle courtyard. It wasn't the sort of thing that Doris would like. It was no use to Baby who, even if she could read, certainly couldn't write. It was no use to anyone in fact, but as small china castles go, it was irresistible.

The emotion that went with the buying of all these presents was a complicated one. In the first place there was the simple pleasure of going into shops and spending money on something that was unnecessary. It was all part of the fairy-tale atmosphere of the seaside—as though, coming from Victoria on the Southern Railway, somewhere about Hayward's Heath the whole value of money changed abruptly and, once south of the Downs, it became simply stuff to be chucked around and played with. Then there was the knowledge that buying presents really meant that the holiday was coming to an end. And, in the result, a kind of urgency crept into the enjoyment of everything. There was at once the sense of the upturned hour-glass and of a strange telescoping of time. It seemed that the moment of arrival had been last night, and also a long while ago; that they had been living at Brighton all their life yet had only just arrived there. Mr. and Mrs. Josser both had this feeling and it translated itself into a rather lofty melancholy. They walked along the front together holding hands and thinking about how long they had known each other.

Mrs. Josser was the first to speak.

"It's the last couple of days that does you good," she said. "Father always said that he could do without the rest of the holiday if he could have the last two days."

It was the last day. Just getting on for lunch-time. Mr. Josser tilted his hat and began swinging his new jungle walking-stick. He felt decidedly peckish and was glad that it wasn't much further to the boarding-house. He was glad too that Mrs. Josser's feet seemed to be holding out.

"Rottingdean this afternoon," he said gloatingly. "Pretty little place, Rottingdean. Mustn't go back to London without seeing Rottingdean."

The gloom of to-morrow's departure had mysteriously cleared a little, and Mr. Josser was secretly looking forward to Dulcimer Street once more. He wasn't thinking of anything very much when Mrs. Josser spoke to him.

"About that cottage of yours," she said suddenly.

Mr. Josser gave a little smile.

"That's all right," he said. "It was only an idea I had. It wasn't anything really. Don't worry about it."

But Mrs. Josser ignored him and went on with what she had been going to say.

"Why don't we look up a few addresses while we're down here?" she suggested. "If there *is* anything going we might as well see it."

"You mean take a cottage down here by the sea?" Mr. Josser asked her.

"Only if it's suitable," she answered firmly.

"Then you mean . . .?"

"I don't mean something that's going to be washed away by the next high tide," she told him.

"But you *do* mean . . .?"

"Only if it's suitable," she repeated.

Mr. Josser did not say anything. He was nearer to getting what he wanted than he had been at any time during the last thirty years.

Between him and Mrs. Josser there existed at this moment a bond of sacred understanding.

They had reached the end of Medina Road by now and were approaching the boarding-house.

"Of course, there might be something at Rottingdean itself," Mr. Josser suggested. "It's worth trying."

"We'll see," Mrs. Josser replied indulgently, as she might have replied to a child. "I don't want you tiring yourself or I shall be sorry I mentioned it."

It gave a pleasant feeling going up the neat gravel path towards the white front door and knowing that there was a meal waiting for them. It was the life luxurious, and Mrs. Josser felt at that moment that she could do with any amount of it.

"There's usually milk-pudding on Fridays," Mrs. Josser said aloud. "Or at least there was last week."

Mr. Josser pushed the door open and, as he did so, they both saw the figure of a woman seated on one of the cane chairs in the hall. It was dark and muffled inside because of the hanging bead curtain and they couldn't see very clearly who it was. But there was something in the lines of the figure to suggest that she had been sitting there a long time. Then as Mrs. Josser parted the dangling threads of beads they saw.

It was Mrs. Boon.

"Clarice," Mrs. Josser exclaimed.

"This is a nice surprise," Mr. Josser began. "Did Percy bring . . ."

But he did not finish the sentence. For he saw that Mrs. Boon had been weeping. Her eyes were red and swollen and her eyelids looked puffy.

"It's about Percy I've come," she said, in a breathless pent-up rush, the words tumbling over each other. "They've taken him away from me. Last night. He's been arrested."

There was a pause. A blank incredulous pause.

"What's he done?" Mr. Josser asked. Then thinking that it might be more tactful, he added: "There must be some mistake."

"They've . . . they've charged him with stealing a car. A Bentley car. . . ."

But Mrs. Boon could get no further. She began crying again. Crying in a forlorn helpless fashion that had lost all reticence. "I had to tell somebody," she managed to jerk out. "That's why I came."

Mr. Josser cleared his throat and tried to sort out the chaos of his mind.

He looked down at the sodden figure of Mrs. Boon in front of them and across then at Mrs. Josser.

"Mother," he said. "We'll have to go back. Straightaway."

CHAPTER 32

I

IT WAS the simple fact of their premature return that betrayed everything. When, accompanied by Mrs. Boon, they arrived home in Dulcimer Street, the day before they were due, it was obvious that something disastrous had occurred, that prearranged and inviolate order had been dislocated. No. 10 was mystified.

Mrs. Vizzard for a start was taken completely off her guard. And so was Connie. She was just going out to her night-club when the three of them came in together. And it didn't need anyone with her uniquely sensitive nose to detect at once that there was a catch in it. Mr. Josser, looking sunburnt and swarthy, wore a strange anxious expression on his face, and he had his arm round Mrs. Boon, vaguely as though he was guarding and protecting her. Mrs. Boon herself seemed to have been crying. And as for Mrs. Josser, she barely even said good-evening to Connie. More tightly lipped and grim-looking than ever, she went straight on up the stairs as though she were late for something.

"It's all a mistake, a horrible mistake. I know it is," Mrs. Boon was saying. "It couldn't be what they said. It's a mistake. I know it is."

But the strain had been too much for her. All that she could do was to lie back in the chair smearing her face with the wet shapeless handkerchief with which she had been sponging at her eyes in the train.

"And you say they won't allow him bail?" Mr. Josser enquired wearily.

The real trouble was that they had been over all this conversation before. There had been hours of it by now, and there was nothing that could be added.

Mrs. Boon stopped crying for a moment. In defence of Percy, she was almost indignant.

"He . . . he wouldn't know how to ask for it," she said. "He's never been in trouble before." She paused. "He will be all right, won't he?" she asked, appealing suddenly to Mrs. Josser.

Mrs. Josser, however, merely pursed up her lips again.

"I'll get some tea," was all she said. "Fred looks just about done in again."

It was with positive relief that she found herself away from Mrs. Boon for a moment. There is something about another person's grief that is at once strangely exhausting and unshareable. And Mrs. Josser was angry. Angry that the thing had happened at all. Instead of being sorry for Percy, she was furious with him. It seemed that simply through Percy's carelessness, his folly, his wickedness, Mr. Josser's holiday had been ruined, and that magical, health-restoring last day had been snatched from him. Mrs. Josser wasn't going to forget it.

Before she had done more than put the brown enamel kettle on the gas stove, she was joined by Mrs. Vizzard. Down below, the suspense had been too much for flesh and blood to endure. And Mrs. Vizzard was human. Finally putting down the size eight sock that she had been knitting, she mounted the stairs wearing the expression of a woman, who, though too well-bred to ask outright, was equally not averse from being told. She stood at the door, smiling in polite surprise.

"Have you got everything you need, Mrs. Josser?" she asked. "We weren't expecting you home so soon."

"I wasn't expecting it either," Mrs. Josser replied.

This was more encouraging than Mrs. Vizzard had expected. It made the next stage so much easier.

"Why? Did . . . did something call you back?"

"Nothing called *me* back," Mrs. Josser answered. "It was Fred who decided."

"Not . . . not his health?" Mrs. Vizzard enquired.

"Fred's never been better," Mrs. Josser told her. "Or at least he would have been if he could have stayed."

She added nothing to this and went over to the cupboard to get the tea-things. Mrs. Vizzard stood there waiting. It was a strained and awkward moment as, of course, she could not actually ask what it was that Mrs. Josser was concealing from her. That would have been unladylike. And what made it so maddening was that Mrs. Josser was obviously just as anxious to tell her. Only that would have been unladylike too.

Then she could contain herself no longer.

"Is . . . is there anything the matter?" she asked.

And at the direct question Mrs. Josser put down the tea-cups that she was holding and faced round so suddenly that Mrs. Vizzard looked up in astonishment.

"Anything the matter?" she said after her. "Don't ask me. You'd better ask Mrs. Boon. He's her son."

"Mrs. Boon?" Mrs. Vizzard repeated. She really was getting somewhere now.

"That's what I said," Mrs. Josser told her. "And it's all I'm going to say. She may tell you herself, or she may not. That's for her to decide."

"Not . . . not in trouble?"

"I've said my say," Mrs. Josser declared stoutly. "It's out of my hands now."

Mrs. Vizzard smoothed down the pleated folds of her black dress, and waited.

"And where is Mrs. Boon, pray?"

"She's in my sitting-room," Mrs. Josser told her. "And that's where Fred is too."

The kettle had suddenly boiled itself over and was threatening to put the gas out. To conceal her real feelings Mrs. Josser snatched it up and made tea violently, pouring in the water as though she were destroying a wasps' nest. Then she stood back and caught Mrs. Vizzard's eye. The two women understood each other perfectly.

"I'll get you some milk," Mrs. Vizzard told her. "Coming back suddenly like this upsets things."

"That's very kind of you, Mrs. Vizzard," Mrs. Josser told her. "I've put an extra cup out."

2

Mrs. Vizzard was back downstairs in her sitting-room again. She sat there, clenching and reclenching her hands.

"The disgrace of it. The utter disgrace of it," she was saying. "First Connie. And then this. To think that it should have happened from my house. Whatever would poor Mr. V. say if he knew?"

And at the thought of the departed Mr. Vizzard's feelings her self-control left her and she had to search for the handkerchief in her waistband. The fact that she was crying humiliated her: it meant that she could no longer despise Mrs. Boon for doing so.

And the fact that it was now after ten o'clock upset her still further. The horrible Percy, it seemed, had ruined everything. Until the moment of the return she had planned to spend the evening quite differently. She had been going to invite Mr. Squales to drink cocoa and eat seed-cake with her. It would have been the fourth time in three weeks that it had happened. And really it was a kindness. He was so much in need of building-up and nourishing, poor man. But now, thanks to Percy, it was impossible. It is one thing to have a man in one's room at eight-thirty in the evening. It is quite another to have him there at ten o'clock at night.

Besides, she was a sight. She couldn't have allowed anyone to see her looking as she was. That sudden fit of angry tears had left its mark on her. She crossed over to the mirror and peered in. It was only lately that she had taken to studying her face in this way. And she knew everything about herself. Knew everything, and hated those pale eyes and hard, high cheekbones. With a gesture half of disgust, half of weariness, she turned away from the mirror and began removing the pins from her hair. A moment later a stiff plait fell down her back and, jerking it over one shoulder, she started to undo it. The mass of it was greater than seemed possible. The hair must have been wrenched and twisted into its braid. When she drew a brush through it, it spread and expanded, covering her back. Only at the temples was it streaked with grey.

She pondered for a moment whether she should make herself the cup of cocoa that she would have drunk with Mr. Squales. All day she had been looking forward to it. But now at this hour and in these circumstances, the stuff seemed sickly and revolting. Even the idea of seed-cake was unattractive. She would go straight to bed. Perhaps in the morning she would feel better, would be reconciled to the scandal that Percy had drawn down upon Dulcimer Street.

"Thank God it hasn't got into the papers," she told herself. "That's something I could never have borne."

She raised her hand to extinguish the light. But as she did so she realised that it was foolish. There was far too much passing through her head for her to be able to sleep. It was useless to attempt it. So, instead, she sat herself upright in the chair beside the table, took up this week's copy of *The Spirit World* from the shelf beside the fireplace, and began to read.

"When those whom we have truly loved depart from us," the writer informed her, "we are aware of their presence in unexpected ways—in a chance shadow cast upon a sunlit wall, in an eddy of dust in the road before us, in a pool's ripple, in the fall of an autumn leaf. . . ." She gazed up from the magazine for a moment. "A thief in my house. It'll never seem clean and wholesome to live in again." She shuddered, and read on. "From these simple manifestations of an unseen personality, to the hearing of voices and the actual *seeing* of the visitant spirit garbed for a moment in earthly form, is but a step." She looked up again. "Of course, he's guilty," she told herself. "He's a wastrel. Anyone could see that, except his mother. He's nothing but a common car thief. He'll be sent to prison for years and years, and it'll be in all the papers." She shook herself and tried to concentrate on *The Spirit World.* She had turned to the advertisements by now. "More than a thousand grateful students of my method, PSYCHIC STEPS, can testify that with application and patience SECOND SIGHT CAN BE OBTAINED BY ALL," she read. "My yellow shilling booklets (third edition) have given eyes to the blind. . . ." Her thoughts were wandering again. "If only he could prove himself innocent, it would be all right. There'd be no scandal then. At least nothing that we couldn't live down. But if they find him guilty, she'll have to go. I won't have Mrs. Boon living here. It's all her fault. She ought to have brought him up differently. She . . ."

It was a knock at the door that interrupted her thoughts. She started. It was nearly midnight and everyone else in the house was asleep by now. Must surely be asleep. Suppose that those three knocks did not belong to anyone of this world at all. Suppose that when she opened the door there were no one standing in the passage-way outside. To be blind and not to have been given eyes . . . she attempted to speak, but her voice sounded faint and unnatural.

"Who's there?" she asked at last. "Who is it?"

"It is a friend," the deep voice of Mr. Squales answered. "I was sleepless and something told me that you were unsleeping too."

She paused. This was more disastrous than ever. If it had been impossible at eleven o'clock, it was unthinkable now. An unmarried gentleman and a lady in a negligée. . . .

"May I come in?"

Her heart pounded. She realised that what she was doing was madness.

"Come in," she said.

As she rose she became conscious of her hair loose about her shoulders. But Mr. Squales himself remained superbly unconcerned. He was dressed in his morning clothes, with the braided black jacket and pale trousers. He had evidently just retied his cravat, which made Mrs. Vizzard's undress seem more mischievous and wanton somehow. She blushed.

But Mr. Squales merely crossed over to Mrs. Vizzard's chair as though it already belonged to him, and sat there gazing broodingly downwards at his feet. It was obvious that there was something on his mind. For a moment he raised his head to look in Mrs. Vizzard's direction, and his dark eyes penetrated into her grey ones, and then he looked away again.

"Would . . . would you like anything?" she asked. "A cup of cocoa? A piece of cake?'

It seemed the moment that she had been waiting for. But Mr. Squales simply shook his head.

"Not to-night," he said sadly. "Not to-night, thank you. It would be too painful."

"Too painful?"

Mrs. Vizzard was staring at him now.

"I have come to say good-bye," he said sadly. "I wrote you a letter because I did not think that I could bear the actual parting. Then I discovered that I could not bear informing you by letter. And so . . . I am here."

Mrs. Vizzard sat at the corner of the table facing him. She was motionless. Transfixed by what he had just told her.

"You are going away?" she said. "Why?"

Mr. Squales dropped his head deeper on to his waistcoat.

"I have my reasons," he replied, and added after a pause: "Personal ones."

Mrs. Vizzard drew in a deep breath.

"Going away for . . . for good?" she asked.

"Or ill," Mr. Squales answered. "I am seeing you for the last time."

Mrs. Vizzard changed her position. As she leant forward, her hair, her dark thick hair, fell across her outstretched arm.

"Tell me why," she said. "We know each other too well to separate like this."

Mr. Squales stroked his cravat with that slender olive hand of his.

"You'll not be angry with me?"

Mrs. Vizzard shook her head. How could she be angry with this wonderful, distinguished-looking creature?

"I have lived in your house for a quarter of a year," he said. "You have shown me many kindnesses. I've grown to look upon you as my friend. My only friend. There is nothing that I could ever do to repay you. Nothing. But my private affairs have not prospered. I am not wanted by the world. In short, I cannot afford to live *anywhere*."

Mrs. Vizzard made a sudden movement as though she were going to speak. But Mr. Squales stopped her.

"During the past month," he went on, "I have pawned everything that I possess. My dressing things gone. My lighter has gone. My ring has gone. My watch had already gone when I came here. Even my dinner-jacket has gone. Sitting before you at this moment is someone who is destitute."

Mrs. Vizzard sat there watching him. She longed suddenly to throw her arms around him and tell him that she loved him; that she wanted him to stay by her for ever; that she would give him a new dinner-jacket, a new watch; that without him she would be doubly widowed. But it was the disability of womanhood not to be able to speak first.

"It . . . it doesn't matter," was all that she finally trusted herself to say.

Mr. Squales, however, shook his head.

"It matters a great deal," he said rising. "To a gentleman it is the *only* thing that matters—not to be a burden. Not to take advantage of the more fortunate. In fact, it is why I have come to say good-bye."

He crossed over to her and held out his right hand.

"You will find the rent for my room on my mantelpiece," he added. "It is complete except for sixpence. I am sorry. But that was all the pawnshop gave me. It was for my propelling pencil."

"I won't take it," Mrs. Vizzard said in a low, half-throttled voice. "It's yours."

"Good-bye," Mr. Squales repeated.

Mrs. Vizzard turned her face away so that he shouldn't see that in her eyes were tears.

"Don't go away," she said.

There was silence after she had spoken. A deep significant silence. And it was Mr. Squales who finally broke it.

"You mean you need me, *too*?" he asked.

He was looking down at her sideways as he said it, looking down with what might have been the faintest of smiles playing round the corner of his mouth. But the smile was possibly no more than nervous tension. It had obviously cost him a great deal to make this frank admission of his state.

Mrs. Vizzard nodded. She could not trust herself to speak.

And, as she stood there, Mr. Squales's arm went round her. Mrs. Vizzard, the widow of Dulcimer Street, the woman who had fought to keep her capital intact, was gathered up against the braided jacket. Her tears were on his cravat and the dark olive hand from which the signet ring was missing was stroking her hair like a lover.

"If you need me I shall stay," he was saying. "It was only that I could not ask. . . ."

The clock on the mantelpiece struck one. One o'clock in the morning. It was a thin, tremulous *ping,* remarkably different from the full-throated *boom* of the Jossers' clock upstairs. On the table were two empty cocoa-cups and a seed-cake with a wide angle wedge cut out of it.

Mrs. Vizzard roused herself. Into the rosy bliss of the present the sordid reality of another way of life was impinging.

"There's one thing I wanted to ask you," she said softly. "It's about Percy. . . ."

But Mr. Squales only kissed her forehead.

"Don't let's talk about Percy," he told her. "Let's talk about ourselves."

3

Even though it was late, there was someone else still awake in Dulcimer Street. And that was Mr. Puddy. Awake, but not well. Practically dying in fact. He'd eaten something that had disagreed with him, and he couldn't move. All that he could do was to groan. As soon as he could get about again, he was going back to the shop that had tried to kill him and he was going to make a row. It was a pretty serious thing to sell something called "Home-Made Farm House Pork Pie" that should have been labelled "Poison." Supposing a child or a baby had got hold of it? Indeed, judging from the effect on Mr. Puddy, any less experienced eater would simply have been carried off after the first bite of it.

Threaten damages and the Food Inspector—that was what he was going to do when he was strong enough. In the meantime, he could only lie full length on the bed and avoid turning over. There might have been red-hot pins inside him.

And it was a pity because the pie had certainly looked all right. Very fresh and crusty, with a nice bit of hard-boiled egg, like a yellow eye, bang in the middle of it.

BOOK THREE

LOVE IN A BASEMENT

CHAPTER 33

I

Anyone with half an eye could have seen that Doreen's and Doris's studio arrangement couldn't last for ever. And it didn't. They had just had their first row. And, as it was a big one, it was also their last. They had both known for some time that it was coming. All the same, when it broke, it was out of a clear sky.

The row divided itself neatly into two parts. The first part took place between seven-fifteen and eight o'clock p.m.: the second roughly two and a half hours later, and finished up about eleven. There had been a slight disagreement at breakfast because Doreen took all the milk—but that affair had entirely blown over. They had ridden down together in the bus afterwards in that almost arm-in-arm intimacy that sharing a double seat imposes.

Lunch, too, was perfectly normal and everything passed off quietly until Doreen announced that Mr. Perkiss had phoned her up and that she had invited him round that evening. Doris didn't like Mr. Perkiss and told Doreen so. She said that she would go out somewhere, to the flicks probably.

But, now that Doris had made the suggestion, Doreen wouldn't hear of it. Simply wouldn't hear of it.

"Oh, you can't," she said hurriedly. "You really can't. Not to-night. You know how he is about me. He goes absolutely crazy if we're alone for a moment. I'd never have asked him if I hadn't been sure you'd be there."

So it was finally agreed: Doris would be there to protect Doreen from the advances of the passionate Mr. Perkiss. And on the way home they went into a *delicatessen* shop and bought a tin of mushroom soup, some ham and a carton of potato salad with which to help assuage this elderly satyr in a fawn suit. Doreen protested vigorously that it wasn't right that Doris should pay for *anything* as Mr. Perkiss was *her* friend, really. But, she pointed out, Mr. Perkiss was sure to bring something with him. And as they'd all have some of it, it would come to the same thing in the end, wouldn't it?

It was while she was laying the table that Doris remarked that she wished she'd thought of it and she'd have invited Bill to come along too. The remark annoyed Doreen, who was in the small cubicle-like bedroom making up her face. Bill, she pointed out, was her friend, not Doris's. If she had wanted Bill, she was perfectly capable of inviting him herself. Indeed, if it hadn't been for her, she went on, Doris would never even have met him.

It was because this was true, and because of the obligation that it implied, that Doris resented it so much. She slammed down the butter-dish that she had been holding and addressed the empty doorway in the corner.

"Well, anyway, he's more my friend now than he is yours," she answered defiantly.

As soon as she had said it, Doreen appeared. She was smoking a cigarette and wearing an old flowered dressing-gown. Her face glistened with cold cream and her hair was gathered up in a red silk handkerchief. On each cheek a small disc of rouge that had not yet been rubbed in burned fiercely. Altogether, she looked like something large and sticky from the back row of the ballet.

"Listen, my pet," she said. "I don't like little girls who go about stealing other girls' friends."

"I didn't steal him," Doris retorted.

"Well, that's all right then," Doreen told her, smiling in a deliberate theatrical sort of way through the cold cream. "It's only just that I'm warning you."

Doris turned her back on her and went through into the absurd tiny kitchen. And it might still have been all right if Doreen had left it at that. But instead of going back into her bedroom and doing something constructive with her face, she followed Doris into the kitchen. And even when they were on the best of terms there wasn't really room for two of them in there at once. And to-night it seemed simply suffocating.

"Really, my pet," Doreen said, "I can't bear to see you making a fool of yourself like this. If you've gone and fallen for Bill in a big way, you'd better watch your step. He just isn't your type."

Doris was standing back from Doreen, right up against the little sink as she said it. It was the first time that she had ever found Doreen repulsive. But now everything about her—her shiny, dolled-up face, the cigarette hanging out of the corner of her mouth, the smeary flowered dressing-gown, her habit of calling other people her pet—all repelled her.

"And how do you know whether he's my type or not, might I ask?"

Everything about the row was proceeding along perfectly classical lines: Doris had now reached the stage of extreme formality.

As for Doreen, she remained more frankly rude.

"Because I know you better than he does, my lamb," she answered. "Or don't I?"

"What do you mean by that, pray?"

Doreen smiled her carefully calculated smile again. And she held on to it all the time she was speaking.

"You surely can't want me to actually say it," she said. "You *must* know." She paused. "Bill comes from such a different sort of home."

"And what's wrong with my home?"

"Oh, nothing, darling," Doreen assured her, still smiling. "Nothing. If you can't see what I mean, I can't explain it to you. It only just proves what I'm saying." She paused again. "Not that I mind, of course. I understand."

"I think you're perfectly horrible."

Doreen came a step nearer. The smile had gone by now.

"Don't be rude, cherub," she said. "That would be so—common."

She turned her back on Doris as she said it and made her way to the bedroom. She hadn't meant to have a row with Doris. It had just turned out that way. Her nerves were jangling anyhow: they had been all day. If there were any of Doris's aspirins left she'd take a couple. Not that aspirins were what she really wanted. They took away the headache but they left you feeling so flat and stupid. It was a drink she needed. But until Mr. Perkiss arrived there was only orange squash and lime juice in the flat.

"Oh, God," she remembered suddenly. "I'll have to make it up with Doris before Mr. Perkiss arrives. Otherwise it'll be too awful."

She was thus quite unprepared for what happened. She hadn't reached the bedroom by the time Doris caught up with her.

"If you think I'm common," she said. "Let me tell you what you are. You're just a greedy man-hunter. You'd go after anything. Even after Mr. Perkiss. You haven't got the slightest self-respect where a man's concerned. Oh, no. You're not common. Of course not. And let me tell you something else as well. You're lazy. Bone lazy. You don't do anything in this flat. If I left it the way you do, you couldn't have any of your wonderful boy-friends here, because it would be like a pig-sty. . . ."

It was at that point that Mr. Perkiss arrived. And as Doreen couldn't possibly see him, it was Doris who had to let him in. She sat him down in the easy chair, gave him the evening paper and left him. It was nearly half an hour before the girls came through to him. And it didn't make matters any easier that they weren't on speaking terms. Doreen had spent the first fifteen minutes crying and she still was shaky and on edge.

But Mr. Perkiss didn't notice it. He was too much preoccupied with being delightful. He had brought gin and roses. And he kept referring to them as his little offering. But in his manner of making the presentation he blundered. Instead of simply dumping the things down on the table and then standing well back, he gave them each the presents in person. It was the gin he gave to Doreen, and the roses to Doris.

"A picture," he said, as he watched her holding them. "A perfect picture. You belong to each other, you and the roses."

There was nothing about the remark that need have annoyed Doreen. It was simply Mr. Perkiss's way of talking. And she would much rather have had the gin. But she had only just recovered from a rather violent fit of wanting to commit suicide, and was in a mood when quite little things upset her. At the thought that Mr. Perkiss's compliments were being directed at Doris she was ready to start *howling* at any moment.

And Mr. Perkiss, not conscious that he was being anything other than a very charming success, went on being untactful. He admired Doris's ear-rings. Then, not content with that, he told Doreen that, poor dear child, she looked tired. He wished, he said, that he could tear himself away from his office if only for a long week-end just to take her to the sea somewhere and bring back the colour to her cheeks. He mentioned three times in all that she was looking worn out.

And—or was it only that Doreen was imagining it?—he was paying particular attention to Doris. He gave her his glass of gin-and-lime because he said that the glass—they were all odd glasses in the flat—matched her dress. And then, turning smilingly to Doreen, he assured her that it was wicked, absolutely wicked, the way young girls were worked in offices nowadays. The proper place for girls, he said, was out in gardens gathering flowers. . . .

Considering his smallness—he was just a little grasshopper of a man—he made a surprisingly good meal of the mushroom soup and the cold ham. And he talked food as well as ate it. He remembered other delicious meals that he had eaten on the Continent. And the only thing that seemed wrong about them in retrospect was that the girls had not been there to eat them with him. To make up for it he began planning other meals in London. When Doreen said that she adored oysters and didn't mind what the rest of the meal was like so long as there were oysters, Mr. Perkiss promised to take them to Pruniers. Then, not wishing to miss an opportunity of being skittish, he explained that he would take Doris another time, adding that no gentleman in his position could afford to be seen with *two* pretty girls at the same time. It was another piece of untactfulness, and it hurt Doreen terribly. She saw how right she had been in what she had said. Doris was stealing her boy-friends, stealing them one after another.

But she tried to pretend that she hadn't noticed anything. She just fixed a social smile on her face and went on sipping her drink, as though she were enjoying herself.

Then Bill came. They didn't hear him coming up the iron staircase because he was wearing crêpe rubber shoes. But they heard him all right as soon as he got up on to the veranda. And that was because he fell against one of the little brightly painted tubs that Doreen had placed there. It went careering all over the place with Bill after it.

And apart from arriving at an awkward sort of moment just as the meal was nearly over, Bill was poor company. He was both loving and despondent. His Finals were in the morning and the Examining Board of the Faculty would decide whether he really should be allowed to become a doctor or not. At the moment, he rather feared not. Until half an hour ago he had resolved to spend the evening quietly in his room in an orgy of last-minute revision. He had decided to check up on everything—the bones of the ear, the nervous system, the symptoms of scarlet fever, the classification of blood groups, the sulphonamide reactions, Materia Medica, morphology, anæsthetics, pathology, midwifery; the whole bag of tricks in fact, five years' medicine packed into a single desperate evening's reading. Then, quite suddenly, just as he was getting down to things he had realised that he simply must see Doris. Stopping abruptly in the middle of cardiac stimulants, abuse of, he got up from his chair and came.

It was Mr. Perkiss's gin that helped to revive him. He poured himself out a long solemn drink, and felt better. Under the influence of it he became genial and silly. He began testing everybody's reflexes, including his own, and was delighted to discover that Doreen was at the top of the list and Mr. Perkiss was at the bottom. Bill kept hitting Mr. Perkiss's knee over and over again, but nothing happened. Mr. Perkiss had simply no reflexes at all. Perhaps that was why he seemed to dislike the whole experiment.

But what was far worse that Bill's coltishness was the way he behaved towards Doris. He went across and sat on the arm of her chair, leaving Doreen alone on the divan and Mr. Perkiss perched on the coloured wicker Sit Easy that creaked even under his weight. Doreen watched him with tears starting up in her eyes. Somehow Mr. Perkiss, absolute darling though he was, looked so small and desiccated beside Bill. And because Doris looked so happy and comfortable and because Doreen herself felt so miserable and out of it, she simply had to say something.

"Tell Monty about what's happened to Percy," she said. "He's been *so* interested in him ever since that night he came here."

Doris shook her head.

"I'll tell him some other time," she replied.

"Oh, but you must," Doreen went on. "It's so tremendously exciting. Monty adores crime."

Mr. Perkiss leant forward and raised his little marmoset face, pleadingly.

"Please, please tell me," he said. "Such an intriguing young man. I'd never met anyone quite like him before."

"Some other time," Doris repeated.

It annoyed Doreen that Doris was behaving in this cold off-hand manner to Mr. Perkiss. But it was not surprising. Everything about Doris annoyed Doreen to-night. And her head was swimming. That was Bill's fault. She had started drinking all over again when he came. And she had told herself even before then, that it was time for her to stop.

"What a long time ago it seems since I first met Percy," she said. "It was over at Kennington." She paused. "Do you remember, my pet? It was the night the gas went off at supper because your father had forgotten to put a shilling in."

"I remember," Doris answered. Her voice was dangerously calm and level as she said it.

Doreen continued to lie there, staring up at the ceiling. Then she turned to Mr. Perkiss.

"You'd never have thought it to look at him," she went on, "but he's just been arrested for stealing cars. It was in the paper. You wouldn't have guessed Doris had friends like that, would you?"

Mr. Perkiss raised his fair, almost invisible eyebrows.

"Well, well," said Mr. Perkiss. "How remarkable!" He leaned across and smiled charmingly at Doris. "I shall hear next that you're a girl-bandit yourself. Just like the moving pictures."

As he spoke, he extended the first finger of both hands and gave a genteel imitation of someone firing off two revolvers simultaneously.

But this was just one more piece of untactfulness in the course of this deplorable evening. For it didn't amuse Doris in the least.

"I think you're being perfectly horrible," she said. "You seem to forget that Percy's in prison."

As she said it she saw Percy very plainly. He was in his purple suit and yellow shoes and he was sitting beside her in the Toledo, a foolish dreamy look on his face. He was eating ice-cream out of one of the little threepenny cups and listening to the organ. . .

The effect of Doris's remark was to make Mr. Perkiss withdraw sharply into himself like a snail that has had its horns touched. If there was one thing that he couldn't bear it was for a young lady to think him horrible. He drew in his breath with a small sucking sound, and said nothing.

It was Doreen who replied for him. She threw out a cloud of cigarette smoke and addressed the ceiling.

"It's all my fault," she said. "I ought to have remembered. They meant a lot to each other once."

She dropped her face a little so that she was regarding Doris out of the corner of her eye.

"You weren't actually *engaged* to him or anything, were you?" she asked.

Doris sat up very straight.

"You know I wasn't. There was never anything like—like that."

Doreen did not move. She was lying back against the cushions, her arm folded behind her head.

"I'm so sorry, I quite thought there was," she said. "You were always talking about him. And then when he dropped in that night everything seemed so natural."

"Don't be silly," Doris said.

It was really a very mild little answer. But in Doreen's state it was disastrous. She had been called silly in front of other people.

"How was I to know he was just another of your boy-friends?" she retorted.

"I didn't have any boy-friends." Doris was sitting bolt upright now.

Doreen smiled. It began as a sort of prolonged smile. But it became instead a slurred and untidy laugh that, for some reason, she could not stop. The sound of it alarmed her. Could it *possibly* be, she wondered, that she had really drunk too much of Monty Perkiss's gin?

"That isn't what you told me earlier," she said.

Doris got up and came over to her.

"I didn't tell you anything," she said. "I don't know why but you're trying to be beastly. I think you're loathsome."

Doreen sat up herself abruptly. Her head was swimming.

"When I want a lesson in manners from you I shall ask for it," she answered. "Just because your Percy's been put in prison you needn't go about trying to get someone else."

The words as she said them sounded perfectly dreadful. They astonished her. But she hadn't been able to stop saying them. They were what she had been keeping right at the back of her mind, and suddenly they had just come pouring out. Then, to her further astonishment, she found that she wasn't saying them to Doris any longer. Doris had left them and gone through into her bedroom. She was left speaking to herself. She got up hurriedly and followed her.

Bill and Mr. Perkiss exchanged glances.

"What a sad affair," Mr. Perkiss said, shaking his head nervously. "I'm afraid our little Doreen isn't quite herself to-night."

Bill didn't say anything. He went and leant up against the painted window-sill on the far wall. He wanted to have a private word with Doris—and then another private word with Doreen afterwards. He was still wondering how he could contrive it, when Doris appeared again. She was carrying a suitcase—and she went straight past him to the front door, without speaking. As she passed him, Bill saw that she was crying.

"What's happening?" he asked. "Where are you going?"

But she didn't answer. And even if she had answered it would have been difficult to hear her because Doreen was apologising at the top of her voice from the bedroom. She would kill herself, she kept saying, if Doris went.

Mr. Perkiss was the only silent one. He remained perched up in the wicker Sit Easy, a frightened look on his face, trying to appear oblivious of the commotion that was going on all round him.

As Doris slammed the front door behind her, Bill snatched up his hat and without saying good-bye to anyone, jerked the door open again, and followed her.

2

It was late by now; really late. After midnight, in fact. Across the table with all the text-books lying on it, Bill and Doris sat looking at each other.

"Feel better?" Bill was asking.

He had just poured out the last of the beer and had insisted that Doris should drink it. "Beer's best," he said. And Doris had drunk it. She didn't like beer, and she felt a little sick at the moment. But she nodded dutifully.

"You'll feel better still in the morning," Bill told her.

"I ought to go now," she said slowly.

But Bill wouldn't hear of it.

"We've had all that out before," he said firmly. "Can't go home at this time. Just upset 'em. You have the bed and I'll take the couch." He sat there looking at her for a moment, as though turning something over in his mind, and then picked up his cherry pipe in the corner and began filling it.

"In any case," he said, "I've still got some reading to do."

On the table the whole unfamiliar theory of modern medicine lay there to be absorbed.

Doris, however, was apparently thinking of something else.

"Do you think Doreen will be all right?" Doris asked suddenly. "She won't kill herself or anything?"

Bill looked up again.

"At this moment," he answered, "Doreen is probably making Mr. Perkiss a very happy man."

He paused.

"Like me to go while you get into bed?" he asked. "Have to be a bit quiet because the landlady's one of the old-fashioned sort."

"That's all right," Doris answered. "I'm just going to lie down as I am."

She kicked her shoes off and stretched herself out on the bed. Then she lay there staring up at the ceiling. It was not a particularly bright and comely ceiling. But Bill's shadow from the reading-lamp on the table beside him spread itself over her. It was larger than life-size, and somehow comforting.

After a while Bill turned to her.

"Like the light out?" he asked.

"When you're ready," she answered.

"Ready now," he told her.

In the darkness the room seemed smaller. And as it contracted it grew more intimate. Through the faint light entering from the window Doris saw Bill arranging the cushions on the couch for a pillow. Then he drew up a chair for his legs. He was very businesslike about it and had the air of a man who had been sleeping on couches all his life.

"Good night," he said.

"Good night," Doris answered.

They lay there without speaking. One of the churches in Hampstead struck one.

"Are you still awake?" Bill asked.

"I'm awake."

"So am I. I'm lonely."

CHAPTER 34

As CELLS GO, it was one of the more comfortable ones. There were two chairs as well as a table. And there was a bed in the corner. The bed was two foot six inches wide and six foot long exactly. It was made up on the simple principle of spreading a very thin straw palliasse over a shelf of very thick boards. At the foot of the bed were two rough blankets and a pillow, thin like the mattress, and stuffed with the same creaky straw. Altogether it was the kind of bed to be slept on rather than lingered in.

Over the end of the bed, and so high that even standing on the bed itself you couldn't look out, was the window. Six massive metal bars like park railings ran up and down across its width and there was a wire mesh stretched across the bars so that birds couldn't fly in and things couldn't be thrown out. It was not the bars alone that made the window depressing; it was the thickness of the walls the alcove of the window revealed. If you stopped and thought about it, it wasn't like being in a room at all. It was like being buried in a solid block of stone.

But there was more than an extra chair that distinguished this cell from the others in the same gallery. There were the privileges that went with it. For a start, there were the meals. In all the other cells, the food was the same. It was prison food. There was none of the Bisto smell about it. But in a remand cell there is no kind of restriction. You simply have your meals sent over from the restaurant opposite. Or from the Ritz or the Savoy, for that matter, if you can afford it.

And it is not only a question of meals. There is the business of visitors. Within reason there is no limit on the number of visitors a remand man can receive. And this is as it should be. A man in remand isn't guilty. He's only suspect. And he can't be kept in prison too long either. The Barons had all that out with King John years ago. So there he is, the man on remand, not yet in Hell and certainly not in Heaven. It's a kind of well-ventilated, carefully supervised, rather chilly Limbo that he inhabits.

Percy had only just seen his last visitor. It was Mr. Barks, his solicitor. He seemed a nice man, Mr. Barks. He had been picked on in court and made to represent Percy, just like that. He was all right, he was. What was more, he was Mr. Barks of Barks, Barks, Wedderburn and Barks—though which one of the Barkses, Percy wasn't quite sure. Top dog of the whole lot of them probably, from the look of him. Very much the gentleman, with horn-rimmed spectacles and a watch-chain and an umbrella with a gold band round it. And, considering he was doing it practically for nix, very conscientious and helpful. He'd been along twice already, and this was his third visit. The only thing about him was that he was a bit brusque. He didn't treat Percy very nice. When Percy told him, naturally, that he'd never set eyes on the Bentley that They were talking about, and that he'd bought the Lalique Lady and the coach lamps and the bedside rug in an all-night coffee-bar from someone he didn't know, Mr. Barks had been quite rude to him. If Percy wasn't going to tell him the truth, Mr. Barks said, he'd chuck up the whole case. He was there to help Percy, he went on, not to listen to a lot of lies that wouldn't deceive a child. And the way he went on you'd think he'd got a right to speak to Percy like that. But Percy saw through him. Mr. Barks wasn't there really to help him. That was simply his line of talk. Underneath it all he was just one of Them. After he had heard Percy to the end, he said that they were going to plead guilty. And when Percy said that he didn't want to, Mr. Barks told him quite curtly that he knew more about the law than Percy did. So that was that. Percy was guilty because Mr. Barks said he was. That was justice.

"Just you wait till I'm on the level with a solicitor of my own I pay money to," Percy kept telling himself. "Then we'll see. No more pleading guilty then. Not guilty, m'lud: that's what it'll be when I've got a solicitor of my own, someone I pay money to."

All the same he couldn't help laughing. It wasn't half funny the way Mr. Barks talked about it all. He didn't say "you," he said "we." "We're going to plead guilty," was what he'd said, just as though it was Mr. Barks with his rolled-up umbrella who was pleading guilty to stealing the Bentley.

Then an unpleasant doubt crossed Percy's mind. Suppose Mr. Barks were pleading guilty only because it was the quickest way of getting things done. Suppose he had said to himself: "There's nothing in this for me. Let's plead guilty and get back into the money." That wasn't a nice thought, was it? It still seemed possible that for twenty-five pounds or so, Mr. Barks might be persuaded to change his plea. Percy decided to put it to him next time he saw him. He hadn't actually got twenty-five pounds. But he could find it.

Not that he was worrying. Luckily for him, he wasn't the worrying sort. Mr. Barks had promised to try some sort of First Offenders racket that he said he knew how to operate. It sounded all right the way he put it. It just didn't sound likely, that was all.

The funny thing was that Percy had got Them foxed. From the way They behaved you could see that They didn't know anything. They'd got him there, where They wanted him, the man They were looking for, the non-stop car bandit, and They were so dumb They didn't know Their luck. He wanted to laugh at Them for it. It was funny, wasn't it, when you came to think about it?

"In any case I'm O.K. this time," he told himself. "If it's First Offenders, I'm O.K. And if it's three months, who minds that? Do it on my head. I'm O.K. either way."

Three months! The words came back to him as a kind of echo. Who minds? Well, there was one person who'd mind all right. And that was him. And also Jackie. She'd be wondering whatever had become of him. She'd think he was unfaithful or something. He couldn't bear that. Not when he wasn't. And how did he know what Jackie would be doing with herself? There were a lot of very undesirable characters round Victoria way. She might get herself into bad company with him not there to protect her. *She* might be unfaithful to *him*. That was what hurt. That was what maddened him. Not to be able to get out even for five minutes to explain.

Through the iron grille of the door he saw the blue back of a warder passing.

"They don't know the harm they're doing keeping me here," he told himself. "I'll go after Them. I'll get damages. They don't know the harm They're doing."

CHAPTER 35

I

IN THE MORNING—the morning after the row—Bill's landlady took matters into her own hands and gave him notice for having had a "person" in his rooms. Nothing like it, she said, had ever happened in any house of hers before. She spoke as though it were something which, left unchecked, would contaminate the rest of Belsize Park, spread across London, and ultimately corrupt Society as a whole.

They were both there when the landlady knocked at the door and delivered her ultimatum. Doris stood over by the window looking into the street and trying not to listen while Bill and the landlady had their discussion in the passage outside. But she was too much dazed by everything that had happened to take proper notice of it. The whole of yesterday evening was tangled and distorted in her mind as though all the brightest colours she could think of had suddenly run into each other. It had been a slashed, fork-lightning kind of evening. Looking back on it, it was like an evening in somebody else's life. . . .

They left the house together, arm-in-arm, shortly after half-past eight and found a little restaurant near the Underground station where they could get some breakfast. It seemed a specially providential little restaurant when they reached it, because the only other source of breakfast in Belsize Park was the dining-room of Bill's boarding-house—and of course he wasn't allowed in there any more. It was a pretty silent sort of breakfast, however.

"I do feel awful," Doris said at last. "Your Finals to-day, and being turned out of your digs just because of me."

Bill only laughed. To-day looked like being the end of everything so far as he was concerned, and he couldn't take the business of the landlady seriously enough to mind about it.

"Wasn't going to stop there anyhow," he told her. "Never really comfortable, you know."

Then because it was late Doris said that she had to be leaving, and Bill insisted on going all the way to the office with her. It wasn't until he had said good-bye to her in Clifford's Inn that he properly realised the state he was in. Here he was on the way to the Examination School, when he should have been composing himself for the ordeal of Finals, and all that he could think about was the feel of Doris's head on his shoulder and his arms wrapped round her.

It was like that, too, in the Examination School. He found himself one of forty-five young men, all about his own age. The invigilator, a hushed, respectable consultant who wasn't above picking up an odd hundred guineas by marking examination papers, told them that they could begin, and sat back in his chair on the dais reconciling himself to the boredom of the next three hours. It was the fifteenth examination in clinical medicine over which he had presided, and it did not differ in the minutest particular from the fourteen preceding ones. Two Jews and an Indian wearing a sports coat and turban, started writing immediately as though conscious that with all the stuff bottled up in them they were heading straight for Harley Street. And the rest read their examination papers closely and anxiously, turned over, and then hurriedly re-read the first side, fidgeted with their fountain pens, coughed, gazed upwards at the ceiling, wrote slowly and laboriously.

At the end of half an hour the invigilator, because he had pins-and-needles in his leg, got up and began to move about. It was then that he noticed a young man sitting towards the back, who didn't seem to realise that the examination had begun. He had a vacant, moony expression on his face, and was apparently drawing with the back of his nib on the blotting-paper. In the course of his rounds the invigilator paused discreetly to have a look. The young man's blotting-paper was covered with a dense pattern made up of five letters. There was "Doris" in large Roman capitals; in cursive script; in small italics; in a high, backward hand with extra serifs to all letters; and in what looked like cuneiform. At the moment the engrossed young man was decorating a large capital "D" with a design of ivy and holly-leaves.

At one o'clock the invigilator called a halt, and Bill looked gloomily at the numbered pages in front of him. He didn't seem to have written so much as some of the others. By now, the two Jews and the Indian had great dossiers in front of them. And that wasn't all. Bill had his own views on the quality of what he had managed to do. "I only wish I knew how I'd been spending the last five years," he thought gloomily. "I only wish I knew."

He forgot his gloom, however, at the thought that he'd at last be able to phone Doris. And because he couldn't wait to get to a proper call-box, he used the telephone in the porter's desk in the front hall. It was an awkward, cumbersome instrument of the old candlestick kind. And it was very public with the porter standing there beside him, and the lobby full of people. But it worked: that was the only thing that mattered. He was able to catch Doris before she went out to lunch.

"I was hoping you'd phone," the voice at the other end said. "I've got to talk to you."

"But I want you to," Bill said. "I want you to more than anything, my little. . . ." He remembered where he was and stopped himself. "Come and meet me as soon as you get off. I'm through here at five."

"You won't like what I'm going to say," Doris told him.

Bill felt a large cold patch in the middle of his stomach as though an ice-pack had been placed there.

"Then don't say it," he told her, trying to sound light and carefree. "Don't say it. Just come. See you at the Tea Kettle at six."

"All right," Doris's voice answered. "I'll be there. But you won't like it. . . ."

Her voice trailed off and it ended in what sounded suspiciously like a swallow.

"Cheer up," Bill told her. "Don't worry. I love you."

He couldn't help about the porter this time. He did love her. And he felt distinctly better now that he'd told her so again. They were three words that he'd been wanting to say all the morning.

2

Altogether, it was a day of telephoning. First, Doreen phoned up the office to say that she had a migraine and the doctor wouldn't allow her outside the flat. Then, later in the morning, Mr. Perkiss rang up Doreen. And only just in time, too. She was just on the verge of another nasty bout of suicide when the bell rang.

Indeed, she could hardly have been in lower spirits. The fact that she had lost Doris for a friend wasn't the only thing that was worrying her. By nine-thirty when he still hadn't phoned, it seemed that she'd lost Mr. Perkiss as well. She'd made two perfectly good attempts to phone him herself and each time, though she was *sure* that he was there, his secretary had said that he wasn't. It was no wonder that she had a migraine. And if it got any worse she really would have to call a doctor. After all, it wasn't her fault that things hurt her so. It was just the way she was made.

And then everything cleared up magically when Monty rang her. He sounded so calm and experienced that she couldn't help simply *loving* him. She didn't know that he had been plucking up his courage for a whole three-quarters of an hour beforehand, reaching out for the receiver at one moment and thrusting it away from him at the next. When he did finally get through to his little Doreen—she was twice his size really, but he always thought of her as "little Doreen"—he had made his mind up. He told her that he couldn't bear the thought of her leaving the flat where they had been so happy together and offered to take care of Doris's share of everything. When Doreen had accepted—and she didn't see what else she could *possibly* do in the circumstances, even though she *hated*, simply *hated*, the idea of being a drag on anyone—Mr. Perkiss suggested very delicately that as he was closing his flat anyway she might let him come up to the studio for a few nights so that she shouldn't be lonely. In her present state, Doreen accepted that, too. And in his snug cosy office in Duke Street, Mr. Perkiss sat back, rubbing his small pink hands, and feeling what he really was—Edwardian.

Ever since he had separated from Mrs. Perkiss fourteen years before, he had been imagining some really daring piece of naughtiness like this.

3

The Tea Kettle, where Bill and Doris met, was one of those half underground tea-rooms with orange-topped tables arranged corner-wise, and horse-brasses and pictures of cats on the walls, and pale lady-like waitresses in long overalls the colour of the table-tops. The waitresses all looked the same—slim, long-nosed and fair-haired; and the elderly lady—slim, long-nosed and white-haired—who sat behind the cash-desk at the door was an example of what the younger waitresses might eventually become if only they stuck at it and didn't get too familiar with any of the customers. The elderly lady wore black—an obvious promotion from orange—and a large butterfly-wing brooch. Altogether there was an air of dignified and frustrated gentility about the place, as though waiting at table were beneath the waitresses and taking cash was rather belittling to the cashier.

Not that the Tea Kettle was any different from a hundred other little tea-rooms all of the same kind in various parts of London. It was the kind of sub-restaurant that abounded—the Five O'Clock, Polly's Pantry, Kate's Café, the Robin Tea Rooms (with a coloured cut-out of an outsize robin in the window) and Queenie's. There was a whole flock of Blue Birds as well fluttering over the city and even nesting quite far out in the suburbs. The only thing that was wrong, from a man's point of view, with some of these feminine tea-cabins was that as the slim young ladies never—on account of their figures—ate anything more sustaining than two pieces of cinnamon toast at a sitting, they had no idea of an appetite like Bill's.

Bill had been there for some time, reading a rather worn copy of *Scottish Country Life*, when Doris arrived, and he saw at once that she looked tired. She was paler than usual, which made her seem fragile and forlorn. He wanted to soothe and caress her. The professional side of him also thought of prescribing an extract of hog's stomach for anæmia. But, in the end, all that he did was to squeeze her hand before she drew it away from him, and pass her the menu which had been written out in hand by one of the long-nosed young ladies.

"I'll have an *hors d'œuvres*," she told him. And because she was a girl the sight of a sardine with a yellow and white segment of hard-boiled egg and a half-tomato backed up by a few leaves of pale lettuce appeared in her eyes to be entirely satisfying. Bill surveyed the menu from top to bottom as though hoping to find a portion of roast beef and Yorkshire, or a chump chop, lurking somewhere on it, and then ordered scrambled eggs on baked beans.

But even though it was in a way her favourite kind of food, Doris made no attempt to eat it. She tailed the sardine, took a speck of black off the hard-boiled egg, and pushed the plate away from her.

"I want to talk to you," she said.

There was something in her voice that Bill didn't like; the ice-pack returned to its place in the centre of his stomach. But he was determined to get in his word first.

"So do I," he said. "I want you to marry me. Straightaway. At once."

"That's what I want to talk to you about," she told him.

"Go on then," he said doubtfully.

"I've been thinking," she said. "I don't want to get married. Not yet."

"Don't want to get married?" he repeated. "Not want to?"

"It isn't exactly that," she explained. "It's different somehow. I just don't want you to feel you've got to marry me because of what happened last night."

The ice-pack melted as she was speaking, leaving a wet sticky feeling in its place. He leant forward and managed to get hold of her hand again.

"But I want to marry you," he said.

"You know it'd be silly," she answered. "It wouldn't be fair. You aren't even qualified yet."

"I shall be by the autumn."

She broke off suddenly.

"Oh, Bill," she said. "I meant to ask you as soon as I saw you. How were the Finals?"

Bill grinned.

"Oh, them," he said. "They're jam. They're a walk-over."

"But you ought to get established first," she went on. "You know you ought. It's a frightful drag on a young doctor being married."

"Who said so?"

She was right, of course. He'd known several men who just hadn't been able to make the grade and had drifted away into East End panel practices.

"Doreen said it. She said . . ."

"And what the hell's Doreen got to do with it?" he asked. "She doesn't know anything about anything."

It surprised Doris to think that Doreen didn't know. It had always seemed to her that she knew everything.

"You know you wanted to go on and be a surgeon," she continued. "That'll take years."

Bill paused and began stirring his coffee with his free hand.

"You've got your job," he said. "We could manage."

Doris shook her head.

"It isn't only that," she said. "It's a lot of things. It's me and my people, and the way I've been brought up, and where I come from. It's lots of things. I might be just about right as a doctor's wife. But a surgeon's different. You'll be in Harley Street, and you ought to have someone awfully grand."

She removed her hand from his for the second time and began searching about in her bag for a handkerchief.

"You'll make a marvellous surgeon's wife," he told her. "You'll make the most bloody marvellous surgeon's wife in the world."

"Oh, Bill, you're crazy."

They sat for a moment without speaking.

"Then you will marry me?"

"Not yet."

"Better hurry up," he told her. "There'll be war at any moment. No sense waiting till I'm sent abroad."

"Do you mean it?"

"I do," Bill answered, suddenly feeling about twenty years older than she was. "I do. And I mean that we shouldn't see each other for years. I may be sent anywhere. I may go to India, I may go to Singapore. I may go to Hong Kong. And in the meantime we've got to snatch at every minute we can get."

"Are you *sure* you'll be sent abroad?"

The single possibility seemed the climax to everything. The news on the wireless and in the papers, General Ironside's going to

Moscow, the row in the Danzig Senate, the Indian troops reaching Suez, all the rubbish that Uncle Henry was always talking, seemed to culminate in this one awful thought.

"Certain," Bill told her. "They'll want all the doctors they can get."

"Doctors don't go right into the firing line, do they?"

Bill grinned.

"No," he said. "They send the ambulance men."

Doris put her hand in his again. "Oh, Bill, I do love you so," she said. "There won't be a war, will there?"

"Not a chance of it," he told her. "I was only joking."

There was a pause.

"What are you going to do to-night?" he asked.

"I'm going home."

"To Dulcimer Street?"

"Yes, of course. I can't go back to Doreen now."

"Have you told them?"

"Not yet."

"Well, let's go somewhere first."

And it was his second evening of revision—Pathology to-morrow—that went down the drain as he said it.

CHAPTER 36

MRS. JOSSER was taking the daily paper down to Mrs. Vizzard. It had gone on for so long, this habit of lending her the daily paper after the Jossers had finished with it, that Mrs. Vizzard had come to regard it as a kind of right. And it was even better now that Mr. Josser had left the City. It meant that instead of having to wait until the evening, she got the day's news in the afternoon while there was still some of the morning sparkle left on it.

As Mrs. Josser descended the dark staircase the thought crossed her mind that it was sad that anyone of Mrs. Vizzard's background should, through the impeccable accident of widowhood, have been reduced to a front basement in her own lawful house. She felt sorry for her. Not deeply sorry, just regretful. Taking everything into consideration Mrs. Vizzard had made a remarkably efficient job of widowhood.

There seemed, when she knocked on the door, to be something oddly hesitating about Mrs. Vizzard's reply. It was preceded by something that sounded like whispering. And then, when she went inside, she saw why she had been kept waiting. Mrs. Vizzard was not alone. In front of the fireplace, in a very new-looking pale grey suit, Mr. Squales was standing. He was fingering a fresh and shiny tie. His dark eyes fixed themselves on Mrs. Josser and he smiled in that deep, enigmatic way of his as though he were either about to say something or conceal it. But, after one glance, Mrs. Josser scarcely noticed him. It was at Mrs. Vizzard she was staring. Something remarkable had happened. It was not the same Mrs. Vizzard who faced her. Instead of the dark blue serge cut very high at the throat, which she usually wore, she was decked out in a smart black dress with a large bunch of artificial flowers pinned on to her shoulder. It was the sort of dress that a lady—even a young lady probably—in Bond Street might wear. But most astonishing of all was the change which Mrs. Vizzard had wrought in her own person. Since Mrs. Josser had seen her earlier in the day she had remodelled *herself*. Even her hair-dressing had changed. Instead of screwing her hair viciously into a small hard roll that she pinned remorselessly to the nape of her neck, she had wound it round the top of her head in two plaits. In the result, it made a kind of halo so that her face seemed set in a tall frame. And the high cheek bones that had appeared so disfiguring before, now appeared positively distinguished-looking. Her temples, which had not been visible when the hair had been dragged across them, now showed themselves; and they were beautiful. Mrs. Vizzard looked ten—fifteen—even possibly more—years younger.

Mrs. Josser stood there still staring. She looked from Mrs. Vizzard to Mr. Squales, and back to Mrs. Vizzard again. And as she did so Mrs. Vizzard intercepted her glance. She blushed.

"We've been buying clothes," she announced stupidly.

"Buying clothes?"

Mrs. Josser repeated the words as though they had no meaning for her. She turned to Mr. Squales again. Under his pale grey suit, he was wearing a bright mauvish shirt with cuffs that came right down over his wrists. Mauve cuffs over hickory-coloured wrists. She could bear it no longer. She looked up at him for an explanation. But Mr. Squales only smiled back at her. She was unpleasantly aware of a double row of strong white teeth in a lean dusky face.

"You see," he said, "this is rather an important occasion. Kitty—that is Mrs. Vizzard—and I have just become engaged."

"Engaged!"

In her amazement Mrs. Josser had done it again. She was repeating everything that was said to her.

"Engaged to be married," Mr. Squales said slowly and distinctly after her as though there were something magical in having the words uttered for the third time.

He paused.

"And I feel sure you'd want to be the first to congratulate us," he continued in the same deep purring voice. "The first to share our joy."

Mrs. Josser tore her gaze away from Mr. Squales and looked across at Mrs. Vizzard. The expression that she saw there startled her. Mrs. Vizzard wasn't smiling in the least. Her face was set. She was looking hard at Mrs. Josser as though daring her *not* to congratulate them.

Mrs. Josser moved her lips. She was trying, trying hard, to say something. But what? She could think of nothing that she would like to hear herself saying.

It was Mr. Squales himself who saved her in this moment of confusion. He appeared suddenly beside her, a wine-glass in his hand. Mrs. Josser glanced up and saw that on the sideboard—the respectable mahogany sideboard where the tea-caddy and the biscuit barrel had always stood—a bottle of white port and a row of glasses were standing.

"You will drink to our health?" he asked her.

But before she could answer, he had transferred his smile, fixed and gleaming as ever, to Mrs. Vizzard.

"And you, too, Kitty?" he added. "A glass of port wine to celebrate?"

"Thank you," Mrs. Vizzard replied.

She spoke faintly, like a child, as she thanked him for her own port wine.

Then Mr. Squales turned to Mrs. Josser. She felt the wine-glass being pressed into her hand. The stem was smooth and icy cold. She drew back instinctively.

"No. No, thank you," she said.

"You won't drink to our marriage?" Mr. Squales enquired.

His smile increased in intensity until it was glowering at her.

"It's . . . it's not that," Mrs. Josser told him. "It's simply that I can't stop. I want to . . . to go and tell Mr. Josser."

The smile reached its uttermost limits.

"Of course. Of course," he told her. "You must invite him down. Then we will all four drink together."

As soon as she reached her own living-room upstairs, Mrs. Josser sat down herself on the corner of the couch. Then she burst into tears. "It's horrible, that's what it is," she said. "Just horrible."

Mr. Josser put down his paper and came over to her.

"Don't take it to heart so, Mother," he told her kindly. "I know just how you feel about Percy."

CHAPTER 37

I

It was boring, waiting. And that was all Percy ever did nowadays, wait. There had been a second remand, and he was getting fed up with it. If They didn't know Their own mind, if They were regretting having collared him, why didn't They come clean and let him go again? He wasn't doing Them any good just sitting there, was he?

"They wouldn't treat me this way, not if I was a rich man," he told himself. "They wouldn't dare." Bail allowed on two sureties of five hundred ... there were paragraphs like that in the paper every day. If he'd had his own Rolls-Royce he could have driven away in it the same day they'd come for him. Talk about one law for the poor and another for the rich, somebody ought to get up in Parliament and do something. He paused and ran his pocket comb through his hair. "They wouldn't treat me this way, not if I was a rich man," he added. "They wouldn't dare."

Then the other thought, the warm comforting one, swept into his mind, sweetening it.

"The laugh's on Them if They only knew it," he went on. "If They knew anything about me They'd do something. They're just wasting their time trying to fix a Bentley on me. It's an Austin they ought to be busy about."

But he remembered suddenly what he was really waiting for. It was his mother. She'd be along at two-thirty. It must be nearly that now. He hadn't got his watch, so he couldn't tell the time. And there weren't any clocks. Why weren't there any clocks? There wasn't anything wrong about wanting to know the time, was there? It was just another of those pin-pricks.

Thinking it over he wished that his mother weren't coming. It would only upset her. And he didn't like to see her that way. What was the use of it anyhow? She didn't understand. Prison wasn't in a woman's line. It was a man's job. A man's job right through. He was in a bit of a jam, that was all. And it was up to him and Mr. Barks to get him out. Women were simply in the way in a thing like this.

He didn't like thinking about what would happen to Mrs. Boon with no money coming in from him. But she'd saved something. He knew that because she'd told him so. And Mrs. Vizzard would never turn her out. She'd know that Percy would square things when he got back. Square things for everybody. He'd make things all right for his old mum, he would. He'd buy her a fur coat. He'd give her something to wear like jewellery. He'd take her to Brighton for a summer holiday. He wouldn't disappoint her.

Then he forgot all about his mother and began wondering about the others. Connie was all right. She'd been in plenty of jams herself. She wouldn't turn up her nose. And Mr. Squales. Well, he was potty anyway. He didn't matter. He'd just burrow his head in all that astrakhan and sleep out the winter. Mr. Puddy was O.K. too. And Mr. Josser was O.K. Very much O.K. It was Mr. Josser who had arranged for the meals that were being sent in.

Why was he doing it? Percy wondered. And then, of course, he saw why. It was because of Doris. Mr. Josser must have seen the way she'd thrown him over, and felt ashamed about it. The price of those meals was conscience money really. All the same it was nice of him to feel that way.

It was Mrs. Josser he wasn't so sure about. She'd always disliked him, he could feel that. But why worry? Disliking was something that two could do. What he was really concerned about was Mrs. Josser getting together with Mrs. Vizzard, and plotting behind his back. He wasn't quite clear what harm they could do him. But he didn't like it. In his present helpless, unprotected state he was aware of a general unpleasant foreboding. Things were happening. And he didn't know what things.

But quite suddenly it wasn't Dulcimer Street that he was thinking about at all. It was the Blonde. Not even Jackie, but the Blonde. That was the worst of being shut away from life like this—your brain kept on working and you couldn't stop it. It played tricks on you. Very unpleasant tricks sometimes. This was one of them. She was just as she had been when he'd first fallen for her. He kept seeing her very smart and dolled up with plenty of lipstick on and her hair swept up in front *à la* West End. And she was smiling at him as though she could eat him. It was all just as though nothing had ever happened.

He was still thinking about her—not because he wanted to, but because he couldn't stop—when there was the sound of footsteps in the corridor outside. Keys jingled and after one of those clumsy pauses that were always occurring in prisons, the door opened.

" This'll be Mum," Percy told himself. "This is where things get difficult."

He got up and stood there ready, a grin of uncertain welcome spreading itself across his face. He knew just how she'd look, with her cheeks sunken from all the worry—his worry, really—she'd been through, and tears waiting in her eyes ready for the moment when she actually saw him.

But it wasn't Mrs. Boon at all. It was the warder with the thick black eyebrows like George Robey's and a Police Inspector and an ordinary copper and a quiet elderly man in a dark grey suit who looked like anyone in the corner of a first-class railway carriage. He was the Deputy-Governor. But Percy only found that out afterwards.

The warder, who couldn't help looking as though he were about to say something funny, stood himself up at attention beside the door and then closed and locked it after the others had come in.

Just to show that They hadn't got anything on him, that They couldn't bounce him round as They wanted, Percy went over and leant against the table, his hands in his pockets. He was grinning.

"Stand up properly, Boon," the quiet elderly man told him.

Percy stood up.

"Now pay attention and listen carefully," the Deputy-Governor went on. "The inspector wants to speak to you."

Percy's grin came back again. But it wasn't the same grin. This was something quite different. This was pure nervousness.

"I'm listening," he said. And because he wanted to show that he wasn't being difficult, that he was on Their side really, he added, "Sir." He was trying hard to make everything go easily.

But the inspector didn't seem to notice.

"You are Percy Boon?" the inspector asked, in a heavy flat-footed sort of voice.

" That's me," Percy answered.

To his surprise the copper was writing down his answer in a notebook as though it were all new and important.

"Of 10 Dulcimer Street in the Borough of Kennington?"

"That's me," Percy said again.

"You are charged," the inspector went on, in the same expressionless voice, "with the murder of Lily Ann Watson, otherwise known as Rosa Sinclair, on the night of June third, 1939, in the Borough of Wimbledon."

There was a pause.

The inspector stopped, and Percy answered: "I never." Even that went down in the notebook.

Then the Deputy-Governor spoke again.

"Anything that you say may be used in evidence."

But Percy wasn't listening any more. He was trying hard to keep control of himself, and not cry or anything. Trying to behave sensible in fact.

"I never done it," he said firmly. "I can prove where I was at the time. I got witnesses."

The policeman was writing hard and Percy realised that perhaps he had said too much.

"I decline to make any statement until I have consulted my solicitor," he said, remembering that those were the classic words in these circumstances. "I'm not saying nothing," he added.

The inspector stepped back, the policeman—the ordinary copper—closed his notebook, and the Deputy-Governor came forward.

"You fully understand, Boon?"

"Yes, sir," the words came faintly.

"The warder will make the necessary arrangements for your solicitor to see you."

At this mention of him the warder drew himself even more sharply to attention and his eyebrows arched themselves even higher as though he were about to utter the wisecrack of the whole performance. But he said nothing. And the Deputy-Governor went on.

"You are still at liberty to write any letters that you want to write," he said.

Percy nodded. He couldn't speak at all now. He was just thinking desperately.

"I'll be O.K. when I've seen Mr. Barks," he told himself. "I'll tell him everything. I won't keep nothing back. Not now, I won't. I'll just rely on him. He'll know what to do. He's clever. I'll be O.K. when I've seen Mr. Barks."

He kept on telling himself that. Had to keep on telling himself. But he couldn't help feeling a bit doubtful.

Things had got a lot worse suddenly.

2

Despite all Mrs. Josser's warnings, Mr. Josser was back on the job again. He was rent collecting. But his heart wasn't properly in it any more. He was too much upset about Percy's having got himself arrested.

Besides, there wasn't the same permanent feel about rent collecting that there had been before he went away. He was really only filling in time. And it is always hard to be interested in something that you aren't going on with. Not that the Building Society didn't want him back—they were always ready for elderly reliables who were content to work for what they were prepared to pay. No, it was Mr. Josser who didn't want them. And that was because of the change in Mrs. Josser's attitude. From being a Londoner, born in London and bred in it, she had now definitely decided to try the dangerous, even reckless experiment of living somewhere in the country. The only thing that she still persisted in was that it was for the sake of Mr. Josser's health that she was doing it. Otherwise, it would have looked as though she had changed her mind.

The arrangement in any case suited him admirably.

"Just see Mrs. Boon through her bit of trouble," Mr. Josser told himself. "Then off we go."

But in the meantime, of course, there were the rents to be collected as usual. And Mr. Josser made the same old rounds with the same old thoroughness. It was astonishing the way nothing had altered. The kitchener in 23 Birkbeck Street was out of order again, and the rent was withheld in consequence. Mr. Josser made a note of it in the rent book as he had done before, and warned the tenant that there might be court proceedings. The tenant (who was a bit short-tempered from doing all her cooking for a family of five on a single-burner oil stove) threatened Mr. Josser's Society to go ahead with the summons and said that she'd hire a van to take the kitchener into court to show the magistrate. Mr. Josser smiled sadly and went along to 143 Arkley Rents. As usual, the rent book was missing. They were a cheerful, feckless lot at No. 143. The wireless was kept playing at full blast all the time so that it was like stepping into a band contest when they opened the door to you, and, in the general uproar, they preferred paying half a crown for a new rent book—they had had two already since the beginning of the year—to putting the old one away in a safe place. Then on to 17 Guinevere Street. As Mr. Josser expected, there was no one in—it might have been a family of ghosts who inhabited the place. He'd have to come back later. So, even though it meant retracing his steps, he went round to No. 1 Cranmer Terrace first, and knocked. Knocked loudly, as he remembered he had to. No. 1 Cranmer Terrace was getting deafer as she grew older. Mr. Josser brought most of the street out before she opened the door to him.

Because it was no use returning to Guinevere Street until after seven, Mr. Josser bought an evening paper and took himself into a tea-shop. It was one of Lyons's little local palaces, all marble and mirrors and bright chromium. Mr. Josser liked Lyons's. For quite trifling sums like threepence and fourpence-halfpenny, you could go into a Lyons's out of the surrounding drabness and bask in its more than renaissance brightness while gay little Nippies brought you your order on a near-silver tray. Mr. Josser had made up his mind as to what he would have. He wanted a cup of tea and two pieces of chocolate Swiss roll. For a man of his age, he was still very fond of fancy things.

As he sat there munching, he was in a very comfortable and contented frame of mind. The tea was hot and rather sweet as he liked it, the chocolate cream came oozing out of the sides of the roll, and he had undone his waistcoat. He felt so well that he might almost have been back in Brighton again.

Then in the corner of the evening paper, in the Stop Press, he saw something that made him stop drinking and put the cup down so hurriedly that it spilt onto the glass table-top.

Car Bandit Murder: Man Charged, it said. And underneath came two short paragraphs, a bit sideways across the column. "Percy Boone, motor mechanic, of Dulcimer Street, S.E., already in custody, to-day at Brixton Prison charged with the murder of Rose Sinclair, on June 3rd. Murdered woman had been employed as cashier in a fun fair."

That was all the space it got. But it was enough. It turned Mr. Josser quite sick at the sight, so that he had to push away the rest of the chocolate roll uneaten.

"Can't be Percy," he said. "They haven't spelt his name right. All the same, I'd better be getting back," he told himself. "Can't leave Mother alone at a time like this."

So far as he was concerned they could go on living rent-free in Guinevere Street for ever.

3

Even so, he was beaten to it by Connie.

She had been round to Madame Marie's Dress Agency to change her best frock—her summery-mummery—for something a bit more generally useful. And, for the transparent chiffon, plus seven and sixpence, she'd picked up a rather nice piece in moire with a nearly new sailor collar. It was an attractive little dress, even though it had gone a bit under the arms. As usual, the chief trouble in choosing it had been the size. At five foot one she didn't even come into Small Ladies. In the eyes of the trade, she was still a Juvenile. The new frock had got a label that said "Business Miss," sewn into the back.

But she was excited about more than the dress. Clutching the paper carrier from Swears and Wells that Madame Marie had given her, just as though the dress had been a new one, she was hurrying back to Dulcimer Street as fast as she could go. She was almost running, in fact. And the reason for this was that she had an evening paper in her hand. She had seen about Percy, too.

She had her first success sooner than she expected. Just as she was going in, she met Mr. Puddy coming out. He'd been resting all the afternoon, with his handkerchief spread over his face to help him concentrate, and he hadn't seen anything about anyone. Connie was therefore able to knock him all of a heap right on the doorstep.

He read the paragraph all the way through twice—it was the *Evening News* that Connie had bought, and there was more about it in there—before speaking. Then he shook his head and drew his breath in noisily between his teeth.

"He's god himself broberly in the soub, he has," he said thickly. "He'll have to wodge his steb."

"Isn't it terrible?" Connie asked him. "Can you think of anything worse?"

Mr. Puddy paused.

"Does his buther know?" he enquired.

"Don't ask me," she said, still a bit breathlessly. "I'm just going to find out. I only knew myself five minutes ago."

Mr. Puddy would have liked to be able to turn back and go in with her. But he couldn't. He was late. And he hadn't yet made any preparation for the night watches. On his way to the factory he had got to do a bit of shopping. He wanted a tin of baked beans, some cheese and half a pound of rich fruit cake. If he left things any later he might not be able to get them.

"God to be booving on," he said apologetically. "I'll buy a baber beself."

But Connie wasn't bothering any more about Mr. Puddy. As soon as he had left her she went bolting on up the stairs to Mrs. Josser's. She hurried so much, in fact, that when she got there she couldn't even speak. And in her agitation she had quite forgotten to knock. All that she could do was to push the evening paper under Mrs. Josser's nose and point.

For a moment, Mrs. Josser had great difficulty in adjusting herself to Connie. She had been sitting quietly thinking about Mrs. Vizzard and Mr. Squales, and was unprepared for sensation. The paper had been folded carefully into three, and it was a flat sword-like object that came thrusting at her. Connie's finger hovered somewhere over the middle of it.

And then she saw. "RUNAWAY KILLER," she read. "Percy Aloysius Boon, aged 18, garage-hand, of Dulcimer Street, S.E.11, already in custody on another charge, was to-day at Brixton Prison charged with the murder of Rose Sinclair, cashier in a fun fair. The murder took place on Wimbledon Common on the night of . . ."

But Mrs. Josser read no further. She handed the paper back indignantly as though she didn't want to be caught holding it.

"I don't believe it," she said.

"Don't believe it?" Connie repeated incredulously. "It's him all right. There aren't two Percy Boons in Dulcimer Street."

Mrs. Josser seized hold of the paper and re-read it.

"Whatever makes you think Percy would want to go and do a thing like that?" she demanded.

Connie shrugged her shoulders.

"That's just the seamy side of it," she explained. "You can't ever be sure with men."

There was a pause. Then Mrs. Josser looked up sharply.

"Does Mrs. Boon know?" she asked.

Connie moved towards the door.

"I'm on my way up there now," she told her. "I only just dropped in here first."

"We'll go up *together*," Mrs. Josser said firmly.

Percy Boon arrested for murder! Young Percy charged with killing someone! she kept on repeating it over to herself incredulously as she climbed the stairs. It was going to be bad enough for Mrs. Boon to have the news broken to her, even without Connie doing the breaking. But Mrs. Josser need not have worried. Mrs. Boon's room was empty. On the table of the dining-room was a dirty plate with the knife and fork still crossed on it and a half-eaten piece of bread resting against the side. In the bedroom the wardrobe door had been left open. It was as though at the very moment of finishing a simple meal something urgent had called Mrs. Boon away.

Connie and Mrs. Josser looked across at each other.

Then Connie put her thumbs down.

4

Mr. Josser had got back. Had got back nearly half an hour ago, in fact. But he still gave the appearance of having only just arrived. His hat and attaché case were on the table beside him, and his umbrella—his new one—was crooked over the back of a chair. They made a small, mournful group, the three of them. And, at the moment, nobody—not even Connie—was saying anything.

Mrs. Josser was the first to pull herself together.

"Mrs. Vizzard ought to be told," she announced suddenly. "It's only fair."

Mr. Josser glanced up from the spill that he was rolling. It was a spill made with the same paper that had contained the news.

"Why?" he asked.

Mrs. Josser's lips were drawn in and determined.

"Because she'll have to hear sooner or later, and I'd rather she heard it from me," she replied.

There was a pause. Connie raised her eyebrows, but didn't say anything. It was Mr. Josser who spoke. He put down the spill and got up.

"You don't want to face this alone, Mother," he said. "I'll come down, too."

But Mrs. Josser wouldn't hear of it.

"You go and sit down," she said. "You look tired enough already. Sit down and talk to Connie."

With that Mrs. Josser left them. They heard her footsteps descending the stairs, and there was silence again. At the thought of the bombshell, *her* bombshell—well, properly speaking, *Percy's* bombshell—that Mrs. Josser was about to deliver single-handed, Connie sat there writhing. For two pins, she'd have gone down with Mrs. Josser herself. But she could see that she wasn't wanted, and she didn't want to cause unpleasantness now. Something told her that this wasn't going to be the end of the evening.

All the same, it called for self-control having to sit there doing nothing while things were happening. Somehow Mr. Josser didn't seem to count. He was absorbed in thoughts of his own, fiddling absent-mindedly with the spill again, folding it in half, rolling it sideways, doubling up the ends. It quite startled her when he spoke.

"I wonder if there's anything he'd like," he said.

He had not said who "he" was. But it was obvious.

Connie gave a little titter. It was one of her inevitable moments of bad taste.

"He'd like to get out, that's what he'd like," she answered.

But Mr. Josser only shook his head.

"I meant something to read. Or some cigarettes, or something. Something to take his mind off things."

Connie thought.

"No harm in cigarettes," she said. "He can smoke all he wants to now. It's later on he'll miss it."

Mr. Josser looked across at her.

"Then you really think he did it?" he asked.

"It doesn't matter what I think, it's what they think," Connie answered. "They've got to prove it, that's all."

There was silence again after that until Connie started humming in a distant preoccupied sort of way.

"Do you reckon she knows, or doesn't she?" Connie asked with a jerk of her head in the direction of the ceiling.

"I don't like to think," Mr. Josser answered simply.

Connie paused.

"Just imagine if she doesn't," she said. "What a sad, sad home-coming."

It was the sound of voices on the stairs that interrupted them. Mrs. Josser's voice and Mrs. Vizzard's. As they reached the door they stopped suddenly. Connie swung round in her chair, expecting they were getting somewhere now. It wasn't Mrs. Josser's bombshell any longer. Then the door opened. And Mrs. Josser, very red in the face, and Mrs. Vizzard, very white, stood there.

Under the shock of events Mrs. Vizzard's transformation had half slipped from her. The black dress with the artificial flowers was still as smart as ever. But to-night it looked simply out of place. Under the new hairdressing, the expression was hard and angry.

"Mrs. Vizzard had heard," Mrs. Josser said shortly.

There was a little gasp from Connie as she said it. She had never really liked Mrs. Vizzard. Had disliked her on and off for years in fact. But this was too much: knowing something like that, and keeping it to herself!

"Did Mrs. Boon tell you herself?" she asked.

"Mrs. Boon?" Mrs. Vizzard answered. "I've not spoken to the woman."

Mrs. Josser turned towards her husband.

"Do you hear that, Fred?" she asked.

Mr. Josser felt uncomfortable. For no reason that he could think of, all three women were looking towards him at once.

"I don't know what you're talking about," he muttered.

"Mrs. Vizzard's going to give Mrs. Boon notice when she gets back," she said. "She thinks it'll get the house a bad name if she stops."

Connie gave a little whistle. She had never imagined any circumstances in which Mrs. Boon could be disreputable and she herself respectable. But if she was surprised at what Mrs. Josser had just said she was far more surprised at Mr. Josser's answer. He put his pipe down and, even though he was only quite a small man, he got up looking the way Connie liked to see men look. Almost big and commanding.

"If she goes, we go too," he said.

As Mrs. Josser didn't speak, it was clearly Connie's cue to say something. It was a big moment. A positive build-up.

"Me, too," she declared. "On the dot."

Mrs. Vizzard's face wrinkled up, almost as if she were going to cry.

"It's all so horrible I can't believe it," she said weakly. "We thought . . ."

"Who's we?"

"Mr. Squales and I. We have been discussing it ever since we heard."

Mrs. Vizzard did not raise her eyes from the floor as she was speaking.

"And who's Mr. Squales to say what's to happen to Mrs. Boon?" Mr. Josser asked her.

"He was only thinking of the rest of us, thinking about No. 10, as a whole," she answered faintly.

"That's right, Kitty. That's all it was," said a deep soft voice from the doorway. "For myself, I'm sorry for her. Deeply sorry."

It was Mr. Squales himself who was standing there. He must have come upstairs on those pussy, panther feet of his and been listening to them. His presence seemed to infuriate Mr. Josser.

"So this was *your* little idea, was it?" he asked.

Mr. Squales's smile left him for a second.

"N-o-o-o," he said doubtfully. "Not entirely, that is. But . . . but the publicity, and all that. It just seemed better what we were suggesting."

"Much better," Mrs. Vizzard echoed him.

"If you turn her out," said Mr. Josser, "she comes and stays with us until she's got somewhere else to go. Then we go, too, like I said we would."

"Sshh!"

Mrs. Josser stopped him. She raised her hand warningly. In the sudden silence, they heard the front door shut below them. They held their breath. There was only one person whom it could be.

As they listened, there was the faint noise of footsteps on the stairs.

Mr. Squales took Mrs. Vizzard's arm.

"Kitty," he whispered. "We'd better be going down."

But Mrs. Vizzard only shook off his hand.

"Quiet," she said.

Then, in a flash, it was all over. There was the Jossers' living-room with the door open and everyone standing there. The light streamed across the landing, lighting up the stairs. And the figure of Mrs. Boon walked straight past them, like a shadow. They had one glimpse of her, bowed, secretive, silent. And then she had gone on upstairs to her empty flat. She was shading her face with her hand.

Mrs. Josser took out her handkerchief.

"She knows," was all she said.

5

It was midnight. The last of the twelve strokes of Mr. Josser's Westminster chimes had just floated up through the floor-boards, round, pulsating, and tremulous like soap bubbles filled with sound.

There were no lights burning any longer in No. 10. But that didn't mean that everyone was asleep. The evening had been too disturbing for that. In their separate and individual ways there were five of them awake in the house at this moment.

Mrs. Vizzard, for instance. She was lying face downwards on the pillow as though she had been crying.

"Oh, God, the shame of it," she was saying. "The awful, awful shame. And just when there seemed to be so much happiness. I've never been like this before. It's only because I love him so. I didn't want anything like this to happen in my house while he was there. Why couldn't it all have been beautiful and pure, the way it was? I hate Percy. Hate him! Hate him! Hate him! And Mr. Squales so good and gentle."

And at the thought of that gentle, good man, and of what his presence in the house meant to her, she shuddered. Before going to bed she had locked her door on the inside. Not to protect herself from him. But to protect him from his own desires. She knew that if at this moment he had been able to come to her, she would not have had it in her to resist.

And Mr. Squales himself, the cause of this profound disquiet? He was lying on his back with his hands behind his head and his dark fingers laced together. He was not in the least enthusiastic about things. He had stopped thinking about Percy and was thinking about himself.

"So this is what it's to be," he pondered. "This is what I've come to." He remembered other women he had known, other prospects, and the promise of earlier years. It was like sitting in the sunset of a day that had dawned too brightly. "It's really remarkable," he told himself philosophically, "that with all my talents I shouldn't have been able to support myself. Men with half my brains manage to make quite a good thing of it. It's simply that with me there's something somewhere that doesn't always click." The sunset feeling came over him more strongly than ever and blackened slowly into night. He lay there in the darkness, counting his tragedies. Then, in his own private midnight, the moon, full and triumphant, rose over the pattern of his thoughts. "All the same," he told himself, "it might be worse. Might be a lot worse. It *was* worse last week. I couldn't see my way then. Now, at least, I'm provided for. I don't have to worry about to-morrow's dinner."

And the Jossers?

They were a good deal nearer sleep than either Mrs. Vizzard or Mr. Squales. They were lying, as they had lain every night for more than thirty years, back to back with just the middle of their spines touching. It was an attitude that was at once comfortable, intimate, and in winter—with a little more pressure—distinctly warming.

Mrs. Josser herself was very nearly asleep. The gates were fast closing, and her thoughts no longer belonged entirely to her. "I ought to get him away before he's too much mixed up in it. I hope he finds that cottage," she was telling herself. "Poor Clarice. I'm sorry for her. She never deserved it. She'll have to stay with us *when it's all over*." Only a chink of light filtered in through the gates by now. In the dim obscurity of the interior the figure of Percy had been lost somewhere in the shadows, and the whole grim business had become exclusively Mrs. Boon's affair. It wasn't Percy's murder any longer. "Poor Clarice," she repeated once or twice more. Then she fell asleep.

Mr. Josser was still half awake. A little earlier, he'd given up hope of ever getting to sleep at all. During the hour in which he had lain there he had gone over the whole of young Percy's case-history. And he saw it all quite clearly—his latenesses, his extravagance, his unreliability, his vanity. "I suppose in a way it's my fault," he told himself. "I ought to have done more for the boy. What young Percy needed was a father. . . ."

If you could have seen No. 10 Dulcimer Street in cross-section, opened clean through the middle like a doll's house, you would have realised how narrowly separated in space the various family existences fulfilled themselves. Mrs. Boon, for instance, was within fifteen feet of the Jossers at that very moment. But utterly cut off. When she had closed her own door the separation was complete. At that moment, she was probably the loneliest woman in London. Lonely, but surrounded. And it was because she was surrounded that she had stuffed a handkerchief into her mouth so that other people shouldn't hear her crying ". . . now and at the hour of our death," were the words she had got to.

There was someone else from Dulcimer Street who was nearly asleep. And that was Connie. Only *she* shouldn't have been nearly asleep: she was on duty. But it's very easy, when the cloakroom is empty, and no one wants to be pinned up behind because a shoulder strap has gone, and there isn't even anyone in the lavatory, just to nod for a few seconds. Connie was nodding now and her thoughts were not noticeably different from those she'd been having while she was still properly awake. "Business Miss, indeed," she was saying to herself. "Business Mischief. I'd like to know what she'd been up to. It isn't just gone under the arms; it's rotten. Not that they'd hang anyone of his age. Not actually hang him. Twenty years more likely. He'll come out looking like Rip Van Winkle. I ought to have taken it over to the light before I bought it. You can pull the stuff apart with your fingers. Connie, you fool, you've been sold a pup. That seven and six has gone straight up the spout. Not that they'd actually hang him."

And Mr. Puddy, don't forget Mr. Puddy. He was wide awake and on the job. Well, not exactly on the job, perhaps, but wide awake all the same. As a matter of fact he was taking a few minutes off in which to snatch a meal. Not a sumptuous meal, admittedly, but something to help to keep him going. A tin of baked beans, in fact. And he was sitting hungrily watching them as they came to the boil in a tin saucepan on the gas ring in the caretaker's little office. They wouldn't be long now: the print band had already detached itself from the tin and was swirling round in the water.

"There's nothing like a few Heinzes if you just want a snack," he said half aloud—talking to himself had become a habit in these long night watches. "They're quick and they're tasty." He paused. "And if he dud it," he told himself, "*if* he dud it, I say, he ought to bay the benalty. You can't go about burdering people."

But nothing about Percy? He's a bit of Dulcimer Street, isn't he? He's a Number Tenner. Hasn't he got the right to any views on his own position?

Yes, he has. But they're shaky views. Decidedly shaky. He's sitting up in the trestle thing that they call a bed and he's arguing it all out with himself. They've had him up in Court twice already. Once for stealing a car. And once for murdering a blonde. It's enough to worry anyone.

"I wonder if I'll be O.K.?" he's thinking. "Mr. Barks said not to worry. And he's smart. He knows the ropes. I think he likes me. I'm his big break now, I'm headlines." He paused. "It's me it's not so good for. I'm the one to take the rap." His stomach turned over inside him at the thought. "I wonder if I'll be O.K.?" he asked himself again.

It is about the hundredth time that he's asked himself that question. And each time the answer seems farther away and more dubious than before.

"I wonder if I'll be O.K.?"

CHAPTER 38

I

A WEEK passed. A gnawing, insistent, sleep-defying sort of week. And the strain of it proved too much for Mrs. Boon. She collapsed under it.

Nor was this really surprising. Refusing everything that Mrs. Josser sent up for her, she had simply shut herself in her room, fasting. In consequence, she grew weaker and weaker. And then, just when she had realised that she must eat *something* if she meant to keep going—when she was actually on her way to the shops, in fact—she fainted.

There is after all nothing very exceptional in the simple act of fainting. It is something that has happened to most women and they have not been noticeably any the worse for it. And nothing especially disastrous occurred in the act itself. Even the situation of the faint was fortunate—just outside Littell's, the chemist's, in the Walworth Road. Two men, a postman and a van-driver—strong, unemotional fellows both of them—lifted her up with ease and carried her into the front shop. Mr. Littell came forward, mixed a dose of sal volatile, and waved a bottle of smelling-salts under the unconscious woman's nose, while the two men, the postman and the van-driver, stood around wearing the strained, slightly self-conscious expression of rescuers.

But when the smelling-salts had no effect, and when Mr. Littell, supporting Mrs. Boon's head in the crook of his arm, found that he couldn't force any of the sal volatile down her throat, he surrendered his charge to higher authority. Laying her down flat, he informed his two hearers that he was going to phone up for an ambulance. To cover up his failure he uttered the single word "Heart," indicating on his own body the position of the affected organ as he did so. He said the word impressively as though to indicate that it was no inadequacy on his part, but merely professional etiquette that was involved.

Because there was clearly nothing else that they could do—indeed, they hadn't been doing anything for the last five minutes—the postman and the van-driver went off on their individual jobs. And a policeman turned up and took over from them. But it was different for the ordinary passers-by who had only just noticed what was happening. They were naturally fascinated by the presence of an elderly woman in black lying stretched out flat in a small lock-up shop. A crowd formed itself around the doorway. And this inevitably shut off the newcomers. In consequence rumour began to spread among those who arrived late. The woman was mortally injured. She was dying. She was dead already. . . .

There was one person in particular who was anxious to see anything that was going, and this was a small woman in a very tight blue dress with a design in sequins all down the front. She had been almost at the other end of the Walworth Road when Mrs. Boon had her attack, but her sixth sense, or whatever it was that told her where to find excitement, had brought her along just in time. She wasn't engaged on any particular business; just cruising, as she called it. And when she got to the doorway things looked pretty hopeless. There were a dozen spectators already, and they none of them seemed to have seen enough. Even saying that she had called round for a prescription that was being made up for her little girl had no effect on them: they were a stubborn, obstinate lot. And small as she was she couldn't ferret her way in because the doorway was too narrow.

"Silly lot of rubbernecks," she thought to herself contemptuously, as she stood there watching them. "Proper pack of nosey-parkers. It probably isn't anything anyway."

The sound of the ambulance bell urged her on, however. Evidently it was something, and she wasn't going to get so much as a peep at it. Then, as the big white Talbot drew up smoothly at the curb and the two attendants and a policeman jumped down, she had an idea. It was something that she had worked before in similar circumstances. And it worked again this time. When the two attendants got out their stretcher and walked importantly through the middle of the crowd, Connie followed them closely like a kind of plain-clothes nurse. She was inside the shop as easy as kiss your hand.

And, once inside, there was the surprise of her life waiting for her. At first she stood back politely near the doorway knowing that in a crowd policemen quite often have a habit of kicking out backwards just like a horse. But as one of the attendants lifted the victim's head Connie caught sight of her face. She shot forward.

"Just in time," she exclaimed. "I couldn't get here sooner."

In the result, she was accepted. And more than accepted. She went off victoriously in the ambulance, climbing up the little collapsible ladder at the back like a Lady Mayoress. She had always liked Mrs. Boon, especially since IT had happened, and she was glad that she was there in case there was any little thing that she could do for her. But so long as Mrs. Boon's coma lasted there was nothing. So she made herself pleasant to the policeman who had got in with her. Dropping her voice in case Mrs. Boon should come round again while she was still speaking, she touched him on the shoulder.

"Name of Percy Boon, car bandit murderer, convey anything to you, Inspector?" she asked. "Because that's his old mum you've got there."

2

They were ever so nice to Mrs. Boon in the infirmary; couldn't have been nicer, in fact. Everything was of the best—the food, the service, the medical attention. There was even a pair of headphones over the bed in case she wanted a bit of music or a sports commentary. But, for the present at any rate, all that she seemed to want was just to be left alone. She still cried a lot.

When visiting day came round, Mrs. Josser managed to get the Sister to herself for a moment. The Sister was inclined to be cagey at first. But Mrs. Josser persisted, and finally she got it out of her. It was just as she had expected—a stroke—and it was going to be a Long Job. All that Mrs. Boon could do, the Sister explained, was to lie there taking things easily and not worry. That was why it was so important that the things they talked about when they came to see her should be bright and cheerful.

"Keep her spirits up," the Sister said firmly. "It's the little things that count. Just let her feel that everything is going pleasantly—here and at home."

The ignorance of the Sister's remarks amazed Mrs. Josser. Either the Sister was a very stupid woman, or else Connie had somehow or other overlooked her. The explanation turned out to be quite simple: the Sister was only a temporary relief while the regular was away. The regular knew all about Mrs. Boon's secret, and she appreciated it. In nearly twelve years' nursing Mrs. Boon was the first interesting patient that she had ever had.

In point of fact, Mrs. Boon didn't give Mrs. Josser very much opportunity of talking. She merely lay there with her eyes closed, occasionally reaching up for the handkerchief that was under the corner of her pillow. Only once did she emerge from her lethargy—after her first grateful smile to Mrs. Josser for having come at all—and that was to beckon her over and whisper in her ear.

"Ask Fred to keep an eye on Percy," she said. "He can see him any Thursday. I'm afraid he may be missing me."

"We'll look after him. Don't you worry," Mrs. Josser promised.

She drew in her lips, however, as she said it. She was not at all anxious that Mr. Josser should get himself drawn any deeper into Percy's affairs.

What was more, it would be the first time that any member of her family had ever been inside a prison, even on a visitors' day.

CHAPTER 39

I

BUT Mrs. Josser couldn't be expected to keep her mind on Percy. Not entirely, that is. Because Doris was already taking up a large part of it. Without asking anybody's advice or permission—behaving, in fact, exactly as Mrs. Josser herself had behaved some thirty years previously—she had become engaged. In other words, within a fortnight of having her safely back home after the fiasco of that Hampstead flat of hers, they were going to lose her again.

Like all important things, it had seemed sudden. Less than a week ago—last Tuesday to be exact—Doris had announced what was going to happen. And to-day—the day on which Mr. Josser was *supposed* to be seeing Percy—the Jossers were to meet Bill's people. It promised to be an overcrowded sort of day—prison in the afternoon and an engagement party in the evening.

Because of the engagement party Mrs. Josser was on edge. She recognised the occasion for what it was—a full tribal evening; and she steeled herself. It was to be their first opportunity of talking over rival taboos and enquiring—not openly, of course, but discreetly and by innuendo—into the strength of the young man and the dowry of the maiden. The Trocadero at seven sharp had been chosen for the ritual ceremony.

Mr. Josser wasn't particularly looking forward to it either. He knew Bill and that seemed to him enough. But Mrs. Josser, who was looking forward to it even less, insisted. It was just one of those things that were required. Even if one of the Jossers didn't know the first steps in the marriage dance, there was another tribe, her tribe, the Knockells, that did.

What was worrying her was the question of clothes. She didn't know what to wear. And she was afraid that Mrs. Davenport would know only too well, and wear it. In the result, her plans alternated between something black and no hat, and her blue costume with her felt hat turned up in front. She wished now that she'd been in the habit of dropping into the Trocadero more often so that she could have seen what other people habitually wore at seven sharp.

The dilemma had been facing her for nearly forty-eight hours. But it was only as the day itself came round, that she grew really worried. On the very morning when she should have been looking forward to a pleasant evening in town with some nice new friends, and a bottle of wine on the table and a foreign-looking waiter asking her if she'd take her coffee black or with cream, she woke up feeling very nervy and depressed. And, by breakfast, the anxiety had increased to a fever.

Only last night, she had been certain that of course her blue costume was all right—she had even pressed it carefully with a damp cloth in readiness. But in the harsh early light she saw things differently. She owed it to Doris, she told herself, to wear something different. A fine tribal impression it would make if Mrs. Davenport and her brave turned up all covered in feathers and wampum, and she and Mr. Josser were only in their second-best blanket.

The real trouble, however, was that she hadn't got a best dress What with Mr. Josser's illness and one thing and another it mus have been . . . good gracious, it was nearly five years since she'd bought herself a dress. There had been blouses, of course; and an odd skirt or two. But nothing, absolutely nothing, which she would ever have cared to catch sight of in one of the Trocadero mirrors.

During breakfast, she finally argued herself into a fierce state o justification. She had left it far too long, *far* too long, she told herself It was positively ridiculous having nothing newer than 1935. She was so much preoccupied with the matter that Mr. Josser noticed it and looked across at her.

"Everything all right, Mother?" he asked.

The question annoyed Mrs. Josser: she was on the verge of decid ing, and this wasn't a moment when she wanted to be interrupted Moreover, turning to him suddenly in this way she couldn't help noticing that quite a lot was wrong with him, *too*.

"You've got to go and get yourself a haircut, that's what you've got to do," she told him.

Mr. Josser got up and examined himself in the mirror.

"I've known it longer," he said.

"Well, just you know it shorter," Mrs. Josser told him tartly "You're not coming out with me looking like that."

She had got up and began clearing away as she said it. Mr Josser would have liked to sit there longer, with the breakfast thing still on the table, and the possibility of another cup of tea if he fel like it. But he recognised that this was evidently not one of those mornings. Rather reluctantly, he put his cup on to the tray that Mrs Josser was loading, and saw it whisked away before his eyes.

A note of extreme urgency was now discernible in all Mrs. Josser' actions. No sooner had she cleared away than she came back, with an apron tied round her, and went about putting the room to right Mr. Josser eyed her silently for a few moments and then wen through into the bedroom because he was so obviously in the way in the other room. But at once Mrs. Josser finished what she was doing and shot into the bedroom after him. Displaced from there Mr Josser went into the kitchen and started to do a little desultory wash ing-up. Within five minutes Mrs. Josser was beside him, snatching things out of his hands and drying them. Then, while the last cup wa still swinging to rest on its hook in the dresser, she announced tha she was going out. She didn't say where or for how long—merely that if she weren't back by lunch-time, Mr. Josser was to give him self a meal, and not wait for her. She added that he was also to have a haircut and that, above all things, he was not to get back late from seeing Percy.

They were starting for the Trocadero at six sharp, she told him. And she wasn't going to be rushed for anybody.

2

Because she wanted to do things properly she took the bus straightaway to Oxford Street. There were other shops south of the river that would have done quite as well—Brixton and Clapham, for instance, were full of small, select dress-shops called Yvonne and Sybille St. Clair and that sort of thing. But to-day Mrs. Josser wanted to be sure of a real West End cut. Sometimes the little shops skimped you under the arms, or tried to get away with a false hem if the stuff had been running a bit short. She was taking no risks and went straight to Bourne and Hollingsworth's. So long as she could remember she had always gone to Bourne's when she wanted something that was good. The only reason why she wasn't better dressed was that she didn't go quite often enough.

But even at Bourne's it wasn't easy. There was such a selection. The assistant unhooked a likely half-dozen and then, when Mrs. Josser was still undecided, went back for more. The little alcove of mirrors in the fitting-room revealed Mrs. Josser in a variety of guises—as a very elderly schoolgirl, as a young matron, as a rather skittish dowager. In the end Mrs. Josser decided on the first one that the assistant had shown her. It was a simple little blue two-piece, and could be had in two styles, one with a white ornament on the left bosom, and one with a red. Mrs. Josser tried on both and came down on the side of the white one.

Then, because the dress was only three guineas, and she had brought five pounds with her, she decided that she would have a look at hats. She hadn't even made up her mind yet that she was going to buy a hat, and she sidled warily into the hat department, like an enemy, avoiding the eyes of the assistants and trying to look as though she were a woman with a whole cupboardful of hats. Right up to the moment of going over to the ten-and-sixpenny counter, she and Bourne and Hollingsworth were of no use to each other. Bourne and Hollingsworth were trying to sell hats and she was trying to resist. And she would probably have succeeded if, purely to see what the thing looked like, she hadn't furtively slipped one of the half-guinea models on her head for a moment. As it happened, it was perfectly dreadful. It gave her a sallow sideways appearance, and she snatched it off again. But, by now, the young lady in charge of the ten-and-sixpenny counter had turned up and offered to help her. Then she was really trapped. She couldn't admit that she didn't want to buy a hat because the young lady had just seen her trying one on—it would seem almost like ringing at a door-bell and running away again. And she couldn't say that there wasn't one that suited her because on that enormous counter there were obviously hats that could suit anyone. Moreover, once she was actually there with the smell of felt in her nostrils she wasn't by any means so sure that she didn't want one. In the end, it was the nineteenth, a hat remarkably like her old one, that she bought. It was in hard black felt with the brim turned up in front, and a sort of buckle, also black, set flush in line with the ribbon.

And that, she told herself, would be all. She had gathered up her two parcels and set off for the door, pleased and self-confident, when the idea of gloves crossed her mind. This time the struggle was more brief. She went straight back to have a look at them. And there was her size, right on top waiting for her. They cost four and eleven, and were guaranteed real kid. All the same, it gave her a little pang as she paid for them. During the past hour she had fairly been flinging money away. She now had only a one-pound note and a handful of small change left.

Altogether, by the time they were all gathered round the ceremonial spot, the evening of tribal customs looked as though it would have cost some of them a nice packet.

3

Mr. Josser had been feeling a bit self-conscious about his visit to the prison. But when the time came it passed off all right. It was only when he got near to the prison that it was rather embarrassing. And that wasn't because he was the only one going there. On the contrary, the whole street was full of quietly dressed men and women—women mostly—going in the same direction. There must have been twenty or thirty of them, all planning to arrive punctually at two o'clock when the gates opened. And the sight of them gave Mr. Josser a pained, sad feeling again.

He took another glance at his companions. They were an extraordinarily respectable-looking and mouse-like crowd. Somehow he would have expected them to look different—if he had expected them at all. It seemed impossible that these sedate, quiet-looking folks should be the wives, mothers, daughters and intimates of burglars, coiners, gangsters, murderers even. Then a taxi, with two men in black Homburgs and a woman with a fur coat, passed him and drew up outside the prison. The woman had a veil over her hat and drew it down as she got out. They weren't at all mouse-like, these visitors. These must be the belongings of someone of importance, someone who had side-slipped in the City or run amok in Mayfair.

There were still a few minutes to go, and the visitors lined themselves up in a rough queue, avoiding each other's eyes. Mr. Josser took a sideways look at them and noticed something else extraordinary about them—they were all in black. It was like an outing of widows and mourners. Then he glanced down at his own legs. He had put his best suit on and he was all in black, too.

It was evidently a very efficiently run sort of prison because punctually at the hour the door opened. But it was a slow business getting in. There was a policeman standing at the gate and two warders in flat caps. They scrutinised everyone as though they didn't like the look of them, and there was a veiled suggestion about their attitude—colder and more sullen somehow than that of policemen on point duty—that if there were any attempt to rush the gate they'd open fire. In consequence, there was no pushing or jostling. The mourners, or visitors, or whatever they were, filed in slowly and silently.

Then they arrived at a door. It was a good thick door studded with nails. Mr. Josser was still thinking about the thickness of the door when the policeman touched him on the shoulder and pointed down at the bag.

"Open up," he said briefly.

It had been an innocent little caseful when it was packed. But under the policeman's eyes everything assumed a sudden guiltiness. The Gladstone bag might have been full of skeleton keys and dynamite from the way the policeman went through it. He turned over the two clean shirts and the pair of underpants, fingering the seams as though to make sure that there weren't any files or lock-saws concealed in them, and then he came upon the packet of cigarettes that Mr. Josser had bought.

"Any matches?" he asked.

Mr. Josser shook his head. He saw now how silly it was of him to have forgotten the matches. You could hardly expect a prison to provide little things like that.

"You'll have to hand these over," the policeman said. "No tobacco allowed inside a prison without a permit."

"I'm sorry," Mr. Josser replied. "I didn't mean any harm by it."

He was suddenly afraid that his action might have compromised Percy in some way.

But the policeman, being treated with respect, became temporarily quite jovial.

"You haven't done any yet," he said.

When the cigarettes had been handed over, Mr. Josser was directed into the waiting-room. It was a long, cold apartment with a dark green dado waist-high running round it, and three small windows set almost flush in the ceiling. Mr. Josser noticed, with a slight sinking of the heart, that the windows were barred as though even visitors tried to escape sometimes. At either end of the room an electric light bulb in a plain china reflector was burning. The lamps were low-powered and you could look at them without blinking. Two wooden benches down either wall comprised the furnishings. Altogether it was rather like a waiting-room in a railway station that had given up expecting any trains. The whole place smelt strongly of carbolic.

It had a clean rather than a friendly smell, carbolic. And it may have been the carbolic, or the iciness of the air, or the barred windows, or the rattling of keys somewhere in the corridor, or the combination of all of them together, that made Mr. Josser shudder. Whatever it was, he became uncomfortably aware of a new and overpowering quality about the room that swamped all the others, a unique and distinctive quality—oppressiveness. To his immense surprise, after only about five minutes of prison life, Mr. Josser found himself looking forward to getting outside again.

The efficiency that he had noticed earlier at the gate was discernible inside as well. It might have been an out-patients' department in one of the big hospitals that he was watching. The patients were called in a very strictly arranged rota. When the warder was ready for them he came inside and called out, "Waiting for 13796," or "27345," whatever the number might be. Most of the visitors simply went along to the special visitors' room where they saw their loved ones through a screen of rabbit-wire. Mr. Josser, however, was taken right along to the cell because Percy wasn't a convicted criminal yet. He was still Percy Boon, Esq., a British citizen with all his rights. There wasn't anything actually against him yet. It was simply that They had certain doubts.

It was quite a distance from the waiting-room. The smell of carbolic persisted, and the way led down a long stone corridor—an endlessly long corridor it seemed—past the doors of cells from which Mr. Josser feelingly averted his eyes in passing. The waiting-room was something free and open to the outside world compared with this stone corridor. Here was the very heart of the prison itself, and the weight of the surrounding stone had borne down on it, crushing and flattening. Then the corridor opened—another door; another unlocking—into a wide hall that was arranged like the inside of a gigantic pigeon-loft. There were three tiers of the pigeon-boxes, all round the sides. And, in between the tiers, sheets of wire-netting were slung. There were no short cuts that way.

Mr. Josser paused and looked upwards. The roof was arched in a high V and had windows let into it. But the glass that they were made of was thick and yellow. And there was another piece of the same wire-mesh spread across them. In the result, the light came through strained and pallid. It made the whole place seem as though a cold wet mist was filling it.

But they were there now, they'd reached Percy's private bed-sitting-room in this enormous block. The warder selected an out-size key and thrust it into the outsize key-hole.

"Why don't they use Yale locks?" Mr. Josser found himself wondering. "Safe enough, aren't they?"—and opened the door.

But the warder didn't give him much time for stray thoughts.

"In you go," he said.

It wasn't an easy interview.

Percy seemed pleased enough to see Mr. Josser. But he was preoccupied. Preoccupied and restless. And the boy didn't look well, Mr. Josser thought. He'd had a haircut in the prison, and the barber had made a strictly regulation job of it. It was short at the back and sides and on top as well, with a broad fringe left in front for parting. The barber, who had been on this work for years, had only two styles up his sleeve. There was Percy's kind, and the other kind. The other kind, for the men actually under sentence, didn't have any fringe. Because his hair was cropped, the lines on Percy's face stood out all the more strongly. And somehow they weren't young lines any longer. The skin across the cheeks were drawn tight, and the skin under the eyes had dropped into little pouches. If Mr. Josser hadn't known where he was, he'd have said that Percy had been giving himself a few late nights.

"I brought you some cigarettes, but they kept 'em downstairs," he said by way of an opening.

Percy gave a kind of self-conscious grin.

"That's right," he said. "Ten a day. Doctor's orders."

"Well, I'm . . . I'm glad they're looking after you."

It was Mr. Josser's turn to give a self-conscious grin.

"How's Mum?" Percy asked.

"Fine," Mr. Josser told him. "Just a bit run down. She's got to rest. That's all it is."

"Is she asking after me?"

"All the time, Percy boy. All the time."

There was a pause.

"Anyone else asking?"

Mr. Josser considered.

"They're all asking," he explained. "All of 'em wanted to be remembered to you."

Another pause.

"Who's all?" Percy asked.

Mr. Josser considered again.

"Well, there's Mrs. Josser," he said. "She's always asking."

"Anybody else?"

"Oh, yes," Mr. Josser answered. "There's Connie. And Mr. Puddy. They both ask."

"Why doesn't Mum write?"

"They won't let her. I told you—she's got to rest."

"It isn't like Mum, not to write. She isn't bad, is she?"

"Oh, no, she's not bad," Mr. Josser said hurriedly. "Just got to take things easy."

"The last time Mum wrote the Sister wrote for her," Percy observed.

It was in a flat detached sort of voice that he said it, as though he weren't talking to Mr. Josser directly. It was rather as though he weren't talking to anyone in particular, just stating a personal grievance.

"Any of the others ever ask?" he said at length.

"Well, there's Mr. Squales: he does. And Mrs. Vizzard, of course. She's always asking."

"It isn't Mum's hands, is it?"

Mr. Josser pulled himself up. He'd been intending to mention Mrs. Vizzard's engagement. All the way up in the train he'd thought that Percy would like to hear about it. But the boy didn't seem interested in anything ordinary like that any more.

"Oh, no, her hands are all right," he said. "It's simply that she's lying down."

"Any of the chaps at the garage ever ask?"

This stumped Mr. Josser.

"I don't rightly know," he said. "I don't come across 'em. I guess they ask all right."

Then he thought of something else.

"Doris asks," he went on. "She's come back to Dulcimer Street now."

This piece of information seemed to annoy Percy.

"What'd she do that for?" he asked.

"She's come home to get married," Mr. Josser said.

And as soon as he'd said it he was sorry. It seemed callous to talk about getting married to a man who was in Percy's position. And he was right. Percy didn't answer.

"I've left you some clean clothes," Mr. Josser said at length. "If there's anything special you want you've only got to let me know."

Percy sucked in his cheeks and thought.

"I'd like some more papers," he said. "I don't see any papers here. Not new ones at least. Anything in them?"

Mr. Josser thought for a moment.

"You've seen about the Pact?" he asked.

Percy shook his head.

"The Nazis and the Bolshies have signed a non-aggression pact. At least it isn't signed yet, it's only just been announced." Mr. Josser paused. He'd forgotten about Percy for the moment and was wondering how he was going to explain that one away at the next Sitting: he couldn't help looking as though he, as Foreign Secretary, had let things slip pretty badly. "It's pretty serious," he went on. "There isn't anything to stop Germany. . . ."

But Percy wasn't listening.

"I didn't mean that sort of thing," he said. "I meant anything about me."

4

Mr. Josser forgot all about the hairdresser until he was nearly home. And, because it was late already, he couldn't risk the extra journey on to the Oval. There was nothing for it, therefore, but to go just across the way to Epson's.

It was clearly a mistake, because he wasn't one of their regulars. They didn't know him, and he didn't know them. Or perhaps he didn't make himself quite clear. Or perhaps it was an inexperienced assistant. Or perhaps it was just Epson's way of turning out a haircut. Whatever it was, they pretty nearly cropped him. He might have been Percy. Before Mr. Josser could stop the man, he had run those galloping electric clippers all round the back and sides, and then he settled down in a grim determined sort of fashion to level off what remained. Even the little quiff of hair in front disappeared. Ten minutes after he had gone into Epson's, Mr. Josser emerged looking like a choirboy.

He was so alarmed, indeed, by his appearance that he wouldn't let the barber do anything about his moustache. His own man on the other side of the street would have known exactly what to do—three quick clips and it would have been finished. But here, Heaven knows what might have happened. He might have found himself with a Charlie Chaplin or a Ronald Colman or anything.

Because he couldn't get it attended to properly, it would have been better if he had simply left the thing alone altogether. But when he came to have a look at himself in the big mirror of the dressing-table, he didn't like doing that because the rest of his hair was so short. He was like an almost bald man with a great ragged moustache hanging down in front. After regarding it carefully from all angles he took out a pair of Mrs. Josser's cutting-out scissors from the drawer and began making a few cautious snips.

It was probably because the scissors were so large that he took off more than he had intended at the first operation. He was so busy with the part of the blade that he was looking at that he didn't notice what the point was doing. And taking the thing as a whole it wasn't a straight cut either. It made his entire face look lop-sided. After that, there was nothing to do but to cut the other side level. And this made the moustache too shallow for its width. After studying it carefully again for a few minutes he decided to bring in the sides a bit. By the time he had finished it was a very tidy but also a very small moustache.

It was like a small white moth resting there on his upper lip.

CHAPTER 40

As IT turned out, they were early; very early. It was only about twenty minutes to seven when they arrived at the Trocadero. Mr. Josser was for killing time by going round the block once or twice. But Mrs. Josser insisted on going straight in. It was her shoes that were troubling her again.

There were plenty of people about, of course. There were at least a dozen other diners who had turned up round about half-past six for seven. And because all the others had ordered themselves a drink

Mr. Josser did the same. When he asked Mrs. Josser what she would have, however, the offer caught her at a disadvantage: she was unfamiliar with every one of the cocktails on the list in front of her. And, in the end, when Mr. Josser decided to have a pink gin, Mrs. Josser said that she would have one, too. Mr. Josser's familiarity with pink gin rather surprised her. It was a side to his character that she had not known before.

But, in comparison with the change in his appearance, this new revelation was nothing. She still could not look at him without being surprised. It was like having a stranger, who in certain lights looked oddly like her husband, sitting there beside her. And he had a more than usually far-away look in his eyes. That was because he kept on remembering about Percy. He just couldn't help it.

Mrs. Josser, however, had more than Mr. Josser to look at. She was doing what she described to herself as "keeping her eyes skinned" for the Davenports. Some psychic sense told her that, though she had never seen them, she would recognise them at once. And, indeed, she recognised them several times in quick succession. There was a large man in black coat and striped trousers, very obviously a doctor, accompanied by several ropes of pearls with a thin pale lady inside them; there was a broad, ruddy-faced countryman with a jolly, closely shingled woman in a rough tweed costume—just the sort of thing that the wife of a rural medical man might wear; there was a tall melancholy man in dark grey—clearly a specialist who made his living by keeping people off red meat and spirits—and a shrivelled little woman who might have been under the treatment for years. It was all very exciting and very disconcerting as the imaginary Davenports, one after another, passed before her.

Then, when she was least expecting it, she saw something that made her blood run cold. Through the swing doors in front of her a woman came in wearing a new-looking dark blue dress with a white ornament on the left bosom. A man might have seen it and experienced no concern. Mr. Josser did, in fact, glance at the woman and then glanced away again. But for Mrs. Josser it was disaster. It ruined everything. She felt as though, instead of being nicely dressed for the evening, she were in a kind of three-guinea uniform. The price ticket might still have been sticking to her. The other dress was identical.

Mrs. Josser was still hoping that the woman would eventually be given a seat on the far side of the restaurant when Bill and Doris came in. They had picked each other up somewhere on the way, and they were wearing the idiotically happy expression that they habitually wore when they were together. It might have been som private unexplainable joke that they were sharing. Bill came straigh over to Mrs. Josser and kissed her. They were still in the early stage of kissing. And they were awkward about it. Mrs. Josser put he cheek up as though she were avoiding him. Then Doris kissed he father, and the evening was ready to begin.

"We'd better order a drink," Bill said. "I bet my people'll b late."

"Not for me, thank you," Mrs. Josser said firmly. "I've just ha one. Fred can have another if he likes."

But Bill wouldn't listen to her. He ordered White Ladies al round. And because they had actually been paid for before Mrs Josser realised what was happening, of course she had to drink hers She liked it rather better than the pink gin.

She was still sipping it when the identical dress entered the loung again. Mrs. Josser was feeling better after the White Lady. Sh merely averted her eyes, and waited for the woman to go away. Bu the woman didn't go away. She stood surveying the circle of face and then came straight towards them.

"Oh, there you are, Billy," she said. "I told Father I was sure w were waiting in the wrong place. He's through there by the door.'

As soon as he had introduced his mother to everybody—h noticed, without having any idea why, that she seemed to be staring rather hard at Mrs. Josser—he went off in search of his father. He re-turned a moment later with a diminutive white-haired man in a nea blue suit, with a Masonic emblem dangling from his watch-chain The newcomer had evidently spruced himself up specially for the occasion. His hair, recently cut very short, was brushed out flat on to his head.

There was no difficulty about conversation at first because they all had to admire Doris's ring. It was a small single diamond set in a thin band of platinum, and the novelty of the design quite overcame them. They passed Doris's hand round and round the table to re-examine it. Then, when Bill had ordered two more White Ladies for his people, and Mrs. Davenport had nibbled a few of the salted al-monds in the little dish in front of them, they all passed through into the restaurant.

The conversation by now was not so easy. They couldn't go on talking about Doris's ring for ever, and apparently there was nothing else that even mildly interested them. Mrs. Davenport was a quiet faded woman who left most of her sentences unfinished, and Dr. Davenport had a habit of referring everything to her in a way that made other people superfluous. As soon as they were seated, he beamed across at his wife—the Jossers could see now that he was one of the beaming kind—and addressed her.

"We don't often dine out nowadays, do we, Mother?" he said.

Mrs. Davenport shook her head.

"No, dear, it must be nearly . . ."

"I expect you're used to it," Dr. Davenport went on, turning the beam in Mrs. Josser's direction. "That's because you live in London. We're just country mice, aren't we, Mother?"

The waiter, like the younger son of an Italian count, hung over them and they ordered what he told them to. Then the wine-waiter, like the count himself, came along and Dr. Davenport got out his glasses. He was evidently a man who understood the subject because he went right through the wine-list from the champagnes on the first page, through the hocks and moselles, to the clarets and burgundies, and only looked up when he came to the liqueurs at the back. But the result, after all that, was disappointing.

"Well, what would everybody like?" he asked, as though they'd all been reading the list over his shoulder while he was holding it.

When nobody spoke, Dr. Davenport passed the wine-list over to Mr. Josser.

"Here," he said. "You take it. I expect it's more in your line than mine. We aren't great wine-drinkers are we, Mother?"

They took so long in deciding that the wine-waiter went away and came back again. But Mr. Josser hadn't been wasting his time. He'd been thinking busily. And he had cause to: he'd just remembered that he'd only got two pounds on him, and it hadn't definitely been decided who was going to pay for the dinner. It had sounded like Dr. Davenport's party in the invitation. But if Mr. Josser started ordering things how was he to know that the waiter wouldn't give him the bill at the end of it all?

So he decided on Moselle to be on the safe side. Everyone always liked Moselle and it was only eight and six a bottle. He pointed to it victoriously.

"No. 86," said the wine-waiter meaningly. "One bottle?"

Mr. Josser nodded.

"One bottle," he said.

At the words Dr. Davenport looked up sharply.

"Better ask him to make it two," he said. "This is a celebration, remember."

Even though it was evidently meant nicely, Mr. Josser didn't altogether like the sound of what Dr. Davenport had just said. It still left the question of payment in abeyance. From the way Bill's father had put it, it might have been either a generous invitation, or a kind of nagging reminder not to stint people who'd come half-way across England for their dinner. Mr. Josser became frightened again.

But Dr. Davenport was happy enough. He'd taken charge of things with an easy professional heartiness. He was rubbing his hands together.

"Well, well," he said, "we want to get to know our new friends don't we, Mother? And I expect they want to get to know us. Do you live right in the centre of town, Mrs. Josser?"

Mrs. Josser drew in her lips.

"Just a bus ride," she said. "Kennington."

"I used to know Kensington when I was a young man," Dr Davenport went on. "Had a friend there. Used to walk over to him."

"It isn't Kensington. It's Kennington," Mr. Josser told him.

Dr. Davenport seemed surprised.

"I could have sworn that it was Kensington," he said. "I used to go there quite often. Through the Park, y'know. He's a surgeon now."

"They're different places," Mrs. Davenport interrupted. "Kensington is over by Harrods' and Kennington is . . . it's the other place your friend used to . . ."

But Dr. Davenport was drinking his soup hastily because the waiter was hanging round them again.

"Well, it's a small point, isn't it?" he asked. "Everybody can't live in the same place. We're all here together and that's the great thing, isn't it, Mother?"

He leant over and patted Doris's hand.

"I'm sure we're going to be great friends," he said. "Bill's a very lucky man, I can see that."

There was a pause for a moment because it was really Bill's turn to say something. But he couldn't help because he was sulking. Ever since he and Doris had become engaged he'd been trying to avoid this dinner party, but his mother and father had insisted. At the moment he was just sitting there, eating gloomily.

Then there was a movement from the other end of the table. Mrs Davenport was trying to say something. She was making those little signalling motions—slight raisings of the eyebrows and wordless lip movements—with which partners, long married, seem to address each other as though by some prearranged code. And as soon as Dr Davenport became aware of it he lost all that easy confidence that he had been displaying earlier. He began to dissemble, and instead of looking anybody in the face he talked down at the table-cloth.

"Of course," he said, "it'll have to be some time. Can't be at once, you know. No runaway marriage or anything like that. Bill isn't even qualified, remember. Great mistake for a young man to tie himself down before he's properly got going. May affect his whole career."

He paused for a moment, and Bill took hold of Doris's hand under the table and squeezed it. But before Dr. Davenport could say anything further, Mrs. Josser had spoken for him.

"*We're* not pressing it," she said.

Dr. Davenport looked up. He had entirely misunderstood the remark, and thought that Mrs. Josser was on his side and behaving very generously.

"There you are, you see," he said. "We're very pleased to have our Bill marry the young lady, aren't we, Mother? But not just yet. That's all it is—not just yet. Say in a year or two."

But Mrs. Josser was far from satisfied.

"How do we know what his prospects will be in a year or two?" she asked.

Dr. Davenport was beaming again.

"Well, they'll be better than they are now, won't they?" he replied.

"That's as may be," said Mrs. Josser. "But they mayn't be good enough for our Doris."

"Oh, Mother, really!" Doris had removed her hand from Bill's and was facing Mrs. Josser across the table.

"Well, what have I said that I shouldn't?" Mrs. Josser asked her.

It was all turning out just as Bill had known it would. He'd warned Doris as they came what his father would say. He'd said it already by letter, and his mother had written the same things by the same post. He couldn't let it go any further now.

"It isn't as bad as all that," he said. "Plenty of fellows get married as soon as they qualify. It's all a question of what you're going to do."

"You were going to do surgery," his father said firmly. "That's another two years."

"I'll wait," Doris said.

For a moment it seemed as though the point had been settled. Dr. Davenport even tried a faint, rather flickering beam on the company. But he was reckoning without Mrs. Josser. As soon as his eye caught hers, the beam died out again.

"And what's going to happen at the end of two years, I'd like to know," she demanded. "He'll only just be qualified even then."

"Bill's a very clever doctor. He's going to make a lot of money. He . . ."

It was Mrs. Davenport who had spoken. Her voice died away half-way through, but, even so, it indicated a remarkable change of attitude on her part. From opposing the whole proposal she was now actually defending it. She appeared to be trying to sell her son, in fact. Her duplicity shocked Dr. Davenport profoundly. Everything that he had said had been what Mrs. Davenport had told him to say. He felt suddenly isolated and betrayed.

Altogether it was a very awkward moment, and Mr. Josser did his best to make things easier.

"He's clever all right," he said. "When I had pleurisy he operated on me a treat . . ."

But Mr. Josser wasn't allowed to get any further. Dr. Davenport turned to Bill immediately.

"You did what?" he asked in amazement.

"Only a paracentesis," Bill told him.

"*Only* a paracentesis," Dr. Davenport repeated.

He was obviously shaken. "And what would you have done if anything had gone wrong, may I ask?"

"Nothing *did* go wrong," Bill told him.

"But suppose it had. Only suppose it had," Dr. Davenport went on. "Where would you have been then?"

"And where would my husband have been?" Mrs. Josser demanded.

This time Dr. Davenport ignored her. His professional sense was so deeply shocked that he could think of nothing but Bill's crime.

"You'd have gone to prison," he said. "That's where you'd have gone."

Then Mrs. Davenport joined the conversation.

"You shouldn't have done it, Bill," she said. "You ought to have remembered."

"Remembered what?" Bill asked her.

"Why, all the money your father's been spending on you," she explained.

Mrs. Josser raised her head sharply.

"Money . . ." she began.

But Mr. Josser stopped her.

"It was all my fault, really," he insisted. "He could see I was in pain and I . . . I . . . asked him to."

"No, you didn't, I did," Doris interrupted.

"It wasn't either of you. I asked myself," Bill said emphatically. "He'd have been dead if I hadn't."

"And you let him do it knowing he wasn't qualified?" Dr. Davenport asked Mr. Josser.

"I didn't tell him," Bill replied.

A thought flashed across Mrs. Josser's mind.

"Did you know, Doris?" she asked.

"Of course I knew."

"And you let your young man experiment on your own father?"

Dr. Davenport sat back for a moment and wiped his forehead. For the time being the centre of the storm had passed outside his own family. It was a matter for the Jossers now. And Mr. Josser tried to save things. He gave a rather nervous little smile and pushed his plate away from him.

"Well, I don't see what the trouble is," he said. "It all turned out very nicely. I'm better and . . . and it gave Bill a bit of practice. It's all over and done with now."

As he said it, the original Dr. Davenport returned to the table. He was a man of peace himself, and he recognised just such another in Mr. Josser. He began beaming more brightly than ever.

"That's right," he said. "No good crying over spilt milk. I'm sure Bill's learnt his lesson. And no harm's been done. Let's all have another glass of wine." He paused. "We don't often come up to town for the evening, do we, Mother?"

But in her present mood Mrs. Davenport appeared to be quite capable of contradicting him. She seemed on the point of telling him that they were always coming up to town. She rose from the table and said rather shakily, "I'm just going to leave you all for a moment."

Mrs. Josser rose simultaneously.

"I'm coming too," she said.

In a strange way the two women seemed to be on each other's side now. It was two keen-witted and far-seeing women ranged against two stupid and easy-going men.

They left Bill and Doris out of their calculations altogether. And Bill and Doris left them out of theirs. As soon as Mrs. Josser and Mrs Davenport had gone Bill got up and took Doris by the hand.

"How about a bit of dancing?" he asked.

Then, when they had gone, too, Dr. Davenport looked across at Mr. Josser. They grinned rather sheepishly at each other.

"What do you say to a cigar?" Dr. Davenport asked. "A cigar and a spot of brandy? It's my little dinner, remember."

The party broke up affectionately on the pavement of Shaftesbury Avenue at eleven-fifteen. Mrs. Josser and Mrs. Davenport were bosom friends by then. And so were the two husbands. Between the four of them, they'd got it all fixed up. Bill and Doris could go on being engaged, of course—they saw clearly that there was no way of upsetting that—but there would be no more talk about getting married until Bill was a doctor.

Anything else, it was agreed, wouldn't really be fair to either of the two young people.

CHAPTER 41

THERE WAS a letter for Mr. Squales. The first letter in fact that he had received for weeks. It was sudden and unexpected. Also, strange and beautiful—like sunlight penetrating into a closed room.

Mrs. Vizzard looking up from the basement saw the blue-and-gold trousers of the postman as he mounted the front steps, and went upstairs at once to see what he had brought. She had made it a regular and rather pleasant duty for years to see what letters the other residents at No. 10 were receiving. It was her way of keeping her finger on the pulse of things. She was thus the first person in the house to touch Mr. Squales's letter. And, for some reason that she couldn't understand, she didn't like it. It frightened her. She wanted to tear it up. Tear it up and burn it and not say anything about it.

As soon as the thought came to her, she was ashamed of it. She recognised it for the piece of insane jealousy that it was, and it served to remind her how obsessed she had become. Really it was things like that that alarmed her about herself. It wasn't a straightforward alarm either. Not simply concern for the way in which Mr. Squales had disturbed the smoothness of her life. No, it went much deeper and further back than that. There was guilt and conscience, and remorse and all the rest of it mixed up there. Every episode of this kind —and there were tiny instances daily—brought it back to her that she had never felt this way about Mr. Vizzard. It was a new sensation, and it savoured terrifyingly of unfaithfulness.

She had put the letter face downwards on the hall-stand because she didn't like holding it. Now she lifted it up again and studied it closely. It was written on large expensive notepaper that bent rather than creased as she handled it. It reminded her of a five-pound note that the bank manager had once passed to her. And it was large, expensive-looking handwriting, with the address heavily underlined with an oblique indented slash of the pen. Obviously the handwriting of a woman.

With a start she realised that she must have been standing there for the better part of a minute with the letter still in her hand. Almost in a trance, in fact. Giving a little shudder, she braced herself and began to descend the dark stairs again. Now that she had quite got over this sudden fit of silliness she wondered whether she should go straight in with the letter or wait until she took Mr. Squales his breakfast at eight-thirty.

The breakfast on a tray had been her own idea. It had been born on that day when Mr. Squales had first put his arms around her. He was hungry and he was hers, and that had been sufficient.

As she got this morning's tray ready—the small teapot that she had bought specially for the purpose, the three thin slices of bread and butter, the freshly-boiled egg under its knitted cosy like a pointed pixie cap—she recognised this for the most delicious moment in the day. Sometimes as she stood outside his door she could scarcely bear to knock and destroy the suspense. She was waiting, she realised, for the occasion when, in answer to her knock, he would throw the door open and embrace her. But up to the present it hadn't happened that way. Usually by the time she got there Mr. Squales wasn't up. Sometimes he was sitting up in bed smoking, his dark eyes fixed on her. But almost as often he was still asleep. If anything, since he had been getting his breakfast in bed in this way his hours had become rather later.

Balancing the tray one-handed, Mrs. Vizzard raised her right one to knock. As she did so the old fluttery excitement came back again. And then, staring up at her from beside the toast-rack, she saw the letter. The horrible thing had succeeded even in ruining this moment, in coming between her and her betrothed.

It was one of Mr. Squales's more wakeful mornings. He was alert and watchful, sitting up against the pillows, a thin spire of smoke rising from the drooping cigarette between his lips. And, as soon as he saw her, he smiled—that slow melting smile of his that made Mrs. Vizzard want to drop the tray that she had been carrying so carefully and rush and place her head on his bosom.

"I've been waiting for you," he said softly, almost reproachfully. "Lying here, waiting."

As he spoke, it seemed to Mrs. Vizzard that they were the most beautiful words that she had ever heard. Then she happened to glance towards the clock. It showed twenty minutes to nine. Evidently the affair of the letter had taken up more of her time than she had realised.

She placed the tray on his knees and she quivered as his hand brushed against hers. When the tray was securely balanced—Mr. Squales wasn't really sitting up straight enough to be comfortable—he reached out and caught hold of her hand again. This time he raised it to his lips and kissed it, and Mrs. Vizzard experienced that same shameful quiver again as she felt the rough texture of his unshaven cheek.

Then his eye caught the letter and he dropped her hand, abruptly it seemed. He picked up the envelope and examined it.

"There's a letter for you," Mrs. Vizzard said foolishly.

But Mr. Squales did not reply. He only frowned. That letter—and he recognised the writing in a flash—was a piece of his private life. About the only piece left, indeed. It was his, and his alone. And he didn't want to have anyone else butting into it. So he merely put it back on the tray again and poured himself out a cup of tea.

"And did my dear one sleep well?" he asked. "No bad dreams?"

Mrs. Vizzard didn't reply immediately. She stood there looking down at the letter.

"Sleep?" she said with a jerk. "Oh, yes, I slept well."

Mr. Squales nodded his head approvingly as though she had slept well specially to please him. He began tapping the white crown of the egg with the back of his spoon.

"I often wonder," he said between the taps, "what I have done to deserve this? Why should I, a wanderer, suddenly find such kindness—such love—when I was by the wayside?"

The egg broke and Mr. Squales hurriedly began chasing a rich yellow rivulet which was coursing down the side of the egg-cup. Mrs. Vizzard stood there watching him. She had never before seen a man crack an egg while he was smoking a cigarette.

"You haven't forgotten this afternoon, have you?" she asked.

"Forgotten this afternoon? Indeed, no!"

His mouth was full as he was speaking, and his voice was blurred and muffled. He took a sip of tea and wondered, despondently, what it was that was happening this afternoon. If anything, his days from being too empty had suddenly become too full. Mrs. Vizzard was always thinking up something new for him—something for both of them. His afternoons, so far as he could see, were degenerating into a series of rather feminine birthday treats. He was only glad that there weren't any relatives of Mrs. Vizzard's whom she might want to take him to see.

Then a happy subterfuge came into his mind, and his face fell.

"There is only one thing about it that makes me reluctant to go. Would you understand it, I wonder, if I told it to you?"

Mrs. Vizzard's hand strayed across her bosom.

"Tell me," she said faintly.

"It is the question of money," he explained. "Your money and my pride. How can I go on letting you spend so much on me? A theatre . . . a cinema . . . they all cost money."

"But the Tate Gallery doesn't cost anything. It's a free day," she told him.

The Tate Gallery! Of course, now that she mentioned it, he remembered perfectly. It was the Blakers that she wanted to be taken to. There had been an article in *The Spirit World* that had said that Blaker was a man who dipped his earthly brush on to a psychic palette, drawing trance pictures that only the Inner Eye could have seen: Mrs. Vizzard had made him read it and he recalled how, at the time, he had reflected that there might be an opening in spiritualist papers for that kind of writing. But the recollection did nothing to encourage him. Mr. Squales had never really cared for picture galleries.

"Everything costs something," he said at last. "You are so good to me. How do I know that before I come back we shall not have taken food somewhere?"

There was a pause.

"Will you come if I promise that we don't spend a penny?" Mrs. Vizzard asked him.

Mr. Squales's heart sank as he realised what it was that he had done. Simply by being too clever, he had committed himself to the pictures and ruined any chance of tea.

But already Mrs. Vizzard was speaking again.

"Will you come if we *walk* there and come *back* to tea afterwards?" she persisted.

She stood there on the rug—it was a rug that she had brought through from her own sitting-room—appealing to him.

"Do say you'll come," she said.

She was ashamed of it as soon as she had said it. There she was, a responsible adult woman behaving like a schoolgirl. The sheer nakedness of her attitude appalled her.

But Mr. Squales was smiling again.

"You didn't think that I didn't *want* to go?" he said. "It would make me unhappy, very unhappy, if you had actually thought that. We will go together as we said, and if"—here Mr. Squales took another spoonful of egg—"we find a place where we can drink a cup of tea, and talk and forget the world, who am I to stop it? This afternoon we will see the Blakers."

Blaker? Blaker? Was it really Blaker or was it just plain Blake? He didn't know because he'd never heard of him before. Not that it mattered. His afternoon was done for, anyway.

Now that Mrs. Vizzard was happy again she could afford to go back and get on with the rest of her duties. In the anticipation of the outing she had even forgotten the letter.

Mr. Squales made no attempt to stop her. He watched her go from the room, and then as soon as the door was shut after her and he had heard her footsteps die away in the passage, he snatched up the envelope and ripped it open. To his surprise he found that his fingers were trembling with excitement.

And no wonder! The letter was from Mrs. Jan Byl and was written in her own imperious hand. Her blunt majestic nib had raced across the paper, leaving the crosses to the t's streaming like a comet's tail. And in the result it was considerably more like painting than mere writing. But it was the substance of the letter more than the characters that roused Mr. Squales. He drew in a deep breath and reached out for another cigarette.

"*Dear Professor Qualito,*" the letter ran, "*I have done you an injustice. A grave injustice. The things you told me while your spirit was far away were terrible. Terrible.*" Mrs. Jan Byl had underlined this word so heavily that the nib had divided itself. "*But I know now that they were true.*"—"True" was also underlined.—"*One cannot afford to be petty in Spiritualism—there is no place for littleness. Will you, therefore, consent to enter the trance state again in my house? If you come I feel that we may be on the verge of great discoveries. Important discoveries. If we could obtain proof*"—likewise underlined—"*you would be famous. It is not in our powers to deny such an opportunity. Come to-morrow, Tuesday, if you are not engaged. I need your help.*

"*Yours inquiringly,*

"*Hermione Jan Byl.*"

Mr. Squales drew in a deep draught of cigarette smoke and lay back holding his breath until his lungs were near bursting-point. He was in ecstasy.

"There you are," he told himself. "I knew I'd make an impression. I'm not usually wrong about women."

Then, as the first flush of mental conquest ebbed away, he reflected in a kind of golden haze on the financial aspects of the thing.

"She sent me away. Now she wants me back. I'll go. But this will cost her something."

Within reason, he could charge her anything. It wasn't even as if he were relying on it now—that always kept the price down. Thanks to Mrs. Vizzard he was independent. And he was better dressed than he had been the last time he had seen Mrs. Jan Byl. He had to thank Mrs. Vizzard for that, too—it was she who had made him a present of the clothes that he was wearing. In his new light grey he could look the part as well as play it. He only wished now that he had shown more confidence in himself in the choice of the suit. He ought to have chosen something darker and more professional. The only thing that comforted him was that he had stipulated a double-breasted waistcoat at the time of ordering.

"To-morrow, Tuesday,"—that meant to-day. And he remembered Mr. Blaker! It was Mr. Blaker who stood between him and his five—possibly even ten—guineas. He crushed out his cigarette angrily in his saucer. Blast Mr. Blaker.

"Opportunity only knocks once," he told himself. "This is where Mr. Blaker goes down the drain so far as I'm concerned. I'll have to square it first with my intended. There may be trouble. There may be tears. But go I must. And go I'm going to."

2

But Mr. Squales wasn't the only one—not even the only one in Dulcimer Street—whose afternoon had been arranged for him. Mr. Josser was just such another.

There he was, all keyed up and ready to spend a couple of pleasant hours doing nothing in particular while Mrs. Josser went over to the infirmary to see Mrs. Boon, when the worst, the very worst, the worst possible, occurred. Mrs. Josser got one of her headaches.

She had suffered from them before—the very word "her" denoted this—and Mr. Josser knew exactly what it meant. Knew exactly, but still did not realise how deeply he would be involved. It just didn't seem possible that he should be asked to go over to the infirmary instead.

For one brief moment when Mrs. Josser put it to him in the bedroom he very nearly refused point-blank. He was fed up; fed up, he confessed inwardly, with the Boons and everything about them; fed up with Percy and the murder and with Mrs. Boon too. Then the feeling passed as rapidly as it had come and he was himself again, with a fierce attack of conscience into the bargain. Of course, he'd go and see her; he couldn't leave Mrs. Boon just lying there half paralysed and with no one to talk to her. Besides, he was the one person she'd really want to see. He'd be able to sit at her bedside and tell her all about Percy.

"And take her some flowers," Mrs. Josser told him as he was leaving. "Take her a bunch of something bright."

He'd got right over to Walham Green where the hospital was before he actually bought the flowers. And that irritated him. Because on his way in the bus he'd been passing barrow after barrow laden up with stocks and marguerites and sweet-peas—just the sort of thing to brighten up a sick-ward. And now that he wanted a flower-seller there wasn't one in sight. Walham Green might have been visited by locusts for all the blossom that was about.

He found a shop finally, a small retail corner of the cut-flower trade, tucked away in a corner beside a tobacconist's. The proprietress, a pale fat woman in black, was finishing off a sheaf of arum lilies when he went in and over her head hung a black-edged notice that said WREATHS AND CROSSES MADE TO ORDER. It seemed irreverent to disturb her. And the result was disappointing when he did so. On the more frivolous side of her practice there was nothing but roses and carnations to be had—all the cottage flowers, as the woman called them, had been sold out earlier. So in the end Mr. Josser chose carnations. He bought half a dozen of them and they cost him three and threepence—three shillings for the carnations and threepence for the asparagus fern that went with them. As he came out of the shop Mr. Josser caught sight of himself in a long mirror by the doorway. Despite the asparagus fern, the flowers made an extraordinarily small bunch. A small, elongated bunch. They might have been a bouquet for an only moderately successful concert-singer.

The infirmary—the infirmary of the Little Sisters of Compassion—to which Mr. Josser was going, was a forbidding, impregnable-looking sort of building. As though fearing riot or assault, or possibly only the big outside world, the Little Sisters had hidden their good works away behind a high brick wall. Mr. Josser had to pull out an old-fashioned bell-handle beside a green front door and stand on the pavement as though he were a tradesman waiting to deliver something.

The door was opened almost immediately, however, and Mr. Josser found himself face to face—or rather face to what was left showing of face—with a nun wearing a gigantic overhanging head-dress of black cashmere, secured by very large pins on to a starched framework as stiff as a man's dress-shirt. It seemed quite astonishing to hear a normal, and rather pleasant, female voice issuing from such a contraption.

"I've come to see Mrs. Boon, if it's convenient," he said, and added rather lamely by way of explanation. "I . . . I'm a friend."

The Sister did not seem to need any further explanation. She accepted him. Closing the door behind her, she indicated a little waiting-room with a glass door, and a row of hard, upright chairs. Mr. Josser went in and sat down rather self-consciously underneath a highly-coloured plaster statuette of Our Lord with the heart picked out in gilt oddly enough in the *middle* of the chest, and the wounds painted in very vividly in vermilion. Feeling awkward and Protestant and out of place, he looked down at his shoes and tried to avoid catching the eye of the other two visitors who were waiting with him.

Then a girl in the plain grey dress of a ward-maid came along and told him that Sister had said that he could see Mrs. Boon if he came now. Holding the flowers in front of him, Mr. Josser followed.

The walk seemed in a way to be a continuation of his walk inside the prison. Between the prison and the infirmary there was very little to choose. It was as though by his simple inability to manage his own affairs, young Percy had sentenced the Boons, mother and son alike, to a life of bleak walls and long, echoing corridors and barred windows. Even the infirmary had metal grilles across the skylights.

When he actually reached the ward, Mr. Josser's embarrassment increased. The young ward-maid handed him over to another of the nuns, and in the wake of that prodigious bonnet Mr. Josser followed right down the centre of the ward as though he were a procession. There must have been twenty beds at least. And as he walked he was aware of sick womanhood all round him. Old ladies with wispy plaits of hair like bleached straw, and young buxom things in tight pink bed-jackets, lay in two long rows; lay in two long rows and watched him. He was a thoroughly self-conscious Mr. Josser by the time he had reached Mrs. Boon's bedside in the corner.

Things were not made any easier by the way in which Mrs. Boon devoured and consumed him. It was not merely that she wanted to hear about Percy. She wanted to hear *everything* about him—how he was looking, what he was wearing, if he had enough clean clothes, whether they were nice to him, when the . . . but she broke down before she got to it and could not actually utter the word "trial."

The rush of questions overwhelmed Mr. Josser and flurried him. And everything that he said seemed faintly wrong somehow. It all sounded callous and impersonal when it was for Mrs. Boon's ears that it was intended.

"He's . . . he's looking fine," he assured her. "Plenty to eat and . . . and early to bed. I've never seen him looking better. He's . . . he's fine. Not worrying a bit."

"And are they nice to him?" Mrs. Boon persisted.

"Couldn't be nicer," he told her. "Real nice, that's what they are. He's a proper favourite."

Mrs. Boon smiled.

"That's my Percy all over," she said.

She paused, and Mr. Josser saw that there were large tears trickling down her cheek. The stroke had affected only one side of her face, leaving the other untouched and even fresh-looking. And the puckered side—it was as though under the skin there were elastic that somehow had been drawn tight—was away from him. If he kept his head low he could scarcely notice any difference.

"Did he ask after me?" she went on as soon as she could speak again.

"Did he ask after you?" Mr. Josser repeated. "Talked about nothing else. Just his old mum the whole time. That's all he wanted to hear about."

It wasn't quite true. Not the sort of truth that you'd speak on Judgment Day. But it was true enough for the present occasion. Better than the truth in fact.

Mrs. Boon was silent for a moment.

"He's very fond of you," she said at length. "He never really knew his father. That's why he looks to you for everything. He was only little, remember, when George died."

Mr. Josser didn't answer immediately. He was uncomfortably aware that he was being drawn deeper and still deeper into the disaster that was Percy's life. Having had to come along to the infirmary to-day was only another part of an expanding pattern that was steadily and remorselessly enveloping him.

But already Mrs. Boon was speaking again.

"There's something I want you to do for me," she said.

There was no excuse, no pleading in her voice as she said it. She simply spoke with the assumed authority of an invalid. It wasn't even a request that she was making. It was an order. And it was obvious that she expected it to be obeyed.

"Any . . . anything you say," he promised her.

"I want you to go along to the solicitor," she said. "It's important. There's a lot depends on it. I want you to go along and fix things up for Percy."

Mr. Josser gave her hand a consoling little squeeze.

"Don't you worry," he said. "Everything's being done that can be. They fixed him up with a solicitor. There's nothing more we could do. Things have just got to . . . to take their course."

"But you don't understand," Mrs. Boon said wearily. "I want Percy to have the best solicitor he can get. I don't want a free one."

Mr. Josser shook his head.

"It isn't as easy as that," he said. "It may cost a lot of money. May run into hundreds, you know."

Mrs. Boon gave a sort of nod—a nod with her head still on the pillows.

"I can pay," she told him.

Mr. Josser looked at her in astonishment. Percy had been doing nicely at the garage. Very nicely, in fact. And Mrs. Boon was the careful sort. She obviously wasn't the kind to spend money when it could be avoided. But hundreds. It amazed him

A Sister, half hidden under the towering black coif, came along to the next bed and Mrs. Boon placed her finger warningly over her lips. She did not speak again until the Sister had moved away.

"I don't want *them* to know," she said in a whisper. "If they knew, I'd have to pay for being here. And I don't want that to happen. I want it all for Percy."

"I understand," Mr. Josser answered.

"It's two hundred pounds," Mrs. Boon continued, still in a whisper. "It was George's insurance money. And it's all in the post office. I've never touched a penny of it. It'll be more than that by now. There's the interest."

"And you want to spend it all?" Mr. Josser asked.

It sounded cruel, put that way. But he had to be quite sure. He was thinking that if anything—"anything" was the way he always referred to it, even to himself—happened to Percy, Mrs. Boon would need that two hundred. That two hundred and a good deal more besides.

But Mrs. Boon seemed surprised at him.

"Of course," she said. "What else should I want it for?"

"And you want me to give it to Mr. Barks?" Mr. Josser said slowly, checking every point as he went along.

Mrs. Boon inclined her head.

"I don't want him to spare a penny of it," she said. "I want him to get all the best people and fix things up just as though Percy was a rich man's son. I know that it's what George would have wanted. He was so fond of Percy when he was a little boy. He thought the world of Percy when he was a little boy."

The tears came again and she had to stop talking for a moment. Then she recovered herself. "And if there's anything over he can keep it for all his trouble," she continued. "I don't want him to have to think of money."

She paused. Then suddenly she reached out and grasped Mr. Josser by the hand.

"Tell me it'll be all right," she said. "You don't think he did it, do you? Tell me so that I can hear you saying it. I get so frightened just lying here. That's why they give me sleeping draughts."

"He'll be all right," Mr. Josser told her, tryng to make his voice sound full and convincing. "He'll be all right. Just you see."

The Sister came up the ward again placidly and efficiently telling the visitors that their time was up and that they'd have to be going. Mr. Josser was relieved to see her. He got up and began pulling down his waistcoat.

As soon as she saw what was happening, Mrs. Boon started fumbling with the round neck of her nightdress. A moment later she withdrew her hand and held something out to Mr. Josser. It was a thin gold chain with a cross dangling from it. On the cross was the pigmy image of a body crucified.

"Give this to Percy," she said. "It's mine. He'll recognise it. It'll . . . it'll help to keep him safe."

"I'll give it to him," Mr. Josser told her.

He took the rosary. It was still warm.

Then Mrs. Boon tried to shift herself towards him again.

"You haven't told me what his room's like," she reminded him. "Are you sure they're looking after him properly?"

"Couldn't be more comfortable," Mr. Josser told her for the second time. "And he's got one of the biggest cells there is . . ."

The Sister touched him on the elbow and he said good-bye to Mrs. Boon. Said it hurriedly and awkwardly, and escaped. "Cells!" Why had he used the word? He'd been trying all the time to avoid any mention of where Percy really was. And then at the last moment it had slipped out just like that. Mr. Josser wanted to kick himself.

But how was he to know that Mrs. Boon was going to talk about Percy as though he were in a convalescent home somewhere?

3

Mr. Squales had been less wise than Mr. Josser: he had attempted to argue about this afternoon. And, in the result, he had been quite right about the tears. Mrs. Vizzard was so upset about the sudden cancellation of her little outing that she had broken down and told him that he didn't really love her. But it was all over now, and she was nestling in his arms again on the straight-back horsehair sofa. She had forgiven him. And he had forgiven her. Forgiven her, but made it plain that he was still terribly, terribly hurt by what she had said about not caring.

"So my little kitten is happy, is she?" he asked tenderly. "First we go together to the Tate to see the Blakers, and then I go on to my appointment—alone. You mustn't be a selfish little kitten, remember."

"You won't be late, will you? Not later than supper?"

She regretted the words as she said them. They were fatal, silly words. They showed how absolutely, how disastrously, she relied on him.

"I shall only be as late as I have to be," he told her severely.

And that was all the promise that she could get from him. He was still a trifle cold and aloof in his manner. And remembering how unforgivably she herself had behaved she could not press him. She was lucky, she told herself, that he was even on speaking terms with her at all. Her feeling of contriteness—and gratitude—remained. And, when they finally set out arm-in-arm, Mrs. Vizzard kept wishing every time she glanced at Mr. Squales that she were a brighter and more dashing companion for such a man. But he still hadn't told her where he was going afterwards.

The Tate Gallery was not really a success. Not so far as Mr. Squales was concerned, that is. All the time he was in it, he kept wondering what he would do with it if it were his. There were obvious possibilities in those magnificent halls if only one could think of a *purpose* for them. The position of the gallery, of course, was against it. It was situated on the Embankment just where Westminster stopped and Chelsea hadn't yet begun. Unless there was a collision on the river, or something, you could never collect a crowd in a place like that. Could never make a *popular* success of a place on a site like that.

On the other hand, it clearly need not remain the obvious failure that it was now. And no wonder it was a failure. It was the pictures themselves that were at fault—that much was apparent at a glance—and Mr. Squales suspected that something had gone wrong on the buying side. There was nothing that you could rightly call an Old Master in the whole place. And a picture gallery without Old Masters was just absurd—rather like a circus without elephants. No: in the race for Rembrandts and Landseers, the Tate Gallery had simply been scooped.

There were some Turners admittedly, but Mr. Squales after one look at them decided that they couldn't be his best. He even wondered if they were genuine. Scooped again, in fact. And the stuff that they had bought up to fill the space was a positive disgrace. Somebody ought to have lost his job over it. "The Resurrection," for instance. And the portrait of Lytton Strachey. You had only to ask yourself the simple question of how they'd look in a room if you actually *had to live with them* to see where they came in the scale of art.

And it wasn't simply a matter of age. The Blakes—Blake, it was: Blaker, he remembered, had been a tobacconist in Brighton—weren't new by any means. But they were bad, too. Shockingly bad. The man obviously couldn't even draw. And the colours! And the number of exhibits. So far as he could judge almost everything that Blake had ever painted was there. Putting two and two together it looked to Mr. Squales as though someone, the widow probably, had pulled a pretty fast one.

Tea was better, except for the decorations on the walls of the tea-room. Now *there,* Mr. Squales spotted at once, was an opportunity. Nicely arranged, with period furniture and the waitresses in costume and one or two good pictures—hired if necessary—on the walls, the room *could* have been made attractive. But Mr. Squales did not bother about it unduly: he was too much preoccupied. Time was getting on, and though he didn't want to be early for Mrs. Jan Byl—that would look gauche and flustered—he certainly didn't want to be late either.

As he was drinking his second cup of tea he noticed that Mrs. Vizzard was looking at him. It seemed somehow that she was always looking at him. It made him feel uncomfortable. And then he remembered that he hadn't spoken to her since they'd entered the tea-room. To be honest with himself he'd got so much on his mind that he'd entirely forgotten her. Leaning forward, he pushed the hot-water jug a little to one side and inserted his forefinger into the open V at the wrist of Mrs. Vizzard's glove.

"A penny for your thoughts," he said at random. "My own were on having to leave you."

"I was wondering if you had eaten enough," she said simply.

Then she pushed a florin towards him. And after Mr. Squales had paid they walked along together as far as the Vauxhall Bridge Road.

"You've got enough money on you? You're sure you're all right?" she asked diffidently.

Mr. Squales squeezed her arm.

"There goes my kitten again," he told her. "You lent me five shillings last Thursday. You aren't going to have a spendthrift for a husband."

A tram was coming over Vauxhall Bridge and Mr. Squales stepped into the gutter to be ready for it. Mrs. Vizzard summoned all her courage in this final moment.

"You haven't told me where you're going," she reminded him reproachfully.

He bent forward and taking hold of her hand he kissed it.

"Right across London. Into *terro incognito*," he told her. "My tram."

And with a final pressure of his lips on to the stitching of her glove, he had left her.

Then a mood of madness took possession of Mrs. Vizzard. A second tram, following close on the heels of Mr. Squales's, drew up in front of her. And, mounting it, she followed him.

The impulse was sudden and irresistible. But, in the result, a fit of violent shivering attacked her.

"Why am I doing this?" she asked herself. "Why? Don't I trust him?"

She slumped down into the first available seat and remained there, her two hands clasped together to restrain their trembling. When she held out the penny for the fare her fingers quivered ridiculously.

But absorbed in the importance of her purpose she overcame her agitation. She had work to do, serious engrossing work. There was Mr. Squales, in the tram in front, blissful, unsuspecting, unalarmed. Here she was, in the tram behind, alert, suspicious, implacable. And the appreciation of the situation gave her a gratifying, God-like sensation. For the first time in her life she felt superior to Mr. Squales. And for the first time in her life she realised how agreeable the life of private detectives must be.

For the next few minutes at least there was very little that she could do. The tram was trundling down the Vauxhall Bridge Road and it did not seem in the least likely that her quarry would be getting off before he reached Victoria. Mrs. Vizzard, therefore, sat back and tried to compose herself. There were moments of anxiety, however. At one moment, for instance, a brewer's dray came across the track and the tram had to slow down for it while Mr. Squales's tram went dwindling dizzily into the distance. But it was all right. By the time they had got to Victoria they were almost on top of each other again. The two trams, in fact, were so close to each other that Mrs. Vizzard was quite nervous as she got off hers. She wondered what Mr. Squales would have to say if in the crush around the Clock Tower she should suddenly bump into him.

Mr. Squales, however, was oblivious of his pursuer. A conspicuous figure in his light grey suit, he made his way through the crowd, moving with that easy, slightly swaying movement that seemed to make his walk different from other men's. Like . . . like an Indian, she told herself, not being quite clear in her own mind what it was that she meant.

And he certainly moved quickly.

She had the utmost difficulty in keeping up with him. Round the corner by the Windsor Castle he went and across the station yard like a man hurrying to catch a train. Mrs. Vizzard was about fifty yards behind him and, for a moment, her heart started beating louder from a fresh anxiety. She feared that he was going off by train somewhere. Going off! Never coming back again. . . .

The fear proved groundless, however. Mr. Squales passed the station without even glancing at it and went straight on to the bus stop in Grosvenor Gardens. It was open country here with no natural cover and Mrs. Vizzard dared not go any further. She remained up against the Grosvenor Hotel watching him. And then as a stream of buses, released suddenly by the traffic lights, surged round in front of her, she realised that she would have to act rapidly if she were to avoid losing him altogether. Darting in and out of the traffic like a whippet she crossed the road. And it was fortunate that she did so. Mr. Squales was already getting on to a No. 19 that was moving. Without waiting to see the number of the bus behind she leapt on to it.

This part of the ride was agony to Mrs. Vizzard. In her haste there had been no time to notice where her bus was going. For all she knew Mr. Squales might be swept off to Cricklewood while she was being carried away to South Kensington. She took a twopenny ticket and remained on her toes.

But her fears proved to be groundless. Both buses, Mr. Squales's and hers, turned west at Hyde Park Corner and went along past Knightsbridge Barracks. Then things began to go wrong. Her bus began to race Mr. Squales's. Nosing out more quickly from the stopping-place, it got away well ahead. Soon Mrs. Vizzard was looking out of the back window to keep the other bus in sight. And this, of course, meant that she had no idea where she should get out. She was well and truly trapped. Buses, she realised, were less reliable than trams for shadowing.

Then, fortunately, as though sensing the competition, Mr. Squales's driver put on a spurt and caught up with them again. For a moment they ran side by side. And through the window in that agonising instant, Mrs. Vizzard saw the back of a very light grey suit making its way towards the exit. At the next stop she got off and hid in a doorway.

Then Mr. Squales did an astonishing thing. He signalled to a taxi. He was too far away for Mrs. Vizzard to hear what he said to the taximan. All she could do was to stand there watching her plan and strategy collapse before her eyes. But she had come a long way to be beaten. She was—apart from this abominable infatuation—a woman of determined will. And without hesitation she did something equally astonishing. She hailed another taxi.

"It's my friend," she said hurriedly. "He's gone off in that taxi. Please keep up with him—I've . . . I've forgotten the address."

The taxi swung round and began the chase. The driver entered into the spirit of it from the very start. He might have been pursuing other taxis all his life. Round the corner of Kensington Palace Gardens he went like a racing motorist. The taxi, squat and unathletic like all London taxis, creaked and rattled. The driver was just letting her out on the straight when Mrs. Vizzard saw Mr. Squales's taxi already drawing up. She tapped frantically on the glass.

"Stop here," she said. "You needn't go any further."

The driver braked hard and they jerked to a standstill.

"Didn't go far, did he?" he asked pleasantly.

There was only ninepence on the clock. But because he had helped her, had rallied to her cause, in fact, Mrs. Vizzard gave him a shilling and told him to keep the change. The driver did not thank her.

It was late now, very late.

Supper-time was long past and the supper that she had prepared was cleared away again. Only the second chair still drawn up at the table indicated that, earlier, there had been a meal in readiness for two. Not that she could have waited any longer. By the time she had sat down by herself and begun eating, the food was already dried up and ruined. After a few mouthfuls, she had pushed the plate away from her and remained there looking at the clock that she had been watching ever since seven. It was now twenty minutes past nine; and in her imagination she saw the clock hand moving on to half-past, to quarter-to, to ten o'clock. Ten o'clock and still no sign of Mr. Squales.

Even so, she had not yet made the tea. The tea-things stood on a little tray beside the fireplace. Like Mrs. Vizzard, they were waiting. And, though she wanted her tea, she hadn't the heart to pour on the boiling water. Somehow, without Mr. Squales there to drink it with her, it wouldn't seem like having tea at all.

"I'll give him ten minutes more," she told herself. "Ten more minutes exactly. And if he isn't here by half-past I'll have it without him."

Having made this resolve she felt better for it. It made her feel strong and independent again. She was just congratulating herself on the victory over her weakness, just enjoying the sensation of being a sensible woman once more, when she heard footsteps on the pavement outside. They were not heavy footsteps. They were, in fact, the kind of footsteps that are made by rather light-soled shoes. Faint, flickering footsteps. But Mrs. Vizzard recognised them at once. And, as she recognised them, she realised what nonsense it was to pretend that she was either strong or independent. At the mere awareness of his presence near her, she was trembling almost as much as she had been on the tram. But even in her excitement, her presence of mind didn't entirely forsake her. She poured the boiling water hurriedly into the pot and sat back again. Her pride made it impossible for her to run up to the front door to greet him. That would cheapen her even more than she had cheapened herself already. But at least his tea would be ready there for him.

She didn't doubt for a moment that he would come straight in to her as soon as he got down the stairs. And she was right. She heard those thin-soled shoes on the front steps, heard the key in the lock and the door closing after him, heard him descending the flight of stairs to the basement. Then, without even knocking, he had thrown the door open and was standing there in front of her. He was pale and his hair was a little dishevelled. His dark eyes seemed darker and more penetrating than she had ever known them.

"Why did you follow me?" he asked.

CHAPTER 42

I

It was a mistake, clearly a mistake, on Mr. Josser's part not to have written for an appointment. Or even to have phoned up. But he had never had much experience with solicitors. He thought they were like doctors: you just called on them.

That was why he was annoyed at first to be told that Mr. Barks was too busy to see him. And it made no difference when he said that he had come about Percy Boon. Then he saw the funny side of it and Mr. Barks's indifference merely amused him. He thought what a fool Mr. Barks would feel when he realised that he had only to open the door and put out his hand for two hundred pounds to be thrust into it.

So Mr. Josser said quietly that he'd wait; wait all day if necessary. And he said equally quietly that it was Mr. Barks himself he wanted, and not just one of the clerks. He was rather pleased with the phrase "one of the clerks"; it had a curt, decisive ring to it. Besides, it wasn't too bad, waiting. He'd been given a chair in the outer office and he wasn't in a draught because even though it was still a fine, hot day, none of the windows was open. The words BARKS, BARKS, WEDDERBURN AND BARKS, SOLICITORS, painted in gold across the panes showed up strikingly in reverse and served to emphasise the long-standing gulf between the legal profession and fresh air. There was an atmosphere about the place—chilly in summer, twilit in the sun—that was reminiscent of a church. Mr. Josser sat there looking at the gilt letters, his umbrella between his knees and his hat perched on the crook of the handle. When at last he grew tired of the name of the firm he transferred his gaze to the names of its clients. These were neatly inscribed in white letters on a series of black japanned boxes ranged along shelves all round the walls. And in a mild, unexciting fashion they were entertaining enough: F. D. SHUTTLEWORTH, Esq.; J. RIGBY MORTON (1928), LTD.; DOWNMARSH ESTATE; MRS. HINKSON, Dcsd.; HOPEJOHN TEN-MINUTE CLEANERS; KIDD, CHUTNEY & SONS; The REV. E. R. H. SIMPSON-FAWCETT; A. LOVECHILD, LTD. He was only surprised that there wasn't a box labelled PERCY BOON, Esq.

Then suddenly Mr. Barks emerged. He had his bowler hat on, a shiny brief-case in his hand, and a glossy rolled-up umbrella hung over his arm. Mr. Josser could scarcely suppress a gasp of admiration at the sight of him—everything about Mr. Barks was so beautifully finished-off and polished.

Mr. Josser rose to his feet politely, but Mr. Barks had evidently forgotten all about him. Either that, or not been told. He tried to walk right past Mr. Josser without taking any notice of him. But that was impossible because Mr. Josser stepped into his path.

"Josser's the name," he said diffidently.

"Josser, Josser," Mr. Barks repeated, as though he either didn't like or didn't believe it.

"I've come about Percy," Mr. Josser explained. "Percy Boon, you know."

"Percy Boon, that's different," Mr. Barks conceded. He eyed Mr. Josser suspiciously. "You a rel'tive?"

"Oh, no," Mr. Josser answered. "I'm not a relative. I'm . . . I'm nobody."

Mr. Barks looked towards the door.

"Only see clients by 'pointment," he said.

Then, remembering that he had built up his large practice of trifling cases only by grasping at every bit of business within arm's length, he softened.

"'s it urgent?" he asked

"Matter of life and death," Mr. Josser told him. "That's why I'm here."

Mr. Barks took out his gold half-hunter, snapped it open and glanced up at Mr. Josser.

"Give you five minutes," he said. "Can't possibly spare more now."

They went back into Mr. Barks's office together and Mr. Barks put down his hat and umbrella and brief-case on his desk in front of him, so that he could snatch them up again as soon as this unwelcome interview was over.

"Yes?" he said.

"It's about Percy," Mr. Josser explained.

"Percy Boon, y'mean?"

"That's right," said Mr. Josser, "you're acting for him, aren't you?"

"Witness?" Mr. Barks enquired.

Mr. Josser shook his head.

"Me a witness?" he asked. "I never saw him do it, if that's what you mean. I've just come along to make sure that everything's going to be all right."

Mr. Barks took a quick glance at his hat and umbrella.

"Ver' busy man, remember," he said.

"Well, it's this way," said Mr. Josser. "I've just been seeing his mother, and she's worrying about him. Afraid he isn't having the best of everything. So she asked me . . ."

Mr. Barks got to his feet.

"No use," he said. "You tell her that everything's being done. Mus' excuse me now. Got another 'pointment."

"But you haven't heard what I've got to say," Mr. Josser complained indignantly. "I've come along to help you."

"Tell me 's quickly as you can then."

"I've come along to finance the defence," Mr. Josser said slowly. "I've got two hundred pounds to put up."

That naturally altered things, and Mr. Barks sat himself back in his chair again. He picked up a pencil and began playing with it.

"So we want you," Mr. Josser continued, "to get the best man you can to defend Percy. We thought of Patrick Hastings. But if you've got your own man, of course, we'll leave it to you."

"How much d'you say you'd got?" Mr. Barks asked.

"Two hundred," Mr. Josser told him. "And there may be more. There's some interest, you see."

Mr. Barks tweaked at his eyebrows.

"Can't do anything with two hundred," he replied. "Wrong sort of sum. Wouldn't attract a silk at all. Lot of work in a murder case. Might get a junior."

"Pay a junior two hundred pounds?" Mr. Josser repeated, incredulously.

"Not all of it," Mr. Barks told him. "My fees too, remember. I'm doing this practically free at the moment. Can't go paying out money to other people and doing all the work for next to nothing. Most irreg'lar. Not et'quette."

Mr. Josser paused.

"How much would Marshall Hall cost?" he asked.

"Marshall Hall?" Mr. Barks said. "Out of the question. Dead long ago. Top rank man cost you a thousand guineas." He paused. "Plenty of smaller ones, though," he added. "Might even get a name if you're lucky. Someone like Veesey Blaize."

"Is . . . is a name important?" Mr. Josser asked.

"Nat'rally," Mr. Barks replied. "Get someone nobody's heard of. May be all right. May not. May be a coming man. Can't tell. No use running risks."

Mr. Josser paused. A silly thought, one that he was still hoping to suppress, had come into his mind.

"How much do you really need for a case like this?" he asked.

"Much as you can get," Mr. Barks answered. "Big thing murder."

Mr. Josser followed up his silly thought.

"Would . . . would three hundred be any good?"

"Better than two hundred," Mr. Barks told him. "Hundred pounds better. Have y'got three hundred?"

Mr. Josser drew back.

"I'm not sure," he said. "I'll have to think about it."

Mr. Barks looked at his watch again. Then he picked up his brief-case and his umbrella.

"My 'pointment," he said.

But the sum of two or three hundred pounds floating in the air had changed his attitude appreciably. He put his arm round the small of Mr. Josser's back as he edged him from the room.

"Come round and see me in the mornin'," he said. "Talk about it prop'ly then. Find out how you stand. No good going to anyone like Veesey Blaize with two hundred. Just leave a bad taste in the mouth."

2

It was the crash of the cupboard as it collapsed that gave Mr. Puddy away. In the cupboard were twelve tins of baked beans, eight tins of condensed milk, six of salmon, six flat ones of sardines and three 2-lb. tins of mixed-fruit jam, as well as ten pounds of sugar and two and a quarter pounds of tea. It was the whole of Mr. Puddy's reserve larder, the iron rations that he had been laying in against trouble in Europe.

The cupboard was a little affair that he'd put up himself on the landing over the gas ring where he did his cooking. It had seemed a good strong sort of cupboard when he'd erected it. And even now it wasn't the cupboard itself that had given way. It was simply that the wall-brackets had come clean out of the plaster. But, naturally, when the cupboard hit the floor it burst open.

The crash could hardly have come at a worse time, because Mr. Puddy had got a small stew cooking on the gas ring at the time. And, of course, that went, too. At one moment, there was Mr. Puddy with his collar off, and in his stocking feet, sitting quietly in his own arm-chair, reading the evening paper and waiting for the stew to warm up, and at the next there was a noise on the landing as though the foundations of Dulcimer Street were giving way. Mr. Puddy ran out, still in his stocking feet, and trampled on burst sugar-bags.

It was really a pretty alarming sight that met him. The gas ring, knocked off the upturned biscuit tin on which it generally stood, lay on its side still burning brightly, and trying to set the stairs on fire. Because of the sugar scattered over it, the flame was spluttering in a blaze of blue fireworks. Mr. Puddy made a plunge for the gas key and as he did so, the searing pain of scalding stew came up through the feet of his stockings. And it was only when he had averted the danger of the fire that he noticed another extraordinary side to the whole affair. A whole series of smaller crashes were going on. Mr. Puddy stood there aghast, listening to them. But they were nothing really. They were only tins of salmon and baked beans bouncing from step to step as they plunged downstairs.

The clatter naturally had roused everyone. But Connie was easily the first to get there. As soon as she heard the first rumblings of disaster she put down her *Detective Magazine*, and came running out to see. She was closely followed by Mr. and Mrs. Josser; by Doris and Bill; and—at some distance—by Mrs. Vizzard and Mr. Squales.

Connie and the Jossers were so much on top of each other that one explanation did for both parties. But when Mrs. Vizzard and Mr. Squales arrived, Mr. Puddy had to begin all over again.

"Dothing to ged alarbed about," he said sullenly. "I've 'ad a naccident, that's all."

Meanwhile, Connie was down on her knees, surveying the mess.

"All that beautiful sugar," she said. "You can't waste it. I'll get a cup."

"There's wud of by gubs ub there," Mr. Puddy told her. "Bedder use it."

He was annoyed that a crowd should have gathered. It was bad enough having met with misfortune without having to excuse himself for it. He was relieved when Bill and Doris, anxious not to lose a moment of the bliss of each other's company, removed themselves. But the others intransigently remained.

"Oh, my!" said Connie. "The tea."

"Leave it where it is," Mr. Puddy answered shortly. "It's dud for now anyhow."

"And my wall? What do you propose to do about that?"

It was Mrs. Vizzard who had spoken. She was standing at the back of the group, looking up at the great jagged rents in the dark red wallpaper.

"Look! There! That's where I mean," she added, her voice shrill-sounding in its agitation.

Mr. Puddy looked up.

"I'll blaster it up on Sunday," he said. "Thad's whad I'll do. *I'll* blaster it. Blaster it beself."

Mrs. Vizzard would have said more. But she became suddenly aware that Mr. Squales was no longer with her. He had thrust his hands into his trousers pockets and was going downstairs again, sick at heart by the sheer sordidness of it all. It wasn't merely that Mr. Puddy, standing half clothed in the midst of so much chaos, was distasteful to him. But that his betrothed should have started railing like a fishwife. That was horrible. He couldn't help comparing the nastiness of the whole event with the sort of life—all pink lampshades and maids in frilly uniforms—that went on at Mrs. Jan Byl's. Then, half-way down the stairs, he trod on one of Mr. Puddy's tins of salmon that was lying there like a little treacherous wheel, waiting for a foot to be placed on it. It was the second big crash of the evening.

Mr. Josser and Mr. Puddy picked Mr. Squales up between them and helped him down to Mrs. Vizzard's room. He leant heavily on Mr. Josser's shoulder, complaining between gasps that his leg was broken. Considering the pain, the agony, that he was in, his self-control was remarkable. It wasn't until he was actually in Mrs. Vizzard's armchair that he allowed himself the question that had been burning in his mind.

"What the hell happened to me?" he asked.

Mr. Josser glanced at Mr. Puddy.

Mr. Puddy coughed.

"You trod on a sabbod," he said.

"On a what?" Mr. Squales exclaimed.

"On a sabbod. A Sailor Slice," Mr. Josser explained.

"How did it get there?" Mr. Squales demanded.

Mr. Puddy looked down at his feet.

"I bood id in the gubbud along with the rest of me things," he said stoutly. "It god oud."

Mr. Squales's leg was still hurting him and he was in a very bad temper.

"You can bloody well thank your stars that I didn't break my neck," he said.

"No, no," said Mr. Josser. "That's what you can do, Mr. Squales."

He gave a little laugh as he said it because he was a great believer in a joke when things were looking really nasty.

But, in any case, Mr. Puddy couldn't afford to stay there much longer. His granary, his nut-store, the one thing that might stand between him and famine, was now open to the world with no one to protect it. And more than open. The sounds of blatant pillaging came down to him.

"God to see how Gonnie's gedding on," he said. "God to look after things."

3

Bill had just gone. And, in consequence, Mr. and Mrs. Josser were able to go back into their sitting-room. Up to that moment they had been spending the evening in discreet discomfort on the nearest thing to easy chairs that the bedroom possessed. Mrs. Josser had occupied the tub-like piece in sprayed wicker-work, and Mr. Josser had taken the one with the cane-bottom.

It had been Mrs. Josser's idea to leave the young people to themselves in this way. But, having had the idea, she afterwards resented it. She held it against Doris in some way that she had, thoughtlessly and callously, evicted her father from his own armchair. "I shall be glad when she gets married, I declare I will," she had said on three widely separated occasions on discovering that she was in the bedroom and that everything she wanted was in the sitting-room.

Mr. Josser, however, was too much preoccupied to take much notice. He had been sitting up in his uncomfortable little chair, remembering Mr. Barks. He and his silly thought were still with him. Looking across at Mrs. Josser, he wondered more than once what she would say if she knew what he was thinking. And in between the hours of silliness he found himself pondering on men to whom two hundred pounds was merely a bad taste in the mouth. It was a sober and chastening reflection.

Then suddenly Mrs. Josser addressed him. She had the evening paper in her hand—the absence of the evening paper had been one of the things that were irritating her in the bedroom—and she was leaning forward eagerly.

"Read that," she said.

Mr. Josser took the paper, and his eyes followed her pointing finger.

"Unique Tudor cottage, ½-acre," was what he read. "3 bedrooms, large lounge, sitting-room, usual offices, indoor san. 45 mins. town, high ground. Wonderful views. £500 or near offer."

Mr. Josser gave a gulp. What was the use? Unless he were able to curb that silly thought of his, he wouldn't have £500 any more. He'd only have four hundred. And four hundred wasn't a near offer. It would be for someone else—someone who didn't have silly thoughts—for whom those wonderful views would be spread out.

"Sounds like what we're looking for," Mrs. Josser remarked, evidently pleased at having found it herself. "I should write before it gets snapped up."

There was a pause.

"Don't forget," she went on. "I'm never really sure with you unless I can see you actually doing it."

Again Mr. Josser didn't answer immediately. Percy might have been there beside him, he seemed so near. Percy and Mr. Barks and Mrs. Boon and the rest of them.

"I won't forget," he said at last.

4

Uncle Henry was at his worst. His absolute worst. He would keep talking about the war. And nothing that you could say would persuade him that there wasn't going to be one. He gave the peace another month at the outside.

He'd arrived, as usual, very late. Just as the Jossers were going to bed, in fact. Mrs. Josser was actually reaching up her arm to extinguish the gas when there was the sound of a bicycle wheel scraping up against the kerb outside and the faint tinkle—as though its owner had accidentally touched it—of one of those revolving bells.

Mr. and Mrs. Josser exchanged glances.

"That's your brother," Mr. Josser remarked.

He always called Henry Mrs. Josser's brother when he was particularly annoyed with him. It was a simple and easy device for passing on the irritation.

And Mrs. Josser did her best to pass it back again. She faced Mr. Josser squarely, while they were waiting for the knock at the door, and addressed him.

"And don't you start any of your arguments," she said. "Just let him say what he has to say and seem to be agreeing with him. I don't want it to be midnight before I'm in bed."

A clatter on the knocker downstairs indicated that Uncle Henry was really there. He always announced himself as though he were a telegram.

"You go down, Fred," Mrs. Josser said. "I'll put the kettle on."

From the moment Uncle Henry came inside the front door Mr. Josser could tell that he was going to be difficult. There was a wild cantankerous look in his eye and his hair was even more unruly than usual. He scarcely answered when Mr. Josser remarked that it had turned quite chilly and looked like rain. Instead, he went straight on upstairs, looking like a tall gaunt schoolboy in those ridiculous knee-breeches of his, and sat himself down in the centre chair. Even before Mrs. Josser had rejoined them with the tea he had started off about Hitler and the writing on the wall.

And the tea did nothing to calm him down. On the contrary, it roused him and made him more eloquent. Under its influence he became inspired and Cassandra-like and sat there, with his cup suspended, prophesying disaster. His customary historical sketch—Manchukuo . . . Abyssinia . . . Albania . . . the Spanish Civil War—was just over, and he had reached the present moment. It was now to-day, August 24th, 1939, that was under discussion.

"At this very moment," he was saying, "there is the sword of Damocles hanging over our heads. The Pope's broadcast to-day. That means war if anything does."

Mr. Josser nodded his head sadly.

"One by one," Uncle Henry went on, "the lamps are going out all over Europe—like in 1914."

"Certainly looks that way," Mr. Josser admitted.

"And in Downing Street," Uncle Henry continued, "there is a dead hand at the helm steering us to disaster."

"We're getting Winston back," Mr. Josser reminded him. "That's something."

"Winston's no dove of peace," Uncle Henry retorted.

Mr. Josser was about to say something when he caught Mrs. Josser's eye. She was reminding him. Mr. Josser allowed himself to go limp again.

"Perhaps you're right," he said weakly. "Maybe he isn't."

The conversion of his brother-in-law to his point of view was so sudden that for the moment it caught Uncle Henry unawares. Then he recovered himself.

"Do the common people want war?" he demanded.

This didn't seem quite fair. It was easy enough to agree with a man who had just said something. But it wasn't nearly so easy to be sure that you were giving the right answer to someone who had merely asked a question. Mr. Josser was on his guard.

"No-o-o," he said warily.

"And what'll happen when their lords and masters in Whitehall tell them to go out and fight?" Uncle Henry continued.

Mr. Josser took a pull at his pipe before replying. Unless he were careful this was going to be Uncle Henry's big opportunity. Mr. Josser glanced at the clock—it showed five minutes to eleven already—and gave his answer. It was a brave one.

"Not this time," he said. "They've had their lesson. 1914 taught it to them. They've seen what it's like living in a land fit for heroes."

They were almost Uncle Henry's own words that he was using, and Mrs. Josser was afraid for a moment that he was rather overdoing it.

His own words or not, however, the answer didn't please Uncle Henry in the least. He dismissed the whole thing out of hand as nonsense.

"Bah!" he said. "They'll go all right when the trumpet calls. They'll go like a lot of bleeding sheep."

Mr. Josser suddenly found his brother-in-law even more vexing than usual. Vexing and silly. He wanted to tell him that sheep were quite unresponsive to trumpet calls. But he kept control of himself very carefully.

"You know best," was all he said. He was very tired.

The very meekness of the answer seemed to stir up something in Uncle Henry. He felt that he was losing his grip on his audience. And, like a touring actor playing to a flat house, he gathered himself up for the attack across the footlights. Setting his cup down on the small table beside him, he stroked his moustache down over his mouth. Then blowing it up again, he began.

"Yes," he said slowly and deliberately, "I do know best. And perhaps if you read a little more you'd know, too. If you knew what was behind the Arcos case, you'd know the sort of people that were running this country. Only you don't know and that's what's wrong with you. Well, I'll tell you: Big Business. Vested Interests. Show me an M.P. and I'll show you a Vested Interest. Cartels and combines—bah! Join the Left Book Club, and then you'll know. There's only one thing that may stop this war, and that's a deal with Hitler. And let me tell you that there's plenty in the City—and up in Birmingham for that matter—that'll be ready to do a deal with him."

"Meaning Mr. Chamberlain?" Mr. Josser asked.

He was leaning forward a little in his chair as he put the question.

"Meaning Mr. Chamberlain," Uncle Henry replied.

"And meaning that he'd sell out to the Germans?" Mr. Josser went on.

"Meaning exactly that," Uncle Henry told him. "Him and his kind like him. Profit motive, that's what it is. Give them plenty of nice cheap labour and plenty of unemployment to keep it cheap and that's all that they're interested in. If they thought that Hitler was coming between them and their profits they'd sell their grandmothers to buy him off. That's what England's come to—profit before principle."

Mr. Josser got up from his chair and going over to the mantelpiece, set his shoulders against it.

"The trouble with you, Henry," he said, "is that you've been reading too much. It's gone to your head because you're the excitable kind. If Hitler does anything else he's for it. And he knows it."

"And what are we going to stop him with, I'd like to know?"

"With our hands," said Mr. Josser, who was surprised to find that his own hands were trembling. "With our hands because a lot of blooming cranks like you tried to do away with the whole bleeding army."

In the end it was nearly one o'clock before Uncle Henry left. The night was fine and very beautiful. Mr. Josser stood on the top of the steps and watched Uncle Henry pedalling away down the long avenue of lights that the street lamps made. It seemed strange that in a world so peacefully sleeping there should be even one man as mad as Uncle Henry. Except that you didn't have to go up in a steel-lined, bomb-proof lift, there wasn't very much to choose between Uncle Henry's book-lined bedroom and the Führer's tapestried study at Berchtesgaden.

Uncle Henry's rear-lamp flickered and was lost to sight round the corner.

"Just the bomb-proof lift. That's the only difference," Mr. Josser repeated. "The bomb-proof lift. And the view."

5

Dr. Otto Hapfel, the little Nazi visitor, was taking a course in English Phonetics and Elocution. The lessons were held in an Acting Academy off Baker Street and Dr. Hapfel, sitting very upright on a small gilt chair with his notebook open on his knees, was facing his teacher attentively. She was a large duchess-like woman who still played character parts when she could get them.

"Remember, the 't' is almost entirely elided in colloquial speech," she was saying. "Try this one: 'Wozzatime?' "

"What is the time?" Dr. Hapfel repeated carefully.

"Again: 'Wozzatime?' "

"Whatisthetime?" Dr. Hapfel intoned faster than before.

"Say: 'duzbin.' "

"Dustbin."

"No: 'duzbin.' "

"Dustbin."

"Say: 'brembutter.' "
"Bread and butter."
"No: 'brembutter.' "
"Brem-and-butter."
The teacher took a deep breath and went on.
"Pickcher."
"Pic-ture."
"Pickcher."
"Picture."
"Pynter milderbitter."
"Pint of mild and bitter."
The old actress sighed. The intense little man was . . . was unproduceable.
"Don't move your lips. Don't move your tongue. Don't move your jaws," she told him. "Just say it. Try: 'Hammernegs, rollerbutter.' "
"Ham and eggs, roll and butter."
"Arjerdoo?"
"Pliss?" asked Dr. Hapfel, puzzled.
But the old actress had given him up.
"Yoowerd," she said.
Dr. Hapfel understood that one.
"You heard," he repeated delightedly.
Really he was trying very hard, because it was important that he should be able to speak this extraordinary language as well as write it. Otherwise he would not have been making the maximum use of his opportunities. All the way back in the bus he was saying over to himself "Wozzthetime?" "Pynter mild and bitter," "Arjer you do?"
Really the study of High Cockney could be most interesting. It was only the idea of actually having to speak the language that appalled him.

CHAPTER 43

I

THEY'D known for a long time—for twenty-one years, in fact—that Doris's twenty-first birthday was coming. But somehow when it came they weren't ready for it. Or, at least, it wasn't what they had expected. After the engagement, it was an anticlimax. And there was so much else in the air—Percy's trial and troops moving on frontiers and gas-mask inspections—that they didn't really get down to the serious business of presents. Not until the last minute, that is.

All the same, the birthday party was a success. There was only one thing that spoilt it. And that was an unfortunate remark that someone made. But by then the evening was nearly over anyhow, and it was only for a passing moment that the whole evening seemed to have been ruined by it.

Admittedly, so far as Bill was concerned, the birthday had come at the worst possible moment. He'd been taking Doris out a good deal lately—nearly every night, in fact—and it had all been steadily eating up money in a quiet unspectacular fashion with nothing big and exciting to show, or even remember, for it. It was simply a succession of two-and-fours, and even one-and-nines, at the Regals and Orpheums and Lidos that had conspired to break him.

What was more, he didn't feel like asking his father for a special loan at the moment. The last time he had written—the time after asking for money for the ring—the old man hadn't shown himself particularly understanding. All that Bill had got was a long rambling letter promising him a practice of his own one day, complaining of income tax at five shillings and sixpence in the pound and enclosing three one-pound notes. It was the three pounds that hurt. Five was what he had expected and he felt as though he'd been docked somehow of the outstanding two. There is, moreover, something magical about five which is entirely lacking from a sum like three. Three, though generous in the circumstances, had all the elements of meanness about it.

But somehow the three pound notes had gone long ago. For all the good that they had done him, his father might just as well have posted them straight off to the Regal or the Orpheum direct. As for himself, he was high and dry again. By the time he'd paid for his room he had twenty-two and sixpence a week all told. And that wasn't a lot of money when it came to evenings for two.

He had, as a matter of fact, been pretty badly depressed about himself lately. Being in love had something to do with it. But not all. He had carefully taken stock of himself and had decided that he was a failure. Nothing dramatic or sensational. Not a wrecked life—no morphine, no gambling, no mysterious women. Just a large, easy-going failure of twenty-five with no qualifications, and no prospects.

He had even given up looking forward to the result of the Finals because he was so perfectly sure of what the result would be. And rather than wait for a slap in the eye from the Bursar, he decided to do something about it now. That was why he got out his suitcase, packed it full with text-books and took it down to Lewis's in Gower Street.

They are good people, Lewis's, a kind of dignified Medical Faculty with commercial book-selling as a sideline. Like the serious-minded academic beings they are, they care for second-hand books almost as much as new ones, and they bought the whole suitcaseful without argument.

Then, with five pounds ten shillings in his pocket, Bill went straight along to Oxford Street and bought Doris a wrist-watch for four guineas. It was a nice little thing in chromium about the size of a small trouser-button, and life began again for Bill from the moment he'd bought it. He spent another five shillings on a dozen roses, and armed with the two birthday presents he set off to meet Doris with all his self-respect restored.

The watch and the roses weren't the only presents that Doris was getting. Mr. and Mrs. Josser had bought her a string of imitation pearls. It was really Mr. Josser's present, and Mrs. Josser hadn't had much to say in it. For as long as he could remember Mr. Josser had looked forward to the day when he could give his wife a pearl necklace: and for as long as she could remember Mrs. Josser had resisted it. She had finally told him that if the pearls were good ones she'd never know another moment's peace with such a piece of extravagance in the house; and, if they weren't, she wouldn't be seen dead wearing them.

So that was that. And, in the result, Mr. Josser packed nearly forty years of pleasure into the purchase of the pearls for Doris. He paid thirty-five shillings for them, and that included a snap-over morocco leather case with the name of the jeweller on it. Every time he took the pearls out and looked at them, Mr. Josser became a reflective and philosophic man: his feelings as a father were all mixed up with his emotions as a husband, and he found himself going back over the years in a great flood-tide of sentiment. Doris looked at times very much as her mother had once looked, and Mr. Josser derived a lot of simple satisfaction from the fact.

There were other presents as well. A pair of paste ear-rings arrived from Dawlish together with a note from Bill's mother. Ted and Cynthia between them gave Doris a new handbag. And Uncle Henry, rendered indulgent by the occasion, posted her a fountain pen. It was rather a good fountain pen, specially labelled "Lady's Model" on the box. The only thing against it was that instead of a clip it had a ring on top; it was the sort of thing that was meant to be carried on the end of a long ribbon. Mrs. Josser, however, wouldn't hear anything against it. She said that Uncle Henry had meant it very nicely, and that Doris might be glad of that kind of pen some day.

Apart from the family, No. 10 itself showed up pretty handsomely, too. Mrs. Vizzard sent her up a handkerchief sachet that she'd embroidered herself. Mr. Puddy wished her many happy returns of the day when he met her on the stairs. And Connie passed on a lipstick with a new refill that she happened to have picked up at the Club. Added to all this, the girls in the office had collected together and given her a large box of chocolates.

The only person who didn't send her anything—not that she really expected it—was Doreen. As the birthday drew nearer Doris had found herself thinking quite a lot about Doreen. And not forgivingly, either. She told herself that if Doreen should send her a present of any sort she would send it straight back again. And she meant it. All the same, when the morning arrived and there was nothing, she was disappointed.

Everything else, however, was perfect. For a start, there was Bill waiting for her down on the pavement in Lincoln's Inn when she came out of the office. He made her put on the wrist-watch straightaway despite the fact that she was already wearing one. He even insisted on breaking one of the roses off short and giving it to her to wear. She'd never known him gayer and more lively and it all seemed a part of the evening when, bulging with money as he was, he insisted on taking a taxi all the way home.

The party started from the moment they arrived. It was Ted's half-day at the Co-op., and Ted and Cynthia had arrived early. But Ted was preoccupied. His only thought was for his wife. He just sat there silently worshipping her. There were dark romantic places in his soul that no one would ever have suspected from his appearance, and it still seemed to him miraculous that the golden-haired usherette of the electric torch, she who had once seemed so aloof and goddess-like, should now be the mother of his child. He encouraged her to wear that idiotically unsuitable little bow in her hair because it reminded him of the first time he had seen her, and made the present moment seem more wonderful still.

Doris was very fond of her brother. He was so sensible and unworrying. He was the sort of person you could always go to if you were in trouble. She saw him as someone—almost as something—that would be there for ever, solid, untalkative, and very, very reliable. She wished all the same that he would be a bit more free and easy in his dress. Beside Bill's sports coat and grey flannels, Ted always looked so frightfully formal and unrelaxed.

It was the black coat and striped trousers and stiff collar that did it. And it was even worse when he wore his bowler as well. But it would have made no difference even if she had spoken to him about it. He knew what he was up to. The Co-operative Movement is a steady-going unflashy affair with a nonconformist tradition and no frills in it. And Ted dressed carefully to match.

When they sat down at the table Mr. Josser, who'd seemed rather quiet and preoccupied at first, sprang his little surprise on them. He'd bought a bottle of South African sherry-type wine and they all had a glass. It was good strong stuff with the sun-baked heat of the *Veldt* in it, and it rather took your breath away if you weren't prepared for it. Cynthia choked, and even Bill said "Ah" when he'd had a mouthful. But it was just the stuff to set an evening going. Within five minutes they were all chattering like natives.

The only thing was that the conversation took a wrong turn from the start. When Bill's glass had been filled for the second time, he insisted on drinking toasts. And one of the toasts was, "To the cottage in the country, to the honeysuckle over the door."

It seemed an innocent enough sort of thing to say because he and Mr. Josser had spent a lot of time in talking about cottages: by now he knew almost as much about the sort of cottage that Mr. Josser wanted as Mr. Josser did himself. And, when he said it, Mrs. Josser raised her glass at once and looked affectionately across in Mr. Josser's direction.

"Have you found anything yet?" Ted went on.

"We're on to a little beauty," Mrs. Josser said enthusiastically. "We're going down to see it, together. Aren't we, Fred? Have you heard from the agents yet?"

Then the extraordinary thing occurred. Mr. Josser went very red and bent low down over his plate.

"Not yet," he said at last.

"You did write, didn't you?" Mrs. Josser asked him.

Mr. Josser shook his head.

"Not write!" Mrs. Josser said in amazement.

Mr. Josser only shook his head again.

"But it was Monday I showed you."

"I know."

He did know only too well. And the tragic thing was that even though he knew he couldn't explain. He couldn't get up in front of everyone and say that it was on Monday that he'd had a silly thought about Percy. Besides, he didn't want to be reminded. He wanted to forget all about it for this evening at least. And by then perhaps he'd have been able to sort things out in his mind a little better.

But Mrs. Josser was mystified and indignant.

"It's a downright shame," she said. "That's what it is. It was on a bus route and everything. And now someone else has probably got it. I've always said you didn't get after things."

It was only the fact that they had finished the veal-and-ham pie and were now waiting for the fruit salad that interrupted her. She got up angrily and began clearing away. It didn't help things that Mr. Josser was angry with himself as well.

The meal brightened up again, however, with the fruit salad. It very nearly brightened up too much, in fact. There was apparently only one thing that Bill and Ted had in common—and that was usherettes. Bill had made a dead set on Cynthia right from the start, even though it was Doris's birthday. He even showed her how to drink water out of the wrong side of the glass as a cure for hiccoughs. And Cynthia, like the silly little thing she was, of course responded. She had made quite a mess on the table-cloth before Mrs. Josser put a stop to it.

But Mr. Josser was relieved by the distraction. Even a little tension and unpleasantness between Bill and Mrs. Josser was preferable to talking about cottages. And, though he didn't know it, there was another distraction already on its way. It was Connie. She'd been timing things to the minute, fitting in a social call before she had to go along to the night-club. She would have liked to come down earlier. But how could she? She hadn't been invited. All that she could do was to pay an unexpected fleeting visit, and stop on. So she tiptoed down and stood at the door listening. Then, with the look of surprise all ready on her face, she knocked on the door and peeped inside.

"My, I'm sorry," she said. "I didn't know it was a party. I only looked in to see how Doris liked the lipstick."

Doris looked up.

"Oh, Connie, it's simply lovely," she said. "Thank you so much."

Connie remained hanging in the doorway.

"What a relief," she exclaimed. "I was afraid about the colour. I thought perhaps it was too . . . too . . ." She had succeeded in disengaging herself from Doris and catching Cynthia's eye. "And how's the little baby?" she asked. "She's getting to be quite a big girl now, isn't she?" Then it was Bill that she managed to fasten on to. "So your young lady's grown up at last," she observed. And turning to Mrs. Josser she added, "You'll have to look out now. You never know what may happen."

There was silence when she had finished and Connie thought for a moment that she had lost—that they weren't going to invite her to join them. It looked as though Connie, sixpence out of pocket over the refill, would simply have to make her way to the night-club, solitary and uncheered. But it was Mr. Josser who rescued her.

"Why don't you come in for a minute?" he asked. "We've just finished."

Connie paused.

"Well, I really don't know if I should," she answered, closing the door behind her and going over to one of the vacant chairs. "But just to drink Doris's health as it were."

It was Bill who helped her over the next stage. He winked across at Mr. Josser.

"But you haven't got anything to drink it in," he said.

Mrs. Josser looked at him hard. She was still annoyed with Bill because of that piece of silliness about water-drinking. And this open hospitality to Connie, coming on top of Mr. Josser's indiscretion in having invited her in, was intolerable. But, without being openly rude, there was nothing that she could do about it.

"Pour her out a drink, Fred," was all she said.

"Well, I didn't expect *this*. I certainly didn't," Connie replied exultantly.

She raised the glass gaily to her lips and smiled across at Doris. And then something happened that even afterwards Connie couldn't excuse in herself, much less explain. It was simply that a little trigger in her mind ticked over and she remembered an earlier evening in the same room, when Percy and his mother had been there, too. The rest just followed naturally.

"To absent friends," she said.

She tried, of course, to laugh it off. But the laugh wouldn't come. Not naturally, at least. And no one else laughed at all. From the silence, the perfectly horrid silence, it was obvious that everyone knew exactly whom she meant.

There was nothing for it, therefore, but to drink up and get off. Within five minutes of going down there she was back upstairs again, putting her hat on. She stood quite still in the centre of the room looking round at the bleakness of it.

"You're getting old, Connie," she said. "You've lost your touch. You're breaking up. . . ."

2

It was the dream that did it. Just when Mr. Josser had finally put his silly thought right out of his head—and it *was* a silly thought, flinging away a hundred pounds of his own money on Percy's defence, which had all been arranged for anyway—he had to go and have a dream about Percy. As it turned out, it was a very expensive, almost a crippling, sort of dream.

Not that it was a nightmare, or anything grisly. But it woke Mr. Josser up, and after he was awake, he couldn't get off to sleep again. It started innocently enough in just the sort of cottage that Mr. Josser had been wanting. It was white. With lots of honeysuckle. And a dove-cot. And one of those great overhanging trees of the kind that spread their arms in dreams. It was four o'clock—for some reason or other Mr. Josser was very sure about the time—and they were all having tea on the lawn. There was Mrs. Josser, and Ted and Cynthia and Baby, and Bill and Doris with a baby of their own by now, and even Connie in her summery-mummery. All of them, in fact. There was lettuce for tea. And some freshly made rock-cakes. And there were wasps round the jam. Altogether it was a perfect garden tea in summer. Perfect except for one thing, that is. And that one thing was Percy. He was walking round and round the cottage outside the thickset hedge that marked the limits of the garden. In places where the hedge was high they could only see his head or his head and shoulders. In other places, they could see nearly the whole of him. He was wearing his light check suit and his pale grey hat and he was smoking. The cigarette hung out of his mouth as it always did, almost as though it were on a hinge. And all the time Percy was walking round, he was looking at them. Looking at them as though he wanted to say something. As though he wanted to join them. But not saying anything. Not attempting to lift the latch of the little wicket-gate and come in to them. Finally, it was Connie who said what they were all thinking. And she said it in between bites of rock-cake.

"He'll feel better when he's been dead a bit longer," she remarked. "Naturally he feels a bit strange at first. He hasn't got any other friends. And probably no one's told him that we aren't expected to take any notice of him. Not after he's been hanged. . . ."

Mr. Josser woke up with a jerk. "Better when he's been dead a bit longer. Not expected to take any notice of him," he kept repeating, until Mrs. Josser woke up, too, and asked him why he was muttering.

At breakfast there was only one letter for Mr. Josser. And that was a bill. A bill from the caterer for Percy's meals in prison. Judging by the size of it, too, Percy must have got his appetite back. It was the biggest bill yet. Three and sixpence more than last week. And, studying it in detail, Mr. Josser saw why. Percy had been having puddings. They must have been Percy's own idea, the puddings, because Mr. Josser hadn't said anything about them.

The sight of the bill temporarily banished the memory of the dream. At the sight of the one pound two and sixpence that he would have to pay, Mr. Josser grew angry. It was one pound two and sixpence that he should have been spending on his own family. And apparently there was to be no end to it. He had paid five weeks' bills already, and still the trial didn't look like coming any nearer. Mr. Josser felt he'd had enough of it.

Mrs. Josser glanced across at him for a moment.

"It ought to be the Government that pays, not Clarice," was what she said.

Mr. Josser did not attempt to explain. He hadn't done so earlier and it seemed a bit late now.

The amount of the bill was still rankling inside him when he set out on his rounds to go rent collecting. The amount of the bill, and the dream. Particularly the dream. For some reason it had come back clearer than ever. And this annoyed him. Because in the ordinary way he rather enjoyed getting on with his own private thoughts while on the Building Society's business. Mr. Josser was the only one who knew how little his mind was really on his work. While one part of him was padding from doorstep to doorstep picking up the seven and sixes and ten shillingses, the other part—the more important part—was training wisteria up the sides of little thatched cottages or holding a warm brown egg in his hand and admiring the chicken that had just laid it.

But now, because of the dream, all that was impossible. He kept remembering, very plainly, how things were. If he had the cottage, Mr. Barks couldn't have the extra hundred pounds. And if Mr. Barks didn't have the extra hundred, Percy was as good as done for. It knocked all the fun and sparkle out of the cottage thinking about it like that. And it didn't seem fair to have his cottage spoiled for him in this way before he'd even got into it. It didn't seem fair. Especially not now when Mrs. Josser was so keen on it, too. It didn't seem right.

In the result, Mr. Josser was sharper and more brusque than he had ever been. He simply pocketed the half-crowns and sixpences, scribbled his initials in the right-hand column and went away again. He didn't even stop to ask after people whom he knew perfectly well were ill. And as for excuses about non-payment, he came down on them with both feet. No. 23 Birkbeck Street was so surprised that it paid up without objection.

Mr. Josser was in such a vile temper, in fact, that he was rude to the girl in the Express Dairy where he had lunch. It wasn't in the least the girl's fault. Mr. Josser recognised that. It wasn't even anything to do with the cabinet pudding that had custard with it instead of white sauce. It was simply the old business of Percy and the cottage. Mr. Josser was so much ashamed of himself that he tried to apologise to the girl before leaving. But it was no use. He didn't remember properly which waitress had served him and he picked out the wrong girl to apologise to. She couldn't make head or tail of what he was saying and thought that he was complaining again. She was rather a rude girl.

Mr. Josser came away from the tea-shop more out of sorts than he had gone in. And all the time on his afternoon calls the figure of Percy went with him. Not side by side. But some distance ahead. His cigarette hanging out of his mouth, and his head half turned over his shoulder as though he wanted to say something. As though he wanted to wait for Mr. Josser to join him.

"He'll feel better when he's been dead a bit longer," Mr. Josser found himself saying. "Nobody's told him we aren't expected to take any notice of him."

3

Taken altogether, it was Mr. Puddy's bad week. First, the collapse of his store cupboard. And now—a sharp difference with his employers. As a result they'd parted. It hadn't been any of Mr. Puddy's choosing and he was frankly sorry about having to go. But there was a point of principle at stake. And, from the way they had put it to him, there was nothing for it but to resign. It all began over the matter of a few boxes. They were empties, admittedly. But in size and awkwardness they were crates. And they had a habit of turning up on a van just after the works had closed for the night and Mr. Puddy had taken over.

On the first two occasions, the foreman had put it to Mr. Puddy as a favour that he should shift the boxes so that the workpeople wouldn't go falling over them next morning. And, as a favour, Mr. Puddy had agreed. But only as a favour. For it soon became apparent that the thing was going to be a pretty serious imposition. If Mr. Puddy didn't look out he realised that he'd very soon find himself shifting boxes all night instead of just quietly going on his rounds, or sitting in his little room waiting in the manner of his profession for something to happen so that he could go and attend to it.

And when the foreman got nasty, Mr. Puddy got nasty, too. He refused. So the whole matter was referred to the manager. And that didn't do Mr. Puddy any good. The manager was a rough, unpolished sort of man who said that for the better part of thirty years he'd wondered what night watchmen did to keep awake, and suggested that a bit of lifting and carrying would be good for Mr. Puddy's figure.

This was too much for Mr. Puddy. He said that two people could be personal if one started it, only he didn't propose to make himself the other one. He also said that if the firm wanted a heavy labourer to work right through the night, they ought to advertise for him instead of trying to get the work done on the cheap by someone who'd been engaged for something else. Keeping dignity on his side and declining to bandy so much as one further word with the foreman, Mr. Puddy just walked out. It made in all the seventeenth different job that he'd seen the back of.

Not that there was any real cause for despair. Only for a sort of general depression. Seventeen was an awful lot of jobs to have got through. But this time he had been let down gently. Just opposite the gate was the warehouse of the United Empire Tea Company. There was a little frame hanging up beside the front door announcing vacancies. And one of the vacancies was for a night watchman. Within one hour of resigning—on principle, remember—Mr. Puddy was fixed up in a new job. The pay wasn't quite so good. It was five shillings a week less, in fact. But there were compensations. The United Empire Tea Company gave their night watchman a nice little room of his own with a proper stove where he could do his bit of cooking. Mr. Puddy quite looked forward to the evenings that he would spend there. Apart from the money—and no man likes earning less as he gets older—the only difference in the two jobs was that he was now guarding the south side of Larkin Street instead of the north.

So far as he was concerned, the north side which he had previously been guarding could be burgled or burnt down or thrown wide open and he wouldn't be expected to raise so much as a finger to stop it.

4

There was a man coming down the steps of Mr. Barks's office block. He made a small dejected figure as he emerged into the roadway, and anybody catching sight of him and noticing the company that he'd been keeping might have taken him for someone caught up at the wrong end of a judgment summons. But it was nothing of the sort, really. He wasn't a debtor: he was a benefactor.

He was Mr. Frederick Josser. And all because of a silly thought and a dream, he'd just made himself responsible for the extra hundred pounds of Percy Boon's defence.

CHAPTER 44

I

CONNIE had got two gas masks.

Not that there was anything dishonest about that. The second one had been practically forced on her right back at the time of the Munich scare. Simply because her head was so small she had been asked to go over to the other, the children's queue, and they'd given her a different gas mask, case and all. Naturally she didn't grumble. She simply said "Thank you" and walked out with the kid's model hanging over her arm and the misfit stowed away inside her coat. The little straps and all that beautiful rubber still looked as though they might come in useful sometime.

She had taken a lot of care of the one that really fitted her. She had put moth-balls in it. That was why every time she tried it on she nearly choked. But it was worth it. She didn't intend to find the mask full of holes just when she needed it.

It was time to try it on again to-night and she'd put it out on the table for an airing. When her eye caught it, she shuddered. There was something sinister and skull-like about it resting there. It gave her the creeps. But only for a moment. When she had actually got it on, she couldn't help laughing. She didn't recognise herself with that grey, pig-like snout in front. And it was rather fun going boogie-woogie at her own image—at the grey pig's image, that is—in the mirror.

But while she was standing there, a thought that crossed her mind took all the fun out of it. She remembered Duke. Snatching the mask off her head the way the man at the distribution centre had shown her not to, she went over and stood underneath the cage.

"Poor little Dukey-bird," she said. "If the nasty stuff comes, Auntie'll hold a handkerchief over Dukey's beak so that he shan't smell it. Auntie won't let little Dukey-bird get frightened."

But it was one thing to be cheerful to a canary, and quite another to believe what you say. She'd only been talking that way so that Duke shouldn't start worrying. It didn't help her any. She *was* frightened. And it was no use pretending that she wasn't.

Not being frightened of being hurt. Or knocked unconscious. Or losing a leg. Or anything like that. Just frightened of dying. And this was odd because the older she got and the less she had to live for, the more frightened she became. "I'm no dewy rose-bud. You couldn't cut me off in my prime if you tried," she told herself. But it didn't help. She still didn't want to die. She had only to close her eyes and see herself stretched out cold on the bed, so small that it might have been a dead child lying there, for tears to overcome her.

And that was largely because of the funeral. There wasn't a soul in all London, not one out of the eight million—except perhaps Mr. Josser—who would take the trouble to go to the graveside. There wouldn't even be any graveside. She had once after bronchitis joined a burial society. But the payments had lapsed years ago—as soon as she really got better, in fact. When her Maker called, it would be the Parish that would have to take over, unless the Actors' Benevolent stepped in. It wasn't a consoling thought, was it? Not at Connie's age.

There was a footstep outside, and she paused for a moment to listen. It was Mr. Puddy. There was something about his footsteps—slow, ponderous, majestic—that intrigued her. It was like the County Hall coming downstairs. Behind that tread was weight, and an imperturbable solidity. It was sheer mass in motion.

Then an idea came to her. Slipping her child's gas mask over her head again she pulled the door ajar and stood behind it.

"Boo," she said at him as he went past.

She hadn't forgotten that he'd accused her to her face as it were of trying to steal his sugar that time the cupboard fell, and she'd been looking forward to getting her own back on him.

2

Percy was seeing Mr. Barks for about the six hundredth time. It was rather flattering in a way having Mr. Barks turn up at all hours. But it was a strain, too. Mr. Barks took notes of everything you said, and if you didn't say the same thing twice running Mr. Barks caught you out on it. Just to show how clever he was. But not so clever as he thought. Percy was beginning to see through him.

To-day, however, everything had passed off very smoothly. Mr. Barks was in a good humour. In a new blue suit and wearing a buttonhole, he looked more like the best man at a registry office wedding. He didn't tell Percy straightaway what it was that had made him so obviously pleased with himself. Instead, he lectured him on the virtues of truthfulness.

"No r'p'tble s'lic'tor ever undertakes a case 'less he's satisfied as to the acc'racy of his client's story," he insisted. "Simply isn't done." Mr. Barks sucked in a quick mouthful of air and continued: "B't 'isn't only that," he said. "It's the jury. They're the people who notice. One slip—just one little slip—and you're out. That's the one thing a jury looks out for—inconsist'ncy."

The jury! Percy felt a little trickle of cold run down his spine. He'd got nothing to worry about. Mr. Barks had told him so. All the same he couldn't help feeling nervy. It was having to say the same thing over and over again to Mr. Barks that made him feel that way.

"I'll remember," he said.

"Not that you've got anything to worry about," Mr. Barks went on, using the same comforting phrase that Percy clutched at every time he heard it. "I've got Veesey Blaize f'you."

Percy looked blank, and then he grinned politely.

"Veesey Blaize, y'know," Mr. Barks repeated.

Percy grinned again. Evidently Mr. Barks had done him a good turn.

"Heard of Veesey Blaize, haven't you?" he asked.

Percy shook his head.

This display of ignorance seemed to annoy Mr. Barks, and he *tt-tt*ed with his tongue against his teeth.

"Ver' big man," he said. "Ver' big man, indeed. Leadin' counsel, y'know. S'pose you know what a leadin' counsel is?"

Percy nodded. He couldn't go on admitting that he didn't know what things were. If he did, Mr. Barks would lose his respect for him. In any case, whatever it was, if Mr. Barks was pleased about it, it suited him.

"Only just agreed. Needed p'suading. Ver' busy man."

Percy grinned again. It made him feel a fool having Mr. Barks going on talking like that without explaining himself. Perhaps it would have been easier to follow him if only he didn't talk so fast.

He hadn't even understood at first that Veesey Blaize was a man. He sounded more like a sort of patent fire-lighter.

"What's he going to do?" he blurted out.

And then he was sorry he'd said it, because it made him sound silly.

"Goin' t'do?" Mr. Barks asked in amazement. "He's goin' t'defend you. That's what he's goin' t'do."

A doubt came into Percy's mind, and that unsettled nervy feeling returned to his stomach.

"D'you mean you're . . . you're chucking it?" he asked.

"Chucking it?" Mr. Barks repeated. "I'm 'structing him."

"O.K.," said Percy. "I get you."

Mr. Barks, however, could see that he hadn't got him. He was just getting ready to leave. But he stayed long enough to give his client a short course in criminal law.

"Small cases, police court stuff," said Mr. Barks, dismissing nine-tenths of his practice with a wave of his hand, "s'lic'tor appears in person. County Court, take your choice. Sometimes one thing, sometimes t'other. High Court and Central Crim'nal Court, quite different. S'lic'tor doesn't appear at all. Not allowed. Wouldn't be proper. Only counsel."

Percy tried to get the blank look off his face. Things were getting clearer.

"Is . . . is the man you said just now the judge?" he asked.

But Mr. Barks was too much engrossed in trying to make the two flaps of his brief-case come together to explain any further.

"You'll find out soon enough," he said. "You'll find out. May want to come here. May not. Ver' busy man. Trial's not so far off, you know. Haven't got long to wait now."

Mr. Barks tapped loudly on the cell door with the cap of his fountain pen and the warder came along to let him out.

In the half-open doorway Mr. Barks turned and looked back again.

"Don't worry," he said, "and try to remember about the catch on the car door. If it was loose, you'd remember it. In a case like this ev'rything's 'portant. Try to remember by next time I see you. Don't worry."

And Mr. Barks was gone.

Try to remember! That's the one thing you can't try to do. Either you remember, or you don't. You can't just sit down and start remembering things you've forgotten. It doesn't make sense. Of course, if Mr. Barks wanted the car door to be loose, he could have it that way. Percy didn't mind. Mr. Barks could have the bloody thing clean off its hinges so far as Percy was concerned.

And so could Mr. . . . Mr. . . . the man Mr. Barks had said.

Mr. Barks had just been passed through the last of the locked doors and he had given the curt but friendly parting nod with which a prosperous solicitor salutes a policeman. With his black Homburg hat tilted a little to the back of his head because the weather was so hot, he looked a pleasantly robust sort of figure in the shabby surroundings of the prison. He was stumping along, his shiny shoes twinkling.

"Elementary education," he kept saying to himself. "Elementary education. What does the tax-payer get for it? What does anyone get? What do the teachers do with themselves? Look at Boon. Left school at fourteen and never heard of Veesey Blaize. Never even heard of Veesey Blaize."

3

Mr. Squales had found it very hard to forgive Mr. Puddy the incident of the salmon. Not merely the sordid indignity of it, but the sheer physical injury as well. His ankle, if not actually broken or sprained, was at least badly twisted and he could get about only by resting his weight heavily on an ebony and silver cane that had once been Mr. Vizzard's.

Not that it mattered so far as looks are concerned. There is something oddly attractive—with a hint of bravery and old war-wounds about it—in a well-dressed, well-built man having to support his weight on a walking-stick. Mr. Squales practised sitting down with the cane between his knees and his two hands clasped thoughtfully on the knob. Besides, he rather liked the stick for itself alone: the knob had got a hall-mark—lion and everything—stamped there. It seemed too good to be kept in the back of a lumber cupboard.

And it was most important that he should learn to use it properly because he had a date with Mrs. Jan Byl on the Tuesday. Not merely a business engagement either. This was something more in the social way of things. An invitation to take tea. Mr. Squales had been slightly disappointed when he had first heard. But Mrs. Jan Byl had hinted that there might be one or two other guests who might be useful to him. Then Mr. Squales tumbled to it at once. She was giving him a break. All that he had to do was to go along and look interesting and see if his luck was in. On the financial side there was clearly nothing for it but to grit his teeth and, with Mrs. Vizzard's help, to hold on a bit longer.

He managed to get out of the house without telling Mrs. Vizzard where he was going. It wasn't easy because Mrs. Vizzard was more loving and solicitous than ever. Almost too loving, in fact. It came at times dangerously close to the cloying. She was all over him. Like a spaniel. But that was simply because she was afraid of losing him. Her anxiety and her infatuation were such in fact that Mr. Squales realised that if he had been the mercenary sort he could easily have taken advantage of her.

"And why the devil don't I want to tell her where I'm going?" he asked himself. "It won't do any harm. It's not an address to be ashamed of—Hyde Park Drive. It's good hunting. Why can't I? I don't know. But I can't."

The words "Hyde Park Drive" made a rather pleasant pattern in his mind and he kept repeating them. "From Dulcimer Street to Hyde Park Drive," he said to himself once or twice. "From a back bed-sitter to a butlered spread."

The bus put him down as usual at John Barker's and he took a taxi round the corner in case Mrs. Jan Byl or any of her useful friends should be standing at the front window as he was arriving. But the taxi couldn't put him down exactly outside the house because there was a pantechnicon there. Mr. Squales's stomach went cold inside him.

And what he found left him stunned and dismayed. Mrs. Jan Byl was apparently moving house. Moving house without having said a word to him about it. The front door was open and a roll of drugget extended up the wide staircase that last time had been carpeted in a very nice piece of rich red Turkey. Coming down the staircase was a bureau, or escritoire or something, supported by two men and with a piece of sacking tied round it to protect the corners. Mr. Squales stood politely to one side, sucking the silver knob of his walking-stick, waiting for them to pass. Then he went up the steps and rang the bell.

Evidently the whole smooth running of the household had been dislocated, and it was a few moments before anything happened. Mr. Squales was just about to ring the bell again when one of the housemaids appeared with a kind of dusterish thing tied round her head.

"Mrs. Jan Byl?" Mr. Squales asked politely.

"I don't think she's at home, sir," the maid told him. "What name is it, please."

"Qualito," he answered. "Professor Qualito."

"Will you come in, sir?" she asked. "I'll see if Madame is in."

"I am expected," Mr. Squales said simply.

She showed him into a small morning-room from which the furniture had gone already. There were now only boxes and packing-cases left. Mr. Squales considered sitting down on one of them but, remembering nails and his own new grey trousers, thought better of it. He remained standing in a dignified, superior sort of fashion, watching bookcases, what-nots and ornamental statuary go past him down the stairs and out into the van.

It had just occurred to Mr. Squales that they had obviously forgotten all about him when he heard Mrs. Jan Byl's voice. He rested his weight on the silver and ebony stick and arranged his face in a polite incredulous smile. But even though Mrs. Jan Byl was coming down the stairs in his direction, she appeared to be somewhat preoccupied.

". . . then they'll have to take them all out again and pack them separately," she was saying. "They might just as well be left here as thrown into a case without sufficient wrapping. Good gracious!"

She had come into the room and found Mr. Squales standing there.

"What are *you* doing here?"

"I . . . I understood that I had been asked to tea," Mr. Squales replied.

Mrs. Jan Byl pinned back one of the curls that had escaped over her forehead.

"Oh," she said, "but I asked my secretary to phone you. She said she couldn't find the number, and I told her to go on trying."

Mr. Squales carefully preserved the smile that he was wearing. But inside he was angry. Very angry. Apparently he'd come tagging half-way across London just to be made a monkey of.

"Didn't your maid announce me?" he asked.

Mrs. Jan Byl was testing the rope round one of the packing-cases.

"Someone did knock on my door," she admitted. "But I sent her away again. I was far too busy."

"I see," said Mr. Squales slowly. "Then I can only apologise. I fear that I'm intruding."

"No," said Mrs. Jan Byl. "Since you're here, you may as well have a cup of tea. You'd better come up into my study. I need someone to talk to."

"I only heard the other night from someone right inside the Cabinet exactly what the Germans intend to do if there is a war," Mrs. Jan Byl was saying. "They're coming over here with ten thousand planes straight away, as soon as it's been declared, if not before, and they're going to destroy London. Of course, Mr. Chamberlain may still be able to do something. But my friend says that he knows for a fact that Chamberlain doesn't really like Hitler any more. And where there's no love, there's no understanding. You see what I mean?"

"Quite," Mr. Squales told her, without either.

"The whole Government's in a panic, all except Mr. Chamberlain," Mrs. Jan Byl continued. "I know that for a fact. There aren't enough air-raid shelters to go round. That's why they're buying shrouds. They're clearing all the big hospitals, too. My maid told me."

"And so you're moving out of London?" Mr. Squales asked politely.

"Only going down to Withydean," she told him. "You're surely not stopping in town yourself?"

Put that way, the question rattled him. It made the security of Dulcimer Street seem somehow less secure. But there was only one thing to do and that was to be big and manly about it.

"I shall remain where my work is," he said.

"Yes, of course," Mrs. Jan Byl answered. "I suppose you'll be called up in any case if there's a war. How old are you?"

Mr. Squales hated these direct questions. They stirred up everything in him that was best left unstirred. So he answered evasively.

"Not too old to fight," he said. "Not too old to do my bit."

"Well," said Mrs. Jan Byl brusquely. "I mustn't sit here gossiping. I've got work to do. You'd better come down to Withydean yourself if the raids get too bad. That is, if there is going to be a war, of course. You don't know anything, I suppose?"

Mr. Squales paused. Obviously this was a big moment. Quite a lot would depend on how he answered. And he was determined not to be found unequal to it. Summoning up his courage he played as big as the moment.

"Something tells me that there won't be any war," he said. "Something tells me that this is just a time sent to test us."

But Mrs. Jan Byl was in no mood for the psychic this afternoon. She was collecting up the little Sèvres ornaments that stood on a side-table by her desk.

"I should never forgive myself," she said, "if these got bombed. All the insurance in the world couldn't replace them."

On the way home in the bus, Mr. Squales thought dark and revolutionary thoughts.

"They're all the same—rich women," he told himself. "There's no humanity in them. They're just Crœsuses"—he liked a classical reference or two in his thoughts. "They smile on you one day and spurn you away with their toe the next. All I ask is one large bomb. Just one. One large bomb on Withydean."

That was why there was such a happy home-coming when Mr. Squales returned to Dulcimer Street. His previous coldness and taciturnity—or had Mrs. Vizzard only imagined it?—had vanished. He was affectionate and even playful.

When Mrs. Vizzard suggested that they should get married in October, Mr. Squales called her his kitten again.

CHAPTER 45

I

Mr. Veesey Blaize's chambers in the Temple were small, dark and inconvenient. They were in Pump Court and the rooms had a north aspect—if you can call the other and identical side of the court, less than twenty yards away, an aspect. Had chambers so manifestly shabby and badly situated been offered to Mr. Veesey Blaize in any other part of London he would, of course, have refused them. But the Temple was different. It had its own standards, and it hadn't departed from them. There was a kind of you-must-take-me-as-you-find-me attitude about the place. New-fangled inventions like lifts and central heating might have conquered the rest of London, but the Temple hadn't been conquered. There was still the sound of foot-leather on stone staircases and coal being stoked on to the fire by the shovelful. In the Temple even the telephone seemed a modern distraction. And it was rather strange, when you came to think of it, talking on the telephone about thousand-pound retainers, and having to share a lavatory with four other men on the same floor.

But that was the Temple all over. And it was simply a part of the overcrowding that went on there. You couldn't have squeezed in even another junior with a shoehorn. There they were packed solid—K.C.s, clerks, devils, bright juniors, and all the rest of them; and some people actually chose to *live* there despite the overcrowding. You had only got to look at the names—rather imposing names, too, some of them—written up on any one of the staircases to see what a pass things had come to. Rows and rows of them. Mr. Valentine Probjay, Sir Aneurin Lewis, Mr. A. Clifton Speldman, Mr. Veesey

Blaize, Mr. E. Predderburn-Goldschmidt and Mr. J. E. A. Ropps—that was the actual list beside Mr. Blaize's own front door.

It was just as bad, in fact, as Harley Street where the doctors lived. And there was nothing except tradition to explain it. Proximity to the Law Courts had very little to do with it because only a little further up the Strand there was a big up-to-date office building like Bush House which would have suited everybody perfectly. No, it was as if the Law, like a lot of lemmings, had suddenly all banded together and then been held up by the railings of Temple Gardens on the way to take their communal header from the Embankment.

Not that there weren't compensations for being there. You had only got to step out of Fleet Street, with its pubs and tobacconists and newspaper palaces, into the Temple to be right out of space and time altogether. It was going back two, three, four hundred years in a hundred yards. Christopher Wren had designed some of the newer parts. And quite a few of the inmates looked as though Sir Christopher had designed them, too. Standing still in one of the courts you could hardly believe that you were in a City at all. The *sound* of London, the deep pulsating roar of the place, couldn't find a way through the crooked alleyways and up the little flights of steps. The only noise that ever got in was the hooting of tugs on the river. And that is something that you couldn't keep out. It was like the river itself. It was why London was there.

Mr. Veesey Blaize had been in his present chambers for nearly eleven years. He'd been there for so long, in fact, that he'd forgotten that there was anything wrong with them. And that was strange because the rest of his life was planned to make him comfortable. He'd got a flat in Knightsbridge beside the Park, and a cottage in Sussex where every week-end—except when there was a rush on—he stopped being a learned counsel and became a two-acre country squire.

Considering the life he led—the public dinners, his late hours and his rages in Court—Mr. Blaize looked a healthy enough sort of man. His eyes were a bit bloodshot towards the end of Term, and his hands sometimes trembled a little. But that was probably only because he didn't get enough sleep. It was really his magnificent physique that had kept him going. He was like a bull; a bull with high blood-pressure. Seen from the back he was a great bulging mass of a man. And so he was from the front and sides. But then you noticed what small hands and feet he had. His face was round and spreading, too. The heavy pink dewlaps fell down over the wide points of the collar. But there was one other thing about him that wasn't round and spreading. Something that was fine and different like his hands. And that was his nose. It was like the beak of a bird. Not large and aquiline like an eagle's. Small and sharp like a razor-bill's.

At that moment he was reading a brief which concerned a big firm which, acting on advice, was resisting a claim for compensation from a workman's widow whose husband while under the influence of drink had been caught up in a piece of the big firm's machinery. It was an involved, tricky sort of case, with the Lords written all over it, and Mr. Veesey Blaize was enjoying it. Really enjoying it immensely. It brought out all that was best in the man. At the thought of what his client, the widow, had suffered, one of his really big Court rages was already boiling up inside him.

But it was not exclusively of the poor widow *v.* Trapleigh Mills, Ltd., that he was thinking. It was of his daughter. She had a most remarkable talent for coming between him and his briefs. And she seemed to have been cultivating that talent lately. There had, in fact, been hardly a day for the last three years—ever since she had come down from Oxford, and that prematurely—when he had been quite sure what was happening to her. For one so young, she was extraordinarily unfortunate. At twenty-two she had been in five night-clubs that had been raided, and had very nearly—and most expensively for her father—been the woman named in a small and no-account divorce case. On the following morning, while her father was pleading for the workman's widow, Celia Blaize was coming up in a different Court on a charge of drunkenness and disorderly conduct in Piccadilly. All the afternoon he had been writing personal letters to the editors he knew, asking them not to report the case. He had never realised before quite how many editors he knew.

Mr. Blaize relit his cigar that had a good four inches to go, and settled himself down to the brief again.

His clerk came in and stood in front of him.

"Mr. Barks to see you, sir," he said. "Case of Percy Aloysius Boon."

"Barks," Mr. Veesey Blaize said angrily, "never heard of him."

2

The South London Parliament was in session. There were thirty-two members present—four more than there were at the moment across the water at Westminster. But there was a reason for it. Down in South London they were having a full-dress debate on foreign policy.

The headmaster of the Church School at Camberwell had nearly finished. He was a small intense man like a kettle that has just come to the boil. His upturned spoutlike nose was raised angrily, and little hot steamlike bursts were coming from him.

". . . and there are some who spend their time trying to make things difficult for this great and good man who has done more to stave off war than anyone else alive to-day. To them I say one thing and one thing only. Where would Britain be to-day if our Prime Minister had not flown to Munich? We should be at war, gentlemen. At war."

He sat down abruptly, his shoulders still rising and falling. But it was obvious that the steam-pressure inside him had subsided: he had boiled himself dry, in fact. Mr. Josser felt rather relieved that he had finished. It was good sense that he had been talking. Good sense, but too much of it. There had been an awful lot of foreign policy let loose since the House had met at seven-thirty. Mr. Josser hoped that Mr. Runcorn, the Speaker, would feel like rising. But even if he did feel like it, Mr. Runcorn was a thorough and conscientious man and, as there was still ten minutes to go, he supposed that there was nothing for it but to give Uncle Henry his chance. He'd deliberately avoided catching his eye earlier, because he hated Uncle Henry.

"The honourable member for Limehouse," he said, without enthusiasm.

Mr. Josser's heart fell. He knew just what it would be like. Uncle Henry had been getting worse lately. He had taken to muttering. All through the last speech Mr. Josser had heard coming from him little snatches that sounded like "soft soap," "crypto-Fascist," ". . . lamp-posts in Whitehall." Even so, Mr. Josser wasn't prepared for what was coming.

Uncle Henry began quite mildly. Suspiciously mildly, for him.

"I've been a member of this House for seven years," he said. "I've watched Governments come and I've watched Governments go. I've seen new faces and I've lost old friends. I've heard some good speeches and I've made one or two myself."

Here Uncle Henry paused.

"And what does it all add up to?" he asked. "What does it all add up to?"

He paused again. A longer pause than last time. Mr. Josser noticed that he had stuck his two thumbs under the back strap of his braces. That was always a bad sign with Uncle Henry; it meant that he was getting ready to kick out at someone. And sure enough he was.

"It means we've all been a bloody lot of fools," he said. (Cries of "Shame! Shame!" from the Church School headmaster.) "If we hadn't been bloody fools we shouldn't have come here," Uncle Henry continued. "Playing Parliament, indeed. Playing ostriches more likely. Wait till the bombs come raining down. Wait till the streets are full of dead and dying. Wait till your wives and children have had their limbs blown off. Wait till Mr. Speaker has got a shell-splinter in his gizzard. . . ."

The cries of "Shame" were so numerous this time, even from Uncle Henry's own supporters, that the Speaker felt bound to intervene. There was only a few minutes to go and he'd hoped that the evening would close quietly.

"I moss arsk the honourable member for Limehouse to restrain himself," he said in a thick, professional voice. "We want politics, not unpleasantness."

But Uncle Henry was off again. His eyes were glazed and staring, and over his forehead his quiff of grizzled hair was standing out like a horn.

"The war clouds," he went on, speaking louder than ever, "are gathering overhead to drench us in a gory deluge. The sea will render up its dead with depth-charge and torpedo. And, on the land, vast armies are about to clash until the rivers of Europe will run crimson to the ocean and the widow and the childless will rend heaven with their cries. And what do we do? What?" Here Uncle Henry raised his voice so much that passers-by in the Kennington Park Road were able to hear him quite distinctly. "We sit down here, a lot of middle-aged men who ought to know better, and pretend we're M.P.s. And a silly old geyser in an armchair tries to kid himself that he's Mr. Speaker. I tell you . . ."

But Uncle Henry had gone too far. Definitely too far. There were cries of "Withdraw," "Chuck him out!" and "Apologise." And it was the latter word, in particular, that annoyed Uncle Henry.

"Apologise for speaking the truth?" he roared. "Never!"

So there was nothing for it but for Mr. Runcorn to assert his supreme authority. He wasn't sorry to do so. He'd been called a silly old geyser with a shell-splinter in his gizzard. And he was angry. Very angry. He rose, trembling.

"I der-clare the honourable member for Limehouse suspended," he said.

"You can't," Uncle Henry shouted back at him. "I've resigned."

Uncle Henry came across to Mr. Josser afterwards. Usually he had sobered up by the time the House had risen. But not to-night.

In his eye there was still that wild look that Mr. Josser distrusted. And he was breathing hard. There seemed nothing for it but to humour him. This time Uncle Henry's suspension seemed final.

"Coming across for the usual?" Mr. Josser enquired pleasantly.

It was an agreeable institution, that weekly migration to the Wrexford Arms. Indeed, without it, the South London Parliament could hardly have continued. There was a dangerous tension, an electric something-in-the-air about these sessions that could not have been sustained week after week without relaxation. The bitter animosities, the feuds that started up on the floor of the House were magically washed away by half a pint of old-and-mild, or a bitter, afterwards.

But to-night Uncle Henry's response just showed how impossible it was to do anything with the man. He simply glowered back at Mr. Josser.

"These are not drinking days," he said sternly. "They're days for action."

"Just so," Mr. Josser replied amiably. "That's what we could do with—action."

Uncle Henry thrust out his hand and gripped Mr. Josser by the elbow.

"Then I can count on you?" he demanded.

Mr. Josser hesitated.

"What for?" he asked.

"To rouse the country," Uncle Henry told him. "To sound the tocsin and awake Whitehall."

He paused long enough to gather up a bundle of papers and, still holding Mr. Josser firmly by the elbow, led him into the street.

"Come," he said. "I'll tell you."

CHAPTER 46

I

THEY'D decided at the infirmary that Mrs. Boon was well enough to be sent away to their convalescent centre. And they'd even fixed up for her to go down by ambulance. All the way to Bournemouth by private ambulance. But she didn't want to go. It was too far from Percy, she said.

And in the end they had to give up. It turned out that it wasn't only the trial that was worrying her. It was Dulcimer Street as well.

She was concerned about the rooms. She was afraid that if she went to Bournemouth Mrs. Vizzard would re-let them and that she would have nowhere that she and Percy could call a home when he came out again. If only she could see Mrs. Vizzard face to face for a few minutes, she insisted, she could explain everything. That, however, was impossible. She had to write. And it is difficult to say exactly what is in your heart when you are dictating to another person. The Sister who took it down was very nice about it, but it wasn't the same thing.

Mrs. Vizzard, however, was far from pleased to receive Mrs. Boon's message about the rooms. She had set her heart on them for herself. She was greedily and extravagantly planning to re-absorb them. They were, in fact, a part of her marriage plans. She would, of course, have preferred to have the Jossers'. Taken along with the basement they would have provided a complete bridal suite. But the Jossers were permanent. And friends. And payers. Anything in the way of dispossessing them was unthinkable.

Then she pulled herself up sharply. How could she think, even for a moment, of occupying more rooms just when every penny, every halfpenny, mattered? She must have taken leave of her senses to contemplate it.

"But surely," she told herself, "it won't always be like this. Rico won't always be . . . be dependent on me. He must as time goes on . . . find something. There must be an opening for him somewhere."

Again she checked herself. These doubting thoughts about Mr. Squales seemed positively disloyal, somehow. It was almost as though deep inside her she questioned his ability to earn his living like other men. But this was absurd, she realised. He was so gifted, so talented. That wonderful presence of his. And the deep rich voice that melted you to jelly when it was turned full on you. Of course he would succeed. Would succeed dazzlingly. And she would have been the one, the woman in the background, who had stood by him while he was still unknown. . . .

It wouldn't be long now. By Christmas they'd be married. And Mr. Squales would have settled down to . . . oh, dear, what was it that he was going to settle down to? Somehow, mediumship—especially when you thought about it before lunch—seemed such a vague, precarious way of earning a living for two. But even so, there was nothing vague and precarious about Mr. Squales. When she had hinted, had declared openly in fact, that with a house waiting for them both they could get married straight away, Mr. Squales had chided her. He had refused. Refused, gently but firmly. He had said that things were too unsettled internationally to be precipitate about a thing like marriage. By January or February, or March at the very latest, they could see how things were in Europe. And then they could wed and set up house with a light heart. In the meantime, as he had reminded her, they were together. They were near, weren't they? he had asked.

But not to-night. To-night they weren't near. Mr. Squales had gone off on a professional engagement. Right over to Finsbury Park where the rival body, the North London Spiritualist Club, held their meetings. He had gone without Mrs. Vizzard. Without even suggesting that she should go with him. And Mrs. Vizzard, stifling her feelings, had let him go. She had felt tears come in her eyes and a large choking lump in her throat, when he had informed her. But she still had some reserve and self-control. She revealed nothing. She even helped him to get ready, ironing him a handkerchief so that he should be compete in every detail. After all, it was his career, not hers, that he was pursuing. She couldn't expect to accompany him everywhere when the engagements eventually came crowding in. And, as things were, it was for her as much as for him that he was building up his connections.

2

Over at Finsbury Park everything was going swimmingly. It was an all-Red Indian evening. Always a safe line, Mr. Squales considered, even if a bit hackneyed. It was his old friend Mocking Bear who had come through, gruff, throaty and pregnant with vision. He was something of an autocrat, was Mocking Bear, and frequently answered only in monosyllables. But that was the keynote of a brave—terse, contemptuous, uncontradictable.

"Is there going to be war?"

The question framed by a pale clergyman had duly been passed on for Mocking Bear's consideration.

"Naw."

"Will Hitler invade Poland?"

"Naw."

"Is Memel still a danger point?"

For a moment, there was no answer because Mocking Bear wasn't quite sure where Memel was. It was one of those things that he'd often meant to look up.

The question was repeated, but when Mocking Bear showed no

inclination to reply they passed on. As it happened, however, the next question was a bit of a stumper, too.

"And Gdynia?"

Gdynia, like Memel, was one of those places that Mocking Bear wasn't sure about. But he couldn't go on not remembering. The reply came prompt but non-committal.

"Uh."

"Will Hitler die a violent death?"

Mocking Bear was on surer ground this time.

"Yuh," he answered.

"How soon?"

No answer.

"This year?"

"Naw."

"Next year?"

"Yuh."

"Before the summer?"

"Naw."

"In the autumn?"

"Yuh."

"September?"

"Naw."

"October?"

"Yuh."

"On the first?"

"Naw."

"The second?"

"Naw."

"The third?"

"Yuh."

Hitler dead on the third of October, 1940! That at least was something established. And it caused a bit of a sensation. Just to check this vital piece of information they asked the same question again. But there was no doubt about the reply. "Yuh, yuh," Mocking Bear answered as though irritated at being cross-examined. He thawed a bit, however, when they asked him to tell them more about the future, the future that looked so sombre yet so shot through with violent colours.

"Mocking Bear says peace in Pale Face Country," came the answer. "War clouds vanish like summer snow. Papooses play and squaws happy. Braves put away scalping-knives and repair wigwam. Much pipe-smoking. Bad eagle fly away with arrow in his breast."

Mr. Squales began stirring because he couldn't lie any longer in that position with the clip of his suspender cutting into the soft part of his calf. The people round the table recognised that the trance state was drawing to a close, and they all unconsciously relaxed a little. Twenty minutes later Mr. Squales with a two-guinea cheque in his pocket was stepping it out in the direction of the Seven Sisters Road.

The secretary had been very nice about it. He had proposed a vote of thanks and asked if Mr. Squales could come along in a fortnight to give them the direct voice for the second time. A fortnight's time. That brought it to the fourth of September. It suited Mr. Squales all right. He'd be able to tell them more about the future by then. Allay their fears. Cast light into the dark places. And he was going to give them value. Something old Spanish, Dom Rodriquez or some such name, was what had occurred to him. Not that Mocking Bear hadn't been a winner. Perhaps it would be a mistake, a disappointment to his public, to change his repertoire.

As he reflected on his success his mind enlarged and expanded. The horizon came near again and he stepped out to meet it.

"I'll give her to the end of the week," he reflected, "and then if I haven't heard from her she'll hear from me. She did say something about my going down there for a week-end and if people don't mean that sort of thing they shouldn't say it."

He was still thinking about Mrs. Jan Byl and about the delights of a week-end there when he returned to Dulcimer Street. His mind was full of it. That was why he was so thoughtless as to blurt it all out quite suddenly.

"Kitty, my love," he asked, without warning, "have you got a decent suitcase? Something that you wouldn't mind being seen carrying. My own is now too battered, too travel-worn. I may have to go away on business."

3

Percy was having company. He'd got Mr. Barks *and* Mr. Veesey Blaize both locked in with him.

It was the first time he'd ever seen Mr. Veesey Blaize. And, looking at him, he wondered how he could have been so much impressed by Mr. Barks. Mr. Barks was a gentleman all right, no question about that. And he was well-to-do and important-looking. But compared with Mr. Veesey Blaize there was nothing to him. Mr. Barks hadn't done more than touch the fringe of what a real gentleman could be. He was just a gent, in a small way. Whereas Mr. Veesey Blaize's gentlemanliness was something that caught you right between the eyes. It was the whole effect that did it. But, coming down to details, the result was still just as good. There was a gold filling to one of his teeth, for instance. And a gold signet-ring the size of a shilling on his left hand. And that wasn't all. There was the butterfly collar with wider points than Percy had ever seen. They sprang right out on either side of him almost as though Mr. Veesey Blaize were proceeding under sail. And the bow-tie was a good bright one, too. It was in silver-grey check and added just that note of dress—almost fancy dress—that Percy admired. It showed that Mr. Veesey Blaize didn't mind being looked at.

But the real fun came from his manner. He treated everyone, Mr. Barks included, like dirt just to show who was the gentleman. Interrupted them before they'd finished speaking, and didn't always listen when they answered. Everyone except Percy, that is. He was very polite to Percy. Polite in front of Mr. Barks, which is what counted. Percy only wished that there had been one or two of the warders in the room as well so that Mr. Veesey Blaize could have been polite to him in front of them, too.

There was an extra chair brought in specially for him, so they all sat down in a semi-circle. Percy was grateful for the extra chair and felt sure that Mr. Veesey Blaize had arranged it. Otherwise Percy would have had to stand, and that wouldn't have been so good. Then Mr. Veesey Blaize opened a great strapped-up case filled with papers tied up in little bundles, and buried his large and purplish face inside one of the flaps. It was only a moment, however, before he found what he wanted. He put the case on the floor beside him, took out a massive pair of horn-rimmed spectacles and began to read.

"There are just one or two points I'm not quite clear about," he said at length in his thick rich voice as though he were talking on the wireless. "Just one or two. The young lady, for instance."

"You mean the deceased," Mr. Barks began.

"Yurs, yurs," Mr. Veesey Blaize answered. "Let Mr. Boon tell me in his own words. We understand each other, don't we, Mr. Boon?"

Percy nodded. He liked Mr. Veesey Blaize. Liked him almost better than anybody else he'd ever met.

"Now about the young lady," Mr. Blaize continued. "You were friendly, weren't you?"

"So so," said Percy guardedly.

"Oh, come," Mr. Blaize objected. "Don't be shy with me. I was young myself once. You used to go about with her?"

"A bit."

"And you looked forward to going about a bit more, eh?"

Percy nodded.

"And I expect she liked you, didn't she?"

"Seemed to."

"Ah. Now we're getting somewhere. She was a very nice young lady, wasn't she?"

"She was all right."

What was Mr. Veesey Blaize getting at, he wondered. It wasn't any good talking about the Blonde, so far as he could see. Too late for that now. Besides, as things were, he wanted to forget her. He didn't like being reminded. But Mr. Veesey Blaize was off again.

"I wouldn't be surprised if you'd had the money if you two wouldn't have got married. Nice little home together somewhere, eh?"

Percy pondered for a moment.

"Might of."

Mr. Veesey Blaize seemed pleased again.

"Now I'm going to ask you a very solemn question," he continued. "Suppose at this moment the door opened and the young lady came in, fresh and beautiful, as she was when you knew her, would you take her in your arms or would you thrust her away from you because of all the trouble you're in on account of her?"

"Wasn't her fault," Percy told him.

"Ah, you see," said Mr. Veesey Blaize turning to Mr. Barks. "Just as I said." He swung round on Percy again. "All we've got to do is to make that clear to the jury and they'll understand that you didn't mean to kill her. Now about the car door. Mr. Barks tells me that it was loose. Very loose. As a motor mechanic, Mr. Boon, have you ever known a car door fly open? You have! Well, there you are then."

Mr. Veesey Blaize shut up all the papers again, stuffed them back into the bulging brief-case, and took off his massive spectacles.

"That's given me all I wanted, Mr. Boon. Mr. Barks will be seeing you. But we shan't meet again until we're together in court. Don't be nervous. Just answer as though you hadn't got anything to hide, and you'll be all right. Just take things easily as it were. And if you've got anything special that you want to tell me just let Mr. Barks know. The more we know, the better. Eh, Mr. Barks?"

They'd gone now, Mr. Barks tagging along like a terrier behind a mastiff. The cell seemed very empty without them. Very empty and very quiet. Percy wished that they were still there. He wished that he could have given them a drink or something. Even tea would have been better than nothing. The only thing that had been wrong had been all that talk about the Blonde. It wasn't good taste somehow. And now that they'd gone it was rather creepy. Didn't they realise that he'd got feelings like other people?

Suppose Mr. Veesey Blaize had done in a girl how would he like to have Percy dropping in on him and asking if he would like to take her in his arms if he had the chance?

CHAPTER 47

Piccadilly Circus may be the centre of London. And some people—enthusiastic provincials mostly—have called it the centre of the world. But you've only got to go about a bit to see that even the first claim is dubious.

Take the Marble Arch, for instance. The crowds at the Marble Arch actually stop where they are—whereas at Piccadilly Circus everyone is always on the way to somewhere else. Choose any fine summer evening and at the Marble Arch you'll find a crowd of several hundred people standing about greedily savouring the simple but tremendous pleasure of merely being there. It's a good spot. As dusk falls, the park in the background becomes vast and mysterious, and the gas-lamps that light your way along the main paths dwindle into the distance like lanterns in Illyria. But somehow or other it remains London, with the buses that cruise up Park Lane twinkling through the railings, and the air filled with roar and rustle of innumerable wheels. Yes, it's London all right. But it's also somewhere right outside it. Sufficiently far out for you to be able to look up into the sky as the dusk deepens and see the gigantic upturned bowl of brightness that the West End has erected above itself. You can, in fact, stand at the Marble Arch and be just wherever you want to be, in London or in the country. That's the magic of the place. Or rather, that's how it was in 1939.

But the magic wasn't working for Mr. Josser because he didn't want to be there at all. He was standing miserably in the forefront of a group of about a dozen people trying to derive some comfort from the reflection that no one was to know that the prophet on the folding pulpit was his brother-in-law.

There was no real cause for anxiety, however. Uncle Henry was conspicuous only to Mr. Josser. Indeed, in all London there was probably no place where he would have been less conspicuous. For there were other Uncle Henries all round him. Just beside his elbow, so close that the two messages sometimes became mingled, was a Kensitite Uncle Henry preaching the straight Bible and no truck with Rome. A little further on was a bi-metallist Uncle Henry reforming the currency. Then came an historical Uncle Henry who proved with bewildering satisfaction that everything important in the world happens in years that are multiples of 13 or 29. But, as a draw, he was a failure compared with young Cousin Henry of the British Union of Fascists who kept telling his listeners to carry a dagger in their belts and keep their weather-eye on Palestine. Further on was another popular draw, a black Uncle Henry with a grievance against doctors. And, in between, came an anti-vivisectionist Uncle Henry trying to whip up his audience of one old man into a frenzy by brandishing a picture of a chloroformed cat. Then, further on still, came Comrade Henry of the Communist Party exposing an ingenious plot on the part of the employers to attack Russia by getting the Government to declare war on Germany. And last of all was old Father Henry, dressed up in the loose black and white robes of the Dominican Order, recounting the miracle of Lourdes.

Indeed, it would have seemed at first glance as though even the most exacting listener could have found exactly what he wanted simply by strolling on until he came to others of his own persuasion. But that wasn't the way things worked. On the contrary, all the audiences were hostile. Communists gathered round the Fascist, and Fascists congregated in front of the Communist. A sworn adherent to Gold stuck himself under the nose of the bi-metallist, and the mere mention of Lourdes brought atheists, agnostics, rationalists and free-thinkers crushing round the Dominican. Uncle Henry's own group was made up to a man of steady-going Primrose Leaguers who supported Mr. Chamberlain.

The day had been hot, swelteringly hot. It had still been hot when Uncle Henry had climbed up into his little pulpit. Mr. Josser had seen the beads of sweat standing out on his forehead as he was speaking. But now, with evening, it had grown suddenly colder. Mr. Josser found himself shivering. A wind sprang up, shaking the branches overhead. And a few drops of rain fell—isolated heavy drops that suggested more. Immediately the crowd, timid as kittens at the approach of water, divided up into small groups and huddled themselves at the foot of trees or made their way in crocodile-streams to the bus-stops or the Underground.

Uncle Henry finally folded up his notes and came down from the pulpit in the manner of an admiral quitting the bridge after a successful engagement.

"I reckon that got under their skins," he said, rubbing his hands together. "That made 'em think."

"G-good," said Mr. Josser, his teeth chattering. "Shall we get this down now?"

He pointed at the folding pulpit as he spoke and began fingering the patent catches. Those two hours had been unpleasantly chilling, simply standing there. And now, with the rain threatening at any moment to become a downpour, he wanted to be getting home. It was different for Uncle Henry, who had taken out his coloured handkerchief and was wiping off the perspiration that was still forming on his forehead.

"What we need," he said, "is hundreds of these meetings up and down the country. Protests. Mass demonstrations. Telegrams to M.P.s."

"J-just so," Mr. Josser answered.

He had just found the secret of the patent catch which was holding the pulpit together. It really needed two people to work it. But Mr. Josser didn't want to bother Uncle Henry at the moment. That was how it was that the whole contraption suddenly came crashing to the ground without warning. It was a multi-jointed affair and it took them both some time to get it up again and shut properly.

Even then they were left with the pile of pamphlets, the "literature" as Uncle Henry called it. There were two large batches, one entitled THE WAY TO WAR and the other WHAT PRICE MUNICH? And they were becoming sodden. Uncle Henry went across and folded his *Evening Standard* over them. As he did so, Mr. Josser could not help noticing that the headlines of the paper were as alarmist as Uncle Henry. They announced that Queen Wilhelmina and King Leopold, as safe as two neutrals can be, were offering to mediate in the impending quarrel between giants.

Uncle Henry looked up suddenly.

"You all right?" he asked.

"Me?"

"For literature, I mean," Uncle Henry explained. "Let me know as soon as you want some more. I'm having another edition printed."

"I'll let you know," Mr. Josser promised.

He felt uncomfortable and deceitful as he said it. There was a whole heap still behind the couch in Dulcimer Street. Or there were, if Mrs. Josser hadn't moved them. She'd been threatening to throw them away if Mr. Josser didn't do something.

"Well, give me a hand then," Uncle Henry said abruptly.

He slung the bundle of pamphlets over his shoulder and Mr. Josser took the pulpit. They didn't have far to go because Uncle Henry's green bicycle was chained against the railings, and there was a trailer attached to it. The trailer had been Uncle Henry's own invention. A picture of it, with Uncle Henry up, had appeared in *Cycling*. Into the trailer went the two bundles with the folding pulpit fitted across the top. Then Uncle Henry squatted down beside it and proceeded to lash up the contraption with straps.

"See you at Parliament Hill on Sunday," he said. "Eleven o'clock sharp."

Mr. Josser nodded.

"I'll be there," he said.

Uncle Henry came closer.

"And keep next Thursday free," he said confidentially. "I may be taking the Prince of Wales Baths. . . ."

They had reached Stanhope Gate by now and Uncle Henry climbed into the saddle. As Mr. Josser, with coat collar turned up, stood watching him, he found that he rather envied the man. He seemed so vigorous, so independent, so inexhaustible.

Even now, as he pedalled off with his trailer rattling after him, across Park Lane and into Mayfair, he was not relaxing. He was calling out "Get rid of Chamberlain. Get rid of Chamberlain and prepare for war" in that high-pitched, slightly mad-sounding voice of his.

Mr. Josser stood looking after him till the words, like the tail-lamp of the trailer, had grown fainter and still fainter in the darkness, and finally were lost amid the rest of London.

CHAPTER 48

I

IT WAS September the first, September the first, 1939.

And a lot was happening. Queen Wilhelmina and King Leopold's offer of mediation had been rejected. Not that there was anything very remarkable in that. Indeed, looking back on it afterwards it is doubtful if either of them really expected it to be accepted. Because, taken all in all, it had been European rejection week. Similar snubs had just been administered to His Holiness and President Roosevelt. In short, the Nazis weren't having any. And, in the circumstances, it seemed pretty sporting and public-spirited of Mussolini of all people to propose a conference.

But, by then, patience had worn a bit thin all round and Whitehall wasn't having any either. It was, of course, nice to know that we still had a friend in Mussolini, but with Herr Forster, a Nazi, already installed in Danzig as head of the state, and Hitler as rude as he had been to Sir Nevile Henderson, it was plain that no good would come of any more palaver. That was why just four hours after the Third Reich began its Blitzkrieg on Poland, the London County Council was busy bundling the first parties of children out of the metropolis for their long holiday in the country.

It nearly broke Connie's heart to think about those poor little kids. And it upset her a bit on her own account as well. The Government would hardly go to all that trouble and expense—special trains and reception committees and what-not, like a glorified Cook's Tour—unless they expected something. And if the balloon really went up what was going to become of Connie, poor thing, with only Mr. Puddy in between her and Marshal Goering's Luftwaffe? The mere thought of it was enough to bring on that sinking feeling.

But it was the schoolchildren that really seared her. And their poor dear mothers. Just think of it—one day a whole quiverful of little blue-eyed darlings with lisps, and on the next just a nursery of empty cots and unplayed-with toys. She wondered how any woman could stand it. There'd be suicides if she knew anything about it. Nice motherly women popping their heads into gas ovens just because they couldn't bear the pain of separation. And little orphaned children crying under haystacks or trying to walk back to London in shoes that were worn through to the tiny feet inside them. . . .

Connie took out her handkerchief and had a good cry over it. She'd always been that way about cruelty to children. And this was funny because she didn't particularly like children when she was with them. But, in imagination, they were heavenly little creatures, golden-haired ones especially. They brought out the best in her. Not that there was anything unusual in that. She was always having her best brought out. Holiday-makers drowned while bathing, brides killed in motor-smashes, sea-birds with oil on their wings, fathers of families getting caught up in machinery, cats marooned on church steeples—she rarely got through the daily paper completely dry-eyed.

But as all these dreadful things were happening, and as these poo little innocents, all weeping and struggling to get back to thei mothers, were going to be sent away, she decided that she might a well go along to Waterloo and see something of it. She'd even stan herself a platform ticket if that would help. It wasn't every day tha there was drama like that going on just round the corner.

She got to the station at about ten-thirty. At first it was difficult t get in because there was so much happening. But she managed it al right in the end even though it did mean having a few words ove her shoulder with a policeman. And, once inside, what a scene it was Not a bit what she'd imagined it, mind you. No screaming, n hysteria, no panic. Just rows and rows of children each with a ga mask, a parcel containing rations and sponge-bag, and a label t prove that the child really was itself and not a totally different chil from some other school. It was all orderly, efficient, disciplined a though the London County Council had been in the business o children's crusades for years. The teachers who were looking afte these enormous families might have been in charge of a mass visi to the Zoo. They merely had about them that look of depresse watchfulness which is common to all adults accompanying schoo outings. The children themselves were blithe, excited and ready fo anything.

For a moment, Connie was almost disappointed. It looked a though she had mis-read the part. Then the artist in her came to th top again and she spotted that really it was worse, much worse, thi way. It meant that the children were simply so many little dum animals being herded into trucks like cattle without realising wha was happening. That brought the lump back into her throat all right and made her old eyes misty. When an infant school of toddler trotted in out of the yard it was too much for her. She took out he handkerchief and cried.

"You're an old fool, Connie," she told herself. "That's what you are, an old fool. If you can't stand it, you shouldn't have come."

But she knew that such advice even from herself was useless. This was something that she wouldn't have missed for worlds.

She hadn't properly recovered when she was moved out of the way quite rudely by a ticket-inspector who seemed to have been put in charge of all the mothers with babies. Obviously a family man himself, he was followed by a long column of large, dejected women with small wrapped-up babies. Connie looked away. Between

Connie and her sex there was no spare sympathy. It was just the children without any mothers who got her every time.

There was one little girl in particular. She wasn't even an especially pretty child. Just one more junior evacuee standing a little out of line. She had a band across her front teeth and wore glasses with a length of cotton wound around the bridge. But, as she stood there, she was hugging her teddy bear and talking to it. The sight quite bowled Connie over. She wondered what the teacher would say if someone, a stranger, started kissing one of her pupils.

Then a happy new idea came to her. She couldn't afford it. But what did it matter? If there really was going to be a war money wouldn't be worth anything, so why not spend now while there was still a chance? Crossing over to the sweet-stall, she bought a Mars Bar. The little girl with the teddy bear was so surprised that she didn't even say thank-you.

But Connie scarcely noticed because there was a big new sensation close at hand. A press photographer was taking pictures of the children, and the children were bunching themselves together to get into the group. Connie didn't stand a chance herself when a well-dressed, determined-looking woman—obviously the headmistress—came striding up to establish order and get into the photograph herself.

Connie was elbowed right back in fact and simply had to stand looking on. The sadness of it all was affecting her again and she pulled out her handkerchief. Some of the children had surreptitiously opened their parcels and started lunch. Little bits were dropping everywhere.

"I'd like to have Hitler here," she reflected gloatingly. "I'd like to have him to myself for five minutes. I'd like to make him go down on his knees and clear up after 'em."

She was disturbed in her reverie by a hand that was placed on her forearm. It was a timid, hesitating pressure, quite unlike the way a policeman grabs hold of you. She turned and saw that there was an old gentleman standing beside her. And such a nice old gentleman—white crinkly hair under a black hat, and a loose bow-tie. Quite the elderly clubman, in fact, with a rolled-up umbrella hanging over his arm and a whole armful of the shiny picture papers. He'd got a suit-case with his initials on it, on the ground beside him. And for some reason or other he was holding out a pound note towards Connie.

"Bless them," he said rather huskily, not even looking at Connie but staring straight in front of him at the children. "It's terrible to have it happening. But they'll be safe and that's all that matters.

I saw you giving them something just now. See what you can do with this."

He thrust the pound note into her hand, and without waiting for an answer he moved off.

For a moment it fairly stumped Connie getting a whole quid to spend like that. But she liked the idea of going right up and down the long lines of children distributing chocolate and buns and monkey-nuts like some perishing Lady Bountiful. She went straight back over to the sweet-stall where she'd first bought the Mars Bar, thinking what a stir her new order was going to make. There was quite a crowd already gathered there, however, and she had to wait while a lot of fiddling small stuff was attended to.

It was while she was waiting that she saw a tiny incident that altered everything. A small boy in the party nearest to her started eating an orange before he'd finished the sandwich that he'd got in his hand, and the master in charge spotted him. He was a rough, brutal type of man, the master—quite the reverse of the old gentleman—and he gave two little hoots on a whistle that he'd been carrying in his pocket.

"Mordyke Road Senior Boys," he said in a harsh, penetrating voice. "Listen to me. There's eating going on again. Stop it. I don't want you all being sick in the train."

Well, that was that. Who *would* want a lot of children being sick all over the upholstery, particularly if you had to travel with them? Not Connie. She saw now that it wouldn't be fair on the teachers to give as much as one piece of chocolate away. It was just one of those things. She looked round for the old gentleman, but he'd gone. There was nothing that she could do about it. She hadn't asked for it: it had been a gift. She stood there, pondering. Then folding up the pound note very small she thrust it deep down into her handbag, and shot out of the station. No loitering.

If this was stealing she'd been wasting her time all these years.

It was next day that she had her big surprise. In the *Daily Mirror*. Front page. There was a picture of the children, and a close-up of herself giving the little girl with the teddy bear a Mars Bar. It made her go all goose-flesh from excitement. She hoped that the old gentleman would see it, too, because in a way it seemed to prove things.

Then she read the caption. And she wasn't so pleased. It was professionally damaging, she reckoned. There might even be a libel action in it.

"Granny gives Her Mite," was what the caption said.

2

There was one further little piece of excitement when she got back. The men had come to measure for the air-raid shelter.

The air-raid shelter had been Mr. Squales's idea. Ever since Mrs. Jan Byl's premature retreat from the ruins of London, he had been worried about Mrs. Vizzard's safety. The house was old, he could not help remembering—it needed only one good push to send the whole stucco terrace shuddering to the ground. And if his intended was going to stay in the danger zone he wanted somewhere below ground for her, somewhere snug where he could creep in and sit beside her so that she shouldn't be afraid.

CHAPTER 49

1

IT'S the next day now. Evening on September the second. To-morrow will bring—what to-morrow will bring. At the moment, to-morrow is just like any other day except for the fact that the Prime Minister is going to speak. The atmosphere is tense, but there are no foregone conclusions.

Let's get away from Dulcimer Street for a moment. Things are going on elsewhere as well. Liners are drawing in at the big ports. Aeroplanes are arriving at Croydon. And, if you feel like it, you can walk into any railway ticket office and book straight through to Berlin. Take a look at Harwich—always a good stepping-off point. At Parkestone Quay lies the night-boat for the Hook. Overhead in the thickening dusk, seagulls wind backwards and forwards in circles as though on strings like children's kites. Despite the rows of suspended lamps—which swing a little in the breeze that comes straight in from the North Sea—the whole place looks bleak, desolate and a little unfriendly as dockyards always look at night. Oyster crates are piled alongside the first-class waiting-room.

On the other side of the harbour, the Royal Naval side, the guards have been doubled and all the destroyers have got steam up. But it's too dark to see anything of that. Everything that's in sight is as normal as the seagulls.

The eight o'clock train from Liverpool Street draws in, the pink table-lamps in the Pullman cars momentarily lending a touch of almost drawing-room comfort to the scene. Porters, the queer half-breed race—part railway servant, part sea-dog—that inhabit every maritime terminus, come forward from a small room that smells of paraffin and cooking. There is new life in the refreshment buffet where the young ladies, wiping their damp red hands on their black dresses, saunter along to take up their positions behind the bar. In the Customs sheds the clerks arrange their cardboard boxes of coloured crayons and hang out their notices about explosives and hashish. Two dim little men—special officers from Scotland Yard—hang around the doorway.

Then the passengers come streaming in. They are a quiet, heavy lot, with very few women among them. Mostly business men with large brief-cases elaborately strapped and buckled. They have about them the air of extreme importance which is the birthright of commercial foreigners. When they stand up in front of their suitcases, to allow the Customs men to go carefully through their pyjamas, their toilet-case, their change of underwear, a row of pink necks bulge out over their hard white collars. Then, innocent of concealed firearms, they raise their furry velours politely, show their passports which are examined as casually as though they were train-tickets, and pass through to the boat for a quick drink before sailing.

The small round man at the far end takes a little longer than the others. Two of the Customs men are bending low over his bag and one of the special officers from Scotland Yard approaches hopefully. But it's nothing. Only the top of Dr. Hapfel's hair-cream bottle that has come off. He borrows a duster to mop up his nice silk dressing-gown and then he too hurries through to the waiting boat.

His thesis on The Leader-Principle in Democratic Government has been accepted and, if the present trouble blows over, it will be published in London as well as in Leipzig. During the three years he has been in England he has discovered many things about the English. The first is their ignorance. Keeping themselves to themselves is the highest virtue. In consequence the entire island race knows nothing of what is happening elsewhere. And no one seems to care very much. Stupidity coupled with comfort has produced a breed that is impervious to anxiety. They sleep at night secure in the arms of the Navy that no one ever sees, supported by an Empire that no one ever mentions.

Puzzling—but, to a philosopher like Dr. Hapfel, also pathetic. There is a lot in England that the sentimentalist in him would like to see preserved; re-modelled, of course, brought up to date and *gleichgeschaltet*, but preserved. But as things are there will be little, very little, nothing in fact, left of the England that he has known. Even the pleasant things, like the young lady with high colouring and a lace bodice in the newsagent's at the corner of the Euston Road, will be swept away along with Mr. Chamberlain and the Archbishop of Canterbury and Mr. Montagu Norman and the Jews of the City of London.

Dr. Hapfel stumbles as he mounts the gangway and someone, a stranger, standing on the quayside helps to steady him.

"Lift 'em up," he says. "It's only for life."

Only for life! It is precisely this attitude that Dr. Hapfel has tried to explain in his thesis. An attitude compounded of cynicism and insensitiveness and impudence. It is the same attitude that has allowed a daily paper this morning, apparently without threat of police action, to publish a cartoon of the Führer, *his* Führer, dressed up in the costume of Charlie Chaplin.

There must, Dr. Hapfel decides as he tries to fit himself into his little cabin, be more to it than either Herr Ribbentrop or the Link have yet discovered. Perhaps English humour is really only a sublimation of the death-urge, the suicide-impulse. Perhaps Mr. Chamberlain actually wants to impale himself.

Perhaps he is certifiable.

Undoing his sponge-bag, Dr. Hapfel, Ph.D., removes his toothbrush and his Odol and proceeds to brush his teeth.

2

The boat has just left and the eight o'clock train for Liverpool Street is being pushed away into a siding. The porters have shut themselves away in their paraffin closet. The young ladies in the buffet have turned out the light and left the washing-up until to-morrow. The Customs men have disappeared to wherever Customs men disappear to between departures. And the special officers from Scotland Yard have gone to a commercial hotel for the night. Only the seagulls are still there.

The boat, with Dr. Hapfel on board, is now no more than a smudge of lights on the horizon.

Take a good look at it. It is the last gleam of brightness that will be seen in the North Sea for quite a time. There isn't going to be a boat-train to-morrow, because there won't be any boat.

By then, it will be war. And England really will be keeping herself to herself.

BOOK FOUR

REX *v.* PERCY BOON

CHAPTER 50

I

A LOT more had been happening.

On the day, the very day, when war had been declared—within half an hour of the declaration, in fact—the air-raid sirens had sounded. And Londoners had been introduced to their new signature tune. It was, as it turned out, only a false alarm. No air raid followed. But on that tremendous Sunday everybody was a bit on edge. Including the aircraft spotters. In consequence, the coastal batteries were opening up on anything in sight. Even on our own planes.

Not that people were jumpy without reason. It was war all right. Out in the September sea off Ireland, the liner *Athenia*, packed as full of children as a day-nursery, was settling down in the water with half her keel blown away by a torpedo. And the U-boat that had fired it was standing by on the surface, shelling the survivors. There was something fateful and symbolic about the whole affair. It was as though the uneasy quarter-century since 1914 had come round full circle, and von Tirpitz was risen from his grave to re-direct operations.

It was the same on the Continent. The Great War had come again. Only this time it was east and not west that the Germans were striking. Belgium was safe in its neutrality. But Poland, sliced like a ham, had been made into a neat sandwich with Germany and the U.S.S.R. squeezing it tighter every day. People, remembering Finland, talked about the Russians being as bad as the Nazis—it certainly didn't look good with the Communist Party standing out against the war—and wise men reminded the world that it is always easier to start a war than to end one. And so it went on. Policemen wore tin helmets and fire-pumps were attached as trailers to the backs of taxis. *Peace News* doubled its circulation and shoppers carried their gas masks in their baskets. Income tax was at seven and sixpence and the National Register was taken. Sandbags were piled in doorways and the barrage balloons floated overhead like silver sheep. There was a black-out all over Britain and Winston was back at the Admiralty.

And all the time, the Law—quiet, methodical and as undistracted as ever—had been proceeding with its briefs and depositions, its summons to jurors and its calendar of trials. Everything was now ready for the case of Rex *v*. Percy Aloysius Boon.

2

There is nothing in the least prepossessing about the Old Bailey, even from the outside. It has none of the complicated Gothic charm of the Law Courts—all Tennysonian turrets and arrow-slits and things—and none of the almost domestic friendliness of the better-class County Courts. It is just a large bleak factory of criminal law with an enormous gilt doll, dressed up as Justice, standing on top of the dome, and a public lavatory and an A.B.C. tea-shop opposite. Old Bailey itself is a miserable thoroughfare, narrowing down at the Ludgate Hill end until it looks as though you could scarcely get a horse and cart through it. The other frontage—on Cheapside—is better. But that isn't where they've put the front door.

For a big murder trial the crowd begins to form quite early. It has to. The Central Criminal Court is so much taken up with the judges and the counsel and the clerks and the witnesses and the jury and the prisoners that there is hardly any room for the public. Just a few benches up against one of the walls. Many quite promising amateur criminologists have been turned away by the "House Full" notice. Of course if you know one of the judges or have had a K.C. to dinner it's different. There are private tickets for the Old Bailey just as there are for everything else. Society ladies can pretty nearly always get in when they feel like it. But the humbler folk, retired civil servants and old clergymen up from the country for the day, can rarely find a seat without a tussle. It's one law for the poor and another for the rich.

Mr. Josser was one of the privileged ones. He'd got a ticket: Mr. Barks had seen to that. But somehow he wasn't looking forward to using it.

"I don't like it, Mother," he said. "I know everything's going to be all right. But I can't help it. I don't like it."

Mrs. Josser made no reply, because Mr. Josser had said the same thing twice already and she had answered on the two previous occasions. There had been a lot of discussion as to whether she should go with him, and she had finally decided against it. She couldn't, despite everything that Mr. Josser had told her about the way Percy was taking it, believe that he wouldn't be embarrassed to see her sitting there. Even the thought of being able to write to tell Mrs. Boon all about it afterwards hadn't moved her. The mere thought of the Old Bailey sent cold shivers through her and she was afraid that she might faint or something. All the same, as the time drew nearer —Mr. Josser was already lacing up his boots—she half regretted her decision.

"They're devils some of those barristers," Mr. Josser observed from somewhere down at knee-level. "They don't mind what questions they ask."

"He's got that Mr. Blaize on his side, hasn't he?" Mrs. Josser answered.

"Oh, yes, he's got Mr. Veesey Blaize all right," Mr. Josser replied. "But, after all, he's only human. He doesn't know what the prosecution may have discovered. It's like that in a law court—you can't tell from one moment to the next. It's enough to tear the hide off a man."

Mrs. Josser regarded him out of the corner of her spectacles.

"Have you ever been to one?" she asked him.

Mr. Josser glanced up for a moment.

"No," he admitted. "If you put it like that, I haven't."

He gave a short tug at his lace as he spoke and said, "Damn!"

His lace, his practically new lace, had snapped off short and he had to start again from the very bottom.

"Poor old Percy," he said at length. "I don't rightly know how I'm going to stand it. Not if anything goes wrong, that is."

That settled it in Mrs. Josser's mind.

"Would you feel better if I came too?" she asked.

Mr. Josser gave a rather sad little smile at the suggestion.

"Do you know, Mother, I would," he said. "It'd make all the difference."

It was just what he had been longing for. And he knew that Percy would appreciate it. It would show that, even in his trouble, Dulcimer Street hadn't entirely forgotten him.

3

They had a bit of a surprise when they reached Ludgate Circus. There just in front of them was Mr. Puddy. With a small attaché case in his hand he was crossing the road in the direction of Benson's.

"D'you see who's there?" Mr. Josser asked.

Mrs. Josser drew in her lips.

"I do," she said. "He's probably going too."

"Oh, no," Mr. Josser told her. "He wouldn't be doing that. Not him. He hardly knew Percy. . . ."

There was no difficulty for the Jossers when they reached the Old Bailey. Mr. Barks's card had seen to that. A policeman, looking rather strange without his helmet, took them straight along as though they owned the place. They were given seats in what seemed to be a kind of family pew.

Mr. Josser looked around him. There wasn't much doing yet because it was early. A junior counsel in wig and gown was undoing a large bundle of papers tied together with red tape, and a small man in a black office coat was sharpening a pencil. Two large policemen with nothing to do talked in whispers. Mr. Josser let his eyes rest on the huge coat of arms above the judge's throne. It was about the most interesting thing in the room. The judge hadn't appeared yet. Nor had Percy.

He was quite startled when Mrs. Josser dug him suddenly with her elbow.

"Look up there," she said.

Mr. Josser looked. Over the rail of the public gallery a small dried-up face under a black hat with a feather peony on it was showing. The face was turned in Mr. Josser's direction, and one eye in it winked. It was Connie. But in his astonishment at what he saw behind her, Mr. Josser scarcely noticed Connie. One row back, and in the opposite corner, sat Mrs. Vizzard, very smart-looking in a new black costume, and beside her was Mr. Squales wearing his light grey.

"Well, if that isn't nice of them," said Mr. Josser.

"They didn't tell me they were coming," Mrs. Josser replied, and drew in her lips.

But at that moment there was a distraction. Mr. Barks, wearing a creaseless blue suit and carrying another sheaf of papers, came bustling in breathing heavily, and at his elbow marched a squat square man whose face under the grey wig was almost mulberry coloured. The junior got up and greeted him politely.

"That'll be Veesey Blaize," Mr. Josser whispered.

They were both looking at him when Mr. Blaize without even putting his hand up to his mouth closed his eyes and yawned. Evidently he had been up into the small hours poring over his brief. All the same, both Mr. and Mrs. Josser were secretly a little disappointed that he didn't seem fresher. He might just have been roused from a rather long after-luncheon slumber. Mr. Josser in particular had a sudden doubt as to whether he was going to get his money's worth.

By now, however, there was too much going on for them to concentrate exclusively on Mr. Veesey Blaize. Already, the jury was filing in. They were not an impressive lot. Indeed, they might have been chosen by an unenterprising casting director who had rung up a theatrical agency and asked for a dozen little puddingy people, eleven men and a woman. At least six of them were completely interchangeable and the other five had the air of being made up of spare parts. They all wore neat dark suits. The identical six wore hard white collars and the other five had dimly coloured ones. Even the woman was wearing a dark dress with a white collar like a governess's. And in character they seemed to have something in common, too: they were wuffly and undecided. Even though there were only three rows of benches on which to sit, the little puddingy people couldn't decide where to place themselves. Then one of them, slightly rounder and fuller than the rest, seated himself in the front row nearest to the judge's throne and undid his coat. He had a thick gold watch-chain with which he started to fiddle. It was obvious that when the time came, he was going to be foreman.

Mr. Veesey Blaize took one glance at them and then yawned again. Altogether he seemed extraordinarily out of sorts this morning. He pulled himself together, however, when another learned counsel came in and said good-morning to him. For a moment he became alert and affable in a big bland sort of way—became, in fact, more what Mr. Josser had imagined him. But this may have been only because the other counsel was such an impressive figure of a man that Mr. Veesey Blaize felt that he simply had to do something to keep up his own dignity.

At first, indeed, Mr. Josser had thought that the newcomer must be the judge himself. He was as tall as a Guardsman and had a large grey face with all the features just a shade too pronounced. When he spoke his Adam's apple, absurdly prominent between the two wings of his collar, rose and fell as though it were on a spring. He kept rubbing his long colourless hands together, alternately stroking first one and then the other.

Indeed, after the sight of him—he was Mr. Henry Wassall, K.C. for the prosecution—the judge himself came as a bit of a disappointment. The usher called something out, the whole court stood up and, emerging from a kind of stage door, on to the bench clambered a tiny pink-and-white man all bundled up in his enormous wig and robes of office. He was such a small and insignificant little body that it seemed impossible that he should be in charge of things. In charge of Mr. Veesey Blaize with that terrifying temper of his hidden away somewhere behind the yawn, and of the big-boned Mr. Wassall with the all-grey face. Even his pink-and-whiteness did not appear to have anything to do with good health. It was of an extreme delicacy all its own and suggested that his lordship on rising had spread a thin layer of peach-blossom porcelain over his old cheeks. Altogether Mr. Justice Plymme cut a disturbingly dainty and fragile sort of figure.

But this was only a layman's view of things. The Law knew Mr. Justice Plymme and respected him. So did the Society of Fine Arts and the English Madrigal Society. Likewise Queen's Club and Shaftesbury Avenue and the Flyfishers'. For Mr. Plymme off duty went everywhere and did everything. He was a kind of respectable bachelor leprechaun who exhibited himself at first-nights and private views and tennis finals. And after dinner his thin voice, high and clear like a choirboy's, had been heard rising in one city hall after another, urbane, cynical and remorselessly witty, in a brittle, brilliant sort of fashion. Mr. Justice Plymme, in fact, was one of the cries of old London.

When Percy was called and stood there in between the two warders, Mr. Josser couldn't at first bear to look at him. And, when he did look, it was all just as he had feared. He looked so out of place there. It needed only one glance at the purplish suit, the coloured handkerchief and his fair wavy hair to see that he belonged to a different world altogether. He'd obviously got himself up pretty carefully for the occasion. But, even so, you could see that he was nervous. A faint smile kept playing round the corners of his mouth as he peered about him.

An astonishing amount of time was wasted at the outset in proving that Percy Boon was really Percy Boon. It suggested that Mr. Wassall had been badly caught that way before. Then the prosecution began calling witnesses. And to Mr. Josser's amazement it was all old stuff. They were simply going over everything that had been said at the police court; checking up on the magistrate as it were. First of all, there was the accountant from Norbury. He identified the car. It was an Austin 12, No. PQJ 1776 that he had bought new three months before. It was practically new. He had taken it to the local Carlton and had left it locked in the car park. When he had come out shortly after eleven the car was missing. Was he quite sure that he had locked it? Quite sure. He spoke in a clipped, busy-sounding kind of voice and Mr. Wassall was obviously prepared to take his word for things. He thanked him in a dead, formal manner and told him that he could stand down.

Dead. Yes, that was it. Mr. Wassall's own voice was like something rumbling round in a tomb. By the time it reached the open court there was a distinctly coffiny and brass-handle ring to it.

The next witness whom Mr. Wassall called was a policeman. The evidence proceeded as smoothly as though it had been rehearsed—which, in the circumstances, wasn't really surprising.

Mr. Wassall: "You are P.C. Lamb?"

P.C. Lamb: "I am."

Mr. Wassall: "Where were you on the evening of the third June, 1939?"

P.C. Lamb: "I was on Wimbledon Common, sir."

Mr. Wassall: "What part of Wimbledon Common?"

P.C. Lamb: "On the main Wimbledon–Putney road. By the Long Pond."

Mr. Wassall: "There had been an accident, hadn't there?"

P.C. Lamb: "There had."

Mr. Wassall: "What sort of an accident?"

P.C. Lamb: "A cyclist had been knocked off his machine and injured."

Mr. Wassall: "Well, what did you do about it?"

P.C. Lamb: "I moved the injured man to the side of the road and sent someone to ring for an ambulance."

Mr. Wassall: "I see. You had moved the injured man to the side of the road. So you weren't causing any obstruction. There was room for, let us say, a car to get past without disturbing either of you."

P.C. Lamb: "There was room for two cars . . ."

Mr. Veesey Blaize rose suddenly to his feet.

"M'lud," he said, "I object. Can the examination really be necessary? This is a murder case that your lordship is hearing, not a running-down charge."

Mr. Justice Plymme turned towards Mr. Wassall.

"I suppose that there is some relevance in the constable's evidence, Mr. Wassall?" he asked.

He spoke in a polite interested voice as though he would not have minded in the least if Mr. Wassall had told him that nothing had got to do with anything.

"Of the first relevance, m'lud," Mr. Wassall replied promptly. "It is quite essential to the prosecution, in fact. I am afraid that I shall have to ask your Lordship's indulgence for a long sitting if my learned friend is to interrupt me further in this way."

"Then pray proceed, Mr. Wassall," Mr. Justice Plymme invited him. "So much evidence that is irrelevant is heard in every court that your assurance is most welcome."

Up in the press gallery the reporters began writing hard. It was the first clash between Mr. Veesey Blaize and Mr. Wassall and also Mr. Justice Plymme's first *bon mot*. Everyone seemed pleased. Mr. Wassall continued louder than ever.

Mr. Wassall: "Yet you were nearly run into, were you not?"

P.C. Lamb: "I was."

Mr. Wassall: "By what?"

P.C. Lamb: "By a car."

Mr. Wassall: "What kind of a car?"

P.C. Lamb: "By an Austin 12."

Mr. Wassall: "Did you obtain the number of the car?"

P.C. Lamb: "I did."

Mr. Wassall: "Well, tell the court what it was."

P.C. Lamb: "It was PQJ 1776."

Mr. Wassall: "How did it happen?"

P.C. Lamb: "I stepped into the roadway and raised my hand."

Mr. Wassall: "How far were you out from the kerb?"

P.C. Lamb: "There wasn't a kerb, sir."

Mr. Wassall uttered a deep, grampus-like sigh. Then he blew his nose and resumed.

Mr. Wassall: "Well, how far were you from the side of the road? From the grass verge or whatever it was."

P.C. Lamb: "About a yard."

Mr. Wassall: "And how wide is the road?"

P.C. Lamb: "Twenty-eight feet."

Mr. Wassall: "Did the car try to avoid you?"

P.C. Lamb: "No, sir. It came straight on in a direct line."

Mr. Wassall: "What did you do?"

P.C. Lamb: "I jumped clear."

There was a noise, half titter half sneeze, from Connie's corner of the public gallery. P.C. Lamb was a large man and it would have been funny to see him jumping clear of anything. But the joke was a purely private one and the court continued without pausing.

Mr. Wassall: "Did you see the person who was driving?"

P.C. Lamb: "I did."

Mr. Wassall: "Was it a woman?"

P.C. Lamb: "No, sir."

Mr. Wassall: "Then it was a man?"

Mr. Josser was staring at Mr. Wassall in amazement. Really, he seemed to have an intelligence of the most obvious kind.

P.C. Lamb: "Yes, sir."

Mr. Wassall: "Was he alone?"

P.C. Lamb: "No, sir."

Mr. Wassall: "Had he got another man with him?"

P.C. Lamb: "No, sir."

Mr. Wassall: "Then his companion was a woman?"

Mr. Josser squirmed. If Mr. Wassall was going on like this he seemed to have forgotten that it might have been a child.

P.C. Lamb: "Yes, sir."

Mr. Wassall: "Did you notice what the driver was wearing?"

P.C. Lamb: "Only that he was wearing a trilby hat and had his coat collar turned up."

Mr. Wassall: "And about the woman?"

P.C. Lamb: "She had fair hair, sir."

Mr. Wassall: "What was the woman doing? Was she sitting there with her hands in her lap?"

P.C. Lamb: "No, sir. She appeared to be struggling."

Mr. Wassall: "She appeared to be struggling!" Mr. Wassall ran his tongue across his lips. "Was she struggling with the driver?"

P.C. Lamb: "She was pulling at his arm and the driver was thrusting her away from him. He had his elbow in her face."

Mr. Wassall: "And what happened after that?"

P.C. Lamb: "The car drove straight on and the lights were switched off."

Mr. Wassall: "I see. You were nearly hit by an Austin car No. PQJ 1776 driven by a man who was struggling with a fair-haired girl . . ."

There was a movement on the bench and Mr. Justice Plymme raised his small white hand.

"Mr. Wassall," he said. "I am quite capable of making any summing-up that the jury may require. Do you wish to examine the witness further?"

Mr. Wassall: "I am finished, m'lud."

Mr. Justice Plymme: "Ah!"

Now it was Mr. Veesey Blaize's turn. He had a warm, rather friendly manner when he started. He might have been discussing a recent round of golf. But his friendliness fell from him in chunks as he proceeded.

Mr. Veesey Blaize: "What sort of weather was it on the night in question?"

P.C. Lamb: "Rather foggy, sir."

Mr. Veesey Blaize: "What does 'rather foggy' mean? I want to know if it was foggy, or if it wasn't."

P.C. Lamb: "There was ground mist, sir."

Mr. Veesey Blaize: "But you said just now that it was fog. They're not the same thing, you know. Which was it—mist or fog?"

P.C. Lamb: "I don't know, sir. The papers called it fog."

Mr. Veesey Blaize: "I'm not interested in what the papers called it. I want to know what you call it."

P.C. Lamb: "Fog, sir."

Mr. Veesey Blaize: "Was it dense!"

P.C. Lamb: "No, sir."

Mr. Veesey Blaize: "Could you see your hand in front of your face?"

P.C. Lamb: "Yes, sir."

Mr. Veesey Blaize: "Did you try?"

P.C. Lamb: "No, sir."

Mr. Veesey Blaize turned towards the jury. There was something at once helpless and appealing in the gesture; it asked mutely how, with witnesses like P.C. Lamb, they could ever hope to get anywhere. Then Mr. Veesey Blaize resumed.

Mr. Veesey Blaize: "Could you see a mile away?"

P.C. Lamb: "No, sir."

Mr. Veesey Blaize: "You're sure?"

P.C. Lamb: "Yes, sir."

Mr. Veesey Blaize: "What was there a mile away from where you were standing? What was there if you had been able to identify it—a mile away exactly, remember?"

P.C. Lamb: "I don't know, sir."

Mr. Veesey Blaize: "Then how could you know whether you could see it or not?"

The police constable was growing sulky and Mr. Veesey Blaize took full advantage of the break. He gave again that you-see-the-kind-of-difficulty-I'm-in glance in the direction of the jury.

Mr. Veesey Blaize: "Was the car in question travelling fast?"

P.C. Lamb: "Yes, sir."

Mr. Veesey Blaize: "Really fast—speeding, I mean?"

P.C. Lamb: "Yes, sir."

Mr. Veesey Blaize: "It bore down on you suddenly out of the mist or fog or whatever it was?"

P.C. Lamb: "Yes, sir."

Mr. Veesey Blaize: "And you jumped out of the way?"

P.C. Lamb: "Yes, sir."

Mr. Veesey Blaize: "Even so, out of the back of your head as it were, you noted the number, the person who was driving, his companion and what was happening inside the car. All that in the fog, remember. I congratulate you . . ."

There was a lot more like that, only Mr. Josser lost count of it. The one thing that consoled him was that Mr. Veesey Blaize was certainly giving them their money's worth; Mr. Wassall and his witnesses looked as though they were in for a whacking. And then, into the midst of these new surroundings, stepped Percy's Big Surprise of the police court. It was a Mr. Jack Rawkins.

It was Percy's turn to stare now and, for a moment, he couldn't place him. And then he remembered him perfectly. Remembered every button about him in fact. He was the man who had been saying good-bye to the Blonde just when Percy had spotted her. But what was really very remarkable was the amount, under examination by Mr. Wassall, that the silly little soak remembered about him. He was able to identify him, to swear that he had seen Percy and the Blonde get into the car together, and to be sure that it was an Austin 12. He had known the Blonde for a number of years, he said; adding only professionally, however. He was a traveller in pin-tables and had met her in the way of business. On the evening in question he had gone along to the Duke of Marlborough to see two men friends and had run into the Blonde purely by accident.

This last piece of evidence was not strictly connected with the case and Mr. Wassall had to arrange for it to be slipped quickly over Mr. Justice Plymme's head. Not that it wasn't important. It was. The tall plain woman in the public gallery was the pin-table salesman's wife.

There were a lot of other witnesses, too. There was the policeman who had found the Blonde in the roadway. The policeman who had found Percy's snap brim trilby. A bone-specialist out of Harley Street. A mechanic to testify that he recognised the spanner. . . . Mr. Wassall was still fiddling about with these odds and ends of witnesses when Mr. Justice Plymme, an inner radiance seeming suddenly to suffuse him, adjourned the court for lunch.

They resumed promptly at two o'clock. Mr. Justice Plymme took his seat looking more pink and white than ever and kept putting his hands together in front of his stomach as though his lunch had been a good one. From the front row of the gallery, Connie was looking down on him. Though Mr. Justice Plymme didn't know it she was feeling sorry for him. She wondered whether, like herself, he was too short for his feet to reach to the floor, and if he was just sitting there with them dangling.

This time the witness called by the prosecution was a very nasty customer. It was someone whom Percy hadn't seen before. But when he did see him he couldn't take his eyes off him. "Mr. Sidney Parker" was called, and a dark evil-looking man with flat hair and dropped sidewhiskers stood up in the box and said that he was the Blonde's husband. He had married her at Portsmouth in 1937, and they had separated ten months afterwards. The Blonde's other name turned out to have been Edith Soper and she'd been in domestic service when Mr. Parker met her. There was a child of the marriage in an orphanage at Wanstead. The marriage had broken up because of the Blonde's friends. Despite his appearance, Mr. Parker was apparently very strict about his wife's friends. Since December 1937 he had not seen or heard of his wife until he saw her picture in the papers at the time of the murder.

The mention of "murder" brought Mr. Veesey Blaize bouncing to his feet.

"M'lud," he said, "this is intolerable. I protest. The witness has just sought to poison the minds of the whole jury against my client. He has used a word that I could not bring myself to repeat in these circumstances."

Mr. Justice Plymme seemed pained. Badly pained. There had been no indication that he had even noticed that anything was amiss. But he immediately turned to the clerk.

"The objection is sustained," he said. "Pray see that the word 'murder' is erased from the evidence." Then he turned to Mr. Wassall. "Mr. Wassall, I must ask you to control your witness. This lapse has been deeply unfortunate."

Having spoken, he picked up his pencil and went on with what he had been doing. He was drawing cats and he was half-way through a large round tabby.

But Percy had scarcely noticed the interruption. The word

"murder" didn't seem to concern him in the least. What had happened to him was far more serious. He'd just had a whole part of his life shattered—shattered by the nasty piece of goods who looked like an Italian waiter. More than once, the Blonde had as good as hinted that she was married but she'd said that "he"—they'd never got as far as using his name—was something in the Indian Army, and had let her down. She'd said that she was from an army family herself and that her name was Evadne St. Claire. It may have been that she had thought that he doubted it, because she had shown him her initials in silver on a packet of mauve note paper as proof. But that wasn't all. Mr. Nosey Parker had suggested that the Blonde had been unfaithful. She might have been to him. But not to Percy. The Blonde was the sort of girl who would stand by any man who was ready to stand by her. Or at least he had thought of her that way. He'd never caught her out. And he didn't like to hear of her being spoken about like that. He'd been in love with the Blonde. If things had been different, he would have been in love with her still.

Mr. Veesey Blaize's temporary defeat of Mr. Wassall had no discernible effect on him. He continued just as he had done after the last interruption, in the same massive voice as before, only louder. He was booming right across the court when he called his next witness.

This time it was a rather shabby old lady who took the stand. She had been the Blonde's landlady. The Blonde had lodged there for about six months, she said. On at least two occasions, she declared, she had seen the prisoner go upstairs—her room was at the top of the house—with the Blonde. On the night when she didn't come home the old lady had sat up for her.

As Percy listened it all came back to him. He recalled now that he had once on the stairs met someone wearing a very dirty apron and carrying a pile of what might have been washing. But he hadn't taken much notice of her—the Blonde had simply said that she was "some old girl." And it surprised Percy that the old girl should have noticed him. But apparently everyone had noticed him. He must have been about the most conspicuous man in London, without knowing it. And what made the landlady's evidence so unreal and puzzling was that she kept on referring to the Blonde as "Miss Watson." At first Percy hadn't been quite sure whom she meant by it. But it turned out that Evadne, or Edith, or whatever her name was, had been using a nom-de-plume. But what was wrong with that? She was free to call herself whatever she wanted to, wasn't she?

He was still defending her in his own mind when to his astonishment he heard the judge saying that the court would be adjourned until to-morrow. Just like that. Adjourned, and he hadn't been given a chance to say a single word. He might just as well not have been there. The sheer injustice of it made him see red. He wanted to shout out things, and tell the judge what he thought of him. If They thought that They could treat him like that They'd very soon find out where They got off. He wasn't going to bring his harp to any party and then not have anybody ask him to play. . . .

His blood was right up when one of the two warders behind him tapped him on the arm and jerked his thumb over his shoulder to indicate that Percy was to follow. Percy got up and followed as obediently as a choirboy.

It seemed to Percy as the Black Maria took him back to the prison that he'd been sold a pup in Mr. Veesey Blaize. Only two interruptions in the whole day and letting that big battle-axe on the other side get away with everything. He supposed that it would be Mr. Veesey Blaize's day to-morrow.

It's a lovely day to-morrow, he said to himself over and over again as the car trundled back to Wandsworth.

4

So to-morrow had come. He hadn't slept much because of the sick, excited feeling in his stomach. That, and the dreams. He'd just been going round in circles all night. And now that he was awake and dressing, he realised that this was the day that he'd been looking forward to. He must have been balmy last night. This wasn't any sort of birthday party that he was going to. He wished that it was still yesterday.

And then he remembered the papers. They'd be something. He'd be headlines all right. Splashed right across the page. "BANDIT MURDERER" and all that sort of stuff. And he would be able to look out for bits of himself without being afraid of what he found. It was funny. The cold sweat of seeing something about It—how the police had got hold of a new clue, or how They expected to make an arrest shortly—all that was over now. He was quite calm inside himself. Had been ever since They'd showed their hand and run him in. No more worries about being picked up, simply because it had happened. It was as though from the moment when the inspector had slipped the handcuffs on him while he was still in a faint on the floor a deep new peace had descended on him. It was the waiting period that had been so killing.

When he'd done his hair and got his coat and tie on he went over to the door of the cell and rattled his fingers across the grille to call the warder. There wasn't any waiting because the man was only just outside.

"Gimme the daily papers," he said. "The whole lot o' 'em. I want 'em all. My s'lic'tor'll pay."

Then he went back and combed his hair again. He had to because he couldn't get the right sort of brilliantine, and he couldn't get the proper glossy finish. Even if Mr. Veesey Blaize didn't mind turning up in court looking as if he'd just had a night out, Percy did. And that was silly, wasn't it? Because a night out was the one thing that he couldn't have had at the moment.

The warder let him have the papers. Or at least all that he could get. There was a *Daily Mail*. And an *Express*. And a *Daily Mirror*. His hands were trembling as he reached out for them. And then . . . and then . . . and then—nothing. He wasn't on the front pages of even one of them. It was just war, war, war, war, wherever you looked.

He felt almost like crying as he put them down. It was all right keeping a stiff upper lip and that kind of thing. But there are limits to what anyone can stand. Especially without acknowledgment. It would have helped a lot to find that the papers were taking a decent interest in the case. A photograph, for instance, would have made him feel somebody. If you're a public figure, you can afford to take things on the chin.

Of course when he went through the papers thoroughly he was there all right. Quite nice little headings, in fact. *And* a photograph in one of them. It was only the placing, the sense of proportion that was wrong. Didn't news editors know that it was a strain having to stand up in court and fight for your life?

He was interrupted by the warder, who came in very officiously and told him that it was time to get cracking. Time to get cracking, indeed. He was ready to bet that they would be half an hour too early, same as yesterday. They seemed to think that he'd got nothing better to do than sit around with a policeman at each elbow until other people were ready.

But it wasn't only of himself that he was thinking on the ride to the Old Bailey. Or at least not directly. He was thinking of the war. It had all gone on over his head and he felt out of it. Of course he'd known it was coming. Some of his friends had been buying up good second-hand cars for more than a year now, getting ready for the day when there wouldn't be any more new ones and the prices would start rising. If only Percy had been outside he too could have done something to help his country. But it just hadn't worked out that way.

Naturally, when the trial was over he could look around. But by then all the fat would have gone. He'd have to content himself with the pickings. Unless conscription came along. He'd missed what they'd said in the papers about conscription. And he was worried. It wasn't going to be any fun for a man of his abilities to have to footslog it with a lot of rookies for a shilling a day. Then he remembered, and he gave a little laugh—on the ride down to the Old Bailey for the second day of his trial he gave a little laugh. He wouldn't have to do any footslogging. Not likely. He'd be at a premium. They'd be all over him. Skilled motor mechanic—he could choose his job just like peace-time. The R.A.F. couldn't have too many men like him.

The line of thought was attractive, and he pursued it. By the time the big blue gates had been opened and the van drew up in the closed concrete yard of the Old Bailey, he wasn't with them any more. He was miles away. Over Berlin. His bomber was caught in a searchlight beam and the guns were firing at him. But he wasn't worried. Not him. This was his sixtieth raid and he was bearing right down on his target ready to drop the secret bomb that he was trying out. Pushing the joystick forward he went into a shrieking power-dive . . .

"Come along there. Look lively," someone was saying to him. "Can't stand here all day."

Not that he need have hurried himself. Mr. Wassall was still fitting the bits together the way he liked them. And when he'd finished Mr. Veesey Blaize began tearing them apart again. Balmy, wasn't it? Because Mr. Veesey Blaize was there to prevent awkward questions.

But Mr. Wassall soon gave him something else to think about. This was the cross-examination party.

It had given Percy a funny feeling, taking the oath. Perhaps that's why They made you do it. To unnerve you. And when you were at the business end of Mr. Wassall it wasn't so nice. He had a cold, superior way with him as though he'd given up even trying to be a human being. He made it quite clear that hanging people was his job and he meant to get on with it.

At first he just asked a few general questions about how long Percy had known the Blonde and that sort of thing. And Percy told him the truth as well as he could remember. But it was difficult even in little things like this. He hadn't really got a head for dates and he'd never kept a diary. Then Mr. Wassall pulled a fast one on him when he wasn't expecting it.

Mr. Wassall: "Were you and this young lady intimate?"

Percy: "Fairly."

Mr. Wassall: "You understand what I mean by intimate?"

Well, everybody knew that, didn't they? You couldn't go to the films, or read a decent book, without knowing.

Percy: "Yus."

Mr. Wassall: "She was your mistress, in fact?"

Percy shook his head.

Percy: "No."

Mr. Wassall: "I will repeat my question. You have just admitted that there was intimacy between you and I asked if she was your mistress."

Percy looked across at Mr. Veesey Blaize. Why didn't he do something to earn his money? Percy certainly needed his help all right. He wasn't going to be trapped into saying that the Blonde had been his mistress. That'd be fatal. Everyone knew that mistresses always got murdered sooner or later. But how could he explain?

Percy: "No. She was just a friend. A close friend. I never paid her anything."

There was a noise behind him that sounded like a snigger, and Mr. Justice Plymme looked up. There was an expression of quite incredulous pain on his face. But it wasn't at Percy that he was looking. It was at a small woman in the front row of the public gallery. She was wearing a black hat with a feather peony in it.

Mr. Justice Plymme: "A murder trial is not a public performance conducted for the amusement of the public. I am not an actor and this court is not a theatre. If I hear any other unseemly noises I shall order the court to be cleared."

Well, that was that, and Connie got her handkerchief ready for future emergencies. She didn't want to be put out.

Mr. Wassall, meanwhile, was continuing. He was the only person who hadn't removed his eyes from Percy's face, and Percy felt uncomfortable under their stare.

Mr. Wassall: "I am not interested in your financial arrangements. I am interested only in the intimacy which you have admitted. Were you aware that this woman was going to bear a child?"

Percy put out his hands to catch hold of the front of the dock. He felt faint for a moment. They'd raised that stunner at the police court.

Percy: "No. She never told me."

Mr. Wassall: "Then this was information that you were expecting?"

Mr. Veesey Blaize was on his feet before Percy could reply. Evidently he had caught Percy's disapproving eye earlier.

Mr. Veesey Blaize: "M'lud," he exclaimed. "I protest. My learned friend is endeavouring to confuse my client. The prisoner has already told the court that he was no more than a close friend of the deceased. These insinuations can have only one purpose."

Mr. Justice Plymme, however, remained quite unmoved by this outburst. He disliked Mr. Veesey Blaize. Disliked him intensely. Had disliked him for years. Cut him quite deliberately in the corridors. And he wasn't going to have him behaving like a jack-in-the-box now.

Mr. Justice Plymme: "Mr. Blaize"—he knew that would annoy him, because the creature loved sounding as though he had been born double-barrelled—"these interruptions are most uncalled for. Mr. Wassall has been conducting his examination in accordance with the best traditions of this court. If it had been otherwise, I should have taken suitable action. Pray proceed, Mr. Wassall."

Mr. Wassall: "Were you or were you not the father of this woman's child?"

Percy: "No, I don't think so."

Mr. Wassall: "But come—you must know. I will repeat my question. 'Were you the father of this woman's child?' "

Percy: "No."

Why didn't Mr. Veesey Blaize help him? Was he afraid of the judge or something? Why didn't he show Mr. Wassall once and for all where he got off?

Mr. Wassall: "How long had there been intimacy between you?"

Percy: "I didn't keep any record. About a year, I reckon."

Mr. Wassall: "About a year. Then it is possible that she might have been about to bear your child?"

Percy: "It wouldn't have been likely."

Mr. Wassall: "I am not interested in what was likely. I said 'possible.' "

Percy: "But we were careful."

Mr. Wassall changed his stance. He caught hold of the two lapels of his coat in a sudden fury as though it were really Percy whom he wanted to seize. His voice was simply enormous now.

Mr. Wassall: "Will you answer my question? Is it possible that this woman was about to bear your child?"

Percy: "Yes, it's possible, I suppose."

Mr. Wassall: "Thank you."

Percy took out his handkerchief and passed it across his forehead. He was sweating. It wasn't easy having to answer a question like that in front of a lot of strangers. Whatever would they think of him? Mr. Wassall had made him blot his copybook all right.

He raised his eyes and took a look at Mr. Wassall. Funny that he didn't show signs of any strain. Less than half a minute ago he'd been bawling at the top of his voice, and there he was looking as though he was standing up in church all the time. But his next question was put in quite a gentle voice. Percy was relieved. He was—why not admit it?—a bit frightened of Mr. Wassall.

Mr. Wassall: "Were you and this woman planning to be married?"

Percy: "No. She said she was married already."

Mr. Wassall: "Did you ever discuss marriage?"

Percy: "No. We just saw each other."

Mr. Wassall: "And how many times did you see her?"

Percy: "I don't remember."

And even if he did remember, he wasn't going to say. Suppose his mother got hold of a paper, it'd break her heart to know what had been going on. He wasn't going to do that just to please Mr. Wassall. He hoped in any case that his mother wasn't well enough to read the papers. Hoped that she was worse, in fact.

Mr. Wassall: "Well, did you see her every day?"

Percy: "No."

Mr. Wassall: "Every other day?"

Percy: "No."

Mr. Wassall: "Well, let us say once or twice a week."

Percy: "Not so often."

Mr. Wassall: "Well, how often then?"

Percy: "More like once."

Mr. Wassall: "You saw her once a week."

Percy: "Not always. At least, that is lately, I'd given up seeing her."

He knew as soon as he'd said it that he'd made a mistake. He shouldn't have said that bit. It was simply playing Mr. Wassall's game. And was Mr. Wassall quick off his mark?

Mr. Wassall: "Why had you suddenly given up seeing this woman?"

Mr. Veesey Blaize jumped to his feet.

Mr. Veesey Blaize: "M'lud, my client did not say 'suddenly.' He merely said that he had given up seeing her."

Mr. Justice Plymme ignored Mr. Veesey Blaize altogether: he merely turned to his notes and addressed them in a quiet voice as though the two of them understood each other.

Mr. Justice Plymme: "At one time I saw her once a week. Lately I had given up seeing her. Those were the words."

Then he turned to Mr. Wassall.

Mr. Justice Plymme: "There has been no suggestion of suddenness that I am aware of. You may proceed, Mr. Wassall."

Mr. Wassall: "I will re-phrase my question, m'lud. Why did this intimacy cease?"

Percy: "I stopped going."

Mr. Wassall: "That is not an answer. I asked for the *reason*."

Percy knew that he'd asked; he'd heard him. But what could he say? He couldn't stand there and tell them about Doris, and about the other blonde at Victoria, because it would sound silly. More than that. It would make him seem a blooming Bluebeard. He wasn't going to have that happen.

Mr. Wassall: "I am still waiting for my answer. Shall I repeat my question?"

Percy: "I got tired of her."

Mr. Wassall: "You got tired of her. She may have been expecting your child but you got tired of her. And when did your tiredness as you call it make you give up seeing her?"

Percy: "About a month before."

Mr. Wassall: "About a month before what?"

Percy: "A month before she . . . died."

Mr. Wassall: "Had you seen her at all during that time?"

Percy: "Not until I met her in the public house."

He was getting confused. He couldn't help it. Mr. Wassall kept banging away with his questions and not giving him time to get his breath between answers. He was like some kind of a machine-gun. And what was worse he was off again already.

Mr. Wassall: "Did you meet her by arrangement?"

Percy: "No, it just happened."

Mr. Wassall: "How did it happen?"

Percy: "I went in to get a drink and she was in there so I went over to her."

Mr. Wassall: "But I understand that you were tired of her."

Percy: "So I was."

Mr. Wassall: "Then why did you join her?"

Percy: "She beckoned to me."

Mr. Wassall: "It didn't give you any particular pleasure seeing her?"

Percy: "No."

Mr. Wassall: "You would just as soon not have seen her?"

Percy: "It was all over and finished between us, like I said."

Mr. Wassall: "In fact her company meant nothing to you?"

There was a movement on the bench and Mr. Justice Plymme raised his small pink face from his writing-pad.

Mr. Justice Plymme: "I am frequently amazed by the number of questions which counsel feel it necessary to put in order to establish a quite simple point. To the best of his ability the prisoner has already told you that the meeting gave him no particular pleasure, that he would just as soon not have seen her and, to use his own expression, it was all over and finished between them. I can see no *progress* in your last question, Mr. Wassall."

It made Percy feel better hearing Mr. Justice Plymme say that. It showed that he was on his side. He wanted to thank him for it, and tried to give a smile in his direction. But Mr. Justice Plymme wasn't having any. He had dropped his head again and was again apparently disinterested in the whole case. But Mr. Wassall wasn't.

Mr. Wassall: "It is a point of the most critical importance, m'lud. That is why I wished to make so certain of it." (Turning to Percy.) "How long did you stay with her after Mr. Rawkins had left?"

Percy: "About half an hour."

Mr. Wassall: "Did you experience any rekindling of your emotions during that time? Did you, so to speak, fall in love with her again?"

Percy: "No."

Mr. Wassall: "Then why did you invite her to drive with you in the car in which she went to her death?"

Percy: "She asked me."

Mr. Wassall: "But couldn't you have refused?"

Percy: "It wouldn't have been polite."

Mr. Wassall: "You are quite sure she asked you?"

Percy: "Yes."

Mr. Wassall: "You didn't suggest it yourself?"

Percy: "No."

Mr. Wassall: "You are sure?"

Percy: "Quite sure."

Mr. Wassall: "I suggest that the invitation came entirely from you. That you proposed that ride for purposes of your own. That you, in fact, lured her into that car."

Mr. Wassall was at his biggest and most terrible as he said it. His voice swept over Percy like a tornado, stunning him. It was silly, he knew: but he felt frightened again. Properly frightened. He hadn't known that things were going to turn out this way. It seemed to have shaken Mr. Veesey Blaize as well. He was on his feet. "M'lud . . ." he began. But Mr. Justice Plymme motioned him to be quiet. Then he addressed himself direct to Percy. It was the first time he had looked full at Percy. And, when he looked, Percy wasn't so sure that he really was on his side after all. He didn't look like a real man. It was just a pair of old haddock's eyes that was peering out from underneath that wig.

Mr. Justice Plymme: "You must answer counsel's questions, you know. Would you like the last question to be repeated?"

Percy: "No, sir. I heard it."

Mr. Justice Plymme: "Then kindly reply."

Percy: "But it isn't true."

Mr. Justice Plymme: "Thank you."

Percy was all hot and sweaty now. He'd have liked a bitter, or a cup of tea, or something.

Mr. Wassall: "Where did the young lady wish to be taken?"

Percy: "Home."

Mr. Wassall: "And where was her home?"

Percy: "Kennington."

Mr. Wassall: "But across Putney Common isn't the quickest route to Kennington, is it?"

Percy: "No."

Mr. Wassall: "Then why did you want to prolong this ride with a young woman whom you were tired of?"

Percy: "I wanted to go the quiet way."

Mr. Wassall: "Ah. And what was your purpose in that?"

Percy: "So as not to be seen."

Mr. Wassall: "It was a foggy night, wasn't it?"

Percy: "Well, misty."

Mr. Wassall: "So whatever route you took, you were not likely to be seen. Even so, deliberately you took the loneliest . . ."

There were still the closing speeches. Mr. Wassall and Mr. Veesey Blaize both tried to score points off each other. That was where the really big stuff came in. It was as good as Marshall Hall after all. Only, by then, Mr. Josser felt sick and couldn't listen.

5

The summing-up was a real triumph. It was long—about forty-five minutes—and beautifully phrased. The *Law Quarterly* called it one of the most artistic and polished performances of Mr. Plymme's career. There was, indeed, a general opinion in legal circles that the whole case of Rex *v.* Percy Aloysius Boon would have been well worth it if only for the summing-up. When his Lordship had finished speaking there was that chastened and slightly embarrassed silence which succeeds the faultless demonstration that something which had appeared very complex and difficult is in reality quite uninvolved and easy.

Its effect was marred only by a foolish question from the little puddingy foreman of the jury. When Mr. Justice Plymme had finished speaking the foreman—he was a corn-chandler—rose respectfully and, after a false start, during which his voice was at first so faint that he couldn't be heard and then so loud that his Lordship drew back involuntarily, he said: "Suppose we decide that the prisoner killed her but didn't mean to, what verdict do we bring in then?"

This question, hesitantly put and indifferently uttered, brought forth the rebuke that was prominently reported in the papers next day.

Mr. Justice Plymme resumed his horn-rimmed spectacles and placed his porcelain-like hand over his little painted face. "There are occasions," he said in his smooth fluting voice, "when it seems impossible to impart information by word of mouth. Perhaps writing would be better: I do not know. The disappointing truth remains that the latter part of my summary was concerned exclusively with answering the very point that this gentleman has just put to me. At the cost of being repetitive in a case where so much has been repetitive already, I will elaborate what I have already said. To administer a blow in anger in a drawing-room may be only an act of common assault. To administer an exactly comparable blow upon a man standing at the top of Beachy Head may be murder. In the case which you have just heard the prisoner has admitted to striking on the head with a spanner his fellow passenger in a fast-moving car. As a result of the blow the passenger fell into the road and was killed either as a result of the blow or as a result of the fall or as a result of the shock caused by both these occurrences. You have heard the prisoner say that the blow was struck lightly. You have heard medical evidence to the contrary. You have heard the prisoner say that deprivation of ife did not enter his mind. You have heard evidence that the door of he car was faulty. You may therefore decide that the succession of vents was out of the prisoner's hands. Nevertheless it remains for ou to decide what set the succession of events in train. And if you lecide that the blow struck within the car, a blow struck by a spanner weighing $3\frac{1}{4}$ pounds, was the cause of the succession of events it vill be your duty to find the prisoner guilty of murder. If on the other hand you regard the delivery of the blow as purely accidental nd the fall from the car as a further accident, then you may rightly eturn a verdict of manslaughter."

Mr. Justice Plymme uncovered his face and fixed his eyes upon the orn-chandler.

"I trust," he said, "that I have succeeded in removing the perlexity which was in your mind."

The corn-chandler cleared his throat and tried to look as though e understood. He was rubbing the palms of his hands up and down iis waistcoat because he was sweating.

"May I ask another question, my lord?"

Mr. Justice Plymme inclined his head politely.

"What about a recommendation to mercy?" he asked.

Mr. Justice Plymme had expected that to be the question.

"All juries," he said straightaway, "appear to labour under the nisapprehension that they have been called to advise His Majesty's secretary of State for Home Affairs in the exercise of his duties. This s not so. Juries are summoned to listen to evidence and to give their verdict on it. Having given that verdict without thought or fear of he consequences their natural humanity may prompt them to utter plea for clemency. The law provides for that, and the plea is passed on to the Secretary of State—who I may add is perfectly capable of howing clemency even without the benefit of advice on that score. That is the right order of events. It is not only misleading but positively mischievous to talk of mercy before guilt has been proved and there can be any possible need for mercy."

Mr. Justice Plymme scrutinised the corn-chandler closely.

"I have made myself plain, I trust?"

"Perfectly, thank you, sir—my lord, I mean," the corn-chandler eplied, looking more mystified and abashed than ever.

"Then the court will adjourn while you consider your verdict," Mr. Justice Plymme announced.

And what about me? Percy was asking. Where do I come in? What do I get out of this? Why wasn't I allowed to speak? I could have told them. I could have put 'em straight. I could have cleared myself. And now what are they going to think of me? Why wasn't I allowed to speak? You can't call answering a lot of ruddy questions speaking. "How would he"—Percy was staring at the door through which the scarlet robes of Mr. Justice Plymme had just disappeared—"have liked it if I'd kept butting in when he was talking? Call this justice! What about me? Where do I come in?"

6

There was one piece of finesse in Mr. Justice Plymme's summing-up which escaped even the *Law Quarterly*. And that was the timing. Without hurrying himself or resorting to any unnecessary padding, Mr. Justice Plymme arrived at his conclusion at exactly five minutes to one—five minutes, that is, before his invariable lunch-hour. And in those five minutes he was able to answer the two foolish questions of the juryman. Punctually to one minute he seated himself at his table in the judge's room, poured himself out a glass of light claret and began dissecting the wing of cold chicken that he had ordered. Mr. Justice Plymme never ate red meat.

On the floor below, the jurymen were settling themselves down to something considerably more substantial. To-day's menu was steak-and-kidney pudding, boiled potatoes and cabbage, and an apple turnover. It was all brought over from a near-by restaurant. A waitress and a boy had made no fewer than three separate journeys with it all. Bottled beer arrived independently from the house opposite. And the jurors, all twelve of them, sat down to the food in a small room with a green dado and closed windows.

Because they were busy men, the jury wasted no time and discussed the case right through lunch. Not that there was very much to discuss. For outside the court, the foreman was a different human being altogether—dogmatic, obstinate and overbearing. He spoke as one who had lived practically all his life in law courts and knew the Criminal Evidence Act, 1898, by heart.

"It's as plain as a pikestaff," he said uncontradictably, pausing only when he actually wanted to swallow. "The judge said so himself. Either he killed her or he didn't, and if he killed her in those circumstances it's murder. Well, she's dead, isn't she? So far as I'm concerned that's all there is to it."

He had finished the steak-and-kidney pudding by now and looked up beamingly to see the effect of his logic. It seemed to have convinced ten of his companions but to have left the eleventh unnoved. A prim, stubborn little man with pince-nez glasses, the leventh evidently had humanitarian misgivings.

"It's a big responsibility," he said. "Suppose he didn't mean to do it."

"Then he shouldn't have tried," replied the foreman. "He ought o have thought of that before."

"But suppose he only meant to stun her?"

"If a person commits an act on another person," the foreman ntoned, "and if the person—the other person that is—dies because of what the first person has done to the other person then the first person, the person who started it all, is guilty."

He sat back, a smile on his face, pleased with his performance.

"That isn't what the judge said," the vague, wispish man complained.

"Then what did he say?" the corn-chandler demanded.

"He said only if the first person was standing on Beachy Head. He said he could hit the other person as hard as he liked in his own drawing-room and it would only be common assault. I heard him distinctly."

"Well, a moving car's the same thing."

"Same thing as what?"

"Same thing as Beachy Head."

"Who says so?"

The corn-chandler undid his waistcoat and cleared a little space on the table in front of him. He gave a little cough.

"Don't let's fall out about small things," he said in a quieter, more engaging tone. "Cases like this sometimes go on for weeks and weeks if that happens. Locked up in here until it's over. Let's be reasonable men."

"That's what I am being," the wispish man interrupted him. "You said a car was the same thing . . ."

"Please!" The foreman lifted his hand and cleared his throat again. "It's not our job to find fault with each other. It's our job to find the prisoner guilty. Now did he do it? Hands up those who say 'yes.'"

Eight hands went up. Then nine. Then, very flutteringly, a tenth. Only the little wispish man remained as he was.

The foreman looked at him fiercely.

"Well, did he?"

"Did he do what?"

"Kill her."

"That's what I'm not sure about."

The foreman put down his spoon and fork and sat back in his chair.

"Would anyone else like to be foreman?" he asked.

No one, not even the vague, wispish man, volunteered.

"No, you just go on as you are," he said. "It's your job to convince us."

"Well, would the young lady be alive to-day if he hadn't hit her on the head?" the foreman enquired.

The vague, wispish man pondered.

"Perhaps she was attacking him," he suggested. "Perhaps it was self-defence. You can't call self-defence murder."

"Nobody's said anything about self-defence," the foreman retorted.

"Yes, they have," the vague, wispish man replied.

"Who?"

"Me."

"We're not here to discuss what you said; we're here to discuss what the judge said."

"It isn't the judge we're trying."

"And it isn't you either."

It was generally felt that the foreman had scored a victory this time. And what was more the other ten were growing a littled tired of the vague, wispish juror. He was prolonging things and raising difficulties—a kind of born unleader of men.

"Tell us again what the judge said," he challenged the foreman.

"If there are two people and one of them does something . . ."

"Which one?" the vague, wispish one asked.

"Either one," the foreman replied. "And because of what he does the other one dies, it's murder."

"What about soldiers and surgeons?" the vague, wispish man asked. "They kill people and nobody calls them murderers."

But that was too much. The vague, wispish man had betrayed himself. He was a crank. And, from then on, the foreman had everything his own way. As soon as the vague, wispish man opened his mouth to raise further objections there was somebody to stop him.

"Then we're agreed, are we?" asked the foreman at last. It was a quarter-past three already and he was feeling tired. "Hands up those who say 'yes.' "

"Not if he's going to be hanged, we're not. Or at least I'm not." It was the eleventh hand—the fluttering one—that had spoken.

The foreman squared his shoulders and glared at his fellow juror.

"So far as I'm aware, the Secretary of State doesn't need any advice on inclemency from us. That's not what we're here for. As soon as I see all hands go up we'll talk about mercy. Not before. Now, is the prisoner guilty? Just that, leaving out being hanged for the moment."

Eleven hands went up, and the foreman began rubbing his own together.

"That's fine," he said. "Capital. And now what about a recommendation to mercy? How about it?"

Eleven hands went up again.

"A strong one," suggested the vague, wispish man who felt that somehow he had been coerced into departing from his principles.

"Hear! Hear!" replied the woman juror.

"Well, that's that," said the corn-chandler. "Guilty. With a strong recommendation to mercy. It couldn't have been anything else in the circumstances."

7

Mr. Justice Plymme was dozing in his chair when his clerk knocked on the door to say that the jury had considered their verdict and were ready. He kept the man waiting while he sat up and straightened his tie.

He was almost pathetically tiny and frail as he stood up in his dark lounge suit, waiting to be robed. His face under the curling silver hair was like that of a small, tired child. The clerk removed the scarlet robe from its hanger in the corner cupboard and held it ready for him. Mr. Justice Plymme vanished into it. Then the starched cravat was produced and placed round his neck. Finally, the horse-hair wig was taken off its block on the writing-desk and, as it was lowered on to his head, the miracle was complete. The little old man was a judge again.

During all this time he had not stirred. Or spoken. The real trouble was that he was not yet properly awake. At least, only half awake. It was a disability which had been growing on him lately—this failure to spring immediately to life when roused. Even in his procession to the court he was still sleep-walking. He mounted the bench, still in the same half-dazed, half-awake condition, and folded his hands in front of him as though praying. Already the clerk of the court was addressing the foreman of the jury. The foreman was standing politely to attention, holding his lapels.

"Do you find the accused guilty or not guilty?" the clerk asked.

The reply was exactly what Mr. Justice Plymme had expected. So exactly, in fact, that his hand was already reaching out instinctively for the small square of black cloth that lay there ready.

"This," he reflected sadly, thinking how old it made him, "is the twenty-seventh time I have done this thing. Here and at Assizes. Twenty-seven times. No wonder the strain is telling on me. . . ."

The clerk turned towards Percy.

"Prisoner at the bar," he asked, "have you anything to say why the Court should not give you judgment according to law?"

So it had come—Percy's big moment. But he wasn't up to it. Simply wasn't up to it. He gave a gulp almost as though he were about to cry.

"Only that I'm innocent. I never meant to."

That also was exactly what Mr. Justice Plymme had expected him to say. Really one murder trial was very like another. He placed the black cap carefully on his head and adjusted it. And as he did so he became grim and terrible for all his pink-and-whiteness.

"You have been found guilty of that crime for which the law appoints one sentence and one sentence only. It is that sentence which I now pronounce upon you. The sentence of the Court upon you is, that you be taken from this place to a lawful prison and thence to a place of execution, and that you be there hanged by the neck until you be dead; and that your body be afterwards buried within the precincts of the prison in which you shall have been confined before your execution. And may the Lord have mercy on your soul."

Then Mr. Justice Plymme removed his black cap and turned towards the jury.

"Gentlemen, I thank you," he said, almost as if he were apologising. "You are exempt from jury service for ten years."

8

But what about Percy? What about him? Hasn't he got any feelings in the matter? Doesn't he count for anything any more?

Oh, yes, he's still the centre of attention in the prisoners' room behind the court. He's a very special person now and they're taking every care of him. Mr. Barks is allowed to see him, but only in the presence of two warders. Percy might be royalty from the way they're guarding him.

Mr. Barks is somehow not quite the same aggressive, cocksure Mr. Barks who came into the court yesterday morning. He looks tired. Even his dapper bow-tie is drooping. Altogether his appearance does credit to his feelings. But appearances after all can be most deceptive. Actually, he is thinking of Mr. Veesey Blaize, and wondering if he realises that professionally he is finished. Thinking of Mr.

Veesey Blaize's failure and his own arrears of County Court work. Nice steady profitable work with no fireworks. Five cases a morning and three more in the afternoon. No wonder that Mr. Barks looks worn.

But Percy is still too much dazed to notice how he looks. Too dazed, and too angry. He feels that, somehow or other, he has been tricked. Tricked by Mr. Barks and by Mr. Veesey Blaize and by Mr. Wassall and by the judge. And, going further back, tricked by Them in general and by the plain-clothes lodger in particular. At the present moment, he sees himself at the end, the very end, of a long road of deception and double-dealing. It was for stealing a car that They first had him, wasn't it? And look at him now. Where is he?

It was the judge in particular who was against him. He could see that now. And he understood why Mr. Justice Plymme had avoided his eye when he had tried to smile across at him.

Not that this was going to be the end of it. Not by a long chalk. He was going to get even with him somehow. It wouldn't be easy, shut up inside like he was. But he'd do it. He'd get Mr. Barks and Mr. Veesey Blaize to complain to the chief magistrate. He'd get even with him somehow. Then just as he has clenched his fists from thinking about it, he bursts out crying.

"I didn't mean to kill her," he bursts out. "I swear I didn't. Why won't they believe me? Why won't they?"

One of the warders tells him to take things easy, and Mr. Barks looks uncomfortable again.

Then a new fear—only it's the old fear, really, all polished and brought up to date—suddenly strikes him.

"They aren't going to . . . to . . ."—the word is slurred over because he is crying so much—"for something I didn't mean, are They?"

Mr. Barks begins fumbling with his brief-case.

"This is only the first stage," he says. "Court of Criminal Appeal comes next. Very important. Fix up early conference with Mr. Veesey Blaize. Clear case of misdirection. Be hearing from me."

"You mean it'll be all right?" Percy asks.

"Strong case," Mr. Barks answers. "Very strong case. Jury prejudiced. Talk all about that later."

With that, Mr. Barks leaves him. But those last few minutes have been as good as a tonic to Percy. He takes out his pocket comb and runs it through his hair. He isn't such a fool as They took him for.

He knows what's what. He'd spotted straightaway that the judge wasn't being fair, hadn't he?

Then one of the warders touches him on the shoulder and Percy follows him.

CHAPTER 51

I

On the evening of the verdict it was a very subdued household that reassembled in Dulcimer Street. If the verdict had been anything else—say manslaughter, for instance—they would probably have foregathered and all gone home together. All except Mr. Puddy, that is: he would anyhow have had to go off to take care of that warehouse of his.

But, as it was, they separated immediately and by instinct. Mrs. Josser took Mr. Josser's arm and allowed herself to be led away from the court weeping. Mrs. Vizzard, who felt faint, had to stay behind for a few minutes drinking water out of a thick glass that the usher brought her; and Mr. Squales remained with her holding her hand and wondering how much longer he could manage without a cigarette. Connie, revolt and *lèse-majesté* seething inside her, went across the road and had a couple.

The Jossers made a particularly sad and broken couple. They didn't say very much. Practically the whole of their conversation was a remark of Mr. Josser's that he made over and over again for no reason except that he couldn't stay silent for ever.

"This is terrible, Mother," he repeated. "We've got to do something."

And whether because of this so frequent reminder, or whether because of its futility, Mrs. Josser went to pieces as soon as she got home. She had to be put to bed, and Mr. Josser gloomily prepared a makeshift sort of meal on a tray. They shared it together in the bedroom, Mr. Josser still remarking at intervals that it was terrible and that they'd got to do something. He didn't add what, because he didn't know.

Then Mrs. Josser spoke. The hot tea had brought her round a bit and the practical side of her nature had risen to the top once more.

"I didn't ought to be here," she said suddenly. "I ought to be round at the infirmary. Someone's got to tell Clarice."

Mr. Josser admired his wife for that remark. It wasn't a pleasant duty that she was suggesting. And he acknowledged that there was no one better to perform it. Nevertheless he resisted it.

"You don't go there to-night," he told her. "You're in no fit state." Then, as an afterthought, he added, "It's Mr. Barks's place really. He's the solicitor."

But that last remark was wrong for a woman of Mrs. Josser's disposition.

"If I thought that she'd hear of it through that man," she replied, "I'd get out of this bed here and now."

"That's all right," Mr. Josser answered soothingly. "He won't do anything to-night."

"He might write," Mrs. Josser pointed out.

"Not him," said Mr. Josser. "He's far too busy appealing."

But Mrs. Josser was not interested in the Law. A woman, her interests lay exclusively among mankind.

"It'd almost be better," she said at length, "if she didn't live to see it."

Mr. Josser shook his head gravely.

"This is terrible, Mother," he said. "We've got to do something." He paused. "It's just as well they didn't send her away, isn't it? Then you couldn't have seen her so easy."

2

They wouldn't let Mrs. Josser in at first because Friday morning wasn't a regular visiting-time. Mysteries apparently took place in the mornings which the uninitiated were not supposed to witness. And even when the Sister heard the object of Mrs. Josser's visit, she wasn't by any means persuaded that it was a good thing at all. She behaved as though by keeping this distressed agitated woman away from the quiet afflicted one she was somehow performing an act of kindness and compassion. Then Mrs. Josser said tartly that in any case the solicitor would be writing, and it would be worse that way. So the Sister let her in. But still disapprovingly.

"It's a great pity this," she said disapprovingly. "It may set her back again."

Set her back again: Mrs. Josser's heart sank at the words. They could mean only one thing—that Mrs. Boon was recovering. Any hope of a quiet release from it all was apparently being denied to her. And, when she got to the bedside, Mrs. Josser found that she was right. Mrs. Boon was obstinately and astonishingly better. She was sitting up a little and had seen Mrs. Josser from the far end of the ward.

"Is there any news?" she asked even before Mrs. Josser had pulled the chair up beside the bed.

"Now you've got to be calm and hear me out," Mrs. Josser told her, her own voice trembling. "The trial's all over now, but there's still the appeal. Mr. Barks is going to see about that straightaway. He'd have come himself—I know he would—only he's so busy arranging things."

She paused and caught the Sister's eye. Under that grotesque black and white head-dress with the starched, side-pieces like a horse's blinkers, anything might have been going on. But, outwardly, the Sister looked quite unmoved. She seemed to belong to a world from which emotion in its cruder forms had been excluded. Mrs. Josser was the only one who was showing any signs of disquietude. Mrs. Boon herself was simply lying back again, eyeing her. Then she spoke.

"You mean they found him guilty?" she asked.

Mrs. Josser nodded.

"The jury made a special recommendation," she added.

But, being a woman herself, Mrs. Boon like Mrs. Josser was interested only in flesh and blood.

"Was he brave?" she asked.

"Very," Mrs. Josser answered. "He just stood there at attention like a soldier."

"Ah!" Mrs. Boon actually smiled. "That's like my Percy," she said. "Always brave."

"Don't tire yourself too much, Mrs. Boon," the Sister interrupted placidly. "Remember what the doctor said."

"I'll remember," Mrs. Boon promised. Then she turned to Mrs. Josser. "Don't *you* worry too much," she said. "He'll be all right. We're all praying for him."

Out of the corner of her eye, Mrs. Josser saw the Sister cross herself. The sight moved and disturbed her. She realised that she resented it. And not only the sign of the cross. Resented the fact that after tearing half-way across London in time to arrive at Walham Green at nine-thirty on an errand of mercy she should be the one who was being comforted. It was as though in a world of terror and anticipation these two women had discovered some special secret composure of which she knew nothing.

There was a pause. Mrs. Boon seemed to be very far away, her eyes staring out over the bed-rail into space which extended far beyond the buff-distempered wall with the brightly-coloured crucifix on it.

Then she turned to Mrs. Josser again.

"Was he wearing the rosary I sent him?" she asked.

Mrs. Josser drew in her lips.

"I couldn't see," she said. "I wasn't near enough."

For the first time, Mrs. Boon seemed to experience some real alarm. She clasped her hands together.

"You're sure Mr. Josser gave it to him?" she asked, craning forward. "You don't think that he might have forgotten it?"

"If Fred said he'd do something," Mrs. Josser answered loyally, "you can be sure of him."

"Ah," said Mrs. Boon for the second time. And a smile, a pale watery smile—but a smile nevertheless—broke out on her face again. "Then he'll be wearing it all right."

Her immediate anxiety removed, Mrs. Boon lay back against the pillows. She closed her eyes, and the Sister gave a little nod to Mrs. Josser.

"That must be all for now," she said. "We mustn't overtire her."

To Mrs. Josser's ears there was just a trace of rebuke in the words. But she got up obediently and put the chair back against the wall.

"Thank you very much for coming," Mrs. Boon was saying. "Thank you for telling me."

Mrs. Josser and the Sister walked back down the long corridor without speaking, but when they came to the head of the stairs the Sister turned to her.

"Next time you come," she said, "can you bring a dressing-gown and slippers? The doctor may be letting her up for a little."

3

Mr. Puddy was fed-up, properly fed-up.

And no wonder. They'd been messing his job about. Nothing less than a revolution, in fact, was taking place in his profession. And by the time it was over and the shouting had died down again, it looked as though everything that had attracted him to such a calling—the quiet life, the regular meals, the absence of bustle, the absolute nothingness of it—would have gone for ever. As Mr. Puddy, in his caretaker's basement, ponderously bent over the two printed handbooks and three roneo-ed sheets issued by the Ministry of Home Security, he felt himself a stranger in his own house; a would-be *émigré* with nowhere else to go.

And all on account of stirrup-pumps. It was easy enough for a man of Mr. Puddy's sober discernment to detect—reading between the lines, of course—that the Government was in a state of panic. And Mr. Morrison in particular had evidently allowed himself to get into a shocking state of jitters about fires. If he hadn't, he would simply have done the calm and dignified thing and said: "In case of emergency, lift the receiver and ask for Fire." He could have left it at that, couldn't he? What was wrong, Mr. Puddy wanted to know, with the blue coats and brass helmets of the London Fire Brigade? Did Mr. Morrison know something that he wasn't saying?

And there was another thing. Mr. Puddy wasn't the build for stirrup-pumps. To keep the plunger going up and down as though pumping up a punctured bicycle tyre called for a shorter and a slimmer man. He wondered bitterly whether anyone in the Government had actually tried to work a stirrup-pump before ordering them in such colossal quantities. Winston, for example. Or Mr. Bevin. He would have liked to have seen either of them after the instruction meeting that he'd just been to. Pumping with one hand and directing the jet with the other. It wasn't dignified.

And stirrup-pumps were only the beginning. There was sand, for instance. The otherwise tidy yard of the United Empire Tea Co. now looked like some kind of a blooming children's play-park. You couldn't even get away from the stuff by coming indoors. There were buckets of it on every landing, alongside the buckets of water that had always been there.

Nor did the Government panic stop at sand. There was sillier still in store. Like special shovels on the end of long brown handles so that you could scoop up the incendiaries as they came down and carry them away to the nearest horse-trough, or the Thames, or anywhere else that looked wet enough. An acquaintance of Mr. Puddy's in the same line of business had been issued with a pair of asbestos-covered tongs. . . .

Mr. Puddy turned back to the instructions par. 3, sub-section 2a:

"*If the incendiary has fallen but has not yet ignited, keep the bomb covered by a fine spray. (For sand, Application of, see Sub-section* 3.) *If the bomb has ignited, press the adjusting switch on the nozzle of the pump over to the right and direct the jet on to the blaze. IN NO CIRCUMSTANCES direct a JET of water on to an unignited bomb.*"

There was more of it overleaf. Another three-quarters of a page of closely typed instructions. There were even drawings of three different types of incendiaries, and a picture of a stirrup-pump with the various parts rather obviously named "HANDLE," "HOSE," "PLUNGER," "NOZZLE" and so on.

Mr. Puddy could see that they'd tried their hardest to explain the thing. But it was no use. He couldn't concentrate because he was hungry. Putting down the leaflet, Mr. Puddy went over to his coat pocket and took out a grease-proof packet containing half a pound of liver sausage.

He pressed his thumb into the middle of it, momentarily screwing up his eyes in suspense as he did so. But it was all right: it gave. Liver sausage was funny stuff. Before now, he'd known it dry up while it was just lying there on the plate waiting for him to get round to it.

CHAPTER 52

It was because of a letter from Mrs. Boon that Mr. Josser was there in Mr. Barks's office. The letter had arrived only that morning. And its urgency was obvious. It must have been written immediately after Mrs. Josser had left.

The Jossers had been discussing the contents all through breakfast, passing the single sheet of notepaper backwards and forwards across the table between them. Not that it wasn't clear enough. It was crystal-clear and pathetic. It said—not in Mrs. Boon's handwriting because she still couldn't write, but in one of the Sisters'—that if the appeal was going to cost extra, would Mr. Josser please arrange with Mr. Barks to auction the furniture and use the proceeds. It was the last paragraph that brought a lump into Mr. Josser's throat.

"*It'll be a shame all those nice things going,*" she wrote, "*and I'm glad that I shan't be there to see them go. Please don't tell Percy, as it would only worry him. It won't matter really because we shall soon be able to get a home going again when we're together once more. But please specially don't say anything to Percy at the moment.*" The last sentence was even underlined.

The peculiar pathos of the letter left Mr. Barks unmoved, however. And Mr. Josser respected him for it. After all, it was only right that he should be giving the whole of his mind to the legal aspects. Nevertheless, it did seem to Mr. Josser just a little unfeeling, especially when it was a friend of the family that he was speaking to, when Mr. Barks dismissed the whole scheme as inadequate.

"What is it?" he asked. "Just three rooms. Two bed and a living. Bedrooms don't fetch anything. Say twenty pounds the two. Living-room another ten. Thirty pounds. What's the use of that?"

"Are appeals *very* expensive?" Mr. Josser asked.

"Depends who you get. Someone like Veesey Blaize'd charge another hundred and fifty. No use skimping. Simply lose appeal."

"Don't . . . don't you think Mr. Blaize might be willing to do it for a little less because of the way it . . . it turned out?" Mr. Josser asked diffidently.

But Mr. Barks only shook his head.

"Wouldn't hear of it," he said. "Probably forgotten the case by now. Very busy man, Veesey Blaize."

"Couldn't you ask him?" Mr. Josser persisted. "Couldn't you put it to him that Mrs. Boon is very ill? It means a lot to her, you know."

Mr. Barks shook his head again.

"Means a lot to everyone," he said. "Means a lot to the prisoner. Means a lot to me. Very bad impression to lose a case. Means a lot to Mr. Veesey Blaize. Won't do his name any good if he can't appeal. But no funds, no appeal. Most unfair to Mr. Veesey Blaize."

"Mightn't there be someone else who's cheaper?" Mr. Josser enquired diffidently.

But Mr. Barks did not take the suggestion in good part.

"Change horses in mid-stream?" he asked. "Throw Mr. Veesey Blaize over half-way through? Very bad business. Very bad business indeed." He paused. "Do it if you want to," he said. "No one to stop you. Find some junior probably. May be someone good. May not. Can't say. Taking big risk. May lose appeal."

Mr. Josser sat rebuked, his hands clasped on the handle of his umbrella. The office was close and stuffy, and he felt helpless. Also trapped. It may have been the effect of the black gauze stretched tightly across the lower half of the windows, or the double lock on both the doors, or the massive hinges of the black Chubb safe in the corner. Whatever it was Mr. Josser suddenly found himself inwardly struggling to escape.

But it wasn't as easy as that. He couldn't back out now. Why couldn't he? He didn't know. He just couldn't.

And to his own amazement he heard himself asking the old fatal question.

"How . . . how much do you need?" he asked.

Mr. Barks took out his gold Eversharp and began making some marks on his blotting-pad.

"One-day affair," he said, thinking aloud. "Quite short really. Say seventy-five for Mr. Veesey Blaize and the junior. Then my fees on top. Lot of work in appeal. May be another seventy-five."

"A hundred and fifty!"

Mr. Josser had spoken the words aloud.

"Near as I can say," Mr. Barks told him. "Haven't asked Veesey Blaize yet."

There was a pause. Mr. Josser's hands were damp inside.

"I'll go up to a hundred," he said.

"And the thirty from the furniture?" Mr. Barks enquired.

"No," Mr. Josser replied firmly. "Just the hundred. The furniture's stopping where it is."

Mr. Barks contemplated his gold pencil.

"Probably no use," he answered. "Cutting things too fine. But we'll see. We'll see what we can do."

And without looking up again he began making crosses and underlinings on the dossier of papers that were on the desk in front of him.

"I'll guarantee up to a hundred." Mr. Josser was still repeating the words to himself as he came away. That meant two hundred in all. And that, in turn, meant that three hundred pounds was all that he and Mrs. Josser had in their old age between them and starvation.

CHAPTER 53

I

Bill had passed his Finals. Astonishingly, had passed them. And the rest had been his idea entirely.

It was simply that a notice had been stuck up on the green baize board in the Common-room saying that qualified doctors were wanted in His Majesty's Forces, and Bill had written offering himself. Not that there was anything unusual in that. For weeks now he had been answering every advertisement he had seen—*locum tenens*, large panel practice in Wood Green; house physician, Stoke-on-Trent Infirmary; anæsthetist, City Dental Hospital: child specialist (vacancy open to a woman), somewhere or other in the Midlands. And one after another they had turned him down. Or rather ignored him. A polite post card from Stoke-on-Trent was all that he had to show for his trouble. And, for the first week, the Army behaved in much the same way. Indeed, by the time he had heard from them, he had already written off to a fever and isolation hospital where a knowledge of tropical diseases was essential.

Then a letter arrived on inferior official stationery asking him to present himself immediately to an address in Victoria. There was something rather flattering about the "immediately." He had understood, from one or two other men who had tried, that this looked like being a pretty difficult war to get into. And it seemed now that he was as good as in it already.

All the same, there was the hospital to be considered. They were paying him £60 a year, and they naturally expected to get their money's worth. He had to fix things up with the resident so that he could skip over to Victoria in the afternoon. And all the morning he kept telling himself that probably the job would be gone by then.

When he arrived it wasn't quite what he had expected. The War Office doesn't waste a lot of money in making its servants comfortable. There is a kind of battlefield severity about everything. In an upstairs room that looked as though it had recently been used for storing things, a major was sitting on a folding chair at a trestle table. There was a makeshift look about the set-up, rather as though the war had caught the Army unawares. The whole place might have been a parliamentary agent's office at some scrap by-election. The major was filling up buff forms with a nib mounted in an unpolished halfpenny penholder. The ink-well was an ordinary bottle with a cork.

He brightened up, however, as Bill entered, almost as if Bill had been his first customer that day. And, for a moment, Bill had misgivings. Perhaps the others had been making a few enquiries before applying. But since he was here, he answered all the questions on the form which the major gave him—whether his parents were both British, where he was born and what his qualifications were. He wrote in "M.B." and "B.Ch." with a flourish, filling in the date when he had qualified a bit smaller—because he didn't want to look too much as if he were rushing things. Then the major told him where to go for his medical examination, asked him whether he'd like to go out East, and shook him warmly by the hand.

The medical examination—also in hospital time—was nothing. Standing stripped, he looked like a prize-fighter. The little doctor who went over him had to stretch up on tiptoe to do so. He had as a matter of fact lost interest right from the start when he found that Bill played rugger.

It was nearly a fortnight after that when Bill received another letter, still on the same inferior stationery. And this one was even more surprising. It told him in rather cold, formal language that he had been granted a commission in the Royal Army Medical Corps, and it enclosed a further batch of forms for him to fill in. Between these forms and the earlier ones, however, there was a subtle but discernible difference. The first batch had been designed to catch him, whereas this lot made it apparent that now he had agreed to come in, had gone too far in fact to be able to back out again, the Army had cooled off a bit. They were full of safeguards, all on the Army's side, just to make sure that they hadn't landed themselves with a dud. The covering letter gave him advice about buying his uniform and told him where to present himself at Sandhurst for an officer's training.

They didn't give him much time and there was a somewhat peremptory ring to the wording.

He hadn't wanted to worry Doris while the whole thing was still in the air. But this looked definite enough. He supposed now that he would have to tell her, and he wondered how she was going to take it.

2

What really mattered, however, was what Mrs. Josser was going to say. And she did not try to disguise her feelings. She was all in favour. But, then, she was prejudiced. With the possibility of Ted's conscription, it seemed unthinkable that any living male should remain. Besides, it wasn't as though—unlike Ted—he had got anything to keep him. There was no job worthy of being called one; no immediate prospects so far as she could see; and, thank God, no wife and family. It was really the fact of Bill's wifelessness that pleased her most. She saw, in this, evidence of her own peculiar wisdom. She had, in short, stopped Doris doing something silly.

And she almost lost her temper when Doris said that she didn't want Bill to go. It would do Bill good, she insisted: it would be the making of him.

Mr. Josser, however, was very nice and understanding about it when he got Doris to himself for a few minutes.

"It's just one of those things that had to happen," he explained. "If he hadn't volunteered now he'd have been sent for in a few months' time. They'll be wanting all the doctors they can get, especially the young ones. As it is, he's gone in on his own terms and that always counts double."

The Davenports on the other hand sided heavily with Doris. Dr. Davenport wrote Bill a long, rambling letter asking him what was going to happen about his Fellowship now; and Mrs. Davenport was so convinced that he was going to be killed straightaway that she could not get further than repeating over and over again that he was her only son and that it was his duty to take care of himself.

The one point on which Mrs. Josser and the Davenports were absolutely agreed was that it was a good thing that Bill and Doris were only engaged and not actually married.

3

Doris took a day from the office, to help Bill buy his uniform. She didn't tell Mrs. Josser anything about it. So far as No. 10 Dulcimer Street was concerned, she left at the usual time. But instead of keeping on the tram as far as the Temple, she got off at Charing Cross and made her way to the hospital.

She found Bill in an engrossed, preoccupied state of mind. He was studying a long roneo-ed list and ticking off such items as "Sam Browne, 1"; "Toilet case, 1"; "Steel mirror, 1"; "Khaki socks, 4 pairs"; "Revolver, 1." There was something strangely medieval about the whole business. Because he was an officer and a gentleman, the Army was providing him with absolutely nothing. It expected him to present himself to his monarch fully equipped for the battle-field, and ready to die in his own clothes. Admittedly, there was the grant. But this, too, had a medieval flavour to it. The thought was kindly, but the amount was not enough. If any officer had presented himself on parade without his socks and forage cap, not to mention things like a swagger cane and kid gloves, the Army would have had only itself to blame for it.

It was Moss Bros. they went to. And Moss Bros. have been in the game for a long time. There is nothing about army etiquette that is not known to the brothers Moss and their descendants. In war-time the shop is practically a government department. Without it, the quartermaster-general wouldn't be able to equip an army in time. As it is, you can rush in at one door, a civilian, and come out of the other, fitted up with a uniform and knee-boots and a pith helmet and a safari collapsible bath and an aluminium water-purifier, a complete soldier, in fact, all within half an hour.

It took Bill rather longer because Doris was with him. She wouldn't let him have the first thing the assistant showed him, even though it seemed all right to Bill. She made the little assistant go backwards and forwards with his arms full of jackets and khaki pullovers and greatcoats. And she made Bill stand up properly and not sag from the shoulders in the way he generally did. If he had to be a soldier at all, she was determined that he should be the neatest, most immaculate modern man-of-war, one pip up, who had ever presented himself at the gates of Sandhurst.

While they were still there another officer recruit arrived. Aged apparently about sixteen, and as innocent-looking as a choirboy, he came in with a large, masterful lady—obviously his mother—and asked nervously if he could look at uniforms. On the whole, the mother seemed the more promising officer material. She might have been playing the Spirit of Knightsbridge in a civic pageant. Doris looked from Bill to the choirboy and back to Bill again. It was going to be a queer war before it was over.

But for some reason or other, the fun of buying uniforms had ended abruptly. They had left Moss Bros. and walked along together arm-in-arm. It was a part of London where the buildings were uniformly dingy and the streets were uniformly full of odds and ends from Covent Garden Market—old sacks, and banana ends and cabbage stalks. She felt dingy, too. Quite suddenly she disliked everything to do with military uniforms—their silly little bits and pieces, the trousers without turn-ups, the sparkling buttons, the catches for the belt—everything.

She simply wanted Bill to go on sagging about in an old sports coat and a pair of flannels for ever.

CHAPTER 54

In the end, when he had heard nothing, it was Mr. Squales who wrote to Mrs. Jan Byl suggesting that he should go down to the country to visit her. He spent a lot of time on the letter, even making a few rough notes on the backs of old envelopes. After all, it was an important letter. A large part—remembering Mocking Bear's inaccurate predictions, possibly the *only* part—of his professional future lay in that direction. That was why he had to be so deucedly careful. One false sentence and he might as well have saved the stamp.

He felt better once he'd actually put the letter into the pillar-box. There was a kind of cheering magic to it, like a bet on long odds or the promise of an engagement. And it went deeper than that. It kindled something right down inside him. Because he was naturally a profound and psychological sort of chap he went on thinking about it. And in the end he saw it all quite clearly. It was only natural really. It was because his fiery independence, that had been damped down lately, was now blazing up again. Some men would have been ready to batten on a woman's love and lose themselves with it. But not, he thanked God, this one. No, he was a doer, not a done-by. He was, he supposed, really more of the Leader Type.

Mrs. Vizzard noticed at once that his high spirits had returned. And she was glad of them. For the last two or three days he had been moody, aloof, preoccupied, and she had been worried about him. But this was the original Enrico Qualito with whom she had fallen in love. He took her hand in his and kissed it before he kissed the face that was put up for him, and his conversation had the whimsical lift to it that she found so adorable.

"Was my little kitten really so worried," he asked her teasingly, "because her big strong man went out for a walk without her? Did she think that he was never coming back?"

Adorable. But, at the same time, frightening. And even sinister. She enjoyed the teasing—Mr. Vizzard, the departed, had never been a teaser—but it was the subtlety of it that alarmed her. It was almost as though Mr. Squales had guessed where her deep fears lay.

But, for the sake of the long delicious evening that stretched ahead of them, she concealed her feelings. The weekly copy of *The Spirit World* lay on the occasional table and perhaps later Mr. Squales would read her extracts from the letter-column. They were wonderful letters—full of glimpses through the veil, and teleportations and proofs of survival—and read in Mr. Squales's rich baritone they were like listening to a *vox humana* that could actually pronounce words.

But before the letters, there was the Guinness. Twelve small dark bottles of the stuff were ranged along the wall of the pantry outside. It had been Mr. Squales's idea, the Guinness. Mrs. Vizzard herself was a teetotaller, an abstainer, almost a Rechabite. Or, at least, had been until a month ago. Then Mr. Squales—practically a Rechabite himself, he had told her—had become worried about her. It was her paleness in particular that was distressing to him. He had thought first of pills, patent medicines, proprietary tonics—but he had dismissed the idea. Then the idea of Guinness suddenly occurred to him. And, in the matter of Guinness, he was inflexible. He insisted. For supper every night she now had half a glass of Dublin stout; and because it was no good since it had been opened, as Mr. Squales explained to her, he finished the bottle for her. It was the first of the third dozen that she was preparing to open for him—no, for her—to-night.

The meal was a simple one. But it included something that was very dear to Mr. Squales—pickled onions. And there was a reason for it, he said. It was a throw-back to his Spanish and Italian ancestors who had practically lived on onions and garlic. He had just eaten the last one and, a thin mist of perspiration across his forehead, he was back in his chair waiting for Mrs. Vizzard to make the tea.

But it was actually a changed and saddened Mr. Squales who now sat beside the fire. All through the meal he had been supported and exalted by the thought of visiting Mrs. Jan Byl. The prospect had expanded and developed itself within his mind. Unless there was a frequent local bus service—which seemed unlikely—she would have to send the car to the station to meet him. And she would surely have to invite him to lunch. And tea as well. And possibly dinner. Dinner: he fastened on the thought. If dinner, how could she avoid asking him to stay the night? And then it would truly have been a worth-while outing, a real buster. "She must surely invite me for the night," he added as an afterthought. "After all, she's sixty miles from London."

Then, quite suddenly a cloud had descended on him. Suppose she *did* invite him for the night, what on earth was he going to wear? And how was he going to explain to Mrs. Jan Byl that Enrico Qualito, the well-known West End medium, hadn't got so much as a dinner-jacket to his name? Or should it be tails? Or hunting pink? How the devil was he to know what guests at country-house parties wore in the evenings until he'd been to one to find out? And by then it would be too late and he might have disgraced himself.

In the end, just as the tea came in, he had decided on a dinner-jacket: a dinner-jacket with a white waistcoat and something a trifle out of the ordinary in the way of ties. A sort of bow-cravat, for example. And possibly a fob. But only possibly. Unsure as to its uses, indefinite as to its method of suspension—was it from a brace-button? he wondered—a fob was nevertheless something that he had always hankered after.

But even the plain dinner-jacket presented a man-sized problem for the moment. He could, of course, ask for it outright, and he had no doubt that Kitty would give it to him. But there was something inside him that made it impossible to ask. No, he told himself, it was just one of those things that he couldn't do. It was the price of pride.

And so, after he had drunk a cup of tea and read a letter from a dead cat taken down in trance state by its mistress in Tulse Hill, he tried a different approach altogether. Leaving *The Spirit World* open on his knee, he addressed Mrs. Vizzard in a thoughtful, far-away sounding kind of voice as though he were speaking his thoughts aloud.

"Would it disappoint you, Kitty," he asked pensively, "if I gave up my calling altogether and entered commerce? A bank perhaps. Or possibly insurance."

Mrs. Vizzard was startled.

"Insurance might be all right," she answered. "I'm *sure* you could sell insurance."

It was the wrong response altogether, and Mr. Squales was temporarily thrown out by it. But he recovered himself.

"Tell me first," he said, "would it disappoint you? Would you feel that I had betrayed anything?"

Mrs. Vizzard paused. Her eyes were shining.

"Not if you went on with spiritualism in the evenings," she told him. "There are plenty of mediums who do other jobs as well. Good jobs, too, some of them."

This was getting worse and worse. Mr. Squales got up from his chair and faced her.

"No," he said decisively. "If I turn my back on mediumship I turn my back on it for ever. I cannot play with my talents."

There was a deep rusty rumble in his voice as he said it, and Mrs. Vizzard's heart began to break. She realised now what a struggle was going on inside him.

"But why should you give it up when you're just . . . just getting started?" she asked him.

Mr. Squales paused.

"That is what I cannot tell you," he replied slowly.

Mrs. Vizzard grasped the arms of her chair.

"But you must," she told him. "Has anything gone wrong?"

"Nothing has gone wrong," he answered. "Nothing that you in your sweetness, or I in my folly, could have prevented."

There was another long pause, and Mrs. Vizzard let go of the arms of her chair to reach for her handkerchief. She was on the edge of tears already.

"But what is it?" she insisted. "What is it that we couldn't prevent?"

This time the answer came soon enough. Covering his face with his two hands he told her.

"My poverty," he said. "My accursed poverty."

And it was the voice of a soul in agony speaking.

"But you've got me," Mrs. Vizzard blurted out between her tears. "Everything that I've got is yours, too."

She rose and tried to fling herself into his arms as she said it, but Mr. Squales repelled her.

"No," he said. "You mustn't. You must let me bear my load alone. You make everything too easy. Too easy, and too difficult."

Now Mrs. Vizzard was really crying. After all, it had come as a most unexpected shock to her. At one moment the two of them had been sitting quietly in front of the empty grate with the Japanese fan stuck into it in place of the coals, and then at the next Mr. Squales was suddenly laying his poor ruined life at her feet and refusing to let her help him to pick it up again. It was enough to make any woman cry.

They stood there like that for some moments, completely separate, like strangers. Then, under the strain, Mr. Squales broke down as well. He came towards her.

"Oh, Kitty, Kitty," he said in a low voice, "how can I ever forgive myself? I've made you cry."

With that he opened wide his arms and she came to him.

After that, the actual matter of the dinner-jacket was really ridiculously simple. He didn't, of course, tell her outright. She had to wheedle the truth out of him bit by bit. But when she learnt it there wasn't a trace of resistance on her part. Rather the contrary, in fact. She had always liked the late Mr. Vizzard best on Lodge evenings when he wore a boiled shirt. And in looks—though she hated to confess it even to herself—Mr. Vizzard had been absolutely nothing, absolutely nothing, in comparison to Mr. Squales.

So that was settled. And Mr. Squales, now that his first embarrassments were over, explained to Mrs. Vizzard that for the best séances, the really serious West End ones which the international mediums attended, everyone wore dinner-jackets. He didn't defend the practice. Privately he even thought it rather silly that Revelation should depend on such things. But there it was. And there was nothing that he could do to alter it.

"It's a sorry reflection of the times we live in," he summed up, "to think that between some of us and the other world, between groping blindly like moles and seeing the bright light like eagles, the only barrier is a mere trumpery matter of dress . . ."

They said good-night very tenderly before Mr. Squales withdrew into his lonely little room. Mrs. Vizzard was like a child as she put up her face to be kissed. But not altogether like one. She was standing exactly under the harsh light of the gas bracket above the mantel, and when Mr. Squales put his arms around her she closed her eyes. He stood there regarding her. Admittedly it wasn't altogether a fair inspection. Crying had done its worst to her. But, even without the swollen eyelids and the redness round the nostrils, it couldn't by any stretch have been called a *young* face. Those high cheekbones had an unmistakably stretched and ageing look about them.

Because the awaited kiss didn't come, Mrs. Vizzard opened her eyes again and their gaze met. He smiled at her—his deep, perplexing smile—and she smiled back.

"Oh, my God, I've got to be careful," he told himself. "She'd half kill me if she knew what I was thinking."

CHAPTER 55

PERCY had grown a moustache. Not just from vanity either. But because he had to have something to do.

It wasn't any fun waiting. Not by any means it wasn't. He'd had too much of it lately. Two of them in a room about the size of a lock-up in a garage—and They called this a civilised country. He hadn't got any personal quarrel with the particular warders who used to come in and sit with him. As warders go, he supposed they were all right. He didn't even think of them as Them. But it doesn't take a thought-reader to calculate how sick you can get of the same faces in the same setting day in and day out. Worked it in shifts too, as though he were too precious to be left for a single moment. When the bald one went off Scottie took over, and when Scottie handed in his ticket there was a dark melancholy one who came in. Then the bald one again, then Scottie, and so on.

On the whole it was the dark melancholy one who was the worst.

But Scottie was bad, too. He told stories. He had a whole collection of them. Seven or eight at least. And he enjoyed telling them. They weren't bad stories, and the first time he heard them Percy thought he was going to enjoy them, too. Even now, they were better than the bald one's attempts at conversation. He was a one man's Brains Trust, was Scottie, and used to begin every fresh incident with "When I was in . . ." He'd been a sailor and was an awful liar, too. Either that or he'd had the same things happen to him over and over again in Johannesburg and Melbourne and Vancouver and Trinidad. Percy tried nowadays not to listen when Scottie started talking.

It was really because of the stories, and Scottie's experiences, and the sheer murky gloom of the dark warder that Percy had started off on his moustache. Not that it was anything new to him. He'd had two moustaches before. One when he was about seventeen just to show that he could grow it. And the second only a year ago when he'd played about with the idea of a toothbrush. But this was something a whole lot more ambitious. This was one right across. Only thin, like *à la* Colman. He'd been working on it for a week now. And the one thing about it that was wrong was that Percy was so fair that it was only when the light caught it that you could see it at all.

In any case, shaving in prison was a funny business. They didn't just give you a razor and a shaving-brush and some soap and leave you to it. Not Them. They were far too anxious about Their razor-blades. From the time you'd got the thing in your hand They didn't take Their eyes off you. Just to tease, Percy used to turn his back sometimes and pretend to start fiddling. It was comic, and it always worked. Trying not to look anxious, the warder used to come sliding round to see what he was up to. . . . On the whole, Percy supposed that They were right to take precautions. After all, there are some pretty desperate characters in every prison. He'd read about men who'd picked their veins open with a pin in the night just so that they should escape what the Law had intended. Plucky all right. But messy to clear up in the morning.

Of course, it was different for him. He was O.K. Mr. Veesey Blaize had said so. It wouldn't be long now till the appeal. And then They'd see. Including the judge. From the way Mr. Veesey Blaize had spoken about misdirection, he wouldn't be surprised if old pie-face didn't lose his job over it. And a good clean-up too. What was the point of having a judge sitting there if he didn't know enough to direct a jury properly? It was a nice safe job, a judge's, with no competition. And it was only natural that some of the elderly ones should get careless after a bit.

It was going to be the Lord Chief Justice himself who would hear the appeal. Mr. Veesey Blaize and Mr. Barks between them had arranged that. No half-measures, no middle-men, for Mr. Veesey Blaize. He'd got everything fixed up. He was probably seeing the Lord Chief Justice at this moment. Telling him where the judge had gone wrong. From the way he talked you could tell that it was going to be a proper show-down once they got into court.

And if anything went wrong and he didn't get a chance to say his little bit at the appeal, there were still other ways of doing it. He'd split the whole thing wide-open in the Sunday papers. He'd give the police the scare of Their lives. He'd expose what They did to you when They got you in prison. Talk about Third Degree! Talk about rubber truncheons! He'd give the public what it wanted all right. There was money, too, in that kind of journalism. Full-page stuff. With pictures. And signed in his own handwriting to show that the revelations were genuine. He'd look all right at the top of the page, head and shoulders, wearing his pin-stripe. Perhaps he wouldn't do it all in one article. He might decide to run a series. Then he'd get his name known, and he could sit back for a bit. He wouldn't be surprised if it wasn't the making of him. FLEET STREET DISCOVERS NEW CRIME-WRITER—that sort of thing. *He* knew the inside story.

Because it was getting on for eight o'clock, Scottie was growing restless. The dark one was due almost any minute now. Then Scottie would be free to go back to his wife. She was an Argentinian that he'd met in the United States, and she was a Canadian who'd fallen in love with him when he'd been a steward on a liner, and she was a . . . but what was the use? He bet she was just like anyone else's old woman really. And you wouldn't get a decent class of girl marrying into the prison trade. Smell of the charnel-house wasn't in it.

There was that awful jangling of keys outside the door and the same silly business of sliding back the peep-hole cover to make sure that everything was all right before coming in. Scottie got up from the chair he'd been sitting on for the last two hours and tried to pull back the creases into his trousers.

"See you to-morrow," he said.

"So long," Percy answered.

They had spent the better part of the last eight hours together, and were glad to see the last of each other.

It was typical of the dark warder that he didn't even say good-evening properly. He just nodded, and then sat down on the chair that was still warm from Scottie. And he hadn't even got an evening paper or a book or anything with him. Which meant that he would simply sit and stare. Percy had had some of that before. And it got on your nerves being looked at as if you were some kind of specimen. He'd decided last time that he wouldn't have any more of it. So he started in to-night while he was still fresh.

"Who you looking at?" he asked.

He put it quite bluntly—just like that, in fact—so that the other man should know that he wasn't joking. After all, Percy could afford to be rude to warders because he'd be a free man again in about ten days' time. They didn't mean anything to him, warders didn't.

But the warder did not reply. Merely went on sitting there, staring. So Percy asked him again.

"Well," he said. "You seen me before, haven't you? Who you looking at?"

It seemed to get home that time, because the warder roused himself.

"I'm not looking at you," he said. "I'm just sitting here."

"Not looking at me! Don't talk silly," Percy told him.

The warder said nothing. Nor did he move. His eyes were still fixed on Percy. Staring right through him as it were. And now that Percy realised that the warder was up to those old tricks once more, he found himself jumpier than ever.

"Take your eyes off me, can't you?" he demanded. "Turn your chair round if you can't stop staring."

"I'm not turning my chair round for anyone," the warder replied quietly. "You go on with what you're doing. I'm not looking at you. . . ."

That was why first thing in the morning Percy asked if he could write a letter to his solicitor. And he didn't care if They read it either. He'd got the jitters and didn't mind who knew it. People would be forgetting him if he didn't do something.

It was cheap stuff, prison notepaper. It looked as if it ought to have been wrapped round something. And the nib! Even a post office would have kicked up a fuss about it. It kept on digging up little tufts of the paper and carrying them along with it like a small inky comet. The ink, too, looked as though They'd been washing-up in it.

It wasn't exactly easy to know how to begin. Even "Dear Mr. Barks" sounded a bit familiar, remembering how important Mr. Barks was. And Percy had got to watch his step: he didn't want to do anything to suggest that he was trying to come it. He sat biting the end of the already-bitten pen while he was trying to work the problem out. But he got started at last.

"*Dear Sir,*" was what he wrote finally, "*Knowing how busy you are I am apologising for bothering you. But I would be obliged if you would kindly let me know that everything is O.K. I am looking forward to the Appeal and if there is anything more that I can do I await your esteemed instructions.*" ("Esteemed instructions" was lock-up garage language to the better class of customers, and there was a pleasantly West End professional ring to it.) "*If you would care to see me, I am in at all times.*" (That sounded funny, but he couldn't help it: he couldn't very well say: "*I am inside at all times.*" It meant the same thing anyway.) "*Trusting that you are keeping well and thanking you for past kindnesses. Yours . . .*" *Yours . . . Yours—what? Sincerely? Truly? Faithfully? Ever?* What he fancied most was: "*Ever so sincerely yours.*" But again that might seem to be coming it. So he compromised. "*Yours respectfully*" was what he wrote.

It was Scottie who was sitting with him at the time. And seeing Percy chewing at his pen reminded him of a piccaninny class that he had once seen in West Africa. "When I was in Lagos . . ." he began.

CHAPTER 56

It would have had to be Connie. Not that it was her fault exactly. In the black-out accidents were happening to other people all the time.

And as accidents go, it was a thoroughly de luxe affair. She was bumped—not much more—by a slow-moving Daimler with a crest on it, at the corner of Jermyn and St. James's Streets. She wasn't even hurt. But luckily she had the forethought to scream and go down flat in the roadway. And having gone down, she kept her head and lay there without moving.

It was a bit risky, of course, with other cars about. But as things happened, it worked perfectly. The Daimler stopped and a man got out. She couldn't see what kind of a man because of the black-out; and in any case she wasn't opening her eyes for the moment. But he seemed a very nice kind of man. He bent over her almost tenderly and tried to lift her up. Then, when he found that she was limp—horribly limp—he began calling out asking if there was a policeman anywhere.

As soon as she heard him do that she knew that she was all right. Positively in luck's way, in fact. He wasn't one of the hit-and-run sort: he was going to stop where he was and see the whole thing through. And every time he called out she got to liking him more. He had just the right kind of voice—loud, commanding and unmistakably upper-class.

The next few minutes were naturally a bit of a strain on Connie. She wanted ever so to open her eyes just for a moment to take one peep at her assailant-rescuer. But she couldn't, because quite a crowd had collected by now and someone was flashing a torch in her face. She could feel the beam of it tickling her eyelids. Then a real busybody in the crowd, a sort of amateur Red Cross specialist, announced that he was going to shift her into a neighbouring doorway and asked for someone to help him. There was nothing that she could do about it—she just had to let them do it. But it was dangerous. From the way they were holding her they might have been going to set her down on her head.

All the same it was interesting to hear the comments of the crowd while this was happening. The general verdict was that she was done for. "She's finished, poor old thing," someone said; and a woman in a high hysterical voice observed suddenly: "Look at her hands, they're dragging." Connie wanted to laugh at first. Then she couldn't because she felt so sorry for the motorist to think how worried he must be. And after that the crowd grew too big for her to make out any further individual comments. It was just a vague murmuring mass of curiosity.

She could tell as soon as the policeman arrived. There was the usual "Move away, there," and almost at once she heard the motorist explaining at the top of his voice that he had hardly been moving when it happened. But that didn't cut any ice with the crowd, and he'd have done better to keep quiet. Connie could tell whose side the gallery was on.

The policeman picked up her arm and tried to feel her pulse. She was surprised how gentle his fingers were—the last time a policeman had had his hands on her he had been trying a half-Nelson. Then the policeman dropped her arm and began putting his fingers down inside her bodice. This seemed to be going just a bit far, especially with a crowd around. But without coming to before she was ready, she couldn't stop him. She just lay there all humped up against the step and let him get on with it. Not that it went on for very long. He soon got tired of it and contented himself with smoothing down her skirts which had ridden up all anyhow. Then Connie felt a warm, heavy coat descend on her and she realised that she was being tucked up. Good class of copper, too, she reflected.

"Move along there," she heard him say again. "There's no good standing round. The ambulance'll be here any minute."

He'd got a nice voice, too. Not a bit like the old-fashioned flatty. This one was real Hendon College. It might have been a deep contralto who was speaking. A deep contralto! Connie felt her blood run cold—colder than it was already from having lain in the roadway. The worst, the very worst, had happened. She had allowed herself to be pawed over by a policewoman. . . .

After that—and she very nearly wept from the sheer shame of it—she didn't properly begin to enjoy herself until she heard the ambulance bell in the distance. Then the old spirit of adventure returned to her In all the years she'd been about, this was the first time she'd ever heard an ambulance bell and known that it was coming specially for *her*.

She opened her eyes just as they were lifting her up on to the stretcher. Opened her eyes and gave the crowd her blessing. "Don't worry, folks," she said in a quavering, feeble voice. "I'm all right. Only shaken." She could have bitten her tongue out, of course, as soon as she'd said it—it was giving the whole case over to the insurance company.

But once an actress always an actress, she tried to console herself. There are some exits which are better absolutely silent and some that need a line or two just to point them. . . .

The hospital was thoroughly up-to-date and efficient on the accident side. More efficient than really suited her, in fact, and somehow not friendly. There was too much white tiling about, and too many unshaded lights. And too many nurses. After her nasty experience with the policewoman she was in no mood to have every stitch of clothing taken off her by a couple of brisk young females who kept finding fresh places to wash. They might have been laundresses, not nurses, from the way they set on her. And she had to remind them that if they'd lain unconscious in the roadway they'd have been pretty dirty, too.

The surgeon who examined her was the cool sort. Cool and aloof and indifferent. He went all over her and then told them—more like an instruction than a good-night kiss—to tuck her up for the night. From his manner she got the impression that he'd cleared the operating-table specially for her and now felt himself cheated out of something.

It wasn't any friendlier in the night ward either. She couldn't even raise a drink before they left her. She said something about brandy. But the Sister only laughed at her, and came back in a few minutes with something in a cup. Because there was nothing else Connie drank it. It was tea, sweetened with glucose, and about the worst cup of tea she'd ever had brought to her.

They let her out next day after the doctor had been round again And Connie made her own way back to Dulcimer Street. She was so stiff at first, especially where the wing of the car had touched her that she began to wonder whether she could really have got out of the gutter if she had wanted to. The whole of one side felt as if a goods-train had run into it. But she put it to herself this way.

"Well, m'old duck, suppose the car had really been moving? Would you still have stayed there and said your prayers? Would you, Connie dear?" And back the answer came: "You bet your sweet life, you wouldn't."

Besides, there was always the insurance claim to console her.

CHAPTER 57

I

Mrs. Jan Byl had replied. And the reply had been just what Mr. Squales had hoped for.

In consequence, there he was in the corner of a first-class carriage, a copy of *Everybody's Weekly* open on his lap. He had been reading it earlier but now he was just toying with the pages.

"In any case, I'll chuck it out of the window before I get there," he told himself. "Bit too popular for this kind of a week-end."

Because he was alone in the carriage he had contrived to get thoroughly comfortable. With his legs up on the cushions opposite he was luxuriating. He had unbuttoned his waistcoat and loosened his cravat. His shoes, his new fashionably pointed shoes, were unlaced and the tongues folded forward on to the uppers. He had been smoking a railway cigar that he had bought at the station and, even though it had gone out in a pungent, unprepossessing fashion, he was reluctant to throw it from him. A cigar, a first-class carriage and a country-house week-end ahead of him—Mr. Squales did not want to forfeit even the least part of the savour.

"It's a long shot I'm taking," he told himself. "There may be nothing in it. But, after all, beggars can't be choosers."

He picked up his hat from the seat beside him and looked inside the lining. It was there. Mr. Jan Byl's obituary notice from *The Times*. Mr. Squales studied it carefully. The need might not arise. But if it did—at a séance or something—he wanted to be prepared. If they were expecting any direct voice stuff from their visitor they'd surely rather have him word-perfect than tongue-tied. After a moment, he restored the cutting to its hiding-place, and continued to stare out of the window.

His mind flitted back and he remembered his parting from Mrs. Vizzard. He shuddered. It had been deplorable. She had behaved as if he had been leaving for the South Pole. Recriminations, tears and finally—as a token of her love—a packet of sandwiches for the journey. It was the sandwiches which he had most resented. He couldn't really feel at his ease as a gentleman until he had been able to pop the small grease-paper parcel into a waste basket on the platform. He kept the little label which said, "To Rico in case he is hungry in the train," simply because it flattered him to think what a masterful hold he had over her.

As a matter of fact, he rather regretted the sandwiches by now. Chiddingly was further than he had expected, and he was beginning to feel hungry. Also, it had somehow been such an ungracious thing to do. After all, as Mrs. Vizzard had advanced the money for the ticket it was not unreasonable that she should have imposed some kind of conditions on the journey.

Imposed conditions! That was precisely what, at the back of his mind, was now worrying him. And such conditions. She had asked him not to be extravagant. Not as crudely as that, of course. But just as meaningfully. When, one by one, she had passed the three pound notes over to him, she had significantly added: "I'm not a rich woman, Rico. I only wish I was. Then I could give you this more often." Nicely put as it had been, the words still rankled. It was the one small, cankerous reminder in what promised to be a beautiful week-end.

It may have been the smooth passage of the train, or the flat featureless countryside, or his own sandwich-hunger—whatever it was, one of his queer fits of abstraction came over him. Suddenly he felt himself slipping. Not bodily, but mentally. He forgot about cigars, first-class carriages, country-house week-ends—everything. His mind went reeling sideways into a somewhere that he did not recognise. He was in the railway train no longer. There were pebbles and coarse sand beneath his feet. And behind him—even though he could not see them he knew that they were there—were bleak jagged cliffs and rolling uplands. And even though, so to speak, he had only just arrived there he knew that he was on an island. What was more, he knew that he couldn't get off: he was a prisoner. At the top of the cliff paths there were strands of barbed wire stretched across the sky and in the shadow of the cliffs behind him an armed guard was standing. . . .

And then, as suddenly, the mood passed and he was back in the corner of his first-class carriage again. But the impact of his experience remained. He was sweating and frightened. Yes, actually frightened.

"It's . . . it's happened again," he told himself. "Just like the other times. I'm always getting these fits nowadays. I must see a doctor. A good doctor. Perhaps it ought to be a specialist."

While he was still recovering from the shock of his discovery, he was aware dimly that the train had stopped, and a porter was calling out "Chiddingly."

Chiddingly?

Chiddingly! Good heavens, it was his destination. And already the train was moving out again.

That was how it was that Professor Enrico Qualito flung himself on the platform for his country-house week-end, with his waistcoat unbuttoned, his cravat undone and his shoes gaping. A crumpled copy of *Everybody's Weekly* was clutched in his hand.

2

It was Mrs. Jan Byl's chauffeur who sorted him out, picked up the big leather valise that had once been Mr. Vizzard's, and recovered the copy of *Everybody's Weekly* when Mr. Squales dropped it.

"I . . . I must have been asleep," Mr. Squales said vaguely.

"Quite so, sir."

He seemed a respectful, deferential sort of man, the chauffeur. And Mr. Squales's spirits returned to him. He retied his cravat and buttoned up his waistcoat. Except that his shoes were still sliding about like small pontoons under him, he felt more himself again. This, after a false start, was more like it. Walking behind the chauffeur he allowed himself, so far as his shoes permitted, a faint swagger, an undefinable something in his gait.

And the car in the station yard fully justified it. The chauffeur opened the door and Mr. Squales stepped into a large, rather old-fashioned drawing-room, upholstered entirely in Bedford cord. He sank back further than he expected so that his feet momentarily rose in the air, and when he had recovered himself the chauffeur wrapped a fur rug round him as if he were delicate.

"Ah," said Mr. Squales involuntarily.

It was some distance to the house and he amused himself by playing with the little cut-glass bottles that were mounted into the side of the car at his elbow. Only one had anything in it and it nearly took his head off when he sniffed it. It was smelling-salts. After that, he left Mrs. Jan Byl's playthings alone and rehearsed his policy for the week-end.

"If there's any suggestion of hunting or shooting or anything like that," he told himself, "I shall just have to be firm about it. It'll be all right so long as I don't seem to be apologising. I'll just go up to my room and stay there till they come back. They can't be gone *all* day. And Mrs. Jan Byl couldn't possibly hunt. Not with that figure."

Bridge? That was another difficulty. Mr. Squales didn't play bridge. "I may have to have a shot at it all the same, just to make up a foursome," he reflected unenthusiastically. "I know the rules."

Or family prayers with all the servants standing in a semi-circle? Another difficulty. He wondered if he would know when to kneel.

Or going-up-to-bed? Did he wait for Mrs. Jan Byl to rise lik royalty? Or because he was the guest would Mrs. Jan Byl wait fo him? He didn't know, and he didn't want the two of them sittin there till morning simply because he was holding things up himsel

"Never mind," he consoled himself. "Nothing's so tricky whe you've done it once."

Besides, he had evolved a formula, an infallible solution to th social maze.

"It's no use pretending to be other than you are," he mused. " will remain a treasure of the great cities on a brief visit to the rura landscape. After all, it's perfectly in keeping—my clothes, m appearance, everything. I'll keep myself a bit apart deliberately. I'l be different. And once I've built the part up a bit I can do anything Anything."

The car slowed down, turned sharply and Mr. Squales foun himself following a winding drive across a small park. An immens inner gratification came over him. He had hoped that there wa going to be a drive. But it was even better than he had hoped. Fo no reason except his own supreme happiness that involuntar "Ah!" slipped out again.

And now the great moment, the moment of actual arrival, was o him. This was Withydean. The car slowed down, drew in and cam to rest beside a large white front door in a big red house. Mr. Squale struggled forward and tried to disentangle the fur rug that wa smothering his knees. Then he stopped himself abruptly.

"Sit back, you fool," he told himself. "Let someone else do th unwrapping. If they put this blasted thing round you, let 'em tak it off again."

It was even more delightful than he had expected. For the larg white front door opened and a butler came out. Like the chauffeu he seemed a decent respectful sort of man. He let the chauffeur carr the late Mr. Vizzard's leather valise as far as the doorstep and the took it from him. Mr. Squales followed, a faint smile of satisfactio softening the hard unsuccessful mouth. Then he stopped.

"My hat," he said. "I must have left it in the car."

The chauffeur shook his head.

"You weren't wearing one, sir," he said.

"Not wearing one?"

"No, sir."

So he had left it in the train, had he? At this very moment sixtee shillings and ninepenceworth of spreading black felt was quietl trundling on across the countryside to an unknown destinatio

Anyhow, he settled it. Without a hat, the creature-of-the-greatities line would be a bit too difficult. He must think up something else. And he had it! The absent-minded professor, of course. It would explain anything and everything.

"No matter," he said. "It's of no consequence."

But wasn't it? Suppose the hat turned up again, handed in by the station-master or something, with Mr. Jan Byl's obituary sticking up inside the lining?

3

It was Sunday evening now. The week-end, golden and blissful, lay behind him. Even the ridiculous episode of the hat was forgotten. He had eaten well, drunk well and slept well. And more than that: he had been introduced to an Honourable and a retired General. Admittedly, Mrs. Jan Byl hadn't made him any actual offers of professional engagements. But she had been affability itself. No, affability wasn't the right word. It was something at once stronger and more tender. Friendliness perhaps. Or even affection. They had enjoyed some beautiful talks together in the conservatory. Talks about the Beyond and the Other Self, with the butler hovering with the silver tea-things in the background. The tea—scented China stuff that was like drinking an actress's handbag—had a profound effect on Mrs. Jan Byl. It broke down all reticence. She became personal and intimate. He heard about the Little One Who Had Died, about Mrs. Jan Byl's own girlhood, about a dream that she had once had, and about Mr. Jan Byl's death-bed. Mr. Jan Byl, it seemed, had died not only openly mocking the spiritualism in which his wife believed, but even doubting that there was another life at all. Had died mocking and doubting, and been convinced *after death*. Within forty minutes of his decease, there he was standing beside the cheval glass in Mrs. Jan Byl's bedroom, holding out his hand as if to apologise. He had remained in that abject position for nearly half a minute, she said, before he faded slowly, like a rainbow.

Mr. Squales said little. There was no chance of saying very much. Mrs. Jan Byl was a great talker and this was her favourite subject. But he listened well. Very well. Mrs. Jan Byl was entirely pleased with him. It was a flower that she had picked specially for him that he was wearing in his buttonhole at this moment.

He sat back, a cigar—a real cigar, not a railway one, this time—between his fingers. He had just drunk two glasses of port in the dining-room and was in the happy condition of feeling inwardly at peace. The sturdy simplicity of country life, he was ready to admit had much to commend it.

That was not to say, however, that Sunday night dinner hadn' come as something of a disappointment. For a start, except for th soup, it had been a cold meal. And Mr. Squales disliked cold meals Moreover, he resented not having been allowed to wear his nev dinner-jacket. But as Mrs. Jan Byl very pointedly said, "We don' dress on Sunday evening," what was there that he could do? Nothing But it was a pity all the same, because the dinner-jacket hadn't, he felt been seen at its best on the previous night. A long mysterious fol had humped itself up across the shoulders and if you weren't carefu how you stood there was a gap wide enough to thrust your han down in between the collar-band and the waistcoat. But all that wa over now. He had discovered the secret of wearing the thing. If yo kept your elbows into the side all the time as though you were ridin a horse it could hardly have fitted better. It was only when yo reached out for anything that the seams at the shoulders gave ou little crackling noises as though invisible fingers were stealthil unpicking them. . . .

But what was specially annoying was that Mrs. Jan Byl herself after telling Mr. Squales not to dress, came down the stairs wearing a mass of beige lace that Mr. Squales hadn't seen before and a necklac of uncut amber that looked like native trophies. Not dress indeed!

And the coldness of the meal had been reflected in the company After the magnificence of the Hon. and the General on the Saturda night, there was a definitely served-up look about this evening' guests—a retired civil servant who had been out East, and the vica from the next village who believed in ghosts. Nor did the solitar lady do anything to relieve the party. The wife of the civil servant she was even more retired than her husband. A vague, wisp presence, she seemed to have lost touch with the world years ago. The vicar, who was a bachelor, kept glancing nervously across at he as though expecting her at any moment to vanish altogether.

The conversation was left mainly to Mrs. Jan Byl and Mr. Squales The vicar had a slight impediment in his speech which led him to abandon most sentences half finished. The vague, wispy woman sai nothing. And the retired civil servant who had been out East, having announced that he had once seen the rope trick but did not know how it was done, relapsed into complete silence, as though reluctant to be drawn further.

For the past ten minutes gathered round the fire in the drawing-room no one except Mrs. Jan Byl had said anything. And she was talking about flowers—a subject which Mr. Squales found boring.

"The beautiful things," he allowed himself to say at last. "Earth spirits is how I always think of them. So fresh, so rare"—dammit, the conservatory next door was positively blocked with them—"and so . . . so pure." He broke off. "Have you noticed," he asked, "how frequently they come through to us from the other world?"

Mrs. Jan Byl's face lit up.

"That reminds me," she said. "Why shouldn't we?"

"Shouldn't we do what?" Mr. Squales asked apprehensively.

He felt sure that Mrs. Jan Byl was going to suggest a séance, and he was equally sure that in loyalty to his profession he should refuse. It was unfair to struggling mediums everywhere that he should be asked to perform on a hearth-rug for nothing except his keep.

"The planchette board!" Mrs. Jan Byl answered. "It's such an opportunity. With you here. It may write anything."

"I knew someone who found some b . . . buried t . . . tr . . . treasure with a pl . . . pl . . . planchette b . . . b . . . b . . . b . . . board," the vicar began. "It told him wh . . . where to l . . . l . . . look."

"In India," observed the retired civil servant, "they use beans."

The vague, wispy lady drew a transparent wrap across her grey hair and said nothing.

And then another of those inexplicable things happened to Mr. Squales as soon as he had got his fingers on the planchette. It was as though a magnet had made contact with its keeper. His fingers seemed fastened to it. He sat down at the green baize card-table with the sheet of paper on it, a smile of sheer ecstasy lighting up his face.

"I shall close my eyes," he observed simply.

And as soon as he had closed them, he was remote from the others. Quite remote. He was floating, distinctly floating. So distinctly, indeed, that he would not have dared to open his eyes again for dread of the chasms that lay beneath him. But all the time he was aware that the planchette was writing for him. Desperately writing words that poured through him.

The change in Mr. Squales was so sudden that the vicar who believed in ghosts grew quite alarmed.

"D . . . d . . . do they always b . . . b . . . b . . . breathe like that?" he asked.

"Only in the trance state," Mrs. Jan Byl whispered delightedly. "Anything may happen now."

The retired civil servant bent forward to study the paper underneath the moving planchette, but Mrs. Jan Byl motioned him back into his chair again.

"Not now," she said. "Afterwards. We mustn't disturb him."

And still the writing went on. Up and down the paper the pencil raced, sometimes dancing about in curves, sometimes merely scribbling but always breaking off every so often to write furiously. Mr. Squales's forehead was covered with a thick beady perspiration. Then the pencil ran off the paper ploughing up the smooth green baize and Mr. Squales abruptly slumped forward in his chair. He was obviously completely exhausted.

It was the vague, wispy lady who was the first to get hold of the paper. She snatched it up almost as though she were stealing it from under Mr. Squales's nose, and held it to the light.

"I'll read it to you," she said.

Then she paused.

"How funny," she went on. "It says the same thing over and over again."

"It may do," Mrs. Jan Byl answered tartly. "But what is it that it says?"

She was annoyed that anyone other than she herself should have been allowed to read it first. Mr. Squales was her guest and she felt that she had a prescriptive right to his spirit writings.

As she spoke, Mr. Squales himself sat up and looked about him. He felt dazed and the first words he heard were those of the vague, wispy woman reading from the piece of paper.

"It says, 'For God's sake don't look inside my hat,' " she answered loudly. "Just that. All the way down the page."

4

They were alone together now, Mr. Squales and Mrs. Jan Byl. The guests had departed early, country-fashion; and Mr. Squales, pleasantly conscious of the whisky and soda that stood at his elbow, was suffused with a rich glow of physical and spiritual contentment. The mystery of the spirit message was forgotten.

It seemed delightfully intimate, somehow, just the two of them. And in a way his conversation only served to make it more so. For no matter on what subject Mrs. Jan Byl started, Mr. Squales always contrived to jerk things round again to the personal and particular.

"What you were saying just now interested me so much," he told her. "About the hours you spend alone. I have been so much alone myself that I know the meaning of looneliness full well."

He always added another "o" to the word because it made it sound so much more expressive.

"Haven't you got any friends?" Mrs. Jan Byl asked him.

Mr. Squales shook his head.

"What are friends?" he answered. "They come, they stay for a short space and they go away again. Life—all Life—is like a pitcher. A jug, y'know. Full at one moment, empty at the next."

"But don't you meet a lot of interesting people in your profession?" Mrs. Jan Byl asked him. "The sort of people that you want to go on knowing."

Mr. Squales turned his dark eyes full on her. She hadn't been looked at in that way for years, and it was positively tingling.

"Mine," he replied, "is a solitary calling. There are the hours, the days, the weeks sometimes, while one is shut away pondering, probing, groping, peering. And then for a short moment one emerges into the harsh limelight. Perhaps one has something important to offer. Perhaps there is only dust and ashes. Mediumship is not a safe bet like other professions."

"A safe bet?" Mrs. Jan Byl repeated.

Safe bet! Had he really allowed himself to use such an expression? He could hardly believe it. The commonness of it, the vulgarity, staggered him.

He smiled.

"You are surprised?" he asked. "I used the words of course in their popular context. An expression of the people, you know. A bit of *hoi-polloierie*."

"Some mediums have been family men," Mrs. Jan Byl observed. "When Stieger was at the height of his powers he married again and had five more children."

"Happy man," Mr. Squales answered. "How happy and how rare. For him the crowded fireside, for me the loonely chair."

He hadn't intended it for a rhyming couplet when he began the speech, and it seemed to spoil it completely. Mrs. Jan Byl would think that he was merely reciting to her.

But it was quite all right as it turned out. And better than all right. It was magnificent.

"You must come down here more often," she said. "This house is usually full of people."

"You are too kind," Mr. Squales answered her. "Really too kind to me." He paused. "It is only my work that keeps me. There is nothing else. Nothing."

Mrs. Jan Byl glanced across at him.

"Why don't you stop down here over Monday?" she asked. "They're not expecting you back, are they?"

Mr. Squales paused again.

"There is no one to expect me," he said. "As I told you—no one."

"It must be strange being quite so alone as that," Mrs. Jan Byl said reflectively. "Haven't you got a secretary or anyone?"

Once more Mr. Squales did not reply immediately. When he did his voice was lower and more vibrating than Mrs. Jan Byl had ever heard it. It was obvious that the poor man was struggling to conceal his feelings, and she blamed herself for being tactless.

"It is probably my fault," he said. "All my fault. When I entered my ivory tower I should have left the door ajar. But I didn't. I bolted it upon the world. Now, still a young man, I am like a hermit. If I were to die to-morrow—to-night—at this moment—there would be no mourners because there would be no one to mourn. I am like a man from Mars, a creature with no ties on earth. . . ."

He took out his handkerchief as he said it and blew his nose. Then he happened to glance down at the rug. Mrs. Jan Byl was glancing down, too. There on the hearth-rug was a little label that said: "To Rico in case he is hungry in the train." Mr. Squales covered it hurriedly with his foot.

"No ties on earth," he repeated.

CHAPTER 58

CONNIE had been upstairs crying.

Just sitting there, on the end of the bed, howling her old eyes out. Perhaps the accident had upset her more than she realised. Perhaps she had really got a claim against the motorist. A nice comfortable maimed-for-life sort of claim running into four figures. She stopped crying for a moment while she thought about the noughts. And then she started again when she remembered Percy. She was in a thoroughly upset feeble state when she could cry about anything. And hadn't she known Percy since he was so high and hadn't she always liked him for his funny cheeky ways? Loved him like a son, in fact. Of course she had loved him. And his mother, too, for that matter. They had almost been like sisters, the two of them. To be lying at death's door in hospital and have your only son sentenced while you lay . . . Well, if Mrs. Boon was strong enough to stand it, she wasn't. Throwing herself forward on the bed she cried louder than ever.

And it wasn't only Mrs. Boon she cried for. She cried for all the strong beautiful young men who were going off to France to be killed. She cried for their wives and their children. She cried for the Poles. She cried for all the shopkeepers who were going to be ruined, and she cried for the Queen Mother. She cried for Mr. Josser because he was taking Percy's verdict so much to heart and she cried for Mr. Puddy who had always been so lonely anyhow. She cried for herself thinking how near to death she had been, and wondered why God allowed so much unhappiness to happen.

It wasn't nice at her age to be reminded of the grave. It frightened her. What she needed here and now was comforting. She wanted someone who would say, "Thank God you're all right, Connie, me old dear! Whatever *should* I have done if you'd gone under?" But there was nobody who cared that much. Nobody who cared at all in fact. And that was what gave Connie the cold shudders. It knocked nine-tenths of the fun out of being alive if there wasn't anybody to care if you were dead.

The nearest thing that she'd got as a friend was Mr. Josser. He was a shoulder of sorts to cry on to when times were bad. And Mrs. Josser, too. She could be difficult admittedly. But Connie knew how to handle her all right. Given patience, she could get anything out of her she wanted. On the day when Connie had got back from the hospital after her accident Mrs. Josser had brought her up some thin bread and butter and a boiled egg done just the way she liked it.

But Mrs. Josser wasn't there at the moment—Connie had peeped in earlier to see. And Mr. Josser was out rent collecting. Mrs. Boon was in hospital. And neither Mrs. Vizzard nor Mr. Squales was exactly what you would call shoulders.

Then she remembered Mr. Puddy. He was better than no one. At least, he'd be *someone* to talk to. He could breathe.

What was more, he could cook. Living just one half-floor below him, she had often wondered what else he could do. There couldn't be time though for much, she reflected. It was one little mess after another going on to the gas ring.

It was a fish night to-night. Unmistakably herrings. She could just picture them, like small oily mermaids, some with soft roes as smooth as custard and the others with hard ones like hundreds-and-thousands. Not that she wanted a share of something that wasn't hers. If she'd wanted fresh herrings she could have bought a couple. And after she'd roped in the kitty from the insurance, she could have them by the truck-load, almost by the catch, if she felt that way inclined. All the same, to a poor lonely woman with no girl-friends and a bruised thigh they did smell something more than somewhat.

She got up off the bed and made up her face from the oddments of rouge and cold cream in the various little jars in the cardboard chocolate-box. Then she re-frizzed the bang of hair in front. And finally she dabbed herself behind the ears, on the back of her hands and under her chin from a nearly new bottle of "Midnight Desire" that one of the young ladies had carelessly left behind at the night-club. Finally she went upstairs and knocked timidly at Mr. Puddy's door.

He was in his shirt-sleeves and carpet slippers when he answered her knock. At any time roused only with difficulty, and particularly averse to interruption when eating, he stood there solid, immobile and resentful. But also impatient. And his impatience was what betrayed him. He was eager, fanatically eager, to get back to his fried herring.

"Gub id," he said. "Gub id and shud the door."

It was the first time that Connie had ever been in Mr. Puddy's room by invitation. But she noticed at a glance that all the old things were wrong with it. It was a woman's hand that was missing. In short, there was no one to arrange the flowers.

Mr. Puddy sat down. He was still puzzled, distinctly puzzled.

"God to go on," he explained. "Geddig gold."

"But of course," Connie assured him. "You go right on just as though I wasn't here. I can have my supper any time."

There was another herring—a third one—in the dish in front of him. Mr. Puddy tried to shield it with the evening paper. He had never felt so tenderly towards any fish as he felt now towards that last herring.

"Well," he said at last. "Dell me whad's ub."

Connie drew her chair a little nearer. Nearer to him and nearer to the table.

"It's your advice I want," she said. "I . . . I wanted a man to turn to."

Mr. Puddy shifted in his seat when he heard the words. There was something distinctly flattering in the first part. He had always prided himself on his advice. But the second part alarmed him. He'd been a widower long enough to know the perils of that state.

"Ubb," said Mr. Puddy to show that he was listening, but not actually committing himself.

"Well, it's like this," Connie began. "There was me quiet as a wren going quietly to work, when suddenly out of the darkness a great big Daimler . . ."

Mr. Puddy listened and ate. Ate and listened. But the more he listened, the slower he ate. Towards the end he was just playing with his food, his eyes bulging. And no wonder. The incident in Jermyn Street had become transformed into something that was worth listening to.

". . . flat out with the driver bent low over the wheel and . . ."

"'Ow did you see id if id was behide you?" Mr. Puddy asked.

"In . . . in a shop window," Connie told him. "That's it . . . I saw its reflection. I tried to leap out of the way but before I could do a thing . . ." She broke off for a moment. "Oh, my," she said, "Don't those herrings smell delicious. You go on before the other one gets cold."

"What habbened then?" Mr. Puddy demanded.

He returned to his meal as he said it. The fish was at the difficult stage now. Only tiny white fragments were left clinging to the ingenious spring framework of fine bones. It was really a full-time job now. And he had lingered too long, The little bits of fish were stone cold and he pushed the plate away from him.

"Like the other wud?" he asked. "I've fidished."

It was while Connie was toying with the cold herring that she took stock of Mr. Puddy. Caught earlier he might have been quite a fine man. There was still plenty of him. But he wasn't exactly the lean cowboy type any longer. And his breathing seemed to get in the way of other things. Like his footsteps, it was slow, heavy, deliberate and sounded as though it might stop at any moment. But there was good sense inside him. He was emphatic about one thing. And that was the hopelessness of trying to get money out of insurance companies unless you had a lawyer to represent you.

"You mide as well give id ub," he said. "Simbly give id ub. Inshuradce is hobeless. You want subwud smard to rebresend you."

He shook his head sadly while he was speaking. Apparently for years he had been coming off second-best in encounters with the Pearl and the Prudential and Lloyds.

"But who?" Connie asked. "They're just as bad themselves, some of them, the solicitors. Wheels within wheels, you know."

Mr. Puddy nodded. He knew.

"Whad's wrog with Mr. Bargs?" he asked. "He did his best for Percy."

"And where's Percy now?" Connie demanded.

"Where he ought to be," Mr. Puddy answered. "Where id's saver for other people."

That turned the conversation on to more general matters. Mr. Puddy liked talking when he was in a mood for it. It was a great restorer of self-respect, was talking. And murders had always been his favourite subject. Next to food, violent death was the one thing that kept him happy and contented.

The Jossers' clock downstairs struck six and Connie rose reluctantly.

"Duty calls," she said. "On with the dance."

Mr. Puddy got up and pushed his chair back.

"Sabe here," he said.

On the whole he was rather glad that Connie had looked in on him. Glad that she had been in an accident, too. It had given them something to talk about.

But Connie wasn't moving. She was looking at a faded enlargement over the mantelpiece. Against a background of pampas grass it showed a large dark woman with a flat sad face.

"Was that Mrs. P.?" she asked.

"It was," answered Mr. Puddy, noticing the picture for the first time for years.

"Don't you miss her?" Connie asked.

"Biss her," Mr. Puddy repeated. "I haven't beed the sabe man since."

He stationed himself in front of the photograph and stared at it lovingly. An expression of cloudy melancholy came over his eyes.

"Whad a wobad," he said at last. "What a wobad, and what a gook. She could gook anythig, she could. Buddings, Bastry, Bobadoes. Anythig."

CHAPTER 59

I

Percy was in people's minds all right. He needn't have worried about being forgotten.

Take Mr. Veesey Blaize, for instance. Very busy man Mr. Veesey Blaize. Very. But also very depressed. And not getting on with his work in consequence. Out of sorts, in fact. Decidedly out of sorts. And why? Because of Percy. This wasn't just ordinary liverish indisposition from which Mr. Veesey Blaize was suffering. It wasn't even because of some new piece of trouble that his daughter had got herself into. It was something that went much deeper. Something had entered the very interstices of his professional soul and spread the misery right through him. There was no part of him that did not feel tired, jaded, harassed and—horrible word—failing.

"Perhaps I've been doing too much," he told himself. "What I need is exercise. Go down to Sunningdale and get a round of golf. Always feel better after golf. But can't manage it to-day. Or to-morrow. In court all day to-morrow. And the next day. . . . Or perhaps it isn't that at all. Perhaps it's that tooth the dentist told me about. Said it was poisoning me. . . ."

He removed his glasses and rubbed his hand across his eyes as he often did when he was thinking.

"And another thing," he went on. "I ought to see the oculist. He told me to come back. . . ."

But what was the use of it? Golf, dentists, oculists—when had he got time for them? He knew what it would be instead. A large brandy-and-soda at the George, and perhaps another one at the Bodega, and back to his chambers again. This wasn't the first time he'd felt this way, and he'd got over it. Or hadn't he? That was just the point. Was he in as good form now as he had been six months ago? A year ago? Five years ago? Twenty years ago when he was still rising? His mind went back over the present term. Reggett *v.* Pawson Collieries; Charleston Investment *v.* Hooper; Anodyne Medicines *v.* Proprietary Drugstuffs, Ltd. In turn he'd been Reggett, Hooper and Proprietary Drugstuffs, Ltd. All big cases and all gone against him.

And now Rex *v.* Percy Boon. Or rather Mr. Justice Plymme *v.* Veesey Blaize. That was the unpleasant part. Somehow or other he'd contrived to set Mr. Justice Plymme against him. And not only Mr. Justice Plymme. But the other judges as well. The way things were he was a marked man. He was caught up in a plot to ensure that he should never plead successfully again.

"We'll win on appeal," he told himself. "Clear case of misdirection. We're bound to win on appeal."

But as he said it an awful doubt came over him. He found himself remembering Reggett, Hooper, Proprietary Drugstuffs, and all the rest.

2

Another person who was thinking about Percy was Doris. She woke up thinking about him. It was as though a bad dream, a thoroughly bad one, had detached itself from the night and waited until morning.

"I know he's going to be all right," she told herself hurriedly. "I know he is."

But that was nothing to go by: it was simply what everyone said.

And it was silly thinking about Percy. Because really she should have been thinking about Bill. Thinking about him blotted everything else out, once she was awake properly. And no wonder. It was his last day. To-morrow morning he was going to a military hospital up North somewhere.

He came round for her, very smart and official-looking in his new uniform, immediately after breakfast and they went off to Richmond together. They were lucky in a lot of things. Lucky in being with each other. Lucky in having the whole day to themselves. And lucky in the weather. The wind had dropped, the glass was rising and the church spires and chimney-pots shone and sparkled.

It was a Sunday and other people appeared to be enjoying it, too. They were out in their numbers. Richmond was crowded with them—men smoking pipes, and old ladies, and dogs on leads, girls in tweed costumes, and nursemaids with babies in perambulators. They stretched up the hill, a bobbing, swaying mass like dancers ascending a long staircase.

Now that Doris looked, she saw that there were other figures in khaki among the crowd. But these were only early days, remember: the war hadn't properly got going yet. Soon, quite soon, the girls in tweed costumes would be taking out the spaniels and red setters alone. All the men in comfortable-looking country suits and those in smartish Sunday ones would have gone. And even some of the girls as well. They'd be getting into uniform like the rest of them and going away Lord knows where for Heaven alone knows how long. It was as though this spectacle of Richmond on a fine Sunday was ready to dissolve in an instant, leaving only the old ladies and the babies in perambulators behind. As though the long shadow of war was creeping up the hill ahead of them.

Bill and Doris walked up the hill themselves because in Richmond everyone walks up the hill. It is the excuse for the place, the hill. And at the top of it, there is the park sitting there. A wide, splendid park. A royal park in a rather public way of business. Admittedly there is nothing in it to set against the Castle in the park at Windsor. But the stucco lodge on the hill is good enough. It has the squat plain look of the houses you see in early water-colours. It is not only English, but English school. It shines away in the distance with an unmistakable touch of the Regency and an equally unmistakable touch of Chinese white. And once you're in Richmond Park you're inside the frame along with it.

Bill and Doris entered the park. They became—Doris's red coat and Bill's khaki—just another piece of the foreground. They walked on without speaking. And, as they walked, they merged. Merged completely. They dwindled into twin spots of colour in the middle distance. Then they went under the trees. And it was dark there. The red coat still gleamed. But it was alone now. The khaki one was lost to sight completely.

It was as though Bill had gone away already.

3

Connie had been thinking about Percy, too. Couldn't help thinking about him. It was all up—that much was obvious. All up, and too sad to let her mind dwell on it. She meant to ask Mr. Barks if there was even one teeny ray of hope anywhere. Because, thanks to Mr. Puddy's advice, she was one of Mr. Barks's clients herself now. Or about to be.

Not that Mr. Barks seemed in any need of further business. He wasn't exactly standing at the front door reaching out his hand for it. Quite the contrary, in fact. Connie had expected to find him rushed, harassed, distracted by telephone calls—for such are the hall-marks of success. But what she hadn't expected—what she openly resented—was that he didn't even seem to want to see her at all. At least not without an appointment. She had, indeed, to put her foot down pretty firmly in the outer office before she could so much as get herself a fair hearing.

"Just you go back inside, young man," she said to the articled clerk behind the counter. "Tell him I'm an old friend of his mother's. Tell him he's on to something good. I'm a client, I am. Not something the cat's just brought in. . . ."

She hadn't really meant to let herself go like that. Not straight away anyhow. She had meant to do a charm school on the young man. And the bit about something-the-cat-brought-in had just slipped out despite herself. It was vulgar and she regretted it.

Not that it mattered. The articled clerk, looking a bit tousled and crestfallen after the second encounter, had just come back to say that Mr. Barks would see her after all, if she would kindly take a seat. For a moment she sat there thoughtfully humming. Then she asked the articled clerk if he really wanted to be a solicitor or if it had simply been his parents' idea.

It was fortunate that she liked big men—she had done so ever since she was quite a girl—or she wouldn't have stood for Mr. Barks's behaviour. There was no pretence about it. He was downright rude.

"May cost you something," he said. "Have you got it? Can't go to law for nothing. All costs money. Suppose we lose. Where do I go for my fees? No speculation cases here. Find some firms to do them. Not this one."

"All right. All right," Connie answered. "What's wrong with me paying for myself if it all goes down the drain?"

"May be ten guineas. May be twenty," Mr. Barks told her. "Impossible to say. Suppose it's more? What then?"

It was an awkward question. And Connie considered for a moment before answering. She gave a little giggle from sheer nervousness.

"I'd better put my cards on the table, hadn't I?" she asked sweetly. "It's like this. If it's more than a hundred I couldn't pay. I just haven't got it. It seems only right I should tell you, doesn't it?" She paused. "I'd never forgive myself if you lost money because of me. Never."

Connie's answer appeared to satisfy Mr. Barks.

"Let's hear all about the accident," he said. "Want to know the details."

He only interrupted her once and that was to correct her when she went wrong.

"Shouldn't say anything about what the crowd said," he advised her. "Not if you were unconscious at the time. Very important point that. Probably just thought you heard it all. Make a bad impression on a jury if it comes to one. Can't be too careful, y'know."

When Connie had finished, Mr. Barks spoke again.

"Any nightmares since it happened?" he asked.

"Nightmares!" Connie repeated, the little nervous giggle breaking through again. "How can you have nightmares if you can't even get to sleep?"

Mr. Barks made a note on his pad.

"Insomnia," he said. "Very important point that insomnia. Have you seen a doctor?"

"Not again," she told him.

"Should do. Go back to the hospital and tell 'em. Make 'em re-examine you. And if they keep you in for the night remember it's insomnia you're there for." Mr. Barks paused to answer the telephone and wrote down £4 6*s.* 8*d.* on his blotting-paper. Then he hung up and turned to Connie again.

"Appetite?" he asked. "Can you still manage your food?"

Connie shook her head.

"I tried to manage a snack the other night," she said. "Just a snack. But up it came. Nothing seems to settle since it happened. It's down one moment and up again the next. Just like a lift."

"Tell 'em that, too, at the hospital," Mr. Barks insisted. "Very important. Insomnia and vomiting. Been back at work?"

"I had to," Connie answered. "I didn't want to find myself out on my ear just because some gentleman couldn't drive his car in the black-out."

Mr. Barks frowned.

"Mistake all the same," he told her. "Bad mistake. May prejudice them. Very dangerous to go on working. No sleep. No food. Oughtn't to risk it. Try and take a holiday if you can afford it. Hope to get it all back later."

"And some over?" Connie asked, smiling up at him.

"Don't know," Mr. Barks corrected her. "Can't say. Won't guess. Great mistake. Better see what happens. May agree to settle out of court. All depends."

"But you'll do your best?"

"I'll handle the case," Mr. Barks replied.

He got up as he said it and held the door open for her. Connie would have liked a handshake just to clinch matters. But Mr. Barks had to excuse himself. His phone was ringing again and the tousled-looking articled clerk was hanging about for him. Through the half-open door—the door into the inner office, not the one straight on to the staircase—she saw the figure of Mr. Josser. He had evidently been fussing about the appeal again.

CHAPTER 60

I

Mr. Squales's glorious week-end was over and he was back in Dulcimer Street again.

At the present moment, he and Mrs. Vizzard were sitting facing each other across the small table on which the backgammon board—the late Mr. Vizzard's backgammon board—was set out. It had been the deceased's one relaxation, backgammon. Evening after evening, he had sat crouched forward in his chair, his flat expressionless face bent over the pieces, studying the lay of the home table, the pieces on the bar, the blots. He had not been a good player—had been a very bad one, in fact—and Mrs. Vizzard had beaten him every time at working off. But there was evidently something in his continued unsuccess which attracted him. It made his work and his play all of a piece.

And now where the pale ineffectiveness of Mr. Vizzard had once sat, Mr. Squales was now sitting. Every time Mrs. Vizzard looked at him she experienced the same extraordinary feeling of inner fluidity. It was as though one glance at him could reduce to nothingness those impregnable walls with which womankind over the ages had surrounded itself. Her own inconstancy, the thought that perhaps she was at heart a fickle wench, worried Mrs. Vizzard. She was sorry now that she had ever brought down the backgammon board from its shelf. It was such a link with the past—and such a barrier. For there was nothing of Mr. Vizzard in Mr. Squales's playing. He had picked up the principles of the game in a single session. By now, he played like a master. His luck with the dice was positively uncanny. Fives and sixes came tumbling out with every throw. And more than once Mrs. Vizzard had wondered if anyone's luck with dice could really be so consistent or whether this baffling fiancé of hers were cheating.

"My game, I think, kitten," Mr. Squales observed at last, and leant over to give her hand a playful pinch.

"Your game, dear," she agreed. "You're too clever for me."

Mr. Squales smiled.

"Not clever," he told her. "Merely lucky."

And he smiled again.

"Lucky at cards, unlucky in love," Mrs. Vizzard remarked absently, and then wondered immediately why she had said it.

Mr. Squales, however, was able to turn the remark easily enough.

"Backgammon isn't cards," he reminded her. "And I'm certainly lucky in love. Pussy wouldn't deny that, would she?"

Mrs. Vizzard did not reply at once. It was being such an agreeable evening that she was hesitant about doing anything that might disrupt it. But if she never spoke, if she never uttered what was uppermost in her mind, she was sure that he wouldn't. Plucking up her courage, she said it.

"Have you thought anything more about going out and getting a job for yourself?" she asked.

The smile which had been still hanging around the deep corners of Mr. Squales's mouth, and in his dark impenetrable eyes, vanished. A look of shock and surprise took its place. It was as though she had hurt him.

"Why? Are you worried about me?" he asked.

She raised her hand and made a movement as though she were brushing away something invisible that stood between them.

"It isn't that," she assured him. "You know it isn't. It's simply that . . . that . . ."

"That what?" Mr. Squales asked coldly.

"That you told me that you were considering it," she finished lamely.

Mr. Squales relaxed a little.

"So I am," he told her. "Constantly considering it." He paused. "And I haven't yet come to any conclusion. That's all it is."

It was dangerous, she knew, to go on any further. She had noticed the change that had come over him when she had first raised the subject. And these few hours alone together were far too precious to be spoiled. But she had to say what was pressing so hard inside her to be said.

"You know why I asked?" she said shyly.

"Because you want to see me self-supporting," Mr. Squales replied brutally.

His voice was cold, and it frightened her.

"Only for one reason," she told him.

"So that I can marry you," Mr. Squales answered in the same hard, unfeeling manner. "Do you think that you need remind me of my own condition?"

Then, just as the evening was threatening to break up in storm-clouds and misery, the other Mr. Squales suddenly broke through. He held out his arms towards her, tenderly, solicitously.

"If I could bring that day a minute, nay, a second nearer, I would go out and tie myself to a desk to-morrow. For your sake I would become a clerk, a commercial traveller, a counter-jumper, anything."

"Oh, Rico."

"But I'm afraid that I shouldn't become a very good one. My kitten must remember that," he told her. "I haven't been trained for that kind of life. I've devoted myself to what I've been proud to think of as the higher things. Sometimes you almost make me doubt whether they really are . . ."

Mrs. Vizzard leaned forward.

"Oh, Rico," she said. "I've been thinking. Why must you wait even if you haven't got a proper job? It's so noble of you—but it's so long. Let's get married straightaway."

Mr. Squales made no reply. But Mrs. Vizzard was too excited to notice. She was carried away by her own shamelessness, by this open declaration of her urgent need for him.

"We needn't live down here," she added as though tempting him further. "We can move up into the Boons' room. They'll never be coming back—either of them."

This time when Mr. Squales still did not reply, she grew apprehensive. And then, as she looked at him, she realised that he hadn't even been listening. His eyes were fixed on the window above her head—the window that showed two foot of carefully whitewashed area wall, then the ornamental pattern of the railings and, through them, the houses opposite. Mrs. Vizzard turned and looked, too.

But when Mrs. Vizzard looked there was no one there.

And by now Mr. Squales was relaxed again.

"I thought I saw someone I knew," was all he said.

2

Mrs. Josser distinctly heard footsteps overhead. She paused in what she was doing and listened. But there was silence. The complete, unnatural silence that there had been ever since the Boons, mother and son, had gone away. Then, just as Mrs. Josser had resumed her mending, she heard the sounds again. They were slow, unmistakable footsteps.

Unreasonably, they alarmed her. For a moment it was as though she had slid back three months in time and Clarice Boon were lightheartedly pottering about upstairs; waiting for Percy probably. Then common sense took over, and she realised that it was probably only old Connie snooping around to see if there were any little trifles that she could borrow. Or Mrs. Vizzard: it may have been that the landlady herself was furtively inspecting her property.

Whatever it was, Mrs. Josser decided to go and see. She put down Mr. Josser's sock, rebuttoned her shoes and went straight up. There was no need for subterfuge and Red Indian stuff on her part. Whoever was in Mrs. Boon's room had no way of escape except across the roof-tops. . . .

The door was closed when she got there, and Mrs. Josser stood outside listening. The same stealthy shuffling footsteps. And then

Mrs. Josser realised something else: that there was no shaft of light rom beneath the door. The intruder, whoever it was, was going bout the room in darkness. Mrs. Josser raised her hand and nocked. The sounds stopped immediately. There was no reply, owever. And Mrs. Josser knocked again.

This time the door opened as though the person behind it had been anding there all the time. And with the opening of the door the ght from the gas bracket on the floor below crept into the room. Mrs. Josser remained there staring.

It was Mrs. Boon who stood facing her.

But it was not the Mrs. Boon who had gone away. This was an lder, a feebler woman. Almost an old one, in fact. The hand that he held out to Mrs. Josser was shaky. And, now that she came out urther into the light, those sagging, frightening lines down the left ide of her face were revealed. Just as they had been in the infirmary.

"Clarrie!" Mrs. Josser said. "Why didn't you tell me?"

The woman in front of her was trying to speak. And it was a ifficult process. There was one corner of her mouth that was idle nd india-rubbery. She made two false, lisping starts before the words finally came.

"I had to come," she said. "I had to be near him."

Mrs. Josser had got her downstairs now. She was sitting in Mr. osser's chair with a cup of tea resting in her lap—the actual holding f a tea-cup was apparently a strain that was too great to be underaken—and her feet stretched out towards the fire. It had not been asy getting her downstairs. Mr. Josser was out—the South London Parliament was still in session—and Mrs. Josser had been forced to do verything single-handed.

Not that she minded. The last thing that she wanted at the moment was interruption. And by keeping Mrs. Boon to herself, Mrs. Josser was able to get quite a lot out of the poor exhausted woman. She earnt, for a start, how it was that Mrs. Boon had been able to climb ll those stairs without anybody hearing her. The truth came umbling out with the unself-consciousness that goes with utter physical fatigue.

"I went up on all fours," she said. "I couldn't have managed it ny other way."

She'd been meaning to come for the past week, it seemed; meaning to come, and planning. But there had been difficulties, big difficulties, to be surmounted first. The doctors had said that she wasn't trong enough. And the Sisters had echoed the doctors. There'd been the fare for the taxi, too: she hadn't got any money left—an money at all—after she'd paid Mrs. Vizzard for her room. So sh had done the obvious thing. Last week she had not paid Mrs. Vizzard. She was quite sure, she said, that Mrs. Vizzard would understand. And it would all come right, of course, as soon as Percy wa working again. Then, between them, they'd be able to pay off an little debts that had accumulated.

Mrs. Boon was so weak that she broke off suddenly in the middl of sentences—even in the middle of words sometimes—and just sa there, her lips moving but no sounds coming. The tea, howeve was reviving her; and with her strength her spirits were returning

"I knew I'd feel better as soon as I was back among friends," sh said at last. "It's what I've been telling them."

She was not so much grateful for Mrs. Josser's attentions as placi and unresisting. It was evident that she had been an invalid for lon enough to expect other people to wait on her. Not that her inne purpose in coming had anything about it that was invalidish o dejected. On the contrary, it was evident from odd remarks that sh let fall that it was for a great deal more than merely to be near Perc that she had made the journey. A very great deal more. She wa going to see everyone—Mr. Barks, Mr. Veesey Blaize, the judge, th Lord Chief Justice, the police, the counsel for the prosecution— everyone, in fact, who was in any way mixed up in this slur upo her son's good name. A ferocious maternal protectiveness emanate from her. She was like a lioness.

In the meantime, however, she was content to be looked after an cossetted. Content even to gossip. And it was the black-out that sh wanted to discuss. This new terror was something that had descended since her time. The London that she had left had been London that met the dark each evening with a million lights an fought it. Then in the infirmary she had watched the Sisters, nigh after night, fitting brown-paper frames into all the windows an drawing the thick curtains over them. But that had seemed n more than a piece of the painstaking pattern of their life. Earlie and earlier each day she had seen the shutters go up and the curtain drawn, and—with the natural egotism of the invalid—never onc had she wondered what it was like outside.

It was not, indeed, until she had emerged that she realised that while she had been lying in her bed, chaos black and original ha come to earth again.

"I nearly turned back when I saw it," she admitted. "Then remembered Percy and I came on."

CHAPTER 61

I

WHAT they had all been waiting for had come to pass: the appeal had been heard.

And it had been dismissed. The last ordinances of the Law had been uttered. And nothing but the King's clemency could now save Percy. In the meantime he was being made as comfortable as circumstances would allow in Wandsworth. It wasn't the same cell, but he still had Scottie to sit with him and tell him about his experiences.

Considering how important the appeal was, it all passed off very quietly. The evening papers, full of a big Finnish victory over the Russians, practically ignored it. APPEAL DISMISSED was all that two of them said, and the third put in a line about MURDERER TO DIE underneath some air news and the latest picture of the *Graf Spee* with only her upper-parts showing above water. The contemptuousness of the treatment depressed Mr. Josser still further. For Percy to have descended from headlines and the stop press to the very bottom of the column served to add a new note of dreadfulness to the whole affair. It was as though murders, instead of being very large and terrible, were really quite commonplace and trivial. As though either No. 10 Dulcimer Street or Fleet Street had been getting the affair of Percy Boon all out of proportion.

Mr. Josser hadn't been along to the Lord Chief Justice's court himself because it had been rent-day. Nor, as it turned out, had anyone else of the immediate circle. When the fateful morning had actually come, all Mrs. Boon's decisions, her determination, her nervous energy, her resoluteness, were seen for the empty, futile things they were. The simple fact was that she wasn't fit to leave the house, and Mrs. Josser stayed in to look after her.

So much for the Jossers. But what about Mrs. Vizzard and Mr. Squales? Mr. Squales himself had been rather looking forward to going. Human nature in the raw, he explained, was one of his hobbies; and about the rawest place that he knew for human nature was in a law court. But Mrs. Vizzard was by now utterly opposed. She wanted to dissociate herself entirely from the whole sordid business. Wanted to give Mrs. Boon notice and forget that such a thing as a murderer had ever lived under any roof of hers. It was, in a sense, a tribute to Mr. Squales's good nature that he gave way. That, and the fact that he was temporarily out of cash again. He hadn't, as it happened, got even his bus fare.

As for Mr. Puddy, he had intended right up to the last minute to cut his sleep and go along. But even that came to nothing. Because of something that he'd eaten—he couldn't rightly name what—he came off duty with a nasty attack of heartburn. And just when all the fun was happening, there was Mr. Puddy sitting up in his room sipping a cup of hot water with a pinch of bi-carb. in it, and thinking about stirrup-pumps.

But Connie's was the saddest case of all. Starting out rather late because she'd been retrimming her dress, she turned up in the wrong court. It was her fault, of course. Nobody else's. It was simply that having seen Percy duly tried in No. 1 Court at the Old Bailey she had assumed that everything else to do with him would naturally go on there. And she had been wrong. The Lord Chief Justice was a bigger man than she had thought him. He didn't go to trials, it seemed: trials went to him. So as soon as she had found out what was happening, she shot off in pursuit up to the Law Courts. But the traffic jam in Fleet Street was so bad that she had to walk. Run almost. And she knew from then on that it was touch and go. As it turned out, it was go. She got there just in time to see them all packing up, and the case over.

They evidently hadn't wasted any time over Percy.

2

Mr. Josser himself was at the Elephant and Castle when he learnt the news. It was about four-thirty when he bought the late night extras from the man at the corner. And he stood there on the kerb-side searching through them. Anyone looking at him would have thought that he was a racing-man with a big bet on, his hands were trembling so. And from the way he tilted his hat back and wiped his forehead when he had found what he was looking for, it was equally obvious that his horse had lost. He didn't move away at once. He just folded up the papers and stood there with them all crumpled under one arm, looking out across the traffic. When he did move away, it was to go straight back to Dulcimer Street.

This, in itself, was a breach of duty. By rights, he ought to have gone back to 23A Tankerville Road, and Flat D, Pewman's Rents, to see if there was anyone in this time. But he didn't. Instead, he opened the two rent books and, in the best writing that he could manage in a moving bus, he wrote: "Out, despite repeated applications," and signed his initials.

It was dishonest, of course. Downright dishonest. In the language of rent collecting two visits don't amount to "repeated applications." But he was glad that he had done what he had. Because things were going pretty badly in Dulcimer Street when he got there. He wasn't actually first with the news. Connie had beaten him to it again. By the time Mr. Josser had arrived, the full impact of the disaster had been received. But it was left to him to put matters right. Everyone looked to him to do something.

And the trouble here was not that Mr. Josser was unwilling but simply that he hadn't got the least idea what to do. So far as he could see, things had gone rather a long way for him to try to intervene. And what made it all so peculiarly difficult was that it was not Mrs. Boon, but his own wife, who kept goading him.

"Well, what are you going to do, Fred?" she demanded. "We can't just sit here doing nothing."

"I know, I know," he answered. "I'm thinking."

Mrs. Josser drew in her lips.

"It's *doing* we want, not thinking," she told him.

"All right," he answered, miserably. "Give me time to get my breath."

He felt rather hurt. Right up to the moment of arrival, it had seemed that merely his presence there would do something to comfort and reassure. And apparently it wasn't so. In inaction, the very sight of him was clearly maddening. And what made it worse was that he was supposed to be at the South London Parliament at eight-fifteen. There was a question about Spain which involved His Majesty's Government pretty seriously, and it wasn't the kind of thing that he cared to trust to his parliamentary secretary. But, of course, he wouldn't be able to go now. And what was more he wouldn't even be able to say that he ought to be there. Merely to refer to the South London Parliament at this moment would have been another of those things that make men despised by women.

And there were not just two women: there were three. For Connie was there as well. She was not actually saying much at the moment because she had constituted herself a kind of sick-nurse attendant to Mrs. Boon and had sunk herself in the part. Everything that she did was in character. She spent her time giving little nudges at the cushion behind Mrs. Boon's head and stroking the poor woman's hand whenever she got an opportunity. Outside night-club hours, the pair—despite one or two pretty terse hints from Mrs. Josser—were practically indivisible.

But Mrs. Boon herself maintained an air of placidness and detachment. Of stupor almost. A damp-looking handkerchief in her lap was all that there was to reveal the desperate present in which she was living. And when Mrs. Josser for the third time abruptly demanded if Mr. Josser had thought of anything yet, it was Mrs. Boon who protected him.

"It's all right," she said. "I shall be better in the morning. Then *I'll* be able to do something. I know I shall be better in the morning."

She didn't say what it was that she proposed to do. And everyone had the good taste not to make things any worse by asking. Finally, Mrs. Josser managed to persuade Mrs. Boon to go upstairs to bed. And she even offered to sit with her. But in Mrs. Boon's present state there was no need for it. The stupor, the merciful anæsthetising stupor, was still on her, and she didn't mind being left. Preferred to be left, in fact. She wanted to pray, she said.

When she returned, Mrs. Josser found Mr. Josser just as she had left him. He hadn't even attempted to put the chairs straight or start to wash-up. He was just sitting forward in his chair, mooning.

Mrs. Josser let herself down wearily into the chair opposite to him. Now that she and Mr. Josser were alone together they had reached the next stage in the tragedy. There was no room for dissimulation any longer.

"There isn't really anything that we *can* do, is there?" she asked.

Mr. Josser shook his head.

"Not a thing," he answered. "Not a blinking thing."

"I was afraid there wasn't," she said. "But it seemed kinder to let her think there might be."

3

They were in bed, really in bed with the sheets pulled up to their chins, when Uncle Henry arrived. The impetuous peal at the bell told them right away who it was. But, even so, Mr. Josser prayed that it wasn't. Getting back into his trousers he went through into the living-room and peered out of the window into the dark street. There in the dim light of the half-moon he saw the shape of a bicycle up against the kerb. And it was Uncle Henry's bicycle all right: there was a bracket at the back for a trailer.

"Coming here at this time of night," Mr. Josser grumbled to himself as he descended the stairs in the darkness. "It's disgraceful."

The hope—only a half-hope admittedly—occurred to him that perhaps Uncle Henry had only come to deliver something. A message, possibly. Perhaps, after a word on the doorstep, he would go away again.

But whatever it was, it was urgent. By the time Mr. Josser got there, Uncle Henry had started ringing again. And ringing vigorously. The bell wires were scraping and flapping against the plaster as Mr. Josser passed them.

"Sshh!" he said as soon as he had managed to slide back the heavy bolt. "You'll wake everyone up."

But Uncle Henry was in no mood to be trifled with.

"It'd do this country good to be woken up," he said. "It's what it needs."

He stepped across the mat as he spoke, and Mr. Josser's hopes of a fleeting message vanished. Uncle Henry passed on up the stairs, stumbling heavily as he mounted.

"We . . . we were all in bed," Mr. Josser told him.

Uncle Henry seemed surprised.

"In bed," he repeated. "To-night?"

"Well, why not?" Mr. Josser demanded. "It's nearly midnight, isn't it?"

Uncle Henry did not reply immediately. He had walked into something. He stood there rubbing his forehead. But by the time Mr. Josser had struck a match and lit the gas, Uncle Henry had recovered. He had reached the door of the living-room by now.

"Do you realise how much time we've got?" he asked. "Do you realise that even now it may be too late to prevent it?"

"Prevent what?" he asked.

"Murder," Uncle Henry answered slowly. "Judicial murder."

"You mean about Percy?" Mr. Josser asked.

He was surprised. Because, so far, Uncle Henry hadn't shown any interest in Percy's trial. He'd been too busy organising protest meetings about something else—the treatment of conscientious objectors, Mr. Josser thought it was.

"I mean a lot of things," Uncle Henry answered.

He took two paces forward, and glared at Mr. Josser. These sudden ferocious advances of Uncle Henry's were one of the most alarming and least predictable things about him. At one moment he was over on the other side of the room and at the next he was right on top of you, glaring. Glaring, that is, with one eye while the other roved moodily, and with no apparent interest, in space.

"This isn't justice," he said finally. "It's class vengeance. Remember what Marx said."

Mr. Josser didn't remember. But he nodded his head just the same. He could tell from his manner that Uncle Henry was preparing to stop, and he didn't want to prolong it.

"Suppose that Percy was the scion of some noble family," Uncle Henry continued, "would he be where he is now?"

Mr. Josser considered the point.

"It all depends on what he'd done," he said at last.

"It depends on nothing of the kind," Uncle Henry contradicted him. "It depends on whether he could have bribed the judges."

"You couldn't have bribed this one," Mr. Josser said feelingly.

"You could—by class influence," Uncle Henry retorted. He paused. "The rulers have got to show their power sometime otherwise they would cease to rule. They have to make an example of someone. That's what Percy is: an example."

"But if he did kill her . . ." Mr. Josser began quietly.

It was extraordinary how, talking to Uncle Henry, Mr. Josser found himself compelled to take the other side.

But Uncle Henry interrupted him.

"Were you there?" he asked. "Did you see him kill her?"

"No," Mr. Josser admitted.

"Neither did the judge," observed Uncle Henry significantly. "Nor the jury. But they found him guilty, didn't they?"

"They were only going on the evidence," Mr. Josser said soothingly.

"And where did the evidence come from?" Uncle Henry demanded. "The police! And were they there?"

"It's very difficult to be certain in a case like this," Mr. Josser admitted soothingly.

But Uncle Henry was in no mood for soothing.

"Not if you understand class structure, it isn't," Uncle Henry told him. "Not if you've read Engels."

Mr. Josser gave a deep sigh. He was wearing only his pyjama jacket and his trousers and, at this time of night, it was chilly. Also, it was clearly one of Uncle Henry's bad spells. He had apparently come along at five past twelve just to give Mr. Josser another lesson on class warfare.

But here Mr. Josser was wrong. Uncle Henry rallied suddenly.

"We're wasting our time," he said. "If we let Percy die we shall have his blood on our hands the same as the judge has."

"I did all I could," Mr. Josser replied, and left it at that.

Remembering his two hundred pounds, he found this new attack on him unnecessarily hurtful.

"But not all you're going to do," Uncle Henry continued. "Your work begins to-morrow morning. At dawn."

"What sort of work?"

"We're going to rescue him!"

Then Mr. Josser became really alarmed. Alarmed for himself. And alarmed for Uncle Henry. The worst, the very worst, had happened. Uncle Henry's madness had developed, and the man was now raving. Mr. Josser saw him up a ladder at Wandsworth, tearing away at the bars with a hack-saw. But he did his best to seem completely calm.

"How do we set about it?" he asked.

"In this street," Uncle Henry answered. "Both sides of it. And then the street next to it. And the street next to that. Until we've got the whole of London on our side."

"You . . . you mean start a revolution?" Mr. Josser asked.

He deliberately kept his voice low and unconcerned. After all, he'd foreseen an attack like this for a long time.

Uncle Henry smiled and showed his teeth.

"Not yet," he answered. "Not till the hour's ripe. Not till the fruit is falling. We won't overthrow our rulers this time. We'll petition them."

Mr. Josser drew a deep breath of relief.

"Ah," he said. "A petition."

"We will petition His Most Gracious Majesty," Uncle Henry went on, "through his servant the Home Secretary. We will present him with thousands and tens of thousands of signatures. And *you* will collect them."

"Me?"

"Certainly, I've got my business to run."

"But do you think it'll do any good?"

Uncle Henry looked at him pityingly. So pityingly that Mr. Josser felt uncomfortable.

"But do you?" he persisted.

"Would you sit easy on your throne if your subjects were rising all round you demanding mercy?" Uncle Henry enquired ominously. "Would you risk your crown for a life?"

"No, I suppose not, if you put it that way," Mr. Josser conceded. "But do you think enough people will sign?"

"They will if you make them," Uncle Henry told him. "Three

weeks to go—that's all there is. Three weeks to go—and every house in London to be visited."

Uncle Henry had to stop there, because Mrs. Josser came in and asked them both what they were thinking about, talking at the tops of their voices when Mrs. Boon just up above needed every scrap of sleep she could snatch hold of.

It was just like two men, she added.

4

In front of the large desk, with the Führer's portrait staring down at him, a young man is standing. He is bolt upright at attention, with each thumb pressed in against the seam of his trousers. And he appears scarcely to be breathing. Even so, he doesn't cut a very military figure. He is too short. And round-faced. And plump. No matter how much he braces his shoulders, he still has somewhat the look of a nursery teddy bear. The man behind the desk is a colonel-general. He is lean and grey. And while he is speaking he keeps his hands clasped round a long ebony ruler. He is very much the high officer. While it is in his hands, the ebony ruler seems to become a baton.

Lean and grey and thorough. He has been interviewing the young man for three-quarters of an hour already. And still he has not quite finished with him.

"Are you in love with anyone?" he asks suddenly.

The young man blushes and shakes his head.

"With no one, *mein General*," he replies.

"Have you a mistress?"

The young man blushes again. He is almost too much ashamed to answer. He feels so immature somehow, so unworthy of his superior's confidence.

"There is no one," he confesses.

The colonel-general leans forward across the desk and points at him with the ruler.

"Then you will not mind if you never come back?"

This time there is no hesitation, no embarrassment.

"I am prepared," he answers. "Heil Hitler."

As he says it, his right hand shoots upwards.

"Heil Hitler," the colonel-general says after him, raising his own right hand above the table-top. Then he gets up. It is obvious that the interview is practically at an end.

"You will say nothing about our conversation," he reminds the young man. "You will not even mention to your family that you've been here. You will go home and continue practising your English studies. Particularly your study of English newspapers. And you will wait quietly until you are called for. The final course of technical instruction is most intensive. It can be learned in six weeks."

He comes round to the front of the desk and places his hand on the young man's shoulder, a colonel-general's hand on Otto Hapfel's shoulder.

"You are fortunate," he says with a smile. "In spring England can be very beautiful. It is a flower garden. The Vale of Evesham is famous and much photographed. So also are parts of Kent and the cottage gardens of Devonshire. At Kew again there are many Oriental plants with much blossom."

CHAPTER 62

I

It was the third day of the petition. And with every hour it was gathering momentum.

Admittedly, the first day had been disappointing. Decidedly disappointing. Mr. Josser had suffered the indignity of having three-quarters of the front doors in Dulcimer Street closed in his face before he had been able even to explain what he had come about. The trouble was that everyone imagined that he was trying to sell something. Either that, or emergency billeting. Or a gas-mask check. Or evacuation particulars.

And when he did manage to establish his real purpose there was the new difficulty that no housewife apparently cared to sign anything until she had spoken to her husband—which meant calling again after seven. By tea-time on the evening of that first day when Mr. Josser returned to No. 10 he had exactly twenty-three names on his scroll of paper. And he was tired—so alarmingly tired—that Mrs. Josser advised him to chuck up the whole thing.

But that was reckoning without Uncle Henry. And things were different when he took over. He arrived as soon after he had closed his shop as the green bicycle could get him there. And he found fault with everything—the hole-and-corner way the campaign was being conducted, the absence of organisation, the unimpressive appearance of the scroll of paper itself, Mr. Josser's own half-hearted approaches.

"Another day lost," he complained. "And only twenty-three signatures to show for it. Not enough to save a cat. What we want is twenty-three million. Something that'll rock the Government."

Mrs. Josser had not said very much so far: she had simply been listening, tight-lipped, while Uncle Henry had been speaking. But she wasn't going to have anyone—even Uncle Henry—criticising her husband. She intervened suddenly.

"Well, it isn't going to be Fred who rocks it," she said. "He's done enough already."

"Do you call twenty-three signatures enough?" Uncle Henry demanded.

"Yes, I do, so far as Fred's concerned," Mrs. Josser answered. "If you want any more you must get 'em yourself. It was your idea."

Uncle Henry did not answer immediately. He was thinking. Not thinking about the petition, but about how rude he could be to his sister without ruining everything. In his own mind he was now calling her the most offensive thing he knew—a petty bourgeois capitalist *rentier*. Also a crypto-Fascist. But these were fighting words, and he dared not utter them. He had set his heart on this petition, and he had to be careful.

"All right," he said finally. "I'll start to-morrow."

"What . . . what are you going to do?" Mr. Josser asked him.

If Mr. Josser hadn't asked him, he would have saved himself a lot of trouble. But, as he listened to Uncle Henry's answer, he was spellbound. Here, on his very doorstep, it seemed, was a vast adventure, a crusade with banners, and it was all going to happen without him. Quite suddenly, he forgot all his tiredness, forgot about the closed doors, forgot about the timid housewives, forgot even about Mrs. Josser. In a flash, he realised that all his life he had been craving for adventures and crusades. He could hold back no longer.

"You can count me in too, Henry," he said to Mrs. Josser's astonishment. "I'll tackle Parliament."

After that everything was easier between Mr. Josser and Uncle Henry. It was only between Mrs. Josser and her brother that a coldness lay. She just sat watching them, the two crusaders, as though at any moment she might have to intervene and call the crusade off. Then she spoke.

"Mrs. Boon had better do something herself," was what she said. "He's her son. Those R.C.s always stick together."

It was only a start, of course. But it was significant. Distinctly it showed softening. In the magnetic field of Uncle Henry's enthusiasm she was being drawn forward irresistibly.

"Not only the Catholics. *All* the churches," Uncle Henry corrected her. "They're our chief ally, rightly handled."

"I'm glad to hear you say so," Mrs. Josser retorted. "I have heard different from you in the past."

"Even opium," Uncle Henry replied coldly, "has its uses in emergency. I shall enlist the clergy personally." He paused. "We've got a lot of work to do," he added, looking hard to Mr. Josser. "Making up for lost time. I shall sleep here. This'll be my campaign headquarters."

2

It wasn't Mrs. Josser but Mrs. Vizzard who objected.

Mrs. Josser herself had become reconciled to having Uncle Henry in his shirt-sleeves sitting at the dining-room table, surrounded by paper, organising. But Mrs. Vizzard would have nothing to do with it. It worried her and she refused even to add her name to the list of signatures.

And, in a way, it was understandable. She still wanted to give Mrs. Boon notice. And all this—this fuss—was still further thwarting and frustrating her. If she attempted to turn Mrs. Boon out now, she would have to face more than Connie and the Jossers. She would have to face Uncle Henry as well.

Nor was Mrs. Vizzard alone in her disapproval. She had company in Mr. Puddy. He had his own views on murder and he was prepared to stand by them.

"If he dud it, *if* he dud it I still say," he declared, "he deserves it. After all, burder's burder."

Mr. Josser, in fact, was in favour of by-passing Mr. Puddy altogether. But Uncle Henry wouldn't hear of it. He went up himself. And he was lucky. Mr. Puddy was just sitting down to a cooked tea and he was so anxious to get on with it while it was still hot that he would have been ready to sign anything.

Even Mr. Squales signed eventually. He slipped up quietly, without telling Mrs. Vizzard, and added his name in his broad backward-sloping writing. It looked rather well on the page and he stood back for a moment studying the effect. With the right pen and the right coloured ink he could toss off a signature second to none.

And Mr. Squales's signature, together with Connie's and the Jossers', accounted for the whole of No. 10. No one had approached Mrs. Boon for her signature. That would have seemed somehow indelicate, and they let the list go out without it.

As it happened, Mr. Josser very nearly stepped off with the wrong foot when he came to tackle Parliament. He tried to introduce something about the petition at the end of an answer to a question about the relations of His Majesty's Government with Turkey. Th Speaker, however, flatly ruled it out of order. After that Mr. Josse simply had to sit there patiently on the Front Bench for another half hour while one by one the members slipped away to their home taking their signatures with them. In the Wrexford Arms after wards Mr. Josser was able to assemble the few that remained, and h got their signatures without much difficulty. But there were onl eleven of them, including Mr. Speaker.

But he need not have worried: Uncle Henry was doing wel enough for two. Like Mr. Josser he had met with his rebuffs. Bu Uncle Henry had buffeted back. In his crusade of the churches h had started rows with a Methodist lay-preacher, a low Churchman a Roman Catholic priest and a Plymouth Brother. And throug sheer perseverance he had at last found what he wanted. He ha found the Rev. Headlam Fynne, the Vicar of St. Jude's.

Fanatic recognised fanatic, and the two of them went into a corne straightaway to discuss things. They made a strange pair, Uncl Henry in his cycling knickers and the Rev. Headlam Fynne in th nearest thing to a monk's habit that the Church of England woul stand for. But between them they certainly got things going. Th vicar announced that he would preach on capital punishment at bot Mass and Benediction on Sunday and have the petition at the churc door ready for people to sign as they went out. He also offered t speak at any public meeting, hall or street corner, that Uncle Henr cared to arrange. He spoke mysteriously, too, of detailing ke members of the Junior Guild of God, of which he was secretary, t set up centres of outcry, as he called them, in other parts of London

"If we are prosecuted for what we do, at least we shall have th thrill, the joy," he said, "of knowing that we have dared. It i something to be a dare-devil for once in His name."

When Uncle Henry came away from the Rev. Headlam Fynne h had that peculiar satisfaction which only born organisers know—th satisfaction of having got something started. In consequence, he wa in a good temper, almost jocular in fact, over supper. He becam human and intimate and told them about other campaigns that h had conducted—campaigns against the eviction of a widow and he four children, against the destruction of an ancient doorway, agains the closure of a footpath, against Sir Samuel Hoare, against the sal of song-birds in cages. All his life he had been campaigning agains something, and he recognised in this, the campaign for a human life the ultimate challenge to all campaigners. Uncle Henry, in short was in clover.

The only thing that rattled him was Mrs. Boon. Mrs. Josser insisted on having her down for companionship's sake; and Mrs. Boon obediently came. Supported into the room she sat down in Mr. Josser's chair apparently oblivious of everything that was going on around her. She was not excited. She was not grateful. She was not even—so far as he could judge—disturbed.

"Everything'll be all right," she said several times. "I know it. Don't you worry."

3

If there was one person with a right to worry, it was Percy. There was a small pocket calendar that Scottie had lent him, and he had been marking the days off. He knew just where he had got to by now.

But at the present moment there was nothing wrong with him. He was dreaming. And a very nice dream, too, while it lasted. He wasn't doing anything much, just waiting at a bus-stop. Then a piece came along, walking slowly like she wanted to be followed. He went after her. And, sure enough, it was the Blonde. They had a drink together and talked about everything that had happened to them both. The struggle in the car and the fatal blow and all that. And it turned out that the Blonde didn't mind a bit. She'd forgiven him completely. Just to prove it she kissed him full on his lips. And he was surprised to find how a dead girl could kiss. Because, of course, he knew all the time, the way people do know things in dreams, that she was dead. It was because of the kiss, the first kiss he had been given for more than two months now, that he woke up crying. Woke up crying, and went on crying even after he was awake.

Scottie didn't take any notice of him at first. Just left him so that he could get over it. Then when it didn't stop and Scottie couldn't stand it any more, he got up and went over to him.

"Don't take on so," he said kindly. "It isn't going to hurt. It's all over so quickly you won't feel anything."

CHAPTER 63

Mr. Puddy had cut his hand. On his birthday, too. And with a tin-opener. He had been levering away at a prime cut of Alaskan salmon when the metal shaft of the opener went clean up through the wooden handle, and lacerated him. What made it so peculiarly maddening was that the tin, except for a small corrugated indenta-tion in one side, was practically as it had left the canners. Whic meant that Mr. Puddy, one-handed—and left-handed at that—ha been forced to sit down to plain bread and margarine, while his fis course stood on the table beside him as inaccessible as if the salmo were still alive and jumping the falls of its original Columbia River

"What a bishap," Mr. Puddy told himself sadly. "On be birth day, too. Fifty-dide and no sabbud."

And, because it was three o'clock in the morning, he was cut of from all hope of assistance. A night watchman's is a solitary calling He has to be practically as self-supporting as a trapper. There h was, right in the centre of London with ten millions of people al round him, and he couldn't so much as borrow a tin-opener fron one of them.

The sense of separation—simply because, when he was on the job everyone else was off it—played upon his nerves sometimes, and lef him jumpy.

"Subbose I was to fall ill, boisoning or hard-addack or somethig like that," he reflected. "I should just lie here till bordig. I should b on the floor when the gleaners cub id."

It was because of these grim fancies that Mr. Puddy always tried to break up the silent monotony of watching. He was careful to keep his mind off himself. And he did it mainly by spacing out his eating. Coming on duty, winter and summer alike, he always began by getting himself a drop of something hot. And it was the simple fact that it was hot that rendered him so estimable. His predecessor in the basement cubby-hole, and his predecessor before him, had both lost their jobs precisely because it was a drop of something cold that they were always taking. And that in watch-keeping circles is ruination. A drunk night watchman—even a night watchman with liquor on his breath—is professionally finished. Once discovered, he is unemployable.

But Mr. Puddy had got it all planned out. First, there was the cup of something hot, the freshener. Then, because it is a long stretch from six o'clock to midnight, he always had a snack round about nine—say a small pie of some sort, or a few sausages, and an apple—and then his sandwiches at ten to twelve. The real sit-down, the tinned stuff, came on at three, when the human spirit is at its lowest. He took a drop more of something hot—cocoa usually—at six just to keep him going. And, with a parting cuppa for the road at seven-thirty, he was through. In between, he made his rounds and washed-up.

The washing-up was all right, because he was used to it. It was the hours of inspection that got him down. There was something positively eerie about patrolling that enormous building all alone at night. And not only eerie, but fatiguing. Imagine yourself doing it: nearly an acre of floor-space, four storeys and a basement, and no lifts working after six-thirty. No lifts, and fifty-eight stairs.

It was partly his weight that did for him. Whereas a little fellow could have nipped up and down those stairs without noticing it, Mr. Puddy climbed slowly and suffered. Climb he had to, because there was a blasted clocking-in device on every floor that had to be punched when he got to it, and wouldn't punch itself if he didn't get there.

So, punctually at twelve every night, he would set out, ready for action, carrying the full regalia of his office—his electric torch, his bunch of keys, his police whistle. If any burglar had been about Mr. Puddy would certainly have alarmed him. There was nearly fifteen stone of him, remember. And his bowler hat on top seemed to carry with it something official, a touch as it were of the plain-clothes man.

But rats are no respecters of even a bowler hat; and the rats are one of the big chief worries in tea importers'. Sometimes in the night Mr. Puddy had to take a stick to them. Then the silence, the unnatural, unearthly silence of the tea warehouse would be shattered by the sound of blows. That would be Mr. Puddy banging on the side of one of the packing-cases to scare away the vermin. He rarely came to closer grips with them than that, rarely hit out at one of the rats themselves, because they were too nimble for him.

But, for the most part, these patrols of Mr. Puddy's were uneventful. It was, indeed, precisely this uneventfulness that rendered them so uncanny. He would open the heavy sliding door at the end of one of the storage bays and there, stretching before him in the tunnel of light from his torch, would be the endless double row of cases, all the same size, all neatly stacked one on top of another, all glittering along the reinforced metal edges. It was the unvarying sameness that got him down. For, at the end of the long bay, there would be another corridor of cases just like the first one. And another after that. And another after that.

Sometimes the cases threatened to come together and crush him, so that Mr. Puddy—on one of his bad evenings, that is—would simply walk as fast as he could to the clocking-in machine at the far end, punch it and examine the next bay without actually walking the length of it. Not that you could blame him. It *was* a queer business, being the one living creature, except for the rats, among these multitudes of boxes. And, in the light of his torch, the boxes cast long fantastic shadows. All connection with the tea trade disappeared, and then Mr. Puddy, night watchman no longer, might have been exploring the deserted midnight ruins of Thebes or Karnak.

There was, of course, always the smell. On the first floor you were greeted by rich Darjeeling and ripe Assam; on the second by the cheaper Chinas; on the third by the really aromatic stuff, the Pekoes and Lapsangs; and down in the basement by dust, sweepings and dried grass-stalks. Even if you shut your eyes you could still tell what floor you were on. But when Mr. Puddy had a cold even that clue went, too.

To-night, his birthday night, had been a particularly bad one for him. Low-blooded and out of sorts when he had started work, the incident of the salmon had depressed him more even than he had realised. It seemed yet another piece of unsuccess with which to taunt himself. Shuffling along the bays, torch in hand, he couldn't help comparing the present with other and better birthdays that he had known.

"Whad I ought to have by rights," he grumbled to himself aloud, "is a bilk-round. A bilk-round with a norse. Something on wheels. And a little shob. A shob with an assistant. Then I wouldn't be here now. I'd be in bed. And asleeb."

He turned the corner and his torch alighted on a large red notice that said: "DANGER OF FIRE: NO SMOKING."

In his present state, the notice annoyed him.

"Thad's another thing," he told himself. "No smoging. Might as well be in brison. I can tell the gompany this mudge—wodgeman or no wodgeman, if the warehouse gadges fire, it gadges fire. I'm not going to stob here and put it out for adywud."

He had reached the last bay by now and his tour, save for one small extra excursion, was over. Once during the night he was supposed to go outside and examine the main gates to the yard. And this was something that he always did.

Except when it was foggy.

Or very cold.

Or raining.

CHAPTER 64

I

THE extraordinary thing about the petition was that it wasn't Uncle Henry's petition any longer. It was the Rev. Headlam Fynne's.

Within twenty-four hours of the enrolment of this formidable new recruit, Uncle Henry had been thrust to the wall; the character of the street-corner protest meetings had changed beyond recognition—they now opened with a prayer and had a hymn to end them; and even the campaign notepaper had altered. The heading now read: A PETITION FOR CHRISTIAN CLEMENCY ADDRESSED BY THE OBEDIENT CITIZENS OF LONDON TO THE KING'S MOST GRACIOUS MAJESTY. Admittedly, it had taken hours of hard committee work to get Uncle Henry to agree. But the fact remained that he *had* agreed. He had, in short, been talked down, overruled and trampled under.

Even so, had the Rev. Headlam Fynne been content with a prayer here and an amendment there, the petition would probably have gone the quiet unheeded way of most petitions. But he was not content. During the terrifyingly short time that remained, he forsook everything—Bible classes, Zenana teas and whist drives—and, like the Good Shepherd, strove for the one strayed lamb. He lived the part, and he dressed the part. In particular, dressed the part. He didn't wear his lounge suit once. His flowing black robe and his buckle shoes were set out beside his bed each night and he emerged each morning in full habit. Not that it was vanity that prompted him. The Rev. Headlam Fynne had lived through that stage long ago. It was sheer showmanship and common sense that prompted him. He knew from long experience that there is nothing that collects a crowd quicker than a clergyman in a habit. It awakens whole centuries of prejudice.

But it was the scarlet cross that finally did the trick. Nearly eight feet tall and made of plywood, he had previously carried it with him only when preaching in the open. Now he took it with him everywhere. And the sight of an athletic priest—his college oar was hung alongside the crucifix in his little study—dressed like something out of the Inquisition and carrying an eight-four cross as bright as a pillar-box, naturally caused a sensation. As soon as he left the vicarage, crowds of children—all that the L.C.C. scheme had left—

followed him. By the time he reached Dulcimer Street it was like the arrival of the Pied Piper.

The first time Mrs. Vizzard saw him through the basement window she could not believe it. She thought that it must be medical students from St. Thomas's, collecting. Then, when the black-gowned figure swept up the front steps—*her* front steps—and into the house—*her* house—she realised that this was one more indignity that the Boons had heaped upon her. And there was worse to it than that. Even after the front door had closed again, the roadway and the railings outside remained littered with unevacuated urchins. And she couldn't go up and chase them away because that would have been unladylike. Nor could she stay where she was because the sight was unbearable. In the result, she withdrew. Shamed and humiliated, she threw herself upon her bed.

But not to rest. She had been lying down for hardly ten minutes when there was a knock at the door. She rose, smoothed herself and went upstairs. It was the Press. She was just on the point of sending the reporter away again when the door above opened, and Uncle Henry came down, hurrying. He was brusque and agitated, and his manners were intolerable. Without asking her permission, scarcely even acknowledging her indeed, he took the little man by the arm and led him upstairs.

Mrs. Vizzard turned. On the first landing a great black shape was standing, and she heard a rich baritone voice say: "Ah, a friend from Fleet Street. It is the moment for which we have been waiting . . ."

And it was only the beginning. A photographer and a lady feature-writer arrived later. But Uncle Henry was on the alert now. He worked upstairs with the door open and came down every time he thought he heard anything. The letters to editors had been his idea.

With the house full of people in this way, it was not surprising that things went wrong. Connie put on her hat with the feather peony in it and was photographed on the doorstep holding a great bundle of papers, all prominently headed PETITION. But what particularly disgusted Mrs. Vizzard was the fact that Mr. Squales of all people somehow got himself mixed up in one of the interviews. It was only his abnormally good manners, she did not doubt, that had made it impossible for him to extricate himself. Out of her sight only for a moment, she found him pinned to the wall by the lady feature-writer. Her notebook was open in her hand. Mr. Squales's dark eyes were fixed upon the creature, and he was saying, very slowly and distinctly: "Qualito is the name. Q-u-a-l-i-t-o."

Mrs. Vizzard turned away, her eyes filled with tears.

"And I've always tried to keep this house quiet and respectable," she told herself. "It was, till Mrs. Boon came here. This settles it: she goes."

2

But this was unfair. Because the only other person in No. 10 who appreciated all this publicity as little as Mrs. Vizzard was Mrs. Boon herself. Aloof and detached from everything that was going on around her, she remained in her room seeing no one.

And, in this, Mrs. Josser assisted her. Connie, Uncle Henry, the strange clergyman, even her own husband, could answer all the questions that the reporter or the lady feature-writer cared to put to them. But she wasn't going to have Mrs. Boon upset.

"She's sleeping and she can't be disturbed," was what she said whenever they enquired about her.

Not that they would have got anything, even if they had been allowed to see Mrs. Boon.

"It's very kind of them to take all this trouble," she had said earlier that afternoon. "Very kind, indeed. But they really needn't bother. My Percy is going to be all right. I know he is."

But Percy appreciated the petition all right. And the change that it produced in him was remarkable. Moody and apathetic for the past two days, he suddenly perked up when Scottie showed him the papers. The blackness fell from his mind and his face lit up again.

"That's me on the front page," he said. "That's Mr. Barks's doing. Or Mr. Veesey Blaize's. That's me in my pin-stripe."

Then he came to the lady feature-writer's article. There was a whole column of it and it took him some time to read. It was nice seeing his name so often. But it was funny being called just Percy all the way through. It was as though she knew him. And he'd never heard of her. When he had finished it, he turned to Scottie.

"What's she mean?" he asked. "What's an 'Oval-born Lothario'?"

CHAPTER 65

1

THERE was no time to be lost. The calendar on the Home Secretary's desk had the day after to-morrow conspicuously ringed round in red. And there was a special reason for it. Dates with red rings round them were dates set aside for executions.

Not that the preceding days had been unrewardful. On the contrary, the petition had acquired a snowball momentum of its own and every post brought in mysterious bulky envelopes from outlying parts, all containing names, names, more names. Some of them came from the unlikeliest quarters. Even Connie had managed to secure nearly two dozen signatures from the night-club. They were written on rather shiny paper with an Apollinaris heading. And except for one man, a drunk, who had signed twice and for another, only half drunk, who had signed in the name of Nazi Party leaders, the list seemed valid enough.

Under Uncle Henry's supervision, Mr. Josser had been sticking the various bits together. On this point—on a continuous scroll of names—Uncle Henry was emphatic and unshakeable. Because it didn't matter in the least, the Rev. Headlam Fynne gave way.

"If it's in separate pieces they could run through it like *that*," Uncle Henry said with a contemptuous whisk of his hand. "But if it's in one colossal scroll they'll see at once what they're up against. They'll recognise their own winding-sheet."

And so, with paste and the help of six large sheets of brown paper, the petition was prepared ready for presentation. There was now some twenty-two feet of it and nearly four thousand signatures. When rolled up it made a bundle about the size of a small barrel.

Mr. Josser signed it dubiously.

"I suppose we'll have to get a taxi," he said. "Isn't it a pity . . ."

He stopped himself abruptly: he had nearly said that it was a pity Percy wasn't there to drive them.

But the Rev. Headlam Fynne wouldn't hear of a taxi.

"No," he said. "No, no. Not by taxi. No one would notice us. We should lose everything. We must march."

"March!"

The idea appealed to Uncle Henry immediately. Even his sound eye was rolling now. "Over Westminster Bridge and past the House of Commons," he said exultantly. "Into Whitehall and up the steps of the Home Office. Right into the fortress of reaction."

"And one of us carry that?" asked Mr. Josser, pointing at the roll he had just been sticking.

The Rev. Headlam Fynne paused. It certainly was a formidable packet, the petition.

"Well, perhaps *not* carry it," he replied. "*Push* it."

"What in?"

It was Mrs. Josser who had spoken. She had been hovering round the outside of the committee, interested and helpful as occasion demanded, but still frankly sceptical.

The Rev. Headlam Fynne shrugged his broad black shoulders.

"In a pram. Or a mail-cart," he answered. "The exact vehicle is immaterial."

Mrs. Josser looked from the Rev. Headlam Fynne to Uncle Henry, and then on to Mr. Josser.

"Well, Fred's not to push it," was all she said. "Not in public, he isn't."

2

This question, however, did not arise when the time came. Instead of finding someone to do the pushing, there was competition for it. Because it was a bassinette borrowed from one of his parishioners, the Rev. Headlam Fynne felt himself entitled to say who should direct it. But Uncle Henry felt differently.

"You leave this to me," he said. "You've got that cross of yours to look after."

The Rev. Headlam Fynne raised his eyebrows.

"We will take it in turns," he answered. "First one will take the bassinette and then the other."

Uncle Henry shook his head.

"Not me with the cross," he said firmly. "I'll stick to the pram."

There was another awkward pause. The Rev. Headlam Fynne was annoyed.

"As you please," he said. "Time is slipping past us while we argue."

There were seven of them altogether. The Rev. Headlam Fynne went first carrying the cross. Then came Uncle Henry wheeling the perambulator. After him walked Mr. Josser and Connie. Behind them were two lay evangelists from the Junior Guild of God. And, in the rear, marched a pale elderly lady—a stranger—who fell into place saying, "The few of us who feel this way must see that it doesn't happen."

They were joined at intervals by such small boys as were temporarily disengaged and, at cross-roads, by policemen who conducted the little cortege safely over.

In Mr. Josser's calculation it was just half an hour from No. 10 to the Home Office. And so it would have been except for two mishaps. The first was the weather. Dark and overcast when they left Dulcimer Street, it was already drizzling by the time they had reached the Oval. The two lay evangelists were all right: they had umbrellas.

And so had Mr. Josser: he and Connie shared. But the Rev. Headlam Fynne had nothing. Not even a hat. He simply shook the dampness from his hair, held his head high and marched on. He was no worse off, in point of fact, than Uncle Henry. For even if Uncle Henry had been carrying an umbrella it would have been impossible to use it. The perambulator was taking up all his attention. He seemed to be finding difficulty in wheeling it on a straight and satisfactory course.

Then the drizzle changed to rain without warning. At one moment they were walking through light filmy stuff like reduced spray and, at the next, the raindrops were beating on their faces. The Rev. Headlam Fynne kept shaking himself like a terrier and the elderly lady in the rear said, half to herself, half to Mr. Josser: "It's nothing. It's just sent to try us."

But the elderly lady was wrong. It was far from nothing. Almost as she said the words, the real storm broke. The rain came pelting down in monsoon-fashion. The broad black bosom of the Rev. Headlam Fynne was soaking and the folds of his habit collected the water in channels. He turned and addressed his followers.

"This is too much," he said. "We must . . ."

He did not finish his sentence because at that moment he was run into. Uncle Henry, head down, had been ploughing his way through the downpour, stopping for no one. The front of the pram, the hard part, drove full into the leader. Indeed, it was only the plywood cross that saved him.

"Careful, careful," he said. "*Festina lente*, remember."

If he had been irritated earlier by Uncle Henry, he was now downright angry with him. Rubbing himself where it hurt, he led the party to the doorway of a shop. They sheltered there while the swollen raindrops burst like small watery crocuses in the swirling street.

All except Uncle Henry. He was out in the thick of it trying to get the hood up. It seemed a difficult sort of hood. By the time he had fixed it, he was more than ordinarily wet. He was sodden. He came back and stood among them, steaming.

The deluge was not a long one, however. Within twenty minutes, the rain had stopped and they were able to move on again. But those twenty lost minutes were important. They were vital. Instead of being in comfortable time, they were now late. Definitely late. They had to hurry. And it was because of this, directly because of it, that the second mishap occurred.

The Rev. Headlam Fynne was striding on ahead again and the

rest of the procession was following up behind, when suddenly there was a cry from Uncle Henry. He was in difficulties. Appalling difficulties. The perambulator was upright only because he was holding it. And, after a moment, the others saw what was happening. The thing was running on only three wheels. The fourth wheel, the one that had gone careering off on its own like a small hoop, was recovered later by one of the lay evangelists.

This time the delay was really serious. So serious, in fact, that the Rev. Headlam Fynne proposed taking the bundle of names under his arm, and walking. But Uncle Henry wouldn't allow it. He refused point-blank to hand the scroll over. It would be a matter only of minutes, he said, to get the wheel back on again. And in a sense he was right. But only in a sense. For with the hub-cap missing—gone down a drain somewhere, Connie suggested—the wheel came off again. And Uncle Henry would not let them start until it was mended properly. In the result, they were still there ten minutes later, and Uncle Henry was saying that if only he'd got his tool-bag with him everything would have been fixed up by now.

It was the Rev. Headlam Fynne who reminded him of the consequences of this tinkering.

"If this petition means anything," he said sternly, "we must deliver it."

Uncle Henry got up from his knees, and straightened himself.

"I didn't provide this pram," he answered. "I'm only trying to mend it."

"And have you?"

"I have not. It's too old. Too old and too broken. We go as we are. I'm ready."

With that, Uncle Henry gripped hold of the handle of the pram and started off with it. It was not easy. But Uncle Henry was determined. Setting his shoulders to take up the uneven strain, he persisted. The thing fairly rattled along. The Rev. Headlam Fynne even had to double up to get to his rightful place at the head of the procession.

But the half-hour that they had lost in all was irreplaceable. And, as though to remind them of this, dusk was now falling. The little column, cross in front, tramped through darkening streets under a steely sky. And it may have been the grim lowering landscape and grey streets and unlighted houses, or the distance that they had come, or the fear that already they were too late, or simply that they were thinking of Percy—whatever it was, dusk fell on their spirits, too, and they were silent. A small silent crusade with the citadel in sight.

As soon as they had passed St. Thomas's and the County Hall, they could see Big Ben with the hands standing accusingly at ten past five. The Rev. Headlam Fynne instinctively stepped out and Uncle Henry, bent almost double, pushed harder. The wide camber of the bridge, Westminster Bridge, stretched out before them and they began to cross it. As they did so, the sudden wide expanse of black heaven and the smooth sliding water underneath, isolated them. Even to themselves they seemed a pathetically small contingent to go challenging the State.

There was a traffic block at Parliament Square and they had to stand there for a moment, motionless. It was only when they had stopped that Mr. Josser realised how tired he was. Tired and shaky. He took off his bowler hat and passed his handkerchief round inside the lining. He was dimly aware that people on the pavement were staring. But he didn't mind any more. Somewhere on the march, he had ceased caring about anything.

"He'd probably have been better without any of us," he thought. "And so would she. Better for both of them if we'd just let it happen and hadn't interfered."

They were on the point of moving on again when Connie saw something. And because she was the only one who spotted it, she made a dive out of the line so that she could find out for certain. She came back a moment later waving an evening paper in her hand.

"Take it easy, boys," she said. "It's all off."

They crowded round to read the stop-press column that Connie was holding out to them. But they need not have troubled. It was all there in chalk letters on the newspaper board that Connie had first spotted.

CAR MURDERER REPRIEVED, was what it said.

3

The sudden ending of the tension, the snapping of the frightful and burning urgency that had been supporting them, left the little party flat and at a loose end. There they were, useless and unwanted, with a plywood cross and a perambulator, two miles from home, tired and soaked through, and with the sky looking as though at any moment it would start raining again. Nerves and tempers were frayed and jagged. And before Mr. Josser could do anything to stop it, Uncle Henry and the Rev. Headlam Fynne had got into an argument together.

"And do I understand that you still believe in a merciful God?" Mr. Josser heard Uncle Henry saying.

"More than ever," the Rev. Headlam Fynne replied. "Oh, so much more. Look what He's just done."

"Do you call it merciful to keep that poor boy locked up for a couple of months with the threat of the gallows hanging over him?"

"It wasn't God who did that, it was man."

Uncle Henry fixed him with his sound eye.

"And who was it saved him?"

"It was God who guided the Home Secretary," the Rev. Headlam Fynne replied guardedly.

"Then why didn't He guide the judge?" Uncle Henry demanded. "Wasn't He feeling quite so merciful then?"

This time the Rev. Headlam Fynne did not answer him. He was looking at his hands. They were scarlet like the cross. As a result of the rain, the colour had begun to run. The Rev. Headlam Fynne wiped his hands on the front of his habit and then regretted it. Even his black habit bore a broad scarlet streak on it now. He looked as though he had gashed himself. When he found out what had happened—it was his best habit—he lost his temper.

"I refuse to stand here any longer listening to your silly blasphemies," he said. "You're no better than an atheist."

"No better . . ." Uncle Henry began.

But it was too late. One of the lay evangelists had hailed a passing taxi and together they bundled the Rev. Headlam Fynne into it. Without even one word of farewell, and abandoning the pram, the property of one of his parishioners, the Rev. Headlam Fynne was swept away from them.

"Well, that's that," said Connie. "There goes His Holiness."

She screwed her neck backwards so that she could peer up at Big Ben. It was five-thirty.

"Duty calls," she said. "Cheerio, chaps." Then she glanced down at the three-wheeled perambulator up against the kerb, and gave a little giggle. "Can I trust you two lads with the baby?" she asked.

When she had gone, Uncle Henry turned to Mr. Josser.

"Let's park this damn thing somewhere up a side street and go and get a drink," he said. "I'm cold."

CHAPTER 66

I

Mr. Josser found himself put to bed as soon as he got back home. Even the tremendous news of the reprieve was obscured in Mrs. Josser's eyes by the fact that his trouser legs were soaking from the knees down. If he had been deliberately trying to make himself ill . . . she began. But it was no use attempting to argue. There he was tucked up in bed with a cup of hot lemon when he should have been upstairs with Mrs. Josser congratulating Mrs. Boon.

But this wasn't going to be Mr. Josser's funeral. It was Uncle Henry who should have been drinking the hot lemon.

102·5° F.

Uncle Henry stood at the window of his bedroom—that large untidy double bedroom that was littered with pamphlets and manifestoes and cuttings out of newspapers—and looked angrily at the thermometer. It was the first time he could remember ever having used it—the little metal case had remained in the dressing-table drawer undisturbed ever since Mrs. Knockell had left him. But, come to that, it was the first time that he could remember ever having been ill. Certainly the first time he had ever *felt* ill. He had a headache. His heart was hammering. His hands were sticky. And across his chest tight invisible bands had been drawn together. After a further look at the thermometer—which still showed 102·5°—he prescribed himself two aspirins and prepared to open up the shop for Friday's trading.

But it was no use. The faint shiverings which he had noticed earlier grew more intense. His fingers—lean, skilful fingers—felt swollen and stupid. And his eyelids had a disconcerting tendency to close as he stood there. Half-way through the morning he gave up trying to be well, and decided to nurse himself. Leaving the business to the care of the two assistants, he walked over to the chemist's and bought himself a large bottle of special influenza mixture. Then, with two more aspirins and with his overcoat spread across him as he lay down on the bed, he left the shop to the assistants.

It was nearly three o'clock when he woke. But instead of feeling better, he felt worse. Even under his overcoat he was still shivering, and the pain in his chest was worse. He gave himself two more aspirins and a double dose of the mixture and made himself a cup of tea. Before he drank the tea he took his temperature again. It was rising steadily. Since this morning it had climbed to just over 103°. And the tea turned out to be no better than a silly mistake. As soon as he had drunk it, he was sick.

Even so, there is no reason to suppose that the chill, or whatever it was, could not have been checked if Uncle Henry had done the sensible thing and called in a doctor. But in all his life, Uncle Henry had never done the sensible thing. And at sixty-three it is too late to begin. Instead, he took a strong laxative, another double dose of the special influenza mixture, two more aspirins and a thing called a pick-me-up which he had had by him for years. With this mixture of rubbish inside him he retired to bed again and set the alarm clock for five o'clock to be ready for Covent Garden in the morning.

That night—it was the beginning of ten nights and days that were largely indistinguishable—he suffered strange and disturbing thoughts. The shiverings continued, despite the fact that he had crept in under the bed-clothes with his coat and trousers on. But, by now, there was more than shivering to contend with. The bed had somehow become detached from its moorings and was wandering crazily about the floor. After a while, enjoying its new mobility, it did more than merely nose round the corners. It floated. Floated and returned to the floor every so often with a sudden bump. But even this was not the worst. Inside his mind, terrible things were happening. He was being marched over. Lying there in the lonely front bedroom of his shop in the High Street, endless armies in field-grey were tramping across him. He kept tossing from side to side of the bed to avoid the Panzer divisions that kept appearing suddenly from behind the wardrobe.

Sometime during the night he put the light on and tried to take his temperature again. But his fingers were thicker and clumsier than ever and he dropped the thermometer. He heard the tinkle of the glass as it broke on the oilcloth beside his bed. And then, without even switching off the light, he returned beneath the bed-clothes to the world of nightmares. There was an execution in progress now and he was striving desperately to cut the rope.

Then the execution vanished like the Panzer divisions, and he was back in Covent Garden Market again, going through the fragrant lofty halls, buying a couple of cases of apples here, a crate of bananas there, and a box of cut flowers elsewhere. But this didn't last long enough. The alarm clock had roused him before he had finished buying.

Dressing was not difficult because all his clothes were still on him.

And shaving presented no difficulty because he never shaved until he had come back from market—Covent Garden is always an affair of black jowls in the early morning. He even managed to keep down a cup of tea which he made himself. But he felt far from well, very far from well, he told himself, as he began to go down the stairs. There seemed to be things in his way and he couldn't avoid them. He had to hold on to the banisters to support himself. And by the time he had emerged into the little shop, which smelt overpoweringly of earth and onions and the skins of oranges, he could go no further. He made his way at the third attempt into the little cash-desk and picked up the telephone. Then he read the instructions as though he'd never seen them before, and dialled O. After the third attempt, the thing worked and a voice answered.

"This is Henry Knockell speaking," Uncle Henry said slowly and distinctly. "I'm ill and I need help. I'm all alone."

Then when the voice at the other end asked him where he lived, Uncle Henry proceeded to talk it down. He went on about capital punishment and airborne infantry and the Panzer divisions that were in the bedroom.

2

It is an organised community, London. Wonderfully organised. Nothing can ever happen there without other people knowing about it. Take Uncle Henry, for instance. His disjointed telephone call was traced through the exchange. And by eight-thirty there was a policeman on the doorstep to see what was going on. By nine-fifteen the ambulance had arrived and carted Uncle Henry off to the City Hospital. And by a quarter to twelve there was a telegram for Mrs. Josser in Dulcimer Street to tell her what had occurred.

Mrs. Josser wept when she received it. Wept because of the sheer suddenness of the shock. And also because her conscience was troubling her. She reproached herself bitterly. It was all too plain now how short-sighted she had been in thinking only of Mr. Josser. If he had come back home soaked through, it was obvious that Uncle Henry must have been just as wet. And she had never given him a thought. The whole incident was just one more vivid piece of proof that men left to themselves were feckless and unreliable.

Clearly she would have to go along to the hospital at once to see if they were looking after him properly. But how? Mrs. Boon still couldn't be left for a single minute. And Mr. Josser, after his chill, certainly wasn't well enough to look after her. Unless Connie—who had tired noticeably of her role of sick-nurse—could be found, there would be nothing for it but to ask Mrs. Vizzard to sit with the poor woman. And Mrs. Vizzard wasn't on speaking terms with Mrs. Boon.

In the end, it was Mr. Puddy who sat with Mrs. Boon. He brought his lunch down with him and ate it with her. She was a quiet sort of person, Mrs. Boon, and she didn't interrupt him. Indeed, throughout the whole meal, she made only one remark.

"I was just thinking," she said at last, as Mr. Puddy was thumbing up the cake-crumbs. "There wasn't anything to worry about, was there? I knew my Percy would be all right."

After a bit of discussion, Mr. Josser finally persuaded Mrs. Josser to let him go with her. It was the first time he'd been out since his soaking and she gave him permission only if he wrapped up properly. In consequence it was a bulky, muffled figure that sat beside her on the bus.

"Just fancy," the figure kept saying. "Poor old Henry. Let's hope it isn't anything serious."

Even though it was really lunch-time when they got there, they were allowed in straightaway—which, as Mrs. Josser whispered to her husband, just showed how bad Uncle Henry must be.

But they need not have hurried. He didn't know them. Even made no attempt to know them. He was lying on his back—his eyes closed, breathing fast and heavily. The flush on his cheeks was just because of something that the doctor had given him, the nurse said. And she added that they could come again in the evening.

As it turned out, it was only the first of ten similar visits that they were to pay him.

3

But where had Mr. Squales been all this time? Why hadn't he gone along with the rest of them for the presentation of the petition?

The answer is that he couldn't go because he wasn't there. He had left the evening before for Chiddingly. And what was more he was still there. Three whole days of the good life now lay behind him, and he was due to leave to-morrow. In his philosophic way he tried not to think about the return. And, trying hard enough, he succeeded.

At the present moment he was sitting in Mrs. Jan Byl's blacked-out conservatory. The scent of the orchids was a little overpowering, and it made him feel sleepy. But he was blissfully happy. Sitting back almost full-length in the wicker chaise-longue he had that feeling of rich and perfect contentment that comes of knowing that there is a drink all ready at one's elbow, and another one to be had simply by making it clear that the first one has been finished.

He was really doubly content. For this time he hadn't had to *ask* to be invited. Quite unprompted by him, Mrs. Jan Byl had written suggesting it. And Mr. Squales basked in the arrangement.

"N-o-o-o," he had just said slowly in answer to Mrs. Jan Byl's last question. "Not exactly working. Merely experimenting."

"All day?"

"And most of the night," he told her. "It's a long road."

He would like to have added that the pavements were not exactly laid with gold. But the moment did not yet seem ripe for it. Above all, he did not want to give the appearance of trying to rush things. And in any case Mrs. Jan Byl was already speaking.

"But sometimes there is a human life at the end of the road, isn't there?" Mrs. Jan Byl asked quietly.

"Er?"

Mr. Squales was startled. He cocked himself up on one elbow and looked across at her. To his amazement, she was staring at him in breathless admiration.

"Don't imagine that I hadn't read this," Mrs. Jan Byl warned him, holding out a folded newspaper. "I was only waiting to see if you were going to tell me yourself."

Mr. Squales was sitting right up now.

"May . . . may I see?" he asked.

It was the lady feature-writer's article that Mrs. Jan Byl had somewhere got hold of. And, when Mr. Squales saw it, he almost snatched it from her hand. Somehow or other he had missed it himself because he had forgotten which paper she represented and after buying the *Express* and the *Mail* and the *Mirror* at the station he had given up. But there it was. And very charmingly phrased, too.

"Behind this last-minute effort to save the car-bandit murderer," the article ran, "is . . . dark, aquiline, bass-voiced medium, Enrico Qualito. Temporarily forsaking the séance room for the public rostrum, this modern Rudi Schneider's flowing signature adorns the first page of the petition now being presented. . . ."

The rest seemed to be all about the Rev. Headlam Fynne and Uncle Henry, and Mr. Squales lost interest.

"Yes," he said slowly. "Perhaps I did play my part. I may not have been unuseful."

"You saved him," Mrs. Jan Byl replied emphatically. "That's what you did."

"I . . . like to think so."

"But tell me," Mrs. Jan Byl said, leaning over towards him, "after so much excitement, how could you bear to come away in the middle of it? How could you tear yourself away to come down to see an old woman in the country, when you didn't know what the outcome would be?"

This was a bit of a stumper for the moment. Until Mrs. Jan Byl had mentioned it, Mr. Squales had forgotten all about Percy. He shaded his eyes with his hands while he was thinking.

"But I did know," he answered at length. "I came down knowing that my work was done."

"*Knowing* it?"

Mr. Squales nodded.

"I often think," he said, "that Time is like a wheel, really. It revolves and what was once the past becomes the present. We have only to turn it backwards and there is the future facing us, doncher know?"

Why had he said "doncher know"? It was little vulgarities like this that were always spoiling even his best remarks. But Mrs. Jan Byl was apparently ready to overlook it.

"You really are a most interesting man, professor," she told him. "That's just what I've always believed about Time. Only I always think of it as a great river. A great river flowing in a circle."

Mr. Squales smiled back at her.

"Wheel or river, it's all the same thing," he said magnanimously. If she had said that it was a moving staircase he wouldn't have contradicted her.

Mrs. Jan Byl shifted her chair imperceptibly towards him. It was more of a gesture than an actual movement.

"Sometimes I think that I shall never go back to London," she said. "Not even after the war's over. Living here among the birds and the flowers one is somehow so much closer. To the spirits, I mean."

Mr. Squales yawned. The odour of the lilies all round was practically anæsthetising him. And then he realised what it was that she had said. In a single sentence she had all but obliterated his whole professional future.

"It's certainly a very nice little bit of property you've got here," he agreed unenthusiastically.

"Boanerges tells me to stop here," Mrs. Jan Byl said simply.

"Boanerges?"

Mr. Squales squared himself. He smelt a rival.

"My spirit guide," Mrs. Jan Byl explained. "He often comes to me. It was Boanerges who told me to ask you here."

Mr. Squales sighed.

"Dear Boanerges," he said.

"And you must come down more often," Mrs. Jan Byl went on. "Perhaps you'll bring Boanerges back to me. Sometimes he's naughty. He stays away for weeks."

"Boanerges'll come all right," Mr. Squales told her. "I . . . I feel it."

And beneath his breath—at least he hoped that it had been beneath it—he added: "Come? He'll practically live here."

As he said it he remembered Dulcimer Street. Remembered Dulcimer Street, and remembered Mrs. Jan Byl's remark about coming down more often.

Why couldn't he be like Boanerges?

CHAPTER 67

I

Considering the delirium that had gone before, Uncle Henry's end was peaceful enough. After another bad night dreaming of total war and tall priests in black habits, he had rallied. The mists cleared away and he knew himself for what he was—a very sick man. Even a dying man. He asked where he was, how long he had been there and what was the matter with him. He also asked for Mrs. Josser, and didn't seem surprised when he was told that she was expected along at almost any moment. His rationalness and sanity quite startled the little nurse who had known him only when he was damply raving. He looked about him for a few minutes and then addressed her.

"Do these screens mean that I'm for it, young lady?" he asked.

She told him pertly that screens didn't mean anything of the sort—that they were only put there to keep the other patients from disturbing him, in fact. And she fastened a fresh piece of sticking plaster on to his lip to keep the little oxygen tube in place. Then she tried to slip away to tell the Sister that No. 18 was back in his senses again.

But, on the way, Uncle Henry stopped her.

"And you might bring me a piece of paper and a pen," he told her. "I shall want witnesses."

The Sister came along as soon as the nurse called her. She recognised this sudden recovery for the bad sign that it was. She wouldn't hear of pen and paper until Uncle Henry himself had explained things to her. Then she sat down and wrote to Uncle Henry's dictation.

"*I, Henry George Knockell, greengrocer and fruiterer,*"—Uncle Henry insisted on the "greengrocer and fruiterer"—*of Dalston High Street, being in my right mind,*" he said slowly, and distinctly, "*do hereby bequeath everything of which I die possessed, both moneys in the bank and my aforesaid business, to my sister Emily Josser of* 10 *Dulcimer Street in the Borough of Kennington, subject only to that she pay my two assistants Alfred Armitt and Charles Evans the sum of twenty-five pounds apiece if they be in my employ at the time of my decease. Signed . . . Witnessed . . . Witnessed.*"

Then he closed his eyes and lay back exhausted. He was too weak for the moment even to sign his name at the foot of the piece of notepaper. But suddenly the eyelids flickered and a trace of colour returned to his cheek. At the thought of being able to score off organised religion he had rallied.

"And put in this bit," he said. "*I want no clergyman and no religious service. Nor do I want flowers or any mourners. My body is to be cremated and the ashes scattered. . . .*" He went on to say something that sounded like "superstitions and unhygienic Christian burial" but his voice trailed off and the nurse could not follow him.

This time he was scarcely breathing at all. But he was pleased with himself. Very pleased. He had always entertained a deep and burning contempt for all lawyers, as well as for all clergymen, and it was gratifying to know that on his death-bed he could beat them at their own game and in their own language. The will, very formal-looking with its signatures and the date—the Sister had put that in as Uncle Henry had overlooked it—was left at his request propped up against the water-jug. He felt no false shame in the matter and he wanted to tell his sister how much to ask for the business. In his impulsive, enthusiastic fashion Uncle Henry was quite looking forward to dying as soon as he could get the details settled.

But Mrs. Josser was still not there. And the strain had been too much for him. That simple piece of dictation had drained him dry of energy. His breathing quickened and he lay there, his eyes closed, picking at the hem of the sheet.

"Tell—her—to—hurry—up," he said at last. "I've—got—a—lot—I—want—to—say—to her."

Then he went off to sleep. A deep gentle sleep that made him feel like a little boy again.

Mr. and Mrs. Josser had been with him for some time before Uncle Henry woke again. His mind was still fresh and clear—he was able to handle with professional keenness one of the oranges that Mrs. Josser had brought him—but he was noticeably weaker. The young nurse, who was unfamiliar with death, wanted to cry a bit. He couldn't say more than one or two words at a time. In fact, the advice about the business was something that was definitely beyond him. After one or two attempts he gave it up as hopeless, and just repeated the name of Swales & Hunter as being reliable agents for the kind of sale. But even this served no useful purpose. He said it too faintly for anyone but himself to hear.

There was nothing more that anyone could do. It was now simply a matter of waiting. The Sister increased the oxygen a little—but it was only a gesture, not a service. And the young nurse fetched another hot-water bottle. Uncle Henry, however, was far away from oxygen and hot-water bottles. He was drifting slowly and peacefully on a great warm tide that was carrying him further and further away from war and hangings and the stranglehold of Covent Garden. It was like free-wheeling on his green bicycle down an endless gentle hill. And as there was nothing but darkness, thick velvety darkness, surrounding him there seemed to be no point in opening his eyes again.

At twelve-fifteen, they decided that he had stopped breathing.

The Sister wouldn't let Mrs. Josser take the will away with her because it had to pass through the Almoner's Office first, to be put on record. But Mrs. Josser was in that strange exalted mood which proximity to death produces, and the thought of touching Uncle Henry's money seemed at the moment abhorrent and even sinful to her. She went out of the ward, her handkerchief to her eyes and her arm through Mr. Josser's.

"It's just too much," she said. "First of all Percy. And then the war. And everything."

Mr. Josser tightened the grip on her arm.

"Don't take it to heart, Mother," he said. "Henry was happy anyway. The war turned out just the way he said it would."

2

The man who was really depressed by Uncle Henry's death was Mr. Puddy. Not that he had seen much of him. Or even liked him. It was simply that Mr. Puddy was in his sixtieth year himself. And, judging by Uncle Henry, the sixties were pretty dangerous years for widowers. In consequence, he became more moody and morose than ever. He ruminated. He spoke to no one.

And all the time, had he only known it, he had got a piece of good luck coming to him.

It wasn't his good luck, really. It was Connie's. Because of Mr. Barks, she had just pulled off her claim against the driver of the Daimler. And it had all been just as she surmised—the motorist was a real gentleman, with the best sort of insurance company. After only a short exchange of letters with Mr. Barks—who was always at his best in running-down cases—the other side had agreed to settle out of court.

And no wonder. With each letter of Mr. Barks's Connie's state had grown more alarming. By the fourth, she was half paralysed down one side and her power of speech was failing.

Sixty-five pounds, and costs, was what Mr. Barks finally got out of them. Simply by asking for it, as you might say. And when Connie heard the news she broke down and cried. There in Mr. Barks's office, on one of his Rexine and Chippendale chairs, she wiped her old eyes from sheer happiness. While it wasn't quite so enormous as she had first imagined—not ten thousand pounds, or anything like that—it was still a pretty good round sum. With the great advantage over any other round sum in her life that this one didn't have to be imagined. Even fifty pounds would have had the same quality. And here was an extra fifteen thrown in for nothing.

No wonder that she had been too much preoccupied with her own affairs to give more than a passing thought to Uncle Henry. Usually a death bowled her clean over. But with this one, she hadn't turned a hair. Not that Connie was one of the mean ones. Not our Connie. She wasn't going to keep the whole of it for herself. There was Mr. Puddy's share, remember. If it hadn't been for his advice about putting the case in the hands of a solicitor she might still have been writing to the nice gentleman on her sixpenny mauve writing-pad. And in all probability she wouldn't even have got so much as an answer.

"I'll give him half," she promised impetuously. "Thirty-two pounds ten something just for thinking of it."

It wasn't quite so easy as that, however. Not straightaway at least. Mr. Barks insisted on giving her a cheque, and there remained the question of what to do with it. She couldn't simply cut it in two and give Mr. Puddy one end. Clearly she had to open a banking account.

Connie with a banking account! The idea tickled her so much that, like a fool, she let them put it on deposit. She had the foresight, however, to keep back five pounds while she still had a chance. And with the five pounds rolled up inside her little moire bag she came out of the bank feeling that somehow she'd been swindled. Five pounds wasn't very much to have kept back out of a fortune.

But still, it was something. It was more than she'd had on her since her gay days. And all out of the makeweight, too. Leaving the solid capital untouched.

"I suppose I ought to buy Savings certificates," she reflected. "Save your money and shorten the war."

But the idea was not attractive. Compared with what a war cost, five pounds wouldn't even shorten it by much. Besides, it meant a lot to her, that five pounds. There were so many things that she needed. Things that she'd been getting along without for years.

Like a new cage for Duke, for instance. Poor little thing, his old cage wasn't fit for a sparrow. It was lucky for the pet that he could fly because, with the bottom of the cage as loose as it was, he might have had to save himself at any moment.

The thought of a new cage filled her with the happiness of sheer unselfishness. And she wasn't going to lose any time about it, either. Duke had roughed it long enough. But bird-cages, good ones, aren't the sort of thing that can be picked up just anywhere. She remembered a pet-stores over at Balham. Suppose, however, that when she reached it they hadn't got what she wanted. What about Duke then, sentenced by her carelessness to spend another night in his present contraption? Thinking over the risk, she decided that it wasn't fair to him and resolved to go straight off to Gamages.

It was quite a journey from Kennington. And she had plenty of time to think about things on the way. Up in the top front seat of the bus, she mused. She realised now how silly it would be to give away half the damages to Mr. Puddy. After all, he hadn't really done anything. And whose accident had it been? His or hers? No, thirty-two ten was out of the question. He'd think she was balmy if she gave him all that. And so she would be. On the whole, half the amount—say the odd fifteen—seemed about right. She could just see herself presenting it.

"A little token of my appreciation, Mr. Puddy. Don't open the envelope now. Keep it till later. And please don't trouble to thank me. It is I who should be thanking you."

Pretty, wasn't it? But, as she said it, the thought of what fifteen one-pound notes would actually look like made her blood run cold. It still seemed a terrible lot of money. . . .

There was a moment's trouble when she reached Holborn because the conductor had just rung his bell when Connie got to the bottom of the stairs, and he had to stop the bus again specially for her. He asked her to make up her mind next time she was going anywhere. And Connie had to tell him that she'd take good care she never went anywhere with him. She added from the kerb-side that it was lucky for him that he was such a little man as otherwise she'd have seen to him.

"Little whippet," she said to herself. "How much does he think he's worth, anyway? He'd fall off the bus if he knew what I'd got on me."

Once inside Gamages, however, she forgot about him. It was like being transported into an everlasting Christmas bazaar going into the shop: it was the lighter side of life organised on the scale of heavy industry. There was everything—cricket bats, air-guns, conjuring-tricks, card games, bicycles, dolls' houses, teddy bears, tropical fish—and bird-cages.

She wished for a moment that she could have brought Duke with her so that he could choose for himself. But as that was impossible she went ahead and bought a glittering wire creation with two porcelain dishes for his food, for twenty-five and six. The assistant offered to send it for her, but she wouldn't hear of it. And then, just as it was all wrapped up, she saw the one she really wanted. The moment she spotted it, she knew that it was the one that Duke would have wanted if he only could have come along, too. There was just something about it. And it made the twenty-five and sixpenny one look like prison. This one was a whopper with coloured glass sides down low where the wires started and a perch made out of a bit of real branch. The shape, too, was more imposing: there was a sort of double dome to it that suggested it might have been designed by an architect. And, finally, to protect the little occupant from the ill effects of its own jumpings, there was a big coil spring on top to cushion the shock.

"Bless his little yellow head," Connie told herself. "He'll think he's swinging in the tree-tops."

It was three pounds two and six; and Connie paid the difference. She even went further and bought a packet of proprietary bird-seed, some grated sea-shell, and a piece of cuttle-fish bone for Duke to clean his beak on. She could hardly walk as she came out of the shop with the enormous bird-cage banging against her knees with every step she took. But she was happy. A sublime ineffable radiance filled every part of her.

"Was the accident worth it, or was it?" she asked herself.

During tea at the Corner House, with the bird-cage under the table where the Nippies wouldn't trip up over it, she thought more about Mr. Puddy. And she rebuked herself.

"After all, Dukey, if it wasn't for your uncle you wouldn't be having a nice new home. Mustn't forget your manners just because you're all excited."

It struck her now that perhaps it would be better to give Mr. Puddy a present of some sort rather than the actual money. There was something about a lady's giving a man money that, no matter how delicately it was done, wasn't quite the thing. Now, a gold watch or a pair of enamel cuff-links would be different. Any book of etiquette would allow her that in the circumstances.

She looked in one or two jeweller's afterwards. But it wasn't much use. She saw nothing she liked. And, besides, she hadn't got enough on her now to buy anything. Before Mr. Puddy could come into his bit of luck she'd have to make another expedition to the bank specially for him.

She had got back as far as the Oval before she remembered that she'd got nothing in the house for supper. She'd need something else before she went on to the night-club. And she blamed herself for not having had one of Lyons's Specials when she'd had the chance. It was all because she'd been so eager to see Duke in his new cage that she'd come rushing out of the place again.

It was only a snack that she wanted, and she went into the Payantake stores at the corner to buy a tin of soup. Then, realising that her station in life had altered, and that she could afford anything in the place, she bought another one for to-morrow night. They made an awkward sort of parcel in their flimsy paper bag, and she wished that she could have put them inside the bird-cage along with the bird-seed and the cuttle-fish bone. But it wasn't far. And the thought of Duke's face when he saw his present. . . .

She'd transferred him. And apart from some silly fluttering on his part when she first put her hand in the cage—wouldn't he ever trust her? wouldn't he ever realise that she was the only mother he'd got—he seemed to like his fresh surroundings. She sat there, her old face pressed up against the new bars, while Duke went up and down his bit of real branch and put one of his feet into the bird-seed.

Mr. Josser's clock boomed five times—five separate reverberations that filled the whole of No. 10—and Connie straightened herself. As she did so, a sharp splinter of pain ran through her left side at the point where the car bumper had hit her. The twinge appalled her. Suppose the hospital had blundered and she really had hurt herself! For all she knew she might really be half paralysed before the month was out. Someone with only sixty pounds in cash between her and destitution.

It was hard on Mr. Puddy that she should have felt the pain at that moment because it knocked on the head all hope of that fifteen pounds. Or of the watch. Or of the cuff-links. Instead of a well-provided old age, it was penury that she now saw facing her. She'd known that it was a gamble right from the start. But it was only now that she saw so clearly that it was her life, her precious darling old life, that she had been gambling with.

But even so—even with death standing in the wings—she didn't forget Mr. Puddy altogether. On the contrary, she decided quite spontaneously that she'd give him the second tin of soup that she'd brought back. She'd make him, in fact, a present of to-morrow night's supper. But when it actually came to it, when it was time for her to go upstairs with the tin held in her hands like a perishing bouquet, she just couldn't do it. If she'd attempted it, she'd have died laughing.

"*Dear Mr. Puddy,—In recognition of your kindness in securing for me the sum of sixty-five pounds here is a tin of soup as a token, price fourpence. Yours gratefully, Connie.*"

It wouldn't look good on paper, would it? And besides there *was* something a bit odd in the notion of giving a grown man a tin of soup. Then the happiest of solutions came to her. She decided that she'd *make* the soup for him and take it up in a cup all ready. That was quite different. It was still generous. And, somehow, charming and ladylike as well.

When she actually got down to mixing the soup, however, she found that, with just a splash of water, it was easily possible to get two cups of strong nourishing soup out of one tin. Indeed, that was what the label recommended. So there was no point in opening the second one.

Pouring the hot soup into a cup, she wiped the edge round with her hanky to give that well-turned-out restaurant appearance and carried it carefully upstairs.

She knocked and waited politely for Mr. Puddy to open the door for her.

"I had some of your supper the other night," she said brightly. "Here's a bit of mine to make up for it."

Mr. Puddy turned a blank astonished face in her direction. Then he sniffed, savouring the fragrance of the steam.

"Bulligatawny," he said. "A dice gub of bulligatawny."

And he reached out his hand for his reward.

BOOK FIVE

DISSOLUTION IN DULCIMER STREET

CHAPTER 68

I

THE EPISODE of Uncle Henry was over. The business had been sold, his collection of books and pamphlets had gone to salvage and Uncle Henry himself had gone to his hygienic and fiery burial. All that remained of him was the green bicycle. Mrs. Josser had kept that in case there was a bus strike or something. You never knew in wartime.

It was Mrs. Boon who was now the problem. There she was shut away in her room, and nobody knew what to do about her. She hadn't any friends. She hadn't any occupation. And, once the rent had been paid, she hadn't any money. She simply sat there, thinking about Percy.

Inevitably, she was a burden on Mrs. Josser. She ate all her meals with them. All except breakfast, that is. And that, Mrs. Josser carried up on a tray to her bedroom. It was nearly six weeks since the reprieve. And, from the way Mrs. Boon was behaving, it might have been only yesterday. She had no plans. No proposals. Not even any apologies.

In the result, she drove Mrs. Vizzard nearly demented with anxiety. All during the trial, and during that awful period afterwards, Mrs. Vizzard had tried to close her eyes to her. Had sought to forget that Mrs. Boon existed. It was merely a matter of waiting, she had told herself, until everything was over. But she was not now so sure. Mrs. Boon's vagueness baffled and defeated her. And what was so peculiarly infuriating was that Mrs. Boon herself was apparently quite unconcerned. The only time Mrs. Vizzard had mentioned the subject to her, Mrs. Boon had spoken vaguely about doing something when she felt a little stronger. But she had not said what or how soon. And meanwhile the bridal suite—Mrs. Vizzard's and Mr. Squales's bridal suite—was as far away as ever. It was excruciating for Mrs. Vizzard in her own house not to be able to make even the most elementary preparation for her own wedding.

She had her own private reasons for urgency. Reasons that she could confess to no one. Least of all to Mr. Squales. But they were there, goading and terrifying her. The simple fact was that she was jealous. In those professional visits to Chiddingly—visits which she herself had financed for him—she smelt something sinister. His behaviour alternately saddened and angered her. To-day in particular—with Mr. Squales out at the Public Library looking up something about the habits of the Incas—she was in despair.

"I don't trust him," she admitted. "That's the whole point. I love him, but deep down something tells me not to trust him. It's only when I've got my eyes on him that I know what he's doing. When he's out of my sight he . . . he . . ." But she could not complete the sentence because she did not know what it was that she feared when he was away from her. It was merely a vague all-embracing dubiety that surrounded him. "It may be simply my money he's after, the wretch," she said fiercely. "And he's had a lot of it already. I don't trust him. I shall never see any of it back. He'll just go away and leave me when he's bled me dry. That's what he'll do. He'll go out of this house one day and never come back."

Then that mood, too, passed and she was back in her earlier one —the mood of prostrate helplessness. "Oh, but I love him so. I do. I want to take care of him always. I want to save him from himself. I want those two rooms upstairs so that we can get married."

She had shifted the chair in which she was sitting, so as to bring it closer to the fire. And, with the warmth of the blaze playing upon her legs in their neat lisle stockings, she sat gazing emptily into space. Gradually, the space resolved into a wall. Then the wall as gradually became a picture frame and picture. Scarcely aware of how the change had come about, she found it was at the portrait of the late Mr. Vizzard that she was staring. He was gazing down at her with a peculiar fixity that was due in part to the conventions of cabinet photography and in part to the expression that had been natural to him. As in life, he seemed perplexed, anxious and gloomily conscious of his own frustration.

The only difference was that there was a frown there that she had never seen before.

2

And then something happened that, at least so far as Mrs. Josser was concerned, took her mind off Mrs. Boon completely. It was

Ted who was responsible. Quiet, steady, reliable Ted who had never given a minute's trouble to anybody. He received his calling-up papers.

There was nothing extraordinary in that. Everyone was getting them. It was the way he was behaving that was quite inexplicable. He just accepted it. With the Co-op. ready to do everything in its power to apply for his reserve—and conscientious young men like Ted were the very backbone of the business—he expressed the view that if everyone got himself reserved we should lose the war anyway. There was nothing heroic or vainglorious in the attitude. It was simply blunt common sense. Having assured himself that the Co-op. would make up the difference in his income, he was unbudgeable. Even Cynthia's tears couldn't dissuade him. He muttered something about it being his duty, and left it at that. And by then, of course, it was too late to do anything. The Ministry of Labour had got his papers and were working on them.

What was more, judging by the speed with which the papers came through, they must have been working overtime. It was settled already, in fact. What a month ago had been no more than a vague threat was now right on top of him. He had to go to-morrow.

In consequence, there was a lowering of spirits all round. And the weather seemed just right for it. There was fog. Scarcely much more than shadowy drifting skeins of it so far. Merely skeins that hung at the end of streets and gardens like gauze transformations. But it promised to be thick, really thick, later. By six o'clock London would be lost somewhere in the gloom at the bottom of a pit, blacker than its own black-out.

Not that the black-out needed any blackening. It was black enough in all conscience. And gloomy enough. Night in England wasn't ordinary night any longer. It was the original Egyptian Plague temporarily redescended. It had a sinister, almost solid, quality of its own, this black-out, so that you felt you had to carve your way through it, scraping and scooping out a passage as you went along. Even frivolous sociable people, restless inveterate gad-abouts, would stand in the shelter of their own front doorways looking out into the evening where there should have been street lamps and the headlights of passing cars and bright interiors of shops and living-rooms; and seeing nothing in all directions but the same unending ebony blackness, without a crack in it anywhere, they would turn and go back indoors again.

Thin fingers of the thickening fog had found their way into No. 10 Dulcimer Street, with the result that the Jossers' gas chandelier seemed to be burning less brightly than usual and the mirror over-mantel looked as though it had been rubbed over with a damp cloth. But it wasn't only the fog that made everything seem so dismal. It was the occasion. This was a farewell party they were having. Ted and Cynthia were both there, of course. And, because there was no one with whom to leave Baby, Baby was there as well. Mr. Josser was sitting in his favourite chair beside the fireplace. And Mrs. Josser and Doris were bringing in the tea.

At first glance, everything might have seemed to be set for a normal pleasant evening. But, when they drew up round the table, it was obvious that there was something wrong. Nobody said a word. And, now that she had come into the circle of light, you could see that Cynthia had been crying. She was silly, giggling little Cynthia no longer.

Mr. Josser tried his best to introduce a lighter, more carefree sort of atmosphere. But he wasn't very successful. He contrived to strike a wrong note right in the first bar.

"Better have another cup, Ted," he said. "You won't get tea like this in the Army."

A faint, rather sickly smile spread across Ted's face. But there was no smile on Cynthia's. Even Mrs. Josser was shocked by her husband's callousness.

"You don't have to go on reminding us, Fred," she told him. "It's bad enough as it is, without that."

Mr. Josser looked across at his son.

"*You* didn't mind my little bit of fun, did you?" he asked.

He put the question appealingly. But he didn't in his own heart feel very funny this evening. He kept remembering how he had felt himself back in 1915 when he'd left Mrs. Josser with Ted as a baby and Doris not even born then.

Ted didn't reply to Mr. Josser's question. He merely shook his head. There was nothing actually surprising in that, however, because Ted had always been the silent sort. But all the same it didn't serve to make the party any merrier. It only set Cynthia burrowing into her handkerchief again.

Then Mrs. Josser suddenly put her cup down and addressed no one in particular.

"I haven't said anything before," she observed, "but I'm going to say it now. I think it's a downright shame Ted having to go off like this, with the streets still full of fellows only half his age. If they'd known their business at the Co-op. they'd have made him get himself deferred. He's essential. That's what Ted is, essential."

"That's what I told him," Cynthia said, emerging for a moment. "I begged him."

"If they'd played their cards properly," Mrs. Josser continued, "Ted needn't have gone for months yet. Perhaps he wouldn't ever have to go at all."

"But he wants to go," Cynthia said. "He told me so."

She began crying again as she said it. Really crying, not just wiping her eyes. They all turned to Ted for him to answer the accusation.

But what could he say? He couldn't get up and explain that between Dulcimer Street and the Germans there was only a thin red line of tried reliable men like himself. Couldn't do it, because he wasn't made that way. All that he could manage was a very halting "I didn't, Cynthie. You know I didn't."

Before Cynthia could reply, Mrs. Josser had taken over. She began to blink very rapidly behind her spectacles, and her lower lip quivered. A moment later her head was on Ted's shoulder and she was crying.

For the next five minutes Cynthia was completely out of it. It was his mother, his own mother, who told Ted how precious he was, how proud of him they all were, how he was to take care of himself, how he'd be sure to win a medal, how big Baby would have grown by the time he got back, and how lucky it was he'd had all that training in the Boy Scouts. She was not in the ordinary way a demonstrative woman, Mrs. Josser, and she was surprised to find how much better she felt towards the war as a whole after this complete breakdown in public.

Because Ted was fully occupied, Mr. Josser got up and went over to Cynthia.

"It . . . it won't seem so bad once he's actually gone," he told her. "We'll look after you."

"I know you will," Cynthia answered, with a gulp.

She liked her father-in-law, and generally he seemed to understand her. It was only on matters connected with Ted that he couldn't be expected to know how she really felt.

"It'll be so lonely in the evenings when Ted's gone," Cynthia explained after a pause. "So terribly lonely. And I shan't be able to go out because of Baby. I shall just be stuck there."

Mr. Josser put his hand on her shoulder.

"You'd better come round and live with us," he told her. "We'd make room for you."

"But I don't want to leave my home," Cynthia answered. "I want to keep it like it is all ready for when Ted comes back."

At emotional moments like this, Mr. Josser was always a bit awkward. He hadn't got any flow of small talk. He looked from Cynthia to Mrs. Josser, and from Mrs. Josser to Ted. But he couldn't find any assistance anywhere.

It was Doris who saved things.

"I tell you what, Cynthia," Doris said. "I'll come round and live with you. You'd like that, wouldn't you?"

"What's that?" said Mrs. Josser, turning away from Ted for a moment.

"I'm going round to live with Cynthia while Ted's away," Doris told her.

"You're going round to live with Cynthia!"

Mrs. Josser repeated the words, and then stopped herself. She simply didn't trust herself to go on. It would be bad enough to have Cynthia round in No. 10 Dulcimer Street where she could keep an eye on her for Ted's sake. But it was something entirely different to have Doris and Cynthia setting up house together somewhere else. Even though she no longer referred to the lamentable experiment with Doreen, she hadn't forgotten it. Nor had she forgotten that Cynthia had once been an usherette.

"It wouldn't work," she said firmly. "You're neither of you old enough."

"Well, I think it's a jolly good idea."

It was Mr. Josser who had spoken. And, having said so much already, there was nothing to do but go on.

"Don't you think it's a good idea, Ted?" he asked. "It'd be company for Cynthia, having Doris round there."

Ted nodded his head. There was a pause while he seemed to be thinking.

"Fine," he said. "I couldn't ask for anything better."

And that coming from Ted was a lot. It settled things, in fact.

3

Ted and Cynthia and Baby were back home again. Back home for the last time. Baby was asleep already. But Ted and Cynthia weren't asleep. They were just lying there in the big double bed together. Her head was on his shoulder and there was a damp patch, warm at first but now chilly, on the arm of his pyjamas where she had been crying.

"Don't take on so, Cynthia," Ted said in a whisper—he had to speak in a whisper because of Baby. "I didn't mean it that way."

"But I promised," Cynthia told him in a small choking voice. "I won't look at another man whilst you're gone."

"If I found you going about with another man, I'd kill him," Ted told her.

A shiver ran through Cynthia at the words. They were adorable. This was the way she liked Ted best.

"You're spoiling everything going on like this," she said. "You're frightening me."

Ted didn't answer. Instead, he drew his arm tighter round her. Cynthia snuggled against him.

"Oh, Ted," she said. "You are silly not trusting me."

It was heavenly lying there like that with him jealous, for her sake, of all the other men in London.

"Kiss me, Cynthia," he told her.

They kissed. But Cynthia stopped him.

"You mustn't, Ted," she told him. "Think of Baby. She'll hear."

They lay after that without speaking, simply holding each other in an embrace that left Cynthia breathless. When Ted's arm loosened, she whispered something.

"I'll think about you all the time," she told him. "Every hour and every minute. And at nights I'll just sit looking out of the window at the moon, thinking that it's shining down on you somewhere."

It was, for the moment, the usherette rather than the wife who was speaking. But the two of them were so mingled that even Cynthia did not know where one left off.

"Every night," she went on, "I'll look up at the moon and dream about you. . . ."

But outside the fog had thickened. There wasn't any moon. London was groping about in the depths by now, and if it was going to be a long war—say two or three years of it—there were bound to be further moonless nights before it was over.

CHAPTER 69

I

Life in Larkspur Road with Cynthia was strikingly different from the way things went in Dulcimer Street.

For a start, everything in the flat was so up-to-date and modern.

Ted had spent a lot of money on the furniture. From the low couch and the duplicate easy chairs, each with a gold tassel hanging from the front of the arms, to the new-looking antique dining-room suite it was all of one style—1937, Co-op. Even the centre light in the bedroom was Co-op. It was a chromium box made up of orange-coloured glass strips. Admittedly some of the pieces had lost their first freshness. One or two of the tassels—there were tassels everywhere in the drawing-room: on the corner of the cushions, on the edge of the standard lamp shade, on the curtain sash—had been pulled off by Baby, and Cynthia had been too busy to sew them on again. Indeed, considering the shortness of her life, Baby had been responsible for a surprising lot of damage in those four rooms. Every time she pushed her toy pram around the dining-room, the legs of the chairs became a bit more antique-looking.

They didn't use all the rooms, of course, now that Ted wasn't there. The drawing-room was kept shut up and the remaining tassels just dangled vacantly for nobody. In the result, the dining-room came in for heavier and heavier wear. It had passed from Late to Early Tudor in a space of weeks. And, unless the war were over pretty soon, and Baby could have somewhere else to bang about, it would be old Gothic by the time Ted got back to it.

Another difference was in the sound of the place. No. 10 had always been a quiet house—especially after Percy had gone. But Larkspur Road was a racket. It was a kind of sub-station of the B.B.C. At seven-thirty when Doris got up, Cynthia would call out to her to turn the set on. And, once on, it played right through the day, even when Cynthia went out shopping with Baby and had forgotten to turn it off. Not that Cynthia listened very much. The set was kept low and talked away and read news and hummed and crooned and saxophoned all by itself in a corner, like a lunatic relation. But if Doris ever turned it off for a moment, Cynthia went over automatically and turned it on again. To Cynthia, the wireless was like the air you breathed. Something that you didn't notice unless it wasn't there.

But she was an easy sort of person to live with, quite different from the exacting Doreen. There was, however, one thing that they had in common: in the house Cynthia did practically nothing. She divided her time into two roughly equal parts. The first part she spent in writing to Ted—carefully marking the envelope with the letters S.W.L.A.K. across the back of the envelope to show that it was sealed with love and kisses. And the second part was spent in waiting for his reply. In the intervals, she read papers called *Poppy's*

Own and *Real Life Romances* and *Film Close-Ups*, sewed new collars and cuffs on to her dresses, and shampooed her hair—her cherished ash-blonde hair that had brought Ted to his knees.

"I've got to keep myself looking nice for Ted," she kept on saying, not as though there were any special point in mentioning it at that moment, but simply as though she were uttering what was uppermost in her mind. In consequence, the house and Baby were neglected.

And, in the face of this neglect, Baby flourished.

2

But to-night her emotions didn't matter. At least, not beside Doris's they didn't. She was so excited that she forgot all about herself and Ted. So excited that she could only sit there in her pink quilted dressing-gown—an idiotically extravagant indulgence on the part of the infatuated Ted—in front of the gas fire, and gaze at the telegram that Doris had passed to her.

"Don't you feel *thrilled*?" she asked.

She was tingling all over as she said it: it was just like a *Real Life Romance* with Doris's face on the cover.

"It's typical of Bill," Doris said slowly.

"I know."

Cynthia closed her eyes for a moment and leant back. Invisible organs were playing to her the kind of music that is heard in cinemas.

"It's all ever so romantic," she added, and bit her lip to show that she meant it.

"He doesn't give me long, does he?" Doris said musingly.

"And you've got to wire him, he says so," Cynthia answered. "Will your ears be red when you go into the post office."

She was reliving, as she said it, the ecstasy of her own courting. Those last few months before marriage had been charged with everything in sex that is sublime. The flat was just being furnished and the tassels hadn't yet come off.

"It's bound to upset Mother," Doris broke in on her. "Dad won't mind. But Mother'll be awful."

"No, she won't be," Cynthia told her. "Not with a war on. That makes all the difference. She'll understand. And just think how you'd feel if he went out there and anything happened to him. Suppose he was . . ." She stopped herself abruptly. "Killed" was a word that she couldn't use until Ted was back safe in her arms again.

"Wounded," she added, as soon as she had recovered from her own little private anxiety.

"I know," said Doris. "I'd thought about that."

Cynthia took a sideways look at her as she spoke. She had never really understood her sister-in-law. Not deep down, that is. She seemed so cold and unfeeling, somehow. Not a bit like Ted. Admittedly she'd shared the telegram. And that was something. But she hadn't cried. Or gone and lain down. Or anything like that. It might have been just an ordinary invitation from the way she was taking it. Then a sudden doubt took possession of her.

"You are going to, aren't you?" she asked anxiously.

"Yes," said Doris slowly. "I think I am."

As she spoke, she picked up the telegram and re-read it: GOING OVERSEAS, it said. WHAT ABOUT GETTING MARRIED AT ONCE SPECIAL LICENCE IF NECESSARY WIRE ANSWER OCEANS OF LOVE BILL.

Cynthia was still staring hard at her. She was shocked. "I think I am": she repeated Doris's last words. That was no way to talk about love. Then she noticed that Doris was crying. Not much. But still just enough to make everything all right. She realised that she had misjudged her.

All the same, it seemed funny, the idea of anyone getting excited over Bill. He just wasn't that sort. Not like her own compact and shining Ted, for instance.

3

Now that Doris had told Mrs. Josser, it wasn't Doris's wedding any longer. It was Mrs. Josser's. And Mrs. Josser didn't believe in hole-and-corner affairs. She wanted something in white satin and a veil. And bridesmaids. And a three-tier cake. Apparently, ever since Doris had been quite a little girl, Mrs. Josser had been looking forward to a church—almost a cathedral—wedding for her daughter. Marriage without Mendelssohn seemed to Mrs. Josser scarcely to be marriage at all.

And what made it all more difficult was that Bill and Doris had decided on a registry office. In disposing of their separate and individual futures, they were brisk and business-like. And they discussed the whole occasion with a casualness which was appalling. They even spoke of having the wedding at ten o'clock in the morning—as soon as the place opened, in fact—so that they could have the rest of the day to themselves.

Having been defeated in the matter of the church—and only she, Mrs. Josser persisted, knew what the loss meant to her—she was adamant in insisting that Doris should be married from Dulcimer Street. She wasn't having any nonsense about Doris setting out for the registry office, only half done up, from Cynthia's flat in Larkspur Road.

But, on the whole, Mrs. Josser raised very few objections. She detected fatalistically that things had gone too far for her to be able to prevent the calamity altogether. It was merely that she suffered certain misgivings. These misgivings were of two kinds. In the first Mrs. Josser saw Bill maimed, blinded, crippled, with Doris, still young, beautiful, marriageable, having to support him. And in the second she saw him as dead, with Doris, as young and beautiful but less marriageable, having to support his children. Either way, it didn't seem fair on Doris.

"And what's he offering her?" Mrs. Josser demanded. "Just a change of name, that's all. She's got to go on with her job, hasn't she?"

"It isn't Bill's fault there's a war on," Mr. Josser said soothingly. "It's just the way things are."

"Ted provided a home for Cynthia, didn't he?" Mrs. Josser went on. "He did the proper thing."

"But the war hadn't begun then," Mr. Josser replied.

Mrs. Josser drew in her lips sharply.

"He'd have done it, war or no war," she answered. "He's like that, our Ted."

"Well, Bill isn't Ted."

Mr. Josser was becoming exasperated by now.

"And Cynthia isn't Doris, let me tell you that," Mrs. Josser responded hotly. "Why should she have a flat on her own, with furniture, when Doris . . ."

But the logic of the argument had thinned and evaporated. Only the argument itself remained. And it had been like this ever since Doris had first broken the news. Mrs. Josser was heroically fighting a rearguard action in retreat.

CHAPTER 70

As IT turned out, it was Connie who was the sensation of the wedding. Or, at least, one of them. Uninvited, unannounced, undesired and unexpected, she turned up at the Kennington Town Hall just as the sacred moment—if there is a sacred moment at such ceremonies

—was approaching. And, simply by being there, she helped to banish that note of Civil Service greyness that somehow hangs over all State marriages.

It was her clothes that did it. Romantically conceived, they clashed violently with the buff distemper of the walls. But clothes like that would have clashed with anything—even with themselves. The magenta blouse and hat, the bunch of yellow artificial flowers, the brown handbag, the red shaggy fur of the coat—they seethed in a disharmony that was all their own. It may, of course, have been simply that the various bits and pieces hadn't yet had time to settle down together. For they were all new—new for the wedding, in fact. On Doris's account, Connie had been making some pretty serious inroads into what was left of the cheque for damages.

She was easily the most elaborately dressed person present. The respective mothers had turned up in severe matter-of-fact tailor-mades like schoolmistresses off duty. And Doris herself was in a plain blue dress that a nursemaid might have worn. No pleats. No Empire sleeves. No *chic*. Nothing. Connie was disappointed.

Connie had managed to give the company a quick all-over as she sidled in. But it was only now when she had taken up her position in the happy group that she was really able to study details. And they were a shoddy-looking lot, she decided. No use concealing the fact. The puffy little man in the dark suit with his tie riding up over his wideawake collar was evidently Bill's father. And no beauty, either. "Five foot seven and moulting," Connie said to herself, and passed on.

Not that Mr. Josser was any better himself. But she liked him and wasn't going to make jokes about his appearance, even to herself. It wasn't his fault if his clothes just hung on him: it was simply because he'd lost a lot of weight over that last illness and hadn't put it back again.

With Bill, it was different. She kept herself shifting backwards and forwards so that she could get a better look at him. And was she surprised? It was wonderful, downright wonderful what an improvement uniform had made. If he'd grown a moustache she wouldn't have known him from a soldier. But it was the best man, a brother-officer, who really took her fancy. He was a proper little beauty. A bit on the short side, he had a cocky air about him that appealed to her at once. And close crinkly black hair. Now if Doris had gone after him, Connie could have understood it.

She stood back modestly while they were all signing the register with the Registrar's own fountain pen; and by doing so she saw the whole proceeding in perspective. It was just as though they'd been grouped there on a stage. Connie the Thespian took over from Connie the lodger and she saw it all in terms of tragedy—the window sandbagged outside because of air raids, the notice about what to do in case of gas, the two young men in uniform. It was heart-breaking, downright heart-breaking. Toppers, silk stocks, photographers, floppy hats, bunches of flowers—everything, in fact, that goes to make up the spiritual side of marriage was missing. And it was only Connie apparently who could see how much was wrong.

"My God," she thought, "the offers I had. The chances I've turned down. Including one Frenchman. If only I'd wanted to. If only I had. Queen bees weren't in it with me. . . ."

The Registrar had got his fountain pen back by now, and the kissing had started. Dr. Davenport was kissing Doris, Bill was kissing Mrs. Josser, and Mrs. Davenport and Mr. Josser brought suddenly face to face wore the embarrassed expression of two people conspicuously placed who wondered if something were expected of them too. It was Connie who saved the situation. As soon as Doris was free, she sank her feelings, pushed her way in and kissed her too. And Bill. Then just to liven things up she kissed the best man as well. And that so far as she was concerned was where things ended for the moment. She wasn't, even for old friendship's sake, going to make a martyr of herself and kiss Dr. Davenport. Or Mr. Josser, for that matter.

Mr. Josser, indeed, seemed surprised to see her there. Surprised, but friendly.

"Hallo, Connie," he said. "I didn't know you were coming along."

"Nor did I," added Mrs. Josser.

But there was no time for any unpleasantness because, at that moment, the second sensation of the day occurred. The door opened and a rather timid little man in a black coat and striped trousers peeped round the door. He hadn't finished peeping when a large fur coat appeared behind him and he was given a push from behind.

"Do get on, Monty," a voice said. "I know we're *hideously* late. I can *feel* it."

Then the little man was thrust to one side and Doreen pushed her way up to Doris.

"My pet," she said, "I only heard yesterday. And I felt I had to. I simply had to. I couldn't have endured it, if I hadn't been here."

Then she turned to Bill.

"Bill darling, you look *marvellous*. I've quite forgiven you. You two are simply made for each other. Really you are."

Connie recognised Doreen, and she was glad to see her. She and the little man in the striped trousers—her father, possibly?—added something that up to now had been missing. They introduced just the right note of St. George's, Hanover Square, or St. Margaret's. But she gave up thinking about them because she was too much concerned with her own little surprise. She'd planned something and she wanted to be sure that it would go off just right. She'd had a hunch—the old stage instinct—that she'd be needed to do her little bit. And all that she was waiting for was her cue.

The cue came when Bill and Doris were getting into the taxi. The door was wide open when Connie whipped out the first of the little parcels that she'd been carrying in the bosom of her coat. It was rice. And with a happy shriek she scattered it over them. But that was only the beginning. She'd got two other packets as well. The second contained confetti and she managed to make it go all round even though it was only small size. Everyone—even Doreen and the little man in striped trousers—got some. And finally to cap everything she scattered the contents of the last lot—small silver-paper bells and horseshoes—on top of the load she had already distributed. It was a proper festive mess by the time she had finished. But it did, at least, give a lift-up to the proceedings.

It turned out afterwards that there was a notice up about throwing confetti, let alone silver horse-shoes—and rice, which was rationed anyway.

The porter at the Town Hall turned quite nasty about it.

2

In the general attitude of goodwill which prevails at all happy weddings, Doris forgave Doreen and asked her to bring Mr. Perkiss back for the reception. Mrs. Josser was amazed. But it was all right. They couldn't stop long. Only just long enough for Doreen, in a whisper, to tell Doris all about the *wonderful* things that had been happening to her. She was expecting to get married herself, she said, as soon as Monty's divorce had come through. He had been absolutely *sweet* about everything, she explained, and had kept her name out of the divorce altogether. Throughout the conversation, Mr. Perkiss stood there smiling politely. He had caught the word "sweet" but had no idea what such sweetness implied, and was trying to look like a model family man.

The early departure of Doreen and Mr. Perkiss, who left wing-to-wing as though looking for a nesting-box, did not break up the party. Indeed, it went on for some time after Bill and Doris had left, too. But by then there was no real life left in it. To some extent that was Mrs. Josser's fault. It was the saddest day of her life. And she made no pretence of concealing it. Rather red about the eyes and with the corners of her mouth tightly drawn in, she sat next to Bill's mother saying nothing.

With the hostess thus eliminated, the party naturally disintegrated. Dr. Davenport and Mr. Squales got together and found that they both knew Brighton. It was the only thing they had in common. Nevertheless it was a difficult conversation because Mr. Squales kept referring mysteriously to his profession. After Dr. Davenport had established that he wasn't a doctor, he decided that he must be some sort of dentist; a smart American dentist with a Far Western diploma. And thereafter he talked to him about dentistry. The South Downs and the Black Rock became all mixed up with caries and transparent fillings.

Over by the window Mr. Puddy was standing. He was talking to Mrs. Vizzard. And this was unusual. It had taken a wedding to bring it about. In the ordinary way, they didn't exchange more than a sentence or two in the whole week.

"Id all debens on whad you bean by alarbig," Mr. Puddy was saying. "In by brofession we can't afford to take risks. We've god sand and shovels on every floor. And water danks."

"Mr. Squales said something about our shelter not being strong enough," Mrs. Vizzard said nervously. "Not in front, he feels."

"Dot strog edough," Mr. Puddy asked. "I don't subbose it is. They're dud of them strog edough." He gave a shudder as he stood there. "Bud the real thig is fire. Thad's whad we've god to wodge oud for, fire. They've issued a friend of bine with an asbestos suit all over. Had, goat, gloves, everythid. . . ."

Mr. Josser came up and joined them. He smiled engagingly across at Mrs. Vizzard.

"Well," he said pleasantly. "It won't be long now, will it? You'll be the bride next time."

He was aware as he began speaking that he wasn't quite himself. Not that things were bad enough to make him slur his words. Only bad enough to make him bold and familiar.

Mrs. Vizzard smiled and her eyes slid over anxiously in Mr. Squales's direction.

"He was hæmophilic, remember," Dr. Davenport had just said,

"and the whole lot of them had to come out then and there. What would you have done?"

"But really, my dear sir, you mistake me . . ." Mr. Squales began. Then he caught Mrs. Vizzard's eye. "Forgive me," he said hurriedly. "I am wanted. I am called away."

His mind was reeling with abscesses and laughing gas and wholesale extractions, and he came gratefully, obediently. He was smiling as he approached them.

"My honey needed me?" he asked.

Mrs. Vizzard smiled back at him.

"Mr. Josser was just saying that it wouldn't be long now. Doris isn't the only person in Dulcimer Street who'll be getting married, is she?"

The smile on Mr. Squales's face died away and was replaced by something tenser and more drawn.

"No-o-o," he said slowly. "Not the only one. Not by any means."

And the smile, to Mrs. Vizzard's great relief, returned. It was richer, blander even than before.

They all had gone now.

All except Mrs. Boon, that is. She still sat on there, just as she had sat right through the party, saying nothing. She had been with them. But not of them. And, in an odd way, her presence was disturbing. With her there they couldn't forget what had happened. Even quite little things like taking another lump of sugar in a cup of tea seemed, in her presence, callous and unrespecting. In consequence, silence fell over all three of them. Mr. and Mrs. Josser simply sat facing each other, thinking.

Then Mrs. Boon suddenly said something. Raising her head she addressed Mrs. Josser.

"Every time I looked at Bill," she observed, "I could see my Percy standing there. That's who she ought to have married—Percy."

CHAPTER 71

I

IT SEEMED that the authorities had got hold of Ted only just in time. Because, over on the Continent, things were certainly moving. The

Germans had suddenly and astonishingly turned everything they had got on to Denmark and Norway—anyone with half an eye could see that Sweden was due to go next—and it seemed as though this extraordinary war might have to be fought out amid frost and ice instead of in the usual sodden fields of Flanders.

The worst of it all was that it had been so entirely unexpected. A couple of days ago—on April the eighth, that is—nothing, absolutely nothing, had been happening. It hadn't been like war at all—more like a particularly unpleasant kind of peace. And by now there were landings and bombardments everywhere—at Narvik, at Trondheim, at Bergen and Stavanger as well as at Oslo and Kristiansand. At Narvik, in particular. The radio said that destroyers of the Royal Navy had sailed right up the fjord, their guns blazing. There was evidently the father and mother of a row going on up there. And—with typical official silliness—the War Office had sent Ted over to *France*. He was now actually further off from the scene of the trouble than he would have been if he had stayed at home.

Even so, he'd been in France for nearly a week now and Mrs. Josser hadn't received so much as a line from him—not so much as a line despite the fact that Cynthia had heard twice. It had come to something having to learn about her own son from an ex-usherette.

Then, on the morning of the eleventh, a letter came. It was from Ted all right. But somehow it was the wrong kind of letter. Come to think of it, it wasn't really Ted's sort of letter at all. There was none of his natural steadiness about it. Not that it was deliberately alarming or hysterical—he was incapable of that. It was simply that in a dogged and undemonstrative way it assumed the worst.

"*Dear Mum,*" it ran, "*I've been thinking a lot lately and if anything happens to me would you look after Cynthia. I know she can look after herself, but with Baby it is a lot and I should feel better if there was someone looking after her. I'm glad Doris is there but two girls together isn't much when it comes to facing things and if you could have Cynthia and Baby with you I should feel a lot better—only if anything happens to me of course. I'm sure Dad wouldn't mind, and I think you would like it too after you'd got used to it. The weather is very hot now and I met one of our chaps who used to be in Hosiery. He's a corporal.*

Your loving son,

Ted.

P.S.—It wouldn't cost anything because Cynthia would have my pension. It's just that I should feel better if I thought that there was someone taking care of her."

It was breakfast-time when the letter came and Mr. Josser had already started his meal when Mrs. Josser went down to see if the postman had brought anything. She was so excited when she found who the letter was from that she tore it open straightaway and started to read it. Started to read it, and then all the strength went out of her and she couldn't go back upstairs again. She finished the letter leaning up against the wall beside the hat-stand in the hall. After she had finished reading it, she suddenly folded the single sheet up small, and thrust it into her pocket.

Mr. Josser didn't notice at once that there was anything wrong. He was quietly and innocently engrossed in one of his old copies of *The Homefinder* propped up against the loaf of bread.

"Was there anything?" he asked.

Mrs. Josser shook her head.

"It's about time we heard from Ted," Mr. Josser went on, without looking up.

He had only been aware of the head-shake, not actually seen it. After thirty years of marriage you don't always have to look across at your partner to know what is happening.

Mrs. Josser sat there without speaking. The half-rasher of bacon on her plate was getting cold. But she was too much upset to eat. Nobody—least of all, Ted—had ever said anything about his not coming back. And she wasn't prepared for it. No, that was wrong. She was prepared. Had been, right from the start. But hadn't been able to face it. And more than that. By not facing it she had made it seem as though it couldn't happen. Now all that would never be the same again. By putting it down in black and white Ted had made it practically certain.

And why was Ted so concerned about someone looking after Cynthia? Did he know something, or did he mean that he just didn't trust her to look after Baby properly? And if he was really thinking of getting killed why couldn't he spare even one thought for his own mother? It was just Cynthia, Cynthia, Cynthia all the time. The very idea of Cynthia in her house, right under her feet all the time—and no Ted—made her want to cry. It was horrible.

"Why, what's the matter, Mother? Anything wrong?"

Mr. Josser had looked up from his *Homefinder* and was staring hard at Mrs. Josser. The corners of her mouth were drawn down and her eyes were moist.

"It's nothing," she told him.

But that was absurd and Mr. Josser got up and went over to her. He put his arm round her. To his surprise, her arm went round him as well. He knew at once that there must be something pretty badly wrong.

Without a word, she recovered Ted's letter and gave it to him. It was folded up into a small creased oblong, just as she had pushed it into her pocket out of sight.

Mr. Josser sat down again and read the single page through slowly and carefully.

"Isn't that just like Ted?" he said at last. "Always thinking of others."

"But nothing's going to happen to him, is it?" Mrs. Josser demanded.

"No, of course not," Mr. Josser told her. "Not a chance."

"Then what was the point of writing and upsetting us all?"

Mr. Josser considered for a moment.

"Oh, just that he was feeling a bit cut off, I suppose. It hits a lot of fellows that way."

"Do you think it means that he's going up into the lines—patrols or something?"

"I shouldn't think so," Mr. Josser answered. "They're too busy up in Norway to start anything in France for the moment. It's quiet enough over there." He paused. "Do you remember what poor old Henry said one night when he was here? 'Keep your eyes on Scandinavia' were his words. He wasn't far wrong, was he?"

2

But it is always the things nearer home that count. And No. 10 Dulcimer Street next morning wasn't thinking about the fate of Copenhagen and Oslo, or even about H.M.S. *Hunter* sunk, and H.M.S. *Hardy* beached in Narvik fjord. Or, at least, not very much. It was thinking about Mrs. Boon. And that was because she had disappeared.

Simply and mysteriously disappeared.

It was Connie who had first discovered what had happened. She had been lying awake for some time—her ear cocked curiously for even the least movement. And suddenly she became interested because she realised that there just wasn't anything.

Then and there she decided that as soon as she was up she would start investigating. And, when she did so, there was no Mrs. Boon. The front room was tidy, beautifully tidy, but it had about it an elusive deserted look quite different from the look of a room that at any moment will be occupied again. And there was something else about it that Connie noticed. One or two little things—a pair of small brass candlesticks, a photograph of Percy as a baby, an electro-plated perpetual calendar—were missing. So was Percy's big brass ash-tray that Mrs. Boon had given him because of all the burns that kept appearing everywhere.

She gave a little whistle and peeped into the bedroom. It was all just as she expected. There was the same beautiful tidiness and the bed had not even been slept in. Also the dressing-table was bare, quite bare. The brushes and combs and the wooden box of hair-pins and clips and odds and ends had all gone. That was a sure sign. The sort of thing that would strike a woman at once.

"Gone with the wind," said Connie, admiringly. "She's flitted."

Naturally she went straight downstairs and told Mrs. Josser, because Mrs. Josser and Mrs. Boon had always been such friends. And secretly she was rather pleased when Mrs. Josser refused to believe her and insisted on going up to see for herself. If Mrs. Josser wanted to make a fool of herself in front of an audience of one, it wasn't for Connie to stop her.

It all worked out just as Connie knew it would. Mrs. Josser looked first in the living-room and then in the bedroom as though she expected to find Mrs. Boon sitting there all the time. Finding no one she took a deep breath and drew her lips in sharply.

"I don't like the look of this," she said. "Not a bit, I don't."

"Perhaps if we'd been nicer to her she'd have stayed. . . ." Connie began.

But Mrs. Josser ignored the suggestion.

"She's got too much on her mind," she said. "She didn't ought to be going about London by herself."

Connie put her finger up to her eye and wiped something furtively away.

"Poor dear thing," she said. "Just fancy ending up like that."

"Like what?" Mrs. Josser demanded.

"Nothing. Nothing in particular," Connie admitted. "Only my imagination. I just thought of Westminster Bridge and the river and . . ."

"Well, don't think about it," Mrs. Josser told her tartly. "She may only have gone out for a . . . a walk, or something."

Connie raised her eyebrows.

"In her condition? All night?" she asked.

Mrs. Josser did not reply immediately. She had just noticed that the small suitcase that Mrs. Boon usually kept on top of the wardrobe was missing, too. People don't go out on midnight walks carrying suitcases if they have any reasonable intention of returning in the morning.

"Mrs. Vizzard'll have to be told," she said.

"And the police," Connie added. "It's a crime not to report a disappearance. It's an accessory after the fact."

"Mrs. Vizzard first," Mrs. Josser insisted.

"Have it your own way," said Connie. "She won't like it. But I suppose she's got to bear it. After all, it's her house."

On the way downstairs, they told Mr. Josser. He was washing up the breakfast-things when they broke in on him. He put down the cup that he was drying, and listened. At first, he was inclined to pooh-pooh the whole idea. Then, finding that they were serious, he was shocked. Shocked and incredulous. He wanted to go up and look for himself. But Mrs. Josser stopped him. If Mrs. Boon could be found simply by looking they wouldn't be on their way down to Mrs. Vizzard, she said. The logic was unanswerable, and Mr. Josser gave up. He followed them.

That was how it was that they all went down to the basement together. The visit was an entire surprise to Mrs. Vizzard. She was not prepared for visitors and the room was in disorder. Spread out on the table was a collection of Mr. Squales's old silk cravats that she had been mending and ironing. A bottle of grease remover stood on the table beside them.

She listened in silence to what Mrs. Josser had to tell her. And then the injustice of it, the mean sordid injustice of it, ignited something within her. She remembered the rent, the nine weeks' rent that was owing to her—remembered that, and how desperately she needed every penny now—and her temper flared.

"I might have known it," she said suddenly. "Like mother, like son."

"Meaning what?" Mrs. Josser asked coldly.

"Meaning that I was a fool not to put her out when I wanted to."

Mrs. Josser paused.

"It isn't Christian to talk about her like that," she said.

Connie shrugged her shoulders.

"I don't know what you're all worrying about," she said. "The furniture's still here."

"That's right," said Mr. Josser. "It's all there. She may be coming back."

"Not so long as I'm here, she doesn't," Mrs. Vizzard answered. "She's done enough to lower the tone of No. 10 already."

Mrs. Josser got up abruptly.

"You've got no right to speak of her that way," she said. "She's one of the nicest women who ever breathed."

This was too much for Mrs. Vizzard. Already her nerves were on edge because of Mr. Squales's absences. And she was worried, desperately worried, by the amount of money she'd been spending. Only last night she had calculated that, including train fares, this precious fiancé of hers had, since the engagement, cost her nearly twenty pounds. And now to have Mrs. Boon, her runaway lodger, the mother of a convicted murderer, called nice to her own face.

"If that's your idea of niceness, it's not mine," she said. "They're rotten through and through, the Boons; both of them. Nine weeks at ten-and-six—that's what your nice friend owes me."

And then, having said it, she regretted it. Even in her present state of agitation she recognised that it sounded something less than ladylike. She sat down abruptly, gripping the arms of the chair.

"Don't . . . don't tell me any more," she said feebly. "I'm in no fit state to hear it."

As soon as her visitors had gone, Mrs. Vizzard slumped forward on to the table, her head buried in her hands, simply lying there sprawled among Mr. Squales's cravats.

Why had she said it? she asked herself. Why, in front of Connie, of all people? If only Mr. Squales, and not just his cravats, had been there to comfort her. Mr. Squales, however, was in the country again. A professional engagement with a fee attached, he had told her.

But how, Mrs. Vizzard wondered desperately, could any professional engagement last three whole days?

CHAPTER 72

I

ON THE following day, Mrs. Vizzard was still as much upset, as much shaken and bewildered, by the abrupt and unexplained departure of Mrs. Boon.

Her own outburst still sounded disgracefully in her ears and she knew that because of it she was shunned by her own household. To be shunned by the Jossers was one thing: it hurt. To be shunned by Connie was quite another: it humiliated. Mrs. Vizzard saw herself as someone who is vile, heartless and mercenary. A leper. Worse, even. A landlady. And still there was no sign of Mr. Squales. Just when she most needed his support the very foundations had removed themselves.

Her only visitor was Mr. Puddy. She recognised his footfall immediately. It was slow, deliberate and elephantine. There was something consciously majestic about it as though with Mr. Puddy the act of walking were a carefully worked-out and ingeniously executed operation. There was nothing in the least light-hearted or tripping about it. But to-day Mrs. Vizzard thanked God for that muffled, ponderous tread. It was reassuring to know that she still had one friend—no, perhaps "friend" was too strong a word: one neutral—in No. 10.

His visit, as usual, was strictly a business one. He was simply coming down to pay his rent. There was an invariableness about his behaviour that made him the ideal tenant. On this occasion, however, even after Mrs. Vizzard had entered the eight and six in the cash-column, filled in the date, added her initials and handed the book back to him with a business smile, Mr. Puddy seemed inclined to linger.

"I hear Mrs. Bood's god," he said slowly. "Stebbed oud on us."

Mrs. Vizzard nodded. She still couldn't trust herself to say anything about it.

Mr. Puddy stood there thinking.

"I doad wonder," he said at last. "Berhaps it's juzzazwell."

Mrs. Vizzard sat there at the table fiddling with the lid of the ink-well.

"Berhabs it god too budge for her," he suggested. "Couldn't stand the straid."

"There's no strain now," Mrs. Vizzard answered tartly. "All that's over."

But Mr. Puddy only shook his head.

"Not for a buther," he explained. "Not when id's her own sud." He paused. "Bore drouble," he said. "We'll have the bolice in agaid before we're through."

"They're looking for her now," Mrs. Vizzard told him.

"Bay they find her," Mr. Puddy replied devoutly. "Rather theb than be."

He restored the rent book to his inside breast pocket and got ready to go.

"All the same," he added, "I still think it's juzzazwell. Gave me the greeps, she did. Good bording."

"Just as well." The words cheered Mrs. Vizzard and comforted her. There was something so essentially calm and masculine about them. They reassured her. So she hadn't been alone in her feelings after all. It was—not to mince words—distinctly unpleasant to have the mother of a murderer living in the same house with you. And she remembered what it had cost her.

"Not a stick of furniture leaves this house until I've got what's owing to me," she told herself. "Not a stick. I don't want to profit out of misfortune. But I do demand justice."

It was the sound of the postman that interrupted her thoughts. And her response to the double knock was extraordinary. She bounded. "There may be . . . there will . . . there must be something from Him," she told herself.

And the sight of the japanned metal post-box behind the front door convinced her. The square glass spy-hole showed the box to be nearly full. It seemed that after Mr. Squales's entire silence during the past three days he had suddenly written her not merely one love-letter but a whole batch of them.

That absurd weakness of the knees that made her despise herself came over her again. Her hands trembled as she hastily scooped up the jumble of envelopes.

She saw her mistake immediately, however. Though the handwriting was all the same, it was not Mr. Squales's. She knew at a glance that he would never have tolerated the cheap notepaper and the watery blue-black ink. His taste was for vellum-wove and violet. Moreover, it was shaky, a feminine hand at which she was looking—quite different from the broad strokes of the oblique nib that Mr. Squales always used. And the top letter in the pile wasn't even addressed to her. It was for Mrs. Josser. She looked below. The second letter was for Connie. It was the third one that was for her. They were all written in the same shaky, straggling hand.

There was nothing from Mr. Squales.

When she got back downstairs to her room, she studied the envelope before opening it. But the postmark was blurred: it told her nothing. It might . . . could it be? . . . was it from . . .? Her hands were trembling as she ripped the flap open and began to read.

"*Dear Mrs. Vizzard,*"—the letter ran uncertainly across the page, the last words in the line crushing themselves helplessly against the margin, "*After you been so good to me in all my trouble I know that I shouldn't have done anything to upset you. I do hope that you weren't worried, if you noticed that I'd gone. About the rent, I've asked the Jossers if they will make arrangements to sell the furniture and pay me the balance after you've deducted what's owing. I hope that will be agreeable and I'm sorry to have kept you waiting so long but with Percy away and all those expenses things have been very difficult. Please don't think badly of Percy. I'm sure he never meant to do it. I'm going down to the country, to be near him: I'm sure he will feel better if he knows that he isn't too far away from someone who loves him. When is the wedding? I'm sure that you and Mr. Squales will be very happy. As I shan't be able to send you a wedding present would you please choose any little thing you fancy before the Jossers arrange about the sale. Yours gratefully,*

Clarice Boon."

Mrs. Vizzard sat there holding the letter. There was no address; no clue to where it might have come from. But Mrs. Vizzard was not reading any longer. She was staring over the letter into the empty grate beyond. Suddenly she put her head down on her two hands and started crying again. And having started she could not stop.

She cried on and on, not caring who heard her.

She was still sobbing, helplessly and uncontrollably sobbing with Mrs. Boon's letter clutched crumpled in her hand, when a voice spoke to her. It was a rich vibrating voice.

"*Not* my kitten in tears?" it asked. "Did she think that her Rico was never coming back to her?"

And there behind her stood Mr. Squales, his arms outstretched. That wonderful smile of his was all ready and the sunburn and tan of three days in the country on his cheeks.

2

As things turned out, it was really Connie and not the Jossers who was in charge of the sale. Expressing the view that second-hand dealers were merely so many spiders lying in wait for fat innocent flies, she urged that the whole affair should be placed on a competitive basis. In consequence, large numbers of shabby little men in bowler hats with a pencil tucked away behind their ears came clambering up and down the staircase of No. 10, casting glazed expert eyes over everything and prodding at the upholstered pieces with blunt stained thumbs.

The generosity of Mrs. Boon, her open invitation to Mrs. Vizzard that she should choose a little something, had not been without difficulties. She had made the same offer to Connie. And to Mrs. Josser. But she had not thought of mentioning it. In the result, an atmosphere of vigilance and suspicion prevailed from the moment when little things first began to disappear from the Boons' two rooms.

There was no key to the flat and, naturally, they all three took it in turns to glance inside to see how everything was getting on. Mrs. Josser was the first to spot that there was something wrong when she noticed that a tall blue vase, with a painted damask rose on it, was missing. Inevitably, she suspected Connie. And inevitably, Connie suspected Mrs. Josser. It was a tribute to the character of Mrs. Vizzard that neither of them even for a single moment suspected her of having taken it. It did, however, occur to Connie—and to Mrs. Josser—that Mr. Squales, going out for an evening stroll in his loose grey overcoat, might have been concealing a vase somewhere about his person. It was a handsome vase and, even though the other one of the pair was missing, it was probably worth five shillings if you chose your shop carefully.

Then, to Connie's and Mrs. Josser's amazement, they saw the vase openly displayed on Mrs. Vizzard's mantelpiece. Mrs. Josser said nothing even to herself. She was too badly staggered. But Connie recovered more rapidly. "My God," she thought reverently. "It *was* the old girl after all. She swiped it."

The fact that the vase was there at all had been the outcome of a long struggle on Mrs. Vizzard's part. At first, she had felt insulted, actually insulted, by Mrs. Boon's suggestion. The whole letter had been couched in a humility more wounding than wrath. For a moment, she had even thought of telling the unfortunate woman to go her own way and keep her debt and her wedding present. Then the folly of that plan revealed itself to her, and she became anxious for her rent again. But, if she took the rent without the wedding present, it would seem as though at heart she really were cold and inhuman. And so, in the end, she chose something large, flamboyant, practically valueless. It stood in its new home, against the mirror of the overmantel, as much a token as a gift. And, because of its presence there, Mrs. Vizzard was able to write back a letter that entirely cleared her conscience.

"*Dear Mrs. Boon,*" she replied. "*It came as such a relief to get your letter and know that you were all right. We were most disturbed by your departure. Please don't mention what I did for you. It was only what any Christian*"—Mrs. Vizzard prided herself on the use of that word: it added dignity—"*would have done. Thank you for inviting me to choose a wedding present. I have decided on the beautiful blue vase that used to stand in the centre of your sideboard. I'm sure that it will be much nicer for both of you if you're near Percy. Trusting that you are in better health, Yours sincerely,*

Louise Vizzard."

Mrs. Vizzard took the opportunity of showing the letter to Mrs. Josser before posting it. They had scarcely spoken since the incident and Mrs. Josser recognised the gesture for what it was. An armistice at least. Even peace, possibly.

Also, the bit about the wedding present had come as a relief. Like Mrs. Vizzard, Mr. and Mrs. Josser had at first been reluctant to accept anything. But from a different motive. "She'll need every penny she can lay her hands on," Mrs. Josser said firmly. "If we choose anything we've got to pay her a fair price for it." And with this in mind, they had gone round the flat inspecting. Somewhat to their disappointment, they found that the only things that they really wanted were the sideboard and a cushion with a red silk cover. But the sideboard, of course, was too big—even if they paid her for it, it would look as though they were trying to pick up a bargain at her expense—and the cushion wasn't permanent enough. So in the end, they compromised on a Birmingham-Benares brass tray with a criss-cross design on it and a deckled edge. It was large, and kept falling over, with the noise of stage thunder, as soon as they had got it downstairs.

But the person who was most relieved by the openness with which things were being picked up was Connie. Not for any reason other than that it had seemed a shame to see the whole home broken up among strangers, she had paid one or two little visits herself already. She had got a pair of nail-scissors, a little china elf, and a bed-table stand on which to hang a watch—only without the watch, of course. The things weren't of any value. But because other people might not understand, she had kept them shut away in the bottom of her drawer. Now they could come out and be worshipped openly.

As it happened, however, Connie had picked up her little trifles before the letter had been delivered. And so, in a way, the letter itself was of the manner of an anticlimax. All the same, it had regularised things. And it made Connie think.

She thought quite a lot, in fact. And, after a while, she got the letter out and re-read it. ". . . So if there is any little thing you fancy before the sale please take it for a keepsake . . ." Any little thing:

Connie turned the words over in her mind. What she had taken already was hardly worth mentioning: they certainly wouldn't have justified a letter. So she decided that she would return them and start again.

This time, she chose the gramophone and the box of records. And half an hour later she went back for the knick-knacks.

CHAPTER 73

I

It was just as well when the time came that Connie was in charge of the sale. Because Mr. Josser turned out to be no good at bargaining. He had already let six of the likeliest sort of buyers go off without getting any offer over twelve pounds ten, when Connie turned up with her own find. He was a soiled decrepit sort of man with sharp steel spectacles, and he jabbed at everything with the stump of a pencil before estimating it.

"Fifteen pounds the lot," he said finally.

Mr. Josser seemed pleased. But there was only a low whistle from Connie.

"Why not just steal 'em?" she asked. "It's quicker."

"That's my price," the auctioneer answered.

"Sorry you've been troubled," Connie told him.

The auctioneer did not move.

"We've been offered twenty-five pounds already," Connie observed, looking hard at Mr. Josser. "Haven't we, Uncle?"

It was awkward for Mr. Josser. But the auctioneer spoke for him.

"You were lucky," he said. "You take it."

"Can't," Connie answered. "We turned it down."

"Fifteen pounds is my price," the auctioneer repeated.

"Twenty," Connie told him.

"Seventeen ten."

"Twenty."

"Eighteen."

"Nineteen ten."

"Eighteen. That's my last word."

As he spoke, he produced a bundle of creased, dirty notes. It seemed as though in his world even the money was second-hand, too.

"O.K.," said Connie. "Have it your own way. You'll be wanting my gramophone next."

She hadn't actually meant to say anything about the gramophone. It just slipped out. Not that it mattered. She'd just got Mrs. Boon three pounds more than Mr. Josser could have got for her. And she was glad. Her conscience had been troubling her about those knick-knacks.

2

The decrepit auctioneer moved the stuff out on the following day. And Mrs. Vizzard set about refurnishing the rooms straightaway. She had wanted the whole suite redecorated first. For its bridal purpose she would have preferred something brighter than the chocolate brown of the paint and the sea-weedy blue-green of the wall-paper. Even something in off-white, possibly. But she was too terrified to spend the money. The permanent loss of rent that Mrs. Boon's departure represented, the uncertainty of the war and the chronic unemployment of Mr. Squales all combined to dissuade her from spending anything.

"If I once *start* eating into capital . . ." she told herself—but the thought was so frightening that she was unable to pursue it.

It was on a Sunday morning when the first of the furniture was moved upstairs, and before they were through with the dressing-table the whole of No. 10 was helping. Mr. Josser himself was in the thick of it right from the start. Mrs. Vizzard had approached Mrs. Josser—the breach between them had tacitly been sealed—and asked if Mr. Josser could lend a hand. Nothing heavy, she had explained; just helping Mr. Squales with one or two of the rather awkward pieces. On those terms, and on those terms only, Mr. Josser was allowed to help. But shifting large old-fashioned bits of furniture up five flights of stairs is an unpredictable affair. And when it became apparent that Mr. Josser was positively and securely trapped behind the dressing-table in the right-angle bend by the first landing, there was nothing for Mrs. Vizzard to do but to go for assistance. She went upstairs and asked Mr. Puddy if he would mind helping—only for a moment, she said.

When she came back down, there were four of them there all told—only Mr. Josser didn't show because he was concealed by the dressing-table. The other two had arrived in her absence. Mrs. Josser was there because she had sensed that something was wrong. And Connie was there simply because she was Connie.

As Mrs. Vizzard and Mr. Puddy got there, they heard a voice

from behind the dressing-table saying that it was slipping. The information alarmed Mrs. Josser. She assumed that her husband was being crushed beneath it. But it was Mr. Squales who answered the voice. He told it to push. Push hard, and keep on pushing, he said. He had been doing all he could, he explained, by *pulling*. And evidently Mr. Squales must have been exerting himself quite considerably. Because as soon as Mr. Puddy appeared he let go altogether. He stood there wiping his forehead with a fancy bordered handkerchief, and sighing.

Urged on by Mrs. Josser and Mrs. Vizzard, Mr. Puddy threw his weight in. This was considerable. And, in the result, it overcame everything. With a sharp rending noise, the dressing-table suddenly rushed forward. Mr. Josser was released.

"I'b afraid id bay be dabaged," said Mr. Puddy. "But I dud it."

He seemed rather pleased with himself because, without further asking, he insisted on remaining in charge of the dressing-table until it was actually in place. And he might have been ready for more—even though moving heavy things wasn't at all in his line really—if Mrs. Josser had not abruptly removed Mr. Josser altogether. She told Mrs. Vizzard—the breach between them was widening visibly again—that if she wanted any other removals done, she would have to make her own arrangements. Mr. Josser wasn't equal to it, she said.

This setback was serious because the overcrowded rooms in the basement were like a ripe seed-pod ready to burst open. Mrs. Vizzard had done a lot of preparing. She had emptied all the drawers and, for protection, she had even tied a rug over the long mirror in the wardrobe so that it shouldn't be splintered on the way upstairs. And now it seemed that everything was to be at a standstill until Monday. Unless she unloaded the bed of its boxes and encumbrances she would have literally nowhere to sleep that night.

But Mrs. Vizzard was not a woman to take defeat easily. Even if the furniture itself were immovable, there were still the oddments, the bits and pieces. Carrying these, she made fifteen journeys in all. Fifteen journeys up and down twenty-seven stairs.

The odd thing was that Mr. Squales himself was so useless. Still with the bloom of his three days in the country on his cheeks, he seemed nevertheless to be fatigued at the slightest exertion. In consequence, he chose none but the lightest objects. And, even so, his betrothed did two or three journeys to his one. To a casual observer—or to Mrs. Vizzard for that matter—it was as though he weren't really trying. Not trying, and not caring very much, either. It was as though his own wedding preparations didn't really mean a thing to him.

Unlike a casual observer, however, Mrs. Vizzard knew the reason for it. Or suspected that she did. It was because of a long and painful conversation that she had had with him the night before. Ever since his return, her fiancé had been more moody and preoccupied than usual. And in the end Mrs. Vizzard had been able to stand the nervous strain, the perplexity, no longer. She had asked him outright whether he was regretting it, whether he didn't really want to marry her at all.

The effect of the question had been remarkable. Never in her most foolishly romantic moments had Mrs. Vizzard expected to receive such assurances. She was, he told her, his life, his very life, his one hope, his star. It was so entirely unqualified a declaration, in fact, that she was able to lead up to the second ultimatum. She explained what Mrs. Boon's departure meant to her, referred to the Jossers' back room—the room the detective had occupied—which was still vacant, and showed him a cutting about the way London was emptying and how for the first time since the war, the Great War, there were more rooms than tenants. Laid all her cards on the table, in short, and told him that he would have to find himself a job.

It was all just as Mrs. Vizzard had feared. The move had been postponed. She had repacked the drawers—so that she could have somewhere to sleep—and had taken the rug off the front of the wardrobe. The room was in disorder, but habitable.

Because the attempt had been abandoned, Mr. Squales was a free man again. Or, at least, if not exactly free, he wasn't wanted at the moment. In consequence, he was lying on his back in bed, resting. He allowed his eyes to rove round the room for a moment, taking in everything—the cross-legged bamboo table with the red fringed cloth on it, the bamboo-and-marble wash-stand, the wicker-and-bamboo easy chair—and then stared again at the blank expanse of ceiling because it was less distasteful.

He was remembering those three days at Mrs. Jan Byl's.

"Blast Boanerges," he said half aloud. "He might as well have stayed away altogether for all the help he was. She didn't give a damn for his advice. And it was pretty straightforward. If I'd put it any more bluntly she'd only have suspected me."

CHAPTER 74

I

THE END of the episode—the deliberate and calculated sundering of all Mrs. Boon's connections with Dulcimer Street—left Mrs. Josser depressed and unsettled. Throughout the arrest, the trial, the appeal, she had remained self-possessed and purposeful. Had managed to keep on top of things. But there was no doubt about it: the sale of the furniture had been the climax. Everything else was now anti-climax. She was living in the trough of things at the moment.

And it wasn't about her own feelings that she was worrying. It was about Mr. Josser. The events of the past three months hadn't done him any good, either. He was ageing visibly. And rapidly. Having looked the same for as long as she could remember—at times it almost seemed that it had been a small grey-haired man whom she had married—he was suddenly changing before her eyes. His hair was wispier now and thinner. And he was growing absent-minded: twice, lately, he had gone through to the kitchen to put a kettle on and then come back without having done it. He seemed, too, to be missing Doris. Missing Doris more even than he missed Ted. He spoke about her longingly as though she were part of a remote, delightful past. He was content to sit for hours—whole evenings, in fact—just smoking and remembering. It was a vague, shaky sort of existence, not like real life at all. And in Mrs. Josser's present state it was getting on her nerves.

It was lucky in a way that there was the matter of Uncle Henry's will to distract her. And it was lucky, too, that she had placed the whole matter into Mr. Barks's hands because he seemed to be so very efficient about everything connected with the law. It was only a bit strange—and a bit ironic, when you came to think of it—that it was Mrs. Boon herself who had recommended Mr. Barks.

In her present reduced condition even remembering Uncle Henry, however, upset Mrs. Josser. She still had occasional qualms of conscience that she hadn't loved him more and been nicer to him. But finally she had to admit to herself that really Uncle Henry was far easier to love in retrospect than he had been in reality. As a family figure there had always been something uncompromisingly prickly about him.

All the same, she had found tears coming into her eyes more than once as she had sat in Mr. Barks's office going over the details. It was the side of life that Uncle Henry himself would have despised most. And at times she had an uneasy feeling that Uncle Henry with his Socialist views must somewhere at this very moment be feeling that, will or no will, she hadn't got any real right to the flourishing business that he had left her. His greengrocery and fruit connection should have reverted to the State or something.

It came, therefore, as a shock, a positively breath-taking shock, to learn what Uncle Henry had been worth. Somehow she had always thought of him as one of themselves. Not poor exactly, but certainly not of the moneyed classes. And she had been wrong. Astonishingly wrong. Uncle Henry, with the sports shirt and his cranky views and his green bicycle, had fairly been rolling in it. By the time the whole estate had been wound up there would be something, Mr. Barks said, between eleven and twelve hundred pounds.

The effect of the news when he told her was to leave her first staggered. Then excited. Then sick. If it had been a decent moderate sum like two hundred and fifty, or even three hundred, she could have borne it. But the immensity of eleven hundred pounds alarmed her. And in a strange way she felt ashamed. Ashamed, because Mr. Josser after having worked hard for nearly forty years had managed to scrape together only just enough to think of buying himself a cheap cottage. Whereas she, by just sitting back and not doing anything, had suddenly become a rich woman.

A rich woman! She turned the words over in her mind all the way back from Mr. Barks's. A rich woman! It put her at once into the Mrs. Vizzard class. Instead of merely renting three rooms in No. 10, the Jossers could buy the whole place outright if they felt inclined. They could expand. It was only a passing thought, however. Because Mrs. Josser knew perfectly well that they didn't want to expand. And the idea became modified to refurnishing the three rooms that they already had. Then that, too, was seen to be the foolish notion that it was, because the three rooms didn't need refurnishing. And the spectacle of Connie frittering away her little nest-egg rose up before her eyes. At all costs she must avoid that. And she recognised that it was just as easy to squander eleven hundred as it had been to squander sixty-five: it was only that it took longer. And with actually spending the money out of the question, Mrs. Josser, to her surprise, found herself wondering what she should do with it. It seemed that, after all, she didn't really need it.

Then the solution, the perfect solution that she should have thought of straightaway, came to her. She would keep it intact, not touching a penny of it until the war was over and then give it to Ted to buy a business. And what was more she would write and tell him so. It would give him something to look forward to during all the time he was away. Only one thing left her unhappy about that —Cynthia. It was monstrous, positively monstrous, that simply because Uncle Henry, despite his odd ideas, had been a hard-working, painstaking sort of chap, a silly, giggling, little ex-usherette should reap the reward of it.

She was still thinking about Cynthia when she reached Dulcimer Street. And her thoughts were so unsatisfactory that she couldn't bring herself to talk about them. In consequence when Mr. Josser got back that evening from his rent collecting—and he was looking whiter and wispier and more frayed than ever—she didn't tell him a thing about it. She merely got him his supper and sat watching him while he ate it without so much as a hint. She was, if anything, rather quieter than usual, and Mr. Josser asked her if she was tired.

She had no answer ready and so she ignored the question. She merely told him to hurry up with his meal so that he could get to bed early. It was a funny business becoming an heiress at sixty-four. Funny, and unnerving.

2

Isn't there any news of Percy? Has he faded right out of it now that the prison doors have closed on him? Doesn't he exist any more?

Oh yes, Percy still exists. You can see him if you want to. Only you wouldn't recognise him. Not at first glance, that is.

He's the one standing at the end of the room. It is a long room with bars at the windows. He is standing to attention with his heels together. But the clothes that he is wearing are so shapeless that he might as well be standing easy. Only his shoulders, where the jacket is a bit on the tight side, show that he has drawn himself up for the occasion.

In front of him is a short grey-haired man, a kind of foreman. He is dressed in a double-breasted blue uniform with black buttons rather like a park-keeper's. Percy is in grey. Grey with clumsy black arrowheads stamped on to it.

Come round to the other side so that you can see his face. It's Percy all right. But you'd never have guessed it from the rear view. That's because all his yellow hair has been sheared off. The wavy and shining halo that he used to go about with has gone completely.

And in consequence his head looks much smaller. In fact, it looks definitely a small head. Perhaps it is. And the moustache that he was just getting started has gone, too. It is just a very ordinary, rather weak sort of face that is left.

"Ever made a pair of shoes before?" the foreman park-keeper asks suddenly. He has to shout because there is so much noise going on right down the length of the bay.

Percy shakes his head.

"No." And after a pause. "Sir."

"Feel you can learn?"

Percy grins. It is the same old grin. Or very nearly. Perhaps it is a bit feebler about the corners.

"I'm a trained mechanic, I am."

The grey-haired man looks up sharply.

"Not here, you're not," he says. "You're a beginner, same as all of them are when they start. And if you don't make the grade you go back to manual work with the rest. See?"

The grin has vanished by now. Percy is looking for an opportunity of saying "Sir" again. He's become very respectful since he came here. It's the only thing they understand.

"You'll start on soles, you will," the grey-haired man goes on. "You'll keep on that until you know it. And if you don't seem to be learning you'll go back like I said."

"I see, sir."

"And no talking. There's enough noise without talking. If you want anything step back from the machine one pace and I'll attend to you when I come round. No. 9's your machine. There's someone on it now. You can stand by and watch. Don't get in his way. And don't talk."

"No, sir."

"That's all. Get going."

Percy stands watching. It's easy. He can see that at once. Just kid's play. Like fretwork. There's a revolving knife, a moving band of metal, at one end of the bench. And, when the leather goes up against it, the knife cuts through like a bacon-slicer. All that the man in charge has to do is to twist the leather round a bit so that the shape comes. But that's easy, too. It's all marked out in blue pencil. You couldn't go wrong. The only thing is the speed. The man at the machine works as though he had become a part of it. The rough soles keep piling up in a wooden box at his side where he flicks them with one hand while the other hand is getting the next piece of leather ready. He is a drawn, elderly man, a pretty ancient sort of workman, though in that awful uniform he might really be any age. Silently, without even looking up to see who is watching him, he goes on turning the leather and flicking the finished soles to one side.

"Wonder he doesn't go barmy," Percy thinks. "Doing that all day. Wonder he doesn't go barmy."

Then the foreman comes round.

"Seen enough? Think you could do it?" he asks, speaking close up to Percy's ear because of the din.

"Yes, sir," says Percy.

"I shall be watching," says the foreman. "Don't you forget that. I've got eyes in the back of my head, I have. And on both sides as well. Stand back, No. 4382."

The elderly workman steps back, still without looking up.

"Hold the leather in your right hand and steady it with your left," the foreman says. "And mind your fingers: they're the only ones you've got. Don't hurry. Take your time and be careful. Remember: you're learning something."

"Yes, sir."

The foreman and the elderly workman move off. Percy is left alone with the machine. The fact that it *is* a machine is something. It belongs to his order of things. Only of course it's primitive. Crude and primitive. Percy can think of a couple of improvements straightaway by just looking at it. But perhaps he'd better leave improvements till later. He's got to get on with things as they are now. Very gingerly he puts the piece of leather up against the spinning knife and the blade cuts quickly deep into the blue pencil line.

"I said 'careful,' " a voice at his elbow reminds him. Percy looks round.

"One of them bearings is loose, sir," he says. "I could fix it for you."

But the foreman is not pleased by the suggestion.

"If I want anything fixed, I send for a real mechanic," he says. "And if I want to know what needs fixing, I ask. If I don't, it's all right as it is. You're learning, not teaching. See?"

"Yes, sir," Percy answers, twisting round the piece of leather so that the snick in it shan't show any more. "I see, sir."

CHAPTER 75

I

Mr. Puddy had got a germ. Or something. It couldn't, this time, have been anything that he'd eaten because, ever since the last bout, he'd been very careful about his food. He'd been avoiding all made-up dishes. But the result was just the same. Whatever he ate, Mr. Puddy suffered stabbing pains, fits of giddiness and a sense of profound dejection.

This had been going on for nearly a week now and he was growing morbid. He even began to fear that he might be losing weight—always a dangerous thing in a man. And his mind recoiled. It was a horrible thought, dying of starvation in the midst of a world of plenty. He got so worried at last that he spent a penny at a weighing machine. The long red hand on the dial finally came to rest at 13 stone 5 lb. But, as he couldn't remember what it should have been, this didn't really console him. And still the pains, the giddiness and the dejection continued.

He had tried all the patent medicines, of course. But they weren't of any use to him. By now he was taking two or three different kinds of tablets and a tablespoonful of this and that, and six drops in water of the other every two or three hours. And he might just as well have saved himself the trouble. It looked, indeed, as though after a lifetime of serious eating he was simply going to waste away and lose himself.

So, in the end, he went along to see a doctor. It was a terrifying experience. Terrifying, because his own father—a profound, hearty eater like himself—had been carried off at about the same age by apparently the same mysterious ailment. He had dwindled away to less than ten stone before expiring. And as Mr. Puddy sat in the stuffy little waiting-room he heard in his ear ancestral voices prophesying . . . prophesying what his father had died from.

The doctor went over Mr. Puddy slowly and carefully. There were wide pale expanses of abdomen to be thumped and prodded, and he prodded hardest where the pains hurt most. When he had finished he stepped back and Mr. Puddy gripped the hard sides of the surgical couch while he was waiting for the verdict. But all that the doctor said was that Mr. Puddy needed exercise. And he said it in such a callous and unfeeling kind of voice that, instead of feeling relieved, Mr. Puddy was offended. He got up with as much dignity as a man can muster when his braces are down below his knees, and addressed the doctor.

"The deed for egcercise is wud thig," he said coldly, "and these sybtobs are adother. I shan't waste any bore tibe here. I'll go roud to the Gederal Free. Good evedig."

And with that he went, his pouchy heroic head carried high, and his body rumbling and protesting as he moved.

It was the five o'clock surgery that he had attended; and even now it was not yet five-thirty. From the moment he had stripped down to the moment he had buttoned up again, it had not taken ten minutes in all. And the fee, because Mr. Puddy wasn't on the panel, was five shillings. Sixpence a minute, he told himself morosely, was what the doctor's impertinence had cost him.

After the gloom of the dingy little surgery, the brightness of the early May evening dazzled him. He stood on the pavement outside, blinking at the sky through half-closed eyes, like a large grounded bat. The real trouble was that he didn't know what to do with himself. There was no point in arriving at the warehouse until seven. There was no point in climbing up all the stairs at No. 10 only to come down again. And he didn't feel strong enough to go along to the hospital to be thumped and prodded again this evening.

After a bit, he began to move off. Not to anywhere in particular —because he hadn't got anywhere in particular to move off to—but simply because he couldn't stand there any longer. And, as a doomed man, he walked slowly: he mooched. His own coroner, he passed along the street, his eyes fixed on the pavement ahead of him.

The real trouble was that something told him that his number was up. Or, if not actually up, at least due to go up shortly. The way things were, even if the doctor happened to be right about Mr. Puddy's stomach, it only meant that he was being preserved from one kind of dreadful death for another that was just as dreadful. Indeed, what was the matter with Mr. Puddy was probably this haunting presentiment of disaster.

Through brooding over it for so long he knew just how it would happen. It was round two in the morning when it was going to occur. The Germans at last would have turned their furious eyes on London, and the bombs would fairly be raining down by then. He would be at the warehouse at the time, of course. Sitting in the middle of the tinder-pile, so to speak. There would be explosions all round him as though the earth were giving way. And fires, huge unquenchable fires. And choking, asphyxiating smoke. And the lights would go out. And he would be left somewhere in the centre of the furnace with the last precious drops of water dripping from the nozzle of his stirrup-pump, and the bucket empty. . . . Even though it was a warm night, Mr. Puddy's teeth were chattering at the thought of it. He had only to close his eyes, and he could see the actual bomb—a big fat one shaped like a porpoise—with his name written in white letters right round the side of it.

"High exblosive," he said aloud. "High exblosive and idcediaries."

And he shuddered.

It was a fine pearly evening, and the high upper storeys of the buildings were glowing back at the retreating sun. Even the buses as they darted out from the shadows of the buildings shone with more than their own natural scarlet. A barrage balloon resting idly on its cable was pure gold.

But Mr. Puddy was oblivious to it all; it might as well have been foggy. With his hands clasped despondently behind his back so that the attaché case containing his dinner bumped against his knees with every step he took, he mooched on. He had come quite a long way by now and already the fresh air had done him good. He was breathing more deeply and the spots before his eyes seemed fewer. His thoughts, too, took on a gayer tinge. After a while he began recalling better times, old meals that he had eaten, the kind of stuff that even now he had got stowed away in readiness for his recovery. In the midst of dissolution, his spirits returned to him and he remembered what a lot of firemen there were in London nowadays. Trained men—quite young men, some of them—whose whole job it was to mop up incendiaries as fast as the Germans cared to send them down. There was even an emergency water-tank, like an elevated duck-pond, just opposite the main entrance to the warehouse.

"So log as I'b dear a telephode, I'b all right," Mr. Puddy told himself. "It's only if I'b cud off, I'b for it."

He had unclasped his hands by now and was walking upright. Really walking this time, not just mooching. And suddenly an idiotic and astonishing thought came to him. He decided that he would walk all the way to the warehouse. His self-respect depended on it. It would prove that he wasn't the sort of man who needed any surgery doctor to tell him when to take exercise. And as he stepped out he seemed to be entering his prime again. The wraiths and spectres had been left behind in Kennington.

All the same, it was a long walk. A very long walk. Nearly four miles, in fact. And for the last half-mile, Mr. Puddy proceeded more slowly. Much more slowly. Finally, he stopped entirely. Stopped and raised first one foot off the ground to ease it, and then the other. Each time that he lifted his foot and the remaining one had to take all his weight, he winced. The walk had been just that much too long.

Mr. Puddy's arches had fallen.

2

Back in Dulcimer Street, Mr. Squales was in a bad way, too. The worst possible, in fact. And that was because he was cornered. Positively cornered. There was, he realised gloomily, no other word for it. No other word. And no way out. It was appalling.

What was so awful was that it was all Mrs. Vizzard's doing. With that nagging and inhuman persistence which is one of the most irritating things about women—especially loving ones—she had been quietly and secretly plotting behind his back, apparently for weeks. It was for his sake, his good, that she had done it—he knew all about that. And, even if he hadn't known it, she had told him so to his face. The fact remained, however, that he didn't thank her for it. Not deep in his heart he didn't. At the time there had been nothing for it, of course, but to smile back and say thank-you. He had even added that he was quite bowled over by the news. As, indeed, he was. And to prove his gratitude he had gone so far as to kiss her hand. But this was a mistake. Because, after all the trouble that she had been to on his account, she was holding up her face for a proper sort of kiss.

The cause of his depression was that she had found a job for him. And the absurd part of it was that the job suited him perfectly. If he had found it for himself before he had given his heart away to Mrs. Vizzard he would simply have wolfed it up. Not that the salary was anything. That was only four pounds a week—the sort of wage that good typists get. It was the sundries, the asides, the perquisites, that made the job worth considering.

The post was that of organising secretary to the North Kensington Spiritualist Union. It was a new body, the Union, and its headquarters were in Portobello Road. The premises had been an undertaker's before the Spiritualists had taken them over, so the clientele hadn't changed so very much. The place was completely redecorated, of course, and Mr. Squales rather liked the chaste, fumed oak with which the interior was now furnished. There was a large circular table with copies of *Light* and *The Spirit World* and *Beyond* and *The Great Divide* spread out on it. And there was a sectional bookcase containing the classics of the cult—lives of famous mediums, records of scientifically controlled psychic experiments, and books on fairies. He'd seen them all when Mrs. Vizzard took him over.

Not that there was any money for the Union in this side of it. The books were there more for their educational value than for anything else. The North Kensington Spiritualist Union, in fact, was really a kind of information bureau. And, as such, it kept open for deucedly long hours. From nine-thirty in the morning until seven o'clock at night it was there to solve every kind of supernatural problem that might have presented itself suddenly to the residents of Notting Hill. The times of its own séances and those of affiliated bodies—the Tulse Hill Psychical Research Society, the Ponder's End Spiritual Temple, the Golders Green Group and so forth—were displayed in frames around the wall. It was, as a matter of fact, because of one frame containing the names of mediums prepared to undertake private séances that Mr. Squales finally accepted the post. As he stood there he saw his own name invisibly over-printed across the lot of them.

But nine-thirty to seven! He shuddered. To arrive at Portobello Road by nine-thirty would mean leaving Dulcimer Street at about quarter to nine. And leaving Dulcimer Street at a quarter to nine would mean getting up at eight. Even, possibly, at five to. It would be bad enough even now with the summer coming on. In winter, in the black-out, it would be unthinkable. He might as well be a milkman or a postman.

But that was not the worst of it. There was an additional peril attached to the job—one that he couldn't very well talk about. At least not to Mrs. Vizzard. And that was that there was now nothing, absolutely nothing, to hold up the wedding by even another day. Previously, it had been simple. He had told Mrs. Vizzard outright that he wouldn't marry her until he was self-supporting. Now, thanks to her he was going to be. The job was open from next Monday. And if he took it, he would be entirely vulnerable. Today was Thursday. Only three clear days. That was what made him so jittery.

What was more, the rooms upstairs were all ready. There wasn't a thing more that needed doing to them. And it all happened just as Mrs. Vizzard had threatened. She insisted on showing them to him in their finished state. With fingers laced romantically—it was Mrs. Vizzard who thrust her hand in his—they went up and inspected them together. It had not been Mr. Squales's idea, this visit, and it had got him down. It had saddened him unutterably. The little room at the side—Percy's room—that had been made into a dressing-room for him, was bad enough. All Mr. Squales's clothes, the clothes that Mrs. Vizzard had given him, were now arranged so neatly, so methodically, that he realised gloomily that in future even if he mislaid a sock or a tie it would be missed immediately. As for pawning anything . . . It was the end of all privacy and personal pride, that room.

But it was nothing to the bedroom. That was terrific. No sooner had he peered inside than he felt himself sweating. A ponderous sepulchral magnificence hung over the apartment. Standing there in the doorway, he realised that it was really the late Mr. Vizzard's bedroom that he was regarding. That peep was really a glimpse into the dead past. The furnishings had about them a genuineness, a solidity, that could only have come from within the trade itself. The big mahogany double bed with its massive claw-feet looked cold and ominous like a converted sideboard.

"Aren't . . . aren't you going to say anything?" Mrs. Vizzard asked softly.

Mr. Squales pulled himself hurriedly together.

"What is there left for me to say?" he asked.

Mrs. Vizzard caught her breath.

"You might say that you're looking forward to the day," she reminded him. "It's not long now."

There was a pause. An awkward pause. Then he recovered himself.

"Looking forward to the day," he repeated, very low in his throat like a church organ pealing. "I think of nothing else."

CHAPTER 76

BILL had got embarkation leave. That was why Doris was there at King's Cross waiting for him.

The train was late. Very late. Nearly two hours out of the forty-eight had gone already in simply standing at the barrier of the arrival platform. Not that Doris was the only one who was lounging about like that. The gloomy cavern of the station was full of tired men and drooping women all waiting patiently for someone. On one of the seats by the indicator there was a woman with a baby. She had been there since seven.

And it was after ten o'clock already. Outside, the light had faded from the evening sky and King's Cross was settling down to its nightly black-out. The platform lamps, like so many blue inverted night-lights, had been turned on by the stationmaster and made a melancholy and futile star-shine of their own. Through the murk, the word "BUFFET" on the tea-room door showed up magically in six-inch letters cut out of cardboard. Every ten seconds or so the word would disappear altogether as a soldier, carrying the war on his back, pulled the door open and went inside.

It was the same wherever you looked. Tired, thirsty soldiers. Soldiers going, soldiers coming. The tramp of their boots mingled with the smell of train oil and the hiss of high-pressure steam. It might have been the Tottenham Court Road and not the Siegfried Line that they were going to storm at any moment.

Doris had drunk her third cup of coffee and didn't want another one. It wasn't anybody's fault that it was bad coffee: it was just that things worked out that way in war-time. A thin scalding stream of something that tasted of nothing gushed out of the urn into the chipped cup, the girl behind the counter popped in a chip of sugar with her fingers, and gave a whisk round with a captive spoon. And that was that. All the other spoons were missing.

At ten-twenty the train was signalled and Doris took up her place at the barrier again. It would probably still be some time before the train was actually in. But she was too excited to wait anywhere else. Absurdly excited. And in consequence she felt slightly sick. But that may have been because she hadn't eaten any lunch. She had been so sure that she would be having dinner with Bill that she stayed in at lunch-time so that she could be sure of getting off early. And now it was supper-time already. Just when every second was precious, when things like honeymoons and normal married life were being handed out by the thimbleful, the railways went and poured a whole evening down the drain for you.

The lights on the front of the engine appeared suddenly at the far end of the platform and the crowd came to life again. The women stopped drooping and ticket collectors turned up professionally from nowhere in particular to safeguard the interests of the shareholders.

As soon as the train stopped, the doors opened and out poured—soldiers. With gas mask and knapsack and tin hat and water-bottle and bayonet and bandoliers slung about them, and clutching a rifle and a kit-bag, they came lurching through the murk like ghosts from Passchendaele.

At first Doris could not see Bill anywhere. Then she spotted him. He came right towards her but, at the last moment, the woman next to her claimed him. And that happened again. Bill, unmistakably Bill, turned into someone quite different. In those uniforms everyone had mysteriously been transformed into one and the same person. The platform was full of Bills, all in khaki and all lugging a floppy oversize valise.

When Bill did at last come up to the barrier, Doris wondered how she could ever have mistaken anyone else for him. His arms as they went round her had the old familiar feel and it was the same voice that was in her ears again. She clung to him. But for some reason or other she was crying. Large, disconcertingly wet tears were running sideways down her cheek into her mouth. "God, what a fright I shall look: I shall look *awful*," she thought. And as she stood there she was aware that the gloom all around her was full of other figures embracing. Small women were being absorbed in great bear-like hugs, and raw-looking privates, in uniforms which didn't fit anywhere, were fastening themselves in an orgy of reunion on to promising young ladies with a lot of fair hair worn over their shoulders. The sound of big smacking kisses came through the darkness from all sides.

But that was only half the story. Because in the darkness there were just as many other couples saying good-bye. It was all part of the crazy pattern of the thing. One train full of soldiers came rolling in from the North and deposited its garrison in London while from another platform another train, also full of soldiers, was drawing out to keep up the occupation of the North. Altogether it was as though someone who had a grudge against home-life had thrust a large ladle into England and given the place a stir. It was the Schlieffen plan itself in operation inside England.

But with Bill's arms round her, Doris had given up thinking about other people. He was there, and that was all that mattered. The magic of having him had worked and she had stopped crying now.

"Oh, Bill, it's heavenly," she said. "It's just . . . just . . . heavenly."

"Come on," said Bill. "Let's go and eat something."

There wasn't a taxi. And it was in the Underground that she noticed what was wrong with him. Bill had grown himself a moustache. A neat clipped moustache like a colonel's. It didn't seem to belong to him. And what was so puzzling was that in some ridiculous way he appeared to be proud of it. He kept running his thumb down it as though, now that he had it, the thing had to be petted. The moustache made Doris cross. It was something that he had done without telling her. And it contrived to separate him from her. From certain angles he simply didn't look like Bill at all. And there were other changes, too, Doris noticed. The uniform which she had bought with him no longer looked like someone else's: he was filling it entirely. And the Sam Browne had lost its first newness. Altogether, he was the complete soldier, in fact. The Army had got hold of him, and he belonged to it.

It was only his voice and his hands that remained the same. They were strong, competent hands and Doris sat looking at them because they were the one thing that really seemed to belong to her.

"Those are my husband's hands," she kept on telling herself. "Those are my husband's hands."

And then another disquieting thought came to her.

"Perhaps I'm not the same either," she wondered. "Perhaps he sees differences in me."

But Doris need not have bothered. Bill had one knee pressed up hard against hers and the fingers of her hand were laced tightly between his. He was in high spirits and he kept on squeezing her fingers until it hurt.

When they got to Piccadilly Circus, he seized hold of her and picked up his case.

"This is where we get something to eat," he announced.

They pushed their way to the door of the carriage and forced a passage through the crowd on to the platform. It might have been the evening rush-hour instead of eleven o'clock at night from the way people were lined up there. And they weren't just ordinary people, either. It was as though a new war-time race of sharks and trollops had suddenly invaded London and made the Underground their headquarters; as though the Passenger Transport Board had called in Hogarth and Daumier, to choose their passengers for them. From one end of the platform to the other, the place had the air of a thieves' kitchen into which hot, confused men in uniform had irresistibly been lured. It might have been Port Said outside, and not Piccadilly.

Bill, however, did not appear to be unduly troubled.

"God, it's good to be back," was all he said.

They went up the escalator behind a Canadian sergeant with his arm round a girl who looked as if she wouldn't go down too well back in Saskatchewan, and came out in the packed booking-hall. A couple of sedate policemen patrolled the place seeing nothing, and all round them the armed forces struggled manfully to forget the war. The telephone kiosks were full of soldiers urgently ringing up improbable numbers.

The blackness of the street outside was sudden and unpleasant. At one moment you were climbing a few concrete steps under a row of dimmed electric lights. And, at the next, you were in the open air, and everything was as dark as the tomb. It was as though someone had slipped up and put a blanket over your head.

"Where do we go from here?" Bill asked. "I can't see anything."

And then gradually the darkness opened up and unfolded and they could see the portico of the Atlas Assurance and the vague curving outline of Regent Street. Under the arches, women with the eyes of owls and electric torches which they kept on flashing down at their legs, were assiduously hunting.

"It's this way," Bill told her. "There's the Regent Palace."

It was bright and cheerful again as soon as they got inside, almost like stepping out of war-time into peace again.

"This is more like it," Bill remarked. "This is what I came up for."

He left Doris for a moment and went over to the reception desk. She thought that he was taking rather a long time when he came back, grinning.

"It's no use," he said. "They don't trust me. They want to see your identity card, too."

"But we're not stopping here . . ." Doris began.

"Yes, we are," Bill told her. "I've got it all arranged. We've had enough hanging about for to-day."

"But what about Cynthia?" Doris began. "She'll be expecting us. So'll Mother."

"Fortune of war," Bill answered. "Hold-up on the railways. Direct hit with a bomb. Lost our way. I was drunk when you met me. Anything you like, only for Pete's sake stop here with me. This is the rest of our honeymoon."

They were in bed together in the darkness. Bill's arm was under her neck and his other thrown loosely across her.

"Seems more like two years than just a couple of months," he was saying.

His voice was sleepy now and his whole body was placid and inert. It was Doris who was wide awake and sleepless. She tried to rouse him.

"You don't think anything did . . . did go wrong, do you?" she asked. "It would be awful if I had a baby with you going away."

Bill held her close for a moment and kissed the back of her head. "Shouldn't worry," he said sleepily. "Only one chance in a million. I'm not such a rotten doctor as all that."

Then his embrace loosened again and his breathing became slow and regular. Bill was fast asleep by now.

But Doris was still awake. Wide awake, in fact. She lay there staring out into the darkness. It was a funny world. You married someone and you weren't allowed to live together. You spent a night in a hotel and you had to prove that you really were man and wife before you were allowed to go upstairs to your room. And finally the possibility of having a baby, which is what you had married for, was the most alarming thing that could come into your mind. It didn't make sense living life that way. The more you thought of it, the less sense it made.

CHAPTER 77

I

DORIS need not have worried about Cynthia. She was all right. When they didn't turn up she guessed that they had planned to spend the night together somewhere in town because it would be so romantic that way. She dropped off to sleep thinking about them. And in the morning there was a letter from Ted.

It was a lovely letter. Everything that a letter from an absent husband could be.

"*My own darling Cynthie,*" it ran, "*I love you more than ever. All night, I think about you. You are my only girl. Don't be angry if I tell you that I have got Veronica Lake's picture over my bed. It's only because she has got hair and shoulders like you. Honest it is, Cynthie. Sometimes I think I can't bear it any more not having you with me. After the war I want you to have a tight black costume with a white blouse, and I've seen some lace nightdresses like I've always meant to give you but couldn't get in London. Have you still got the red shoes with the open toe-caps? Don't wear them out before I come home. And don't have any of your hair off, not even if it's ever so long. I want to see it right over your shoulder when I get back to Blighty. And now, darling, don't be angry with me if I say something. Some of the chaps out here can't trust their wives once they're away from them. There are two cases in our camp. If I ever heard that there had been anyone hanging round you I would know what to do about*

it. I would kill him—I mean it—if I found that you had let somebody else come into your life while I wasn't there. I have bought you a pair of French slippers with real swansdown on them. They're pink and they'll look pretty under your pink dressing-gown. As they're fives they ought to be all right but I expect they'll get pinched like everything else. The post is awful. One man had a letter saying his father had died and it took seven weeks to reach him. Two of your letters arrived at once so you can guess how I'd been worrying. Take care of yourself and don't stop up too late reading. All my love, sweetest, Ted.
P.S.—Kiss Baby for me and tell her I'm going to buy her a present as soon as I can find anything decent. Keep cheerful and don't forget what I said."

Because it was such a beautiful letter she wanted to read it again. And she didn't want to re-read it out there in the kitchen with the washing-up all round her. So she went through into the drawing-room. She hadn't been in there yet this morning. But she didn't trouble to draw the blinds. She just put the light on and sat down on the couch beside the crumpled evening paper that was left over from last night. Then she started on the letter for the second time. She didn't mind a bit about Veronica Lake if that was only why Ted had her picture up. She wanted a black costume, too. It was something that she had always wanted, only somehow or other she'd always bought a bright one when the time had come. And the bit about her hair. Ted had always loved her hair. She used to tease him sometimes by saying that she was going to have it shingled.

When she came to the bit about what Ted would do if anyone else came into their lives, she cried. Cried like anything. But she enjoyed crying over that sort of thing. It was thrilling having a husband who was as jealous as all that. It made life worth living even when he wasn't there.

But it was silly, too. What chance had she got to give him any cause to be jealous, even if she wanted to? She'd only been out with a man once since Ted had been away. And that had been to the Co-op. dance with someone from Ted's department. What was more Ted had asked him to take her. There had been three of them because he had to take his own wife, too. She wished now that Ted hadn't said what he had done about being faithful, it made her feel cheap. What right had he got to tell her how to behave? If he didn't trust her he shouldn't have married her. Come to that, how did she know that Ted had been faithful to her? She *did* know, of course, because Ted was the sort who would always be faithful. Always and for ever and for ever, because he was built that way. But it just showed that he shouldn't have written such things. Because then she wouldn't have had thoughts of that kind about him. . . .

She'd remember that bit about the red shoes. But it wasn't really as simple as that. It was just like a man to think that it was. Even if she wore them when Ted came back, she wouldn't be the same. Her hands were getting awful with all the work she had to do. And looking after Baby, even though she was such a darling, was beginning to tell on her. If Ted wanted to find her as she had been when he went away the best thing that she could do would be to get herself a job as soon as possible so that she could see someone sometimes.

It was Baby that was the difficulty, of course. But she knew other girls with babies who managed somehow. There were crèches, weren't there? She'd seen pictures of them in the papers. Hundreds of happy babies all playing under artificial sun-lamps, while their mothers made munitions and had lunch-time concerts and things. It wasn't, as a matter of fact, really munitions that appealed to her. She wanted to be an usherette again. And usherettes were wanted just as much as munition workers. They were advertising for them at the Granada and the Astoria and the Ritz. She could walk into a job anywhere. And then she'd be able to see some decent films while she was actually doing a war-job, and it wouldn't seem so much like being buried alive with Baby.

Only what would Ted say? He didn't like the idea of her working. He'd rather she just sat at home waiting. It was so unfair, this business of having to consider somebody else's feelings, when it was her life that was affected. So unfair that she started crying again.

She cried for quite a long time. And then she felt better. There wasn't any sense anyhow in just sitting there when she had got things to do. And it was gloomy with the electric light on and the daylight coming in through the chinks in the black-out curtains. So she got up and began putting the room straight. When she pulled back the curtains, she shook up the cushions and pulled the covers into position. She wanted the room to look nice if Bill was coming.

A whimper—half cry, half grumble—from Baby sent her running. Baby was sitting in her high chair in the kitchen where she had left her. She snatched her out of the chair and started cuddling her.

"Mummy won't ever send Baby to a creesh," she said. "Mummy loves Baby far too much for that. Silly Daddy made Mummy cry, but Mummy always got Baby to make her happy."

All the same, it wasn't much to ask—just to get out of the flat and see a decent film again *sometimes*.

2

Bill and Doris—Bill thoughtfully carrying a new doll for Baby—got back to Larkspur Road after lunch. Bill had wanted to spend the rest of the afternoon in the West End seeing a show. But Doris wouldn't let him. She reminded him that, after they had been to Cynthia's, they would still have to go round to the Jossers. Her mother, she said, would be waiting for them. It would look rude if they left it any longer.

But again Doris was wrong. Mr. and Mrs. Josser were entirely preoccupied. In their present mood they wouldn't have noticed if Bill and Doris had stayed away altogether.

"I never thought Henry would be the one to go first. It still doesn't seem possible it's happened."

It was Mrs. Josser who had spoken. And Mr. Josser, paper in hand, looked up from the paper he was reading. There had been no preliminary conversation leading up to Mrs. Josser's remark. No bridge. It was simply one of those observations that occur suddenly, isolated and unannounced, as though a portion of the speaker's mind has become detached and is drifting away into space.

Mr. Josser considered the point.

"Pneumonia's a funny thing," he agreed at last. "You can never tell with it."

As he was speaking he raised his eyes to the mantelshelf. All that now remained of Uncle Henry rested there. His ashes scattered, his business sold—even the name Knockell above the shop had been changed to Skyte & Son—his library of alarming yellow literature dispersed, the one monument to the man was contained in the large foolscap envelope leaning up against the presentation clock.

Not that it wasn't an impressive sort of envelope. Mr. Barks knew the etiquette in such matters and he used only the best law stationery. Getting at the letter inside was like ripping armour. It had come that morning, the letter, and Mr. and Mrs. Josser had both of them read and re-read it. They had known all about it, of course. Even been expecting it. Nevertheless, now that it had come, they were dazed. Distinctly dazed. And in consequence they had done nothing about it. Mr. Josser hadn't liked to suggest paying the cheque into his account because, after all, it was addressed to Mrs. Josser.

And it was such a thunderingly big cheque. It dominated everything. Despite all his Socialist views, Uncle Henry must have been steadily piling it on in the greengrocery line for years. A halfpenny on the peas here and a penny on the Blenheims there—and it had all added up to something pretty terrific. The cheque that Mr. Barks had sent to Mrs. Josser was for more than a thousand pounds. One thousand one hundred and twenty-eight pounds, six and fourpence to be precise.

"We ought to pay it in, you know," Mr. Josser said finally. "Just supposing there was an air-raid, for instance. We shouldn't have anything to show for it if this house got hit."

Mrs. Josser drew in her lips sharply.

"If that happened, we shouldn't be here either," she observed grimly. Then she paused. "I haven't done anything about it because I don't like to touch it," she added. "I can see it's silly, but I just don't like to touch it."

"I know how you feel," Mr. Josser told her. "It seems a pity poor old Henry didn't get more fun out of his money himself."

"Henry had all the fun he wanted," Mrs. Josser replied sharply. "It was just that he was made that way."

The subject of Uncle Henry was still a delicate one, and Mr. Josser didn't attempt any answer. Ever since his death, Mrs. Josser had defended her brother's memory with fierceness and asperity. And in consequence the character of Uncle Henry was perceptibly changing. In retrospect he had become a kind of very nearly Christian saint with a flair for cycling.

"It was a lot of money he left," Mr. Josser observed neutrally.

"Well, why not?" Mrs. Josser demanded. "He worked hard for it, didn't he?" She paused. And another, a new, aspect of her brother's saintliness suggested itself to her. "If he'd wanted to," she added, "he could have had a whole chain of shops like that, instead of just one of 'em. He could have been like Waltons."

Mr. Josser got up and knocked the ash out of his pipe.

"Think I'll make a cup of tea, Mother," he said. "I expect we'd both like one."

He was rather relieved that the incident of the tea provided an opportunity for changing the subject from Uncle Henry. He'd had rather a lot of Uncle Henry all day. And it wasn't the Uncle Henry he recognised. He had a suspicion that Uncle Henry wouldn't have recognised himself either.

When he got back with the tea, Mrs. Josser was going round the room tidying up. This was always a sign with her. Whereas other people went for long solitary walks or wrote letters to the papers or retired to bed with a headache, Mrs. Josser did an extra round of tidying. It was a sure indication that there was something on her mind.

"We'll drink the tea now it's made," she said as Mr. Josser entered. "And then we'll go straight off to the agents. We'll start looking to-morrow."

"To-morrow's Sunday," Mr. Josser reminded her.

"Well, there are just as many cottages on a Sunday as there are on any other day, aren't there?"

So that was it. Because of Mrs. Josser's reticence, he hadn't liked to raise the subject of cottages himself. In the circumstances it would have looked as if he were trying to spend her money for her. And it was always possible that she had changed her mind. For all he knew she might have decided to give the money to one of the societies to which Uncle Henry during his lifetime had devoted his activities. Already, he had half seen her as the patroness of the North Hackney Anti-God Committee.

But there was no more doubt about it. Mrs. Josser was decided.

"We'll go to the agents to-day and then start looking on Monday," she announced. "And we won't skimp ourselves. We'll buy just the sort of cottage Henry would have wanted us to have."

And this was strange. Because the only time they'd discussed cottages with Uncle Henry, he'd been opposed to them. They ought all to be condemned, he had said. Condemned, and blocks of agricultural workers' flats put up in their place.

They were still talking about cottages when Bill and Doris arrived. It seemed to Doris callous and unfeeling to go on with such a topic when Bill was due to go overseas in twenty-four hours' time. But Bill seemed rather relieved about it. And he said something that brought Mrs. Josser nearer to liking him than she ever had been before. What he said was that it was nice to think that if the air raids got really bad Doris would have somewhere out of London to go to.

BOOK SIX

THE COTTAGE IN THE COUNTRY

CHAPTER 78

As a matter of fact, Mr. Josser was rather relieved, too. Only he was thinking of Mrs. Josser. London wasn't the sort of place in which to leave any woman these days.

Everything had been going so badly over on the other side. The remains of our army in Norway—the one that had gone out complete with skis and white coats for warfare in the snow—had re-embarked at Namsos leaving its skis and white coats behind it. And there were rumours—admittedly only rumours so far—about German intentions in the West. Belgium was to be the next one, people said. Not Holland, because the dykes would make fighting impossible. And whether it was true or not about Belgium, the Belgians themselves certainly believed it. Mr. Josser had read in the paper that morning that all traffic on the Albert Canal had been suspended. Altogether, it seemed a funny sort of morning on which to go out choosing a country cottage. It was either very frivolous or only just in time.

It was getting on for ten o'clock when the Jossers finally emerged. And there was just a hint of peril hanging over the expedition. Mrs. Josser kept on referring mysteriously to her feet as though they were a pair of scarcely convalescent invalids who, for better or worse, had decided to accompany them. If they let her down, she emphasised, Mr. Josser would have to go on without her.

It was unfortunate, therefore, that Mrs. Josser should have decided that they should make Crouch End their destination. She had been there once as a girl. And she remembered it, from that one afternoon forty-eight years ago, with a sentimental enthusiasm amounting to nostalgia.

"Don't want to go and bury ourselves miles from anywhere," she explained. "There's lovely country all about Crouch End. We'll just go and look round."

"May have changed a bit since you were there, Mother," Mr. Josser warned her.

But Mrs. Josser would not hear anything against the place.

"Not Crouch End," she said confidently. "You don't know Crouch End."

Nor did she when they got there. They took one look at the shops and the rows of houses and the buses, and decided to go on still further into the unknown.

There was something rather terrifying in having come so far only to find themselves still somewhere in the heart of London. So Mr. Josser suggested a cup of coffee in a Lyons's before they went on. The Lyons's was an exact replica of the one at Kennington and this simple fact depressed them anew; it was as though they hadn't yet even left home. While they were sitting there, Mr. Josser kept muttering something about having told her so until Mrs. Josser asked him sharply what he was saying. But as Mrs. Josser hadn't heard him properly, no real harm had been done. And a remark which she made quite casually changed the whole complexion of her blunder.

"It must have been longer ago than I thought," she said simply. "I was sixteen at the time."

The effect on Mr. Josser was remarkable. He put down his cup, and leaning forward gave Mrs. Josser's hand a squeeze.

"That was just before I met you," he said. "I wish I'd known you then."

Mrs. Josser went on drinking.

"You've known me quite long enough," was all she said.

It was easy, however, to see that she was pleased. She looked at him sideways and gave him a little smile, and Mr. Josser forgave her for Crouch End.

Then they set out again. Still in search of the undeveloped hinterland that Mrs. Josser remembered, they penetrated further and further into an endless desert of identical little red houses. Even the names of the roads—Grove Road, Windermere Road, Alexandra Road, Hillside, Elm Avenue, Victoria Terrace, Balmoral Gardens—seemed identical, too. They were travelling on relays of bus by now. And when they reached Edmonton, it was time for lunch.

It might have been better if they had turned back from there. But Mrs. Josser was in no mood for turning back. After the rebuff at Crouch End she now saw the whole expedition in terms of a challenge. With Mr. Josser following, she pressed on. By three o'clock they were at Waltham Abbey. And, because in between the houses little patches of green had started to appear, their spirits rose. They went into every estate agent's they could see and began collecting orders to view. It was a firm called Sprackett and Clutt which seemed the most promising.

Between them, Mr. Sprackett and Mr. Clutt seemed to spread a pretty wide net. Waltham Abbey was really only the beginning of things. The properties caught up in their mesh were mostly in the countryside behind Waltham. There was one in particular, Conservatory Cottage, Ditchfield, that the clerk recommended. It belonged to a Mrs. Marble and had come on the market only that morning. He advised the Jossers to see it at once. He didn't conceal that it was a pity that they had come to Waltham first because it was a roundabout way to get to Ditchfield. But he was a friendly, almost fatherly sort of man. He explained that when they actually lived in Ditchfield they would have a station of their own only two miles away.

As it was, the Jossers had to go by bus. It was a small single-decker. And it did not hurry. It rumbled. It waited for people. It stopped at cross-roads to deliver things. And by the time they reached Ditchfield they had been right across the steppes and tundras of Essex. And it was now after five, and they wanted tea. But Ditchfield did not seem to be the kind of village that provided teas. The hamlet—or as much of it as could be seen at a glance—stretched for nearly half a mile along a perfectly straight road. There was a public house, The Plough, closed as only an English public house at tea-time can be closed; a petrol pump without a garage; a post office in a converted villa with an enamelled sign over the front door advertising HOVIS, and on the gate a poster of a sinking ship and a warning against careless talk. But it seemed a long way somehow from Ditchfield to the North Atlantic.

After the post office the houses petered out a bit. There was an elm tree with no branches, a small patch of grass worn threadbare like an old carpet, and a pond so low that it seemed to have a leak in it somewhere. In a field opposite rested the upper part of a small delivery van from which the engine and chassis were unaccountably missing. Altogether Ditchfield was a representative corner of unspoiled rural England. The sort of place that tourists miss.

The bus driver had never heard of Conservatory Cottage, and by the time Mr. Josser had finished speaking to him the other passengers had all disappeared. So they tried the post office. The postmistress was of the compassionate kind. She seemed worried at the idea that anyone should want to walk as far as Conservatory Cottage. She agreed, readily, however, that there was no other way of getting there and came out to the gate to show him the way. It was not difficult. Straight on down the road would get them there, she said, and there were no turnings. It was the last house on the left, after the sandpit.

For the first half-mile, they chatted as they walked along. Then Mrs. Josser grew silent. Grim and unsmiling, she proceeded. She was peering anxiously ahead for what looked like a sandpit. But Mr. Josser was enjoying himself. He was walking like a man in a dream. For the better part of half a century he had been awaiting precisely this moment when he and Emily should be passing down a country lane together, looking for a cottage. It was just such a day of heat and bright sunshine that he had always imagined. And now, magically, the moment had come.

"Shouldn't be long now, Mother," he said encouragingly.

Mrs. Josser still said nothing. But it was obvious that she was in bad condition. In really bad condition. It wasn't a trifling thing like her feet either. This was altogether more serious. The danger zone had shifted upwards. It was one of her headaches that Mrs. Josser expected any moment to be getting. The way things were working out, Mrs. Josser judged that she wasn't going to like Ditchfield.

And then came one of those magical surprises, those sudden transformations of which even the flattest of English countrysides is capable. The road behind them was as straight as a ruler, but the ground on either side had begun to drop away slightly. And through a gap in the hedge a view appeared. It was like coming on an open door in a long corridor. As far as they could see across the heat-haze of the late afternoon the green and brown pattern of the countryside was spread out before them. And it looked good.

Even the sandpit turned out to be beautiful. It was an old one. The notice-board about "Truck-loads to order: distance no object" was half covered up by branches and the pit itself was simply a bowl of willow-herb. Mr. Josser would have liked to stop there for a bit and take a look at it, but Mrs. Josser made it quite evident that if she paused for so much as a single moment she would never go on again.

And then behind a little copse, Conservatory Cottage appeared. It was white and clean-looking, and the hedge in front of it had been cut into a neat green battlement. A double border of flowers led up to a green front door.

Mr. Josser stood for a moment at the gate appraising it all. But Mrs. Josser urged him forward.

"Just so long as there's somewhere I can sit down, that's all I ask," she said.

"We don't know if there'll be anyone in," Mr. Josser warned her. "We didn't say we were coming."

But Mrs. Marble was there all right. A large, vague woman in a flowered overall, she was standing in the window watching them. She came to the front door wearing a pleased, rather puzzled expression as though she were afraid that she must have invited them and then forgotten all about it.

"Oh, dear," she said. "I wasn't expecting anybody so soon. If I'd known you were coming I'd have had things ready. But do come in. I'd better get you some tea."

After the heat and glare outside, it was cool and dim within the cottage. Mrs. Josser loosened both her shoes and said "Ah." A pleasant smell of bees-wax and old furniture filled the room, and Mr. Josser felt sleepy. There was no opportunity of any rest, however, as Mrs. Marble kept asking them questions. She asked them twice how far they had come and was astonished each time to find that it was London. She told them that the station was really only half a mile away if you went across the fields. She asked whether they'd ever lived in the country before. She asked how they'd heard that the cottage was for sale. She asked if they'd like lettuce and then remembered that all hers had run to seed. She asked how far they'd come, and was astonished to hear . . .

The tea did Mrs. Josser good. After drinking it, a light perspiration broke out on her forehead. And, after she had furtively and politely wiped it away with her handkerchief, she felt better. It was her turn now to begin asking Mrs. Marble questions. Was the cottage dry? How long had Mrs. Marble lived there? What was the water supply like? When did she propose to leave? Was an Elsan easy if you weren't used to one?

Mr. Josser did not say anything at all. He just sat back admiring his wife. She might have been buying cottages all her life. Mrs. Marble was impressed, too. She asked again if Mrs. Josser had ever lived in the country before.

While the two women went upstairs, privately and mysteriously on their own, Mr. Josser sauntered out into the garden. It wasn't a large garden. There were bigger gardens in many of the suburbs. But after one look at it, Mr. Josser decided that he'd never seen a nicer one. There were two fruit trees, and a well, and a kitchen plot and a bit of a lawn with a rustic seat at one end of it. When he came to the conservatory he saw why the cottage had been named after it.

The conservatory was very nearly as large as the cottage. It had been put up in the best style with a length of ornamental metalwork running along the top of it, and there was a handle for winding up the windows at the sides. It was quite the most beautiful conservatory that Mr. Josser had ever met.

He had been in the garden for some time when Mrs. Josser and Mrs. Marble came out. Mr. Josser looked up eagerly. He hoped that Mrs. Josser liked the upstairs.

But even if she did, Mrs. Josser was being guarded.

"We'll write and let you know," was all she said.

When they got as far as the gate a happy thought came to Mrs. Marble.

"If only we were on the phone we could phone up for a car," she called after them. "But I doubt if it would be any good. You ought to order it the day before really if you want to be sure of getting it."

They went round by the road because Mrs. Marble had left them confused about the route across the fields. And Mrs. Josser didn't say very much.

"How that poor woman manages I can't imagine," was all that she remarked. "Nothing but oil to cook with and lost her husband at Easter. It was his idea the conservatory. They had it built for them."

"But what . . . what did you think of the cottage?" Mr. Josser asked, trying to keep the note of excitement out of his voice.

"You didn't go upstairs," Mrs. Josser told him. "Or come down again. If you had, you'd know what breaking your neck meant."

It was after eleven when they got back to No. 10. And Mrs. Josser was too tired by then to discuss anything further. Her attitude was one which suggested that she could not understand how anyone who had been wafted by Destiny into a haven like Dulcimer Street could ever think of going to sea again.

CHAPTER 79

I

But don't forget that some of the other occupants of No. 10 had cut themselves adrift already. And, if we want to keep them in sight, we shall have to follow.

For instance, the doctor's wife at Chelmsford is worried about the new housekeeper whom she has just engaged. Wouldn't it have been better, she wonders, to have waited and seen if the London registry office were going to send someone after all? Not that anything would have come of it—she consoles herself with that thought. It's really just like 1914 all over again. From the very moment war was declared all the good maids threw up their jobs and rushed off anywhere to make munitions or aeroplanes. And the salaries these workers get! Only that morning the doctor's wife had read about girls of sixteen getting five and six pounds a week simply doing piecework—whatever piecework might be.

It isn't as though there is anything actually wrong with the new housekeeper. She isn't as young or as strong as she might be; and she is rather slow in consequence. But she is careful, very careful, and conscientious. She isn't a smasher. She doesn't drink. And she doesn't seem to want any time off. Nor is it the fact that she is a Roman Catholic that upsets the doctor's wife—though naturally she would have preferred that the new housekeeper should have been Church of England like other people. No, it isn't any of those things. It is simply that the doctor's wife is afraid that the new housekeeper is perhaps a little mad.

But the new housekeeper is too tired to notice her employer's suspicion. All that she is concerned with is giving satisfaction. She was lucky to get the job at all in her state of health—she knows that. And even if the work is heavier than she had reckoned on—"working housekeeper" was the expression the advertisement used—she tells herself that there are other people who are working harder. Above all, it is the money that counts. And thirty-two and six a week and everything found is wonderful. The new housekeeper is secretive and has plans of her own. So long as she can hold the job, she reckons that she will be able to save sixty-five pounds a year easily.

At the moment she is standing at the window of her bedroom looking towards the city. She spends a lot of time alone in her room and sometimes she is heard talking to herself. It is partly this that makes the doctor's wife think that she *must* be mad.

But she isn't. Not a bit of it. The cause of all the trouble is merely that the person she is speaking to, the only person she cares about, isn't there. That is why morning, afternoon and evening—and sometimes at night as well—she peers out across the garden in the direction of the missing one.

"Don't worry, Percy boy," she tells him. "Mother's here. She's watching. Everything's going to be all right, Percy. Just try to forget what's happened, and remember to say your prayers. Be a good boy, Percy, that's the main thing. And don't fret yourself about money. There'll be some more ready for you by the time you want it. Mother's near you. She'll see that you'll get everything you need."

Then with that expression of sadness that she has worn for years—the expression that she wore before she had any real reason for it—Mrs. Boon goes over to the bed and kneels there, her rosary in her hands and the patchwork showing in the heels of her darned stockings.

2

Mr. and Mrs. Josser made two more trips to Conservatory Cottage. And after their second visit, they went along to Sprackett and Clutt and paid their deposit to the kind fatherly clerk.

There was some little difficulty about this because the money, Uncle Henry's money, was all in Mrs. Josser's name, and she had never written out a cheque before. Mr. Josser had to stand over her to show how it should be done and even so she signed herself "Mrs. Josser" before he could stop her.

But there was really more to her hesitation than mere inexperience. She was suddenly appalled at the enormity of what she was doing. The purchase price was seven hundred and fifty pounds, and here was she solemnly writing away a tenth of it, a whole seventy-five pounds, with a flick of the pen. And seventy-five pounds was something she could get her mind fixed on to—the whole seven hundred and fifty was too large to be imagined. She had never really pictured herself actually paying away that amount.

"Couldn't you do it, Fred?" she asked quite humbly after the second attempt. "My hand's all trembly: I've been doing too much."

And she was still shaky when they came out of the estate agent's. Still shaky and still appalled.

"It'll be Ted's some day," she said, suddenly. "That's one comfort."

Mr. Josser was rather taken aback.

"Don't say that, Mother," he told her. "We'll have a bit of time there ourselves first."

He was disappointed in this sudden change in Mrs. Josser's attitude because, right up to the very moment of writing out the cheque, she had been so eager and enthusiastic about it all. Almost girlish, in fact. She had brushed difficulties and disadvantages aside impetuously.

For example, when Mr. Josser had said something about its being rather a long way from the station, Mrs. Josser had suggested cycling. And when Mr. Josser had reminded her that she couldn't ride a bicycle she had been offended.

"I suppose I could learn, couldn't I?" she had demanded. "Other people of my age go about on bicycles. Hundreds of them. . . ."

But now everything was different. She was timid and unsure of herself.

"I hope we've done the right thing," she said twice over in the bus, as much to herself as to Mr. Josser. "I do hope we've done the right thing."

All Mr. Josser's assurances, however, counted for very little until she herself thought of Doris.

"It's Doris I did it for as much as anyone," she said. "It's what that girl needs, plenty of fresh air and sunshine. It isn't really healthy living with Cynthia the way she does." She paused. "She'll get used to the ride," she added complacently. "There's no harm in a great strapping girl like Doris cycling to the station every morning."

And having convinced herself that it was for her children that she had bought the cottage, Mrs. Josser felt better. She recovered all her old excitement. On the way up in the train she kept on telling Mr. Josser where the various pieces of furniture were to go. It was rather a one-sided conversation, however, because Mr. Josser with a man's natural vagueness on the practical side of things hadn't thought about furniture at all: he had been too busy simply thinking about the cottage. But Mrs. Josser was ready to arrange the furniture for both of them. She gave her whole mind to it. And she gave it so decidedly when it came to Doris's room that Mr. Josser had to warn her that Doris might want to have some say in it herself.

The warning annoyed Mrs. Josser: it seemed to suggest some division of taste that she refused to admit existed.

"If I don't know what Doris likes, I'd like to know who does," she answered. "I'm her mother, aren't I?"

She paused. Another aspect of it all had crossed her mind.

"And the first thing in the morning I'll go down and tell Mrs. Vizzard," she said. "I didn't want to worry her when we were only looking. But she ought to know now. It'll be a shock when she hears."

CHAPTER 80

I

THE DATE for Mr. Squales's wedding had been fixed. It was to take place on Wednesday week.

In consequence, with time so short, Mr. Squales had been nearly distracted. His face showed unmistakable signs of the strain. It was pale—a kind of chalky, milky paleness—under the olive tan, and his eyes had pouches under them like a parrot's. Also, he was smoking much more. From the moment he woke up in the morning until he went to sleep at night, even during meal-times and while he was dressing and undressing, he had a cigarette clutched nervously between his fingers or hanging feebly from his lips. It now required the better part of three packets of twenty simply to keep him going from one daybreak to the next.

But it was all right now. He had got what he wanted. That was all that mattered. With less than a fortnight to spare he had got it. The future was all golden. And with the sudden lessening of the tension, he was almost light-headed. He began talking to himself aloud. Not loud enough for anyone else in the house—Mrs. Vizzard, for instance—to hear. But loud enough for him to be able to savour the unique satisfaction of hearing of his own success.

"So I *was* right," he told himself. "I haven't been wasting my time. I thought I hadn't been. But I couldn't be sure. And all the time the noose was closing. Another ten days and I'd have been dangling there."

He sat back in his chair and stretched his long legs out in front of him.

"Just fancy her letting herself go like that," he went on. "Talk about Merry Widows."

He gave a little chuckle and took out of his pocket the wallet that Mrs. Vizzard had given him for his birthday. From the inside pocket, the very private part under the flap, he took out a letter and began to read. He had just got to the bottom of the first page—there were nearly five pages of it in impulsive-looking royal blue ink—when there was a coy, dainty tapping on the door. He shot up instantly in his chair and shoved the letter all crushed up in his hand back into his pocket.

"Come in, my kitten," he said. "Come in. . . ."

He scrambled to his feet as he said the words and thrust back the loose lock of hair that trailed across his forehead. He only wished that he weren't trembling. Trembling was so conspicuous somehow. And, above all things, he wanted to avoid anything that was even in the tiniest degree conspicuous. He just wanted to be himself. Not that it was going to be easy. Before the evening was over, it would have called for more poise and aplomb even than poker playing. But because he was so anxious that everything should pass off smoothly and without a hitch, he rose obediently and followed Mrs. Vizzard into the front room where the cold meat and salad was already spread out for him.

The ordeal of meal-time was worse, however, than Mr. Squales had even imagined possible. Mrs. Vizzard was at her most playful. She had moved her chair to his side of the table and, at intervals, her hand kept stealing across the table to nestle confidingly in his. Each time it arrived, Mr. Squales obediently squeezed it. Once or twice to keep up appearances it was his hand that went out first. But there was no warmth, no passion in the grip. Only a hard, unyielding muscular pressure like a man wringing something out.

"I've arranged with the photographer," said Mrs. Vizzard softly. "A cabinet study."

Mr. Squales started.

"The photographer?" he said. "Ah yes, the photographer."

"And will you do something for me?"

Mr. Squales turned a baleful, bloodshot eye in her direction.

"Anything you ask," he answered.

"It's your collar," Mrs. Vizzard explained. "I know it's silly. And I suppose it's just that I'm made that way. But I've always loved men in butterfly collars. So I wondered if just for once, just for the wedding, you'd wear one. It'd be in the photograph, too. I'd love to have you in the photograph in a butterfly collar."

Mr. Squales shifted in his chair and the letter in his pocket crackled like a five-pound note. He shuddered.

"This is dreadful. Positively dreadful," he told himself. "Why must the woman go on? Can't she see that I'm not enjoying it?"

But he was not a man to give up simply because the part was difficult. He braced himself.

"Butterfly or Oxford," he said. "It's all one to me. And if it means anything to you . . ."

He broke off with a little gesture of accommodatingness, leaving the rest of the sentence expressively unfinished. He felt so sure that he had got over that hurdle all right that he even allowed himself to relax for a moment. Slumping back in his chair he started to whistle idly through his teeth. He soon found, however, how wrong, how disastrously wrong he was. Something told him that all was not well with Mrs. Vizzard. And when he looked toward her he saw that she had her handkerchief pressed against her face.

"Don't . . . don't you mind what *I* wear on Wednesday week?" she asked.

Mr. Squales cast one quick, agonised glance in her direction. Then he looked away again. Really it seemed as though she were doing her utmost to embarrass him.

But once more he controlled himself. Controlled himself, and smiled.

"For my part," he said, "I would like nothing better than what you are wearing now. But you're a woman. You must decide when the time comes. . . ."

2

It was nearly eleven when Mr. Squales escaped to his own room. And by then he was about knocked up. He took off his coat and opened up the front of his shirt because it was sticking to him.

"Phew," he said. "What an evening."

And it wasn't over yet. The really delicate and dangerous part was still coming. That was why Mr. Squales made no attempt to undress. Instead, he lit another cigarette and lay on his back on the bed with his knees up, gazing at the ceiling. Twinges of something that might have been conscience but clarified themselves each time into foreboding kept passing through him.

"It'll about be the end of her," he reflected silently. "She's the type that takes things badly."

After half an hour spent cogitating on the future, Mr. Squales got up off the bed and removed his shoes. Then when he could move about without being heard, he went round the room in his stockinged feet.

There was a lot that he had to do even though he had all night, or practically all night, in which to do it. First of all he got out his night things, the brocaded pyjamas and frogged dressing-gown that Mrs. Vizzard had given him, and folded them carefully for travelling. After all, he could hardly arrive at his destination and begin by asking for the valet service, could he? Then he took out his old suit —the suit that he had been wearing when he came to Dulcimer Street—and folded that up, too. He was already wearing the still almost new light check that had been an earlier present of Mrs. Vizzard's. Beside it the old suit looked so pathetically shabby that for a moment a lump came into Mr. Squales's throat. Nothing looks worse than a double-breasted black cashmere that shines like a mirror across the seat and shoulders.

It was the overcoat that presented the real problem. It was so enormous; lined with bear and trimmed with astrakhan, it hung like a hunting trophy on the peg behind the door. And the inside of the overcoat was as saddening as the outside of the black cashmere. Moths had made their meals there. And a cigarette-end dropped carelessly in a railway carriage had burnt clean through the massive skin itself.

"To think," Mr. Squales reflected, "to think that if I'd got there before the moth I could have raised fifteen pounds on it."

But partially devoured or not, the coat was unfoldable. Mr. Squales tried it all ways—folded in half, folded in threes, rolled up like a mattress. And still it remained a sprawling mass of skin and fur. In the end he recognised that there would be nothing for it but to carry it over his arm.

"People'll think I'm mad," he told himself. "A fur coat in this weather."

Mr. Squales was very sensitive about appearances. And there was something else that played on his sensitiveness. Considering that it was all he had, there was really embarrassingly little to pack. It went into one old suitcase. And when it was full Mr. Squales stepped back and regarded it.

"It's a queer world," he told himself. "Whatever way you look at it, it's a queer world. If the late Mr. Vizzard knew what his suitcase was being used for . . ."

But even though he had finished his packing, the evening's work wasn't yet over. The worst part of it, in fact, was still to come. Mr. Squales went over to the mantelshelf and got down the twopenny bottle of blue-black ink, the plain schoolboyish penholder and the packet of cheap writing-paper. That, however, was about as far as he was able to get. With the sheet of fancy vellum-wove spread out on the table in front of him he just sat there staring at it. Instead of writing he began drawing designs on the packet—hearts and anchors and true lovers' knots.

It was the chimes of Mr. Josser's presentation clock seeping down wall and ceiling that finally roused him. Squaring his shoulders and dipping the nib into the bottle right up to the cork finger-guard, he began. "Dear Friend," was how the letter started. But to go on was still difficult. He dried up completely once or twice. But he struggled on, filling the page with his bold backward sloping writing, with the downward strokes of the g's twisted round like monkeys' tails. And the end of the letter proved as difficult as the beginning. He pondered long over the subscription. "Yours sincerely"—too prosaic; "Yours faithfully"—too cold; "Yours truly"—too formal; "Yours ever"—unthinkable. In the end he decided to strike the note of friendship again. "Your sincere friend" was what he wrote.

And when he came to read the letter over, he was pleased with it. It was calm, detached, dignified. Only one thing worried him.

"How the hell do you spell forgiveness?" he asked himself at last. "Is there an 'e' or isn't there?"

The letter, propped up against the piece of Bangor china on the mantelpiece, seemed to dominate the whole room, and Mr. Squales glanced back at it nervously.

"She can't miss it there, poor dear, that's one thing," he told himself.

He was stiff from sitting in the chair for so long, simply waiting for the time to pass. But now he stretched himself. He was ready. It was four a.m. and that gave him comfortable time to make his way quietly to Victoria. He would have breakfast at the station and then pick up the 9.15.

He opened the door of his room carefully. Very carefully.

"No need to rouse everyone," he said under his breath. "This farewell is private."

It wasn't easy, however. The suitcase was all right. But the fur coat behaved as erratically as if the bear had still been living. It tried to sweep things off stands as it passed them. And in the end Mr. Squales had to go out backwards, leaving the coat to trail after him. It was safer that way, but not dignified.

Opening the front door was difficult. And he had to put the suitcase down before he could manage it. But the relief, the blessed relief, when the door at last was open and he could stand on the doorstep a free man. He took a deep breath.

"Thank God," he said aloud. "That's over. Too close to be comfortable. . . ."

The sudden transition from strain to placidity was so great that he nearly screamed when someone spoke to him. He turned round, his eyeballs staring. There on the step beside him stood Connie, the night-club girl, just returning from her evening's work. She looked at him, at the suitcase and at the huge fur coat. Then she gave a large grin.

"Taking the dog out?" she asked.

CHAPTER 81

I

IT WAS on the same morning when Mrs. Vizzard had discovered Mr. Squales's letter that Mrs. Josser went down to give notice. Only Mrs. Josser, of course, didn't know anything about the letter. She was, indeed, so much concerned with the problem of how to give notice nicely—eleven years is, after all, a long time to have spent in anybody else's house—that she couldn't imagine that Mrs. Vizzard could have any preoccupations of her own. That was why she started right in by telling Mrs. Vizzard how comfortable they had all been at No. 10 and how, for her part, she would have preferred to stay where she was for ever. But there were other considerations outside her control, she explained. Mr. Josser's health, for instance. It was that which had decided her.

"With his chest what it is," Mrs. Josser went on, "if I kept him here in Dulcimer Street against my better judgment, I should be a murderess. That's what I should be—a murderess."

She paused for a moment, and looked up in Mrs. Vizzard's direction. Up to the present, Mrs. Vizzard had not said anything. And Mrs. Josser wanted to make sure that she wasn't offended. But what Mrs. Josser saw astonished her. So far from being offended, Mrs. Vizzard apparently *wasn't even listening*. She was sitting back in her chair with her head cocked over on one side staring vacantly into space as though she were seeing ghosts.

Mrs. Josser coughed.

"It's been a weekly tenancy," she said stiffly, "and we should be in our rights to give a week's notice. But naturally we don't want to put you to any inconvenience. Not after the way things have been. So I'm saying that we shall want to go at the end of the month. Not before, but not much after."

"Go at the end of the month?"

Mrs. Vizzard had roused herself suddenly and was gazing incredulously at Mrs. Josser.

"That's what I said," Mrs. Josser told her.

"Why?" Mrs. Vizzard asked blankly.

It was obvious that she hadn't heard a word.

So, as it turned out, it was Mrs. Josser and not Mrs. Vizzard who was offended. And if Mrs. Vizzard weren't prepared to show her the courtesy of attending, Mrs. Josser certainly didn't propose to go on explaining. The limit of her patience had been reached. And exceeded. She got up.

"You'll probably like to have the house more to yourself anyhow," she said pointedly. "It'll be different when it's really a home for you again."

"A home again!" Mrs. Vizzard repeated half an octave higher.

Then, to Mrs. Josser's amazement, she said the words a second time.

"A home again!"

This time her voice had risen still further. It was shrill and tremulous. And still the phrase seemed to hold some hidden fascination for her.

"A home again!"

She was almost shrieking the phrase by now. And she was laughing as she uttered it.

"You . . . you don't know what you're saying."

She could not say more, however, because she was laughing too much. It was quite low, ladylike laughter at first—not more than little chuckling giggles. But, like the words which she had just spoken, it grew louder. It grew into a hoarse boisterous gust of laughter with nothing in the least ladylike about it. And it became continuous. Soon Mrs. Vizzard was sitting there holding her sides. And laughing. Laughing. Laughing. Her hair, which she had been wearing on top of her head in the halo which Mr. Squales had admired so much, came undone and slid down in a sort of noose.

Now that Mrs. Josser suspected hysterics she realised that she would have to do something about it. The difficulty was in making absolutely certain. Even after she had half-filled a cup with water at the tap she came back and stood there with the cup poised, uncertain whether or not to throw. It was only when she heard the words ". . . home again," inextricably mingled with the laughter, that she let go. The contents of the cup hit Mrs. Vizzard a hard, fluid slap.

And the effect was magical. The laughter stopped instantly. Mrs. Vizzard paused and gasped for breath. It was, of course, some little time before she had recovered herself completely. But she was in her right mind again. She remained where she was, whimpering freely and trying to mop up the icy streams that were running all down her. . . .

It was over the tea, brewed by Mrs. Josser to revive her, that Mrs. Vizzard told everything. And Mrs. Josser listened tight-lipped and aghast. Not until Mrs. Vizzard implored her: "Don't tell Connie and Mr. Puddy. I couldn't bear the shame of it," did Mrs. Josser allow herself to interrupt even for a single moment.

"They'll have to know sooner or later," she said firmly. "You can't conceal it beyond Wednesday week."

"My wedding day!" Mrs. Vizzard said under her breath, almost as though she'd forgotten that she was still speaking to anyone. "Oh, the scandal, the disgrace. And after everything I'd done for him."

Mrs. Josser drew in her lips tightly.

"You ought to thank yourself you've been spared," she said. "It was merciful Providence. Nothing less."

But Mrs. Vizzard was past listening to her.

"The cruelty. The horrid cruelty of it," was all that she could say. "Look what he wrote to me."

She handed the fatal letter—a little crumpled by now—over to Mrs. Josser as she spoke and sat back to see the effect on her companion. Mrs. Josser read it through carefully and then, with the tips of her fingers, passed it back as though she didn't care to handle it.

"He's not a man at all," she said. "He's a monster."

And then perhaps the most extraordinary thing of all occurred. Mrs. Vizzard indignantly contradicted her. Spurned, jilted, humiliated, she remained faithful.

"It's not his fault," she said miserably. "He's just been weak. Weak and foolish. It's some she-devil who's lured him. He . . . he's such a lovely man in himself."

2

All the time while Mrs. Josser was in with Mrs. Vizzard, poor old Connie was in agonies. She was so much upset that she nearly cried—cried because suddenly she was on the outside of things. Last night, or rather early this morning, on the doorstep, everything had been heavenly. She had poked her nose in at exactly the right moment. A few seconds either way and she and Mr. Squales might have slipped out of each other's lives without so much as a nod in passing. Thinking over the perfect timing of the episode she had gone to bed, chortling.

And, naturally, she had proposed following it up as soon as she had snatched a wink of sleep and a bite of breakfast. The trouble was, however, that she had unaccountably overslept. With the treat of a lifetime hanging over her, she had just gone on sleeping peacefully like a baby. Right on until nearly ten a.m. It was actually the sound of Mrs. Vizzard's hysterical laughter that woke her.

Considering that she was only just awake it wasn't bad—getting up and dressing all inside eight minutes. She didn't attempt to do her hair, of course. Instead, she simply wound a bright red handkerchief round her head in a turban, hooked on a pair of rolled-gold ear-rings, and emerged looking like a small, frowsty pirate on a private boarding party. The distressing part was that when she got downstairs, it—whatever it had been—was over. All that she could hear through the closed door was the clink of tea-cups and the sound of voices. It was Mrs. Josser who was with Mrs. Vizzard all right. She could detect that much even though she couldn't make out so much as a word of what they were saying.

"Mumble, mumble, mumble," Connie muttered to herself angrily. "What's the use of that to me?"

Her instinct was to knock on the door, make some excuse and go right in. But she checked herself. After all, it was *her* treat and she didn't want to share it with anyone. So she decided to check up on things first. For a start, there was Mr. Squales's door standing invitingly open just to the left of her. Knocking on it quietly so that she shouldn't be heard, she turned the handle and peeped in. It was empty and smelling of stale tobacco, just as she had expected. Even the cupboard was wide open—and bare.

She closed the door again behind her and gave her skirt a hitch upwards.

"Oh, well," she said. "Here goes. Into the breach, dear friends. . . ."

Before her head was properly round Mrs. Vizzard's door she started speaking.

"Hail, shining morn," she began. And then stopped, stopped in sheer surprise at seeing Mrs. Josser there. "Too many bridesmaids," she said, shaking her head coyly.

But at the sight of Mrs. Vizzard, all tear-stained—and more than that: *drenched* apparently in her own woe—Connie suddenly wondered if she would be able to go through with her little act. Right up to this moment it had seemed that she could settle up all old scores in a few hurtful words carefully chosen. But now she doubted it. Mrs. Vizzard was the landlady no longer. She was simply a middle-aged woman who had had it. As Connie stood there she underwent a change of heart. And that automatically meant a change of plan as well. She turned to Mrs. Josser, her eyes starting.

"Don't tell me it's happened like you said it would," she asked in an incredulous whisper. "Not about Mr. Squales, I mean."

By the time Mrs. Josser had denied to Mrs. Vizzard that she had ever discussed Mr. Squales with anyone Connie felt secure enough. Conversation was general by now. She had succeeded in inserting the thin, unwanted wedge of her company into their midst. Emboldened, she drew up a chair and sat down. The rest was easy. She was one of them. And more than one of them. She was their leader.

"You could get *him* for breach of promise," she declared confidently. "And you might be able to get *her* for enticement. That's harder, but Mr. Barks would know. As for *him*, he's finished: he's practically hanged himself by going off with the suitcase. . . ."

Before she left, Connie gave her oath that she wouldn't breathe a word to a soul.

It seemed, in the circumstances, the least that she could do. She gave her oath readily and without reservation, and what was more, she meant it. She even passed her wetted forefinger across her throat as proof.

It was all the more surprising therefore that, a couple of hours later, Mr. Puddy should stop Mr. Josser on the stairs and address him in a hoarse enraged whisper.

"The dirdy foridder," was what he said. "Ledding dowd a lady. Breege of bromise. Thad's whad id is. If he things he can ged ub to Dago triggs in Dulcimer Streed, just led him waid till a jury geds hold of hib."

CHAPTER 82

I

But, by next morning and for several mornings to come, there was —even in No. 10 Dulcimer Street—more than the singular defection of Mr. Squales to think about. It was May the tenth. May the tenth, 1940—the day on which Mr. Churchill took over from Mr. Chamberlain. And just across the Channel every single gloomy prophecy of Uncle Henry's looked like coming true. The Germans were pouring across Belgium and Luxembourg, as though it were all just some big military manœuvre. Even Holland—apparently the

Wehrmacht had taken the matter of the dykes into consideration—was being overrun with the same precision. The Third Reich was really on the move at last, and Europe had been slit wide open.

Now that it had actually started everybody agreed that it was what they had all been waiting for. Even expecting. Everybody except the War Office, that is. The British Army, the army of Ted Josser and Lord Gort, was moving forward. But it was obviously too late. Neutrality had seen to that. And worse than neutrality. There were queer things happening. Bridges that should have been blown up were left standing. Tunnels that should have been blocked remained clear. Parachutists disguised as nuns were being dropped like black snowflakes. And the centre of Rotterdam was being bombed to rubble, not because Rotterdam had offended the Germans in any way, but simply as a warning to wantons not to interfere.

It was all very sudden and terrible. And now that the war was coming this way it was all uncomfortably near home.

On that same morning, May the tenth, as soon as Mrs. Josser had listened to the radio and read the paper, she went straight round to Cynthia. It was her duty—nothing less she told herself—to be with her at such a moment. If she knew anything about Cynthia, she would find her either in tears or in hysterics. And that kind of thing wasn't fair on Baby. It was, in fact, really for Baby's sake that she was going. For Baby's sake. And because of the letter that Ted had written. He'd asked her to look after Cynthia and that was what she was doing.

All the way in the bus—it was a twopenny fare to Larkspur Road—she tormented herself. Preparing for the worst, she planned exactly what to do if she found Cynthia prostrate and incapable. First she would get her to bed—*put* her to bed, if necessary. Then she would send a telegram for her mother. And, as soon as Cynthia was seen to, she would remove Baby to Dulcimer Street for safe keeping. Anything so long as Baby didn't get upset as well.

It was just nine-thirty when Mrs. Josser got there. And Cynthia wasn't yet dressed properly. She came down to the door in a kind of kimono with her hair done up in a fish-net. The sight offended Mrs. Josser. In her house, particularly when the children had been little, she herself had always been clothed and presentable from seven o'clock onwards. She didn't approve of housewives who made a late start. Also, she wished that Cynthia could have looked a little more pleased to see her. Pleased. Not just surprised.

"Oh, do come in," Cynthia urged her after a pause that was just a moment too long. "Everything's in an awful muddle. But do come in."

Mrs. Josser went in. And she saw straightaway what Cynthia had meant about a muddle. The remains of Doris's breakfast—an empty egg-shell and a dirty cup and saucer all piled together on a plate—stood beside Baby's brightly painted teddy-bear mug and another cup and saucer that were evidently Cynthia's. Through the open door of the bedroom an unmade bed was visible, with what looked like clothes left lying about on the floor. And Baby, dressed only in pyjamas and dressing-gown like her mother, was imprisoned inside the play-pen banging industriously with a little wooden hammer. . . . Mrs. Josser's heart bled when she thought of the home-life that Ted had so gallantly been concealing from her all these years.

"What a day to come and see us," Cynthia said with a little giggle. "We all overslept."

Overslept! Mrs. Josser drew in her lips.

"I'm glad you could," was all she said.

She had gone over to the play-pen by now and was stroking Baby's hair. Thanks to Ted's share in the child's inheritance, Baby's hair wasn't going to be the same ridiculous colour as its mother's. There were darker shades in it already.

"What time did you hear?" she asked at last.

"Hear what?" Cynthia asked her.

"About the Germans."

"What?" Cynthia asked, arching her eyebrows film-fashion. "Have they signed an armistice or something?"

It was then—only then—that Mrs. Josser realised the dreadful truth that Cynthia didn't even know. And the realisation shocked her just as much as the unmade beds and unwashed dishes. It was everything that she had told herself that she mustn't believe about her daughter-in-law. With Ted away and fighting for his life against the entire German Army, Cynthia couldn't even take the trouble to listen properly to the wireless and find out what was happening to him. It was monstrous.

"They've attacked," she said tersely. "At dawn."

"Oo-er."

Cynthia gave a little giggle as she said it. But Mrs. Josser could detect, however, that it was sheer nervousness. Perhaps the hysterics were developing. But somehow she had never imagined herself actually breaking the news. Only coping with it.

"Where does it say so?" Cynthia asked.

"It's in all the papers," Mrs. Josser told her. "The man on the wireless . . ."

"Isn't it awful?" Cynthia said.

"It's awful for the Belgians," Mrs. Josser replied. "They've attacked them first."

Cynthia squeezed her two hands together. They were thin delicate hands and the blue veins on them showed clearly.

"That's the way Ted always thought they'd go," she said simply.

"Well, now he knows," Mrs. Josser replied shortly. She paused. "They're sending our Army right up into Belgium," she added. "It said this morning . . ."

"Sshh!"

Cynthia had turned her back on her and was addressing the play-pen.

"Quiet, darling. Granny's saying something."

She turned and faced Mrs. Josser again.

"I'm so sorry," she said. "Only I was afraid she'd break it."

"It doesn't matter," Mrs. Josser answered.

She was offended and she didn't mind if she showed it.

"You break everything you get hold of nowadays, don't you, Baby?" Cynthia went on, over her shoulder, ignoring Mrs. Josser completely. "You're just mummy's naughty little smasher, that's what you are."

That decided it. Mrs. Josser took one more glance round the room. Then she got up. It was only five minutes since she had got there.

"Well, now you've heard, I may as well be going," she said.

Cynthia rose hurriedly.

"Oh, don't go *yet*," she implored her. "Do stop and I'll make some fresh tea. This is all cold."

"No tea for me, thank you," Mrs. Josser answered. "I'm not in the mood for it."

Cynthia's forehead wrinkled up.

"You're not worried, are you?" she asked.

"Of course I'm worried."

"About Ted, I mean."

"That's what I mean, too. He's there, isn't he?"

"Oh, dear."

Cynthia's whole face was puckered now. She looked as though she might be going to cry.

"He'll . . . he'll be all right, won't he? Tell me he'll be all right."

This was more than Mrs. Josser could stand. She had been ready for it when she came in. But she wasn't nearly so ready now. That was the trouble. She'd got herself all worked up in the meantime.

"You know as much as I do," she snapped back at her. "He's your husband. Not mine."

And, with that, she left. It was no use trying to be nice to Cynthia. She saw that now. The girl was just a common usherette. That's what she was. An usherette.

Back in the flat Cynthia was standing at the window with Baby in her arms. The breakfast-things were still on the table and Cynthia's hair, her wonderful golden hair, still tucked away in its hair-net. She was staring vacantly into the street.

"Ted's mother's a funny woman," she was thinking. "Coming over here like that and upsetting me."

Then the thought of why she had come and what was behind it all grew too much for her and she began to cry. Cried helplessly. Still holding Baby in her arms, she stood there, the tears trickling down her face.

Only by then, it was too late. Mrs. Josser's visit of consolation was over.

2

Altogether, as things turned out, it was Mrs. Josser's bad day. Even when Doris dropped in to see her on the way home from work, it didn't improve matters. And that was because Doris said the wrong thing. Not about the war, but about something else. Said it quite casually, too, just before she was leaving. It was, indeed, the very casualness that Mrs. Josser found so particularly wounding. Without so much as a thought for Mrs. Josser's feelings, she said that she'd been thinking matters over and had decided that she'd rather stay on with Cynthia than come down to live at the cottage. Cynthia needed someone to be with her, she said.

And when Mrs. Josser tried to expostulate, it was too late. She wasn't listened to, in fact. Doris had to rush away again. With the extreme cruelty of youth, she added that she had to go back so that she could write to Bill. She kissed her mother lightly and perfunctorily. And withdrew unaware of the agitation she had left behind her.

"That settles it," said Mrs. Josser firmly as soon as Doris had gone. "It's just a white elephant now, that cottage."

Mr. Josser tried hard to reason with her. But it was difficult. And more than difficult. It was impossible. Mrs. Josser had set her heart on having Doris with them and nothing else would satisfy her. She hadn't said very much about it, she explained, because she was so sure that Doris would do what she wanted. And she added that she wasn't the sort of woman who would go away into the country in times like these and leave her only daughter behind her.

"I tell you flat," she said. "I'm not going to live there without Doris."

"She . . . she could come and stay," Mr. Josser suggested.

He was being cautious and conciliatory in everything he said. He liked Conservatory Cottage. Liked it a lot. And he didn't want to lose it before he had even had a chance to have it.

But Mrs. Josser only shook her head.

"Not her," she answered. "You can see she's set her face against it."

Mr. Josser thought.

"If Bill came home on leave, it would be nice to have somewhere for them both to come to," he said tentatively. "They haven't got anywhere now, remember."

Mrs. Josser drew in her lips.

"It was Ted I bought that cottage for, not Bill," she replied briefly.

Then Mr. Josser thought again. It was a happy thought this time.

"Perhaps Cynthia and Baby . . ." he began.

But that was altogether too much for Mrs. Josser. She sat bolt upright at the suggestion.

"That's where I do put my foot down," she said. "We may have to live at the cottage ourselves without Doris just because we've bought it. But I'm not going to have Cynthia with us. Ted can take her down there if he wants to. That's his affair. But I'm not going to share any house of mine with Cynthia, thank you."

3

Not, by any means, that everyone in London was taking the morning's news so much to heart as Mrs. Josser had done.

There were still plenty of people, the steady ones, who didn't quite see where we came in so long as it was only Holland and Belgium that had been invaded. Or France for that matter. There was the Maginot Line, wasn't there, a great subterranean fortress stretching from the Alps to the English Channel? And with our Army ready and waiting on the Continent, the same Army that had won the last war—only, of course, fully mechanised this time—it didn't seem likely that the Germans would be willing to risk another clash with it. May the tenth was admittedly a shock after all those months of inaction. But there was nothing actually *dangerous* about it yet. It wasn't as though we hadn't got a Navy and an Air Force.

Take a cross-section of opinion. Take Mr. Josser's view of things, for instance. Though perhaps it's not quite fair to compare him with Mrs. Josser because he had the natural advantage of a man's understanding of things. He didn't personally pin his faith on the Maginot Line—he'd never had much faith in the French anyhow. But he did pin his faith in Lord Gort. It was from him that the Germans were going to get their lesson. Invading a few small neutrals was one thing. Coming up against the B.E.F. was quite another. So far as Mr. Josser could see, it was going to be 1914 all over again. That was why he felt so sorry for Cynthia. Judging from the way things were going it would probably be years before Ted was home again.

But he didn't really worry. Not much, that is. And that was because of another of those masculine advantages that he had over Mrs. Josser. He had something else to think about. Rent collecting. The Germans unwittingly had chosen a rent-day on which to open their offensive. And no matter what happened on the Continent —even if the Panzers drilled right through to Paris in one go— those rents would still have to be collected. Mr. Josser was unassailable.

In this he was luckier than Mr. Puddy. Admittedly, Mr. Puddy had his own job to occupy him. But the nature of the job was less protective. It left too much time for thought. And it had too much to do with what was happening. Reading between the lines in the A.R.P. pamphlets, Mr. Puddy was practically front line already.

"It's cubbig," he told himself gloomily. "Idcediaries. Stirrub-bumbs and shovels and everythig. . . ."

Or, take Connie. Her moods had been fluctuating. Since she had first heard the news, she had experienced fear, horror, jubilation and a profound relief. "Just think," she kept on telling herself. "Just think if I'd got that job with ENSA. I might have been on the boards in Brussels at this moment. Imagine me in my scarf dance with all those Germans raging outside . . ."

Or Mrs. Vizzard. She was actually one of the lucky ones. In the desolate and abject misery of her betrayal nothing new could now impinge upon her. Gazing out from the ruins of her life she surveyed the staring headlines and went on thinking about Mr. Squales.

4

And Mr. Squales himself?

He shuddered when he read the news. Shuddered and turned away. A man of peace, he asked nothing more of life than that it should cease to disturb him. Just when everything seemed to be going right at last it was irritating having all this happen. Because, after the strain of the last few weeks in Dulcimer Street, the quiet and calm of the past forty-eight hours in Chiddingly had been delightful. An oasis. It had been like a dream, a smooth luxurious dream. Indeed, looking back on it, Mr. Squales decided that in many ways those two days had been among the very happiest of his life.

Of course, his arrival at Withydean could have been embarrassing. Beastly embarrassing. But he had handled it so well—and Mrs. Jan Byl had responded so handsomely—that even that had passed off easily and without a hitch.

"You take me as I am," had been his opening words to her. "Penniless."

And Mrs. Jan Byl, not batting an eyelid, had replied, "The price of genius, my dear man. Don't ever refer to it again."

Not that it could really be dismissed as simply as all that. He had, of course, been *compelled* to refer to it again. He couldn't go around with only two and three in his pocket like a schoolboy. But even that had passed off happily, too. As soon as she had realised that he really meant what he said, Mrs. Jan Byl opened the formidable green steel safe which stood in the corner of her bedroom—as she did so, Mr. Squales craned his neck a little to one side from sheer curiosity, but she closed the massive door again before he could see anything—and removed ten one-pound notes. Mr. Squales's face softened into a rich bland smile.

And some of the smile—the part around the mouth—remained there after Mrs. Jan Byl had re-counted the notes and popped half of them into her own handbag. She handed the other five to Mr. Squales.

"There," she said archly. "Now genius can be self-supporting."

Five pounds, admittedly, was five pounds. And he appreciated the readiness of her response. It was no use, however, concealing the fact that he had hoped for something more. Say a banking account opened in his own name. Or a big block of war-bonds. A marriage settlement, in fact. But in the meantime, with all found, five pounds was very pleasant to go on with.

It had come as a bit of a shock at first when he found that Mrs. Jan Byl wasn't expecting to put him up before the wedding. He had been looking forward to the pink guest-room with the inlaid light above the shaving-mirror in the private bathroom. It had just that touch of home—Mrs. Jan Byl's home—that he relished. But apparently such glories were not yet to be. On the subject of having her fiancé staying in her own house she was adamant. It wasn't the thing, she said; it might start the servants talking. Accordingly she had made arrangements for Mr. Squales to stay as her guest at the little A.A. hotel in Chiddingly.

Her guest—Mr. Squales heaved a sigh of relief when he heard the words. And he heaved another sigh as soon as he saw the place. It was a large modern road-house, and the room that had been reserved for him had an inlaid lamp over the mirror just like the other one. Right up to the last moment when the car put him down at the hotel door he had been fearing something picturesque and old-world with the light in one corner of the bedroom and the bed in the other.

As it was, he couldn't really have been more comfortable. Mrs. Jan Byl's chauffeur brought the Rolls-Royce round to the door at ten o'clock each morning and deposited him back at about eleven o'clock at night. Not that it mattered within a few minutes either way. As a resident, he could get something sent up to his room whenever he wanted it.

Altogether, it promised to be a very pleasant stay in Chiddingly, a graceful interlude between the grey months of Dulcimer Street and the magnificence of Withydean. The banns had been read once already and it would not be long now before Mr. Squales, supported at last by the rich wife that he had been looking for, would be able to devote himself entirely to himself. But, remembering how close he had run it, how for weeks on end it had been touch and go, he sweated. Fate and he had been seeing rather too much of each other lately.

"Just one twitch of her cruel fingers," he told himself, "and I might have been another's. I might have been sentenced for life to that flea-run in Dulcimer Street."

Then his face softened.

"How she must miss me," he reflected. "I was everything she had."

CHAPTER 83

I

DORIS or no Doris, victory or defeat in Europe, Mr. Josser had ordered the moving-men for next Thursday. And unless he did something about it, they would be turning up round about ten-thirty.

The trouble was that he didn't know what Mrs. Josser really wanted. She had told him so many times to cancel the move altogether and then, at the last moment, had withdrawn the cancellation, that Mr. Josser still had an uneasy feeling in his mind, not knowing whether he was going or staying. Thursday was simply a glowing question-mark set in the uncertain future. At the moment, it looked like going. Mrs. Josser had spent the whole of the morning turning out a cupboard and examining, with the peculiarly rapt expression of a woman who is planning something, the curtain lengths and odd bits of carpet that she found there. But he couldn't be sure. It might simply be the apartments in Dulcimer Street that she was thinking of doing up a bit.

There was, he supposed, always the possibility that the moving-men might solve everything. Simply by forgetting about it. After all, it was some time now, over three weeks, since he had written to the firm—and in those three weeks such a lot had been happening. Enough to put things like furniture removals out of anybody's mind. And at this rate, Lord only knew what things would be like by the time next Thursday came along. There wasn't a Holland any more. The Dutch C.-in-C. had simply given up. And Queen Wilhelmina and Princess Juliana were in London. Not that Belgium looked like lasting much longer. Or France for that matter. You could tell the way things had gone from bad to worse in those four days because already Mr. Eden had spoken on the wireless and made an appeal for volunteers—Local Defence Volunteers. It was obvious that even the steady ones were getting rattled now.

And in the face of all this, Mr. Josser had a strange deep guilty feeling about leaving London at all. It was too much like those people who had packed off to America at the beginning of the war. At this moment, there seemed something faintly disloyal and rattish about even going out as far as Essex. It was like walking out on your own family just when things looked as though they were going wrong.

2

Thursday had come. It was a question-mark no longer. Mrs. Josser had made up her mind—a night-time cough of Mr. Josser's had been decisive—and they were going. The farewells had all been said and the loaded moving-van was waiting outside. Mrs. Josser, her hat on, was ready to depart.

Now that the moment for leaving Dulcimer Street had actually come, she was feeling completely flat and dispirited. She couldn't imagine why she had allowed herself to be persuaded into this thing. The bare floors of what had once been the comfortable living-room sent up echoes when she walked across them. And the discoloured shapes on the walls where the pictures had been, brought tears into her eyes. The whole business of moving seemed once more ridiculous, untimely, ill-advised. For two pins, two pins, she repeated, she would cancel everything even now, send Mr. Josser a wire, telling him not to stand about waiting at the cottage for her to arrive, and ask the removers to carry the stuff back upstairs.

She wished now that she hadn't let Mr. Josser go on ahead. It had seemed such a good idea at the time that he should hare off immediately after breakfast and have the rooms aired and a kettle boiling. It had been his idea, anyway. She recognised now, however, that she needed him. If Doris could have been there it would have been all right. But that was out of the question because Doris was at the office. Even Cynthia would have been better than no one. Or would have been up to last night.

As it was, things in that quarter had finally come to a head with faults no doubt on both sides. At the last moment, on the very eve of departure, in fact, Mrs. Josser had suddenly decided that Mr. Josser had been right and that it was her duty to have Cynthia and Baby at the cottage with them. Overcrowding or not, it was her duty: and Cynthia had refused. Refused point-blank. The rejection of the offer and, above all, the reason for the rejection had hurt Mrs. Josser profoundly. She told Cynthia as much. Then Cynthia said that Baby wouldn't feel free in anybody else's house. And Mrs. Josser's visit, embarked upon in a mood of Samaritan compassion, ended in recriminations. The memory of it came back to her at this moment and raising her hand she brushed away a tear. She had, after all, only been trying to do her duty.

She was still standing there by the bare window without its curtains, looking down at the large deck-like top of the moving-van, when there was a knock at the door and Mrs. Vizzard came in. Mrs. Josser felt both relieved and ashamed. Ashamed because she had been crying and relieved because it was another human being. She faced Mrs. Vizzard.

"I think you'll find it all in order," she said. "There's some paper in the grate. But apart from that I've cleared up everything."

"I'm quite sure you have, Mrs. Josser," Mrs. Vizzard answered. "It wouldn't be like you not to."

"Thank you, Mrs. Vizzard."

It was a formal, absurdly formal, conversation for two women who had known each other for as long as they had. And it was one of those conversations that cannot easily go on.

"I'm sorry to be going," Mrs. Josser said at last. "Very sorry in a way."

"I'm sorry to lose you," Mrs. Vizzard answered. "It'll leave a gap."

There was another pause.

"What I really came up about," Mrs. Vizzard explained, "was to ask whether you'd come down for a cup of tea before you go off."

"That's very kind of you. Very kind indeed."

There was still the same formality about the conversation. Altogether, it was more like two strangers meeting than two old friends parting. And there was a reason for it. In her present state, Mrs. Josser didn't trust herself to say very much. She took one last look round the room, and silently followed Mrs. Vizzard downstairs.

It was the hot tea—served, Mrs. Josser noticed, in Mrs. Vizzard's best china—that broke down the awkwardness and restraint. The conversation got round at last to Mr. Squales. Over the second cup, Mrs. Vizzard looked up suddenly.

"Thirty-seven pounds ten was what he cost me," she announced. "Thirty-seven pounds ten, including three loans and the dinner-jacket."

Mrs. Josser drew in her breath.

"It doesn't bear speaking of," she said.

Mrs. Vizzard dropped her eyelids.

"I often wonder," she said, "what Mr. V. would have thought of me. It was his money."

As she spoke she lifted her head and regarded the three-quarter portrait of Mr. Vizzard. But there was nothing there to provide a clue. The face with its half-rainbow of moustache wore the same expression of stolid failure that it had worn for nearly thirty years.

There was even a suggestion in the hang-dog look of the eyes that he was past caring.

"You can only thank Providence it wasn't more," Mrs. Josser told her.

"It nearly was," Mrs. Vizzard answered. "He wanted an overcoat."

"The peacock!"

The words slipped Mrs. Josser's lips almost before she was aware of them.

But Mrs. Vizzard didn't hear. She was simply staring into space, her lips moving. It was almost as though she were silently adding something up. Then suddenly she spoke.

"Not that I shan't get it back when I find him. And more besides. If his lady friend wants him she's got to pay."

Mrs. Vizzard checked herself abruptly. It was difficult to sound vindictive without also sounding vulgar.

But Mrs. Josser only looked across at her admiringly.

"I respect you more than I can say," she told her. "Most women in your place would simply have gone to pieces."

Mrs. Vizzard was looking at her husband's portrait again.

"So should I if it hadn't been for *him*," she said. "I owe it to his memory to get every penny I can. Mr. Barks thinks so, too."

There was a pause. Mrs. Josser glanced up uneasily at the cabinet clock on the mantelshelf.

"It's time I was off, Mrs. Vizzard," she said. "That cup of tea was just what I needed. But I really must be going now. I don't want Fred putting all the things in their wrong places."

"I'll come up with you. Just to see you off," Mrs. Vizzard answered.

In the hall, they met Mr. Puddy. He was just coming in from shopping. He presented a blurred, indefinite outline because of the paper bags. He stood back for Mrs. Josser to pass.

"Da-da for the last dime," he said.

There was a sinister note of finality, of doom almost in his voice that disturbed Mrs. Josser.

"Not the *last* time," she said. "You're going to come down and see us."

But Mr. Puddy only shook his head doubtfully.

"If the drains are still rudding," he said. "If id isn't dodal war by then."

To cover up the gloom of Mr. Puddy, Mrs. Josser turned and kissed Mrs. Vizzard. It was the first time that the two women had ever kissed. And in normal times they would probably never have done so. But these weren't normal times. Mrs. Josser and Mrs. Vizzard had faced a lot together. And, remembering Mr. Puddy's words, Mrs. Vizzard might still be facing it. It was terrible leaving her there alone, betrayed, ageing, defenceless. Mrs. Josser pulled herself together.

"Say good-bye to Connie for me," she said. "Tell her I'm sorry to have missed her."

"Bissed her!" Mr. Puddy repeated incredulously. "She's god ahead."

There was silence.

"She's done what?" Mrs. Josser demanded.

"God ahead," Mr. Puddy answered. "I saw her. Id the vad. Ub with the driver."

CHAPTER 84

I

IT WAS silent nowadays in Dulcimer Street. Suddenly and unnaturally silent. The tall, pale stucco house was full of echoes and bare rooms. It might have been a household of ghosts over which Mrs. Vizzard was presiding.

Not that she wasn't doing her best to repeople it with flesh and blood. On the contrary as soon as she had properly realised that the Jossers were going—her mind at the time still had the utmost difficulty in apprehending even the simplest of facts, and kept returning inescapably to Mr. Squales—she had advertised the rooms. And she had taken the precaution of re-curtaining the Jossers' front windows and the Boons' so that the house shouldn't appear to be going downhill. If the place once looked the deserted human derelict that it was, it might—and this was her real terror—become unlettable.

But in May 1940 it needed more than curtains at the windows to let rooms in London. Everyone who could get out—the aristocracy of places like Streatham and Golders Green, the real local cream—was going. It was a new evacuation. A second Exodus. And those who remained, the real Londoners who belonged there, weren't in any mood for moving. They were just holding their breaths and sitting tight.

And there was another difficulty so far as No. 10 was concerned: there was such an awful lot of it to let. Mr. Squales's room. The

Boons'. The Jossers'. She couldn't, Mrs. Vizzard decided, insert just one advertisement to cover the whole lot—it would make her look wholesale like an agency. That would be fatal for the kind of tenant that she wanted. There was nothing for it, therefore, but to advertise the suites one by one with discretion. And that was terrible. Advertisements simply ran away with money.

It was because of her panic about money that she was so implacable in her pursuit of Mr. Squales. No, not of Mr. Squales himself. Of the rich woman who had enticed him. If Mrs. Vizzard, jilted and unprotected, was to be forced to sit out the war in Kennington alone, she was going to make somebody pay her for it. That was why she made those frequent visits to Mr. Barks to see how his investigations were getting on. But, like the advertisements, it all cost money. She returned each time from Mr. Barks's office, her palms damp and sticky, thinking of the bills to which her impatience was committing her.

Taken all in, however, it was the silence—particularly at night when both Connie and Mr. Puddy were at work—that was the worst. It was then that Mrs. Vizzard remembered how full, how lively, No. 10 had always been. Remembered and wept. She might have been living through the first days of widowhood again. And from the way she recalled the Dulcimer Street of last month, it was as though Mrs. Josser, tight-lipped and steel-spectacled, had been accustomed to keep the whole household awake right into the small hours with lyrics and snatches of gay song.

Without the Jossers there was desolation.

And with only three of them—Mrs. Vizzard, Connie and Mr. Puddy—in the whole house, they tended irresistibly and inevitably to come together. In some mysterious fashion—prompted possibly by a consciousness of the brooding universal danger—they cohered. As the news from France got worse—and this was happening all the time—they became one family. Within a fortnight of the Jossers' departure, Mrs. Vizzard to her own astonishment found not only that she could now tolerate Connie's company but that she actually looked forward to her visits. And to Mr. Puddy's. She sat there in her front basement sitting-room listening for a step on the stairs, either a mincing, tripping one or a good solid monumental tramp.

It was naturally Connie who came the more frequently. She looked in most mornings round about eleven when there was usually a cup of tea and perhaps a dry biscuit going. And it is a tribute to her common sense that she did not abuse the privilege. Recognising her new status for the promotion that it was, she carefully kept the conversation to painless and uncontroversial subjects. Like the war, or the Jossers' country cottage. For the time being, she avoided all reference to Mr. Squales.

In the result, Mrs. Vizzard had heard half a dozen times already how Connie, if she had her way, would land the whole British Army and Navy and Air Force right on the coast of Germany and tell them to fight their way to Berlin instead of trying to defend France; and how she was convinced that the walk to the village was going to be too much for Mrs. Josser.

On the latter, she spoke as an expert and an authority. Mr. Puddy was quite right: it was Connie he had seen on the van that day. Defying everyone, even the driver, she had gone the whole way to Ditchfield. And had Mr. Josser been surprised to see her! She had stopped there as long as she could. And it was only that she had to get a lift back in the same van as soon as it was empty that prevented her greeting Mrs. Josser on arrival. That, and the fact that she didn't know quite how Mrs. Josser would take it.

But even if Connie's repertoire was limited, it was better in a way than what Mr. Puddy had to offer. He always had something fresh. Something fresh and disquieting. Sitting up there in his top flat, his ear pressed against his wireless set for any scrap of battle-news that the thing would impart to him, he terrified himself. And when it was too much to be borne alone he would come down to tell Mrs. Vizzard.

"Id's all ub," he would announce, breathing heavily and emphatically. "You cad dell thad frob whad Widstod says. He's over there dow. Id was a dent. Dow it's a bulge. There's dothing cad stob them. The French aren't drying broberly any longer. Id's all ub. Our durn next."

Despondency and Mr. Puddy had become practically synonymous.

2

It is dark. And drizzling. And bitterly cold. The sea, which was choppy earlier, has quietened down by now. But the little waves still slap spitefully against the windward side of the vessel.

In the lee, another and smaller vessel is moored. It is a rubber dinghy. Two seamen are trying to hold it in position while a third lowers something into it. This isn't easy. In the first place, the side of the submarine bulges so far outward that the dinghy is at more than arm's length from the stanchion that the seaman is holding on to. Secondly, because it's dark and because he isn't allowed to show even a glimmer from a torch, he cannot see what he is doing. And, finally, the thing that he is holding is awkward and intractable. Part of it keeps swinging round and hitting him. It is a bicycle. A second-hand B.S.A., with a Brookes saddle and Dunlop Magnum tyres.

Then up the ladder of the conning tower climbs the captain. With Otto Hapfel after him. Otto Hapfel is muffled up in standard-issue oilskins with a big sou'wester and rubber boots. Underneath it, he's got on a Burberry raincoat, a suit with a Simpson's label, a pair of Lilley and Skinner's shoes and Wolsey socks and underwear. His hat comes from Dunn's. Everything about him is typically English. And everything has a carefully well-worn appearance. He wore his going-away clothes right through the intensive six weeks' course. They're a bit bulky under the oilskin. But they're his uniform now. It's going to be no picnic in that dinghy. And even with the tide in his favour all the way he's got a three-and-a-half-mile row ahead of him. Also he's got exactly two hours in which to do it. Two hours until dawn, that is.

Before he climbs in he checks the contents of the dinghy. But he need not worry. The Navy is always efficient. Everything is there. His rations. His compass. His little parcel of belongings in the fibre suitcase. His smuggled copy of last Wednesday's *Daily Mail*. His bicycle. He's got all that he could need for his English holiday.

Then he turns and shakes hands with the captain. "Auf Wiedersehen," he says.

"Auf Wiedersehen," the captain answers.

"Heil Hitler."

"Heil Hitler."

Both arms go up, and Otto Hapfel turns away. He is momentarily glad that it is dark. That is because he is so much moved. There are tears in his eyes. And he does not want the captain to see them.

It is very tricky getting into the dinghy. But not entirely unfamiliar. He's been attending special dinghy classes. Though naturally this is a bit different. This is the real thing. And he is trembling as he takes up the sculls.

With one of them he pushes himself away from the side. And immediately the outline of the submarine fades into the surrounding darkness. Otto Hapfel is alone. Alone in the German Ocean. The Scottish coast lies somewhere ahead of him. He wonders whether he will ever get to it. And, if he does get there, he wonders if he will ever get away again.

In the darkness and the rain, with the spray freezing as it flecks on to him, he remembers—not his mother, or his Führer, or the mission that brings him here, or even his own danger. None of these. He remembers the colonel-general's last words to him.

"In spring England is very beautiful. It is a flower garden . . ."

He says the words over and over to himself as he trys to prevent the dinghy from going round in circles. It seems such a long time since war was declared and he was sitting up in the gallery making notes on the South London Parliament.

CHAPTER 85

I

THERE WAS still, however, at least one man in England without a care in his head. There was Mr. Squales.

The improvement in his condition since his stay in the country had been remarkable. Truly remarkable. For a start, he was sleeping better. And, because of all the exercise he was getting going round the garden with Mrs. Jan Byl, he was eating better. He was even drinking better. His appearance, too, had improved—though that may have been simply because Mrs. Jan Byl had persuaded him to wear his hair just *a little* shorter. It was now only a two-inch lock that fell over his forehead when he leant forward. And, in the result, both she and Mr. Squales had been repaid. He looked a new man. Almost like his own younger brother.

In face of such rejuvenation why *should* he worry? It was like being twenty again, and there wasn't a hitch anywhere. The banns had been read the three necessary times, and no one had objected. The church had been booked. And the matter of the ring, which might have been awkward, had been solved by Mrs. Jan Byl's generously insisting that it should be ordered from her own jeweller and put down to her account. In the circumstances, he had gone all out for platinum. But it was the thought, he told himself, rather than the value of the thing that mattered. And in this he found it strangely touching that Mrs. Jan Byl should have shown such understanding. But there it was. She adored him, and there was no blinking the fact.

She had even spoken of building him a little den, a kind of Swiss chalet in the grounds so that he could continue with his work undisturbed when visitors came. The idea still amused him but he had thanked her at the time for thinking of it. Indeed, life at the moment was one long thank-you. He positively had to be careful not to admire too much things that he didn't like because they were almost invariably given to him.

But the sense of freedom, the escape from want, was marvellous. It was this that made him feel so much better in himself. Better and ready for anything. Ready even for to-morrow.

2

Because of the occasion Mr. Squales took particular pains with his toilet. He had bought himself a bottle of Rosebay Scalp Stimulator and he spent nearly five minutes rubbing the stuff into his scalp before he started shaving. Then he began lathering himself, patiently and laboriously like a barber. In consequence, it was a good shave the first time round. But not good enough—with hair as dark as his, he looked like an Italian ice-cream vendor if he wasn't careful. So he re-lathered and started again. And it was this time that he cut himself. A great three-cornered snick came out of the centre of his chin, and he had to staunch the wound with a tuft of cotton wool.

"We'll have to do something about this," he said, examining himself in the mirror. "Can't turn up at the church looking like the Snow Queen."

The cut gave him more trouble than he had expected. By the time he had finished dressing, he had spoilt the pale silk necktie which he had bought specially for the wedding, and ruined his two good collars. In the end, there was nothing for it but to trim up one of his old ones by going round the edge with a pair of nail-scissors, and wear the tie that he had come down in. He didn't like doing so because it made him feel rather a cad. That tie had been one of the first presents that Mrs. Vizzard had given him.

The unwelcome memory of Mrs. Vizzard at such a moment unnerved him, and he shuddered. Between his past fiancée and his present bride there was such a gap—such a vast, unbridgeable gap. It was really quite extraordinary to think that they were both women. Not that he felt unequal to his new station in life—the station of a country gentleman. He was quite sure of himself there. Before the month was out, he would have cured the butler of breathing down his nose every time he looked at him. No: it wasn't that. It was simply Mrs. Jan Byl's *size* that was worrying him.

When he was actually with her he didn't notice it so much: it was all of a piece somehow—large house, large car, large woman. But, looked at in prospect, she was enormous. Simply enormous. Marrying her seemed to take on a new significance. It was like uniting himself for life with the Taj Mahal or the Leaning Tower.

It was a bit late, however, for any misgivings. Mr. Squales recognised that. Already it was nearly nine o'clock, and he went downstairs to breakfast. Usually he ate a good breakfast—porridge, kidneys, toast and marmalade—everything. But this morning his mind was too full to concentrate on his food. Too full to concentrate on anything. Sitting with the untasted wheat-flakes in front of him, he found himself drifting off into one of those dangerous psychic states of his. It seemed that Mrs. Vizzard was very near to him again. Right up beside his elbow, and trying to say something. It was as though he could feel that her lips were moving, yet not hear a syllable that she said. He roused himself finally with a groan which startled the waitress, and went outside to walk in the garden. It was only a small garden and he went round and round it several times.

"Poor woman," he kept repeating to himself as he walked. "I can understand just how she feels. It must be terrible for her. Especially at her time of life. I must make it my business to see her sometime if only to console her."

Mr. Squales peered in at the clock in the dining-room as he passed—Mrs. Jan Byl was giving him a watch for a wedding present—and saw that it was nine-thirty. The car was coming for him as usual at ten. And it was his business to be ready for it. Leaving the placidity of the garden behind him—"They could easily bung on another quid or two a week if they had an orchestra or a loud-speaker and served meals out here under little umbrellas," he told himself—he went back upstairs to his bedroom.

Mr. Vizzard's Gladstone bag, limp and rather sinister-looking, stood on the rack at the end of the bed, and Mr. Squales bundled his things into it. Then he caught sight of the tuft of cotton wool adhering to his chin. It had slipped down a little and now rode there like a small goatee, giving him the air of a swarthy Federal general. He whipped it off in irritation. And, in consequence, he was still mopping at his chin when the car came for him. What was worse was that he'd used his last clean handkerchief.

The fact of this upset him—it seemed so absurd not to have a clean handkerchief on his own wedding day. What upset him more, however, was that it was the Morris, practically a market-wagon, driven by the gardener, that came to collect him: the Rolls-Royce driven by the chauffeur was standing by to carry Mrs. Jan Byl. And his best man—he had arrived in the Morris with the gardener—was enough to upset anyone.

To begin with, he was practically a stranger. When Mr. Squales had told Mrs. Jan Byl that he was literally friendless in England because he had spent so much of his time abroad—and compared to Withydean, Brighton *was*, so to speak, abroad—he had not imagined that, in addition to everything else, she would go to the length of giving him a friend. But that is what had happened. She had rounded up someone simply to be Mr. Squales's companion on the day. So far as Mr. Squales could make out, all that was expected of the newcomer was that he should stand at the altar-rail and pass the ring over at the right minute. But even that seemed something of a tax on his powers.

He was a small, sallow-complexioned colonial servant who had been invalided home. And the reason for this premature retirement was obvious to Mr. Squales at a glance. There was something slightly wrong with the poor fellow's brain. He didn't speak very often. He just sat looking on, and smiling. His only hobby, so far as Mr. Squales could discover, was playing bridge. And when Mr. Squales, trying to be friendly, said that he was thinking of taking up the game himself and asked for a few tips, the ex-colonial servant only smiled again.

Not to put too fine a point on it, Mr. Squales hated him. Had hated him from the first. And he hated him still more this morning when he saw that he was wearing tails. Tails was the one thing in which Mr. Squales's armoury was incomplete.

"Do I look all right in a lounge suit?" he asked, just as they were setting out. "My morning dress is in town. I forgot to send up for it."

But the invalided wallah did nothing to reassure him. He only smiled. And such a broad smile, too. It was almost as if he were not smiling at all, but laughing.

3

The wedding was pretty as only country weddings can be. The little church had been decorated throughout with Mrs. Jan Byl's favourite flowers—dark red roses—and, as Mr. Squales noted appreciatively out of the corner of his eye, there was hardly room for another bloom anywhere. They were in vases on the window-sills, hanging down in baskets in the chancel, crawling in spirals round the pillars. The whole church resembled a mock ecclesiastical side-chapel in a high-class West End florist's.

But it was not at the flowers alone that Mr. Squales was looking. After the first flattered glance, his eyes fastened themselves on the assembled congregation. So far every man there was dressed in shapely black tails with a vivid white rim of collar showing. Mr. Squales, radiant in his pearl grey, turned his head away and took up his place inconspicuously behind a screen in the side-aisle. He was still thinking bitterly about the array of tails.

"I'll bet they're all hired, the whole damn lot of 'em," he told himself in an attempt at consolation.

As there was nothing to do for the next few minutes Mr. Squales, whistling almost silently between his teeth, took further stock of the interior. Judging from the music spread out along the choir-stalls, the service was going to be fully choral. Evidently Mrs. Jan Byl had seen to that. He was still feeling grateful to her for all the trouble she had taken to make the whole thing a success, when an enormous peal from the organ—he was practically leaning up against the side of it—made him jump backwards. It had the alarming note of doom, that organ-peal. Mr. Squales wasn't prepared for it, and his nerves were all on edge, anyway.

While the organ was playing, more and more cars kept drawing up outside, and more and more men in tail-coats, accompanied by women with remarkable hats, came trooping in. Mr. Squales was still the only man present in a lounge suit.

It was while he was standing there that a little incident occurred that, despite his polish, he found difficult to pass off smoothly and gracefully. It had to do with the seating. Up to now, only the pews on one side had been occupied. And these were getting unhealthily congested. As soon as anyone fresh arrived the others had to move up one. When things had clearly become impossible, the verger came creeping up the side-aisle and plucked the best man by the sleeve.

"Excuse me, sir," he whispered loudly, "but there isn't any more sitting room on the bride's side. Are any friends of the bridegroom's coming?"

Where he was standing Mr. Squales couldn't help hearing every word that the verger had said. And he couldn't help hearing the best man's reply.

"Better ask the bridegroom," was what the friend whom Mrs. Jan Byl had picked for him replied. And that inane smile broke out on his face again.

Ask the bridegroom! Mr. Squales half closed his eyes and put on his wonderful two-piece smile, first the cheeks wrinkling and then the lips opening slowly.

"Put the guests wherever you please," he said magnanimously. "Any friend of Mrs. Jan Byl's is a friend of mine."

But the humiliation of the episode remained. There seemed to be something so ridiculously *naked* in not having even a single friend in the whole company. It was like being an orphan. Anyone would have been better than no one. For two pins he would have asked Connie.

Connie? Mr. Squales's stomach went icy inside him. In the third pew on the bride's side was a fairy-sized figure in bright georgette trimmed with tufts of white rabbit wool. On its head was a schoolgirlish straw hat supporting a bobbing bunch of red cherries. And beneath the hat showed a fringe of frizzed magenta hair. Mr. Squales, his jaw dropped, stood there staring at the vision. And, to his horror, he realised that the vision was beaming back at him. Before he was able to step back behind the cover of one of the pillars the vision had even managed to blow a rather saucy kiss in his direction.

"My God," Mr. Squales reflected wildly. "I know what this means: this is blackmail. She's been shadowing me."

There was no time for further thought, however. With a whirr from the electric bellows, the organ started up again. *Ti-tum, ti-tum, ti-tum, ti-tum,* it went. Eight scrubbed and polished urchins from the village opened their lungs. The best man gave Mr. Squales a nudge —rather an unnecessarily hard nudge, Mr. Squales thought it. And Mrs. Jan Byl, in white satin, followed by two tiny morsels also dressed in white satin and with dark red rose-buds in their hair, forged up the aisle.

In white satin, Mrs. Jan Byl looked absolutely prodigious.

4

The reception was held at Withydean afterwards. The french doors of the morning-room had been thrown back making one large salon. And through the gay throng—bowler-hatted generals, pensioned civil servants and retired City men—Mr. Squales passed, sagging, his bride upon his arm. It was a bit of a strain this, he didn't mind admitting—meeting all these friends of his wife's for the first time. So much depended on the kind of impression that he made. In consequence, he decided to be quiet, genial, self-depreciating. It was difficult because really he was still thinking about Connie and wondering how much she wanted.

"To the bride and bridegroom!" suddenly said a large well-meaning man whom Mr. Squales had never seen before.

Immediately all glasses were raised. There was a generous unanimity about the gesture. It meant that now they could all take a good long drink of the champagne instead of simply sipping it surreptitiously.

"Mr. and Mrs. Squales," they said in a chorus.

With everyone standing facing him, Mr. Squales recognised this for his moment. It was now or never that he would be able to convince them what a decent unassuming sort of fellow he was. He took his wife's arm in his.

"No, no," he said modestly. "Mr. and Mrs. *Jan Byl*."

CHAPTER 86

I

At Conservatory Cottage the Jossers were really moved in at last.

The sideboard had been tried in three different positions and was back against the wall opposite the fireplace. Which was where they had first put it. And the curtains—both the black-out and the ordinary ones—had been made to fit. There had been some slight unpleasantness about the curtains. Because, though it was Mrs. Josser who had actually done the cutting, it was Mr. Josser who had done the measuring. And between the two of them they had miscalculated. When they came to put them up, there was daylight showing along the bottom of every window. But all that had been seen to by now. Mrs. Josser had found a roll of old braid which she sewed along the hem. And the local warden on his nightly patrol passed the cottage scarcely knowing that it was there.

The other sign that they were moved in was that Mr. Josser had got to work on the garden. He had shifted a small white-painted tub round from the back door to the front. And planted nasturtiums in it. Also, he had made himself a new rustic seat at the other end of the lawn so that he could have somewhere to sit quietly and smoke a pipe and survey his property. As seats went, it was not a very good one. He hadn't, he told himself, got the uprights in deep enough. And he couldn't get them in any deeper until he had bought a spade.

There was a kind of see-saw, rocking-horse motion to the thing unless you sat back in the dead centre.

But it wasn't only the workmanship of the seat that made it so difficult to sit still in these early summer days. There was too much happening. The whole business of being alive was now split up into chunks, waiting for the B.B.C. at eight o'clock, at one o'clock, at six o'clock and at nine o'clock again. And what you heard meant that you were all jumpy and on edge until the next bulletin came round. You couldn't get down to anything properly in between.

It was at night, when there wasn't any news, that it was worst. Like to-night, just lying there, listening to aeroplanes flying overhead. And wondering. Wondering about a lot of things. Whether Ted was all right. Why the dent had ever been allowed to become a bulge, and why the bulge hadn't been squeezed back before it had burst open into a gap. How Doris and Cynthia were getting on in London. What Captain Ramsay and Sir Oswald Mosley had done to get themselves arrested. Whether Bill was in a base hospital or up at the front. When the French were going to start fighting in earnest. What Sir Stafford Cripps was up to in Moscow. Whether Mrs. Josser would get the knack of oil-cooking after she'd been doing it a bit longer. Whether Winston knew more than he was saying and when he was going to say something again. Whether it was true that the B.E.F. was surrounded and trying desperately to fight its way to the coast, or if that was only German propaganda. Whether the L.D.V. would be of any use if the Germans really did come, and whether the fact that he wore glasses meant that they were going to turn him down.

Without telling Mrs. Josser, he'd been along to the L.D.V. headquarters in the village. And he was still waiting for their answer. He was bound to admit that they hadn't seemed awfully keen about him. From his reception it was obvious that they thought him too old. Well-meaning, but too old. And this rankled. It was a fine state of affairs just being expected to sit back and take it easy while his country was being defeated. It practically made a traitor of him. He had already more than half decided that if they wouldn't have him in the L.D.V. he'd offer himself for a special constable. Or a warden. In either case, he reckoned, there ought to be plenty of minor duties, like seeing schoolchildren across the road at breaking-up time, or blowing a whistle when incendiaries were falling, that could still be faithfully performed at sixty-four, by a burning patriot a bit on the short-sighted side and a trifle dicky in one lung.

"They don't know me. That's what's wrong down here," Mr. Josser told himself. "Now if I was still in Dulcimer Street . . ."

The real trouble was that he was feeling out of it. Right up on the shelf again. It was like reliving the blankness of that first awful morning after he had retired from Battlebury's. There was just the same air of uselessness hanging over him, the vague sensation of being a ghost that still required three square meals a day. Mrs. Josser's original instinct had been right after all. They ought never to have left London. Least of all at a time like this. London was where their home was. At this very moment he ought to have been up there by the Thames alongside Winston and Mr. Puddy and Connie and Mrs. Vizzard and the rest of them. Standing by in case they were needed. Not playing about with tubs of nasturtiums in the country.

There was a movement in the bed beside him.

"You awake, Mother?" he asked.

"Of course I'm awake," Mrs. Josser answered. "I haven't closed my eyes yet. What time is it?"

Mr. Josser struck a match.

"Nearly one o'clock," he told her. "Just after five to."

There was a pause.

"I didn't like what it said on the wireless to-night," Mrs. Josser remarked. "Ted'll be all right, won't he?"

"Be all right?" Mr. Josser repeated. "Of course he'll be all right. Trust our Ted. As a matter of fact I thought things sounded a little better. You can generally tell from the tone of voice they use."

With that there was silence. Even the aeroplanes had stopped now. There was the deep heavy silence of the countryside. Mr. Josser reached out in the darkness and found Mrs. Josser's hand and squeezed it. Then they lay there, awake. But not speaking. Simply sharing the same thoughts.

The single arrowhead of Mr. Josser's presentation clock striking the hour pierced through the floor-boards from the dining-room beneath. Mr. Josser got up on one elbow.

"It's no use, Mother," he said. "I'll have to take one of my indigestion tablets."

It was the thirtieth of May by now. One a.m. on the thirtieth of May 1940. Quite a famous date on which to be lying awake and staring at the ceiling. Already in the creeks and tidal estuaries of England the pleasure-boats and paddle-steamers were casting their moorings for the day trip to Dunkirk.

And, over on the other side, Ted stood as good a chance as anybody else.

2

Mr. Josser wasn't the only person, awake and away from home, whose night thoughts included Dulcimer Street. A little further out into the country, and just as homesick, was Mrs. Boon. She had actually been crying—which wasn't usual with her. Crying, with the corner of the pillow stuffed into her mouth so that the doctor's wife shouldn't hear her.

What had started her off was thinking about the old days. It had all been so happy and carefree then. Such a blissful life with Percy making a name for himself at the garage. And giving her big expensive presents like a rug. And going out at all times of day to meet his friends and enjoy himself. There hadn't seemed anything more that she could ask. That was why Percy's arrest had come as such a shock to her. It had been like a nightmare in the middle of a warm night's sleep.

For a time she hadn't been able to understand how God could ever have let it happen. And worse than that. It was as though He weren't listening to her prayers. As though, suddenly in the midst of things, she were cut off. But she was beginning dimly to see how foolish she had been. How foolish and how wicked to have doubted. It was all becoming clear to her.

Because, even though she didn't read the papers or listen to the wireless very much, she knew how terrible things were over in France. There wasn't a woman's son over there whose mother could be sure about his safety. And, if Percy had been free to volunteer, she knew that he'd have been one of the first to go. But he wasn't free. That was the whole point. While others were being maimed and giving up their lives, he was being shielded from it all. Kept away and intact. Preserved, she didn't question, for something important. She put her two hands together.

"Oh, Holy Mary and all the Saints," she began, "praise be for having spared him . . ."

And this was odd because she'd always imagined Percy as a hero. A real hero. A V.C. or something. She'd seen his name that way when he was still quite little. And now she supposed that could never happen.

He would just be plain Percy Boon, for ever.

3

And there was at that moment a third person, awake, away from home and remembering Dulcimer Street. But with one big difference in his case. Ted was busy. He was holding up the German Army.

Come across to the other side and join him for a moment in the small hours of that day as May is departing and June preparing to come in, flaming and full. It's noisy. And it's dangerous. But it's history.

Ted is tired. You can see that at once from the way his eyes are fixed and bloodshot. And the hands that fumble with the cartridge-clips are trembling. Not from fear. Just from fatigue. Sheer fatigue. He hasn't had any sleep for forty-eight hours. In fact, if you hadn't known him as a member of the family circle you probably wouldn't have recognised him. He's so dirty. It's days since he shaved, and he's got a rough unsightly stubble all over his chin, with the dust clinging to it. There's more than dust on his forehead. There's a long half-moon of a gash, dried almost to mud-colour. And he doesn't know what caused it. There were such a lot of things flying about where he has been. His uniform is torn and dishevelled. It's even scorched in one place where the lorry next to him caught fire. He is still lying there in the chassis embers. He moved back again for protection as soon as the metal parts had cooled down a bit.

It isn't dark where Ted is. Because more than the lorry has been alight. Behind him where the port lies there is a big crimson glow the shape of half a grape-fruit. Sometimes there are yellow and vermilion streaks in it when an ammunition dump goes up. And even while it is just glowing quietly it is bright enough to light up the bushes in front of him. Altogether, it's been military bonfire night. The Germans are igniting everything British that they can see. And what is left over we are setting fire to ourselves, so that it shan't fall into German hands. A moment ago there was a great whoosh as a whole convoy went up like Guy Fawkes night. The vehicles are just burning quietly now, the flames lap-lapping over steering-wheel and dashboard. And it's still lively round about because a battery is shelling the spot.

The one thing that worries Ted is how long he is expected to stay there. He can't ask the sergeant because the sergeant has been killed. Those are his legs just showing over the edge of the ditch opposite.

And there isn't anybody else to ask because there were only the two of them to start with. No wonder Ted's anxious. He's one stripe up already and he doesn't want to do anything silly. As soon as it's a bit lighter he's going to make a reconnaissance. Edge down toward the sea-front somewhere. He and the sergeant were making for the "English Spoken" quarter when the sergeant had his accident.

He looks at his watch. It is a fat, old-fashioned Ingersoll. And it's been standing up to things remarkably. Trodden on, left under water and finally the glass smashed, it has faithfully recorded every moment of the retreat. Right up to now, that is. Because the strain of the last two days must have been a bit too much for its old works. It is stuck at a quarter to two. Which is what it was when Ted looked at it he doesn't know how long ago.

The failure of his watch depresses him. It's his last friend gone. Now he is really alone. He doesn't know where he is. He doesn't know what's in front of him. Or behind. Or on either side. He doesn't even know the time. There is nothing for it but to stay where he is by the lorry until it's light enough to move on. And with his watch ruined in his own keeping, how does he know what's happened to the other things he left behind him when all this trouble started? Somewhere or other there is his knapsack with a diamanté ear-clip for Cynthia and a little toy bedside table complete with chamber-pot for Baby. The chamber-pot is a bit vulgar perhaps. But the whole thing was only 8 francs 50 and Cynthia can throw the chamber-pot away if she doesn't want Baby to have it. Or could have done. Perhaps she won't ever get it now. Some little Nazi baby will play with Ted's present. And some little Nazi mother will let it.

The battery that had been shelling the convoy turns its attention to the road a little higher up. And Ted has to lie lower than ever now. One shell in particular, a regular stinker that he knew somehow was coming, covers him up with earth and sand and bits of twigs and bushes after it's missed him. It leaves Ted half smothered. To see him at this moment, the Co-op. wouldn't have believed it of him. Not that Ted is worrying about appearances. He's got such a roaring, buzzing sound inside his head from the concussion that he doesn't care how he looks.

It's getting lighter. Distinctly lighter. There's a glow in the sky that isn't simply burning stores this time. The sergeant's legs show up quite plainly. He might merely be resting there in a rather unusually comfortable position. But Ted can't hang around for him. Slinging his Bren-gun, he begins to move off. It's certainly a proper mess all right. He picks his way gingerly by other burned-out lorries, tanks, ambulances, field-kitchens. And by other sergeants, a bit past it, like his own. First of all, there's a flat scrubby field to cross. Then a six-foot ditch so deep that he has to push himself off from his side and swim for it. One stroke and then a scramble up the bank opposite with his clothes all dripping.

"I could have jumped it," he tells himself. "And I probably would have done if I hadn't been so tired."

The stupidity that comes from tiredness is rather alarming. It means that he's practically sleep-walking.

But he's getting on. There are some of his own chaps in front of him, sheltering up against a barn. About thirty of them with a bandaged major who is blasting someone for having let the maps get wet. Ted salutes him and passes on. The going is easier. Ted does a mile in half an hour. And he isn't lonely any longer. There are quite a lot of the boys about. None of his own fellows. No one he can recognise. But he's on the way. It's English Spoken everywhere. Out of the half-light comes a company of Guards. They're marching perfectly. Long strides, perfectly in step. The young captain with them carries a little cane. The only thing that strikes Ted is that there are so few. Not more than a couple of dozen at the most. And half these are wounded. Even the officer has got his left hand in a sling. Ted waits at the side of the road for them to pass and then follows up the column. But the pace is too much for him. He falls behind.

At a cross-road there is a military policeman standing. Ted goes up to him. The man is calm and imperturbable. He scarcely looks in Ted's direction. He just says, "Stragglers straight on. Beach muster." So Ted's a straggler now. The thought depresses him. He can see his one stripe going.

Another half-hour and he's there. It's quite light by now. And what a sight. The beaches of Dunkirk are like Blackpool in Wakes week. Only everybody is in khaki, of course. Men standing in ranks, lying in the sand-dunes, squatting by breakwaters, wading out to rowing-boats. And the sea beyond them is just as full. The junk Armada is standing off the shore, tramps, coasters, trawlers, steam-yachts, everything. And a ferry-service is plying across the surface of the sea like beetles.

"So the sergeant was right," Ted tells himself. "They are getting us off."

And he needn't have worried about being a straggler. There are about ten thousand other men there already and he isn't conspicuous.

A provost-major genially tells them all to hang around and wait for transport. It's being organised, he promises. It's a little difficult, however, to hear what he's saying because the beach is under such heavy shell-fire.

There's another trouble. Now that it's lighter the dive-bombers are back again. Ted can see them out of the corner of his eye. But he's so used to them that they don't trouble him. He simply wonders what they're going for. As they string out, a light ack-ack somewhere down by the port sends up a solitary shell a hundred yards behind them. Some of the chaps cock their Brens instinctively ready to take a pot-shot at anything.

Then Ted knows what the dive-bombers have picked on. It's the beach muster. In line now, they're pointing straight at it like a ruler. "Down flat," the provost-major tells them, and he lies down himself with his legs spread out as though swimming.

There are six Stukas and they've got the whole thing marked out like a chess-board. Ted hears the first two bombs as they come down. And as they go off. But not the third. He only hears that one coming down.

When the smoke from the last one clears away—not that a little smoke more or less is really noticeable on those beaches—the provost-major gets up again. There still seem to be plenty of soldiers left all round him.

And, in the general hubbub, he's to be excused for not noticing that Ted isn't there any longer.

BOOK SEVEN

LONDON LIGHTS THE CLOUDS UP

CHAPTER 87

I

It was August.

The Jossers had been in Conservatory Cottage for three months now. And looking back over that quarter of a year it seemed that their lives had been divided sharply and brutally. Cut clean through, as it were, so that the portion which they were now living hadn't got very much to do with anything that had gone before. One by one, the links binding past and present had been severed until, in its total effect, the change added up to something more like a re-incarnation than a move.

Mr. Josser still spent a lot of his time thinking about Dulcimer Street. And you could tell from odd remarks that Mrs. Josser let fall that she was remembering the old days, too. "It can't be easy for Mrs. Vizzard on the tea-ration. Not with just the one of her," she would say. Or: "Nothing from Clarice. I hope that doesn't mean she's ill or anything." But it was no use. It was a different Mr. and Mrs. Josser who had lived in those comfortable first-floor rooms in No. 10. Those Jossers had had a son who was coming home to them.

Naturally, as soon as they had heard that Ted was missing—and it was Doris who sent the telegram on to them from town—they went up immediately to be with Cynthia. Mrs. Josser didn't lose a minute. Simply piling the breakfast dishes unwashed in the kitchen sink, she left them there. And Mr. Josser did not attempt to argue with her. There was, he recognised, something sacred and indisputable about such a moment. Not that it was the slightest use. Five minutes saved now wasn't going to be any good to Ted. But, somehow or other, not saving it would have meant that they hadn't done all they could.

And on the whole it was a good thing that they went up when

they did. Because Cynthia was obviously in a bad way. In a very bad way. Though not half so bad as Mrs. Josser had expected. And the fact that she was not prostrate was for the terrible, the futile, reason that she didn't believe her news.

"He'll come back. I know he will," she said cheerfully. "He told me so before he went away. Ted's always done what he said he would . . ."

Only, at this stage, she broke down. And it was then that Mrs. Josser was so useful. Because she was able to distract Baby and amuse her so that she shouldn't notice that anything was the matter. And while Mrs. Josser was looking after Baby, Doris was able to comfort Cynthia. Not that it was easy for any of them. Because Baby, with the all innocent torture of childhood, insisted on going on with the conversation. She said "Daddy" over and over again, pausing attentively in between as though waiting for an answer.

Because of her resolute faith in Ted's return, Cynthia refused even to consider leaving Larkspur Road.

"Suppose he comes back and finds me and Baby gone . . ." she said every time Mrs. Josser raised the point. And in face of reasoning such as that Mrs. Josser did not press it. Not for the moment, at least. It was obvious that any appeal she made would pass unheeded. And she had no strength left with which to be persuasive. It seemed that with the telegram all her powers had gone out of her. There was just nothing of her left. And, in the end, she had allowed herself to be brought back to Ditchfield, empty, broken and exhausted. And conscience-stricken. She'd promised Ted that if anything happened she'd look after Cynthia and Baby. And she wasn't doing it.

But all that seemed a long while ago now. Cynthia and Baby, despite all the visits she had paid them, had detached themselves and become separate. Even Doris, her own child, was separate, too. She didn't belong to them any more. When she might have been coming down to Ditchfield she was going instead up to Carlisle where Bill was stationed. Because Bill had been one of the lucky ones. Unhurt and undefeated, he had taken the same road that Ted had taken. Only Bill had taken it further.

And with no Doris and no Ted, it was only Mr. and Mrs. Josser who were left. Just the pair of them. A rather elderly couple in a pleasant country cottage. And being alone so much there was a lot of time for thought. The same thought. A thought that neither of them would admit. More than once, their eyes had met when they were both wondering what was the meaning behind it all. Why should Bill have been spared and Ted taken? Simply that.

And each time they had looked away again, before the other could possibly admit it.

The truth, though Mr. Josser wouldn't have admitted it, was that he had severed quite a few of the old links himself. Had just let them slip from him without troubling. Links like the South London Parliament, for instance. Right up to the day of the move, he'd intended to go on with that. Not as a member of the Cabinet, of course. He couldn't keep that up from a distance. But simply as an ordinary working Conservative M.P. And, in the result, what had happened? He hadn't been up there once. Not once.

Astonishingly enough, there was such a lot to do where he was. In Ditchfield, he was practically one of them by now. Admittedly, the L.D.V.s had turned him down. And so had the Special Constabulary. And the wardens. But in offering himself, he had met a lot of useful people. And, being the one entirely free man among the lot of them, all the odd jobs naturally came his way. In one week, he had collected for the cottage hospital; helped to move a whole family of evacuees—whole, that is, except for the father whose presence would have solved everything; organised a newspaper-delivery for the members of the local searchlight battery by the simple means of taking the papers over to the site himself; and assisted in the building of the Ditchfield anti-tank trap.

The last was by far the biggest undertaking. He didn't have to do any of the heavy work on it himself. The sawing and digging was reserved for the L.D.V.s. In consequence, Mr. Josser's own task was comparatively light. Light, but responsible. He was stationed a hundred yards or so ahead of the actual spot, just round the bend so that he could warn oncoming motorists. As it happened, nobody, not even a pedestrian, came along while Mr. Josser was on duty. But they might have done. And half an elm tree mounted on a disused cart-wheel wouldn't have been a pleasant thing to run into. It wasn't meant to be.

Another thing that kept Mr. Josser busy was that Mrs. Josser was out such a lot. And that was something altogether new. In Dulcimer Street she had practically never gone out. Except in emergencies. And here in Ditchfield it was as though there were an emergency practically every day. For a start, on Tuesdays and Thursdays there was the Women's Institute—Tuesdays for a Make-and-Mend Class, and Thursdays for Economical Cottage Cookery. The vicar's wife had persuaded Mrs. Josser to be one of the demonstrators. And the classes were certainly well attended. Which was strange because the pupils who came toiling across the countryside on foot had every one of them been making and mending and cooking economically in cottages all their lives.

It wasn't even as though the rest of the week were free. There were bandages to be rolled. And on Mondays there was the inspection at the Rest Centre, and all the blankets had to be taken down and shaken out and then folded up again. Mrs. Josser had been put in charge of the amenities. In a locked cupboard there were two tins of condensed milk, a thermos flask, a primus stove, a canister of tea, and a tin kettle. So that if any household in the village were unlucky enough to be bombed out all that they had to do was to move across the road, send for Mrs. Josser and, in a jiffy, they would find themselves tucked up between aired sheets and sipping something hot.

In fact, by August 1940 Ditchfield like the rest of England was remaking itself. Practically overnight, the old notion of the family had been discarded and the still older motive of the tribe had come back into its own again.

2

A tribe's O.K. so long as you're a member of it. Then the rest can carry you. And you get things for nothing. And, if you're smart, nobody notices. And if anything goes wrong there's all the rest of them to draw on. A tribe's O.K. So long as you're a member of it.

But what about Percy? Yes, *what about Percy*? We saw so much of him at one time. Something almost every day, in fact. And now he's passed clean out. Not so much as a glimpse of him. Has anything happened? Is he all right? Is he still there? Is he—to put it bluntly—a member of the tribe? Or isn't he?

Well, he's still there. And, in a way, he's all right. But he isn't a member of the tribe any more. Not really. When other people were getting out their spears and smearing on the war-paint, he got left behind. And the funny thing is that, though the warriors are some of them far away by now, their names are on everybody's lips. Whereas you never hear Percy mentioned. The tribe's forgotten all about him, even though he's still at home. Forgotten entirely. By all except Mrs. Boon, that is. She still prays for him night and morning. And talks of him, too, when the doctor's wife isn't listening.

The plain fact is that there's been too much happening for Percy to be remembered. And, if you must know, Percy never was as important as he thought himself. It was really only by chance that he happened to hit the headlines at all. And by then the mischief had been done. After the palaver was over, the women-folk just shrugged their shoulders and returned to their cooking-pots.

Percy was out.

But not to himself. With Percy, Percy still counted for a lot.

And he was getting on O.K. He was on uppers now. And he hadn't made any mistakes yet. At least not bad ones. Not bad enough for the foreman-warder to have spotted. And if they got past him, why worry? Percy hadn't got to wear the boots, had he?

He wouldn't have believed that he could get so interested in boots. Not just in three sizes of them. But he had. He could tell which size he was cutting by the shape of the curves as he went round them. Could have told it in his sleep. And if he knew as much as that in four months, he'd be on to stitching before the year was out. And that wasn't bad. There were some seven-year men who'd never worked up to stitching. Seven years, and never got beyond soles. Percy was getting on O.K., he was.

The prison chaplain thought so, too. He was pleased with Percy. Very pleased. He was such a bright intelligent lad compared with most of them. And polite. He always got up when the chaplain entered. And called him "sir." That was one of the best of signs. It showed respect for authority.

If only Percy had got a bit more of a voice, the chaplain would have given him a place in the choir. Because music, properly handled, could work miracles. But as the choir was impossible, the chaplain tried his other approach—Association Football. The great thing about soccer was that it taught that it was the team and not the individual that mattered. And the team-spirit was everything. That was why he encouraged an intelligent interest in the professional side of soccer as well. Not to bet on, of course. No pools. But simply because soccer was fought between teams. And the best man in the team was the man who was the best for the team. There was a sermon in every cup final.

So that Percy could keep up the conversation on Wednesdays, which was the day when the chaplain had his private time with him, Percy read all about soccer in the marked cuttings that were provided. It wasn't difficult, memorising the fixtures. And the chaplain never noticed that he didn't care for the game really. Too tame. Not enough in it. No excitement. Dogs were better. Or boxing. Or exhibition dancing with a partner you took round with you. But if the chaplain liked to talk soccer, that was O.K. by him. It was better than some of the things the chaplain talked about.

But with nothing to talk about but soccer and nothing to read but what was in the prison library—and those books were a proper disgrace: no thrills, no sex, no love-interest, even—no wonder Percy had to fill his mind with other things. When the key turned in the door at night he used to go over the same old story every time. He was eighteen now. Be nineteen in September. And a life sentence like his only meant fifteen years really. That would make him thirty-four by the time he got out. Things would have changed a bit by then. Couldn't help it. Progress was like that. Houses would be all-plastic, he wouldn't wonder. And television in every room. Tune in to New York for hot crooners whenever you felt like it. Or go across there. Atlantic taxis. Sixty-seaters. With stewardesses wearing sailor-hats. Come to think of it, it wouldn't be motor-cars people would be stealing then. It would be autogyros. Pick up a plane in an airfield and get chased through the clouds by cops in rocket-helicopters. And no shooting when they caught up with you. Just tickle your ribs with a death-ray. . . . Percy extended his forefinger, his lethal death-ray finger, and made a low whirring sound with his tongue. His finger toured the four corners of the cell, exploring it. Percy was doing a death-ray hold-up.

He'd told the chaplain once about how funny everything would seem when he came out again. And the chaplain had got it all wrong. He'd been sorry for him. But that wasn't what Percy meant. Percy was looking forward. There was nothing in the least old-fashioned about Percy.

Besides, he was O.K. He'd been lucky being put inside so early. Suppose he'd waited a bit, and then gone inside. Where would he have been then? He'd never have caught up again. As it was, he'd still be on the right side of forty when he took up the reins again. And even forty wasn't old. Not for a man. He knew a lot of girls—quite lively ones, too, some of them—who preferred men that way. He hadn't got anything to worry about. He was lucky having gone in so early. He was O.K.

It was only his mother that he was worried about. He'd have liked her to be O.K., too. But somehow he didn't know whether she'd care for things the way they'd be when he came out. Plastic houses, and things.

CHAPTER 88

I

And Mrs. Vizzard?

Poor woman. For her, they had been difficult, perplexing months as well as lonely ones. She had made up her mind, unmade it, made it up again. And not once merely, but a succession of times. The pattern of indecision had looked like being extended indefinitely right along the entire fabric of her life.

There had been no uncertainty in Mrs. Vizzard's mind at the outset. When she had first learned of Mr. Squales's duplicity—and it seemed now she had never really doubted it—she had been resolved upon revenge. Nothing less than a writ, and damages, and the creature's dishonoured picture in all the papers, would satisfy her. During those weeks of mystery while Mr. Squales's whereabouts were still unknown, she had been one of Hell's leading Furies.

But when Connie, rosy with mischief, had returned from Chiddingly on that May evening to boast that she had done what Mr. Barks's sleuths had failed to do, Mrs. Vizzard began to experience her first misgivings. The image, Connie's image, of Mr. Squales as a winkle and herself as a pin, had displeased Mrs. Vizzard. Was it possible, she had wondered, that in going through with this thing, in baring her poor bleeding heart in a court of law, she was simply appeasing Connie's insatiable appetite for sensation? Was it really her wish to destroy publicly everything that in private had seemed so delicious, so desirable? To sum up, was it ladylike?

But ladylike or not, she didn't fancy letting the wretch get away with it. Every time she closed her eyes if only for a moment she remembered—could see as plainly as if the various items were written there—the list of presents that she had showered on him. It was a long list. A list ending with the valise that he had showered upon himself.

As for Mr. Squales, he had practically forgotten Dulcimer Street. Forgotten Dulcimer Street. And forgotten Mrs. Vizzard. Even forgotten what it had felt like to be hard up.

It was really astonishing quite how rapidly the spectre of poverty had receded. Something strange and wonderful had taken place inside him, and he was transformed. Metamorphosised. The shabby back-room chrysalis was now a pretty full-sized sort of butterfly.

He was, as a matter of fact, nearly a stone heavier. He had put on twelve and a half pounds in just over three months. And his wife was delighted with him. Absolutely delighted. Admittedly, so far as his mediumship was concerned, this was one of his Sabbatical periods. The days and weeks were passing without so much as one psychic flicker through his whole thickening figure. But wasn't this the case with all mediums? Hadn't the great Schneider had his wintry seasons long before his prime? Mr. Squales saw no cause for anxiety. Not yet.

And what was so gratifying—and so surprising in a man of his temperament—was that he had proved himself such an adaptable kind of husband. When Mrs. Squales, after she could stand it no longer, had asked him cautiously if he were really attached to his light grey cashmere with the double-breasted waistcoat—the one that Mrs. Vizzard had given him for a walking-out suit—he had replied simply that he hated the thing. In consequence, he now had hanging up in his wardrobe two rough country tweeds, a dark blue worsted with an almost indiscernible stripe and a new dinner-jacket.

At the moment, however, because it was so hot he was wearing a sports shirt and a pair of flannels. More than once he had reflected on the irony of it. Because flannels may mean anything. And unless he had gone to the length of showing people the tailor's label sewn inside the waistband at the back there was no way of proving that he wasn't still going about in something cheap and nasty off the peg.

Not that in present company there was any danger. It was one of his wife's tea-parties under the big cedar on the lawn. And only a certain class of person—the class that didn't know about things off pegs—got invited. Mr. Squales always enjoyed these occasions. There was something at once so graceful, yet so informal, about the whole setting. So essentially English. The Prince's Plate teapot merged delightfully into the background of laurel hedges. And the butler's white shirt-front, a sparkling shield of pure ivory, added just that touch of the baronial that the scene demanded. The war seemed very far away.

"There's a gentleman from London wishes to speak to you, sir."

Mr. Squales started. He had been day-dreaming. He hadn't noticed that the butler was already close beside him. Too close, in fact. He was practically crowding.

"I'm wanted on the phone, you mean?" Mr. Squales demanded.

The butler came even closer.

"No, sir. He's here. In the hall. He says he's got something private to deliver."

"Something private?"

The butler dropped his voice still lower.

"He's from the solicitors, sir," he explained.

And then Mr. Squales remembered. It was something to sign. Or something. His wife had warned him all about it. She'd given him a block of shares in a present. Just enough to enable him to vote. And now there was the matter of a waiver. Mr. Squales wondered dimly what was expected of him. He had never waived before. But presumably, he told himself, the solicitor's clerk would know how to do it. Otherwise, why send him all this way?

"Show him out here," he said to the butler. And with an easy smile he addressed his wife's guests: "You will forgive me?" he asked. "Some papers I have to sign. A rather important document."

He caught his wife's eye and smiled lovingly.

It was quite a nice young man who emerged from the house. Even though it had to be admitted that in his black coat and striped trousers he looked oddly out of place there. And in such surroundings he was obviously nervous and ill at ease. Mr. Squales noted sympathetically that the young man's shoes were dusty and cracked across the instep.

"You are from the lawyers?" he asked.

The young man's embarrassment increased.

"Mr. Squales?" he asked.

"Who else?" Mr. Squales replied. "Who else, indeed?"

"I have to give you this," the young man answered, feeling inside the pocket of his coat.

But Mr. Squales stopped him.

"Not yet," he said. "Later. A cup of tea first. A sandwich. You walked?"

"Only from the station," the young man answered with a grin. "Not all the way."

Mr. Squales ignored the gaucheness of the pleasantry.

"We'll run you back in the car afterwards," he said. "Too hot for walking. You take milk? Or lemon?"

"Tea, thank you," the young man answered.

Mr. Squales smiled. Clearly the youth was impossible. Yet, in a way, he felt sorry for him. Even rather liked him. He was so crude, so untutored. Mr. Squales could imagine the tale of the sheer magnificence of this tea-party that he would unfold that evening in some tiny villa in Hackney or Turnham Green. And to give him something else to talk about, Mr. Squales fished out his gold cigarette case—a wedding present from his wife—and offered the young man a cigarette. "Turkish or Virginian?" he asked.

The young man lit his cigarette and looked about him.

"Nice bit of property you've got here," he remarked.

This time Mr. Squales shuddered. They had been his own words once. He decided that he didn't like the young man so much after all. Scarcely looking at him he extended his hand towards him.

"That letter you spoke about," he said. "Hadn't I better have it?"

It was a large envelope of the best quality that was thrust into his hand, and Mr. Squales's fingers tingled as he touched it. He made sure that the guests were watching him and then addressed the young man again.

"I'll only glance at it now," he said. "And then we'll go inside. This needs taking seriously . . ."

He had extracted the letter at last, and began reading it. His voice died away as he did so. The shade under the cedar tree seemed suddenly to be full of eyes. And all devouring him. Then he grew oblivious to them. All that he could see was the notepaper that he was holding. At the top ran the words, "Barks, Barks, Wedderburn and Barks, Solicitors." And beneath, in the smudged blue ink which is peculiar to solicitors' typewriting, ran the words: "*Sir, Our client Mrs. Louize Jane Vizzard instructs us that whereas you promised to enter into a state of marriage . . .*" Mr. Squales's gaze fled further down the page, "*. . . breach of promise . . . damages and compensation . . .*" He closed his eyes. He swayed.

And because his eyes were closed, Mr. Squales did not see that his wife had crossed over to him. The first thing that he knew was that the letter had been playfully tweaked out of his hand, and that she was reading it.

As soon as he realised what had happened, his poise, his good manners, left him.

"Gimme," he shouted hoarsely. "Gimme."

He tried to snatch the letter back as he said it and, out of the corner of his eye, he saw the young man grinning at him again. But it was too late. Mrs. Squales had seen as much as he had seen. She had seen enough, in fact. There was silence. An awful unending silence.

Mr. Squales glanced over his shoulder in the direction of the house. There was something furtive about it as though he might still make a dash for it. His wife's hand, however, was on his arm. It was a firm unshakable kind of hand. And it was digging into him.

Her voice, too, when she spoke, was firm and unshakable. Just like her hand. And it dug in just as deep.

"Would you all please go on?" she asked, turning to the guests. "I'm afraid we must leave you for a moment."

Then she addressed her husband:

"Come, Rico," she said. "Come and read me your letter."

CHAPTER 89

MR. PUDDY had done himself a bit of good.

Simply by keeping on where he was instead of darting about like some points-shoppers, he had got something to show for it. The man at the provisions counter where Mr. Puddy dealt had known him for a long time; and he respected Mr. Puddy's kind of shopping —patient, contemplative, discriminating. He was the same sort of human being himself. And it was because of this spiritual bond between the two of them that he half closed one eye, rubbed his forefinger expressively along the side of his nose and from under the counter passed Mr. Puddy a limp sagging parcel done up in greaseproof paper. Appreciating that any display of emotion was out of place in transactions of this kind, Mr. Puddy merely slid the little packet into his attaché case, inclined his head slightly to show that he understood and left the shop unhurriedly.

Of course, once he was outside, it was altogether different. By then he could afford to be inquisitive. Resting the case up against the lamp-post opposite, he prised open the greaseproof paper and peeped inside. His guess had been right. It was the better part—probably the whole part—of eight ounces of picnic ham. Already sliced. Not too thin. And with no more than a halo of white fat all round it. Mr. Puddy closed his eyes for a moment.

"Hab," he told himself. "Pribe hab."

And, at the thought of so much happiness, he closed his eyes for a moment.

"If I could odly lay be hads on sub tobatoes there'd be dothing else I should deed."

It was getting on for six o'clock when Mr. Puddy left Dulcimer Street for the tea warehouse. And possibly because of the September weather—hot, cloudless and holidayish—or possibly because he'd picked up half a pound of ripe tomatoes, Mr. Puddy was feeling completely at peace with the world.

Admittedly, he still jumped if a motor-cycle back-fired or anything. But remember what he'd been through. During the whole of the Battle of Britain period he'd practically lived on soda bi-carb. His inside just hadn't been able to get along without it. Then, as soon as he'd got used to the vapour trails of fighters in the daylight sky and German planes coming down so fast on top of each other that the Stop Press couldn't keep count—he'd taken the better part of a bottle of milk of magnesia as well on the day when 182 were destroyed—things had started cooking up at night instead. All through the last few days of August he'd had simply shocking heartburn.

The night of the twenty-sixth of August had been the worst. And he hadn't expected to get through it. Bombs with his number on them had fairly been raining down. But here he was, on the seventh of September, still alive. Marshal Goering hadn't been able to do for Mr. Puddy. And even if he weren't exactly smiling, at least he'd got his nerve back. All because of the eight ounces of ham, he was calm and self-possessed again.

He didn't tuck into it as soon as he'd hung his hat up. No rushing at it. Anything eaten before midnight was simply by way of a snack. It was the three a.m. break that counted. And Mr. Puddy had everything ready for it. He'd put the ham out on a plate with another plate over it; and the tomatoes were in the bag at the side. The ham was still intact. All that he'd allowed himself was a tiny nibble that had been adhering to the paper.

His first round of the premises had been entirely uneventful. Simply a saunter past sleeping mountains of tea. Even the rats had been quiet to-night. Unusually quiet. There wasn't a thing to disturb the stillness. And the soundlessness finally began to get on his nerves a little. He might have been somewhere on the moon, instead of inside the City, he was so lonely. So lonely, and so muffled up in silence.

He was standing by the front door when the sirens began. They were faint at first, a mere flickering disturbance of the atmosphere. But Mr. Puddy heard them all right. He had ears in his stomach. And, immediately, a large cold patch began to spread right through him. And this was absurd because sirens as indistinct as that hadn't got anything to do with the tea warehouse. Those sirens were warning the sleepers of Gravesend or Dagenham.

All the same, as Mr. Puddy sat there listening, his heart was thumping so hard and his breathing was so noisy that he had to hold his breath altogether, simply so that he could listen. Then, before he was ready for it, the next rank of players in this queer nocturnal orchestra had taken up their fiddles. London itself was howling and whining away at him. And, next moment, Mr. Puddy's own personal siren, the one just outside the back entrance, went off. It was so near that it wasn't simply a matter of hearing it. Mr. Puddy was engulfed and surrounded by it. His stomach went up and down with the wailings. Mr. Puddy was the siren.

When it stopped, Mr. Puddy went on vibrating for several seconds all by himself.

It was at this point that Mr. Puddy was supposed to go up to the sand-bagged telephone kiosk on the roof and tell the London Fire Brigade about any incendiaries which might come his way. Right up there, with nothing but chimneys and a stirrup-pump and long-handled shovel for scooping up the things when the Germans had dropped them.

And did he go?

Have a heart. There were fifty-eight stairs to the roof from where Mr. Puddy was sitting. And even if he had *wanted* to perch himself right under the bombs, fifty-eight is an awful lot of stairs. What was more, supposing he had gone, how long would he have to stay there? For all he knew, he might still be up there at breakfast-time, a lofty anchorite looking down on the ruins of smoking Babylon. Taking it for granted, that was, that he himself was still all right. And, in air raids, it isn't safe to take anything for granted. That was why he picked up his big box-torch—he had a terror of being left suddenly in the dark—and went down to the underground cubby-hole where the ham was.

Not a moment too soon, either. This wasn't just a siren-raid. Already there was a kind of summer thunder, a rumble in the air, as though the suburbs were being racked by earthquakes. Mr. Puddy didn't wait to hear the drone of planes. What he had heard was quite enough. It was tympanum and double-bass of this ten-thousand-acre orchestra.

"Let's hobe it's odly recodaissance," he told himself stoutly. "Just wud or two plades cub over to sby on us."

But, if it were only one or two, the guns were making an extraordinary fuss over them. Either that, or the gunners had lost their nerve and were simply loosing off wildly. Even down there in the basement it was noisy. Which just showed what it would have been like if he'd gone up on the roof. Mr. Puddy took his steel helmet off the hook and put it on.

Then came the kind of sound that Mr. Puddy liked least of all. The guns were going *woof-woof* in all directions: there was a kind of hollowness about them. But this last noise was quite different. It was a sort of *crrr-rump*. And it came the wrong way. Instead of coming through the air like all the other disturbances, it rose suddenly out of the ground at Mr. Puddy's feet. It was as though the hard concrete floor had growled and then kicked him.

"That's wud," Mr. Puddy told himself. "This isn't recodaissance. This is the real thig."

As he said it, the globe of cold in his stomach expanded and re-iced itself. And, with the rapid changes of temperature inside him, Mr. Puddy began sweating. He passed his hand across his forehead. It was sticky. And no wonder. Because they were overhead all right. The 'cello passage had started. Even from there where he was, with a roof and five floors above him, Mr. Puddy could hear them. Clear and distinct above the general uproar, the *throb—throb—throb* came through the walls as though bees were swarming. Mr. Puddy tried not to think about that sound. To produce it, the night sky must have been practically solid with planes.

But the 'cellos weren't the worst. The bar with the flute and piccolo had now been reached. And it was an altogether new sound. Beginning as not much more than a shrill whistle, it mellowed and rounded and then changed suddenly into a vulgar *whoosh*. As soon as Mr. Puddy appreciated what it was, that he was really hearing a bomb *coming down*, he forsook all dignity and crawled underneath the table—the table with the ham still on it. Even before he had got under it properly, the thing gave a little jump into the air and a lot of dust and cobwebs were dislodged from the ceiling.

But that was all. Even the *whoosh* hadn't meant that it was Mr. Puddy's bomb, the one with his name written on it.

It was while he was still down there on all fours—as it were playing bears with himself under the table—that he suddenly realised that, shut away from everything like that, he mightn't know what was happening until it was too late. Not merely too late to save the building. But too late to save himself.

That was how it was that Mr. Puddy came to leave the security of his cubby-hole for the open draughtiness of the basement corridor. And out there with his helmet on he felt fairly in the thick of it.

All the same, it seemed about the safest place that he could think of. And he remained where he was. Remained there until the gunfire had died away again as though the summer thunderstorm had moved on to another parish and the bees had ceased their swarming. When it was quite quiet, Mr. Puddy looked at his watch. It showed five to two. There was just comfortable time for him to nip up to the top floor, punch the infernal clocking-machine on the fourth landing and get back down to his cold ham.

And perhaps it was just as well that Mr. Puddy should have decided to put work before eating. Otherwise it might have been five minutes, ten, even a quarter of an hour before he smelt the aroma that now filled the tea warehouse. And by then it would probably have been too late.

It was a queer elusive sort of smell when it first reached him. A long flickering feeler of fragrance came out and tickled his nostrils, and went away again. And that was all. There was nothing about it to which you could give a name exactly. It was more the sort of thing that at dawn gets carried on the wind to schooners as they draw near to the Spice Islands. Mr. Puddy stood still and sniffed. Sniffed, and sniffed again. But there was nothing unusual about the smell. In the leaf, tea is always strangely mutable. He'd known a sudden change in the weather to be quite sufficient to set a whole floor of Lapsang exuding so powerfully that you couldn't go in there without sneezing.

Then it reached him again, the fragrance. Stronger than before. Stronger than he had ever known it, in fact. The whole basement now smelt like an open tea-caddy. And there was a roughness about, a harshness, that he had never noticed before. It wasn't a really nice smell any longer. Somewhere in it, there was just a suggestion of an old autumn bonfire.

A bonfire! Mr. Puddy gave a brief involuntary belch of sheer terror. And he started to tremble. He shifted from one foot to the other, wondering whether to go on or turn back. It was not an easy decision to make. Because if it was anything serious, he naturally didn't want to be caught in the building. On the other hand, if it was nothing to worry about—say somebody else's warehouse on fire—he would like to be able to reassure himself.

In the end it was not the smell but the ham that decided him. He wanted to get the second round over and sit down to his main meal. Mr. Puddy went on.

At the top of the stairs, he found the swing doors and sniffed again. He was on the track of the smell all right. It was distinctly nearer by now. And if he just went on quietly as he was going, he ought to catch up with it in about two more flights. There was, however, a nasty surprise in wait for him just round the next corner. Up to this moment, he had simply been pursuing an unplaceable tantalising smell. But as he went past the concrete buttress on the stairs, the beam of his torch suddenly encountered something. It was as though the middle air were churned and milky, and the beam itself took on a shape. It became a long white horn probing the mistiness that lay ahead. Mr. Puddy had got as far as the smoke.

Not that there was anything *very* courageous so far. He could see perfectly well along the full length of the first-floor corridor. And the smoke wasn't anywhere enough to be what you might call choking. It was simply that the atmosphere was slightly tainted.

Then the next shock came. When he opened the swing doors on the second storey a puff of smoke, real smoke this time, came out at him. But there still wasn't much of it. What there was escaped past him up the staircase and he could see the rows of cases, extending in front of him, orderly, peaceful and unfiery. The second floor was evidently nothing to worry about.

"False alarb," he reflected. "Id's subwhere else. The sboke's gedding id frob oudside."

But the third floor made him wonder. He paused when he got there. And not merely because he was out of his breath, and his legs were giving way under him. He paused, because it either was *hot-tish*, or he was imagining it. Those last eighteen steps seemed to have taken him back into the middle of the September afternoon.

He couldn't, for the moment, get himself to go on any further. Suppose the building really was on fire? Suppose the raid started up again? Suppose he fainted? On the other hand he couldn't go back down again just like that. Because he was far too jumpy and on edge to be able to eat anything. Just for his own peace of mind he *had* to continue and make sure.

There was hardly any smoke on the top landing when he reached it. But there was something else. From underneath the door a brilliant shaft of light like a searchlight was streaming. And the air around him was roaring in his ears. When he opened the door and peeped inside, he jumped back. And pretty quickly, too. In the very furthest corner of the floor, the Soochong floor, a fire was raging. The smoke was rolling up from it as though a small volcano had started. And in the tiny glimpse that he had got, Mr. Puddy understood now why the smoke hadn't been thicker outside. In the roof over the volcano a large untidy hole had been scooped out, and there was a straight up-draught like a chimney's.

Mr. Puddy got back down the fifty-eight stairs faster than he had ever moved before. He had seen quite enough. And he wanted to share it with someone. With as many people as possible. The telephone he used was the one on the ground floor just beside the main entrance. He chose that one because it was farthest from the fire. But it wasn't that far, all the same. He stood there banging the receiver up and down and wondering how long it would be before the flames were lapping round him.

The voice at the other end—when at last he got to the other end—didn't seem in the least surprised when Mr. Puddy announced that he was speaking from a burning building. On the night of September the seventh, 1940, there were too many burning buildings in London already to get very excited about one more.

As soon as he had rung off, Mr. Puddy wondered where he should wait until the engine got there. He didn't like stopping where he was because, at any moment, the floor above might come crashing down on him. Nor did he fancy hanging about outside because a tin hat didn't seem much of a protection against the sort of things that might start being dropped again at any moment. In the end, he decided on the alcove under the front stairs. And while he sat there he remembered everything he should have done—like keeping the blaze under control with the stirrup-pump until the engine arrived, and stuffing up the underneaths of doors with a damp cloth to exclude the draught, and moving inflammable objects as far away from the blaze as possible.

And, as he remembered the last, Mr. Puddy laughed. A hollow kind of lonely laugh. Because everything around him was inflammable. If he had tried to do what the handbook said he would have had to shift the whole blooming warehouse and put it down again on the other side of the river. And, in any case, the handbook wasn't all that reliable. If he had been up there on the roof where he should have been he wouldn't have been down here now. The place where the incendiary had come through was exactly where he would have been standing.

By the time the firemen arrived, the whole corner of the warehouse was well alight. Simply by pushing the front door ajar and peeping out into the night, Mr. Puddy could see the reflection of the flames in the windows opposite. And so far as he personally was concerned he would have been quite content to leave it at that. But the fire officer wouldn't hear of it. He was a brusque efficient sort of man and wanted to know everything about the warehouse. He even insisted on Mr. Puddy's going round with him.

During the past twenty minutes things had certainly taken a bad turn. The wind had shifted and the smoke was now curling down the staircase in great wreaths. There were shrill cracklings like a forest fire as well as the roar that Mr. Puddy had first heard. Even the third floor was a bit further than Mr. Puddy really cared to go. But he had reckoned without his companion.

"You'd better lead now," the fire officer shouted at him through the din. "You know the way. I'll follow."

And follow he did, so closely that Mr. Puddy could not possibly turn back. He could feel the fire officer's knee pressing into him. The fourth floor, however, was beyond even the fire officer. Smoke like this needed masks and equipment. The two of them came back down again choking.

And once he was back down, Mr. Puddy remained down. He stood there by the telephone in case he was needed. And he wasn't. The A.F.S. got along perfectly well without him. Mr. Puddy watched fascinated, while an enormous tapelike bandage of hose was unwound and carried up the staircase. And the young men who followed it carried axes, crow-bars, jemmies. . . . Then the fire officer, all blackened and besmirched like a nigger minstrel, came back down the stairs and, pushing Mr. Puddy out of the way, began telephoning. It seemed that the A.F.S. wasn't so self-efficient after all: the officer was appealing for a fire-tower.

Mr. Puddy had only just taken up his place again after the officer had finished with his call, when the top floor gave way. Not all of it, but the north-east corner where the volcano had been. And, as it broke, it scattered the ignited cases of Lapsang into the quiet orderliness of the Ceylon bay. Two minutes later, despite the water that was cascading down from the top floor, the Ceylons were burning furiously, too. The fun, in fact, had really started.

Even the fire-tower couldn't save the building. The huge giraffe-like thing arrived and immediately went into action like a Niagara. And, for all the good it did, it might just as well have stayed at home. The jet of water, heated nearly to boiling-point by the flames, spread across the floors, with the contents of the broken cases floating on top of it. Soon the warehouse was swimming in gallon upon gallon of half-brewed tea.

Mr. Puddy had left the telephone by now because that position no longer looked healthy. He was over by the bicycle sheds. The air raid really seemed at last to be over, and he was breathing more easily. The only thing that worried him was having to explain to the manager how he had come to let the warehouse get into such a state.

So far as he could judge there would be only the four outside walls left by the morning. The whole incident would almost certainly lead to a row. A row. And, of course, a spell of unemployment.

It was while he was thinking these gloomy thoughts that he remembered his ham. Thank God *that* was safe! Right down there in the basement it probably wasn't even warm. The only danger was that some of the water might have leaked through on to it. And so that he could rescue it before it was too late, Mr. Puddy decided to slip in for a moment through the side door that led straight into the basement corridor. From the look of the building he had cut things pretty fine, anyhow.

It was stopping to pick up the tomatoes that was Mr. Puddy's mistake. He had got the plate with the ham all ready, when he tried to balance the tomatoes on top. And in his haste he dropped them. Picking them up again cost him nearly two minutes because one of them had burst. And by then the ground floor, rotten for years and now sodden as well by the weight of water, gave way as well. Admittedly, it was only in one place where it collapsed. But a basement is a naturally confined sort of spot, anyhow. And a great blast of sparks and smoke rushed in a gust past Mr. Puddy's door. It was like standing to one side while a swarm of fiery bees tore by. Mr. Puddy redropped the plate that he was carrying.

He was so frightened now that he ran blindly to get out. The side door was only twenty-five feet away and he reckoned that, full-speed, he could just reach it holding his breath all the time. He might even have managed it, if he hadn't fallen over something. Right in his path, where he couldn't see it because of all the smoke, there lay an obstacle. And Mr. Puddy fell headlong. The bulb of his electric torch was broken, and he found himself abandoned in the basement, with no light except the big red glow at the far end of the corridor. Mr. Puddy screamed. And, at the same moment, the obstacle that he was lying on gave out a long groan. Mr. Puddy screamed again.

It was a man, all right. Mr. Puddy could feel that much. And he was in A.F.S. uniform. What Mr. Puddy didn't know was how badly hurt the man was. Nor did he know that, twenty seconds before, the thing that had tripped him up had been directing a fire-hose two floors above and had come down through the floor with the boiling water and the cinders. The man wasn't unconscious. Mr. Puddy could tell that because his arms and legs were moving. Particularly the arms. After exploring Mr. Puddy's body, they discovered his neck and fastened themselves on to it.

Then began the worst five minutes in Mr. Puddy's life. He was in the dark. He was trapped in a burning building. And he was being throttled. It was now simply a question whether death would come first from strangulation or from suffocation by the smoke.

When he found he could do nothing to make the man relax his grasp, Mr. Puddy began to crawl. With the other man still clinging to him, he groped his way along the corridor as though he was playing bears again. And he was getting on quite nicely when a sudden crash behind him sent up a fresh cascade of sparks and fragments. One of them fell quite near him and lay there glowing like a red-hot coal. Mr. Puddy put on a fresh spurt. Composite and hampered as he was, he scampered.

The stairs very nearly beat him. Steep and awkward at the best of times, they rose up sheer like a cliff now that he had to tackle them on hands and knees. It would have been bad enough if he hadn't got the weight round his neck. As it was, the whole thing was very nearly impossible. Twice on his way up the flight he decided to give in and just die there in whatever way men do die in fires.

But when at last he did manage to get as far as the door, and collapsed forward over the low stone steps, it was worth it. Kind hands took hold of him and one of the helpers—Mr. Puddy was too far gone to notice which one—poured something down his throat.

He learnt afterwards how it was that they were ready for him. Just before he had gone back for his ham, the fire officer had given orders to evacuate the building. Then it was discovered that one of the firemen was missing and a volunteer search-party was trying to break in to look for him. Nobody had noticed at the time that Mr. Puddy was missing, too. He didn't make much difference either way. But when, retriever-like, he suddenly emerged at their feet with his burden, it made the volunteer rescue-party look rather silly.

As he was carried away by two muscular A.F.S. men, Mr. Puddy heard something about his being an example to the entire force. It was the fire officer himself who was saying so.

CHAPTER 90

EVEN though Mr. Puddy knew nothing about it, his old friend, Mr. Josser, had watched the blaze right through.

From the front garden of Conservatory Cottage, he saw the whole thing. Admittedly, from twenty miles away, he couldn't really detect which was Mr. Puddy's particular part of the general flare-up and what was simply the rest of London going up in the flames. So far as Ditchfield was concerned, the new fire of London was just a great red glare in the sky with streamers of bright orange that ran up into it. It was a pretty handsome scenic spectacle, too, because all the while the anti-aircraft shells were bursting—quite silently at that distance—in the midst of it, and the fingers of searchlights waved about and pointed. Because everything was so silent, there was an unreality about it. It might have been some children's party on a prodigious scale, complete with Bengal lights and penny sparklers, that they were watching. But, for a children's party, it was too long drawn out. The clouds over London were still salmon-coloured in places, a good half-hour after the dawn began lighting things up on its own account.

Mrs. Josser stood out there beside him during the greater part of the time. And, while they watched the sky flicker and perform, they both remembered Larkspur Road beneath it. And Baby. And Doris. And Cynthia. And wondered what was happening to them. It was a grisly business just standing there, in the front row of the balcony so to speak, watching the huge funeral-pyre on which at any moment granddaughter, daughter and daughter-in-law might all be heaped.

Mr. Josser was the one to speak first.

"I'm going up in the morning," he said. "Reckon I'll catch the early train. They oughtn't to spend another night there. Not with things like this."

Mrs. Josser, however, had already taken things a stage further in her own mind.

"And if there's any trouble with Cynthia, just you put Baby under your arm and bring her down," she directed. "Cynthia'll come soon enough if she finds Baby gone. As for Doris, just tell her I said so."

"You . . . you wouldn't like to come up yourself?" Mr. Josser enquired tactfully.

But Mrs. Josser only held him in contempt for the suggestion.

"Me?" she asked scornfully. "And what about getting the cottage ready? Somebody's got to do it. If there's going to be three more of us to-night, I've got to do the rearranging."

In a way, it was strange after last night even to be going to London at all. There seemed at least reasonable doubt that the place would still be there. But for the first half of the journey there was nothing to show that last night hadn't been as peaceful as any other night-time in September. Day had dawned on a beautiful silky morning, and the little suburban villas with their small oblongs of garden backing on to the railway looked snug and comfortable. There were children playing in them and here and there a baby taking its nap in a perambulator. No matter out of which side of the carriage Mr. Josser looked, there was still nothing to show for that massed midnight spectacle of star-shells and illumination.

Then, round a curve in the line, he abruptly found himself in the war-zone. He was getting into London by now. And, under the balloons, the little villas were packed and crowded. They were the suburbs of a previous generation. And overnight, they had suddenly been opened out. Disembowelled. A bomb—quite a big bomb, it seemed—had come down in the midst of them. Two of the little villas had disappeared completely. There was simply a large untidy crater filled with litter where they had been standing only eight hours before. So little of them was left, indeed, that it was difficult to feel any sense of loss. It was the houses on either side that brought to mind the damage and destruction. There was something shocking and vaguely indecent about the way they were exposed. The back of one of them had been pared clean off. And a bedroom, complete with bed, was open to the railway. Another bed, upside down this time, rested in the garden. And on the end of a length of lead piping a bath, soiled and abraded by the rubbings of countless bathers, hung straight down over the remains of a staircase. In another little villa there was an iron grate, with a mantelpiece and picture over it. But it was simply a grate set in the open air. There was no room for the iron grate to warm any longer.

The man next to Mr. Josser leaned over.

"Lucky it didn't hit the line," he remarked consolingly.

Mr. Josser nodded politely. He was too shocked to do more. Shocked by the sheer flimsiness of the houses that people had been living in. Before the blast had caught them they had looked ugly, sordid, overcrowded—anything you like. But solid. Undeniably solid. So many dense little lumps of architecture. But he could see now that they were shams really. The bricks that they were made of were nursery bricks and the ceilings matchwood. Against the sky, the broken rafters showed up like fish-bones. The whole thing was makeshift and temporary-looking. It might have been in a native kraal that the bomb had fallen.

It was quite a long time afterwards when he saw the next reminder of last night. The line ran high here and he could see out across the landscape of roof-tops. Against the sky-line stood the openwork girders of what up till yesterday had been a factory. Now

Mr. Josser could see right through it. At one corner the tall chimney stack was still standing, even though there was no smoke coming out of it. But over the whole building there hung an opaque dirty mist. And, as the firemen were still pumping in the water, the mist was constantly renewing itself.

It was not until Mr. Josser reached Liverpool Street that he actually *smelt* burning. But it was there all right. A rank frowsty odour hung over everything as though an incinerator door had been opened. But there was more than a smell of burning to distract him. The streets outside the station were full of scorched paper. Charred embers of what might once have been office ledgers. And large cobwebby smuts that were all that was left of filing-systems and double-entry book-keeping. Under foot there was the crunch and jingle of good plate-glass.

The extraordinary thing was that by the time Mr. Josser got to the Embankment he was out of the war again. The plane trees hadn't lost a leaf and the Thames was sliding peacefully along. There was no sign of misery and desolation there. Either the Germans were very thorough and conscientious and were going to demolish London methodically parish by parish, or the late summer's night hadn't been long enough for them.

The look of the Embankment comforted Mr. Josser. And the thought occurred to him that simply because London was such an easy enormous target, it was safe. The Germans could go on ravaging and tearing away at it. But, at this rate, they'd need a lifetime to destroy it. By the time Marshal Goering was an old man there would still be bits that were recognisably London left standing. And it was the same all the way to Larkspur Road. Except for a church with the roof gone and a few missing windows, and a whole street roped off with a hanging notice that said UNEXPLODED BOMB, Streatham was as calm and normal as Ditchfield had been. The chances of Baby's survival seemed better. They seemed good, in fact. She might even have slept through it.

Even so, when he got to Larkspur Road, it was all far simpler than Mrs. Josser had hinted that it might be. There was no need for kidnapping, and scarcely any even for persuasion. Cynthia didn't have to tell him what sort of a night she had been through. He could see. There were dark circles under her eyes and her hair was all anyhow. It didn't even look so blonde as usual. This was the first time Mr. Josser had ever seen her really close when she hadn't any make-up on, and he was surprised to notice how sallow she was. How sallow and tired and unblooming. Conservatory Cottage with its sunny half-acre was evidently just as much the place for her as it was for Baby. He blamed himself again for not having *insisted* that she should come down there sooner.

And, now that he put it to her, there was no opposition. Cynthia didn't want Baby to spend another night in London. Four or five separate and distinct times last night, she said with a little giggle, she had expected it to be all up with the three of them.

But it was not Mr. Josser who finally clinched it. It was Ted. His authority, calm, sagacious and unruffled, still hung over the little flat. And Cynthia invoked it.

"It wouldn't have seemed right to Ted leaving Baby here with all that noise going on. It couldn't be good for her nerves," she explained. "He'd have been dead against it. Doris thinks he would, too."

So that was decided. And Mr. Josser helped Cynthia to pack.

It wasn't easy because Baby required such a lot of things. Such an astonishing lot. One after another the fibre travelling cases—there wasn't a decent-sized trunk in the whole flat—were filled with dresses, underclothes, nightgowns, toys. But that was only the beginning. Cynthia couldn't reasonably be expected to start a new life in a cottage with nothing to wear herself. And the pile of dresses on the bed grew steadily larger. Grew larger, while all the time Cynthia kept adding little things that she couldn't do without—the case of silver spoons that had been a wedding present, her toilet set, Ted's photograph, the library book she was reading, a packet of jellies for Baby's supper, a box of special shampoo sachets. . . .

While she was going through her shoes to see which pairs were worth taking, Mr. Josser slipped out for a moment to phone Doris. He had more than half expected her to be at Larkspur Road. And it was awkward that she should have gone along to the office just as though nothing had happened. Because people are usually far more independent and obstinate over the phone than they are face to face.

It took Mr. Josser some time to get through. The telephones were evidently still in a bit of a tangle from the raid. And the operator doubted whether it was worth trying. But, when at last Doris answered, it was easier than it had been with Cynthia.

"My, you have been quick," she said.

"Quick?" Mr. Josser asked her. "I just wanted to make sure you were all right."

"Then you didn't get my wire?"

Mr. Josser paused.

"It hadn't come when I left," he told her. "Perhaps Mother's got it."

"Because I asked her if she could have Cynthia and Baby," Doris went on.

"That's what I'm here about," Mr. Josser explained. "Cynthia's packing. I've just been there."

"You are a darling," Doris said.

"It was Mother's idea," Mr. Josser replied firmly. "And she says you're to come down, too. She told me to tell you."

There was another pause. A longer pause this time.

"Oh, all right," Doris answered. "Say I'll be down later."

The voice in which she answered was flat and weary-sounding with all the overtones rubbed out. She hadn't meant to say she'd go. It was such a journey. But, now that she came to think about it, she supposed she *was* rather sleepy. And if the Germans came over again at sundown, she wouldn't be good for anything in the morning. In the circumstances, it was only common sense to take the chance of a good night's rest where she could find it. Besides, if she stayed on at the flat Bill might start worrying. And that was the last thing she wanted.

By the time Mr. Josser got back to the flat he found that Cynthia had thought of quite a lot of other things she needed. The cupboards had practically been emptied in his absence and the contents added to the pile. What was more, there were no spare suitcases. Mr. Josser took off his coat and got down to it.

It was evident that this was going to be a string-and-brown-paper evacuation after all.

CHAPTER 91

I

IT WAS different for Connie. She'd had to stick the raid out, too; her old teeth chattering. And if the Germans came over again tonight or any other night for that matter, she'd have to stick it out just the same. She hadn't got a sugar-daddy to come and take her into the country away from all the nasty noises. She hadn't got anyone.

And it was because of this, or rather because of this on top of everything else, that she was crying. Crying because there wasn't anybody in the whole world who cared enough about her even to send a post card.

But it wasn't only loneliness that was the trouble. If she had been surrounded by loving friends she'd still have felt awful. And not just ordinary awful, either. This was something special. Something chronic. Something that the doctors had never been taught about.

And it was because there wasn't any cure for it, bar one, that she was crying. Her face was all puffy and smudgy from the tears, and the eye-black had run right down her cheeks in two dark tunnels. She'd been like that for hours, just sitting there sobbing, and trying not to think about it. But what was the use of trying not to think about it when you didn't know what it was? There wasn't anything specific or particular about the pain—nothing that you could actually put your finger on and say Ow! It wasn't in any one place. Simply an all-over sickness. Something that was in the bones and in the blood. Something that was eating the lungs and binding round the heart. Something that didn't make her food taste so good any longer, and buzzed and bubbled inside her head whenever she lay down. Something that drew her cheeks in so that there were pockets where the dimples had once been, and made her poor old legs swell so that she couldn't get her shoes on.

She shook her head sadly.

"It's me notice," she told herself. "It's me calling-up papers. It's me cue. Better get ready, Connie."

And, with this premonition, she grew calmer. Tears and all, she was steadier now. Kind of peaceful inside herself as it were. She looked back over her past life almost as though it were somebody else's. And crikey it wasn't half a waste! The money she'd had in her time—and the chances. Talk about chucking opportunities away—she'd fairly shovelled 'em. Offers of marriage. Little places down at Maidenhead. Sovereigns slipped in playfully under the frilly part of her garter. Diamonds. If she'd watched her step she could have been a rich woman by now. Rolling in it. Paying super-tax. And instead of it, what was she? Just the old girl with the dyed hair who sat behind the counter in the ladies' cloakroom and had a saucer, with a few pins in it, in front of her ready to receive the tips.

It wasn't even as if she'd learnt any sense as she'd grown older. Not a bit of it. Her sixty-odd pounds from the accident had gone the way of all cash. There wasn't a penny left out of it. Or out of anything else. She was really high and dry this time. Washed-up and flapping. She could feel her tired gills closing.

She'd been too ill last night to go along to the night-club at all.

They'd had to get through the raid without her. And because she hadn't been along, she was afraid to face them now. Afraid of what they might say to her. Afraid of what she might find when she got there. How did she know there wasn't some new and more glossy pussy-cat sitting there on her cushion already? And why hadn't she phoned up and said she wasn't well? Because, silly, you can't phone up when you haven't got so much as twopence in your handbag and you don't like to borrow from your landlady because you owe two weeks' rent already and would rather that she put it down to sheer forgetfulness. . . .

Connie suddenly screwed up her face so that the wrinkles all ran into one another. The pain had come back again. In her side, and working up towards the middle. In a minute it would start giving her little jabs right under the heart, the way it always did. She couldn't rely on even five minutes' peace and comfort nowadays.

"I wish I was dead," she began again. "Dead and underground. Tucked away somewhere quiet where the pain couldn't get at me. Laid out proper and put to rest. Helping up next year's roses."

Then she sat bolt upright.

"Well, why shouldn't I?" she asked herself. "Who's to stop me? It's my sacred spark, isn't it? Not anybody else's . . ."

She'd done it. Just like that, with no warning. Five minutes before, the idea hadn't even occurred to her. And now she'd booked her passage. Booked the one passage on which there is single fare only and no return. She'd taken ten aspirins and three sleeping-tablets. And when her eye caught the bit about being dangerous to exceed the stated dose she couldn't help laughing.

She was half unconscious already. Just lying there, doll-size, scarcely breathing. One thin yellow arm hung down out of the bed trailing, and the other was folded across her chest with the knuckles up against her eyes as if she had been crying. As suicides went, it had been nothing. Simply swallowing the tablets was easy. She'd gulped them down with some water out of the tooth-glass. And she'd have taken another forty if necessary.

For as long as she could think clearly with all that drug inside her, she argued it all out and the answer still came the same. She was within her rights. There had been no other way for it. It wasn't Connie who was walking out on her part. It was the whole cast that had walked out on her. And she wasn't standing for it.

Then, just as her eyes were misting over and closing, a bright light came to her. She saw how selfish and sinful she had been. And she wanted to be alive again. Wanted it desperately. She tried to sit up in bed for a moment. Sit up? She couldn't even draw her arm in. It was too late now for any misgivings. She was numb all over. Already it was somebody else's feet that were at the bottom of her legs. She'd said good-bye for the last time. That was why—longing for something that she couldn't have because she'd given it away herself—she was crying when she finally passed out.

The bright light that had come to her wasn't an inner one. It was simply the afternoon sunlight catching the brass edge of the bird-cage. But it had been enough. She'd realised in that moment that she wasn't quite alone. There was someone dependent on her. And that was every bit as good as having someone to turn to.

Because of Duke she'd wanted to go on living.

2

Anyhow, it was all over now. She was in heaven. And the realisation astonished her that, even after the Awful Thing she'd done, it was heaven and not the other place. Either the regulations were more merciful than anybody led her to suppose, or somebody had blundered. Whichever way it was, she wasn't going to say anything unless they raised the matter with her.

She didn't know how long she'd been there, because time didn't seem to matter much anyway. All that she knew was that the pain had stopped and she felt better. Felt better and liked the new neighbourhood. It was a bit strange of course—little cherubs sitting about on Vi-spring clouds and choirs of angels conducted by seraphim like Jack Buchanan making music in the corners—but not so strange that you couldn't get used to it. Everyone was so friendly, too. "How are you, Connie? Better?" or "Settled in all right? If there's anything you want, remember you've only got to ask"—she was having that sort of remark made to her all the time. What was more, she seemed to know them all without introduction. "I'm fine, thank you, Luke," she had said before she realised that she'd never really met the Saint before.

The funny thing was her age. As soon as she'd got there she'd naturally gone to tidy herself up in the Ladies' by the front entrance and, when she looked in the big silver mirror that was hanging up there, she scarcely knew herself. She wasn't exactly young again. Not seventeen or anything like that. But she certainly didn't look her age. She was so much fatter. And her hair didn't seem to have been dyed. With war-time lighting she might have passed for thirty-five anywhere.

She wasn't even surprised, though she couldn't help going a bit trembly, when she heard that St. Peter was coming to see her that afternoon. Not Connie going to see St. Peter, but St. Peter coming to see Connie. A sort of royal visit as it were. But it didn't turn out a bit that way. There wasn't any guard of honour, or curtseyings, or trumpets or that sort of thing. In fact, she didn't properly realise that he had come until she found him sitting there beside her, leaning up against the same star. And he wasn't in the least what she'd imagined. There was no long robe or white beard. No saint's crown. No sword. No key. He was simply a middle-aged man in a dark suit and a bow-tie, with a rolled umbrella hanging over his forearm. Altogether, he was just like the nice kind gentleman at the railway station who had given her the pound note to buy Mars Bars for the evacuees. He was so much like him, in fact, that she became quite alarmed for a moment. She wondered if they really could be one and the same person.

It didn't put her at her ease either when St. Peter hung up his black Homburg on one of the points of the star, and began opening the black brief-case that he'd got with him.

"Just one or two points I'd like to run over with you," he said. "I always like to meet the new arrivals personally."

Connie couldn't help noticing that the file he'd taken out of the brief-case had her name on it in full, with "Connie" in brackets afterwards. He even had all her old addresses, one after another, right back to childhood days. Below the last one, 10 Dulcimer Street, S.E.11, a double line had been drawn in red ink with the words FINAL DEPARTURE and the date, September 7th, 1940, added with a rubber stamp afterwards. It was her dossier all right.

"Would you like to say anything first or shall I begin right away?" St. Peter asked her.

And, as he spoke, he opened up the folder with all the pages neatly fastened in loose-leaf fashion and some of the sheets flagged with red adhesive tape. She'd have liked to know what those sheets said, but the way St. Peter was holding the folder that was impossible. It would have looked bad if he'd caught her trying to cheat. Besides, what was the use of it? It wasn't like being up before a beak. You couldn't fool St. Peter—or, at least, she supposed you couldn't. There was only one thing for it and that was to make a clean breast of everything.

"There is just one little thing I'd like to say," she told him quietly.

"I do appreciate being here. It's been very kind of you to take the trouble."

"No trouble at all, Connie, I assure you," he told her. "We'd been expecting you."

Looking back on it she wondered why she hadn't let it go at that. But there was something about him that was so frank and friendly that she suddenly found herself wanting to tell him things—all sorts of things. If only she could get those off her chest, she'd feel better. But when she actually came to it she realised that she didn't know him well enough. So all she did was to mutter something general by way of apology.

"I've led a rotten sort of life," was what she said.

"Oh, really?" St. Peter asked in a surprised sort of voice. "It doesn't say anything about it here."

Not say anything! She whistled. It looked as though someone had been keeping the facts from him.

"I . . . haven't always been good," she said lamely.

"In what way?" St. Peter asked, flipping through the dossier with his finger.

That was rather embarrassing. She would much rather that he had blamed her for it and been done with it. This business of making her tell him was slower than she liked it. She'd rather have had one walloping, break-neck-speed confession that would have left her gasping.

"Oh, almost every way," she said with a little gesture of hopelessness. "I've knocked around quite a bit one way and another. I was only a kid the first time I fell."

"How much of a kid?" he asked.

"Under sixteen," she answered, dropping her eyes.

St. Peter paused.

"Under sixteen," he repeated. "That's a long while ago, isn't it?"

Connie nodded.

"Of course," St. Peter went on, "if you'd come to us then we'd have to have spoken to you about it. We couldn't have overlooked it. But you're practically a different person now. There's no point in going right back like that."

Connie looked up.

"You mean it?" she asked.

"Certainly," St. Peter told her. "It would only make you unhappy."

"And does that go for all the rest of them?" Connie enquired politely. "All my gay days, I mean."

St. Peter didn't answer immediately. He was reading. Then he turned to her.

"Not altogether," he said.

There was a pause.

"You let one man down pretty badly," he went on. "Remember?"

Connie shook her head.

"What . . . what was his name?" she asked faintly.

"Harry."

Then it all came back to her. Came back so clearly that she wanted to cry. She could remember everything about him, even the way his check-suit hadn't fitted properly. And—wasn't it funny?—right up to this moment she'd always congratulated herself on not having lost her head and gone through with it.

"You lost marks over that," St. Peter told her.

Connie kept her head averted.

"How many?" she asked at last.

"Ten," St. Peter answered. "All in one go."

"Out of a hundred?"

"Out of a hundred."

"Phew!" Connie wiped her forehead with a little wisp of fleecy cloud that was floating past her. "Was it as bad as all that?"

"Naturally," St. Peter told her. He was more serious now. Still friendly, but definitely serious. "If you'd married him you'd have had children. We'd got them all ready, and they weren't wanted."

"My children?" Connie asked him.

St. Peter nodded.

"What were they?"

"Two boys and a girl."

There was a pause.

"Was the girl like me?"

"Spitten image," St. Peter answered. "Bit darker perhaps. But no mistaking."

She gave a little sniff.

"What became of them?" she asked.

"Had to go elsewhere," St. Peter explained. "We held 'em back as long as we could, but God wasn't able to reserve them any longer."

"The girl, too?"

St. Peter inclined his head.

"The girl, too," he told her.

She had a good cry then. A real good cry, thinking about what she'd missed. She put her head on St. Peter's shoulder and cried her heart out. When she'd finished St. Peter lent her his own handkerchief because the fleecy cloud had moved on too far from her to catch it.

"You see now what I mean?" he said.

Connie dropped her eyes again.

"I see," she said huskily. And she did.

"Well," said St. Peter, "I didn't want to upset you. So we won't say anything more about it. There's just one little formality and then we're through. Have you got a pen on you?"

Connie shook her head.

"Well, use mine," St. Peter told her. "It works all right if you shake it."

It was a beautiful pen, all rolled-gold and chasings; the feel of it made her better again immediately.

"Now, I just want you to read this," St. Peter went on, "and initial it if it's all right. It's not too late to alter it if any of the particulars aren't quite right."

With that, he detached the last page of the dossier and handed it to her. Connie ran her eyes down it.

There was a long pause. The tears were streaming down her cheeks again and she could hardly see.

"That's me all right," she said at last.

"Then just initial it," St. Peter said. "In the little square at the end."

Connie scribbled in "C. T." and reached for St. Peter's handkerchief again. But she wasn't quite through yet.

"And the date," St. Peter told her.

Then he got up and put his hand on her shoulder.

"Now you're really one of us," he said. "If you want anything you've got my number—Rainbow 1212. And, of course, if it's an emergency, just dial 'O'."

He held out his hand to her as he said it, and Connie took it limply. So limply that St. Peter immediately spotted that there was something wrong.

"Cheer up, Connie," he said. "Don't take it too much to heart, old girl. We get all sorts up here. Free will's a very tricky business."

It was four o'clock on the afternoon of the seventh of September when Connie passed out. And it was not until nearly eight o'clock on the following evening when she came round again. The effect of the aspirins had entirely cleared off by then. And, except that she was a bit light-headed for want of food, she felt marvellous. Not a pain in her. Not even a headache. Just a few head noises. Altogether she was in better condition than she had been for years. Better and brighter and more bounce in her. Quite the old high-stepper, in fact. She got up and went over to the window.

The dusk outside startled her.

"You're late, Connie dear," she told herself. "Time you were getting dressed . . ."

3

It's Scotland Yard again. But not the room we were in before. Not Percy's room. This is two floors higher up. And there is no football group on the wall. Simply rows and rows of filing-cabinets all round the place. All lettered. And all locked.

In the centre of the room there is a large deal table. And round the table three men are sitting. They are leaning forward. And propped up against the ink-well under the low electric light is a row of photographs. All of plain, rather plump young men, all in their early twenties and all wearing glasses. Alongside them is another photograph, the master copy. One by one they keep glancing at it for comparison.

"Isn't doing too badly," one of the group says after a pause. "Not for a foreigner. He's a progress-chaser now. Must have brains."

The man on the right glances up. Even though it's Scotland Yard, he isn't a policeman. He's a lieutenant-colonel.

"Where d'you say he is?" he asks.

"Drayton and Sons, Leeds," the inspector tells him.

"Optical manufacturers?"

The inspector nods.

"Bomb-sights?"

The inspector nods again.

There is a pause.

"When's it to be?"

It is the lieutenant-colonel who has spoken.

"When's what to be?" the inspector asks.

"Bringing him in."

The lieutenant-colonel has only recently been put on special duties. But he's enjoying them. And just to show how much at home he is in Scotland Yard, he likes using the language of the place.

But the inspector looks shocked.

"Oh, not yet, sir," he says. "We don't want to rush things. Find out first who he's working to. Give him a run. There's no hurry. Not now he's being taken care of."

The lieutenant-colonel is a little bit hurt.

"You're quite sure he is this Otto Hapfel?" he asks, pointing at one of the photographs. "No doubt about it?"

"Oh, no, sir," the inspector assures. "Just look at the nostrils. And those lobes. You'll notice, too, that . . ."

The inspector begins to get technical.

CHAPTER 92

DOWN at the cottage, it was a bit of a crush admittedly. Cynthia and Baby had Doris's room. And Doris herself had to sleep on the couch in the living-room. In fact, by the time Conservatory Cottage was tucked in for the night it was the sort of household that a billeting officer writes off as useless.

Mr. and Mrs. Josser still had their own room. At first, they had wanted to give it to Doris. And Mrs. Josser had affirmed mysteriously that they could manage perfectly. She spoke rather as though she and Mr. Josser often slept on couches and easy chairs for preference. But Doris naturally wouldn't hear of taking their bedroom. After all, it was only going to be for one or two nights at the outside, and then she would be going back to the flat again.

All that had been nearly a month ago, however. And there she was still catching the 8.5 from Ditchfield Station in the morning and getting back again at night in time to have some supper, hear the news and go to bed. It wasn't much of a life, really. There were too many hours of it spent hanging about on platforms or sitting, and sometimes standing, in trains. But every time she had got her things ready to go, Marshal Goering had done something else to stop her. There were no two ways about it. At the moment London simply wasn't the right place for a good night's rest.

Mrs. Josser, in consequence, was delighted. Ever since Doris had first left home, Mrs. Josser had been devising means of recovering her. And now, with the colossal accident of war to assist her, she had achieved it. Of course, there was Cynthia to spoil everything. But even Cynthia's presence in the cottage hadn't justified Mrs. Josser's earlier forebodings. Granted, she didn't like the girl. And never would. Cynthia's pair of cherry-coloured slacks was alone enough to make Mrs. Josser wonder whatever people would think that Conservatory Cottage was coming to. But Cynthia did at least have the good sense not to interfere in the housekeeping. She laid tables. She washed-up. She made her own bed. She made Baby's. But that was about as far as her contribution went. After that it simply and unostentatiously petered out. And every afternoon—and very often in the mornings as well for that matter—she would go quietly off to her room and sit there polishing her nails, brushing her hair to bring the lustre back into it and reading the *Film Weekly*. Everything considered, she had settled down into the ways of country life quite remarkably well.

All the same, if it weren't for Baby, explained Cynthia frequently, she would have gone off and got herself a war-job. Something where she'd be doing something.

But this morning it wasn't Cynthia whom they were discussing. It was Mr. Josser. He sat there at the head of the breakfast table, his bacon and fried bread uneaten on the plate in front of him. And propped up against the teapot was the letter that the postman had just delivered.

Mr. Josser was engaged at the moment in re-reading it. Re-reading it minutely and seriously so as to miss nothing. In consequence, there was a respectful hush over the whole room. Nobody had said anything since Mrs. Josser's last remark. And that had been distinctly cold and uncompromising.

"The idea of it. At your age!" was what she had said.

Mr. Josser, however, had not been put off by it. He was far too much excited. So excited, indeed, that he didn't mind what anybody said about anything. And all because Battlebury and Son had invited him to go back into their counting-house:

"*Dear Mr. Josser—On account of the call-up we find ourselves short-staffed on the book-keeping side,*" the letter ran, "*and Mr. Battlebury wonders if you would like to rejoin the firm on your old salary. In the event of your accepting this offer it is, of course, understood that your pension would lapse during your new service with the company. Awaiting a reply at your earliest convenience, Yours sincerely, E. A. Veritter.*"

Mr. Josser looked up.

"Just as I said," he remarked. "They want me back."

"Let me see that letter," Mrs. Josser demanded, tightening her lips ominously.

"Half a minute," Mr. Josser answered. "I haven't finished with it yet."

It irritated Mrs. Josser to be kept waiting. What was more, it was an alarming indication of the state of Mr. Josser's mind: in the ordinary way he passed things over obediently as soon as he was told to. But to-day he was holding out on her. And she didn't like the letter any more when she had got it. As soon as she had finished reading it she drew her lips in more tightly than before. And she kept them drawn in for some moments before speaking.

"Well?" she asked.

"Isn't it nice of them?" Mr. Josser replied, beaming. "Fancy them remembering me."

"And why shouldn't they?"

Mr. Josser looked down at his plate again.

"Well," he said, "there are lots of other fellows that they might have thought of."

"Not in war-time, there aren't," Mrs. Josser told him.

She drew in her breath between her teeth. It made a sharp hissing sound as though a serpent had spoken. She was determined to say nothing more in front of Cynthia, and only wondered if Mr. Josser's idiotic allegiance to his old firm would make it impossible for her to keep to her decision. Apparently the mere words BATTLEBURY AND SON at the top of a piece of notepaper were enough to unhinge her husband. If it had actually been the majestic Mr. Battlebury himself, and not simply one of his underlings who had signed the letter, Mr. Josser would probably have swooned clean away holding it.

"Still some life in the old 'un yet," Mr. Josser said suddenly. "I'll show 'em."

"You won't do anything of the sort," Mrs. Josser contradicted him. "Not with your chest."

"What's my chest got to do with it?"

"Do you imagine I'd let you go back there just because that Mr. Battlebury of yours snaps his fingers at you?" Mrs. Josser retorted.

"But I'm better now. I'm perfectly well again."

"And you're going to stay well. Back to work again at your age, indeed!"

Mrs. Josser's references to his age annoyed him.

"Mr. Veritter's my age," he answered. "He's working."

"Mr. Veritter hasn't got your chest," Mrs. Josser reminded him.

Then Mr. Josser lost his temper. Carried away by the sheer magic of the notepaper, he thumped the breakfast table.

"My chest's perfectly all right," he said loudly. "It's as good as anybody else's."

"Then why are we all down here instead of in Dulcimer Street where we ought to be?" demanded Mrs. Josser. "Don't forget I'm the one who has all the trouble when anything goes wrong with it. Not you."

"But nothing's going to go wrong with it," Mr. Josser persisted.

"Not if you stay here and take things quietly, it isn't," Mrs. Josser replied, her voice rising, too. "I don't want two funerals on my hands inside six months."

Her lips were drawn in tight again by now. And, behind her spectacles, her eyes looked misty.

As it was obviously impossible to make any impression on her for the time being, and as Mr. Josser was always very much ashamed after he had lost his temper, he decided to leave it at that. He got up from the table and went out into the garden. Usually a good smoke soothed him. But this morning he was too unsettled to smoke. He simply stood there in the sunlight, his pipe in his hand, fiddling. The letter had brought the past back to him so closely that he wondered suddenly how he could ever have borne to be separated from it. It was as though merely by dictating the letter Mr. Veritter had invited Mr. Josser to step back into his own youth. All because of this wonderful war, being sixty-five didn't matter any more.

"I wonder about trains," he was thinking. "There must be some good early ones. . . ."

Back indoors Cynthia was trying to gloss over the little incident.

"It's reely me that ought to be getting a war-job," she said with her little giggle. "Something where I'll be doing something."

But Mrs. Josser was still too much preoccupied to answer. She was planning to reply to Mr. Veritter's letter herself. And in the reply Mr. Veritter was going to be given a straight piece of a wife's mind.

CHAPTER 93

As IT turned out, Mr. Josser need not have worried about trains. When he came to enquire at the booking-office he found that there were plenty of them. And as early as he could want. There was even one at ten minutes to six if he had really felt like it.

Not that it was in the least necessary, all this rush. The train that Doris always caught, the 8.5, got to Liverpool Street in plenty of time, and going by anything earlier would simply have been silly. Besides, it was very pleasant travelling up with Doris. This morning it had been rather like the beginning of a holiday, pedalling through the pearly September morning to the station, Mr. Josser on Uncle Henry's green bicycle and Doris on her new one. The Jossers were all three of them cyclists nowadays. And the only thing that Mr. Josser thought was a pity was that Mrs. Josser and Doris should both have left it so late. Because, even though nowadays you paid two or three pounds more for the bicycle, all the bits that should have been bright and shiny were just plain black on the war-time models.

Of course, it had all seemed rather strange this morning, waking up by the alarm clock and having to hurry through with his shaving. Mr. Josser had got up first as usual to take Mrs. Josser an early cup of tea. But when he reached the bedroom he found that she was dressed already. And that was significant. Because it had been agreed between them that Doris should get herself off in the mornings. And Mr. Josser had expected things to happen that way today. But evidently in Mrs. Josser's mind the departure of the two of them was a bigger affair altogether. Something that would have to be handled personally.

And, considering that she was still opposed to the whole notion of his going, she was certainly sparing no pains about it. With one eye on the presentation clock while he was eating his scrambled-up dried eggs, she began questioning him. Had he remembered his scarf? His gas mask? His office coat? His season-ticket? From the way she was behaving it might have been a rather stupid and absent-minded little schoolboy that she was getting off to school for the first time.

And it was the same when she kissed him good-bye. She asked if he'd remembered his handkerchief.

Mr. Josser was sitting in the corner of the carriage feeling important. Battlebury's couldn't get along without him. And he was somebody again. But it wasn't all expectation. There were a lot ot regrets as well. He was older—there was no denying the fact. Even the ride to the station had taken it out of him. And perhaps that was why he was feeling sort of flurried inside himself. As though moths had settled in his stomach. Whatever it was, he couldn't settle down properly. As he glanced across the carriage he caught Doris's eye and she smiled back at him.

"Looking forward to it, Dad?" she asked.

Mr. Josser gave a slightly self-conscious little grin.

"I am rather," he admitted.

He didn't go on with the conversation because Doris had got her library book and he didn't want to interrupt her. Besides, he was full of his own thoughts. Puzzling, unexpected thoughts. About Ted, for instance. And seeing Mrs. Boon in the infirmary. And the night with Percy at the Camberwell Baths. And Uncle Henry's last illness. And the holiday at Brighton with Mrs. Josser. And Duke. And the procession to Whitehall with the perambulator. And the time Mr. Puddy's cupboard gave way. And Mrs. Vizzard's engagement. And Mr. Squales. And Percy's arrest. . . . All muddled up together and out of order. He was going backwards through time. Not forward the way he should be.

The carriage had been empty when they left Ditchfield. But it was filling up now at every station. After Epping there were people standing. And Mr. Josser tried to give up his seat to a little City typist who was swaying about in front of him, her *Daily Mirror* in her hand. But the offer was refused. Rather indignantly refused. And thereafter she ignored him. Mr. Josser sat looking out of the window, pondering. Either manners had changed since he had last been about in the rush-hour. Or else he looked older and more fragile than he thought he did.

The train by now had chugged and puffed its course to outer London, and they were poking their way through the smoke belt. Nosing along under a khaki-grey canopy that stretched ten, twenty, thirty miles ahead of them. Any sentimental nonsense about pearly September mornings had been left somewhere in the country far behind. And so had the country. The houses here were packed up to the railway line, one against the other, like books on a library shelf. Inside the carriage perpetual twilight reigned. And the little City typist who had the air of an inveterate reader had to give up her penny picture paper and console herself with her memories.

Then, as the train slackened speed, Mr. Josser began gathering his things together. He was excited again. Eager and excited. It was like coming home from exile. He got down his attaché case and fastened the cord of his gas mask through the handle. Five minutes before they drew into the station, Mr. Josser was ready to get out.

As he did so, he remembered something. Remembered what it was that he had forgotten. Of all things to forget when he was re-starting his professional life, he'd forgotten his fountain pen. It was in his old brown suit on the hook in the bedroom cupboard.

Liverpool Street being what it is in the mornings, there was too much of a rush once they had got on to the platform to be able to say good-bye really properly. There was no one, Doris included, who hadn't cut things just about as fine as could be. And an uneasy feeling seemed to run through the entire crowd that, by allowing anybody else to get to the barrier first, jobs, pensions, bonuses, everything would be in jeopardy. The whole train-load panicked.

Before she left him, however, Doris managed to put her arm through Mr. Josser's for a moment.

"Take care of yourself, Dad," she said. "Don't overdo it."

Mr. Josser gave that rather self-conscious little grin of his again.

"Don't you worry about me," he said. "I shall be all right."

And that was all. For a moment, father and daughter formed a small stationary eddy in the forward swirl. Then Doris kissed him and ran upstairs to get her bus. Mr. Josser was left alone to face the serious business of the day.

Take care of himself, indeed! Mr. Josser was rather hurt by that remark. He'd never felt fitter in his life.

Mr. Verriter hadn't said exactly what his work was going to be, and Mr. Josser was wondering whether he'd get his old accounts back. "D" to "J" had been his ledgers, and he didn't fancy seeing other pens scratching about in them. Not that it wouldn't be too late already. There wasn't the same pride in penmanship nowadays. And Mr. Josser was pretty sure that, if he searched, he'd find the "D's" to "J's" simply cluttered up with 9's that looked like 7's, and no double underlinings in red anywhere.

It was pleasant to walk for a bit after sitting all hunched up in the train. Pleasant, but difficult. The gas mask, dangling over the side of the attaché case, kept on swinging round and bumping him. And it seemed strange to be about without his umbrella. But umbrellas are notoriously tricky things to get fixed satisfactorily on to bicycles. And before leaving home he'd given up the attempt as hopeless.

His mind was still playing tricks on him on the bus-ride. There was Ted again. Always Ted. And Bill bending over him and thrusting the syringe-thing into his back. And Percy. But, for the most part, the little pictures that came tumbling out were from an earlier volume altogether. And considering the date of them, their age and brightness astonished him. He saw himself, for instance. Away back at the beginning nearly fifty years ago. Saw young Freddie Josser starting out on his career.

And the odd thing was that he was still saying the same thing to himself that he had said then.

"I hope I can give satisfaction," he kept thinking. "I hope I can hold it down."

He had just got off the bus when he stopped abruptly. And that was because the other side of the Row wasn't there any more. The shop where he had bought Mrs. Josser the shawl had simply vanished. And instead of the grey brick cliff-face of offices that had been stolidly sooting itself up for generations, there was now an open vista with the offices of Creek Lane on the far side. Creek Lane itself seemed to be the same as ever. Except for the windows. In place of them, there was now a rather mixed display of wood, cardboard and a kind of thick-skinned cellophane that might have been used for wrapping up monster chocolate-boxes.

He wasn't given any time to think about it, however, because as soon as he got his foot on to the pavement of Creek Lane he heard his name spoken.

"Why, if it isn't Mr. Josser!"

It was a female voice that had addressed him. And turning round he found himself facing the elderly Miss Unsett. An undemonstrative woman in the ordinary way—a lifetime's absorption in *pro-formas* had flattened out all the more feminine curves in her character—she was temporarily thrown off her balance by his reappearance. Miss Unsett was blushing.

And so was Mr. Josser. Or very nearly. After all, it was something—coming back to London like this, one of the eight million again, and being recognised before he'd even got to his own office.

But it was nothing to what was waiting for him in the office. He shook hands ten times in five minutes. And everyone told him that he didn't look a day older. Mr. Josser only wished that he could have said the same about Mr. Veritter. But Mr. Verriter's pale whippet face was more peaky and drawn-out than ever. Even his white collar appeared to have been bought for a bigger breed of dog altogether. It was evident that the bombs and the black-out, coming on top of the call-up, had been getting Mr. Verriter down pretty badly. Either that, or the whippet-strain in him had won and he was in for a bout of distemper.

As soon as Mr. Veritter had finished saying how glad he was to see him, he took him into the inner office—the one with the word YRATERCES written across the glass door when viewed from Mr. Veritter's side—and unburdened himself. It was too terrible, he said. Simply terrible. They were two men short already and Mr. Parsons was due to leave on Friday. Mr. Veritter had been there till nine and ten at night just trying to keep his head above water.

It fairly broke Mr. Josser's heart as he listened. In the first place, it was painful enough in itself. And secondly it was the first time that anyone in Battlebury's had ever confided in him.

"What . . . what do I start on?" he asked as soon as there was a pause.

Mr. Veritter wrinkled up his nose and ran his eye down a memorandum pad on his desk in front of him.

"The 'L's' are behind," he said. "And the 'M's.' There's Lambert's and Maplerose both outstanding."

Mr. Josser hadn't moved.

"Are the 'D's' to 'J' all right?" he asked.

Mr. Veritter looked at his memorandum pad again.

"There's trouble in the 'E's'," he said. "Edwards and Son are disputing."

"Edwards and Son!"

Mr. Josser had looked after Edwards and Son himself for over twenty-five years. And during the whole run of that quarter-century there had never been so much as a bicker. A dispute with the Edwards, either son or father, was as unpleasant as a row in his own family.

"Do you mind if I go over it?" he asked. "Perhaps it's in the brought-forward."

His voice trembled a little as he spoke. It all seemed too good to be true. He didn't know about the rest of them yet. But he'd got the "E to Egg" volume back all right.

He had just taken it down from the shelf when Mr. Battlebury arrived. And that was how it was on the second occasion, the second in all those years, when Mr. Battlebury tried to shake hands with him, and Mr. Josser had his arms full and couldn't do anything about it. But that didn't stop Mr. Battlebury. He had recognised the wisp of grey hair that showed up over the top of the ledger. Recognised that, and the striped trousers protruding underneath. The ledger walking towards him had suddenly become human.

"Why, if it isn't Mr. Josser," he exclaimed.

"E to Egg" gave a sudden lurch.

"Good . . . good morning, sir," the voice behind them said.

"Glad to have you back, Josser," Mr. Battlebury told him. "We all are."

And just to show how warm and friendly everyone was feeling towards him, Mr. Battlebury clapped Mr. Josser on the back. It was a good hearty slap and Mr. Josser felt himself letting go. He sagged involuntarily and then steadied himself against a chair back.

"I'm . . . I'm glad to be back, sir," he said simply.

There was a brief pause. Mr. Battlebury seemed to be thinking about something else.

"Mind you don't go overdoing it now you are here," he remarked at last, as though Mr. Josser's return had been his own idea entirely. "Take it easy, remember. No late hours."

With that, Mr. Battlebury went through into the room marked PRIVATE, and Mr. Josser took out his handkerchief and wiped his forehead. Unlike Mr. Veritter, Mr. Battlebury evidently thrived on war. He seemed bigger and glossier than ever. And busier. The way things were, he'd have forgotten all about Mr. Josser by to-morrow. Would simply be ignoring him as he had been ignored during all those years that had led up to the presentation of the clock. Mr. Josser would have reverted. In Mr. Battlebury's eyes, he would just be the clerk at the end desk in the left-hand corner as you came into the counting-house. And, on the whole, that was how Mr. Josser preferred it.

End desk in the left-hand corner! Mr. Josser glanced nervously towards it. Then he sighed. Sighed from sheer relief. The desk was still there. And what was more, the place was empty. Empty and waiting for him. It had an unmistakable air of having been unoccupied ever since he had left it. Not that Mr. Josser could understand this at all. Because it was easily the nicest corner in the whole room. A regular gem among corners, in fact.

The high stool creaked as Mr. Josser climbed on to it. In the old days it had annoyed him sometimes, that creak. But to-day he liked it. He wouldn't have had anything about it changed. It was his creak. And it was like clambering up on to his mother's lap getting back on to that stool.

"This is where I belong," he told himself. "I belong to London. And London belongs to me. . . ."

But already the desk was behaving in its old familiar way. Now that he had got "E to Egg" on to it, the ledger was doing what every ledger on that desk had always done. It was trying to slide forward on to Mr. Josser's knees. And in the end he had to wedge it with a piece of blotting-paper and a lump of rubber. Then he turned to the page with "Edwards & Son" at the top in as nice a piece of cursive script as he had seen for a long time—it was in 1908 that he had opened the account—and dipped the office pen which Miss Unsett had found for him.

But he didn't write anything. Didn't even begin to check the figures. Just sat there, with the page open in front of him and the pen drying in his hand. Looking out across the smoky roof-tops. And thinking. Not thinking of anything in particular, either. Simply day-dreaming in Mr. Battlebury's time.

And he did a strange thing. Turning his head to the side he made a remark out loud as though someone were standing there. Standing there right in the corner beside him.

"You know, Ted," he said slowly, "you're the one who ought to have been coming back. Not me."

Then he remembered himself. Remembered where he was. And to cover it up he gave a little cough. But it was all right. No one had heard him. The electric adding machine on the centre table was whirring and chattering, and it drowned everything. Those few words between father and son had been entirely private.

A few minutes later, Mr. Veritter looked out to see how Mr. Josser was getting on. But he need not have worried. Mr. Josser was bent forward over "E to Egg" as if he'd never been separated from it. His black alpaca office coat was rucked across his shoulders as it had always been, and over his forehead the solitary wisp of white hair floated triumphantly upwards.

With his left hand he was stroking the leather corner of the ledger.

POSTSCRIPT

Having A Last Look Round

I

It's Christmas Day again. Christmas Day, 1940. And a very different sort of Christmas it is from the one when Mr. Josser brought home the port wine and the cigars, and the box of crackers for Baby. A distinctly whittled-down war-time kind of Christmas, a sort of stepping-stone between Christmas past and Christmas future. A Christmas with penny cards costing sixpence and little things for the stocking just exactly what you can't get. And no mistletoe. Not that it is any use grumbling. There is a war on, and it's the same with everything.

Mr. Josser is spending the holiday quietly at Ditchfield with the family. Now that he's back at Battlebury's he likes a quiet spell sometimes. And it is certainly quiet at Ditchfield. Very quiet. That's because the family has been reduced to three. Just Mr. and Mrs. Josser and Baby.

Doris is in the Forces by now—that's one less. For no reason at all that Mrs. Josser can understand—or ever will be able to—Doris has suddenly thrown up her job with the firm of solicitors in Lincoln's Inn and joined the A.T.S. Has simply walked out on three pounds ten a week and a Remington Noiseless that the firm bought specially for her. But Mr. Josser has guessed the reason straight away. It is because Bill had been posted out somewhere in the Middle East, and Doris can't settle down to anything without him. Probably she feels better, he tells himself, with a lot of other girls of the same age and her own motor-cycle to look after. Doris will be a dispatch rider as soon as she's got her corporal's stripe. And this is funny when you come to think about it. Because Bill's a major already. Bill's been doing rather well, in fact. And Doris is very proud of him.

But even with Doris in the A.T.S. that still doesn't explain why Baby should have been left with the old people. Cynthia isn't in the Forces, too, is she? Well, not exactly. Even though all that talk about getting a war-job proved to be perfectly genuine. It was last November when it came to something. Cynthia is now the balcony usherette at the Rialto in Epping. And it's given her new life, doing something. Her hair is longer than ever and more golden. She is walking out with a Canadian officer. And what with the long hours at the Rialto and trying to see something of the Canadian she is hardly ever at Ditchfield at all. At this moment she is dreamily holding hands in a café in Walthamstow. It isn't much of a café but it is the best that they could find open on Christmas Day.

She hasn't actually taken the man from Saskatoon back to Conservatory Cottage. Not yet. But that's only because she wants Mrs. Josser to get used to the idea gradually. She doesn't want to do anything that might upset her feelings. But she does want to introduce Baby to her new daddy. Baby herself is indifferent. She is enjoying things well enough as they are.

And that completes the Ditchfield set.

2

Before we get on to the Dulcimer Street lot, come up to Central Station, Leeds, for a moment. It won't take long. The London train is just due to leave. And the carriage is full already. The progress-chaser of Drayton and Sons, optical manufacturers, has two days' leave, and he's going to spend it in London. Which is brave, considering the bombing.

Because there are no restaurant cars, he has a thermos with him. And some sandwiches. He also has a *Daily Mirror* and a *Literary Digest*. As well as his private papers—his really private ones—sewn up in a little roll inside the seam of his waistcoat. He is still a bit new to the game. And he feels slightly dizzy with excitement every time he remembers about them. Remembers about them, and remembers where he is to deliver them.

But there is no cause for excitement. No one suspects anything. The guard blows his whistle. The train draws out. And the man opposite falls asleep, his hat down over his nose. Dr. Otto Hapfel relaxes and begins to eat the dried-egg sandwiches that his landlady has made for him. He has a pleasant feeling of well-being.

That's because he's being taken care of so nicely. He is not alone. The man opposite—the one with his hat down over his nose—is a policeman. And so is the man standing up in the corridor outside.

Altogether, it's practically Dr. Hapfel's last ride.

3

Now for Dulcimer Street. Back there, it's sadly changed. A family called Rossiter is living in what used to be the Jossers' rooms. And Mrs. Vizzard isn't any too sure of them. She has her doubts. Nothing that she can exactly put a name to. Just a vague uneasy feeling that somehow they're not quite right. She suspects that Mr. Rossiter drinks. And she doesn't care very much for the couple above them who followed on the Boons. They're both working, and Mrs. Vizzard doesn't approve of women who're out all day.

But the saddest part of all is Connie's room. It's empty. And Duke is downstairs hanging up in the window with only a basement view, instead of the roof-tops, to comfort him. He's been there nearly a month now. Ever since the night when Connie didn't come home. Not that anybody really worried very much at first. It was nothing new for Connie to be detained. Detained all night sometimes. And still fresh as a daisy next day. But this time it was the end all right. A river police-boat found her. Right down by the Pool, too. Though how she got there only Connie knew. Drifted, probably, her clothes spread wide, all the way from Charing Cross or Westminster which was on her beat anyhow. But even then there was no saying how she had come to find herself on the wrong side of the Embankment. She was dead, quite dead, by the time the police-boat got there. Wrapped half round a hawser, her old feet pointing out to sea. All the sheen and slime, the murk and magic of London's river, was drifting past her, agitating the small body so that her legs were moving slightly and she seemed to be trying unsuccessfully to swim upstream, back to St. Thomas's and Lambeth and the parts she knew. The funny thing was that close beside her, practically in her arms, was a large Persian tabby, also drowned. It may simply have been coincidence, of course. But the river policeman was a kindly, rather sentimental sort of chap. It was his view that the little old lady had fallen in trying to rescue the cat. And he may have been right. Either that, or kitty had jumped in trying to rescue Connie. It might have been either way. You could never be really sure with Connie.

Mr. Puddy finds that he still misses her. He hasn't forgotten that surprise cup of mulligatawny that she once took up to him. And the memory leaves a sense of gap. It was partly because it was so quiet upstairs with no one in the room beside him that Mr. Puddy accepted Mrs. Vizzard's offer to shift down to the back basement. Partly that. And partly because it was so much safer. Now, if the house above him catches fire, he can just walk straight out through the french windows into the garden.

Taken altogether it is, in consequence, a rather basementy sort of life that Mr. Puddy is leading. Because his new job is that of Shelter Marshal. Every evening, whether the sirens have sounded or not, he has to go below ground. And stay there until the morning. There is no more nonsense about being expected to climb up on to the roof-tops. Wet or fine, he's on the Bakerloo platform at Trafalgar Square before the planes have even left Germany. And everything considered, he's never been more comfortable. Or had so much to which he can look forward. The rescue of the fireman didn't pass unnoticed and Mr. Puddy is down for a George Medal. He's got to call at the Palace in person to pick it up.

And what about Mr. Squales who had the back basement before him? Poor Mr. Squales. There's real tragedy there. Something that Hitler and Mussolini will have to pay for. It had been touch and go in any case after Mr. Barks's letter had been snatched from him at the garden tea-party. He'd even had his bag packed in readiness with everything he could lay hands on, waiting gloomily for his inevitable dismissal from Withydean. But after a while he was able to make his wife see reason. He even got her to agree to help him fight the case. And he was just on the point of persuading her that it would be better to avoid all that nasty publicity and settle out of court, when Italy declared war. That was the bitterest blow that could fall. Because it turned out that he hadn't been romancing about his name after all. It really was Qualito. And he really was Italian. What was more, the Home Office really meant to intern him. When the police came for him, everything at Withydean was at its most delightful once more and they positively had to prise him out of his partner's loving arms. It was a terrible and tragic scene, with Mr. Squales not helping in the least and Mrs. Squales fainting clean away.

So it's turned out a very quiet Christmas for Mr. Squales, too. He is in the last hut but one, right at the far end of the camp. The Isle of Man climate doesn't agree with him. Nor the food. Nor the sense of confinement. At the present moment he's standing at the window, looking out past the guard at the endless landscape of cliffs, sea and sky. Just now he tried to pass the time by playing Patience. But he gave it up when he found that he had dealt himself a whole row of Spades.

The other prisoner from Dulcimer Street has scarcely noticed that it's Christmas Day at all. He's still on uppers. And getting tired of them. There's a new foreman-inspector, too, who behaves as though he'd got to wear the shoes that Percy cuts out. Takes a pride in finding fault with them. He makes Percy sick. But Percy's got the laugh on him all the same. The foreman-inspector doesn't know that when the spring on the rotary-cutter went, Percy kept half of it. He's got it in his mattress now. And a paper-clip that he found. And a match that was given to him by someone who was just leaving. It's worth something, that match. And so are the pieces of string and the paper-clip. When you're planning your escape anything may come in handy. And Percy's escape is all he's living for now.

It's really rather sad about the escape. Because Mrs. Boon is still sure that *she* is the only thing he's living for. That's why she writes him so many letters—more than the prison authorities will let him have. And she's been saving up for the day when he'll be coming out. She's got fifty-five pounds ten towards it already. And, though the doctor's wife doesn't know it, Mrs. Boon is looking round for another job. Somewhere with more to do so that she can earn more and save faster. All the time she's been in Chelmsford she hasn't spent a penny on herself.

Nor has Mrs. Vizzard. Not since Mr. Squales's departure. Not that she need be so careful. Because, with the new sub-letting of No. 10, she's living inside her income again. Twenty-four shillings a week to the good, in fact. But money doesn't mean as much to her as it once did. She is so wrapped up in her Spiritualism that she scarcely thinks about money nowadays. It's been her one comfort, Spiritualism. And it has brought its own reward. She's developing psychic gifts herself. Scarcely a day passes without a manifestation of some sort—a Voice, or an Impression or even Levitation. Only last Wednesday she had scarcely turned her back when a full milk-jug was whisked off the dresser behind her where she had just placed it and transferred silently through the air to the draining-board by the sink—where she would never have dreamt of putting a milk-jug. Without a drop being spilt, too. And sometimes Mr. Vizzard's portrait smiles at her and the lips move. They seem to be saying something that a lip-reader might have read as "Settle." Just that. Over and over again. She spends a lot of time looking at that portrait. And wondering.

That's what she's doing now. Simply staring at it, waiting for it to address her. The fact that it's tea-time, tea-time on Christmas Day, has entirely escaped her. There isn't even a kettle on. Then suddenly she rouses herself. Not because she mustn't let the picture get a hold on her. But because of the black-out. It's the Rossiters that she doesn't trust. They're just the sort of people to leave a chink in the curtains. Particularly if it was Mr. Rossiter who drew them. And she doesn't want any more policemen knocking on the door of No. 10.

As there's only one way to make really sure about the black-out, she puts on her winter coat and goes outside to have a look. Right outside in the cold. Over on to the opposite pavement, in fact. And it's just as well she does so. A six-inch triangle of light is showing from the first floor. Her eyebrows contract in irritation. She's going straight upstairs to say something to those new tenants of hers.

Before she goes in she glances down the length of the terrace. Except for a huddle of searchlights somewhere over Hammersmith way, no other lights are showing, and everything looks peaceful in the dusk. The war hasn't so much as touched Dulcimer Street yet. Perhaps never will. But you can't be sure. There's such an expanse of it. It stretches, you'll remember, in an unbroken row from Dove Street at one end to Swan Walk at the other.

And they are certainly fine houses.